Backtracking

By

M S Baker

For the Bold Sue

Table of contents

Contents

Chapter One. 5 1
Chapter Two. 17 20
Chapter Three. 31 44
Chapter Four39 58
Chapter Five. 46...70
Chapter Six. 56...87
Chapter Seven.. 65 102
Chapter Eight74 117
Chapter Nine. 84 134
Chapter Ten.. 94 151
Chapter Eleven.. 103...166
Chapter Twelve. 111..179
Chapter Thirteen.. 120 194
Chapter Fourteen.. 129 208
Chapter Fifteen.. 136 219
Chapter Sixteen.. 149..240
Chapter Seventeen.. 161 260
Chapter Eighteen.. 172 278
Chapter Nineteen.. 181 293
Chapter Twenty. 192 311
Chapter Twenty - one. 202 327
Chapter Twenty - two. 212 344
Chapter Twenty - three. 221 360
Chapter Twenty - four231 377
Chapter Twenty - five. 241 394
Chapter Twenty - six. 252 411
Chapter Twenty - seven.. 262 428
Chapter Twenty - eight275 449
Chapter Twenty - nine. 288..470
Chapter Thirty. 302..493
Epilogue. 314...512

Chapter One

Paul Denton scowled as his boss stumbled through the farewell speech. Exasperated, he shifted slightly and gazed through the grime coated window to the yard below. The place had originally been a Victorian soap factory where bones had been rendered to fat, traces of which still clung to many of the soot stained walls. His gaze wandered to a stunted Buddleia which was waiting for spring in order to resume its precarious existence rooted in crumbling brick corbelling on the boundary wall. Wintry afternoon sunlight filtered through the clouds, glancing off the stainless-steel cupolas of The Thames Barrier before dying in the haze of exhaust fumes over Woolwich Church Street. He sighed, turned and gazed round the boardroom.

A dozen or so people, in roughly two groups, were gathered either side of the long, highly polished table. The speaker, flanked by two acolytes, stood at its head. He was a small pink person, slight in build with thinning sandy hair. His most remarkable features were a huge Zapata moustache of gingery tint that was totally out of proportion to the rest of his face below which was a receding chin and an abnormally large Adam's apple. Denton had long held the view that the excessive length of shirt cuff the man habitually displayed was a direct result of him buying shirts of a collar sized to accommodate this abnormality. It was obvious, from the frequent sidelong glances towards Paul and the hurried references to his notes, that the man was nervous. Apart from one or two sycophantic giggles most of his jokes had fallen flat. So much so that Paul suspected that Henfield had decided to then play it straight and in so doing had lost his place in the script.

It was difficult to see what was worrying the man. He was the Boss, although, only God knew how or why. And Paul was leaving. The speaker should have been reassured by the terms of the agreement: Denton was going quietly in return for a reasonable settlement The fact that Henfield was so nervous was either a comment on his lack of bottle or a measure of the effect that Paul knew he sometimes had on people. Probably, a bit of both. Part of the problem, he knew, had been the fact that he was prone to speaking his mind without considering the consequences for himself or others. Strange really, he mused, many people were fond of saying that they took a pride in speaking their minds. They

1

normally said it with a northern accent and what they meant was that they enjoyed being bloody rude. With him it just happened and more often than not he had wished it hadn't. Still, it had been a good job for most of the fifteen years and with his fifty-third birthday looming he supposed he should be grateful that there were now only Stella and he to keep. God knows how they would have coped if they had still had a mortgage or if both kids had been at University.

He glanced over in Stella's direction. The days when his heart stopped when she entered a room had long gone. But still, on a rare occasion, and this was one, she could take his breath away. He knew she was beautiful. She didn't. He'd watched heads turn. She hadn't. In many ways, they were opposites. Her calm, his furies, her neatness and her 5'4" to his shambling proportions. She looked up and smiled uncertainly at him then looked away, quietly brushing her blonde hair away from her eyes as she lowered her head.

Stella Denton knew it was going to be a difficult day. Her husband's redundancy was not the problem. That had been a dot on the card for at least the last two years, since Paul's Company had been bought out by a Northern group looking to expand down South and became part of the NMG; Northern Mouldings Group. She had become used to the idea that their lifestyle would have to change and that there was a chance they would have to move to a smaller house. No! The immediate problem was the embarrassment she felt sure she would feel the minute Paul started his reply. She knew how angry and bitter the last two years had made him and she knew that he would find it very hard not to speak his mind.

Glancing across to where he was now half sitting against the edge of the boardroom table she noted his arms tightly folded across his chest and his head down, seemingly oblivious to the proceedings. He was staring rigidly at his shoes. Like many big men, he had large feet. For years, their size had been a source of family fun. And they'd had fun. Later years had been fraught but the early days with the kids had been good. In those days, his energy, strength and drive had made him seem invincible. There had seemed to be nothing at which he failed. He'd had presence. A big man who made friends easily and enjoyed life. He was still big. Too big. Three stone too big. Still driven but no longer in control. Now he was vulnerable. But he didn't know it. An overweight, unfit alcoholic frightened of what he'd become and

2

terrified of how it might end. As she watched he unfolded his arms, flexed his shoulders, ran his fingers through his mane of grey hair and then put both hands to his face to massage his eyes with the tips of his fingers. As he took his hands away from his face she noticed the deep dark rings under his eyes. She wondered if he was listening and, if so, what he thought of the compliments and thanks that littered the speech. With his sense of humour, she suspected that part of him would be comparing the glowing tributes with the harsh fact of his sacking and finding the irony amusing. She saw him stiffen, perhaps sensing the end of the speech and suddenly rock himself off the table.

Denton swivelled towards Henfield, and with a glare forced a stuttering and abrupt end to the litany of meaningless and pointless drivel. Enough was enough and he was damned if he was going to sit still any longer while this smart arsed little accountant rambled on, searching for appropriate things to say because he was too frightened to stop. He lumbered towards the end of the boardroom where Henfield was trying to lift a poorly wrapped and thinly disguised set of golf clubs. Looming over the struggling man, he gripped the bag with one hand and seized Henfield's elbow with the other. Dropping the bag carelessly onto the polished yew table, he propelled Henfield back towards his colleagues and then swung round to address the small group of Managers that had been with him for years.

'Stella is worried what I'm going to say. But then you all know Stella. She worries a lot.' He threw a glance and a grin her way and then turned back to the group. 'I wasn't going to come today but then I thought,' he paused and smiled, 'why not? Have a drink with the old crew, perhaps a bit of a laugh, few memories and a couple of jokes. A chance to thank you all and wish you well. I was goin' to be cheerful. Then I saw you lot looking about as happy as the boiler room crew on the Titanic and I drifted off into one of me deep desponds. For Christ's sake cheer up! You've all got jobs, you're earning well and you won't have me crashing around and nicking your fags after today.'

This raised brief smiles on the faces of some of the managers and more than one smug grin from Henfield's cohorts. Denton turned his attention to them catching Stella's warning glance on the way. 'Well! You've got what you want and in a strange sort of way,' he mused, 'so have I. I ran this company well. People earned a good living and customers got good service. You lot are going to struggle and I doubt you'll make it. But we'll see. Won't we?' This last barked in the direction of Henfield who took one step back straight onto the instep of one of his more sycophantic subordinates.

In the brief confusion, Denton grabbed the golf bag, swung it onto his shoulder and walked straight at Henfield's crowd, forcing them back against the wall as he strode down the corridor between them and the boardroom table. As he neared Stella he slowed, transferred the bag to his other shoulder, noted the satisfying thump of the bag smacking into somebody and took greater satisfaction from the muttered protest. He placed his free arm round Stella's shoulders and moved her towards the door. Reaching for the handle the door swung open before he could grab it.

Standing four square in, and filling a lot of the opening was a casually but designer dressed man in his mid-thirties. A solidly built man with a face that demanded a second look. It was hard, angular and weathered. The lips were fixed in a thin humourless smile and the eyes had a pale intensity that held the attention. The skin had the lined, yellowing and parched appearance of a forty a day habit and a voice that rasped from a smoke cured larynx, 'hello Paul, you off then?'

Denton glanced at him before moving towards the door, as always noticing the peculiar way that one side of George Webber's face remained strangely immobile. He had long ago assumed that Webber had Bell's Palsy, had suffered a stroke or that the injury resulting in the thin scar that ran down his left cheek had severed a nerve. 'I will be if you get out of the bloody way Webber,' Denton barked.

There was an appreciable, challenging, moment while Webber remained motionless. Then with a slow, knowing smile to Stella and a curt nod to Denton he ushered them both through the door with a mocking sweep of his hand, moving to one side to allow them to pass.

'Come on Stella let's go. We've things to do and its Friday afternoon.'

They walked in silence across the yard towards the Directors' car park. Denton paused and briefly looked back at the place that had, almost, been his home in recent years. He remembered the day he had signed the contract for this Victorian

4

warehouse with its brick elevations and trussed roof structure so typical of that period. The facilities had not been great but he'd fallen in love with the high brick arches to the storey height windows. The acres of storage space with a small but adequate manufacturing area and the fact that it was within a mile or so of the Blackwall Tunnel had seemed to answer all the storage and distribution needs that he'd had at the time. He'd even toyed with the idea of barge deliveries from the Thames which was close enough to smell.

For February, it was a warm afternoon and Denton took off his coat. Stella hit the button in the key fob as he reached for the door. Slinging the golf clubs into the back of her car, he squeezed himself into the passenger seat and reached for the belt. He knew immediately, from the way that she yanked her seat belt from the door pillar, that she was angry with him.

'Was that absolutely necessary?'

'Was what necessary?'

'That bloody performance.'

'What bloody performance?'

'Oh! Paul for God's sake. You know what I mean. You were just plain bloody rude. What was all that business with Webber on the way out?'

'Don't like him. Never have. I've never managed to work out what we paid him for. He came just after Henfield and all he seems to do is travel and run up expenses. I used to think that he was a sort of minder, and then I thought he was there to do the legwork for Henfield. Now I don't know and I don't have to care anymore.'

'He's the Export Manager.'

He turned to her, surprised, 'he is?'

'So I was told,' she added quickly before repeating, 'the Export Manager.'

'Exactly.'

'What do you mean 'exactly'?'

'Stella, we don't export. We import unassembled, prefabricated, modular service units for student accommodation, the Services, Hospitals and anybody else who will buy them. We assemble them, deliver, build and connect them on sites: Ready-made glass fibre bathroom and toilet pods in any colour providing you want no less than twenty at a time and don't mind if they are identical.'

5

'Import export, what's the difference?'

'The difference is that we import from Holland. Webber spends most of his time in Holland! What's an Export Manager doing in the country from which we import?'

'Well! You never made any effort to get to know any of them really. If only you had made some sort of effort. He doesn't seem so bad.' She shrugged, 'he's always been very courteous to me.'

Denton looked at her in disbelief, 'Webber?'

'Paul, forget about Webber, it's us,'

He interrupted, 'Stella, not now, not today,' he sighed heavily, 'please!'

'Yes, now Paul. For the last two years, it's been like living with a madman. You're either asleep, at work or drunk. You don't talk, you don't seem interested in anything that the kids or I have to say and if you do happen to listen you disagree and argue just for the sake of it. What is the matter with you?'

'It's my midlife crisis. Not that you seem to have noticed.'

'Bollocks!'

Denton attempted to stretch his legs in the confined space, sufficient to ease a small cramp in his leg and then resigned himself to the fact that in this car his knees would be jammed under the dash however he arranged his long limbs. He let his mind drift as he gazed at passing scenery he'd ignored for fifteen years. Stella drove through the Ferrier Estate, Lee Green, Verdant Lane and then a short cut through the Downham estate where he had grown up.

He had been born and raised in a small enclave of prefabs on the northern edge of the estate. Recently he had experienced increasing nostalgia for the security and certainty that he had enjoyed there as a boy in the fifties. This prompted a particular poignancy at the lunacy of a two-year-old boy having been abducted the previous day by two children in Liverpool. Life hadn't been easy on the Estate and was sometimes rough but there had been rules. The place had seemed to have a solidity about it, a pattern of chain link fences, narrow alleyways, neat gardens, neighbours and the 'palaces for the people' in which they lived. Shortly after the end of the second world war the estate had filled up with a mix of ex-servicemen and families cleared from the bomb damaged east end of London. Many of the east-enders were market traders or Dockers with access to a still necessary and flourishing black market. The ex-servicemen were a quieter, more responsible group determined not to have their hard-won peace and chance at prosperity undermined by a bunch of spivs. There was an uneasy period of settling down which saw several confrontations culminating in the battle of the Christmas trees.

One of the traders in the week leading up to Christmas had denuded swathes of Kent and West Sussex of fledgling fir trees. These had been cleared at the dead of night on an ex-army lorry and residents of the prefab estate had woken on successive mornings to find their alleyways and sometimes their gardens full of conifers. No amount of asking, demanding or threatening had any effect on the trader. Denton could remember his dad gently explaining to his mother that, despite her fears, something had to be done. Two days before Christmas, when at least half the stock remained unsold and littered through the estate, and knowing that the balance was intended for the last market in Lewisham before the holiday, Denton's dad had made his move. He; ex Para, and two neighbours, Irish Guards and Durham Light Infantry, stole the trader's lorry. Throughout the next day, deprived of his means of transport and desperate to shift the stock, the trader ranted around the estate and surrounding areas. Returning home later that day he found that all the Christmas trees had also gone and a wife with a message to call on Harry Denton. Denton's dad had opened his front door to be confronted by a very angry man.

'Harry, you know where my stuff is don't you?'

'I do Charlie.'

'Well you better tell me before I beat the shit out of you.'

'I've got the lorry and the trees Charlie,' Harry advised insouciantly.

'Harry, so help me, get 'em now or take me to them before I beat you to a pulp.'

Denton's dad, a small man, with an air of natural authority and a disposition honed by five years of shot and shell didn't flinch. Charlie King just couldn't understand how and why this small man didn't seem to be the slightest bit concerned at the prospect of a beating but what had puzzled him more was the gradual realisation that he'd underestimated this man and was now feeling fear tinged with respect.

'Charlie that would be a mistake. You've annoyed a lot of people and you're going to stop doing it. Understand?'

Denton was hiding in the hall behind his dad terrified what this boozy bully might do and was relieved to see the DLI and IG open the little picket gate, stroll down the short path towards the front door and stand a few steps behind Charlie.

'Lads!' Harry greeted them.

'Alright 'Aitch?'

'Yes. Just explaining to Charlie why we took his lorry and trees.'

'How's he taking it?'

'I'll tell you how I'm taking it you thievin' bastards,' Charlie had shouted as he wound himself up to take action.

With parade ground precision, the Irish Guards, 2 Para and the Durham Light Infantry had each taken one pace forward and boxed Charlie into place.

'Charlie' said 'Aitch; 'we've had a year of you. We've had rotten cauliflowers stinking the place out, we've had potatoes you couldn't give away dumped all-round the estate and two lorry loads of nutty slack dumped across the pavement and into the road. The trees are the last straw'.

Charlie began to splutter a protest.

'Quiet and listen' 'Aitch said, suddenly jabbing his extended forefinger to within an inch of Charlie's nose. 'You are going to behave. You can have the lorry back after Christmas.'

'What about me soddin' trees? Just how long do you think I'm goin' to 'ang around waiting for them? I've got to get them to Lewisham for Christmas.'

'That's all taken care of. We've sold the trees. We pick up the money tomorrow which is when you'll get your half.'

'Half,' King spluttered, 'fuckin' half! God help me Harry I'll have you for this! It won't end here 'arry boy. If I have to do you one at a time, I'll do it.'

'Who shall separate us?' said 'Aitch with a smile.

'You've lost it 'arry. What the fuck are you on about, 'who shall separate us?'

'It's the motto of the Irish Guards you pikey little arsewipe and it means that you've got more trouble than you can 'andle. Would you like a taster now?' Without waiting for an answer DLI pinned Charlie to the wall of the prefab with an elbow to the throat.

'I'll fucking 'ave you', gargled Charlie.

'Language Charlie and no you won't.'

'I bloody well will if it's the last thing I ever do.' This, gamely, while rubbing his throat as DLI released him.

There was a long moment of silence during which 'Aitch, again, had moved his forefinger, this time, until it had touched Charlie's nose and he quietly said, 'so, you do understand the risk you'd be taking? 'Cos it would be the last thing you ever did.'

'You threatening me Harry?'

'No, I've never seen the point of giving warnings. I've asked you to think a bit about the other people who live around here and now you know I'm serious. I think we're all going to get on fine in the future. Don't you? Now get off home to your wife, she'll be worried.'

As Charlie, had stumbled up the steps and into the alley Denton, peering over his Dad's shoulder and caught sight of the slight figure of Charlie's son Roy. Fairisle pullover, grey worsted short trousers, National Health wire framed specs and a pinched and frightened little face on a big but undernourished body. As Charlie passed his son he rewarded him with a cuff for his muttered enquiry of concern.

'Spiteful bastard!' Muttered 'Aitch.

Denton noticed that they'd passed the Malaya garage in Bromley Road. He'd never had as much nerve as his dad and was uncomfortably aware that his character had, on occasions been closer to Charlie King and his bluster. He chuckled to himself as he sought comfort in the thought that at least he had brought more in the brains and good humour side to his operations than poor old Charlie could have mustered.

He half turned towards Stella, changed his mind and watched the shops and the crowds going home as Bromley Road drifted past and wondered how he was going to get a serious drink into him without attracting further approbation from his wife. The thing was, she was right. The last two years had been a vicious circle of rows, work, bad news and finally failure. That was the bit that hurt, the failure. Losing, to a pompous little prick like Henfield. Losing the business that had taken so long to build up. It had seemed an ideal solution at the time. His undercapitalized business, joining forces with a capital rich but market poor firm. At the beginning, it had worked well. OK he'd had to meet targets, was limited in the decisions that he could make without consultation and there were strategic decisions made that he sometimes found difficult to accept. But at least he hadn't had the worries about cash flow. Then that little shit Henfield had arrived.

Paul knew that he had been his own worst enemy. If the agenda had been to get him out, then Henfield had played his hand brilliantly while Denton had dealt him the cards he needed. Every decision quietly questioned, every error publicly discussed, while the successful contracts never received a mention or if they did the mention was at the end of a report to the Holding Company signed by Henfield. Each move designed to provoke a response and those responses had become more irrational the angrier Denton had become. To the point where he knew that no reasonable organisation could tolerate his continued employment. What had really hurt was that in his quieter and more sober moments Denton had realised that Henfield's way was actually making a difference and the company was better organised and becoming more profitable. That realisation had come one Friday morning and had resulted in a protracted lunch that finished in the Duke's Head on Sunday evening with Stella having to be called to get him home. Back to the old circle: No fit state on the Monday morning to match the unsullied grey cells and gym toned fitness of Henfield and Co.

Denton heaved a sigh. 'Can you drop me off in the square? I promised a few of the boys that I would meet them in the Duke's and buy them a drink away from the office.'

'Paul if you want to go and get drunk again then do it just don't give me any more crappy excuses.'

'Stella, I've just been kicked out of the company that I founded, I'm fifty-three, I haven't got a clue what to do next and I'm getting pretty pissed off with you carrying on as though it is all my fault.'

She snorted, 'stop feeling sorry for yourself. A lot of it is your fault. OK! Go and have your drink, get smashed into oblivion with that bloody crowd of wasters. You seem to prefer their company to mine anyway. But, when you've sobered up, you and I are going to talk, whether you like it or not. There are things I need to tell you. You getting drunk again isn't going to prevent that. And if I have to get drunk myself to get you to talk, I will.' She turned away from him before adding, quietly, 'I think we're nearly at the end of the line.'

Denton studied her resolute profile and wondered why she had averted her eyes as she'd uttered that last thought. His Stells, looked you straight in the eye, spoke the truth and shamed the Devil. Something had happened. He kept silent. He'd long ago accepted that whenever he was convinced he was right he often behaved badly, particularly when in drink. He lost his temper, swore, said hurtful things and was tactless and intolerant. Stella always managed to reinforce her position and win any argument by remaining doggedly silent in the face of any onslaught. The silence continued while she drove through the outskirts of Bromley. He was wondering whether now was a good time to tell her of his decision to go on the wagon. This was, perhaps, the last working day of his life and was certainly the last day of a hard-worked career. Why shouldn't he finish it in style? He had already acknowledged to himself that his life would change and one of those changes would need to be some serious attention to his drinking problem. On balance, it was probably not the time to mention his plans, such as they were. Stella had heard similar promises before and announcing a programme of future abstinence just before going into a pub was a marketing exercise beyond his skills. The start of every recent year including that of just a few weeks back had seen him resolved to stop drinking. A resolve that the hung-over eyes of that New Year's Day, nineteen ninety-three, had viewed in a different light.

Stella stopped the car at the start of the one-way system and sat motionless staring ahead. Denton took his cue, got out of the car and shut the door. The temperature had dropped during the journey and he put his jacket back on and felt for his chequebook. He didn't like cashing cheques in pubs but Margaret; The Landlady, had long since accepted this as the most efficient way to manage his account. He walked round the square towards the pub. He still liked Bromley, although he was convinced that the recent addition of a shopping mall had been the ruination of the old market town. He had grown up around here. The place had been a building site for the past couple of years and Denton felt that much of its character had been sacrificed to provide more offices and shops. He crossed the road and walked towards the mock Tudor frontage of the little pub briefly reflecting on the difference in values represented by it and the newly opened McDonalds opposite. Inside, he quickly glanced around the circular bar that filled the centre of the pub. Seeing nobody he knew he moved towards the far end of the bar noticing that the banquettes that ran around the outside were only sparsely filled.

'Evening Margaret, how's it going?'

'Hello Paul. Not bad. Busy at lunchtime. Usual thing, no bloody staff.'

Margaret was partly obscured by a cloud of smoke and cigarette ash. She was a short woman in her early sixties. She ruled the pub from a position in one corner of the bar where she perched on her stool surrounded by newspapers carefully folded to the crossword page. Beneath the counter, she kept a small library of dictionaries and reference books. It was rare that she moved far from the stool during a session which, given her steady consumption of lager with brandy chasers, had given rise to the rumour that her enormous girth was all bladder or that she was piped directly to the drain in the cellar. In the absence of any staff, Margaret levered herself to the ground, stuck her biro into her tightly gathered bun, retrieved her glasses from the vast shelf of her bosom by snatching at the cord round her neck, parked the cigarette in an ancient Craven A ash tray and wheezed over to Denton. 'Usual?'

'Yes please. You O.K.? Is Johnny about? Oh! And have one yourself.'

Margaret paused briefly in her attempt to jam the glass under the cross tree of the optic, sighed and theatrically returned to the task in hand with a slow shaking of her head and another sigh as she thumped the glass back under the dispenser for the double that Denton had ordered. She took his money and gave him his change. A cursory glance at the coins in his hand told Denton that he had treated her to a brandy. Margaret returned to the bar hoisted her bosom over the counter, pursed her crimsoned lips, paused a full ten seconds for effect and then unburdened herself. 'I'm OK dear. You do your best dear, don't you? Mind you, it's not easy with Johnny and his problem. He's really not been right since that last turn.'

Denton nodded as sympathetically as he could. Johnny's problems were a lifetime addiction to alcohol that required a daily intake at least equal to any potential profit that the pub could produce together with a passionate dislike of Margaret. Denton had often thought that Johnny only stayed because nowhere else could he live so comfortably in a twenty-four-hour haze while Margaret worked efficiently enough to keep the show on the road, the customers happy and the brewery at bay. Margaret stayed because she had nowhere else to go.

The "turn" had taken place at a Licensed Victuallers Association dinner and dance, when, after consuming several pints before the meal, at least two bottles of wine during and the best part of a bottle of Courvoisier with his coffee, Johnny had collapsed over the table. For some this had enlivened an otherwise dull round of speeches but for Margaret the shame and humiliation were only partly assuaged by the later discovery that Johnny had suffered a stroke. Weeks of hospitalisation and abstinence had gone some way to mending their relationship but the full return of all Johnnie's faculties, seen as an opportunity for a fresh start by Margaret, was greeted by Johnny as a sure indication that he was fit enough to return to his old ways. Things had gone steadily downhill since. Denton had often thought that there but for the grace of God, and the need to earn a living, went he and a good many of the other habitués of The Dukes Head. Certainly, the discipline of work and the demands of a family had often been all that had prevented him from sliding towards Johnnie's level of oblivion. He wondered if the demands of his shrinking family would be enough now that he had no job. Since his daughter, Julie, had gone to Uni his relationship with Stella had deteriorated and he wasn't sure that it was all down to his boozing. He'd been a little surprised at her intensity in the car given the strained nature of their relationship. He'd begun to think recently, so distant had she become, that she had become reconciled to his behaviour. He'd even, very much from his cups, once wondered whether there might have been someone else until his alcohol fuelled ego dismissed the thought.

'He's changing a barrel dear, or at least that's what he went to do an hour ago. Hello! The Rush Hour has begun,' she announced as she moved up the bar to greet her "Gentlemen from Town".

Denton nodded to one or two of the new arrivals but, realising that he was earlier than usual, settled down to wait for the mid-session crowd he met most evenings. He glanced briefly up at the small television bracketed into the farthest corner of the bar and quickly away from the disturbing and blurred security camera pictures of the two-year-old Bulger baby being led off. His thoughts returned to Stella and her threats of a showdown. He knew that he was the type of man who was uncomfortable with any sort of emotional scene. Inevitably in these arguments he found himself floundering and losing his temper. He also knew Stella was far too intelligent to allow any argument to degenerate to that sort of level. He half smiled at the mental image of himself being subjected to the sort of quietly reasoned lecture he was sure Stella would deliver. She would be pleased that he had seen his redundancy as an opportunity for change but he suspected she was as worried as he about their future and the different stresses that it would impose on them both. He had recently decided that what was needed was a change that was sufficiently radical and challenging to force them back to the sort of teamwork they had enjoyed in their early days, together against the world! A new house or even a new business had crossed his mind although he liked the existing house and wasn't particularly anxious to risk it, and what remained of his sanity, to solve a problem that might have a simpler solution. A hearty thump between the shoulder blades stopped his introspection and he swivelled on his stool with a smile already forming.

'What's the craic? And how's life on the dole you aul shister?'

'Different, about sums it up Mickey, how's it going?'

'Busy, busy. But then I'm in a growth market.'

Denton turned away from the newcomer and waved a fiver at Margaret to attract some service. Satisfied that help was on the way he faced Detective Sergeant Michael Joseph McCarthy and grinned. 'Mickey, you have got to be the only detective in the Met that wears a buttonhole.'

'Ah! But then isn't it just the best form of undercover that you could get? Nowadays most of the bad lads are into drugs and they know from the TV that the cops wear baggy jackets, turned up sleeves, very white trainers and loose tee shirts.'

'No trousers?'

'Ever the merry quip Paul. I've told you before, unless you want to work for Special Branch, a soft Irish lilt and the clothes and poise of the horse breeding fraternity are an asset in my line of work.'

'Mickey, and I've told you before. The one thing you're short of is a sense of humour.'

McCarthy stiffened, looked away and then sharply back. 'Paul what I do isn't a joke. There are serious Players out there prepared to go to any length to get more than they have and to keep what they've got. Nowadays that means drugs. Importing and selling. Criminals don't walk across the pavements waving sawn offs these days Paul. They can make more money from the 'loads a money' mob. Some blazered fool of a city broker will pay thousands a week for Crystal, coke and crumpet and these guys will supply his every need for a fraction of the risk they used to take knocking over a wages van and ten times the profit. The demand's everywhere and what's more so's the money to pay for it.'

McCarthy looked away for appreciable moments. Denton, a little surprised at his vehemence nudged him with the glass in his hand and offered the drink as he turned back and for the umpteenth time, marvelled at his turn out. The suit was a four-buttoned high three piece made from the sort of tweed that used to give Denton prickly heat in the crutch when he had been forced to wear similar as a child. The shirt was crisp enough to have just been removed from the box and the tie could only be described as a statement. Not the sort of statement that Denton would have wished to make but one that Mickey obviously felt appropriate. The suit, like all Mickey's suits, had been measured to the stitch. Mickey looked elegant for every inch of his seventy-two. Again, not for the first time, Denton also marvelled that a man older than him could look as young and as fit. This despite incredibly long hours, a thirst of health threatening proportions and contempt for any form of exercise.

'Anything exciting happened since I last saw you?'

'Not a lot boyo. Bit of fun the other night in here though.'

'What was that?'

'Ronnie Allen finally caught up with little Jimmy Waddicker and I had to separate them. Calmed down in the end. After they'd had a few drinks they seemed to have forgotten it.'

Denton laughed. Allen was a well-known local jobbing builder. Part time alcoholic, full time racist, and homophobe and a regular but useless bar brawler. Waddicker was a self-employed car mechanic, slight, sneaky and fleet of foot with a massive eyesight problem that required him to wear glasses with lenses as thick as the bottoms of beer bottles giving him more than a passing resemblance to a captured Japanese general. Allen had acquired a Land Rover that needed work including a re-spray. Waddicker had taken on the job. A few weeks previously the pair of them had been in the pub discussing the work and Waddicker had asked what colour Allen wanted the paint job. Waddicker had explained that the Army seemed to have them in all sorts of camouflage colours from jungle greens, through arctic greys to desert blush. Allen was quite taken with the idea of desert blush perhaps picturing himself in army surplus desert fatigues. Waddicker had duly completed the work and delivered the Land Rover one evening to the pub. Money changed hands and a small crowd had gone out to inspect the work in the late evening light and Allen had driven home pleased with the job. The next morning however, drawing his bedroom window curtains and viewing the vehicle in the harsh dawn light he had seen not the militarily recognisable combat ready hues of the British Army in full desert blush but the feminine hues of the boudoir akin to the gentle flesh tones of Liberace's face powder. Thus, it was that the biggest homophobe in Bromley had been reduced to cruising the streets in a pink Land Rover looking for a short-sighted car sprayer who was either colour blind or had more of a sense of humour than had been previously suspected.

'So! Did the last day go with a bang?'
'I listened to a bloody stupid speech, made a bloody stupid reply, had a row with Stella and wished to Christ that it had gone with a bang. I should have slotted that bastard.'
'Who, Webber?'
'No! Henfield.' Denton looked quizzically at McCarthy. 'How do you know Webber?'
'And didn't you mention him yourself once or twice.'
'Did I? I don't remember.' Denton said thoughtfully.
'Mickey, I didn't mean to upset you earlier you know.'
McCarthy smiled. Gripped Denton's arm just above the elbow and squeezed.
'Sure, and I know that. Been a bad day. It doesn't matter. Look I have a ticket for the match. Will you come? You need some distraction. Kick off in an hour, half hour to get to Selhurst Park so we've got time for one for the road.'
'I don't think so Mickey. I thought I'd see the evening out here, get home in reasonable time and start my life tomorrow without Stella banging on about me being an irresponsible drunk.'
'You've got no chance. The Bulimia Brothers have just walked in.'
Denton glanced behind him as two huge grins appeared around the corner of the bar. Forty-seven stone of muscled good living advanced with playful menace.
'Evening Ron. Evening Don.'

'Denton, you little scamp.'

This, from Ron as he locked Paul's head to his chest with a forearm the size of the hindquarters of a small horse.

'I've been bellin' ya all day. Where ya bin?'

Before Denton could answer, Don had pinched his cheek between the knuckles of two fingers that were the size of Cumberland sausages.

'Allo mate! You bin avoidin' us?'

Denton prised himself free, straightened his tie, shook his jacket back into position and waved another fiver at Margaret. 'I've been expecting you boys. I miss you. I do Don Ron. I do,' he chorused.

The two roared their appreciation.

'Oh! Bon mot, bon mot and mine's a spritzer and Don will have a pint of the tarts juice.'

'A spritzer and a pint of lager please Margaret. Oh! And after this can you cash a cheque?'

'So! How's things in Surrey Street then?'

'Why? You thinkin' of getting' a stall and joinin' us then?'

'Might do. Ideal business. All cash, low overheads and very little intelligence required.'

'Ark at 'er,' exclaimed Don as he took the lager from Margaret, 'and 'im an out of work entrepreneur.'

Denton chuckled to himself. They weren't brothers; they just looked as though they should be. As far as he knew they had grown up together, been in the Navy together, married within weeks of each other and produced children with wives that grew to look more like each other and the 'brothers' as the years passed. He had first met them when his business was thriving and had occasionally helped them out with the loan of trucks or storage in the face of a breakdown or a shortage of space when a bulk bargain buy was in the offing. He had never asked for anything in return and was always surprised, a few weeks later, to have a fold of bank fresh notes slipped quietly into his top pocket.

'Did you slot any of them bastards before you left?'

Denton grinned. The carriage and storage arrangements had ended abruptly after he had sold the Company. Henfield had stumbled into their Aladdin's cave during his first duty tour of the premises and had decided to call the Police in the face of what he obviously considered to be contraband. This had proved to be one of the few occasions when Paul and George Webber had agreed. The Police had not been called. The Bulimias had been told to clear the shed immediately. It had been Ron, long after, who had advised Paul never to trust or cross Webber. He had refused to elaborate but his words had worried Paul at the time.

'I'll be off to the match then,' said Mickey draining his glass.

Denton smiled and nodded and noticed that the Bulimias were staring fixedly ahead with glasses raised and tilted to the tightly clamped lips of un-smiling mouths.

'Yeah! Ok Mickey. Sorry about that. See you during the week.'

McCarthy nodded curtly at the Bulimias and moved away from the bar and through the rapidly filling pub towards the door, chatting with Regulars on the way.

'What's up with you two? Unsociable sods!'

'He's Filth inny. You can't relax with the Law hangin' on every word. Can ya?' Explained Don.

'For Christ's sake, he's a local Copper. He comes in here for the company and the crack. What's the problem with that?'

'Paul, are you thick or what?' Don turned to face Paul, put his drink on the bar and began to tick off his points using the index finger of his right hand to fold back successive Cumberlands on the left as he made each point. 'One, 'e's bin coming in 'ere for months and 'e's everybody's friend.'

'Well, he's Irish.'

'Never mind Irish. Two, coppers drink with coppers, unless of course, they're workin'. Three, 'e don't drink. Oh! There's always a drink in front of 'im but it's like the magic porridge pot: It's never empty. Four, 'e's got ears on elastic, 'e can hold one conversation and listen to three others at the same time.'

'So! Are you saying he's not a copper then?'

'Oh! 'e's a copper all right but 'e's not local, 'e's not friendly and somebody who uses this boozer has got or knows something that 'e wants.'

Denton turned away and looked across the bar towards the entrance where McCarthy was opening the door. He watched him step back to let somebody pass into the pub. Don's shout coincided with the side of McCarthy's face and part of his jaw disappearing in a red misty cloud with ropes of blood looping into the air from his neck. As Paul was pulled to the floor he heard the second barrel cut short screams and shouts and the silence was only broken again by the sound of doors slamming, the high revving of an engine and the squeal of tyres. He became aware that Ron was pulling himself up the bar and peering across the counter towards the door. Paul stood up cautiously as others rose from prone or crouching positions and gently moved through the shocked customers towards the body of Detective Sergeant Michael Joseph McCarthy with the man's words ringing in his ears; "Criminals don't walk across the pavements waving sawn offs these days Paul."

Chapter Two

Andy Starmer sat on the floor boards in the sparsely furnished room with his knees clasped under his chin staring fixedly at the slim dark haired and unconscious girl lying on the bed on the other side of the room. He wondered if he should check or remove the ties that held her wrists and ankles to the bed but decided to wait until the room lightened with the rising sun. He twisted his head to one side, resting his right cheek on his knees and gazed out of the window to his left. If the day proved to be clear, he would be able to see across the roofs of the red-bricked back to backs of Fallowfield to the start of the Pennines on the eastern edge of Manchester.

The girl moved and groaned, Starmer pushed himself to his feet, went to the bed and leant over her. She stirred again but did not become conscious. He tucked the duvet around her and sat back on the floor but this time with his back to the wall. It was now just possible to make out some of the detail of the small room. Student accommodation; makeshift shelving, alcove curtained as a wardrobe, expensive computer and workstation and a collection of full size wall posters with no apparent theme but there to mask mould growth and damp patches. In the corner nearest the window was a used and abused chest of drawers. On top and leaning against the wall was an old thirties enamelled sign advertising the delights of a proprietary brand of gravy with two scruffy but beatific kids sniffing their way to culinary ecstasy. Starmer dwelt briefly on the irony that in a few hours' time some kids, sixty years on from that golden era, and less than a hundred yards from where he sat would be sniffing their way to a more damaging ecstasy courtesy of a plastic bag and a tin of adhesive.

He had met the girl at the first-year cheese and wine induction in the University, some two years ago. It had been one of the formal, fresher week, social occasions designed to effect introductions and start the process of bonding, a concept with which he'd been instinctively uncomfortable. He had tried hard to overcome his uncertainty and diffidence but even then, had been probably the most reserved and isolated person in the room and certainly the oldest. Hovering on the edges of conversations, until, embarrassed by his own silence, he had then moved to the edges of other enclaves of entente. Tiring of the whole business he'd started to edge towards the door with head down to avoid stumbled contact with feet or the odd rucksack. He'd walked straight into her. The apologies were already springing to his lips when he realised, first, that she was grinning at him and secondly, she had quite deliberately positioned herself on a collision course. He'd stepped back, smitten.

'Off already?'

'Yeah, things to do.'

He felt lost. She was beautiful. His nervousness forced his eyes out of contact, around the room and back, and again and yet again. With each circuit, he added to his impression of perfection. She would have stood out in any gathering but in this one she was out there on her own. Not for her the student uniform. She was probably the only woman in the room not in trousers. She wore a sweater, a silky sort of scarf, a pleated skirt and polished shoes. She was a few inches shorter than him, which put her at about 5' 8' and her hair was short and dark. As he reached the end of the next circuit she laughed, looked into his eyes and smiled. There wasn't, then, a power on earth strong enough to protect him from those eyes. They were mesmerising, compelling, challenging, welcoming and when he drew back to risk a glance at the rest of the face, her grin confirmed that they were also twinkling with laughter.

'I'm Julie.'

'Yeah, right,' he mumbled, 'well,' he paused, scanning the room again, as he gathered his bemused thoughts then offered his hand, 'it's nice to meet you.'

She had cocked her head to one side, frowned and put her hand on his chest to halt the beginnings of his side step. 'And you are?' She prompted.

'Andy. Andy Starmer.'

'Are you a Lecturer?'

Andy's spirits took an immediate dive. He'd already been feeling out of place, 'I look that old?'

She looked around the room, 'older than most here, I'd say.' She smiled, 'extended gap year?'

'Sort of.'

'Talkative.'

'Sometimes.'

'So, a mature student?'

He nodded.

'And it wasn't a gap year?'

He nodded again.

'This is hard work, 'she grinned, 'bit like twenty questions. How many have I got left?'

'Fifteen,' he smiled, relaxing a little as he realised that she was trying to put him at his ease.

'Hmm, not a gap year then,' she pulled on an imaginary beard, assumed a quizzical pose and looked him up and down, 'fit, as in butcher's dog, neat and tidy, clean shaven, pressed clothes and very short hair,' she tugged on the beard, turned her head slightly to one side and let a triumphant smile slip into place. 'Military. Right?'

'Correct.'

'Army?'

He nodded.

'Para, right?'

'No.'

'Pity, my granddad was a Para.'

'Good for him. I never managed to work out why anybody would want to leave a perfectly serviceable aircraft mid-air.'

She laughed, 'so what did you do?'

'Driver.'

'Driving what?'

'Heavy Goods Vehicles.'

She clapped her hands, 'ooh, something in common. My dad lets me move the lorries in his yard sometimes. What sort did you drive?'

'Chieftains?'

'Tanks?'

'Correct. Eight left.'

'Were you in Iraq?'

'I was.'

'I protested against that.'

'Well good for you. So did I.'

'I'm serious.'

'So am I. After seventy-two hours locked down inside a hot smelly, noisy piece of kit pushing Jingly trucks off the Basra road, I was dirty, dehydrated and desperate to get home. I protested long and hard.' He laughed, 'they just couldn't hear me.'

'Were you in the err?' she paused, 'did you err?'

'Get any trigger time?' he smiled.

She nodded.

'Why do you need to know?'

She looked at him ruefully with a slight air of embarrassment, 'I don't. How many questions left?'

'Six.'

She threw back her head, ruffled her hair and laughed, 'and I intend to use them all. My starter for ten is, what course are you on Andy?'

'Business studies.'

'And what course are you on Julie?' She prompted again.

'Sorry. Yeah, like and what course are you on Julie?'

'Well, Andy I'll tell you. It was going to be quantum physics but now, well, business studies it is.'

She'd laughed up at him, took his arm and steered him to the door. 'Let's go.'

They'd spent the evening, but not the night, together. He learnt a little bit about her but she, mainly, just listened. Years of introspection and loneliness threatened to terminate this embryonic relationship but he found himself telling his story, well some of it, and she listened. She seemed troubled but interested although he'd had the sense to realise the dangers of complete disclosure. He was pleased when she asked more questions. Later, he marvelled at her patience and whatever quality it was that she possessed that had prompted him to talk so much about himself. Dealing with the professional caring industry had taught him to recognise counselling techniques and he had been able to discern warmth where he had been used to the chill of

23

Professional concern. Julie listened, silently, before announcing that Uni was his fresh start and that she was part of that and was looking forward to getting to know him. He also needed to look forward she advised. If he had simply been in love before, now he was ready to die for her.

His story was a simple and common tale. A one-parent family that had become one parent minus one when his mother had taken off to grab her chance of happiness at the expense of his. That happiness had come in the shape of a local government officer, a house not on a council estate, an MFI kitchen and three recently orphaned children. He had been too young to remember these events but had lived with the consequences and hurt of his mother's betrayal ever since. First there had been a series of foster parents, a couple of attempts at more permanent 'placements' and then a residential school. By that time, he had begun to realise that he was quite a way up the pecking order when it came to brains and that the rest of his life was rushing towards him. Further disruptive behaviour had seen him summarily despatched to the Royal Armoured Corp's Junior Leader Regiment at Bovington. There, for the first time he had felt a sense of family and had buckled down and taken any opportunity he could to prepare for this new world. It was there that he'd found and honed his basic survival instincts of invisibility or instant aggression.

Walking back to his room he had wondered what had attracted Julie or rather what had maintained the attraction past the cursorily physical. He had long since reconciled himself to the fact that his lack of confidence and social skills often prevented him from developing brief involvements to their full potential. He then worried about the burden of trust placed on her shoulders and half resigned himself to deal with betrayal, rejection or worse, public humiliation were she to share his confidences.

The next morning saw his fears vanish and that morning had set the pattern for many to follow. As he collected his cereal from the breakfast buffet in the Halls canteen he heard her call out his name. She waved him over to a table out of the crowd. 'Get home Ok?' She chuckled.
'Oh yeah, up one flight and three doors along.' He grinned 'What've you got today?'

'Statistics, then I've got to go and sort out some paperwork on fees.'

'Fancy the Union this evening?'

'Yeah.'

'Here at seven?'

'Great!'

There had been few days that hadn't passed without this agenda setting over breakfast. It had been some months before he began to question the basis of this relationship and his good fortune. Within a couple of months pretty much everybody else on the campus were shagging themselves silly. He knew that Julie was aware of this because they sometimes remarked on the whirl of Fresher relationships and casually circuitous promiscuity that rendered some liaisons close to incestuous. His tentative approaches to Julie had never been rebuffed but somehow never progressed beyond a good goodnight. He thought by then that she must have known of his love and was certain that she was fond of him but wondered whether she saw him more as a father figure than a suitor. The gap was a few years only but sufficient to cause comment. He was not prepared to risk what he had by pushing for more. He knew that she had rejected more than one approach from both serial shaggers and more earnest suitors. He had once found her standing, frowning, almost pinned to the wall, her arms folding her books to her chest, while two trophy hunters ran her through their limited range of conversation and courtship. He had reached between them, took her hand, guided her past them and begun to walk away.

'Oi! You rude old git. We were talking.' This from the smaller of the two.

Starmer had given his bag to Julie and walked back. He stood a few inches in front of the bigger of the two with his arms hanging down in front of him and his hands loosely together over his crutch. Looking slightly up into the lad's eyes he had very quietly said.

'Go away.'

The lad had glanced to his friend for support.

'Now!'

Time passed very slowly for the lad before he dropped his gaze and walked.

'My God! Where did that come from?'

'It happens.'

Julie had sensed that he didn't want to talk.

When it happened, sex had been puzzling. Physically, he knew, it had been as near to good as either of them could have wished. Neither of them were inexperienced and there were a few months of abstinence to address. He'd engaged in the desperate couplings of the kids looking for they knew not what in a world of institutionalised care and he'd sensed in Julie's responses experience that hinted at previous relationships. Between them there was affection, there was respect, there was even commitment, of a sort, but from her, there was little on the emotional level. Passions spent; there was a hasty covering, a withdrawal to the bathroom and reappearance from the kitchen with a coffee for him, hers she had placed by the desk. No shared warmth. No afterglow. He'd wondered if there was someone at home. A boyfriend and promises now broken perhaps?

Their fun came from their shared experiences and social life; the Union, clubs, parties and the holiday together. As the students settled into the first-year, relationships also settled and he and Julie moved with a group that had begun to make plans for sharing a house in the second year. Five of them had arranged to rent the house in Rusholme. Another couple, Mike and Jo, a computer nerd called Jake and a guy from another course, Leo, in the loft conversion. Leo had been there on trial. Nobody knew him too well but he filled a gap when somebody else had dropped out. He was an oddball in every sense of the word; short, almost spherical with Mediterranean looks and very much a loner.

Starmer, with nowhere else to go, spent most of that summer in Manchester sorting out their rooms and earning money doing bar work while Julie went back home to her family. His work led to a job as an assistant bar manager in a club called 'Slammers' in the town centre. The money was quite good and he got to wear a polyester tuxedo, frilled shirt and bow tie. The hours were reasonable; from eight till late Friday and Saturdays. He was looking forward to Julie's return and a little worried that he had not heard from her very frequently. When they did speak, things had been fine and although she spoke of some worries at home she had not been specific. When she had arrived back, the day before her first tutorial, he had been shocked. She was thin, very thin, looked ill and was distracted.

'Hey! I've missed you. How's it going?'

He hugged her to him, buried his face in her hair and then kissed her neck. She clung to him preventing him from pulling back to kiss her properly and he realised that she was shaking. He prised her loose and held her at arm's length looking down into her face. She was crying.

'Julie! What's the matter? C'mon angel, tell me what's up.'

She just threw herself back into his arms and sobbed. Eventually he got her up the stairs to their room, laid her down on the bed, knelt by the side and cuddled her to sleep. That had been the start of the nightmare.

The next six months brought an accelerating deterioration in Julie's state of mind and health. For at least the first month, or so, Starmer was mystified. He'd assumed that there had been a problem at home during the holidays but no amount of questioning or gentle enquiry ever got Julie to talk. Then her behaviour started to become difficult, irrational and unpredictable. At that point he cursed himself for the unobservant fool that he had been. For God's sake, he had seen it all too often but just hadn't thought of Julie in connection with drugs. Confirmation came when she started spending time with Leo in the loft. There was no way she went there for companionship or conversation and he knew that Leo was a user. Here he made his first mistake. He literally, coldly and deliberately kicked Leo down three flights of stairs pausing occasionally to open cellophane packets of drugs and sprinkle the contents over the man's face. The last packet he poured into Leo's unconscious mouth not the slightest bit deterred by the clicking of a broken jaw. Charges were laid and dropped and Leo had last been seen on a train to King's Cross struggling with his belongings and a surgical cast.

Julie left. Whether out of protest at his vigilante vengeance or because of the increasing difficulties imposed by her addiction he wasn't sure. He knew that she was missing tutorials and avoiding their circle of friends and acquaintances but for a month or so he had no idea where she was. He assumed that she had gone home and, ignoring his pride, he called there and asked to speak to her. It was quickly apparent that his call had caused concern and he had stammered a range of excuses, founded on his own supposed forgetfulness, to calm those fears. Home hadn't heard.

27

Then, just before Christmas he'd seen her in Slammers. He'd then made his second mistake. He was clearing cash from the bar tills and on his way to the main office and the safe to lock the money away. He had two till trays and a bag of notes as he ducked under the security grille at the end of the bar to cross the few feet to the office. She was standing at the edge of the bar with the bigger of the two nobheads that he had confronted in Halls all those months previously. She was brightly, beautifully brittle and blown out of her brains. She saw him and burst into a laugh, which she had then half smothered with the hand holding the drink while the other jabbed at nobhead to point out the source of her amusement. Some people never learn and nobhead was one.

'It's fucking orphan Annie,' he chortled turning back to Julie to share her enjoyment of his joke. Julie was mopping spilt Breezer from her cleavage.

Starmer turned and carefully gave the two till trays to the accompanying Doorman, made sure that he had them securely, slowly balanced the bags of notes on top then walked back towards Julie.

'Hello Julie. Can we talk?'

She turned her back on him.

'Julie. Please.'

He couldn't remember a greater sense of loss and betrayal. Not even his mother's abandonment and the years of growing up alone had hurt so much as her rejection and the knowledge that she had shared his confidences with these idiots. He reached out to hold her arm and gently, very, very gently turned her to face him. She was crying.

'Come on Julie, let's go. You don't want to be here.'

She looked at him and he saw despair and confusion in her eyes.

'Julie, I love you.'

He didn't see the bottle but stunned as he was he knew it could only have been nobhead. He staggered up to see Julie running across the club. Turning to the idiot he saw that whatever had fuelled his bravado had now deserted him. He was backed up to the bar terrified by the realisation that Starmer was still conscious, back on his feet and advancing. Starmer held out his hand for the remains of the bottle. Nobhead passed it over the way he had, in safer times, passed confiscated toys to teachers. He held the broken edge to the boy's cheek, drawing a small bead of blood, then dropped it to the ground before slowly, with an open hand smacking the boy hard. First on one then on the other cheek, once, twice, three, four times slowly and more. He stopped when the boy began to cry and slowly sink to his knees with his arms folded protectively around his lowered head. Starmer spun on his heel, noticed that the doorman hadn't moved, pushed his way through the audience and left the club.

He'd heard later that the doorman and chums, not satisfied with his ritual humiliation of the idiot, had demonstrated staff solidarity by taking him outside and damn near killing him. The inevitable Police enquiries resulted in them being disciplined, new security staff being hired and Starmer being called into the office the next night.

Cecil Woolley was an ardent homosexual who had exploited his position on the club scene since the end of the Second World War to secure both riches and power. Rumour had it that the start of his fortune had been the black market with goods stolen or redirected from the PX on American bases. This had been supplemented by earnings from prostitution, protection and armed robbery of anything from cash to cigarettes. Those had been the days of blagging security vans, jumping Post Office counters and the odd carefully planned attack on Banks with firearms and extreme violence. Bankrolling from the shadows and staying in the background had been a lucrative activity that also served to establish his seniority in the criminal fraternity of Manchester while keeping him at a safe distance from prosecution. The promiscuity and the 'you've never had it so good' of the sixties had very nearly ruined Cecil. The sexual freedom of those times had brought sex from under the Newsagent's counter and cards in telephone boxes, to Festivals with the consequent hit on the profits from his escort agencies, porno and contact magazines. Also a particularly successful run by the Police had seen a sharp decline in income from the 'over the pavement' actions of yore. Facing this serious decline to his business interests he'd had the wit to climb on the back of the 'Liverpool' beat clubs but struggled to make much more than expenses until he stumbled on the wonder of drugs.

Cecil liked to think of himself as a businessman and often bragged of how he came to recognise this market opportunity. In fact, he had arranged for a Turk, who owed him money, to be killed. The man who had completed the commission, had removed a suitcase full of tablets from the boot of the Turks car, mainly to make room for the Turk's body. It had been another, Cecil's passion of the time, who had squealed his delight at discovering this pharmaceutical bonanza. There had been no looking back and Cecil had prided himself on having kept pace, through the years, with demand and fashion, to his present position. He'd experienced considerable annoyance with a recent Government appointment of an ex Chief Constable, to the post of 'Drugs Tsar'. That had been Cecil's title. Since then his passions had come and gone and age and the fear of Aids saw him settled into the comfort of voyeurism and a long-term companion who doubled as his enforcer. Cecil's voyeurism wasn't confined to the sexual, sometimes the companion was allowed to combine his duties with his boss's need to witness the pain of others.

Starmer had also heard all the rumours about Woolley and seen enough to know that there was a strong element of truth in most of them. He had not, therefore, been looking forward to the meeting. He knocked and went straight into the office. Woolley was sitting on a leather tilt and swing chair by the window. The sort of chair advertised in the Sunday Supplements to recline and relax the senior citizen. The shoes must have been a thousand pounds worth and the suit at least twice as much again. Woolley was known for only ever wearing suits of Prince of Wales check and all his suits were identical as were the burgundy silk handkerchiefs floppily arranged to decorate his breast pocket. There had been a rumour that many years back Woolley had arranged to steal a lorry filled with bolts of this now somewhat dated material and had been using it ever since to maintain his wardrobe. Starmer had always marvelled at the style. Woolley was over twenty-five stone and dressed in the fashion of his youth. Bertie Wooster morphed into Cyril Smith. Cecil sometimes adopted the speech and the mannerisms of nineteen thirties Wodehouse, although rumour had it the nearest he had got to that lifestyle was watching films as a boy in the cinema at Cheetham Hill.

The companion, Mister Osman, was sitting on the edge of a Partner's desk flicking through some receipts. He was not a large man and indeed Starmer had always thought that he wasn't a particularly strong man having the pallor and posture of the permanently unwell. Like his master, he also was a slave to the fashion of a bygone era. In his case thirty years farther down the line than Cecil. The two-tone tonic mohair of Dormeuil lived on. Starmer had been aware of this man's reputation for viciousness. He'd always supposed that Osman overcame his physical shortcomings and exercised his predilections by instructing foot soldiers to subdue the victim past the point of effective resistance. Woolley swivelled to face him.

'Good evening Andrew. How are you after your exertions last night? Well?'

'Fine Mr Woolley, thank you. Sorry about that. 'fraid I lost the plot for a minute.'

'Andrew, Andrew, I understand. The folly of youth.' He smiled understandingly.

'I don't know about that Mr Woolley. I,'

Woolley interrupted and Starmer could see that his chubby face had hardened. 'The constabulary came to call Andrew. I am not overly fond of the Constabulary.' The smile had disappeared.

There seemed little point in him pointing out that had the bouncers left it where he had there would have been no Police interest.

'How well do you know that young woman Andrew?'

'She's at Uni Mr Woolley, or was. She's dropped out of sight a bit this term.'

'So! Chum? Or something more serious perhaps?' From the little pink lips of any other homosexual this enquiry would have sounded arch but the snapped shut tight thin line of Woolley's lips below the hardened gaze of his bloodshot and protuberant eyes made Starmer realise that there might be more to this than a staff disciplinary. Something was playing on Woolley's mind. He instinctively thought that somehow Woolley's interest was to do with Julie and that it would be in both their best interests to put distance between them. At least as far as Woolley was concerned.

'Well neither really,' he said, praying that the Doorman on the night hadn't heard his declaration of love. The next few moments would tell. 'It wasn't about her really; it was the dickhead she was with.'

'Oh! My dear boy, one of those strut your stuff thingy's. How lovely!'

Starmer breathed a sigh of relief. The Doorman couldn't have heard or if he had, he'd kept it to himself.

Woolley struggled from the chair, his voice changed, tension tightened the jowls and spittle sprayed from his spiteful little mouth as he hammered home each of his points by taking a step nearer to Starmer. 'Don't strut in my club. You're an employee. Punters strut. Employees don't strut. Don't hit people in my club. You're 'Management'. That means you're supposed to have brains. I pay planks to do the hitting. Don't smack people. Humiliation is not a lasting remedy. A goodly period of pain keeps people in line longer than dented pride.'

Starmer nodded. There didn't seem much point in replying.

'But apart from that Andrew, people who know about these things tell me that you have a certain way with you. A sort of no limit approach to these sorts of problems. That could be a gift Andrew.'

'I've always thought of it as a problem Mr Woolley. Anyway,' he laughed self dismissively, 'I'm not big enough to cause trouble.'

'It's not about size,' this time archly, 'it's more to do with attitude.'

The interview ended when a knock at the door prompted a look between Woolley and Osman, the downing of drinks, the stubbing out of a cigarette, the collection of coats and a move to the door. Turning at the door Woolley waved an admonishing finger in Starmer's direction.

'You could have a bright future Andrew,' he paused, 'if you want it and if you're careful.'

University and the job had settled back into the old routine as Christmas approached. Starmer had spent his spare time barely keeping pace with his studies while spending hours searching for Julie. The idiot from the club would have been the most likely source of information but hardly the most available or cooperative since he was still in hospital.

Christmas brought with it extra hours at the Slammers and he was quite surprised how he became caught up in the festive spirit. He had far from forgotten Julie but she was no longer the first and only thought of every waking hour. At the club, nothing further had been said about the incident and he allowed himself to become engrossed in keeping pace with the bar accounts, cashing up, sorting out the staff rota and the million tasks that went with stock control on his shift. He had also noticed a subtle change in his relationships with the other staff. It wasn't that he was treated with respect but there was now distance where there had been a sort of easy familiarity. He began to take more notice of the club, its' clientele and management. Initially this was academic interest fired by his business studies course, particularly the marketing element. He'd already noticed the absence of drugs in the club. There was little trouble. If it occurred it was quickly, quietly, courteously but very firmly dealt with.

'Slammers' was an establishment that, literally, worked on several levels. The entrance, from the pavement, led onto the main club area. The focus on the ground floor was the stage at the farthest point from the entrance, which tiered up twenty feet or more above the floor. There were two bars, one on either side of the area and three sections of seating. What was left, at least half the floor area, on a good night, was jammed with clubbers. The décor was Maginot Line concrete in purple, blue and black with chrome and plexi glass furniture. Dimmed spots provided running light from behind a suspended ceiling. Depending on the event these were replaced or supplemented by a light show. The bars were front lit with barely sufficient working light to allow the accurate mixing and measure of cocktails. Upstairs was a smaller bar and small lounge leading into a restaurant with loft proportions, un-plastered walls and unforgiving aluminium and oak tables and chairs. It still attracted the minor celebs that wanted to have a meal without being photographed. The basement area contained the kitchens, offices, staff changing rooms and stores with an exit and loading area to a yard at the rear.

Starmer had noticed that Woolley had carefully marketed his enterprise by catering for different interests on different nights. By rotating hip hop, soul and jazz and winding in the gay and grey factor he had created something for everybody on at least one night of the week. That way he avoided the pitfalls of fashion and the dependence on any one part of the market. There was also a regular income from the non-clubbing fraternity. Those that lunched long, those that drank hard and those that worked without benefit of office. Included in this set were Woolley's associates. Hand stitched lapels, cuffs shot over a Rolex and shirts fresh from the box. They tended to be there through from mid-afternoon to early evening. Urgent discussions, sometimes interrupted by more casually dressed men with gold at wrist and throat and some blemishes of battle, leaning in respectfully to impart or receive information and sometimes to leave envelopes or packages. Often, they would all return later in the evening with heavily made up and bejewelled women with more cleavage than class. Other times they would drift in as the club was closing. Woolley seemed to know when this was going to happen and arranged for food and drink to be left out before he sent the staff home. He seemed to be on first name terms with them all while only one or two enjoyed or dared the same familiarity with him. Their presence, in part, gave the clue to Woolley's public disassociation from drugs. If the club was the hub of Woolley's criminal enterprise, then staying "hands clean" and avoiding the sort of scrutiny a drug bust might bring was crucial to his survival. This Policy was rigidly enforced by the door security staff and Starmer had idly realised that he who controlled the doors controlled the drugs.

The night that had led to Starmer's current predicament had begun well. It had been a busy night with the club starting to fill up again after the January lull and he was glad of the activity and bustle. As his shift, had neared its end he'd threaded his way through the dancers on the floor when he noticed Julie, near the door, arguing with one of Woolley's associates. Robbo Thompson was a squat, powerfully built man with a ponytail and an affectation for sunglasses. He was responsible for security in the club and was effectively Starmer's line manager also responsible for locking away the night's takings. Keeping out of sight, in the crowd, Starmer saw that Julie continued to argue with Thompson. He stifled his instinct to interfere but used the crowd to get to a position where he could keep an eye on her. Julie had long ago abandoned the fashion sense that he had so admired and tonight was tottering on six-inch heels in a pair of skin-tight jeans with a low cut diaphanous blouse with long sleeves. The argument seemed to be over and Thompson, quite gently, took Julie by the arm, looked nervously around and steered her towards the basement. Starmer followed. Quietly, he kept far enough back not to be seen or heard. He peered around the corner at the foot of the stairs and saw Thompson insert his keys into the lock on Woolley's office door. He knew that both Woolley and Osman were out and not expected in the club that night. The door closed behind the pair as he crept down the corridor and hovered outside the office uncertain of his next move. He tried listening at the door but didn't expect to hear much through a door fitted for its strength and soundproofing qualities. Whatever he did he knew that Julie wouldn't thank him for any intrusion. On the other hand, Thompson had a reputation for taking his enforcement duties beyond what Woolley had called 'the productive limit'. Specifically, Woolley had pointed out that disfiguring one of his girls had reduced her earning potential to a level from which she could never hope to repay her debts. Starmer got his set of keys out before gently trying the door. Surprised that it wasn't locked he loosened his tie, slipped his watch in his pocket, grasped the keys more firmly and opened the door.

Thompson was resting his buttocks against the edge of Woolley's desk, facing the door, with his legs splayed out in front of him, his eyes closed and his trousers around his ankles. Julie, with her blouse on the floor beside her, was kneeling in front of him. It took Starmer appreciable moments for his brain to believe what his eyes were seeing. The truth finally registered at just about the point his rush across the room slammed him into Thompson and both flew across the desk and landed on the floor behind. Starmer dropped hard onto Thompson whose natural defensive instincts had been abandoned in favour of protecting his exposed genitalia. Starmer clubbed his fist down into Thompson's face at the same moment that the thug snapped his head to one side. The fist, with the set of keys still firmly grasped, and with all his strength behind it, punched into the side of Thompson's neck. The fountain of blood from the punctured carotid artery sprayed up into his face but didn't prevent him from continuing to smash the keys down again. Even through the mist of blood he saw that Thompson was dying with a look of disbelief that he had gone from ecstasy to eternity in less than four seconds.

He extricated himself from the clumsy embrace of the dead man and dragged himself back over the desk to Julie. She was sobbing and retching with saliva and mucus streaming from her nose and mouth and the evidence of Thompson's last stand glistening in her hair. He'd taken in the cellophane packet, spoon and syringe on the desk and some small comfort from the conclusion. He yanked her to her feet, gathered the blouse from the floor and pushed her into Woolley's bathroom. She just wasn't really all there, semi and then fully unconscious. He let her slip from the edge of the bath into it and propped her up so that she wouldn't drown in her own vomit. His mind was racing but he felt very calm. He rushed back through the office and locked the door before going to take another look at Thompson who, by then, was lying in an even larger pool of his own blood. He knew that he had, at most, twenty minutes before he and Thompson would be missed. As the club closed he would be expected to cash up and take the money to Thompson in Woolley's office for him to put it in the safe. Once that was done the security staff would expect Thompson to lock up behind them for the night.

Starmer locked the office door behind and praying that he wouldn't encounter anybody in the corridor, ran to the staff changing rooms, ripping his jacket and shirt off as he went. With these bundled into a ball under his arm he cautiously opened the door. The room was empty. He unlocked his locker and jammed the blood-soaked shirt and tuxedo into his sports bag, ran his head, hair and shoulders under the cold tap of a chipped and stained washbasin and pulled on his street clothes before returning to Woolley's office. He quickly checked on Julie, then his appearance. He realised that he wouldn't have enough time to properly clean up and prayed that the dim lighting in the club would allow him to pass cursory inspection. He ran up the stairs to the main bar floor and waited until a crowd, on their way out, passed across the head of the stairs before mingling with them and making his way to the closed bar. Grabbing the empty bank bags from below the counter he quickly emptied the tills without bothering with a count or the cash forms he was supposed to complete. Clutching the bags, he crossed the nearly empty floor to the other bar and did the same there. As he raised the counter flap to leave the bar one of the security staff held the bar flap up and stepped back to let him pass. Starmer's heart was thumping and his mind racing and as he began to walk away with his shoulders hunched, half expecting an assault.

'Oi! You're in a bit of a rush!' This with a nod to Starmer's street clothes.

His reply had amazed even him. 'Fuckin' right I am. That bastard Thompson's got a strop on. He's got some slapper in tow and wants the office to himself. I'm supposed to count this lot in ten fuckin' minutes, bag it for the safe and take it down to him, complete with a bottle of fuckin' champagne for madam and then lock this fuckin' place up for him.' He'd left it there. And hoped.

'Well, can we go then?'

For the first time since killing Thompson he entertained the thought that he might at least make it out of the building. Something he hadn't thought possible ten minutes earlier. 'Don't see why not mate.'

'Ok Andy. See you tomorrow.'

Starmer locked out the cheery goodnights of the security staff, hit the front of house lights and made his way back down to the basement. He was still surprised at his own calm. He had taken life, yet, while he fully appreciated the potential consequences they were very much at the back of his mind. Citizens that took life faced the full might of the law and a guaranteed period of solitude in which to repent. The plan that had begun to form was accelerated by the nameplate on Woolley's office door.

He wasn't a citizen. He worked for Woolley. A criminal, a man who controlled the demimonde of Manchester, a man who defied the law. A man with his own rules. Starmer reasoned there was no doubt that were Woolley to find out that he had killed Thompson, retribution would be quick and terminal. But, it would be Woolley's retribution not the Law's. Entering the office, he realised that this afforded him a few advantages. Probably most important was that the office would never become a crime scene. That relieved him of any worries about DNA and fingerprints. On that basis, he thought, he could grab Julie and just run. It took all his willpower not to accept the early and easy solution. He forced himself to rethink. With the body left in the office there was a chance that a 'civilian' employee, a cleaner, might be first on the scene, panic and call the police. Visions of blue and white tape and Scenes of Crime Officers had forced him to the conclusion that for Woolley's rules to apply all obvious signs of the murder, including the body, had to be removed. Where to put the body? His gaze rested on the night's takings and he steeled himself to get the safe key from Thompson. Patting the sides of the man's jacket pockets, he struck lucky. He fished out a set of keys. Car keys. In the other pocket, he found the single ring with the two safe keys. He turned to the safe and started to open it when he realised that he had the answer to the disposal problem clutched in his other hand. Thompson's car. It had to be close. With

37

Woolley away for the night there was even a chance that it was parked in the loading area at the rear of the club. He went quickly to the bathroom where Julie was still out of it, and ripped the shower curtain from its rail. It took a few minutes to roll Thompson onto the curtain and drag him from the office, down the corridor to the fire escape doors that led out to the rear yard. Using his back to crack the crash bars he looked over his shoulder and his heart thumped as he saw a Mercedes prominently parked in the space marked 'Mr. C. Woolley'. He hit the button on the key fob and was rewarded with the sound of locks springing and the double flash of the indicators.

With Thompson stowed in the boot he returned to the office with the rest of his survival plan forming as he walked. The next step was to remove all signs of the murder. It took over an hour using mops and buckets of water to clean the blood from the floor and the wall. While doing this, he decided that his biggest problem was buying time to allow him to get as far away from Woolley as possible before the hunt started. That meant Thompson's car couldn't be found in the yard the next morning. He stopped in the act of drying the floor, as it hit him that if Woolley could be persuaded that Thompson had legged it with his takings, then the initial focus of any hunt would be Thompson not him. It occurred to him that two hours earlier he would have had all sorts of scruples about theft. Apply Woolley's rules. Thompson wouldn't just leg it with the night's takings, he thought. If Thompson were going, he'd go big time.

He opened the safe and then sat down. Stacked, like thin glass bricks were packets of used and new notes in cellophane wrappers. In a row of ten with each stack ten packets high. A hundred packets. He picked up one packet, which had a label around the middle advising that the packet contained one hundred ten pound notes. One hundred thousand pounds would have Woolley looking for Thompson with a passion and an industry divorced from the calm reasoning necessary for Starmer to be connected to the loss. At least in the early stages. He didn't hesitate further and shovelled the money into the sports bag. Behind the money, he discovered a plastic bag, which contained sachets of drugs. This puzzled him because he just knew that Woolley wouldn't have taken the chance of keeping drugs on the premises. That sort of quantity would have rated him as a dealer. He decided that they probably belonged to Thompson, put there for safety and a little bit of dealing in Woolley's absence that night. They too, along with a tooled leather filo-fax had gone straight into the bag. He'd cleared the safe.

It was two thirty by the time he'd secured the club, got Julie into the car and started the drive to Fallowfield. Knowing that he had to dump the car and accepting that Julie was in no state to walk he had taken a drastic step. At his flat he dumped her on the bed and secured her hands to the bed legs with strips torn from his sheets just to keep her in place until his return. The last thing he needed right now was to go and have to look for her while trying to stay out of Woolley's clutches. Back in the car he prayed that the ties were strong enough to keep her there while he dumped it and got back to her. The Manchester Metropolitan University halls of residence car park at Pars Wood had been a constant source of complaint from the students because the University would not provide CCTV to dissuade the local idiots from vandalising and stealing the students' cars. The added advantage was that it was not the sort of place that would be high in Woolley's awareness.

Back at the flat he'd reviewed his plan and still reckoned that he had about eight hours before Woolley was aware of the disappearance of Thompson and his money. If the cleaners didn't notice anything unusual, and if, as usual, staff didn't open until ten and no one from the night security team was on the day shift, then he had a chance. He was still confident that Woolley wouldn't involve the Police and would initially assume that Thompson had done a runner. Woolley would then turn Manchester upside down looking for him. When that proved fruitless he would eventually realise that Starmer had been the last person to see Thompson. That would probably happen when the security shift reported for duty at eight thirty that night. Then Woolley would want to see him. Starmer knew that this left only two choices. He could change his mind and report for work and hope to front it out. Or he could run. If he stayed, he might just manage to convince Woolley that he knew nothing of the theft and had left Thompson happily ensconced in Woolley's office with the slapper who by then would have become common knowledge. The problem then would be dealing with the inevitable questions as to the identity of the woman. If anybody remembered Julie having been with Thompson, Woolley might begin to put two and two together.

He looked over at Julie and thought about her and Thompson. He knew little about drugs other than the effect they had on lives. While part of him was revolted by Julie's degradation the part of him that hurt realised that she hadn't exercised choice; she'd acted as her craving dictated. If they ran he might get a chance to address her addiction. Without knowing anything about dosage he was fairly certain that the drugs he had lifted from Thompson and the safe would be enough to keep Julie together until he could get the time and the space to deal with her problem. Looking down at her again he realised how much he needed to help her. It was part of never having stopped caring for her. He had never loved anybody before and all other considerations fell into place behind that crushing need to care for and protect her. They would run. Be together. But how and where? Hiding in Manchester wasn't an option. Woolley's territory. Abroad? For Christ's sake, he had upwards of one hundred thousand pounds in cash. They could go anywhere in the world. That meant passports, security at airports and passenger lists and he had no doubt that Woolley had access to those systems and information. Anyway, after abroad, then what? One hundred thousand wasn't enough to keep them for life. Back to London? But then Woolley probably had his tentacles and connections into most of the bigger cities in England. So! Where didn't Woolley have contacts and influence? Julie stirred. He looked at his watch. Six fifteen. If they were going to run it had to be now.

He pushed himself to his feet and went over to the window. There had been a frost overnight. One tiny edge of the front lawn had lost its crispness to the early morning rays. The rest, in shadow, was crisp and white. His gaze drifted up to the sharp outline of the Pennines profiled against the rising sun. You could get lost out there. Too near Manchester and Woolley though. Stay away from cities. Memories of enforced misery to no apparent purpose on the Duke of Edinburgh's award scheme came back to him. Scotland; well away from Woolley's clutches.

He strode to the alcove, pulled the curtain to one side and retrieved an old rucksack. Into this he jammed the money, drugs and the Filofax and then clothes underwear and toiletries. He pulled an old parka from the hook on the door and scrambled into his fleece. He turned, conscious that he was being watched.

'Andy?'

'Good morning. How do you feel?' He enquired with a great deal more chirpiness than he felt. He released the ties and watched as she struggled with her mind. She dragged herself upright and, unsteadily, swung her legs onto the floor before collapsing back onto the bed.

'I'm thirsty,' she groaned. She sat up, with his support, to take sips from the bottle of water. As she raised the bottle to her lips their eyes met. He could see the memories in her eyes moving in and out of her consciousness and leaving fleeting, haunting shadows of fear and disgust on her face. Then her gaze steadied and her face crumpled. 'Oh! Christ Andy.'

'Forget it,' he barked. 'Two things to concentrate on. One we are in trouble. Two, I can deal with it, but we have got to go. Now!'

'Jesus Andy, what's going on?'

'C'mon, put the coat on. We're moving. I'll explain later.' He got the parka onto her, grabbed the rucksack, hauled her to her feet and guided her to the door. Gently he walked her along the landing to the head of the stairs. She stumbled into him, forcing him to grab the banister and the loose newel post partly secured to the floor with an aluminium bracket. They both jumped at the sound of the front door splintering from its hinges and frame. A sign, if nothing else, that Woolley was looking for him with a vengeance unlikely to be slated by any explanation. Woolley had moved faster than he had thought possible. Who knew, new security staff out to make an impression or a late return to the club with his hangers on? He'd underestimated Woolley. Not a mistake he'd make again if he ever got the chance.

A thug Starmer didn't recognise appeared at the foot of the stairs with the security guard from last night peering over his shoulder. Without speaking they both ran up the stairs. He pushed Julie away from him, dumped the rucksack, put his foot against the newel post and thrust it from its' bracket. In one continuous movement, he grabbed the freed post, lofted it high, swivelled with increasing momentum and caught thug mark one in the throat with three foot of four by four hardwood just as he reached the top of the stairs. Mark two, trying to support the dead weight of his mate, while he teetered on the point of losing his own balance, found himself defenceless to the second swing of the post brought vertically down on the crown of his head from a two-foot height advantage. Both tumbled to the foot of the stairs. Starmer, still holding the post, grabbed Julie and the bag and charged down the stairs with the hope of getting past the two and out the door before either of them recovered sufficiently to prevent the escape. His second victim was struggling to his feet as they reached the hall. Without breaking his stride, he thrust the end of the post into the man's face, turned, once his momentum had carried him past, and, one handed, smashed the timber onto the man's knee, producing a scream of pain that his hands holding his broken mouth together could not muffle. Reaching the door, he paused, shoved Julie into the front garden and went back to the whimpering thug.

'Keys.' He demanded, holding out his right hand, from which dangled the rucksack, while using the newel post to remind the man of the balance of power by gently tapping him on the shin of the undamaged leg.

He knew he wouldn't have to look far for the car. It would be black and BMW. They always were. He opened it, put Julie in the back, ran around to the other rear door, opened that and slung the rucksack on the seat next to her. He hoped she hadn't noticed him spring the child locks. He accelerated down the road mentally running a route map through his mind.

'Andy. What the fuck's going on?'

'Not now Julie. I'm thinking. We'll stop in a minute and talk then.'

'But Andy.'

'Shut up!'

He glanced briefly in the rear-view mirror and was alarmed at the fear and horror clearly showing on her face. Priorities. It was early in the morning. If he used the main roads out of Manchester heading north, there was a good chance that he'd be spotted and have Woolley around his neck before he got halfway to the sanctuary he had in mind up in Scotland. Woolley didn't have to report the murder to involve the Police; he could simply report the stolen BMW and sit back and wait for reports. On balance Starmer still thought Woolley wouldn't go to the police, even if he'd found Thompson's body, but he might have some bent copper run a few checks for him. He grinned. Scotland was the objective and Woolley had to be put off the scent. He swung off the A62 Oldham road, the start of his intended route across the Pennines to the A's 6 & 7 and got back onto the ring road aiming for the M's 56, 6 & 1; London. He'd be there in four hours, park the car where it would be clamped or towed away and then start the journey to Scotland.

Chapter Three

Dee Dee Wilson lazily inclined her head to allow the smoke from her cigarette to rise unobstructed to the draughty roof space of the rehearsal hall. She guessed the room was some forty foot by nearly as much again and caught sight of her own foot-tapping impatience in the one wall of storey height mirrors. Somebody had installed a Christmas tree in a red fire bucket which was sadly seasonal with randomly applied cotton wool balls and a forlorn fairy in yellowing taffeta leaning out from the top of this already wilting spruce. With six weeks to go to Christmas Dee rated its chances of survival only slightly less than hers of completing a successful tour in the New Year.

The poor acoustics resulting from the high vaulted ceiling of the converted church and the mirrors suggested a rehearsal room geared to dance and musical rather than sessions and practice. However, it was available and apparently central being somewhere called 'The Borough' and therefore not too far from her London hotel. She squinted the length of the hall to the source of the noise. It was obviously the singer's big chance, one for which, she suspected, he had practised many lonely nights, probably in front of his bedroom mirror while trying to keep his cigarette ash off his candlewick bedspread. His moody, over the shoulder smoulders, might look good in reflection, a reflection that he checked constantly in the mirrored wall, but they were playing havoc with his attempt to fret the chords and coordinate the group. She sighed as they started a new number. She recognised the intro to 'Country Boy' and prayed that her fellow New Orlean; Fats Domino, never got to hear, even from his grave, of her involvement, however tenuous, with the 'Blue Nuages'. The

Singer's insecurity manifested in his inability to look at his audience, preferring to glance backwards over his shoulder with vaguely rhythmic nods and smiles in the direction of the drummer. She realised that the drummer was getting the full benefit of the carefully prepared stage act because the Singer hadn't got the confidence to face the audience. She turned to the representative from the record company. Her A and R man.

'How many more?'

He consulted a pad on his knee, 'this is the last one Miss Wilson.'

The statement hung between them and the young man shuffled the papers in his lap, hoping against hope that he had made a mistake and that even as he sweated, something, anything, would appear and rescue him from this woman's scrutiny.

'Honey! I done seen nine bands this morning. You've introduced them all as professional hitters with history, some with chart success and all with visiting Artist references.'

'That's certainly my understanding Miss Wilson.'

'Well there's something wrong with your understanding. Just in case it sort of slipped by you, bands two and seven shared half the same line up. Now, that ain't necessarily bad 'cept that in this case it was the worst half. Then, there is the point that I haven't, yet, heard anything that's vaguely simpatico with my work. You capiche 'simpatico' young man?'

Young man died. Dee steadily held his anguished gaze with eyes that gave no hint of quarter. This woman impressed on every level. He reflected briefly on her public image. She had been born to a mother who had viewed her conception as an occupational hazard, raised in an orphanage and made her debut as a bouffant Tamla Motown backing singer for whichever groupette she was assigned in the late sixties. Early success had prompted a solo career that had spiralled on the back of a couple of hits into a drug dusted daydream and inevitable decline. She'd disappeared; dropped from the scene. The disappearance had never been explained, not even on her return, some five years back. She had given one interview to Rolling Stone, during which she had studiously avoided all personal questions speaking only about her music and her professional plans. There had been a minor flurry of interest, some then and now comparisons and little else until the first concert of the US promotional tour. The album

45

had been selling on nostalgia until that concert. Held in a small hall, the nostalgic audience barely filling the seats, her success had grown from that night. Word of mouth recommendation generated interest that defied the lukewarm critical acclaim. By the end of the week she was singing to audiences that had come to see a shiny, sparkly, skinny plastic booted popster and stayed to be enthralled by a mature, statuesque African American who commanded their attention with a voice and presence they knew they were privileged to witness as she smilingly swayed through her set. Concert had followed album had followed concert then once again she withdrew from public life. It had almost been as though proving she could was enough.

Then last year she had decided to tour in the UK. This decision fitted loosely with the need to prove herself theory: Different audiences to sway, cultures to conquer and a new professional challenge. However, her seeming indifference to her career, paradoxically juxtaposed to her passionate commitment to her performance had resulted in tensions that the original band had not been prepared to tolerate. Disagreement had been endemic. Some of the tour management staff and most of the band had returned to the States the previous day.

The young man was, in fact, good at his job. He had analysed the situation and had defined three major problems. The first was a marketing problem. Dee Dee Wilson, her Manager, the record company and the promoter were all selling "a rave from the grave". The young man had watched her perform and realised that when she sang you listened not to the singer but to the woman. The woman didn't come over well in the records because of the material but by God, when she was on song, she made an impact on stage. She vested her history, life and experience in every lyric. It would be a mistake, he decided, to even mention the Tamla thing. This woman was now, not then. She needed to forget the material that had catapulted her to fame and focus on the sort of material that would showcase that cool melodious voice and allow her life experiences into the performance through carefully chosen songs.

The second problem was the range of material she used. There was too much. She was trying to cover all the ground, almost as though to emphasise the differences between her and the high fashion gowned and wigged teenager of yesteryear. She was at her most enthralling when fusing Jazz with the music of Porter or the lyrics of Cahn. Her phrasing and timing were impeccable and she could draw a nuance from a lyric that gave the tune a different direction. She could also cross that tricky rhythmic divide between Jazz and South American music with all the between beat accents, freedoms and melodic variations that went with the genre. Contemporary songs in her repertoire were professionally delivered but lacked the magic of her other work. And Punters wouldn't pay to hear a woman they didn't recognise sing songs they hadn't expected or appreciated from a songbook that their parents grew up with.

There were other problems. Dee Dee Wilson loved the Blues. A lot of her two-hour set was Blues. Good Blues but neither brilliant nor memorable Blues. Just good Blues. As he thought, the young man realised that someone was going to have to point out to Miss Wilson that when she sang the Blues she sounded like the poor man's Nina Simone. When she sang contemporary stuff, she took on the baggage of the earlier hit versions but when she blew Jazz she was airborne. The problem, he knew, was the arrangements. Somebody needed to provide arrangements suited to her and tutor her out of some sloppy habits. The knowledge that he was the somebody did nothing to ease his worries. Telling a black woman singer that Blues weren't her forte was going to be difficult. Very difficult given the attitude she'd exhibited since they met because the final problem was that Miss Wilson either didn't care or had given up.

The click of a cigarette lighter returned his attention to Miss Wilson. He doubted that her eyes had left him during his reverie. She wasn't beautiful by the conventional showbiz standards. She was a big strikingly attractive woman with a full figure and a dominating personality. She was a woman who was aware of her body and he suspected that clothes were one of her passions. Unless he was mistaken the hand crafted, black beaded and appliqué top was Rocha and the blue wool pinstripe trousers were Tommy Nutter whose recent death still concerned the young man and his friends.

While the young man squirmed in discomfort Dee Dee Wilson studied him through the haze of cigarette smoke. He was an unlikely looking representative of a record company. In her

47

experience, they were usually smooth operators and sharks; fulsome to the point of gush in their dealings with the Artist, manipulative and with an overblown sense of their own importance. Most were sharp or fashionable dressers with the air of authority and confidence essential, in their world of wheeling and dealing. This young man was in that same world but not of it. She had wondered, at one point, whether she had been landed with a second stringer and then been briefly concerned about what that meant in terms of her career. He was a pleasant enough young man in his mid-thirties with a shock of black hair that contrasted sharply with the pale and pinched features of his face. He had a cute nose upon which were balanced rimless spectacles that magnified his eyes giving the impression that he was permanently startled. Slight of build and painfully thin he had an air of vulnerability and seemed constantly ill at ease. She leant forward to stub out her cigarette and raised an eye in query as Sinclair searched the pockets of his corduroy jacket for a handkerchief. Taking off his glasses he nervously breathed on the lenses before vigorously polishing them with the handkerchief and delicately hooking the wire frames behind each ear in turn. She looked at the magnified eyes. For the first time since they had met he held her stare. She saw a moment of uncertainty and then a hardening in his gaze that spread across his face into a look of grim determination that quickly masked his earlier vulnerability. Startled, she looked away briefly before swiftly seeking to spitefully regain control.

'Are you gay?' she smiled.

'Yes, I am and my name is Mathew Sinclair and I have an idea. An idea that is going to change our plans, your career and probably get me the sack. And has my being gay got anything to do with it?'

'Nothing at all. I was just curious.' She leant across to him and gently squeezed his arm. 'Mathew, honey. Let's do lunch.'

Dee Dee Wilson was used to being feted and lunch was a time for a light meal; grilled fish perhaps or a light pasta with a side salad and a glass of chilled white in restaurants from St Germain Des-Pres to Rodeo Drive. Having dismissed the last band Mathew Sinclair hurried her from the rehearsal rooms and began to usher her across Borough High Street. He turned as he realised that he had reached the centre island alone. Dee Dee Wilson was just where he had left her. She did not look pleased. He hurried back to her side.

'What's the matter Miss Wilson?'

'Mathew, honey, where are we going and where is the car?'

Mathew realised that what he was about to explain over lunch would have some hard messages for the singer. He was a man who believed in straight talking. This was not something that came easily to him but he had learnt from experience that it was generally less painful in the long run. Dee Dee Wilson, 'B' list celebrity, was about to learn the lesson, that kick starting a stalled career required not only some creative reinvention but also an acceptance of just how far down the pecking order she now was. He could finance his plans but would need to budget carefully and the lesson started now.

'I thought we'd take a stroll to a famous old pub I know just along the road from here and grab a pie and a pint. It's an old coaching house,' he hurried on, 'cobbled courtyard, a bar where Charles Dickens is supposed to have written Little Dorrit and best of all,' he grinned,' they serve Green King. Its seventeenth century, very famous and I thought it might be an interesting place for an American to visit. Also, it'll be quiet at this time of the year and we can talk.' So saying he offered her his arm. There was an appreciable delay during which he thought he'd blown it and with relief he expelled the breath he had been holding as she placed her hand on his arm.

'Mathew, this had better be good.'

Her disapproval of the venue, the food and the drink was all too apparent from her demeanour and her monosyllabic responses to Mathew's attempts at conversation. It had been some time since he'd been to The George and even he had to admit that the service was poor and some areas of modernisation bumped up uncomfortably with the antique atmosphere. Still, he'd often wondered why, in all his dealings with Artists, they all assumed that only they had needs, feelings, talent and the God given right to temperament and arrogant self-expression. Miss Wilson might be surprised to learn that he played a mean jazz piano and had a temper that he had spent most of his professional life trying not to lose. 'I'm not doing very well am I?'

She looked at him, put a cigarette between her lips, lit it, inhaled, exhaled in his direction, picked a speck of tobacco from her bottom lip and said nothing. Mathew decided to go for broke but was stopped in his tracks.

'What do you do for a living Mathew?'

'I'm an A and R man,' he replied, puzzled.

'And what does an A and R man do Mathew?'

Sinclair could see the trap coming and decided to step into it in the hope that the proposal he nurtured might steer her away from such rigid role definition. 'Well, let me see. If we start at the beginning, an A and R man discovers new artists,' he beamed. 'Then there is arranging contracts, agreeing repertoires, finding songs, songwriters, overseeing recordings, promoting the single and marketing the album.'

'And how's that working with me?' Her sniff, accentuated by a raised eyebrow and the down turn of the corners of her mouth, suggested she felt he'd failed to deliver on the defined responsibilities.

'Well, I don't hear a single and I haven't heard enough material to form a view on an album,' he paused, shrugged, leant forward earnestly and hurried on in defiance of the glare prompted by his observation. 'Ok! Here's how I see it. One, you haven't got a band. Two, you've got a tour starting in four weeks. Three, the record company is promoting its backlist. Four, the tour promoter is less than impressed with having to deal with your temperament. Five, your material is not working for you. Six, Tamla doesn't sell tickets these days and seven, you are not Nina Simone. Stop imitating her!'

Dee Dee Wilson slowly, deliberately and viciously stubbed out her cigarette on the congealed crust of a lasagne that was similar in shape, colour and consistency to the adjacent ashtray. 'Call me a cab.'

'You want a cab, you call it, you pay for it. That's star treatment Miss Wilson,' he paused, dropped his head to his hands and ran his fingers desperately and anxiously though his hair. He then looked at her sadly and quietly said, 'you are no longer a Star. Which is the whole point of this conversation. Now I've got your attention let me tell you what you have got going for you, why I'm interested and how we can help each other.'

La Wilson smouldered but didn't move.

'You don't just have a good voice. You have a great voice. Although the cigarettes don't help. You have a way with you on stage that commands attention and a way with a lyric and phrasing that puts you up there with the greats. I've seen you hold an audience enthralled. With the right support, different venues, the right material, new arrangements and a lot of hard work I could move you out of the 'let's do the 60's' tour of provincial England into areas that could get you a grip on the international and world music market and the acclaim you deserve.'

'Just how do you propose to do that?'

'Jazz.'

'Jazz?'

'Yes Jazz. Standards from the great American songbook set to my arrangements with backing supplied by me on piano and some friends that I want you to meet later. A simple quartet to start. Piano, sax, guitar and drums.'

'You play piano?'

'I play very good piano.'

'Jazz piano?'

'Yes. My passion is Brubeck and Monk but here we're talking Shearing to your Peggy Lee.'

'It's been done.'

'Not with my arrangements it hasn't.'

'That's the past. For God's sake, these are dead people.'

'I think Mr Brubeck is alive and kicking but you're missing the point. These are timeless songs that live again with new arrangements. But, I agree, we do need new material for the record.'

'Record?'

'The album we're going to do together. The album with the single we'll write slap bang in the middle of it.'

'You write too?'

'Of course, But I was thinking more of us writing together.'

'Can we get another drink?'

'Of course,' he replied courteously. 'Thank you for listening Miss Wilson. I've thought about this a lot. Will you let me explain the rest of my proposal?'

'Honey, I can't wait, she replied with a heavy sarcasm. 'Oh! And you'd better call me Dee. Seems more appropriate to my new status,' she added ironically.

'Miss,' he spluttered into a smile, 'Dee, I mean Dee, I wasn't denigrating you or your career but I did have to get you to listen.'

'Mathew honey, drink first then let's hear the rest.'

He took the opportunity of the break to review his strategy and progress. She was interested. The next part of the pitch was crucial and, carelessly handled, could expose him for the schemer he was. His partner, David Williams, was something in the city. Mathew had never been quite sure what it was that he did other than it was very lucrative. They had been together for nearly five years and it had worked well. They had both been looking for stability and trust in a world that was traditionally characterised by transience and betrayal. Their love for each other was understated but obvious to their friends who marvelled at the change the relationship had brought to them both. David was wealthy beyond their needs and had, for some time, been trying to persuade Mathew to make more use of his talents and get out of a career that he didn't enjoy and which was going nowhere. David's original plan had been to promote his lover's talents. Mathew had been shrewd enough to know that good as he was, his talents alone weren't sufficient to carry a performing career. Long discussions between them had gradually evolved into a plan to promote and manage a talent that was either fresh or needing new impetus to which they could then hitch Mathew's musical and managerial ideas. David would handle the contractual and financial side of whatever they managed to put in place. Their first attempt had been with a boy band from Ilford. Both David and Mathew had been stunned at the level of greed and demand and total self-delusion that this mediocre and motley mob had brought to the deal. Their refusal to listen, their fascination with the tabloids and their never-ending arguments had ended with David writing off just over a quarter of a million pounds and Mathew reluctant to try again. Mathew had been worried that getting rid of the Ilford band would have involved them with solicitors and more expense but Williams had been very sure that this would not be the case and so it had proved. David was firmly of the view that the plan was good but they needed to work more on the selection criteria. It was Mathew, at work, who had stumbled over Dee. Her decision to come to the UK and the fact that she had talent but a career blighted by poor choices, attitude and reliability issues got her elected. Once she had been chosen the rest had been cynical manipulation. Cynical in the sense that Dee had to be moved to a position where their plan became the only viable option for her in an arena of diminishing opportunity but in a climate where her eventual best interests were also theirs.

It had not been too difficult to sow the seed of discontent in the band. Alienating her pianist and arranger from a regular supply of smack had strung him out sufficiently to make him susceptible to the odd comment about the comparative rates of pay. Arranging for Dee to stay in a good hotel and booking the pianist and the band into accommodation well below that standard added fuel and criticising his arrangements, ostensibly, on Dee's behalf, had finished the poor man off. The band had voted with their feet. Winding in second rate bands for audition had needed to be handled carefully in terms of the obvious comparison of his management skills to the standard of talent being supplied. Dee's truculence, however, had blinded her to their machinations.

'Try this.'

'What is it?'

'Spritzer. Half white wine half tonic water.'

'Ok. So! The plan is?'

'Well, it all hinges on my partner, David and a group of friends that I want you to meet tonight. I've arranged a get together at our place and David and I will explain the proposal and introduce you. These are friends who are hoping to tour with you.'

'This is a set up!'

Mathew was stunned. Not by her prescience but because he had underestimated this woman. If he denied it and failed to convince her, the game was very definitely over. He spent a few moments industriously stirring his gin and tonic with a plastic swizzle stick that had obviously been recycled because the logo on the top was indistinct from at least one spin through the dishwasher.

'Yes, it is. I've been planning it for some time.' He quickly looked away to hide his embarrassment and flushed cheeks.

'You been after me for some time, or would anybody have done?'

'Bit of both really but you are ideal for what I have in mind.'

'Well! How flattering. Where I come from they call that stalking.'

'I can see why you might think that but what have you got to lose? Think about it, I'm offering you a new chance, fresh ideas, a big opportunity and the chance to show the world a different you. Let me ask you, do you really want to be messing around with this crap for the rest of your life?' Mathew waved his hand in the general direction of the rehearsal rooms up the road.

'And what do you get out of this?'

'Oh! I get a lot and the more I get the more you get. I get a chance to be a part of something important and a chance to show what I can do with something that I care about very much. And, don't forget what I'm giving up. A reasonably well paid, if boring career, and the outside chance of failing and blowing David's money and our security. Do you understand the risks I am prepared to take now?'

She viewed him thoughtfully, 'I think so but what about my manager and the record company?'

'Bin 'em. What have they done for you recently? Apart, that is, from getting you involved in a tour as part of a three-ring circus the other two rings of which are occupied by clowns. You're better than that.' He didn't think it was quite the right moment to tell her that both her manager and the record company had been giving off signs for weeks that they would be relieved to see her move on. Dee looked at her watch.

'I'd better get back to the hotel and freshen up if we're meeting tonight.'

'I'm afraid that you're going to have to book out of that hotel. The record company won't continue to pick up the bill once they realise what we are planning.'

'They won't know immediately and I want to see what's on offer before I decide.'

'That's fair enough.'

Mathew and David had thought this through. Working to a budget wasn't the reason for getting Dee out of the hotel. The plan required her to work closely with Mathew for a period of intense rehearsal on the new arrangements. David was also of the view that they needed to find out quickly, given her attitude, whether a working relationship with her was at all possible. The way to find that out was to invite Dee to stay in their riverside loft.

'So where are we meeting and how do I get there?'

This part of the plan had been left for Mathew to deal with depending on how the rest of the discussion had progressed. He tossed the swizzle stick onto the lasagne and for the first time was totally honest with Dee. 'David is as important to the plan as I

54

am. Why don't I get him to come to your hotel, buy you an early dinner and then, if all is well, bring you on to the flat? It will give you two a chance to see whether you hit it off and him a chance to explain the financial and contractual proposals. If you turn up at the flat, I'll know you're up for it. If not, I'll start looking for another job anyway.' He smiled and held out his hand. She took it and returned his gentle squeeze.

'You know Mathew, this might just work.'

Dee was gratified that David Williams didn't seem to share Mathew's hang-ups about the expense of using cabs. On the way from the hotel to the apartment she reflected on their meeting. Williams had surprised Dee. To start with he was older than she had expected. She'd put him in his early fifties. Perhaps, knowing Mathew, she had preconceptions as to his likely choice of partner and, just perhaps, she had allowed herself to be influenced by gay stereotyping. Williams was a bear of a man. Dressed in a dark blue striped wool suit with highly polished oxfords a stiff collared shirt and a club tie, he looked like a banker. He was slightly overweight but could carry it although his face had started to take on the fleshiness of the well lunched but poorly exercised executive. He was softly spoken but with a rasp to his voice almost as though his vocal chords were damaged. Dinner had been a little tense to start and Williams had spent few moments on niceties. Once he had got down to business she had been impressed by his knowledge of her world. She was also impressed by his obvious commitment to Mathew to whom he constantly referred. She had learnt that they had met at a jazz club in Greenwich where they had both gone to see Stacey Kent. As dinner progressed she had realised that where Mathew had hit the headlines with his pitch and explanations, Williams had provided the detail and it was his command of the detail that had finally been the decider. The dinner lasted longer than she had expected and she worried that Mathew and his friends may think her discourteous. Explaining this to Williams she was surprised but relieved to hear that he had cancelled the arrangement. 'Tonight, was probably not the right time.' he explained.

Mathew opened the door to the flat. In her time Dee had known some fabulous houses and hadn't quite known what to expect when the cab deposited them in the narrow-cobbled street in Wapping. Warehouses on both sides towered above her and she noted the old loading bays and gantries at regular intervals at each floor level down the length of the building. David Williams had handed her through the front door to the apartment with a dramatic bow and sweep of his hand that suggested he was used to gasps of surprise and appreciation from visitors seeing the apartment for the first time. He had not been disappointed. Dee estimated that the open plan apartment was close to eighty-foot-long and some thirty-foot in width. The main features of the original structure had been maintained and that the apartment had been a warehouse was obvious. The vaulted brick ceiling had been cleaned and renovated and was supported at regular intervals by two rows of seven cast iron circular columns which, at their heads, butted under rolled steel joists running the length of the room at the springing point of each section of vaulted brickwork. Mild steel tie rods ran between the joists and supported brightly polished aluminium heating and ventilating ducts and a grid of spotlights. The longest side of the room was fully glazed in hardwood frames from floor to ceiling with the head of each frame shaped to fit the semi-circular profile of the brick vaulting. The night view across the river was stunning.

She was certain that there weren't many restaurants that could match the kitchen that ran the length of the wall to her right. In fact, that's what it was; a restaurant kitchen. A stainless-steel heaven for a serious cook. Letting her gaze drift across the stripped oak floor she considered the dining area which was dominated by the longest refectory table she had seen and concluded that food and entertainment were an important part of life in this apartment. Between two of the steel columns ran a bench with two work stations on either side, each complete with a PC and printer and there was a fax and another monitor on the end nearest to her that was scrolling what looked like market information. The farthest corner had three settees, a couple of chairs and some low tables while the longest internal wall was obscured by shelving filled with untidily stored books and magazines. Between the book shelves and the settees at the end of the room was a grand piano the top of which was littered with sheet music.

Dee turned to Williams, 'washroom?'

Williams pointed to the middle of the room and the cast iron spiral staircase to the floor above.

'Four bedrooms, WCs en suite.'

'WCs?'

'Toilet. Complete with bath, shower, and bidet.'

Her initial concerns about placing her career into the hands of two relative strangers began to ease as Mathew clattered down the stairs, bounded over and hugged her.

'Dee. You don't know how pleased I am to see you'.

Chapter Four

Denton eased his buttocks forward in an attempt to, at least temporarily, restore the circulation to his legs where it had been cut off by the unyielding front edge of the polished hardwood bench. He looked left and right down the length of the corridor before returning his gaze to the front and yet another mind numbing read of each item on the notice board. Give blood, support the Neighbourhood Watch, home security. He had supposed that notices exclusively for the eyes of police officers would be more exciting, details of courses on firearms perhaps, instruction on changes in legislation or information about the next issue of body armour. Apart from a poorly designed advertisement advising that PC T. Hughes (456) was anxious to sell his Vauxhall Astra, the board could have been one in any office.

In desperation, he turned again to the abandoned newspaper he had retrieved from a wicker waste basket earlier in his wait. He reflected briefly on the front-page story of the Liverpool football crowd standing in respectful silence in memory of little James Bulger, abducted and killed in their city, and wondered yet again at the violence abroad in the country. It amazed him that only a few hours previously he had chuckled at memories of 'Aitch' and his Army chums and their version of vigilante law. Denton suspected that his father had seen far worse sights than he had witnessed earlier that evening. Indeed, he knew he had, having been present at a drunken retelling, by an old Army colleague, of the retreat to Dunkirk, before 'Aitch' had shushed him into silence, "not in front of the boy!". He hadn't been sorry when his mum and dad moved from the prefab estate down to Birchington on the North Kent coast, having felt that his father's pride and independence were being threatened in his declining years by incomers to the estate who had different rules and values. Values that certainly didn't recognise the respect due to an old soldier and his mates. His mum had thrived in Birchington and he and 'Aitch' had joined the local sailing club, built a dinghy and attempted to race it before his dad announced that he'd watch from the bar. Long summer days had followed over the years, days of beach cricket, picnics and teaching the kids to sail a variety of boats with 'Aitch' taking them off to the crab pool whilst Denton was competing in sailing events. He dragged himself back to the present as, yet again, he realised he was taking refuge in the past.

He had been actively resisting the urge to look at his watch but now felt trapped into assessing just how long it had been since he'd made that decision. It was well over four hours since the murder and at least two hours since he'd been driven to the police station. It was now just past midnight. Denton acknowledged that he could be wrong but it certainly seemed like two hours that he, and other customers, had been kept at the Duke's head.

He'd been the first to reach the body. He had not hurried and was aware that the other customers were frozen into a tableau of stillness and silence. As he neared the corner of the bar by the door and eased around one of the late drinking "Gentlemen from Town", he noticed that the man was covered in white plaster dust from the hole in the ceiling. The Customer's jaw was working as he swallowed constantly in great gulps, dragging air and saliva down to block the upward rush of the contents of his stomach. Denton moved him away from the bar and the last resting place of unrecognisable parts of Detective Sergeant Michael Joseph McCarthy now splattered across the bar and up over the row of shattered optics. He reached down to the gentleman's briefcase tucked behind the foot rail, took the neatly folded raincoat laying across the top and used it to gently cover most of the remains of his friend Mickey. He straightened up to the sound of glass crunching underfoot.

'Stay there Ron. You really don't want to come any further.'

'You all right mate?'

'Get on the 'phone Ron. Three nines. Ambulance and Police.'

'S'covered mate. Margaret's doing it. What's the score? No chance, had he?' This with a nod towards Mickey.

'Never knew what hit him.'

'Fuckin' sawn off. That's what fuckin' hit 'im. One in the face and one in the ceiling to keep our fuckin' 'eads down while 'e scarpered. Classic blagging. Professional.'

More crunching and Denton turned to see Margaret peering from behind Ron.

'Oh Paul!' She wailed. 'God! This,' she paused, searching for words, 'this, this, this is my pub. Oh! What in God's name am I going to do?' She subsided into silence, covered her face with her hands and peered with wide eyes over the tops of her fingers.

Denton glared at Ron and viciously jerked his head towards the rear of the little pub. Taking the hint, Ron gently but firmly ushered Margaret down the bar. Gradually, sound returned. A sob, a question, a curse, small sounds of movement, the trundling of a bottle or glass rolling on the floor and then in the distance he heard the faint sound of sirens. The first policeman through the door had obviously decided that the perpetrators had left the scene as he barged in with no more than blue serge and silver buttons for protection. Visibly shaken by the sight at his feet he immediately took refuge in procedure and training and began to take names and addresses. It had seemed an age to Denton before any attempt had been made to impose order on the situation. Eventually an Inspector, having established that Denton had been the last to talk to Mickey before he was shot, had arranged for him and the Bulimias to be taken separately to the Police Station.

The interview had been courteous, considerate even, with offers of tea and cigarettes. The Officers apologised for having kept him waiting, explained that many people had to be spoken with and thanked him for his patience. Their questions had been straightforward as they had taken him through the evening and the events leading up to Mickey's murder. Once they had established that he hadn't seen the gunman, they seemed satisfied that there was little more that he could contribute as a witness. A uniformed Constable had been detailed to show him out. As they had moved into the corridor, Denton, sensitive to his loss ventured,

'Hell of a way to lose a chum!'

'Chum?'

'Yeah! The guy who was shot?'

'You mean he was Job?'

'Yeah, he was based here.'

'Was he? I didn't know him but then I've not been here long.'

Denton concluded that Mickey had not been quite the high-profile thief taker that he'd implied. As they moved along the corridor, he became aware of a posse of plainclothes in flying wedge formation striding purposefully towards them. The cutting edge of the wedge was a man whose weight problems were accentuated by his lack of height. Sweat, perhaps caused by the exertion of walking, had plastered his comb over to his brow but the misting of his steel framed lenses didn't mask the intensity of his bright-eyed scrutiny of Denton who'd pressed himself back against the wall to allow the group to pass and who then smiled sympathetically at the young PC pinned to the opposite wall. As they both turned again to the exit he was halted in mid stride.

'Mr Denton,' enquired bright eyes. Denton nodded.

'My name is Church. I'd like to talk to you if I may.'

Intuitively but, given the location, inexplicably, Denton asked, 'Are you a policeman?'

The sweaty little man ignored the question, 'we need to talk. Could you bear with me a few moments while we find our quarters and then I'll send someone down?'

That had been over an hour ago, reflected Denton, as he established that PC Hughes was asking an exorbitant sum for his very old Vauxhall Astra. He rose to his feet and jammed a fist into the small of his back, arching, stretching and turning as he heard leather soles clipping the hardwood tiled floor. He glanced to his right and saw Church bearing down on him. He was sure that he had come to collect him although the man was trying hard to give the impression that he wasn't, by studying a sheaf of notes as he walked.

'Ah! Mr Denton. Are we ready?'

'Have been for some time.'

Church ignored the sarcasm and smiled, 'good! Let's make a start, shall we?'

The room was small, about nine feet square, the wall opposite the door had a cast iron radiator running pretty much the full width against which leaned one of the heavy mob from the flying wedge in the corridor. The man nodded to him. The wall to the right was bare and that on the left equally so except for a borrowed light that ran the full length of the room just below ceiling height. All the walls were painted with a gloss coat of magnolia stained by nicotine through the full range of hues from sepia to kipper. In the centre of the room was a wooden table with a green leatherette surface and hardwood edging. On the table was an aluminium ashtray next to which was a packet of Benson & Hedges. Denton moved to the nearest chair, placed his hands on the back and rested his weight.

'Please, sit down Mr Denton.' Church moved around the table took the chair opposite, sat, grabbed the cigarettes, shook one loose, offered the packet to Denton and sat down.

Denton took the proffered cigarette.

'So! How well did you know the victim?'

'You're not a policeman.'

Church concentrated all his attention on searching his various pockets. Finally, triumphantly, he produced a cigarette lighter and flourished it. Denton lowered his head, ignored the offer and concentrated on his cigarette, which he carefully rolled between his thumb and forefinger gently testing the firmness and texture of the cylinder. The click of Church's lighter, a sigh and a blue cloud signalled craving resolved on the other side of the table.

He looked at Church who was holding the cigarette delicately in one hand while examining the fingernails of the other. Church raised his eyes and for an appreciable moment stared straight into Denton's. Feeling threatened by the scrutiny and the sense of power Church exuded, Denton snapped his cigarette in two; to break the stalemate and to make the point that there was no leverage in cigarettes as far as he was concerned.

'That's an odd statement.'

'And the answer is?'

'We'll come to that,' Church wiped the palm of his hand across a brow still beaded with sweat, 'I repeat, how well did you know McCarthy?'

Witnessing a violent and messy murder at close hand had been more of a shock than he had realised and Denton wasn't at all sure that he was capable of coherent thought. There was also something nagging away at him, perhaps something that Mickey had said or something here from his time in the police station.

Whatever it was, despite his state of shock, he was holding together sufficiently well to have realised that there was a lot more to all this than was immediately apparent. 'Shouldn't I have a Solicitor and shouldn't there be a tape recorder and shouldn't you be saying, "For the benefit of the tape Mr Denton looks tired, confused and more than a little pissed off"?'

Church chuckled, pushed his chair away from the table, grabbed the ashtray and went to lean against the radiator.

'You are not under arrest; as far as I know you are not a suspect.'

'So why am I here?'

'Because you knew Mickey. You drank with him. You might have some little bit of information that we need. Something that Mickey said or did which means nothing to you might be crucial to my enquiries.'

Denton sighed and slumped forward to rest his elbows on the table. He put his face in his hands and massaged his eyes with the tips of his fingers. He had no idea what this was about or where it was going but had resigned himself to the fact that the quickest way to get home was to cooperate with Church.

He paused before replying, considering the fact that Church, had gone from "The Victim" to "McCarthy" to "Mickey", suggesting that the dead detective was a little more than just a passing acquaintance. 'I met Mickey in the pub.'

'Did you approach him or the other way around?'

'I can't remember, I'd seen him in there a couple of times and we'd exchanged nods and then one night we got chatting. I think the Bulimia's were there. They might remember more.'

'Ah! Don and Ron. How often did you see Mickey?'

'Most evenings, some weekends.'

'What sort of time did you get in there?'

'Normally I'd get there about six and depending on the company and the crack could leave any time between eight thirty and eleven. Mickey would normally arrive soon after me.' Denton began to wonder how these simple questions were relevant but then supposed that they were preambles to put him at his ease. None of which removed the impression that he was being asked questions for which Church already had the answers.

'What about the Bulimias?'

'They normally got there soon after seven. They weren't too fond of Mickey and I think he knew that, so he'd sometimes finish his drink and go soon after they arrived. It happened that way tonight.'

'Why didn't they like him?'

'They didn't think he was kosher.'

Denton raised his head just in time to catch Church exchanging a look with the heavy on the radiator who'd raised his eyebrows in response

'How'd you mean?'

Denton realised that he had said more than he'd intended but now had no option but to provide some sort of explanation without damaging the Bulimias too much. 'They're Market Traders. They work the margins. Wheeling and dealing. You know the sort of thing. He made them feel uncomfortable.'

Church, appearing to accept this, made a note on one of the papers in front of him, shuffled them and clipped them together with a pink paperclip. For some reason the incongruity of a pink paperclip in this sweatbox of testosterone fuelled masculinity made Denton smile. A smile that brought some relief from the tension that had painfully locked down the muscles in his neck. Church missed the moment and looked up to ask.

'So, what did Mickey talk about?'

For the first time since the murder Denton realised a sense of loss. He'd liked Mickey. The man had been easy company and a born raconteur. They'd talked about anything and everything. There weren't many subjects that they hadn't discussed. A conversation could be prompted by anything from a headline in the Evening Standard to a passing comment from one of the regulars or in response to Margaret's constant queries about crossword clues. They had bounced ideas off each other and there had been times when Denton had beefed about work. Mickey had always listened patiently and sometimes offered good advice. Yes. He would miss Mickey.

'Did you talk about work?' Church prompted.

'Not often. The odd humorous story about someone he'd arrested but nothing much.'

'I meant your work.'

Denton raised both his arms above his head, locked his hands together, arched his back, stretched and slowly stood up. The thug eased himself from the radiator in readiness for Denton knew not what as he rotated his head on his shoulders to ease the muscles in his neck. Shoving both his hands deep in his jacket pockets he slowly paced the width of the room. He had looked forward to his evening encounters with Mickey. His spirits had lifted whenever he had seen the big genial Irishman barge his way through the doors of the Duke's and shout a greeting. There had been days when his spirits had needed lifting and Mickey seemed able to sense this. Those were the times when he had seen a different Mickey. The boisterous, flamboyant character had become quiet and considered: A listener, not an entertainer. It had been Mickey, breaking all the rules of pub lore, who had pointed out that he was drinking heavily and then gone on to dare to suggest that Stella might have a point. Yes, they had talked about his work. Denton's view had been that the pressures and problems with the business demanded that he took some time to unwind, relax and think things over in convivial company. Mickey had thought that the time might be better spent addressing some of the problems. That had caused their only argument. After a heated and very vocal discussion that had frightened Margaret, Mickey had finished his drink and left. Denton then hadn't seen him for a couple of weeks. When he'd eventually returned to the Duke's they'd embarrassed each other with their instant regrets and apologies. Denton's drinking had never been mentioned again but the problems at his firm, NMG, had become a recurring theme in their conversations with Denton's explanations of his frustrations, the problems he was having and the people involved. Yes, they had talked about work. It occurred to Denton that Mickey had probably known more about him and NMG and its operations than anybody else including Stella. Still, nagging away at him was the thought that just wouldn't crystallize. The sensation that something was not right, missing, hidden or so obvious that he simply wasn't seeing it. He needed time to think and he couldn't do that here. 'Work? Yes. But again, nothing much. The odd rant about VAT, staff not turning up. That sort of thing.'

'And what is work Mister Denton?'

Denton sat back down and took a deep breath while trying to decide where to start. In the end, he chose the end of the story. 'Well, actually, I don't work. I retired today. But when I did work I was Operations Manager for a company called Northern Mouldings Group.'

Church shrugged an invitation to continue.

'It used to be my company but I got an offer I couldn't refuse plus the offer of a job. Bit lower down the food chain but good money. I took the offer.'

'"An offer you couldn't refuse"? sounds ominous.' said Church, looking up with a puzzled frown from the papers he had again released from the pink paper clip.

'Not at all. It was just a good offer at the right time.' As he said it Denton wondered, for the first time, at his good fortune. The offer had been very good. Too good?

'What does this company do?'

He allowed his frustration to creep into his tone as he quoted from an old sales pitch in the sort of monotone that made a mockery of the original intent of the words. 'They import, assemble, finish and install prefabricated utilities units in hotels, universities, airports,' he stumbled to a halt, 'that sort of thing.'

'Utilities units?'

'Toilet and bathroom blocks. Look what's this got to do with Mickey?'

Church ignored him and glanced back at the papers on the table before looking up. 'So, who is in charge there now?'

'Well, I was in charge when they took over but a guy called Henfield was put in to run the show after the buy-out and I don't know who is going to replace me but Henfield will make the decision.'

Church turned a page and ran his finger down a list. 'Nothing else? That's it?'

Denton shook his head, Church crossed to the radiator, fished a battered leather attaché case from beneath it, returned to the table, undid the two leather straps, fiddled with the brass catch and fished out a plain white card on which he wrote a telephone number before packing his papers away. 'I'll be in touch but ring me if you think of anything else.'

Denton nodded, took the card and watched Church struggle with the brass catch, which had an intricate design etched onto its face, as he fumbled to close the case.

It was gone two o'clock when he found himself being directed through the police station car park to the exit on Kentish Way. With his mind still spinning he decided to walk the two miles home to clear his head. He set out at a brisk pace enjoying the feeling of freedom and the exercise for his stiff limbs. He wondered whether Stella had heard about the murder. He doubted it; she rarely watched television and often spent the evening with friends. He was sure that, had she heard, she would have eventually arrived at the police station. She was much more likely to have assumed that he was on a bender and gone to bed in disgust.

He strode down through the pedestrianised precinct that had once been Bromley High Street idly looking in shop windows as he went. Nearing the bottom, where the road was open to traffic, he crossed to the centre island and waited opposite a leather goods shop to let the late bus pass. He wasn't sure whether it was the chill of the night air that made him shiver or the realisation, prompted by the window display of briefcases, that Church was a Customs and Excise Officer. The inscription on Church's attaché case lock had been a portcullis: The insignia of Her Majesty's Customs. Denton had seen it enough on VAT documents to be annoyed with himself for not having recognised it earlier. If Church was in Customs and Excise what was his interest in the case of a murdered police officer? He set off again but this time at a pace that matched his slowly churning thoughts. Step by step he ran through the interview, now playing it against the background assumption that Church was a Customs Officer. Denton knew nothing about the lines of demarcation between the Police and Customs and Excise but he was aware that Customs exercised greater powers, particularly of search, over the public than the Police. He was, conversely, certain that murder investigations were well outside their jurisdiction.

So! Why was Church involved? Perhaps he knew Mickey? Denton stopped as the truth slammed into his consciousness and the nagging thought crystallised. Mickey McCarthy hadn't been a Policeman, he'd been a Customs Officer. If that thought stopped him in his tracks the next one forced him to sit down on the wall outside the DHSS building at Bromley South while he struggled to come to terms with the fact that he must have been under surveillance for months. Mickey hadn't worked at Bromley nick. Neither the officer who attended the scene nor the one who had started to show him out had known of him. Mickey had been interested in NMG. Maybe that's what had fuelled his concern over Denton's drinking. He stood to lose a reliable source of information if Denton'd slid down the drain on a wave of booze. His thoughts then turned to his first encounter with Church. Without introduction, he had greeted Denton by name. Denton had never seen him before. Church had also known about the Bulimias. He'd known that Denton was referring to Ron and Don. It was a nickname used only by the few in the

Duke's Head; those friendly enough with Ron and Don for them not to take offence at this jibe on their size. He realised that the Bulimias would have been interviewed but in the climate of an official interview, thought it unlikely that they would have introduced themselves as such. Church could only have got the nicknames from McCarthy. Then there was the question about Denton's work. Church had asked him about work and seemed to be referring to papers on the desk checking the detail he'd provided. He had known the answers! When he'd run his finger down a page at the mention of Henfield he'd found the name there.

Denton set off up Westmoreland Road trying to put his conclusions in order. Church was a Customs Officer and had information that he could only have got from Mickey. But what was their interest in Denton and NGM? The more Denton thought about his meetings with Mickey the firmer became his conviction that, while McCarthy had never obviously pumped him for information, NGM had been a planned and regular topic in their conversations. He was now convinced that McCarthy had been investigating NGM and nearly convinced that his murder was connected to that investigation.

What in hell could have been going on at NMG that, firstly, he hadn't noticed and secondly had drawn the attention of Customs? He decided that it wasn't financial. He knew the books were straight because he still signed off on the accounts as an Officer of the company. He also knew that Henfield was scrupulous about paying taxes and VAT on time. So, that wasn't what had got them noticed. He puffed his way dispiritedly up to Barnfield Wood Road and stopped to catch his breath. When it hit, he breathed out as sharply as if he he'd taken a blow to the stomach and a rising sense of panic swept over him. Mickey had told him the answer. Denton could hear the lilting brogue as the words ran though his mind: "Paul. There are serious Players out there prepared to go to any length to get more than they have and to keep what they've got. Nowadays that means drugs. Importing and selling.". The next thought turned the panic to fear. Whoever "they" were they were associated with NMG. Or at least Mickey & Church had thought so.

He continued down the road to Park Langley golf club and turning wearily into the drive of his house opposite was surprised to see the downstairs lights ablaze. The front door was savagely opened before he could get his key into the lock and a tearful and distraught Stella hissed at him. 'Julie's missing! Where the hell have you been?'

Chapter Five

Starmer was grateful that Julie appeared to be sulking in the back seat as they drove down the motorway to London. It gave him a chance to think. On balance, he thought that the plan to divert attention to London and then to skip from there to Scotland was a good one. As he couldn't think of one better he let that side of his predicament slip from his mind. Of more immediate concern was Julie's addiction. When he'd researched the subject after the incident with Leo he had done so thoroughly. He'd known that Julie was addicted to heroin but had racked his brains for sources of information that might help further.

Help had finally come in the unlikely shape of a footballing mad Jesuit Novitiate studying philosophy at the university. Andy had met him once or twice without realising either his calling or the fact that he regularly counselled students on drug abuse. Getting the Jesuit apart from his post match pint had been the hardest part. Once Andy had hesitantly explained what he wanted and hinted that this was for the inevitable "friend" he'd felt that he had the man's full attention. He suffered a lengthy explanation about drug abuse and the various substances that could be abused before deciding to come clean. He had then explained that he wanted to know how to help somebody get off heroin and he needed to know about the effect of the drug, how it was used and as much as he could learn about withdrawal. The Jesuit had urged him, or his "friend", to seek professional advice: not to go it alone. Witnessing Starmer's obvious exasperation, he gave a graphic account of the pain and anguish that both the addict and anybody helping would experience as well as practical advice for going cold turkey without professional help, concluding with the sobering warning that most attempts at cold turkey failed. Further urgings to seek qualified help and the offer of personal assistance that became more and more insistent prompted Andy to wonder whether the Jesuit knew of his friendship with Julie. He had, therefore, quickly ushered the man back into the bar. Shortly after that discussion Julie had disappeared.

So, he was under no illusions; his decision to get her free of drugs was going to be no walk in the park. What he had learnt was that it was possible to come off the drug but that the first few days were a nightmare of symptoms, cravings, mood swings and the need for twenty-four-hour support for the addict. He'd learnt that this should peak on the third day with things getting slowly better and the acute symptoms largely gone between the seventh and tenth days. The Jesuit had been emphatic though, that once off the drug and free of the withdrawal symptoms the addict still had a long way to go with dependency cravings likely to arise for up to nine months from initial withdrawal. This was called the Protracted Abstinence Syndrome, where the addict still experienced several symptoms and a craving for the drug. Whether the addict relapsed was, during that period, dependent on the sort of support they were getting and their exposure to old ways, places and acquaintances. He felt he'd got the answer to that. Being on the run from Woolley was going to keep them together and away from what one of his old, very Catholic, housemothers used to call "occasions of sin". What he needed to know in the short term was the level of dose and the frequency that Julie needed a fix. He had no idea how much of the stuff he had lifted from Woolley's office and he needed to know how long it could feed Julie's habit. He glanced in the mirror as she fidgeted on the back seat. Her scowl told him all he needed to know about her current frame of mind. He really couldn't be doing with any more arguments and realised that he needed to postpone any serious attempt at weaning her from the heroin until he had thrown off the chase. Sooner or later she was going to need a fix. He decided that he wouldn't tell her about the stuff he had taken from the safe. He'd make her wait. Leave her in the car and pretend to score on the street. Make her dependent upon him: Tough Love.

'Are you going to tell me what's going on?'

As he turned to look back at her he was just able to narrowly avoid being hit in the face by her knee as she clambered over into the front seat. She didn't look at him as she crossed her arms over her chest and vigorously massaged her shoulders. Continuously fidgeting so that no part of her body ever appeared to be still she went on to massage her thighs before running her fingers through her hair and scrubbing her scalp with her knuckles. She was sniffing continuously and occasionally wiped her nose with the back of her hand. The fingers of the left hand picked unceasingly at a sore on the knuckle of her left thumb until both hands returned to massaging her scalp. She'd lost a lot of weight since those happier times and in the clear, harsh, morning light, rather than the less than radiant illuminations of Slammers, she looked gaunt, unkempt and tawdry. And, Andy realized with alarm; she smelt. Not just the smell of the unwashed but the rank and acrid stench of the soiled and uncaring. His Julie had been obsessive about cleanliness, if possible changing clothes at the first sign of perspiration and damn near causing riots at the house because of the time she spent in the bathroom.

'I'm cold.'

Starmer spent some minutes fiddling with the unfamiliar heating controls while he considered what to tell her or rather what she needed to know just then. First, he needed to find out how much she remembered. He also desperately wanted to know how she had got to this pass and what the connection was to Woolley, Slammers and Thompson. Now was not, he realised, the time for that sort of discussion. Maybe if they got through the next few days or weeks and maybe, if he could get her off drugs, they would go there then. Not now.

'How much do you remember?'

She looked at him and then away quickly. He sensed her embarrassment and then knew that she at least was aware that he must have seen her on her knees in front of Thompson. He gently rested his hand on her right thigh. He was surprised at how quickly and strongly she took his hand and gripped it. He kept quiet. She threw his hand back into his lap, leant forward, turned the heater down, looked at him again then turned to stare out of the nearside window while clasping her shoulders and rocking gently back and forth in the seat. Withdrawal had started.

'You were with Thompson', Starmer prompted. Neutrally.

'Andy, have you got any idea what it's like to be addicted to heroin? No, I don't suppose you do.' she sneered, 'mister fuckin' perfect'. It's a treadmill. It's like,' she shrugged, hopelessly, defensively, massaged her scalp again, tossed her head and looked at him defiantly. She yawned, and wiped her runny nose on the sleeve pulled down over her hand before continuing, 'it's like living underwater and having to buy air when you want to breathe. You do what you have to do. Don't you think I have tried to get off it? Every day I wake up I mean to stop. I pick special dates in the future when I'll give up. My birthday, your birthday, Christmas or New Year. The most I've managed is three days. Andy those were the worst three days of my life. Then back underwater. Paying to breathe. You have no idea. Andy, I don't get a buzz from it anymore. Now I need it just to stay feeling half way fucking reasonable. I hate it. I hate myself. I hate what I've become. I'd do anything to get off it.'

He reached over and held her hand. This time she let him and gently squeezed a message of reconciliation. He was encouraged by what he had heard yet still struggled with exactly what to tell her about the events of last night. He took a deep breath, exhaled and noticed from a passing sign that they were seventy miles outside of London before he spoke.

'Julie, last night I killed Thompson.'

'I know, or at least I think I know,' she breathed quietly.

'I thought you were out of it,' said Starmer, incredulously.

'Not at the moment you went for him I wasn't.'

'Then you know we are in trouble. You know we're on the run from Woolley and his merry mob?'

'That's certainly the impression I got from this morning,' she said wryly. She looked at him thoughtfully, 'did you kill Thompson because of me?'

'Not really. I wanted to but I hadn't intended to. It was well,' he tried to gather his thoughts, 'you know I loved you.' He sighed, 'probably still do and well seeing him with you,' he glanced sideways at her, 'like that, well, I sort of lost it. I wanted to hurt him, hurt him badly, but not kill him.'

'What'll happen now?'

Starmer spent the next forty miles until they were on the outskirts of London explaining why he didn't think it would ever become a police issue but that Woolley would move heaven and earth to find them. He pointed out that if he was found it was unlikely that Woolley would leave any witnesses to his murder and that they were, therefore, in the same boat. When Julie asked where they were going and what plans he had he was strangely reticent. A part of him that he was beginning, now, to get used to cautioned him about telling her too much. That same part of him also began forming a plan to test just how much he could trust her. Any feelings from their old relationship, while still present on his side, may have been eroded in Julie by her addiction. 'You can't trust a junkie' he reasoned, and his life was on the line. He needed to know. He could, however, talk about the addiction.

'When will you need the next fix and how often do you need it a day?'

Julie hesitated and covered the moment by turning the car heater back up again. She shivered, clasped her hands and forced them between her thighs as she resumed the rocking motion.

'Like now?'

'How often a day?'

'Two or three times, sometimes more.'

'Ok, in about an hour I'm going to drop you somewhere while I dump the car. I'll be gone about another hour and I'll bring some stuff back to you. While I'm away you are to stay where I leave you. Don't talk to anyone, don't 'phone anyone but most of all don't move from where I leave you. Do you understand?'

'Where would you get horse?' She enquired with a slightly incredulous tone in her voice that suggested a sudden rethink of her 'Mister Perfect' tag.

'It doesn't matter, I'll get it. Trust me.'

Almost exactly 60 minutes later he pulled up in a public car park opposite and just past the Maritime Museum in Greenwich. He removed his rucksack from the car and gently, guiding a, by now, visibly shaking Julie they made their way down Trafalgar Road. They came to a small café that offered 'All day brekfast' carefully painted in near perfect copperplate on the window. He sat her down, ordered the coffee and toast she asked for, pressed a twenty into her hand and reminded her of his instructions. He reassured her that he would be back with the drugs and to collect her in no more than an hour.

He walked past a 'phone box which he used to conceal crossing the road, moved down the other side until he was nearly out of sight of the café and turned into the 'The Victoria'. A public house that looked as though it had last received a coat of paint at the beginning of the reign of that great queen. The barmaid approached, all lipstick and lurex, parchment skin and cleavage weary and wrinkled from weight and too many hours on a sun bed. Her face muscles worked hard against layers of make up to produce the semblance of smile that didn't extend to world weary eyes but did reveal gums in retreat from nicotine stained teeth. He ordered a pint and a cheese roll, which was retrieved from a small plastic greenhouse on the bar, the heat from which had at least softened the cheese while giving it a fine coat of perspiration. He found a stool at the corner of the bar from where he had a clear view of the telephone box and the cafe beyond. He ignored the distraction of a group of middle aged men playing pool near the other end of the bar although he did notice that all had bare arms, tattoos, bellies that smothered belt buckles and shaved heads that glistened through stubble under the table lights. Their language was loud, foul and littered with racist references. So much so that Starmer took a second look. He'd half turned back when the comment came.

'What the fuck you lookin' at?'

Starmer turned back, smiled disarmingly and pointed to the clock on the wall behind the man. He was a large man with a scarred face and some spectacular disfigurement around his cheekbone and eye socket.

'Meeting someone. Just checking my watch is right.'

This was greeted with a look of total incomprehension, a swagger, an injunction to watch his step and brief looks at the rest of the gang to ensure that they had noticed territory had been marked. Starmer smiled again, apologised and returned to his surveillance.

With half an hour to go he had begun to think that his suspicions were ill founded when he saw Julie leave the café and enter the 'phone box. Ten minutes later she went back towards the café. He finished his pint, navigated his way through the pool crowd to the toilet, apologising all the way, and locked himself in a cubicle while he went through the contents of the rucksack. The next part of the plan would need money. The crisp new cellophaned notes from the safe would need a bit of thinking about before he could use them. He checked the till bags from last night and found that they contained about three thousand odd pounds. He retrieved one of the packets of heroin and the drug paraphernalia, put it in his pocket then buried the rest of the packets at the bottom of the bag.

Julie leapt from her seat by the window as he walked through the door of the café and pushed him back out and onto the pavement.

'Did you get it?'

'Yup!'

'Give it to me quickly.'

'Hang on a minute Julie you can't fix up in the middle of the street.'

'Andy this is not like a bad case of PMT, c'mon!'

One look at her told him that she was desperate enough to try. She was shivering uncontrollably. Her desperation gripped him as he handed her the gear and before he had really thought it through he was ushering her through the doors of The Victoria.

'Fuck me. The clock watchers back.'

Starmer chuckled heartily and probably too long, pointed Julie in the direction of the Ladies and pulled her back by the arm before she could move.

'Julie, be careful. Don't overdo this. Just enough to kill the chill. We've got to walk out of here. You listening?' He hissed.

He watched her run the gauntlet of undressing eyes until she reached the safety of the toilet. He turned to order at the bar then noticed that the barmaid was leaning against the wall on the other side of the pool table smoking a cigarette and studiously ignoring him. Two of the players had gone into a huddle in front of her, which had drawn the attention of the group comedian who joined them for a lengthy discussion while throwing frequent glances at Starmer over his shoulder. Starmer was painfully aware that he and Julie were the subject of the whispered discussion. Three men turned towards him and he could just see the barmaid peering aggressively over their shoulders. Their reasons became clear as the harridan hissed 'Junkie'.

Julie emerged from the toilet and Starmer's heart stopped. If the men had suspicions before she went in there would be no doubt in their minds when they turned to see her now. The comedian, Starmer reasoned, was the likely flash point. He wasn't tolerated for his jokes. It was his size that kept his audience laughing nervously and that bulk was now advancing towards Julie. A Julie that was clearly spaced out.

'Fuckin' 'ell 'Chelle! You're right. She's been shooting up in your bog. What the fuck you think you're playing at?' This salivered at full volume inches from Julie's face complete with the self-righteous indignation and ignorance that only the closed mind of a true National Front supporter can muster in the face of the unusual, the different or the vulnerable. The comedian grabbed Julie's arm and propelled her around the pool table towards

Starmer shoving her into his arms. He gently caught her and propped her against the bar. He now knew this prat was going to kick off and reluctantly prepared. The rucksack had to be secured. He lifted it and threaded both arms through the straps took Julie's arm and headed for the door.

'Oi! Where the fuck d'yer think you're goin'?'

Starmer propped Julie back against the bar turned and looked at the comedian again. A fresh look. An assessment. He was big. Too bloody big. Clued up as well. He'd stopped four feet away; giving himself time and space. But that, he thought, works both ways: If you can see your opponent's feet with your peripheral vision you get a split seconds warning of the move. Starmer reasoned that about the only thing he had going for him were the scars and the damaged eye socket. This guy had been caught before and more than once.

'You're not leaving! What you got in that rucksack?'

He held his arms away from his side; palms outward cocked his head to one side and said, 'please leave it. I don't want any trouble.'

'Don't hold yer breath sweetie. You've got trouble'.

From somewhere behind the comediancame a throaty, smoky female chuckle. For the first time in long seconds the comedianmoved. Not a lot. A slight turn of the head and a twitch at the corner of his lips. Playing to the gallery. Starmer placed one hand on his hip, arched an eyebrow and lisped. 'Well, that's not very nice big-boy. I thought you liked me.'

Right on cue Chelle snorted a throaty chuckle of hastily suppressed amusement and the comedianturned to snarl reproof. He'd realised his mistake and did his best. Too late. Starmer had moved. As the Comedian turned back he desperately launched a roundhouse right that lost all point and power as Starmer stepped under it and to his side and powered his right heel into and through the side of the comedian's right patella giving him a split second to realise that he was standing on one unbroken leg before a right elbow smashed oblivion through his temple.

Starmer grabbed Julie and rushed for the door banking on useful seconds of shock freezing the other two players before they realised that he was outnumbered and that they had pool cues in their hands. They'd run no more than a couple of hundred yards with Starmer dragging Julie behind him before he realised that unless he carried her they weren't going to get much further. He urged her around a corner into a narrow street of terraced houses and glancing back behind him cannoned straight into an elderly man half way across the pavement carrying a cardboard box full of paperbacks. He apologised and steadied the man and his burden. They'd just passed an old Sierra with the boot open and he was frantically assessing how far they would have to go before they were out of sight of the main road when it struck him; the engine on the Sierra was running. He turned in time to see the man making his way back up the garden path, presumably for another tray of books. Getting Julie into the car had been the easy bit, stealing the old man's car had been very difficult for him and he resolved to leave it somewhere safe and relatively local. At some point, he had to break the trail between him, Greenwich, where he'd left the BMW and his destination. Stealing the old man's car could be connected. The sooner they hit public transport the better.

A Thames river boat to Charing Cross and the Tube to Caledonian Road would buy them time and distance and a break in the trail. Starmer had assuaged his conscience by stuffing two hundred pounds on the carpet in the boot of the old man's car before parking it with two wheels on the pavement outside Greenwich railway station where it would cause the most obstruction.

He was grateful that Julie dozed for most of the short journey. It gave him a chance to review the next part of his plan. Time was now of the essence. It was past one o'clock and he was aiming for Market Road in Islington, famous for its unofficial market for second hand VW camper vans. Depending on the time of the year, there were often several Antipodeans anxious to sell on their vans to either fund the next leg of their journey or to get the cash for the air fare home. If he could buy a half way reasonable one for cash he'd have an untraceable vehicle, accommodation, independence and privacy while they made their way to Scotland.

They turned left out of the station and right into Market Road. There, down towards the end, on the left, were three VW vans. As they approached they could hear a vigorous football match in progress on the Astroturf pitches adjacent. He briefly reflected on the sound and fury of the game and wondered if there was any activity, these days, that wasn't littered with profanity. Of the three vans, one was an obvious winner. Sitting alongside it, jammed into an aluminium framed, canvas slung picnic chair, was a red headed, big boned, fresh faced and freckled young man wearing chinos and a University of Western Australia hooded sweat shirt. As Starmer greeted him he rose out of the chair, which lifted slightly with him, until he levered it from his backside by pushing down on the arms.

'Good day. You interested in the van?'

'Could be,' he replied, shaking the offered hand. 'Depends how much you're asking.'

'Oh man, it's a steal at seven grand.'

'Yeah! It would be at that price. More like daylight bloody robbery,' grinned Starmer.

'Hey! Come on man. You are looking at a classic '63 two tone split screen. Interior superbly restored, twin gas hob, grill, sink with running water, full width bed, demountable dining table, awning and a pop up roof. It'd be an investment. Come on man you and the lady could be really happy in this.' He grinned again this time in a nudge, nudge way with a wink in Julie's direction. Starmer couldn't help smiling at the look of total disdain on Julie's face.

He got into the van and had to agree that it was as described and in good condition. It was also exactly what he had in mind. The Australian showed him copies of receipts to confirm his claims that a new starter motor, brakes and battery had been fitted and a brief tour around the neighbourhood revealed nothing wrong with the engine or at least nothing wrong that he could find. They haggled about the price during the drive with the Australian claiming poverty and potential enforced separation from his loved ones if he didn't meet him half way. The bargain was eventually struck when he offered six grand cash there and then to drive it away. The fact that the Aussie didn't hesitate for longer than it took to offer his hand made Starmer wonder whether he'd been had. By the time the Aussie had cleared out his bits and pieces, counted the cash and he'd loaded Julie and the rucksack on board they had spent less than an hour on the deal.

Two hours later, having stopped at an army surplus store to buy sleeping bags, clothes, camping gas and loaded up with more tinned food than was commensurate with his normally strict dietary regime, they headed up the A1 and, by nine o'clock were on the outskirts of Newark on Trent. He was so tired by then that he turned right onto the A17 in the hopes of finding a lay-by to park for the night when he saw a sign for a camping park in the village of Stragglethorpe.

After a meal, at which Julie only picked, of baked beans, egg and bacon, during the cooking of which they discovered that only one of the twinned hobs worked, Julie asked for another fix. Counting the one she had had in a service station on their way north this would be the third that day. He fished out another packet from the rucksack and gave it to her. He watched with feelings moving between disgust and dismay as she added lemon juice to the drug in the spoon, warmed it with a cigarette lighter and drew the liquid into the syringe. She placed the syringe to one side as she shucked down her trousers and opened her legs to expose a mottled and bruised area of inner thigh. She pierced the skin with the needle, drew a little blood into the syringe and then smoothly pressed the plunger all the way home. She had barely pulled her trousers back up before the drug began to take effect.

He woke from a deep sleep the next morning to find that she had gone. As had his rucksack. He struggled from the sleeping bag and sat on the edge of bed with his head in his hands. He despaired. How in God's name could she do this to him? For Christ's sake, he'd killed, broken bones, stolen cars and money all because of his feelings and the deep need that he felt to protect her. Now he was stuffed. Thirty quid in his pocket a thirty-year old van of uncertain reliability, short on petrol, and stuck in the middle of nowhere with the Manchester mafia after him. Despair gave way to anger and then determination. If that's the way it was then so be it. He could move faster on his own anyway and he wouldn't have to worry about her or her habit. He hadn't told her where they were going or why and there was therefore no reason why he shouldn't continue on his way. He could lie low for a bit in Scotland and then join the bloody Foreign Legion or something. None of these attempts at cheering himself up or looking for the positive elements in his dire situation dulled the deep sense of betrayal that he felt at her departure.

He was startled from his reverie by the side door of the van clanging open to reveal Julie dressed in the new clothes they had brought with hair still wet from a shower.

'Morning sleepy head.'

'Julie, where the hell have you been?' He shouted.

'For a shower?' She said with the inflexion rising at the end of the sentence to turn it into a question. 'Did you think I didn't know I was dirty? I'd have gone last night if the damn shower block had been open.'

'Why did you take the rucksack?' He growled suspiciously. She looked at him quizzically for appreciable moments before she climbed into the van, dumped the rucksack in his lap and answered, 'because you were asleep and I couldn't work out how to lock the van and I didn't want to take the chance of it being stolen. Particularly after I'd seen what was inside. Oh! And I was looking for the drugs. We need to talk.'

While she had been talking, he had opened the bag to find the remaining drug sachets sitting on top of the clothes she had removed in the shower block.

'Yes, that's what we need to talk about. I've worked out that if that's all you've got there is three days' supply. Andy, when I said that I wanted to get off drugs I was serious. I want to try. For the first time, in a long while, I feel hopeful. I know we're in a lot of trouble and I know that you're only in that trouble because of me. I couldn't get off the stuff on my own but I think I might manage it with your help. You say you love me and I believe you do. I'm not sure what I feel for you now and I realise that might not be enough for you but it's best to be honest. I know that when my system is in balance I trust and value you as a friend. The best friend I have ever had. I'm attracted to you and very fond of you but doubt that my feelings are as strong as yours. I don't think junkies do love. I don't see how they can. So, I want to come off the stuff and give myself a chance at love with you.' She paused and took a deep breath, 'no! Don't interrupt for a minute, I've not finished. I know it sounds like a copout but I want to get a fix just before we leave. Then I am going to try to cut out one fix today. If I can do the same the following day and the day after we'll have used all the stuff you have in that bag. Hopefully we'll be settled somewhere by then and that's when I want to go cold turkey. Will you help me?'

Overcome with relief, Starmer reached out for her and she snuggled into him with her wet hair pressed against his cheek. He gently stroked the back of her neck, released her, raised her head and kissed her gently on the lips.

'Ok! Let's get underway. I'll explain as I go.'

'You didn't answer me.'

'You didn't need to ask.'

This time Julie reached for him. She put both her arms around his neck and held him for a long time before letting go. 'Will you be able to forget Thompson, y'know, the other night?'

'You were buying air to breathe. Right. That's all it was. It's different now and it didn't mean anything,' he lied.

It was while he was folding away the bed and boiling a kettle for some tea that he remembered the 'phone call.

'Julie, yesterday, when I left you in the café you went to make a 'phone call. Who did you call?'

She looked at him eyes brimming with tears, 'I called home. I wanted to talk to my Dad, tell him I was alright. He wasn't there. Mum answered the 'phone. I hung up. Then I realised that she might get a message to him so I rang back.'

'Why did you hang up on your mum?'

'It's a long story and I will tell you but not now.'

'Julie is that the truth?'

'Andy, I left you because I couldn't, wouldn't lie to you.' She stuttered grimly.

By the time, they reached Morpeth he'd begun to question the wisdom of buying the van. Convenient it may be but speedy it wasn't. A gradient of anything slightly more than horizontal saw the speed bleeding off progressively and much shouting and waving of fists from lorry drivers when they eventually passed. Julie had been quiet for most of the journey, seeming to sense that he'd wanted to think. After a brief stop for breakfast she had joined him in the front of the VW. 'So! What's the plan?'

'Such as it is, I'm aiming for a place called Findhorn. It's a sort of new age settlement that's been there for years. I've got a friend lives there.' Out of the corner of his eye he saw Julie pull a face.

'New age?'

'Well, it's a lot more than that really. I suspect that's how it started but now it's an internationally recognised centre for meditation and spiritual retreat. It's got an ecovillage; homes made of straw and grass roofs. They do courses there and everything. It's a really interesting place.'

'Who's the friend?'

'A guy called Jamie. He did one of their community programmes and stayed on.'

'You never mentioned him to me. Where do you know him from?'

There was a long pause and a sigh before he replied. 'We were in a home together and I sort of looked out for him. I stayed with him a few weeks before I started Uni. I was having second thoughts. Wasn't sure I'd fit after the Army. Cold feet. He helped. Listened.'

'How do you mean you looked out for him, was he bullied?'

'Yeah, sort of.'

Andy left it there as distant memories of very bad times drifted through his mind. She'd either work it out or not. If she did work it out she'd either ask, or not.

'You mean he was abused?' She looked over at him and studied his face. Looking for a reaction. 'Were you abused?'

He pulled over to the side of the road, stopped, rested his forearms on the wheel, gripped it hard and rested his head on the back of his hands. Only he and Jamie knew the full story and he wasn't sure that he wanted to tell anybody else. He felt her arm go around his shoulders and her breath on his face.

'You don't have to tell me Andy. I shouldn't have asked.' She whispered.

He took a deep breath. 'Some of the kids from the home went on a sort of outward bound course at a place up near Fort William: sailing, climbing, canoeing that sort of thing. I'd been there a few times before. I loved the sailing. It's nice up there. I thought you and I might head over that way. It's well off the beaten track and in this van, we wouldn't look out of place among all the other outdoor types up there. Anyway, Jamie and I were in the group. The guy in charge was a filthy shit called Randall. Middle aged, scruffy little bastard with halitosis and piggy eyes. All the kids knew he was a nonce. I found out afterwards that he'd been at Jamie for months. Jamie was a beautiful boy. Small, curls, gentle, kind, vulnerable and seven stone, dripping wet. Anyway, about midweek Jamie disappeared. He was gone for the best part of two days. When he came back he was in a terrible state. Poor little sod could barely stand let alone walk and Randall never let him out of his sight. Jamie was terrified. Eventually I got him out of the way and got him to talk. Randall and some of his nonce mates had been with him. They'd had a party.' Starmer felt a sense of despairing bitterness at the recollection and he glanced at Julie to see whether she needed further clarification. He paused, pushed himself off the steering wheel and looked again at Julie with moist eyes. He wasn't sure quite what he expected to see. Sorrow, understanding perhaps? That was there but he was surprised how heavily anger was also written onto her face.

'What did you do?'

'What makes you think I did anything?'

This time Julie leant back and looked at him with one eyebrow raised quizzically. 'Because I know you and if I've learnt nothing else in the last two days I've learnt that when you decide to look after someone there are no limits to what you will do.'

Andy nodded. 'You asked if I was abused. I wasn't. But Randall had tried it on. If he could have had me, it would have been the icing on his little holiday cake. I spent the next day getting close to him. Sending out the signals. He bit.'

That evening I'd suggested we go sailing. He liked sailing, in fact it was him who'd taught me. It was a nice but cold evening with a fresh wind from the west and we had to beat upwind to go towards the end of Loch Eil. I had the helm and I tacked at regular intervals shouting 'lee oh!' every time until we got into a rhythm. When we got far enough away from the Centre, dots in the distance, I tacked again. As he took his feet out from the toe straps and moved towards the middle of the boat I reversed the tack and sheeted in hard. He was caught off balance and went over the side. I luffed up about twenty yards from him and sat there. At first, he thought it was an accident and he was laughing. He started to swim towards me and I sheeted in a bit and moved away. Luffed up again and sat there, saying nothing. He began to realise he'd got a problem with me so he made for the shore. But it was a long way and the cold was getting to him. Towards the end, he was begging. Crying.' He paused, 'just like Jamie had. I sat there and said nothing. I didn't want him to die with the satisfaction of an answer. The water's never warm in Scotland and it was a chilly evening. He lasted about thirty minutes. Longer than I'd thought possible. When he'd gone, I capsized the boat and sat on the hull until they came looking from the centre.'

'How old were you?'

'Sixteen.'

'Christ Andy and nobody suspected?'

'One of his noncy mates did. I just told him to go to the Police, 'cos I had a very interesting story to tell and that if he ever went near Jamie again I'd kill him. He believed me,' Starmer said simply.

'And that was that?'

'Well there were some questions as to why he wasn't wearing a life jacket. He was a very safety conscious man.'

'Why wasn't he?'

Starmer looked sideways at Julie and grinned. 'Because when he got in the boat and started to put it on I said we didn't need them and they would only get in the way. His little piggy eyes lit up. I told the police that he'd it on when he went into the water but that it hadn't been buckled and it must have come off as he went under. In fact, I tossed it into the water after he'd drowned.'

'You killed him!'

'In a way. The post mortem revealed he'd had a heart attack. Which was handy.' He stared grimly and vacantly through the windscreen at the middle distance. 'It had to be done,' he finally announced.

There was a protracted silence while they both considered their new knowledge of each other. Both took comfort from each other's strengths while appreciating the weaknesses.

'Jamie was left alone after that?'

'He was moved on to another place and I was sent to the Junior Leader Regiment at Bovington. We kept in touch and I'm pretty certain he was left alone there but, yeah, the damage had been done. He was very badly traumatised and now he's getting there but he's different. You'll see what I mean when you meet him. He lacks confidence and he can't sustain a relationship. I think I'm the only person he's trusted in his life and I'm hoping that at Findhorn he's found a kind of peace with people who will appreciate him for what he is without questioning why he's that way. Maybe, one day, he'll find someone that will understand and be patient. That's what he needs.'

Not for the first-time Julie wondered at the character of a man that could comfortably move from violence with no limits to the sort of caring and sensitivity that Starmer had just demonstrated.

They pulled into Findhorn late in the afternoon. Starmer disappeared to find Jamie. On his return, he introduced a small shy man, half of whose body was shielded behind him, as though Jamie were seeking refuge or shelter there. Julie offered her hand and the man, a little reluctantly, took it. As they shook hands he timidly averted his gaze but smiled.

'Hello Jamie. Andy tells me you're his only friend. Well, I'm another. Let's compare notes'. So saying she put her arm around his shoulders, squeezed him and walked him off in the direction from which he'd come.

Starmer smiled as Jamie looked back and grinned at him with pleasure.

Chapter Six

Dee was surprised at Mathew Sinclair's approach to their new partnership. She had expected a degree of urgency. Their first morning together in the apartment on Wapping Wall started quietly with Mathew suggesting that they spend some time talking and planning how they were going to work together and, more specifically, what they would be doing. Dee supposed that he'd adopted this strategy to put her at her ease and was mildly surprised to note that it had the opposite effect on her. The hard talk about her career, a few nights back, had hit home and she was anxious to make a start and prove that her talent, while perhaps mismanaged and ill-used, was a least as good as Mathew's expectations. She was also aware that there was a mountain to climb and very little time in which to do it. Williams, she knew, was negotiating new tour venues specific to the changes in her style and the material that they had loosely discussed. She also knew that Williams was talking with a Public Relations company about promoting that new image and there had already been some discussion about publicity appearances on TV and radio shows. It seemed to Dee that they were making promises that they were a long way from being able to deliver unless they moved fast.

She lay back on the settee and stared moodily out across the river. The day was cold, even for January, overcast and squally with gusts of wind throwing rain and sleet against the windows with the sound of birdshot rattling on tin. Somewhere mast halyards were beating rhythmically against their staffs and snapping against their fixings. She watched a Police launch make slow progress upwind and against the tide with the bow occasionally disappearing beneath sheets of spray. A day to stay inside. A day to work.

'Ok Mathew, let's make a start.'

There was a rattle of plates, a crash, a muffled curse and the sound of footsteps behind her as Mathew hove into view carrying a plate of buttered toast. 'Elevenses. Comfort food.'

'Elevenses?'

'Food that you have in the morning at about eleven? Brunch?' He said passing a side plate and offering the toast.

'Mathew, I don't want to eat I want to work.'

Sinclair looked at her a little taken aback. He then placed a piece of toast on a plate and handed it to her. She took it grudgingly. 'Eat', he smiled, 'we can talk while we eat. The thing is', he mumbled through a mouthful of toast, 'we need to get to know each other. Oh, I know your discography and a little bit about your life but I don't really know you. We're going to be spending a lot of time together working, hopefully creatively and that won't work if we're strangers. It's not one-way either. You need to know a little bit about me. More importantly you need to know what I can do. I've told you I play piano and write songs but you have no proof. You should have made me audition. Perhaps you're too polite to ask?' He grinned.

Dee laughed. 'Yeah! Right!'

'No! I'm serious. I need to show you what I can do because you need to have confidence in my ability if we're to get this show on the road. So, this morning I thought we'd sit and chat about life, love and the universe, then I'll take you to lunch and this afternoon you're invited to a concert. Then we'll see what happens.'

'Will lunch be better today than it was in The George?' she goaded.

'No much worse. We're going to a dump down the road: The Prospect of Whitby.'

The rest of the morning's conversation must have had some effect because they walked to the pub with linked arms. Dee had begun to feel comfortable with this sensitive man and found herself warming to him. She enjoyed his old-fashioned courtesy, his thoughtfulness and his ability to put her at her ease with a stream of consciousness chatter that she found amusing, informative and interesting. She began to relax and as she did so was surprised at how much she opened up to this chatterer who was also a consummate listener.

She loved the pub. The barrels built into the bar, the flagstone floor, the old masts used as ceiling supports and the polished, hammered pewter top to the bar. She even enjoyed her half pint of 'Old Speckled Hen'. She had been enthralled to learn that both Samuel Pepys and Charles Dickens had supped their ale here but slightly alarmed when Mathew suggested they try the whitebait, neither understanding nor recognising the dish from his description. She was pleasantly surprised and enjoyed the meal and Mathew's running commentary on the view across the river. Over coffee the conversation drifted back to music. He spoke quietly and informatively about his favourite artists. He preferred jazz piano and she was not surprised by his knowledge and enthusiasm and shared his appreciation for many of his chosen performers. Both liked Bill Evans, Monk and Brubeck, agreed to differ about Peterson and shared a love for Ella Fitzgerald. Dee agreed to listen to some Marion McPartland and he agreed to get an Anita O'Day and a Patricia Barber CD. They argued about the greatest singers and settled on Sinatra for voice and phrasing, Nat King Cole for his unique vocal style and Mel Tomé as a singer, arranger and songwriter. Dee felt she had to adjust the gender balance and tossed in Peggy Lee. Neither mentioned Nina Simone. The couple that walked back to the apartment were relaxed and Dee was looking forward to her 'concert'.

Mathew played for over an hour and she sat entranced. He started with a classical piece that she recognised but couldn't name. He played this with his eyes closed; gently swaying back and forth on the stool almost as if leaning in increased his concentration on the piece while leaning back allowed a moment to reflect on the beauty of the music. She was enthralled. He came to the end of the work and theatrically keyed the last note with a flourish of his hand. She applauded. If he noticed it wasn't apparent as, with eyes closed, he continued to play.

She recognised Brubeck's 'Blue rondo a la Turk,' Shearing's 'Lullaby of Birdland', Gershwin's 'Rhapsody in blue' and Strayhorn's 'Take the A train'. The following medley melded one jazz classic into another with a series of improvisations and sheer virtuosity that set her pulse racing. This time he noticed when she applauded and clasped his hands together and raised them over his head like a boxer celebrating a knockout. 'Mathew that was superb.'

He brushed his nails against his lapel, raised them to his lips, blew on them and then re-polished them in the universal sign of self-appreciation. 'Not bad for self-taught eh! Hey, but all I've really done is prove that I know which keys are which and roughly where the pedals are. We've got to talk yet about arranging and writing. That's where I'll earn my corn. That's the key. Have you ever written anything?'

'Yes, but nothing that'd I want you to hear.'

'C'mon Dee with your talent and experience you must have thought about it.'

She looked across at him, into his earnest and magnified eyes, and thought back to the few bars and a refrain that still haunted her. The bad days. Days he couldn't possibly imagine. Days when she had closed herself off from the world, blurred day into night and life close to death. When she closed her eyes, she could still recall the smells. That of her unwashed body, the cheap scent to cover it and the acrid taste and smell of vomit. She remembered the stench of food rotting in a fridge, because she hadn't paid the utility bill, overlaid with the ever-present stink from a three pack a day cigarette habit. Most of all she recalled the humiliation. Wearing clothes too big for her shrunken and undernourished body and selling prized possessions to a Korean pawnbroker whose cynicism was matched only by his opportunism with his persistent attempts to buy the one thing she wouldn't sell. Neither, would she ever forget the desperation of those days and the attempts that she had made to earn a little money. The agony of being billed under her own name as a star of the sixties in a roadside bar where she eventually realised that she and her fall from grace, not her performance, was the entertainment. It had kept her afloat for a few weeks until the owner had decided that the waning drawing power of her humiliation could be increased if she sang topless.

The good time friends that disappeared with the money and the 'phone that didn't and then couldn't ring because it was disconnected. And the occasional kindness: the piano player from the bar who had given her a lift home the night she walked out and stuffed fifty dollars into her hand as she got out of the car. Most of all she remembered the refrain that came into her head every time she fixed up. Initially a chant uttered tunelessly to the rhythm of the ritual, then a melody as the hit took hold, and on into a song that would take her back to where she wanted to be as the drug carried her to where it didn't matter anymore. The words had become a prayer that sustained her with the promise of better days. Words that had returned to her as she came down and words that fuelled her determination to quit until she could bear the pain of withdrawal no longer. And they had worked. Eventually, when there was nothing else left, the words had worked. With some help.

She paused, hesitated and began to speak softly. 'Mathew, I don't suppose you know about backtracking. Well,' she hurried on, 'when you're injecting heroin, you insert the needle and pull a little blood into the works before you inject. It makes for a clean connection. That's backtracking. When I was addicted, every time I fixed up I had these words going through my head. They became important to me. A sort of mantra. On the face of it the words are about heroin addiction but I want to write about so much more: Life, love, survival. Somehow those words kept me sane. Sometimes I dreamed about writing that song. Writing that song has always been important. It's still important. It's only a few words but I thought they could be the hook. I have little idea of what else I want to say but I do know how the hook goes.'

Sinclair had heard the Industry rumours about her addictions. Rumours that she had always denied from behind hauteur high walls. To have those rumours confirmed with such a personal disclosure was an indication of the trust that she now placed in him. He was moved and got up from the piano, came around to her side, put his arm around her and squeezed. 'Why don't you sing the hook? Let me hear it. I'll think about it and you try and think about what it is you want to say. Then we'll work on it. What do you think?'

Dee took a deep breath and walked to the window. It was nearly dusk and the embankment lights threw orange splashes of colour across the silvery black water on an ebb tide that reflected her sense that she was moving backward in time. Without turning she sang quietly to his refection.

'You take a little pain,
You draw a little blood
You breathe a little air
Rise above the flood
And that feeling starts over again
Backtracking................ooh.............Backtracking.'

She watched Mathew's reflection as it crossed the room. He stood behind her with his arms round her waist and his chin on her shoulder. 'You know Dee you are a truly remarkable woman. It's good. I can use it. The hardest part of song writing is the hook and we have one readymade and perhaps a bit more. The way you lift the last line and hold it is haunting. Though whatever we come up with has got to pick up on the 'life, love and survival angle'. Richards and Jagger might get away with 'Sister Morphine' but it's not really where we want to be. Ok?'

She nodded. "Rise above the flood'. That's the bit that kept me sane,' she muttered.

'How did you get off it?'

'Another piano player I knew helped me out, he was one of the few men I've met who didn't have an ulterior motive. That's if you don't count love as an ulterior motive. He'd been there. knew what it was like and knew it was impossible on your own. He just turned up one day in a truck, put me and my stuff in it, locked the doors and took me out to his place in the desert. Didn't matter what I said or what I did, he just hung on in there. God bless him. We were together for a couple of years and he kept me clean. When he died, I was strong enough to start again. He'd be pleased about that. I still miss him now and then.'

'A fellow pianist no less. I'm honoured.'

'No. A piano player. He played for pennies and pleasure.'

'Don't we all.'

Mathew went back to the piano and Dee joined him, leaning against the side. He played a few chords, tried some others, closed his eyes and accompanied himself as he sang her words back to her. Then he slowed it down, changed key and sang it again. For Dee, it was as though the pain was being washed from her by the music. A few bars but so much history. She'd always thought of Dee the addict in the third person and as the echoes died away part of her wished that the old Dee could be here with her and that she could tell her she had been right; you can rise above the flood.

Mathew closed the piano. 'Is it coming to you?'

'I really think it is Mathew. Thank you.'

'Ok. Well I've enjoyed today. I love having you here and we've made a very good start. Tomorrow though, the real work begins but we'll devote some time to "Backtracking".'

The next morning started early and not to her liking. He made her sing scales and do voice exercises for an hour. She said nothing but inwardly seethed. At the point where her patience was about to snap he handed her a sheet of paper listing some numbers. She recognised them all but had sung less than a handful. She worked her way through the first three very aware that it wasn't going well. Mathew was patient with her but determined and several times stopped and sang a phrase back to her emphasising tempo and accent before asking her to try again. The more he did that the worse it got. Eventually she called a halt for a coffee break. She made it and carried cups over to the piano. They didn't speak. After appreciable minutes of hostile silence, he asked her to start again. The second time he interrupted she exploded. 'For Christ's sake Mathew. I'm the singer, I know how to sing, I just can't sing this stuff. It's just not me. It's not working.'

He crossed his hands in his lap and stared down at his feet for a few minutes before taking a deep sigh and turning to her. 'Dee, it's time for a few more home truths. To start with your voice is out of shape. You'd get away with it on sugar pop or country and western but with this material you won't. Neither will you have the cover of that down-home approach to the blues where 'natural' seems to be an excuse for the sloppiness that lets you slide onto a note. So, that's why we did the exercises and that's why you are going to have to do them every day and twice a day when you're performing. You say that the material is "not you". I thought we'd agreed that this was the direction you wanted to go and this was the type of material we were going to use. If I got that wrong, you need to say so now and we'll call it a day.' He looked back down at his feet and his knuckles whitened when one hand gripped the other tightly as he steeled himself. 'Then, Dee, there's still your attitude. Each of these songs means something, each word, each note and they've all been crafted by masters. You are not listening to what you're singing and if you could hear yourself, and I don't think you're even paying that much attention, you'd be as disappointed as me. You don't just perform on the stage; you need to practise that performance at rehearsal. You've got to get the love of performing back. At the moment, you're on autopilot. You could just 'phone this stuff in for all the feeling you're putting into it. I'm sorry to have to say this but you lack discipline and respect. Without discipline, we're never going to get through the amount of work there is. Finally, you lack respect. Respect for me, respect for what we're trying to do and respect for that talent that you seem to have forgotten which, properly used, may lead to some self-respect. Do you understand?' He shouted the last three words across the piano before very slowly closing the lid and going upstairs.

93

She was stunned, then furious. She'd not been spoken to like that for a very long time. All her good intentions to prove her talent to him lay in pieces around her. She paced up and down the apartment half hoping that the sound of her steps would prompt Mathew to return and apologise. By the time she'd realised that this was a forlorn hope she had calmed down. He was partly right. She hadn't been giving it anywhere near her full attention and for a man of his accomplishments that had obviously been noticeable and very frustrating. The problem she knew was that she resented direction. Always had. It also dawned on her that in a few days she had gone from being fairly imperious in her dealings with him as the record company representative to a role reversal that put him in the driving seat. No, he wasn't partly right he was completely right. She also realised that Mathew had little choice, it hadn't been working and he must have had to summon up all his courage to say what he did. Ok, time for humble pie and a fresh start. She stood in front of the piano and took a deep breath. She started with the scales and then moved on to the exercises. Mathew appeared at the foot of the stairs with a smile on his face.

'Sorry Dee,' he shrugged, 'had to be said.'

'Ok,' she laughed. Too brightly. 'Don't rub it in.'

'I've had an idea. You've been singing to the window. You've had your back to me. That's the way it'll work on stage when you've got an audience. While we rehearse, I'll be the audience. Sing to me.'

The afternoon wasn't good but it was better than the morning. They completed the run through of all the songs with Mathew interrupting less frequently but rather relying on dictating the tempo with movements of his head and demanding emphasis with a widening of his eyes and raised shoulders. When he did have to interrupt, it was now more often to make a point about interpretation not delivery. At the end of the afternoon and after another break he suggested that they try three of the songs one more time: "Misty", "Cry me a river" and "Love for sale".

Dee was impressed. Those were her favourites. She gave it everything she had. There were no interruptions, widened eyes or head movements. Just encouraging smiles and approving nods.

When she'd finished, he closed the piano. 'That's good. So, so much better. I've got a good feel for where you're at and we've got three numbers. I'm going to try a different arrangement for those tomorrow, personalise it to you a bit, then we'll go through another list with some more upbeat stuff in it and see how we go with that. The idea is to have a mix, old, new, ballad, beat but all with new arrangements.' He looked up shyly from the keyboard, 'you know Dee, when I said the other day, that you weren't Nina Simone what I meant was that if you want to sing her songs you need to make them your own. I can help there with arrangements.' He sighed, 'anyway, then I want to try one or two covers that are not standards. When we've got that, I want you to try a couple of my own numbers and then of course, there's your song. Then we rehearse with the group.' He rubbed his hands together in anticipation, 'Shall we work on your song now?'

'No, I'm tired, can we stop now? I'd like to rest.'

During the days that followed they made good progress and Dee was surprised at how much she was enjoying the work. She also noticed that she and her voice were becoming stronger and that she was singing with more verve and confidence. Previously, anytime Mathew had mentioned the first performance date she had become nervous and distracted. Now it no longer bothered her and there were times when she yearned for an audience and couldn't wait for the first concert.

Most of the time they had the apartment to themselves. Williams, when he appeared, was good company and always interested in their progress and keen to update them on his. Tour dates and venues had now given them firm deadlines with which to work and he was an entertaining source of information about the people he dealt with when making the arrangements. Dee had noticed that there was very little open affection between him and Mathew. What there was, however, surprised her because Williams, not Mathew, was the instigator: a hand on a shoulder or across a table to engulf Mathew's long, delicate fingers within his fist. At one point, she had thought she sensed tension between them and some strain in their relationship and as hers, with Mathew, developed, worried that she might be the cause. Mathew had explained that her fears were groundless and that Williams accepted that they were both working under pressure and had elected to spend time elsewhere so as not to be a distraction.

One evening Williams arrived with two other men and a stack of paperwork. He spent time with Dee explaining the contracts he wanted her to sign and asked each of the men to go through their respective specialism in detail for her benefit. While she respected him, and was grateful for his hospitality and endeavour, she realised that it was Mathew she trusted. Not Williams. He sensed her uneasiness and asked the two men to leave. The three of them sat on the settees with coffee and brandies in an embarrassed silence for some minutes. Williams eventually broke that silence.

'What's the matter Dee?'

'I'm not sure,' she shrugged.

'You don't trust us?'

'David, I'm not sure what I think. I'm grateful for all that you have both done and I'm enjoying working with Mathew but I've got nobody to ask about all this and every contract I've ever signed has proved worthless with more of my money going into somebody else's pocket than mine.'

Williams looked at Mathew, sighed, leant forward in exasperation and rasped. 'Dee, let me tell you about Mathew and me. We're gay. Even in a newly enlightened and liberal world that's still not an easy way of life. Despite that we've been together for five years. It works. Now! I don't need this. I need Mathew. Mathew needs this. Therefore, I want it to work. For both of you. I know that this started out as a cynical plan to hijack your career and you have every right to be suspicious but I am not going to steal your money or take advantage of you.'

He paused, turned to Mathew and took his hand. 'But, we've moved on since we met. I'm not a totally insensitive clod. I realise that you and Mathew have become close. That's not a threat to me. It just means that its working better than I could have possibly hoped. Now, I'm a wealthy man but I'd like to see a return on my money and these contracts go some way to ensuring that. But, they also ensure your future and protect your interests. Mathew wouldn't allow it to be any different and in this he sets the rules. He's not had a chance to study the contracts. So, I suggest we let him take them upstairs and look them over. After all he's the A and R man. He should know what he's doing. If he wants to make changes, we'll do it. If he's satisfied I would hope you would be too.'

They signed the contracts the next day.

Dee was still working at her song. She now had a very clear idea of what she wanted to say but a complete block on writing it. She knew it was about despair and hope, weakness and strength but most of all survival. She'd made several attempts to get her thoughts down on paper but with very little result. She'd begun to feel cooped up in the apartment and at the end of one day's work told Mathew she was going for a walk. She came out of the apartment and turned right, passed the Prospect of Whitby and on towards a new development around an open lake that she discovered was called Shadwell Basin. She followed the path around the basin and watched a group of school children helping to put away some sailing boats into a water sports centre. There was a fresh breeze and she shivered at the thought of being out on the open water on a day like this. She had a fear of water and couldn't understand how anybody enjoyed such sports. Eventually she came to a path alongside a canal and after several wrong turns found herself in a main road at the junction with Wapping Lane. Her natural sense of direction told her that this would take her back to the river and she began to stride out.

She felt better for being in the open and found her mind wandering. Sailing, survival, water, floods: Rise above the flood, floating, sinking, drowning, breathing air, struggling, fighting, and living. The words tumbled through her mind and turned into phrases and verse. She hurried on anxious, now, to get back, write it down and talk to Mathew. The song, her song, was coming to the surface.

She entered the lobby of the building to the sound of an argument coming from the stairwell near the lift. Raised voices, one of which belonged to Williams. She waited for the lift nervously.

'I don't care what he says. Sort it out. If he argues make him a better offer, or he's got to go. Do I make myself clear?' The husky voice rasped.

She heard footsteps and turned away, ostensibly to scrutinise the call button panel. She turned back to see a man stride purposefully across the lobby. His profile was presented to her as he turned through the door. The profile of an angry man. An angry man with a thin scar to his face.

The first rehearsal with the group went better than anybody expected. They all knew Mathew and seemed to be friends of long standing. The exception was the drummer. She wondered why it was always the drummer. The saxophonist was a stunning looking woman in her late twenties who, as she was dressed in an immaculate navy blue business suit, Dee had assumed was part of the management team, until she picked up the alto sax. Marie played with the light, lyrical touch of Paul Desmond and she was very sexy. Which, was part of the problem with the drummer. The guitarist was an avuncular balding, pony tailed, grey haired giant with the unlikely name of Percy who had a complete mastery of his instrument. Pete, the drummer, was a truculent young man whose ability didn't come very close to his self-image. He had a tendency to argue and a lunchtime drink habit that Mathew, eventually, had to address. Despite that, after three days of hard work and a week from the first concert date Mathew declared that they were well on the way.

The tour started at the Cambridge Corn Exchange and was initially scheduled to run for six appearances up and down the country visiting cities and towns from Brighton to Edinburgh. Dee had realised that she would be effectively touring for a month at least but was looking forward to the experience. She felt alive. She, Mathew and the band had worked hard and she felt that they had good material and a lot to offer. Now that the time had come, however, she was more nervous than she had ever been before. She knew the material was good but it was different. She knew she was better than she had ever been but very different from what she had been. Sitting in a chair in her dressing room in front of one of four show-biz style mirrors framed with light bulbs and staring back at her gloomy reflection she tried to calm her nerves. She liked the theatre with its high vaulted ceiling, arched windows and timber support beams and prayed that it would not be empty on this important night and then prayed that it would be full to capacity. There had been a lot of work done in the background to boost ticket sales and she was hopeful that it would make a difference.

There had been interviews with the local press and radio and she and Mathew had been pressing flesh and meeting and greeting anyone who was anybody in and around Cambridge for the previous four days. She'd done a guest appearance at Ryles, a local jazz club, where Williams had arranged for the resident artist to pretend to recognise her from the stage and then call her forward to sing three numbers that they had carefully rehearsed together that afternoon. It had gone well and created a lot of local interest. Williams had been working tirelessly in the background and had arranged an after show party in the St John's bar of the theatre to which he had invited several critics and music industry movers and shakers from London. Some of them were already here; she could hear them in the green room just a few yards from where she was sitting. She wished they'd go away. The green room was a place where artists tried to relax between scenes not a place where hangers on should be allowed to intrude on those last few moments of vulnerability before the mask slipped into place and the artist went into the crucible.

She looked around the well-appointed dressing room again. She'd been in far worse. This one had a shower, sink, sofa and the fridge had been well stocked. She thought briefly about opening a bottle of Bud and then remembered Mathew's lecture about the effect of alcohol on the voice. She decided to try the relaxation and breathing exercises that he'd taught her and had begun to feel an appreciable lessening in tension when a knock at the door rocketed her stress levels to the point where she could hear her own pulse in her ears.

'Hi Dee!' he greeted her as she opened the door, 'how's it going? We've got ten minutes. You ready?' Mathew enquired with a brave attempt at a smile that did little to hide his own obvious nervousness.

'Hey! I'm fine baby.' The mask was slipping into place as, appreciating Mathew's nervousness, Dee realised that she had the responsibility for the show and for troupe morale. She pulled him into the room, held his hands in hers, kissed him on both cheeks and looked into his eyes. Gripping his hands, she said, 'Can you feel my strength honey? Take some of my strength.'

Mathew nodded, not entirely convinced by what sounded suspiciously like a new age concept straight from a southern Baptist gathering, but grateful for the attempt and her concern. As Dee closed her eyes to facilitate this transfer of power he was seized by an overwhelming desire to giggle which provided the release from tension that he needed. Dee squeezed again and pulled him into a hug.

'Mathew, we're going to enjoy this. This is what we've worked for. Forget everything but the music. We live for the music tonight, anything else can go hang.'

He smiled.

'Have we got a full house?'

99

'Not quite but it's not bad and it's better than I'd hoped for the first concert.' Silently praying that Dee never discovered that Williams' people had bribed more than a few out of the nearby pubs with free tickets.

'OK! Let's do it.'

Dee marched straight from the changing room into the green room and stood in front of the long mirror next to a coffee machine regarding herself critically while Mathew and the group made their way onto the darkened stage.

From the exquisitely simple opening number, through gently lilting songs from the great American songbook way on down to Latin jazz and Ipanema the emotional authenticity of Dee's distinctly evocative voice held the audience captive and expectant for more. The well thought out and varied programme rang the changes and sustained the audience interest while dictating the pace of the experience and exposing them to images and sounds from the worlds of the salsa clubs in Rio, social clubs in Havana, New Orleans juke joints and the great jazz clubs of the world. Piano centred pieces with Mathew's solo edgy jazz piano breaks saw Dee standing quietly aside with time to appreciate and enjoy his performance. She used the carefully designed, natural breaks in the programme to deliver rehearsed ad-libs about her life, the band, her career and Cambridge. They loved her.

When she got to her song she took centre stage as the lights dimmed. With the microphone held in both her hands against her breasts she lowered her head until the two big Pani follow spots found their marks on either side and just in front of her. She looked up and breathed deeply, expanding her bosom inside the low-cut, burgundy and strapless, silk cocoon of a gown and stepped forward. The spots bracketed her and an ellipsis of light spilled onto the floor at her feet as she dove into the song and swam her way into and around the lyrics. Her words, her life, Mathew's music and a great welling of emotion that drew her spirit from within with words that soared into the auditorium until the dying echoes were swamped by the standing ovation. Her eyes filled with tears as she bowed her appreciation to the audience and turned to invite Mathew to stand and share the moment.

She got drunk at the after-show party though not a drop of alcohol passed her lips. High on the occasion and perhaps a little drunk with the power that she had experienced. The power that she could physically sense coursing through her veins, the power of not just having survived but of having returned in triumph, the power of having attempted and achieved.

She walked into the St John's bar on the arms of a shyly smiling Mathew and a David Williams who couldn't stop grinning as he eased people to one side as they made their way through the throng to the bar. Signalling to white jacketed waiters to begin distributing the champagne and without any apparent effort he hoisted Dee onto the bar and called for attention. Ushering photographers into position Williams raised his glass and announced. 'Ladies and Gentlemen. A Star is reborn.'

Williams had left nothing to chance and kept Dee at his side for the next hour while he methodically worked the room with her. Journalists were greeted effusively, introduced to Dee, plied with champagne, given a press handout, photographed and then introduced to Mathew so that Dee could expand her growing body of admirers and conquests with more of William's introductions.

Eventually the party stumbled to a halt and Dee found time to sit with the band. She hugged Marie and Percy and blew a kiss to the supine form of the drummer. Mathew joined them.

'We did it!'

'We sure did.' Said Dee. 'God bless you all.'

She raised her glass of orange juice to theirs of champagne and looked over at Williams who waved a champagne flute in her direction and winked. She smiled as he, surprised, turned away and lowered his head to listen to the whispers of a man who had urgently sought his attention and who Williams then immediately pulled through the throng and away towards the far end of the room. She recognised the man as the one Williams had been talking to in the stairwell at the apartment block and wondered why she felt alarmed.

Mathew waved over another tray of drinks, took a glass and raised it high for a toast.   'Next stop Manchester.'

'Manchester.' They chorused.

Chapter Seven

Denton powered the big Rover up the ramp from the Dartford Tunnel and settled back for the drive to Manchester. He set the cruise control for eighty, adjusted the rake of the seat, selected the CD player and arrived at the turn off for the M11 to the quintuple rhythm of 'Take five'. As Brubeck's piano vamp was gradually overshadowed by Joe Morello's drum solo he put his foot down. He enjoyed the car, with its two and a half litre engine it had all the power he needed, was comfortable and a joy to drive.

He'd always liked Rovers, right from his days as a kid when his Uncle Fred used, periodically, to turn up at the prefab in his Rover 90 and take the whole family down to Broadstairs for a day by the sea. Fred had been a big pink, portly, pipe smoking gentleman of the old school whose only dress concession for a day on the beach had been to remove his suit jacket, slip his paisley patterned braces from his shoulders and remove his shoes and socks. Attired in a fine cotton, cuff linked shirt with studded collar, rolled up bespoke suit trousers and knotted handkerchief on his head he had organised and taken energetic part in games of beach cricket and rounders. He'd stop only to refill or relight the pipe that was clamped between his teeth throughout. Denton could still freeze frame the picture of a horizontal Fred going for a catch in the slips with the pipe firmly in place, the ball within reach and a tide pool beneath him to soften his landing.

Denton used to divide the day into zones of expectation: the journey down, the first sight of the sea, the first swim and then lunch in a pub. As the day drew to a close he'd begin to look forward to the treasured drive home. Normally his sister would fall asleep, his mum and his aunt would get in the back seat of the car with the little girl stretched across their laps and he'd be promoted to the front seat. Sitting between 'Aitch and Fred he was allowed to grasp the big ivory knob on the top of the long, cranked gear stick and change gear on Fred's command. It had been his first introduction to concentration. He'd held the gear stick until his hand had ached while staring at the diagrammatic representation of the shift positions engraved on the top of the ivory knob, waiting for Fred's instruction.

'Young Paul, you're doing very well but you're not looking where we are going. Look out the front and then listen to the engine.' Fred would then demonstrate the relationship between the engine noise and the gearing while Denton had tried valiantly to take all that in whilst risking quick glances through the windscreen.

'That's it Paul, now you tell me when to change gear.' By the time, they'd reach Faversham on the old A2 Denton had mastered the process. As Dartford hove into view he'd drifted off into a state of half wakefulness vaguely aware that Fred's big hand had engulfed his and the gear knob for the rest of the journey. When, on arriving home, he had been carried from the car still half asleep he always remembered to thank the big man. 'Thanks Uncle Fred. Thanks for letting me drive, thanks for the ice cream and thanks for taking us,' he'd mumble sleepily.

'That's quite alright Paul Old Man. I've enjoyed your company.' Then this courteous man would slip a big pink ten-shilling note into his pocket as he kissed Paul on the forehead. Fred had been one of those people every kid should have in their life as they grew up.

Denton took the turn off from the M11 to the A1 and thanked his foresight in leaving home before dawn. At pretty much any other time of day the A1 would have been solid with traffic making its way north. At this rate, he reckoned, he'd have time to stop off at one of his favourite views for his thermos of coffee. He usually came off the A1 slipped round Barnsley and picked up the A635 through Holmfirth. He'd often stopped at a car park near some grouse butts on Saddleworth Moor overlooking Holme Clough. From there it was no more than half an hour to drop down from the Pennines into Manchester, hopefully getting there just before nine. He pulled into the deserted car park, got out of the car, retrieved the thermos and sat on the bonnet and looked back down the road to a watery sky through which the sun was just about strong enough to draw some shadows on the stark frosted landscape. He had often marvelled that this isolated beautiful desolation of rocky edges and moor could be so close to the cramped city and back streets of Manchester. 'Well Denton', he muttered, 'what now?'

Arriving home in the early hours of the morning to be greeted by an hysterical Stella screaming that Julie was missing after the night he'd already had, was an experience he wouldn't have wanted to repeat. He'd ushered her indoors and through to the lounge while listening as she ranted. He'd poured them both a brandy half expecting her to throw it at him and follow through with a lecture about drinking. She'd taken the glass without comment taken a sip, run her free hand through her hair and taken a deep breath. She'd then slumped onto the settee placed her elbows on her knees, supported her chin with her wrists with the brandy balloon clamped to her cheek.

'Stella, I need to get the full story as calmly as you can tell it with as much detail as you can remember if I am going to be able to do anything,' he said patiently.

'Fine Paul,' she said through gritted teeth. She'd taken another sip from the brandy, leant back into the cushions and closed her eyes. Denton had waited. There was no point in rushing her and she had seemed to be gradually regaining control of herself. 'I don't know where to start.'

He crossed the room and sat beside her, took the glass from her hand, put it on the floor and placed both her hands in his. He then gently pulled her towards him until her head rested on his shoulder. 'It doesn't matter where you start. Just start. When you're ready.'

She nodded, patted his knee and sat back in the settee. 'When she came back home from Manchester at Christmas she was different. Sort of distracted. Almost as though she was here but her mind was elsewhere. You must remember that she was out till all hours most of the time. We didn't see much of her at all. Not that you'd have noticed. You spent most of that holiday pissed.'

'Stella, that's not going to help now. How was she different?'

'Well, I'm not sure but, thinking about it, it may have started at Christmas. When she came home for the summer she was fine to start with. You remember that she talked about that boy she had met? Andy? She was full of that for a few days. Then she started work at your place. By the time she went back to Uni she didn't seem right. She was bad tempered, didn't seem to eat much and didn't want to be in the same room as me. You were working with her. Didn't you notice anything?'

'Well, I wasn't actually working with her. Webber took quite a shine to her.'

Stella looked up quickly, Denton hurried on, 'oh, not in that way. He just thought she was a bright kid. I didn't see a lot of her. She worked directly to Henfield although I think she did some stuff for Webber as well.' He paused, gradually aware that Stella was staring at him and that the colour had drained from her face. 'What's up?'

She didn't answer immediately but got to her feet and made for the brandy bottle. With her back to him, her arms folded across her chest and the rim of the glass resting on her bottom lip she said, 'Webber?'

'What's the problem?'

'I didn't think you liked Webber.'

'I don't Stella, she was just working for him; doing odd jobs, admin and secretarial stuff.'

'And you didn't notice anything out of the ordinary?'

'Stella, as you've frequently pointed out, I really wasn't in a fit state to notice very much. I'm sorry. What did I miss?'

Stella turned to face him, took a sip from the glass, walked to the chair opposite the settee and sat down. 'Well, apart from what I've already told you it's difficult to be specific. I tried talking to her but she either clammed up, became aggressive or walked out. The next time I challenged her she packed and went back to Manchester. Don't you remember? Anyway, in the term leading up to Christmas she became more and more difficult to contact. Paul, she used to write every week. We had one letter that term. I didn't twig it at the time but the fact that her boyfriend 'phoned here a couple of times to talk to her should have made me think. I just assumed that they'd split up and she hadn't told him where she was. I was a bit dismissive of him. I'd 'phoned her house, the Uni office and her friends down here. In Manchester, they'd take a message and promise to pass it on and nobody down here has heard from her. I was getting really worried when she then 'phoned and said she was coming home at Christmas. Paul, you must have noticed how bad she looked when she turned up?'

He shrank within himself as the full realisation of the extent of his deterioration hit home: He hadn't been able to remember or hadn't noticed in what condition his daughter had been.

'Paul, she's on drugs. In the end, I just had to ask her. There was a terrible scene. She denied it of course. So, I got in touch with one of those drug clinics and they agreed that her behaviour was consistent with regular drug use.'

His mind whirled. Up to this point in the conversation he'd been half of the opinion that Stella was being over dramatic and while he had been listening, half of his brain was still engaged on earlier events and how and what he could tell Stella. He could feel himself getting angry. Angry that he had so far removed himself from his family that he hadn't noticed anything amiss and angry that the distance was such that she had seen no point in involving him.

'Why didn't you tell me?'

She shrugged, looked archly at him and raised her eyebrows quizzically with a sad smile on her lips.

'Right' he breathed. 'So! She went back to Uni after Christmas and you thought she was on drugs. What then? I mean I realise that drugs are serious but what makes you think she's missing?'

'She had a letter delivered here today. I opened it. It was from a finance company. She hasn't made a payment on her car for over six months.'

'But I include for that in the allowance I pay into her account every month'.

'Well she's obviously not spending it on her car. Anyway, I've spent the whole day on the 'phone and this time I was determined to get some answers. The upshot is that she hasn't attended a lecture since the summer; she's not living where she told us, she's not with the boyfriend and she didn't have the car when she went back after Christmas. Paul, she could be anywhere and if she's on drugs she could be doing anything.'

Stella started to sob, he went across to her, sat on the arm of the chair and pulled her head down onto his knee. He was worried but had been consoling himself with the thought that while Stella's conclusion was reasonable there could be any number of other explanations to fit the facts. As he'd gently stroked her hair he decided that while it wasn't exactly the most propitious moment he would have to tell her about McCarthy. He could however, sweeten the pill a little.

'Look Stella. I'm going upstairs for a shower, you pack me a bag for a couple of days and I'll leave straightaway for Manchester. I promise you that wherever she is I'll find her.'

'I'll come with you.'

'No Stella, think about it. We don't know where she is. We need someone here in case she rings or comes back here.'

'Where will you start?'

'I don't know, last known address, friends,' he shrugged? 'I'll find her.'

Stella looked doubtful but didn't argue and rose to go upstairs. As she passed, Denton gently held her back by her arm.

'Stella, this is a really bad time but there's something you need to know.'

She looked more irritated than concerned.

'Mickey McCarthy was shot dead in the Dukes Head tonight.'

'Jesus Christ Paul! Are you joking?'

It had taken him over an hour to explain what had happened, have a shower, collect his bags and leave a distraught and frightened Stella to wait for a phone call.

Denton spent some time cruising up and down Wilmslow Road, or "Curry Mile" as he knew it was known locally, before he recognised where he was. He turned into Norman road and cruised to a halt outside a large Edwardian detached house. This had been the last address that Julie had provided and somewhere in the building was the room that Julie had occupied. He walked through the sizable front garden, skirting an abandoned Austin Allegro, a fridge and some sort of sports car beneath a poorly secured tarpaulin. He glanced at his watch and realised that it was a little early in the day to expect students to be up and about. There was an aluminium panel with buttons, speaker and voice grille half screwed to the wall inside the entrance porch. He noted a confusion of wiring spilling from the bottom of the panel where the fixings had come away from the wall and doubted whether the entry phone was operational. He tried four of the six buttons before he got a response.

'Fuck off!'

Despite his irritation, Denton was amused at the man's response. He pushed the button again.

'Are you stupid or what? Fuck off!'

'I'm not stupid and I'm not fucking off,' he jammed the button back onto its contact and kept it there.

'What do you want?'

'Open the door and you'll find out.'

'You the Law?'

'Might be,' Denton grinned to himself.

'Go and stand out the front so I can get a look at you.'

Denton walked down the entrance steps until he thought he was in full view from any room and sat on the tarpaulined sports car. Some minutes later the front door opened.

'Get off my fuckin' car.'

'Good morning.' He skipped up the stairs and slipped a foot over the threshold before the still sleepy student could react.

'Hi, I'm Paul Denton and my daughter Julie used to live here. Did you know her?'

'Got any ID policeman?' the young man smirked.

'You're a suspicious sod,' said Denton fishing in his jacket for his wallet. As the student studied his driving license Denton looked him over. He was probably in his early twenties, medium height, heavily built with a shock of thick brown hair and the puffed, pale features of those that turn night into day. He watched as the student nervously pushed a pair of tortoise shell spectacles back up the bridge of his nose with his index finger and handed back the driving license. He had on a faded tee shirt and a pair of sweat pants and his feet were bare. He shivered, folded his arms, stuffed both hands under his armpits and nudged the door open with his shoulder.

'Yeah! I knew Julie. You'd better come in. I'm Jake.'

Denton followed him down a long dark hallway to the back of the house into a surprisingly large kitchen that also obviously served as a common room. Jake rescued a tin kettle from within a pile of pans without causing the heap to collapse, removed the whistle top and filled it with water. As Denton crossed the floor towards a table and chairs he was uncomfortably aware that the soles of his shoes were sticking to the floor and releasing with audible suction as he walked. He sat down and glanced around

108

the room. The walls were covered from floor to ceiling in bright red tiles and the floor in some type of cushioned linoleum, which in turn had a sheen of grease, interrupted occasionally by islands of dried and encrusted food spillage. To one side of the kitchen table an old door, supported by four columns of empty pizza delivery boxes, was being used as an open larder and was covered with cereal boxes, jars, tins and open boxes of tea bags.

'Sugar?'

'One please, Jake.'

Jake delivered the teas and pulled up a chair. 'How much do you want to know Julie's dad?'

'Everything Jake.'

'You sure?'

'Yes.'

'Ok! When I first met her she was the best! Man, she was something else. Y'know? Not just looks. She was kind, had time for you, listened. Had no side to her. Uni's a weird place specially the first year. Away from home first time people go a little bit mad. Too much drink, sex and of course the drugs.' As he said, "drugs" Jake took a sip of his tea and looked straight into Denton's eyes gauging his reaction. Denton kept all emotion from his face.

'Did she do drugs Jake?'

'Yeah, too much, but it wasn't always like that,' he added hurriedly. 'At the start, she was respected man. You know you get these little cliques; well she was out there on her own. Not a joiner. That pissed a few people off until they got to know her. Then it was like she was a celeb. Welcome wherever she went. Respect.'

'Do you do drugs Jake?'

'Who doesn't?'

'Did you start Julie on drugs Jake?'

'No man. I use, sometimes. I don't deal and I don't pass it around.'

Denton believed him and found himself warming to this young man who had obviously admired his daughter from afar. Jake's concern for Julie was apparent and it couldn't have been easy for him to be the bearer of such bad news.

'So, what happened to turn Miss Goody two shoes into a Druggie?' Denton paused barely believing he was talking about Julie in such a dispassionate and dismissive way.

'Man, you really didn't know your daughter, did you? She was no Goody two shoes. She was just a really a good person.'

'So, what happened?'

Jake tugged at his mane of hair and then scratched furiously at the top of his head with an expression on his face that went from puzzlement to exasperation. 'I'm not sure and that's the truth. She'd linked up with Andy,' he hesitated, thinking.

'You know Andy?'

'Yeah, I know Andy. Andy Starmer. Bit of a loner, nice guy but I wouldn't want to cross him. Older than her; Mature Student. They seemed to be getting on fine. Kept themselves pretty much to themselves but mixed in with some things. We were in Halls of Residence then. Anyway, when we came back to this house for the second-year Julie didn't show up on time and Andy was getting a bit frantic. When she did turn up she was in a state. She was definitely on something but it wasn't just that. There was something else. But hey, what do I know. She'd been down on vacs, holidays. I mean, you'd maybe know better than me what was going on.'

Denton reflected briefly on the irony of that observation before asking. 'Older than her?'

'Maybe five years?'

'Did Starmer get her on drugs?'

'It doesn't work like that and anyway when Andy found out she had a problem he sorted out the guy she was buying from. I mean big time.' He nodded towards the passageway, 'there's still a dent in the wall at the foot of the stairs where the bloke landed. No, Andy's not into drugs.'

'Then what happened?'

'Difficult to tell really. She and Andy had a big bust up and she moved out. Andy was walking around like a dead man for weeks and I think he went looking for her. I know she's dropped out of Uni and I don't think Andy has found her. She was seen once or twice by a few people but she'd become a bit of an embarrassment and was well and truly in with the wrong crowd so people kept their distance.'

'Do you know where she is now?'

'No! But I'd bet real money she's still in Manchester.'

'What makes you think that?'

'Well, I don't know where I've got this impression from but I felt that when she returned after the summer she was running away from something. Here was where she'd run. Plus, the fact that the crowd she was mixing with was heavily into drugs and

Christ knows what else, so my bet would be that she'd stay near to the supply.'

'So, if you're right, where, in Manchester, do I start looking?'

'I'd start with Andy. He's moved from here but I can give you his address if you like, it's not far.'

'Thanks Jake and thanks for being honest with me.'

'Hey man, I did try to help her you know.'

'I'm sure you did Jake,' Denton offered a forlorn smile, 'thanks.' He got up to leave and offered Jake his hand. The student's grip was surprisingly strong and he grasped Denton's forearm with his left hand, looked him in the eyes and grimaced. 'Sorry man.'

'It's Ok. Hey, what was all that business about 'are you the law' when I was outside?'

Jake sighed. 'Nothing really, I've got a few problems. Not drugs. I'm expecting to get a tug. Hacking. See, I'm a computer nerd and a bit of a loner. Didn't mix. If it hadn't been for Julie I doubt that I'd have stayed in Uni. She'd make a point of including me and if you were with her you had a pass to most things. She cared.'

'Then you take care Jake. If I need you can, I ring?'

'Sure man.'

Denton got back in the car and looked at the address scribbled on the top torn from a cereal box. Jake's rough directions sent him off from Rusholme in the direction of Fallowfield looking for a side street off the A34. He noticed that he was moving from what had obviously been a fairly prosperous area at the turn of the century, perhaps for merchants and artisans, to the smaller terraced accommodation of the working class. Detached stucco with porticos was giving way to terraced red brick two up and two downs. The area had all the hallmarks of a student ghetto with a pub on every corner and a kebab shop or a takeaway on every other.

He turned into Brailsford Road and realised that the number he wanted was at the far end on the opposite side. He parked the car wondering briefly whether it was safe to leave it in this part of town and crossed the road. Momentarily, he felt that he was in a Lowry painting with tiny red brick houses on either side of him and a factory chimney looming up at the end of the road. As he neared the house he noticed that the front door was open. Crossing the pavement, he realised it wasn't just open but was hanging from one hinge.   He paused briefly and looked up and down the street. Out of the corner of his eye, he caught the movement of a curtain and the hasty withdrawal of a girl's face, from the light back into the shadows behind an upstairs window opposite. He walked down the four yards of Victorian glazed tiled path to one side of the scruffy patch of front lawn. Standing outside, but leaning into the hall while pushing the door cautiously with the flat of his hand he was startled to see a scruffy, spotty youth frozen into immobility on the stairs with a computer tower and keyboard in his arms, a sports bag hanging from his elbow and a mouse dangling on its lead from the back of the keyboard. The lad was painfully thin and wearing a fawn coloured, hooded sweat top with a draw string at the throat. His emaciated body and a maroon ball cap on his pinhead reminded Denton, once again, of Lowry and his matchstick men.

'Who are you?' barked Denton.

The youth took a step back, juggled the box in his arms as he tried to slip the handles of the sports bag back from his wrist to his elbow and tried desperately to front it out. 'I live here. Who are you?'

'What's your name?'

'What's it got to do with you?'

Denton smiled before patiently explaining, 'Well, unless your name is Andy Starmer, which I don't think it is, you're stealing that computer.'

'What the fuck you on about?'

'The owner has written the name "A.Starmer" with a big black marker pen on the side of that box,' Denton patiently explained.

The youth instinctively turned the box to check, the sports bag slipped back to his wrist, he lost his balance and sat down hard on the stairs. Denton quickly went up the stairs, placed his knee on the PC tower and leaned his considerable weight onto the youth pinning him and the box to the stairs.

'Look', said Denton, not unkindly, 'I'm not interested in you. If you answer a few of my questions as far as I'm concerned you can leave and spend the rest of the day burgling from here to Bradford. But you're going nowhere at the moment and you're definitely not taking anything with you when I do let you go.

Understand? Look, I don't even want to know your name. I just want to know about the people who live here.'

The Youth squirmed under Denton's weight but said nothing.

'Why did you break in here?'

'I didn't.'

'Well someone put the door in and you're the one cleaning the place out. If I was a copper, which I'm not, I might be tempted to put two and three together. Ok, you didn't break in. Who did?'

'Two other geezers.'

'What two other geezers?' Patiently.

'I don't fuckin' know do I? All I know is two geezers pulled up in a big beamer, got out, kicked the door in, went screaming up the stairs and didn't come back down.'

'What do you mean they "didn't come back down"?'

'Well, not straight away. A bloke and a girl came down, nicked the beamer and pissed off. A few moments later the two geezers came out. Someone had given 'em a right pasting.'

'When was this?'

'Hour or so ago.'

There was no doubt in Denton's mind that he had missed Starmer, and perhaps Julie by the narrowest of margins and that if the girl had been Julie she was in more trouble than he had anticipated. It very obviously wasn't just about drugs. 'Ok, give me the computer and fuck off. If I want to talk to you again, I'll come back.'

'Oh yeah, like you're goin' to find me?' Relief moving on to cocky.

'You live in the house opposite dick head. I should get back over there. Your girly lookout will be worried.'

The look in the lad's eyes told Denton that he had guessed right and there was no further protest from him as he took the computer and walked him to the door. He locked the computer and the sports bag in the boot of his car before returning to the house. It wasn't difficult to find Starmer's room he just followed the trail of damaged fixtures and fittings until he got there. Whatever may have been in the room in terms of personal belongings had either gone with Starmer or was somewhere in the pile of rubbish on the floor. The computer monitor lay smashed at his feet, partly covered by the curtain that looked as though it had previously concealed the wardrobe alcove, and splintered shelving and books littered the rest of the room.

Denton sat in the car and pondered his next move. He glanced idly at the house across the street, in time to see the downstairs curtain twitch back into place, and he kicked himself. Spotty, living opposite to Starmer, might know more.

As he neared the front door the curtain twitched violently as though the person holding it had let it go in a hurry and moved away from the window. He hammered on the door repeatedly with the flat of his hand. Peering through the letterbox and down the dark passageway he wasn't surprised to see the back door open and Spotty making a hurried escape through it. Denton realised that in the time it would take him to run to the end of the terrace Spotty would long since have disappeared though one of the back-entry alleys. Discouraged and cursing his stupidity he straightened up.

'Can I help you?'

He turned to see a small, elderly, neatly dressed woman standing in the doorway of the house next door to Starmer's. She was stationed sideways to her front door with a hand on the keys to throw a deadlock into place. She was dressed in a smart navy blue wool coat, a bright scarf at her throat and a fur-trimmed hat on her head.

'Oh! Hello. Yes, you might be able to,' said Denton crossing the road. 'The thing is I think my daughter may have been staying next door to you and I think she may be in trouble. My name's Paul Denton.'

The woman ignored the introduction, withdrew the keys from the lock, unclipped the front of a capacious leather handbag and dropped them inside. She seemed to be considering her reply while she fumbled with the latch on the bag. Once that was closed she retrieved a black prayer book from beneath her arm, clasped it to her chest and looked at him thoughtfully before turning back to the door and twice checking that it was locked.

'Would she have been the girl with Andy?'

'You know Andy? Yes, that would have been her.'

'Is Andy in trouble?'

'Yes, I think he is. But then so is my daughter and he appears to be helping her. I just want to find her. I don't mean Andy any harm. I might be able to help Andy as well.'

'Andy's a nice boy. Did a bit of shopping for me? Often knocked to see if I wanted anything while he was out.' She paused again and looked at Denton long and hard while she carefully pulled some leather gloves onto her hands, smoothing the leather free of wrinkles by intertwining her fingers and massaging the back of one hand with the front of the other. 'There was a disturbance here this morning,' she finally announced in a tone that left Denton in no doubt that whatever had happened was close to sacrilegious in her eyes. 'Two men came here and broke into Andy's house. There was a lot of shouting and thumping and banging and then Andy came out of the house with your daughter, got into their car and drove off.'

'Did you call the Police?'

'There's not a lot of point there are always break-ins around here and the Police don't seem that interested.'

'Had you ever seen these men before?'

'No, but I know the type.' She sniffed.

'What type's that?'

'The type that used to pick Andy up some nights and take him to work. Always smart, very polite but not very nice. I didn't like Andy working in that club.' She sniffed again.

Denton's spirits lifted at the new information. 'Andy worked in a club? You wouldn't happen to know the name of it would you. The name of the club?'

The woman sighed, tucked the prayer book back under her arm, peeled off her gloves a finger at a time and opened the handbag. 'Somewhere in here I've got a card Andy gave me. It was when my husband was in hospital. As he worked nights, Andy said I was to ring him if my husband took a turn for the worse and he'd ask someone to come and get me and take me to the hospital.' She paused and seemed to shrink before announcing. 'In the end, he died in the day.'

'I'm so sorry.'

'No need to be, you didn't know him and even though I was married to him for forty-three years, I didn't like him. He didn't understand my work for The Lord. Ah! Here it is.' So saying she handed over a business card advertising a club on Princess Street called, 'Slammers'.

Denton parked the car, walked through Piccadilly Gardens, down Portland Street, left into Sackville to Canal and down to the corner with Princess Street. He was vaguely aware that this part of the town had become the gay and lesbian centre for the North but he was surprised at the number of bars and restaurants in an area that he suspected must have been a pretty derelict part of the town only a few years previously. He leaned on the stonewall by the canal, gazed down past the buddleia clinging to the red brickwork into the sluggish chocolate brown water and the near perfect reflection of the building behind him, complete to the detail of an external blue cast iron fire escape. He briefly reflected how fast things change. The Rochdale Canal, once an essential trade link between Lancashire and Yorkshire was now little more than a backdrop to a cosmopolitan, hedonistic and consumerist society that would be incredibly difficult to explain to any who had worked the original canal barges for a living. He glanced briefly to his left where a narrow boat was emerging from the tunnel below the buildings of Piccadilly. He watched its stately progress, and although hardly in the mood returned the waves of the couple in the stern. He was a blue fishing smock and a soft peaked cap while she was a yellow heavy wool sweater and unnecessary sunglasses. Briefly he envied their happiness and companionship before crossing the street and turning the corner to the club.

Once he had doubled back sharply into Canal Street he realised that it must have been the sound of the fierce argument that had alerted him. He had been fifty yards from the club, clearly 'Slammers' from the sign hung vertically above the pavement from the first floor. Not close enough to hear words but near enough to be aware that a confrontation was taking place. A very large man, red in the face wearing a check suit was screaming at a calmer, younger man who was half in, or out, of the back door of a Mercedes. The younger man raised his right arm, placed the palm of his hand on the fat man's chest and said something that had either calmed or intimidated the larger man into listening.

Denton had about faced the minute he recognised the man at the back door of the Mercedes. It was George Webber.

Chapter Eight

The developing friendship between Julie and Jamie fulfilled the early promise and then exceeded Starmer's expectations. He'd had no reason to suppose that they wouldn't get on but he had been afraid that Julie's addiction and Jamie's nervous reserve were not the best foundations for a friendship. Jamie lived in a roundhouse, which he shared with two co-workers from the Findhorn foundation. It was surprisingly spacious and comfortable and the fact that his colleagues were away for a few weeks meant that there was no need to sleep in the camper van. The floor was littered with red and brown cushions, there was a pine table with non-matching chairs and an old canvas covered sofa, leaking stuffing, that looked as though it had been rescued from a First World War officer's club where it had been regularly abused.

The pair disappeared into the kitchen area and Starmer judged by the low hum of half heard conversation, interspersed with laughter, that they were at ease in each other's company. He was pleased. While he had never considered Jamie a burden he had been a responsibility that had occasionally weighed heavily. He sat at the table thinking through recent events. Short of getting Julie clean he had no real plan, but, with sinking heart, realised that at some point there would be a reckoning with Woolley. In a perverse twist on accepted moral standards he knew that killing Thompson wouldn't overly exercise Woolley. Stealing so much of his money would. He remembered the Filofax from the safe. Retrieving it from the rucksack he took it back to the table. Opening it he was surprised to find that it wasn't the diary or appointment schedule he had expected. The book seemed to consist of two sections. The first, alphabetical, contained a series of entries in the tiny, neat handwriting that Starmer recognised as Woolley's. Most records contained a date followed by what were maybe coded references to perhaps places or people. It contained sections of different coloured notepaper divided by card separators with an alphabetical referenced thumb index for each divider. Behind that was a similar arrangement but with a numeric card separator index. He flicked through using his thumb to riffle through the pages. The first section containing some detail of which only dates were decipherable, the back section ruled for accounting where the entries were obviously sums of money.

'Move yourself. I want to set the table,' interrupted a grinning Jamie.

'Here it is', announced Julie bearing a huge dish of spaghetti alongside which Jamie dumped a hot saucepan of bolognaise sauce.

The meal was one of the best that Starmer could remember. Good food with good friends and banter that was relaxing and conversation that stimulated. He quickly realised that there were the makings of an unholy alliance between the pair with many of the jokes being at his expense and was surprised at how comfortable that made him feel. In the odd pauses his mind inevitable returned to the problem of Julie and the addiction. He didn't want to frighten him with the full story of their predicament but Jamie would be street wise enough to realise that Julie had a problem when she started to become strung out. He had to tell Jamie something. As the thought occurred he caught Julie's gaze. She was going through the motions of listening to Jamie while looking hard at him. He raised a questioning eyebrow. The look got harder and she nodded firmly. 'Jamie, there's something I need to tell you.'

Jamie, by turns looked startled, expectant, apprehensive and then frightened. Starmer patiently explained Julie's problem and their intentions to get her clean. His friend shuffled in his seat and pushed cold spaghetti around his plate with his fork. He looked hard at Julie and such scrutiny from such abused innocence found Julie looking uncomfortable and avoiding his stare.

'And what do you want me to do Andy?' he said, almost shyly.

'Let us stay here. Help?' He shrugged, 'I don't really know.' Starmer tailed off into an awkward silence.

'Did you think I wouldn't help', spluttered Jamie, 'after what we did?'

'Jamie, we,' he emphasised the word, 'didn't do anything. I did. It's long gone now. A long time ago. Forget it.'

'Andy I won't forget it. Can't. Where would I be now if you hadn't helped me? Besides which I'd like to think that I'd help anybody that was in trouble and helping Julie will not be a problem. I want to help her.' Jamie stood and went to the back of Julie's chair and rested his hands on her shoulders. 'There is one problem though. What do either of you know about drugs and withdrawal?'

Starmer explained about his previous reading on the subject and was gratified to note a sad smile of acknowledgment from Julie. Jamie digested this information for a moment. 'Make yourselves comfortable. I'm going to have a chat with a neighbour. She's a bit clued up on this stuff. It's how she came to be here. We talk. Her name's Melissa and she's my friend. She may be able to help and anyway she'll need to know who my visitors are. How much do I tell her? When do we start?'

Before Starmer could say anything, Julie replied, 'now'.

'If she's a friend you must be the judge of how much to tell her Jamie,' said Starmer.

Jamie smiled but with a slight trace of affronted dignity that the possibility he might have denied his help could have been an issue for the pair. He left the room shaking his head.

As the door closed behind Jamie she turned to Starmer, 'you didn't mention the other business.'

Starmer nodded, 'I can't see the point. I think maybe we're safe enough here. Hopefully it won't be an issue and I really don't want to freak him out any more.'

By midday Julie was in withdrawal and Starmer in the throes of despair. The cocky commitment of the previous evening now had as much strength as the pale and watery sun still struggling to warm the frosted landscape. He felt a mixture of pity and anger but all his resolve to be patient and help her through the process had come to nothing in the face of one, snarled, cruel response. One, spiteful comment from a struggling Julie had seen his commitment waver. Jamie was constantly at her side, solicitous, patient and understanding with never ending, seemingly meaningless, chatter. This had also begun to get on Starmer's nerves and he became more and more aware that he was redundant: The unholy alliance of the previous evening had turned into symbiosis for survival.

Julie had woken withdrawing. The symptoms that Starmer had previously seen became progressively worse as the morning wore on. The sweating and the chills, the yawning, shivering and runny nose he'd seen before. The frequent rush to the toilet, the irritability and the muscle cramping were new to him. The strident demand for the curtains to be pulled shut, the manic laughter, a bout of heart-rending sobs prompted by a newspaper story about starving children in Africa and the truculent dismissal of his attempts to comfort her had left him feeling confused and helpless. At one point, he thought that there would be a period of respite while she slept. She lay down, closed her eyes, briefly, announced that she was tired, and within minutes was walking around the room complaining of a pain in her back. A few moments after that she started to shiver uncontrollably and then to cough, a deep hacking cough that went on for minutes and became worse when she began to choke on her own vomit.

Jamie was instantly in attendance with a bowl, towels, comfort and encouraging words. Without looking at Starmer and with no protest from Julie he removed her soiled top, threaded her arms through the sleeves of the replacement and talked to her quietly. A few moments later he approached her with a large glass of orange juice and some buttered toast. Starmer had fully expected her to throw it in his face but she took it, nodded, and began to eat the toast. She didn't eat it all but when she'd finished Jamie took the plate and glass and set them to one side. He then swung her legs up onto the settee, turned her over onto her stomach and began to massage her shoulders and neck all the while talking to her almost inaudibly. Starmer went out to stand on the porch where Jamie found him a little later.

'Christ Jamie! I had no idea it was going to be like this.'
'What the fuck did you expect? A runny nose and a few aspirin and everything would be hunky dory? She's got a serious problem and she needs serious help and you're just not helping.'
'Jamie, she won't let me.'
'That's because she is picking up disapproval from you. The way you stand, the way you sit, the way you look and the way you talk to her. They all scream disapproval. If you don't get on

120

side soon she's going to quit trying.' He took a deep breath and sighed, 'Andy, since this started you haven't touched her or spoken to her direct and most of the time you can't even bear to look at her. She's in withdrawal. She hasn't had her brain removed. She's the same person she was last night,' he waved his arms in exasperation, 'last year even, same values, and same feelings. Just different body chemistry. She knows you can't stand this but she's in no condition to work out why. What's the matter with you? I thought that this was what you wanted.'

'Jamie, I don't know,' he sighed. 'You're right but what should I do?'

'Christ Andy, you're not in the fucking Army now, start thinking for yourself. In the meantime, go back in there and make a fuss of her. Doesn't matter what she says. Hold her hand, stroke her hair, and tell her you love her. You do, don't you?'

Starmer nodded dumbly.

Jamie smiled with a look of satisfaction that bordered on the smug. 'Good. When you've made your peace, I want you to get out of here for a few hours. Go into Findhorn, have a pint, walk on the beach. Work it out. When you come back be prepared to take over because by then I'll be knackered. We're going to have to do this in shifts and yours starts this evening.'

Starmer walked back into a room that was dominated by Julie's eyes set deep in sockets of sorrow. He pulled her to him and whispered into her hair. 'I'm sorry Julie. I've not been much help have I?'

She hugged him and sobbed, 'It's not your fault. I'm sorry too. It's all such a mess.' She pushed him to arm's length, 'I will do this if you can help me.'

He cupped her face in his hands, 'Give me another chance?'

'That's what you're giving me Andy. Thank you.' She smiled mid shiver. He explained the plan to work in shifts, picked up the rucksack and made for the camper van feeling better than he had but still apprehensive and with an overwhelming sense of helplessness and a little guilt that he still couldn't quite trust her with the rucksack.

Findhorn was pretty much as he remembered and still as enchanting. The village, consisting of a scattering of attractive cottages and houses sat on a spit of land between the enclosed estuary that was Findhorn Bay and the Moray Firth. He gazed across the bay and then turned to look out towards where the village petered out into a short walk through the marram grass and low sand dunes to the beach. Shoving his hands deep into his coat pockets and shrugging his collar up against the chill he headed for the Kimberley Inn: A rendered, sand coloured building that had probably been a pub for years but looked as though it started life as a house. Had it always been a pub, he'd decided, they'd have put the entrance at the front not tucked it up a side street. The Kimberley had been where he and Jamie had spent many of their evenings on his last visit and where Jamie had introduced him to a potent beer with the intriguing name of 'Sheepshagger.' Starmer had, as the evening had worn on, spent memorable minutes speculating with Jamie about the origin of the name. It had been a good evening.

He ordered some food, took his pint and passed along the narrow passage in front of the bar down some steps to the front of the pub so that he could look out over Findhorn Bay while he waited for his chowder. The water seemed to be pretty much at full tide and the brisk wind was whipping the tops off the small waves in the sheltered bay. Culbin Forrest, on the other side of the bay, looked green, deep, dark, dense and forbidding but offered some shelter to a small group of seals huddled together for warmth on the shore where the trees gave way to a wide expanse of almost white sand.

Fishing out the Filofax he began to idly turn the pages without really thinking about the contents. What sort of records, he wondered, would a villain like Woolley need to keep, in code, and in a safe? The Contacts, names and numbers associated with honest enterprise wouldn't need to be coded. So, the first assumption must be that if the code referenced people then these were people that were engaged with Woolley in his crooked dealings. So! What sort of people wouldn't want to be publicly associated with Woolley or they with him? All the half way decent citizens of Manchester, Starmer concluded with a chuckle, hastily banishing an errant thought of Woolley in polite society. He turned to the accounts section and quickly established the connection between it and the alpha indexed section. Each ledger entry had a date and a letter suffix. By tracking the letter back to the corresponding alpha section Starmer found that the dates tallied and cross referenced back the other way with a single number indicating which page held the transaction detail. In a second vertical column, on the right-hand side of the page, there was another set of figures. Some entries in that column had been totalled and when the total equalled the figure in the left-hand column both were crossed through. Transactions. These were transactions. Woolley was recording his deals, payments, debtors and creditors. Instalments.

Returning to the alpha section of the book he checked and noted that the section had eighteen separators to cover the alphabet: Five separators each served two letters of the alphabet but only eleven of the sections were in use. He jotted down the letters. 'A', 'B', 'C', miss 'D' and 'E', 'F' & 'G', miss 'H' and 'I', 'J', 'K', 'L', 'M' and 'N', miss 'O' then 'P' and 'Q' together. With no obvious answer springing to mind he returned to the accounts section. For a while he puzzled as to why Woolley needed thirty-one numbered sections. His earlier thought had been that these were to do with days of the month. Realising that only the first nine pages contained any entries he eventually concluded that Woolley was simply using the pages in turn and the numbers for cross-referencing: There had probably been thirty odd pages in the pack and Woolley had adapted them to his own use. What, though, was the significance of the letter index? He reminded himself that only eleven of the pages were in use. Why those letters? To what did they refer?

He put the thought aside as his chowder was delivered and returned his gaze to the bay. It seemed to be a haven for wildfowl and not for the first time Starmer promised himself that one-day he'd take some time to learn about birds. They'd always fascinated him and he envied them their freedom. He knew, from Jamie, that Osprey and over wintering duck were common in the area but doubted that he could identify them. Something for the future, assuming Woolley allowed him a future. He tipped the bowl away from him to spoon up the last of the hot chowder and was suddenly consumed with a cold anger. His future was his to determine. Not Woolley's. At some point, Woolley, would have to be tackled and the more he knew about him and his operation the better chance he had of coming out alive.

He returned to the Filofax. So, Woolley recorded transactions in code. He wanted to keep a record but didn't want the identity of those involved to be readily available. Again, he thought, who would Woolley want to protect? Criminals? The mob? Maybe? Who else would a criminal have dealings with? Starmer chuckled as he thought of the Police. Only unsuccessful criminals had dealings with the Police.

He shivered as he realised that the opposite was also probably true. Successful criminals could well have connections to the Police that ensured their continuing success. And there was no doubt that Woolley was successful and had been so for a very long time. He shut the book sharply. Frightened to consider the problem further. If Woolley was that tight with the Law, then he could call on resources that would make finding the pair of them a lot easier. He watched some ducks on the near bank fluffing their feathers against the cold and a chill entered his heart as he realised that their protection was probably more effective than any he could currently muster against Woolley.

He went to the bar, ordered another pint, returned to the table and again opened the Filofax. It could be the lever he needed but he had to understand it first. The letters were the key. Eighteen separators, eighteen sections, eighteen divisions. Only eleven divisions in use. Each with a letter but no records after 'Q'. Starmer went back over his earlier thoughts but could get no further. Tired, he put the book back in the rucksack and made his way back out to the camper.

He drove back into the Findhorn Foundation estate and parked. Having a few hours to kill he made his way over to the community centre. From his last visit, he knew that the centre ran several courses one of which allowed visitors to experience the lifestyle for a week and gave exposure to the ideas and concepts that underpinned the work of the community. Those that were interested in joining the foundation could take advanced courses to prepare them for the life if they decided to go further. He'd been very sceptical about the whole thing and only Jamie's entreaties to "behave" prevented him from gently winding up the people he'd met. They weren't his kind of people but he eventually warmed to their innocence and endeavour and found their values interesting even if their company was uninspiring. The visitors to the centre were there to connect to the spiritual side of their nature, which was a concept so far removed from his experience that he found it difficult to relate to them. He had tried though and recalled one unnerving encounter with a grey-haired woman who struggled to explain the significance and importance to her of an experience that she'd had in the vegetable garden.

Every considerate fibre in his body had strained against his natural inclination to make fun of her experience or to suggest that what the world needed now was for everyone to have a vegetable garden experience. When she went on to explain that the experience involved a giant cabbage and the growing of people he had begun to wonder whether there was more growing in the garden than the vegetables.

Despite his reservations, he had found a sort of peace there among the people and the extended sprawl of the eco village, bungalows and offices. The setting was all, everything set just back from the sea and surrounded by miles of silver beaches fringed with gorse covered dunes it was difficult to see how anyone could be anything but peaceful there.

He wandered into the community centre, which was an over extended bungalow used for social functions and some meals for the experience week people, still with its wooden benches and trestle tables he noticed. He well remembered getting inveigled into the Transformation Game in the building they called the "cc". He wasn't sure that he ever really understood what was going on but Jamie had taken a lot away from it. Starmer had appreciated that it was a game played on a circular board symbolising each player's world and that while moving along "life's path" he had the opportunity to address "key issues". More than that had seen him struggle although several attempts were made to explain that it was a useful life tool. He'd reached the conclusion that it was more like mah-jong for the intellectually able but vulnerable and yet could see absolutely none of the claimed similarities to life and its problems. He noticed the old chalk menu board was still in place and posters advertising a shamanic journey: "healing ourselves and the earth" and a festival of "sacred dance, music and song". Not for the first time he wondered how these people earned a living.

He returned to the roundhouse to discover Jamie and Julie at the table poring over the transformation game. Praying fervently that he wouldn't be expected to join in he pulled up a chair and sat down. 'How's it going Julie?'

'She's doing very well but we're into the next stage. We've talked about it and Julie knows what to expect. We're just trying to take our mind off it with the game for a few moments,' replied Jamie on her behalf.

Julie reached across the table for his hand and smiled grimly at him. He returned the squeeze, raised her hand to his lips and kissed it.

'Tough?'

'Ain't that the truth. I've started getting the cramps and you really don't want to know about the by-product of that,' she joked, 'and, right now, I could murder for a fix.'

'Hang on for me?'

Julie suddenly stood up and headed for the toilet. Starmer turned to Jamie with an enquiring look on his face.

'She's doing well but we've really only just started. What I've been trying to do is keep her busy, distracted, talking, trying to keep her mind off it. She doesn't want to eat and that's ok for a couple of days but she must drink. If you get stuck for something to do make tea, it'll help get the toxins out of her body if nothing else. Or,' he added, 'get her to try to make it. Anything to distract. Don't let her have coffee. It's a stimulant. A couple of times she's had to clean herself up and I've put her in the shower. That seems to help a little bit. Massage seems to relax her briefly and talking while you do it helps as well. Melissa recommended that the person withdrawing should try to keep a diary. You know, get your feelings on paper? That went down like a lead balloon. What has been useful though is being able to use the stuff Melissa gave me to prepare her for what's coming. So, she knows that she's got three more days of hell before it gets any better. I took her for a short walk this afternoon. Sort of trying to tire her out. I think she enjoyed it but then she became anxious about you. Sort of panic attack that you wouldn't be coming back. For the last hour, she's had one eye on me and one on that door. It's good your back mate!'

'You're a diamond Jamie. Thank you. You go and do your thing and I'll take over.'

'I'm going straight to bed. Wake me in eight hours. I've got some ideas about tomorrow. Being cooped up here may not be the best way of dealing with this. Perhaps if we take her out for a bit, down the coast. Stay away from the crowds but give her a wider perspective. Might help?'

'Anything you say mate.'

When Julie reappeared Starmer was encouraged to note that she had tidied herself up and combed her hair. He smiled and she walked into his arms. Yet again he was at a loss to know what to do or say but stood gently massaging her back and kissing the top of her head. Apprehensive that the idea might not meet with her approval he decided that nothing ventured meant nothing gained. He released himself from her arms went over to the CD player, selected a Judy Collins recording and gathered her back into his arms. The music washed over them both and the soothing melodies seemed to relax her. They swayed on the spot for a few moments before moving naturally to the sort of boy meets girl at the end of the evening dancing that had initiated romances in ballrooms up and down the country for years. Starmer could feel a change in her. She was still tense but not as intense as she had been. Occasionally she would raise her head from his shoulder look up at him and smile. Each time she did he kissed her forehead. When the CD finished, she asked him to play it again and he gladly obliged. There were moments when she pushed away from him and he noticed that she was shivering but perspiring heavily, though she still held his hands and moved to the music with him. Towards the end of the CD he felt her getting heavier in his arms and surreptitiously brushed the hair from her brow. Her eyes were closing and occasionally flicking open the way a baby's do when it finally gives up the fight to stay awake.

Leaving Julie sleeping fretfully on the old settee he made a cup of coffee and found himself brooding again about the Filofax. The key was in the alphabetical section. The letters on the eleven sections in use meant something. Eleven letters of the alphabet. He riffled through the book again, seeking any inspiration. He reviewed the sections and realised that there could be more than eleven letters in play. Five of the sections, where there were entries, had double letters: 'EF', 'GH', 'IJ', 'NO' and 'PQ'. So, he could be looking for a pattern or reference that connected sixteen letters. What the hell did eleven or sixteen letters of the alphabet have that connected them to Woolley and his grubby little world of crime and deals? Why was the book in those divisions?

He put the book aside deciding to get some rest while he could. It occurred to him that he needed to meet Melissa. Jamie was obviously fond of her and her advice had been useful. It struck him that all his knowledge on drugs had come from a Jesuit novitiate and a woman who had taken refuge in an alternate society; one fighting the addiction of others the other retreating to deal with her own. He chuckled at the thought of them meeting and wondered whether they would get on. The Jesuit had been good company but not the most patient of men. Starmer could remember him arguing fiercely in the bar at the Hough End Centre Police club with a coldly angry Policeman after a hard-fought draw had seen the Uni side being hacked off the football pitch. He'd have thought twice about taking the copper on. He'd the sort of coldly calculating intensity and presence that suggested violence was not far below the surface but this hadn't stopped the Jesuit.

He froze as the memory passed through his mind leaving ripples of alarm behind it. The Police team were the 'A' Division team out of Bootle Street Police station. Police were organised into Divisions and each Division was allocated a letter of the alphabet. He couldn't remember how he knew this but was absolutely certain that he was right and had found the connection. That had to be it. Woolley was dividing his operations up to match the geographic areas that the Manchester Police used to structure their operations. It couldn't be coincidence. It had to be corruption. If so, he and Julie were in more trouble than he had thought.

He pondered what advantage this new information afforded him over Woolley. If it was corruption, there had to be an angle. He could contact Woolley and offer to give the book back on the understanding that he would call off the hounds. That thought was dismissed as quickly as it had occurred; it was a flawed strategy because he couldn't trust Woolley. He could contact the police but realised the obvious danger that he might just pick up on one of Woolley's cronies. His mind turned again to the question of why Woolley kept such accounts. Why did anyone keep accounts? Because they were bean counters? Maybe but more likely because they were accountable! Woolley must be accountable to someone. Would that person, a Boss perhaps, be a better bet for negotiation than Woolley and if so how would he find him? Feeling more in control than he had for the last few hours Starmer settled himself under his coat on a collection of cushions and went to sleep.

He woke, startled, to find Jamie hovering over him with a cup of tea and daylight filtering around the edges of the still drawn curtains.

'Thanks for waking me,' said Jamie shoving the cup into his still sleep-numbed hands.

'Sorry. How's Julie?'

'I came down at about three this morning and she'd gone.'

'What!' Starmer scrambled from beneath the coat and levered himself from the cushions.

'Don't panic. She's back. Said she just had to get some fresh air.'

'Fresh air be damned. She went to the camper. She thinks there's a days' supply of drugs in there.'

'Is there?'

He ignored the question. 'Where is she now?'

'In the shower.'

'Right. Say nothing about what I've just told you. She won't want us to know that she nearly cracked. That idea of yours yesterday, you remember, get her out. I think we should do it.'

'Ok we'll have something to eat and go into Nairn.'

Starmer hadn't been to Nairn on any of his previous visits and was pleasantly surprised by the town. One part of it, towards the west, seemed to consist of large Victorian mansions built in a grey stone with splendid views of the Moray Firth while to the south of the town was a collection of small cottages that looked like the original fisherman's cottages of yore with the two areas connected by a seaside promenade and a large area of open recreation ground sweeping up from the front to the finer mansions. A river wandered through the town into a picturesque harbour and the three of them sat in a café at the harbours edge watching the world go by. They kept a watchful eye on Julie while keeping up a distracting running commentary on the view. Starmer realised that they were plumbing the depths when Jamie drew attention to a stray dog whose mission in life seemed to be to mark his territory on every bollard on the harbour wall.

'Andy, have you got any stuff in the camper?'

He looked sharply at Jamie who went back to looking at the dog. 'No Julie. There's none left.'

'But there was. There should be some left.'

'Julie there isn't. I wouldn't lie to you. It's all gone. Is it bad?'

She looked at him as though he was a simpleton newly arrived in her world of hurt, crossed her arms, hugged her shoulders and rocked back and forth on the chair. Starmer knew that the next move would be the massaging of her thighs and arms and offered a paper napkin pulled from an aluminium

129

dispenser to wipe her runny nose. She snatched it from him, got up and left the café. Starmer hurriedly settled the bill while Jamie rushed after her. He caught them up down one of the side streets in Fishertown. Jamie had his arm looped through Julie's and he fell into step on the other side and put his arms around her shoulders. Thus linked they slowly made their way across the promenade green towards a Victorian bandstand in the middle. A pale sun in a clear sky gave some warmth, which a freshening breeze tried to snatch away. They sat in a row on a bench, in silence, each with their thoughts about the same problem.

'You're doing really well Julie.'

'No, I'm not Andy.' She muttered her voice muffled, as she drew the back of her hand across her runny nose.

'Julie, I know you feel like shit but it will get better and we're about half the way through the really bad stuff,' encouraged Jamie.

'For Christ's sake Jamie, will you just stop wittering on and shut the fuck up?' She screamed.

Jamie looked at her sadly before making matters worse. 'I know you don't mean it.'

'Fuck off Jamie!'

Starmer wasn't shocked he'd been expecting something like this at some point but he was beginning to get angry. Jamie had opened his heart and his home to her and his friend deserved better. Starmer cared for her but for the sake of any future relationships there had to be some limits and she needed to be made to refocus. 'That's enough Julie. Jamie didn't deserve that and you know it. If you want drugs I'll drive you into Inverness, give you some money and you can get a train to Manchester. When you run out of money you can go back to sucking cocks.'

She looked at him with red rimmed and haunted eyes. 'Do you mean that?'

'No.'

She sighed and leant her head against his shoulder. 'I'm sorry but you have no idea how bad this is.'

'No I don't but you have no idea how my life has been turned upside down by the mess you got yourself into. You're totally self-centred. Start thinking about those around you. Give us a break. We're doing all we can.'

She twisted her head around on his shoulder and looked up and grimaced, 'bit of a cow am I?'

He grinned back, 'sometimes.'

They both glanced up to see where Jamie had got to and started walking in his direction. Julie apologised, Jamie forgave and they all decided that they would continue the walk along the front. She surprised them both with a newfound determination that saw her setting a brisk pace and taking a lively interest in the sights of the seashore. They stood for some minutes watching an elderly man and his large black Labrador playing on the sand and all laughed as the man's hat was whisked away by a sudden gust of wind, bowling it across the sands with man and dog in hot pursuit. As they got back to the town Julie surprised them again with the announcement that she was hungry. On the way back to Findhorn they stopped at a small pub and Starmer ordered some sandwiches. She nibbled but at least, he thought, she ate something. Jamie, continuing his programme of distraction, got some darts from behind the bar and started a game. Julie didn't join in but sat silently watching them. Starmer, sensing that her energy and commitment were draining away again, finished the game quickly with all the skills acquired by hours of practice on one of the few durable entertainments there had been in the children's home.

They had stopped off in Findhorn for some supplies so it was close to dusk when they returned to the estate. Jamie bustled straight to the kitchen area laden with plastic bags and began putting the shopping away while Julie sank onto the settee without bothering to take off her coat. Starmer's mind was returning to Woolley and the book when a knocking at the door interrupted him. Opening it he was confronted by the earnest smile and slightly vague expression of the woman who'd had the vegetable garden experience. She looked him up and down in silence for a few moments as if considering whether to acknowledge that they had met previously. He returned her gaze and wondered whether she had left her home in a hurry. She was wearing a sheepskin helmet with earflaps like antennae and a string of purple beads wound around the crown, a purple scarf at her throat in the style of a Palestinian Keffiyeh and hugged a brightly coloured blanket with native designs around her shoulders. She drew the blanket more tightly to her as a slight breeze wafted scents of violets, lavender and mints to him. He decided to break the silence.
        'Yes. Can I help you?'

131

She looked bemused for a few moments and then lifted one of the earflaps.

'Pardon?'

'I said could I help you?'

'Yes dear. Is Jamie there?'

Starmer waved her into the house where she crossed the room with her antennae fully active and picking up on everything until she reached Jamie.

'Hello Melissa. How are you?'

'Fine dear. Fine. Nice to meet your friends. How's it going?' This with a meaningful glance at Julie who chose to ignore what she considered one intrusion too many.

'We're doing fine Melissa'. Jamie smiled.

'Right dear. Well what I came to say was that someone called for you.'

Starmer stiffened and looked at Julie who had half risen from the settee in obvious alarm. They exchanged looks. Woolley?

'Yes. He came to the shop. Bought some candles and was asking about The Foundation. We got chatting and he asked if I knew all the people who lived here. I told him I knew most of them and then he asked if I knew a Jamie.' She looked at Jamie conspiratorially. 'Well dear. Didn't sound right to me. Fishy. So, I said I couldn't recall anyone of that name. Did I do the right thing dear?'

Melissa, Starmer thought, may all your cabbages weigh forty pounds apiece and may your garden grow the sort of people you love. She had bought them time.

Jamie, however, looked puzzled and asked anxiously. 'Melissa, was this today? You saw this man today?'

'I think so Jamie' said Melissa vaguely, 'but you know me. Memory's not what it was. Bit like a sieve. All those good times in the Sixties perhaps; taken their toll on the old grey cells'. She giggled before looking nervously at Julie and blushing.

'Yeah, fine Melissa. I don't know what it's all about but I expect he'll come back if it's important,' said Jamie.

With antennae still on full sweep Melissa made her way to the door and wished them goodnight.

Starmer looked at Julie and then turned to Jamie. 'I'm sorry Jamie but we've got to go. And I mean right now.'

Chapter Nine

Denton checked into the Sachas Hotel on Tibb Street just around the corner from Piccadilly, shortly after midday. He sat on the edge of the bed and stared gloomily at the mini bar. He needed a drink. Trying to put the thought behind him he undressed and headed for the shower. Feeling slightly better he lay on the bed and started to run through the day's events.

More than anything he felt an overwhelming sadness. Sadness at the wasted years and the grief they carried with them. Jake's description of the bright and beautiful girl with all the social skills he had described fitted his memory of Julie. The fact that she had deteriorated into an addict without him noticing moved him through anger to pity. What disturbed him was that it was self-pity. Part of him was relieved that the drug issue had been confirmed. At least he knew what the problem was and, with entirely misplaced confidence, was sure that if he could find her she could be cured. He realised that he had no knowledge of drugs but was convinced that there was an answer. First, he had to find Julie. He took some comfort from the fact that she was with someone who not only appeared to be acting in her interests but also seemed capable of looking after them both. What worried him more was the involvement of what could only be a criminal element and try as he might he simply could not make sense of that but was certain that the answer could be found at Slammers. He was still struggling with the coincidence and the potential implications arising from Webber's appearance there when he fell asleep.

134

He woke a few hours later. Hungry, he dressed and headed downstairs. The restaurant was at a mezzanine level below the reception floor and there was a bar off to one side. As he walked through the reception lobby he was vaguely aware of having to pick his way through piles of luggage and noticed that there were several musical instruments in cases propped against the reception counter. An untidily dressed, slightly effete young man was arguing earnestly with the receptionist, apparently on behalf of a group of half dozen or so people dotted among and on the luggage. A striking black woman in a white trouser suit leant with her back to Reception, her hands holding her lapels and her elbows resting on the counter behind. They exchanged glances. She smiled but before he could respond Denton felt himself falling and cursed for having been distracted as he tripped over a bag at her feet. He swiftly apologised for his clumsiness and bad language.

She smiled as she said, 'that's ok honey, it's not every day a man falls at my feet.'

Embarrassed, Denton went down the stairs and into the bar. Beech, chrome, plate glass and a liveried bar man whose claret waistcoat wasn't that many shades different from his hair which had been dyed, gelled and spiked to a height that must have brought it into frequent contact with the glass shelf above the bar. Denton took his tomato juice and, noticing he was the only person in the bar, took a few seconds deciding where to sit. He wasn't in the mood for company so he moved to the far end of the bar pulled out a chair and sat facing a glass partition overlooking the hotel pool. The pool was empty apart from a middle-aged man, with more hair on his back than his head, who was rhythmically ploughing his way up and down the length of the very small pool and executing perfect racing turns at either end. He sipped his drink and thought again about Julie. He was now very worried. Jake's reference to him not knowing his daughter had really hit home, forcing him, again, to acknowledge that in recent months, with his booze problem, the chances were that she had changed without him noticing. The fact that she had disappeared was worrying enough but that she was last seen in the company of a man who had been involved in a running fight with God knows who, was bringing him close to despair. Where the hell would she go and why, if she was in trouble, hadn't she contacted him or Stella? Then there was the connection to Slammers. Was it simply coincidence that his enquiries had led him there only to find Webber? Again, he reasoned, some of the answers had to be at Slammers. He realised that he was going over old ground and took a sip from his drink.

'Hi! Are you ok?'

Denton started at the interruption and came out of his reverie sufficiently to note that the enquiry had been in made in an American accent. He swivelled and half rose from the chair. The striking black woman in white smiled at him while he blushed and struggled for a reply.

'Hey! Don't look so apprehensive,' she suddenly looked uncertain, as she paused and then blurted out, 'look, I'm not a hooker and I don't want to jump your bones.' She waved a hand at the floor behind her and rushed on to divert his attention from her embarrassment, 'it's just that this place is empty, you look like a man that could use a conversation and I just felt the need for some of that conversation while they sort out that mess upstairs.'

Denton studied her face noting her obvious discomfiture at the clumsiness of her approach, 'no, no, please, please sit down, would you like to join me?' He waved her towards the chair opposite as he rose from his own. 'Paul Denton,' he said, leaning forward and offering his hand.

'Dee. Dee Dee Wilson'

'You're American.'

'Sure am brother, from the deep south.'

'I wouldn't have got that straight away from the accent.'

'What did you expect? A red polka dot head scarf, a few "lawdy lawdies", a rolling of the eyes and some verses of "gimme crack corn"?'

Denton leant back and considered her response, 'Boy, you don't take prisoners, do you?'

She edged forward in her seat, ready to leave and now obviously uncomfortable with the situation she'd engineered.

He smiled, 'hold on! What I meant was that you seem sort of' he paused, 'I don't know, well you look European. I mean you're loud enough for an American,' spluttered Denton finally, deciding that attack was probably the best form of defence with this remarkable woman, 'but your accent's not exactly southern belle.'

'That's possibly because your southern belle was white or at least a pale shade of magnolia. You may not have noticed but

I'm what those southern belles might have called an "uppity niggrah".' She smiled pensively and conceded appreciatively, 'the European thing's interesting though. I've spent time in Amsterdam. I speak Dutch, get by in French and have passable German and "doan hab no truck wid dem damn Yankees."' She tilted her glass of orange towards his tomato juice with one eyebrow cocked in query.

'You on the twelve steps?'

'I beg your pardon.'

'Booze. You look like a guy who enjoys a beer.'

'Twelve steps?'

'AA? The path to recovery? You never heard of it?'

'No. I'm not an alcoholic.'

'You sure?' She smiled.

'Look,' Denton appeared to struggle to remember her name.

'Dee,' she supplied.

'Right. Dee. As far as I know I'm not an alcoholic. I'm under a bit of pressure at the moment and I was sitting here quietly mulling over my options when you butted in. Now you're a bloody good looking woman but I can really do without you and your intrusions right now.'

'Mulling? What the hell is mulling?' She laughed.

Denton paused, leant back in his chair and thought she was a bit more than bloody good-looking. She was a big, strikingly attractive woman with almond eyes that were beginning to hold him spellbound. He grinned. 'Forget mulling I'm in a bad mood. Start again?'

'Dinner?'

'On me!' Said Denton.

Once they were seated and while both gathered their thoughts behind their menus Denton took the bull by the horns. 'I have a drink problem but I don't think I'm alcoholic. I'm just trying not to drink at the moment,' he blurted out before retreating behind the menu.

'Hey, I'm sorry. That's me, in with both feet.' She grimaced, 'you may have noticed it's a bit of a habit with me.'

'No, really?' He laughed, 'it's ok. How about you? How do you know about AA?'

'I'm what you call a recovering alcoholic. To tell the truth, in my time, I've recovered from pretty much anything you care to name. Booze, drugs, cigarettes, love and one serious illness.'

The claret waistcoat, now doubling as waiter, was hovering to take the order. When he had gone Denton, his interest awakened by the reference to drugs, asked, 'how long have you been in recovery?'

'From booze about twelve years, drugs a couple of years or so, cigarettes about a month, love since whenever and the serious illness was some twenty years back.' She paused, 'how long have I been clean? Three hundred and sixty-five days? Yesterday? Tomorrow? You never know.' She smiled sadly.

'Well, recovery suits you. You look good.'

'Thank you. I feel good.'

'Are you a singer?'

'You recognise me?' Dee said as she pantomimed false modesty with a fluttering of her eyes and a dismissive wave of her hand.

Denton looked confused. 'No I just saw you upstairs and there were band instruments and I thought that as you were the best looking you probably fronted the operation.'

Dee made a small moue of disappointment, turned her profile to him, put her right hand on her hip and extended the left straight out at shoulder height, dropped that hand at the wrist and sang the first line of a familiar song. 'You still don't recognise me? No? Dee Dee Wilson? Many years and quite a few pounds back, in the time of Tamla I had a few chart hits.'

'I'm sorry. I do remember. I just didn't make the connection.'

'S'okay. Not many people do these days. Yes, I'm a singer. I'm over here to re-launch my career working with new management; he's the guy who was arguing at the desk. He's got good ideas. This tour was one of them. I'm using different material, writing some stuff myself and it's going well. I'm enjoying myself. It's a Comeback. Someone once said "They were born, they learnt to sing, they made money, bought diamonds, got royalties and died". This time round honey, I ain't gonna die.'

Denton spotted the management threading his way through the restaurant in their direction.

'Dee', said Mathew Sinclair. 'Sorry about all that. I've got it sorted out now. Your stuff has been taken up to your room.

Some of us are booked in and the rest have been transferred to a place down the road just for tonight.'

'Thanks Mathew. I'd like you to meet Paul Denton.'

They shook hands and Denton sat and listened while they talked about a rehearsal scheduled for the following morning and the arrangements for a sound check and the next evening's performance. Sinclair had politely declined Denton's offer for him to join them and wished them a pleasant evening before leaving.

'Now Paul Denton, tell me about this pressure that you were 'mulling'?'

Denton wasn't naturally inclined to disclosure, particularly to relative strangers, certainly not without the benefit of some heavy alcoholic intake. Even with this woman it wasn't easy but then suddenly it was. She coaxed him along with odd questions and added to his understanding about drugs while empathising from a position of obvious experience about his daughter's involvement in that culture. By the time they had moved back to the bar for coffee she had heard the whole story of Julie's disappearance. He'd brought her right up to date to the point where she had caught him mulling. They were sitting side by side on stools at the rapidly filling bar. Denton glanced sideways as deep in thought Dee raised the cup to her mouth. She sipped, lowered it, turned to him and smiled. Denton noticed that his breathing was irregular, picked up his cup and stared straight ahead only to catch her reflection in the mirror at the back of the bar. She was looking straight at him and smiling. The bar had filled up and the crowd was now jostling them both.

'We can't talk here. You want to come up to my suite?' This time the smile wasn't just warm it was challenging.

Denton stopped breathing as he felt the blood rush to his face.

She laughed, 'hey, Denton. Don't go getting a bunch of ideas. I told you I don't want to jump your bones. Well, not tonight anyway. It seems to me that I might be able to help with some of this. For a start, I know how the drug culture works on the streets and I know quite a bit about clubs and the dregs that run them. I've also, once or twice, moved on the edges of the mob scene. You're on foreign territory and maybe I can wise you up a bit and stop you getting yourself hurt. She inclined her head to one side and smiled. 'Shall I get some coffee sent up?'

Denton had got back to his room about three in the morning feeling good but guilty. Dee had certainly helped to clear his mind and focus on what needed to be done. She had also been a mine of information about the drug culture that afflicted most cities throughout the world. When he had been telling her about Julie he had told her of Jake's opinion and affection for her during the early days at Uni. He hadn't been able to get his head round the rapid decline from a young woman on the threshold of an exciting life to that of an addict apparently living on the fringes of criminality. Dee had gently explained the nature of addiction and even more gently got him to draw the parallels from his own life and the changes wrought by alcohol. She'd pointed out that once addicted, reason, scruples and self-preservation became totally subsumed by the need to feed the addiction. She had concluded that the addict could not or rather should not be judged but rather helped. They had agreed to meet for lunch the next day after her morning rehearsal.

The guilt he felt had come partly from the enjoyment that he experienced while in her company and the appreciation that there was a sexual tension between them, of which he was sure she was aware. This became evident as he was leaving. His honest but somewhat over profuse thanks for her help and a lovely evening were cut short by her taking his hand and leaning over to kiss him on the cheek.

'See you tomorrow,' she had whispered.

On reflection, the only downside to the evening had been the residual guilt he felt for not having told her about McCarthy.

He spent the morning killing time around the hotel in a state of nervousness before finally descending to the dimly lit hotel bar and an aroma of stale beer and furniture polish overlaid with a faint whiff of chlorine from the pool. By half past one Denton had been waiting in the deserted hotel bar for sixty minutes more than was reasonable for a man on the wagon. She was late and he desperately wanted a drink. Coffee and fruit juice simply weren't doing anything for him other than fuel his frustration. He began to wonder whether he had completely misjudged the woman. On reflection to have gone from chance encounter to even agreeing to meet to discuss his situation further the following day seemed little short of unreal: as unreal as the world of show business that had claimed Dee for the morning.

He'd woken that morning without a hangover for the first time in years. His first feeling had been a sense of achievement that he had managed twenty-four hours without a drink. Then, in the way of all awakenings, his world had piled back into his consciousness and Julie's problems had brought him back to earth. After that came thoughts of Dee and the previous evening: The first thought had been sexual. Such early morning thoughts weren't unusual but had been remarkably few and far between in Denton's recent life. Then, again he had reasoned, he hadn't had a meaningful conversation with a woman while sober for probably as long.

While he had been showering, and musing on the connection between sobriety and libido his mood had lifted. Dee, he'd reasoned, could help and seemed to want to do just that and he wanted her assistance. He'd briefly wondered what Stella might have made of him spending time with Dee and he'd decided to ring her and bring her up to date. When the answer phone kicked in he left a brief message reporting his safe arrival in Manchester and a promise to ring later. Duty discharged, his thoughts had returned to Dee and he realised that he was very much looking forward to seeing her again. Her brashness and directness excited him. Her invitation to her room had both thrilled and frightened him. Now doubts had begun to creep in and he'd begun to wonder whether it was usual for her to act in that way. Perhaps it was a showbiz thing; perhaps if you spent a lot of your life in hotels inviting people back to your room was as natural as asking people back to the house. But then there was still the kiss. Or had he got that wrong too and in the cold light of day she had reconsidered and wasn't coming.

'You given up on me Denton?'

She was by his side leaning against the bar, smiling. Denton swivelled on the stool while attempting to stand and elbowed his orange juice over the counter. She avoided the deluge and laughed as she pantomimed mopping imaginary spillage from her cashmere polo neck and tan flared trousers. While Denton faffed around looking for bar towels and napkins she leant forward and kissed him on the cheek. 'Steady boy! Order us a couple of booze busters and club sandwiches. We'll be sitting over there,' she indicated to the barman who had been noticeable by his absence until her arrival.

Still mopping himself down Denton watched her turn and walk to a table down at the other end of the bar, sit down, cross her legs, remove her bag from her shoulder, open it, retrieve a note pad and a don a pair of horn rimmed glasses which took her from showbiz to serious secretarial in a second. He joined her. 'Do you think you could call me Paul?'

The almond eyes, magnified by the glasses viewed him seriously for a moment and with her head cocked slightly to one side he had the feeling he was being inspected. She grinned. 'No! I like Denton. Calling you Paul will mark a milestone in our relationship that may be some way off yet. I've decided'

'What have you decided? To call me Denton or that we are having a relationship?' He fired back.

'Maybe both. You wanna talk about Julie now?'

Denton did, but God help him he wanted to talk about the relationship more. 'Last night you kissed me,' he paused, embarrassed, then rushed on, 'and you just kissed me again.'

'You complaining?'

'No, but,'

'Denton, don't tell me kissing is a problem for you. Leastways not kisses on the cheek. Doesn't your wife kiss you?'

'Stella? Only when she's checking to see if I've been smoking.'

'Man, that's so sad. You're in worse shape than I thought. C'mon what's the problem?'

Denton paused and used the sandwiches being delivered as an opportunity to marshal his thoughts. He sighed. 'Ok. I woke up this morning and I should have been worried about Julie and I was but I was also looking forward to seeing you again and wondering how and why it is that you've become a part of my, and now, Julie's life. Why was I sitting on that stool as nervous as a schoolboy on his first date? Why am I sitting here instead of searching for Julie and why do I have such confidence that you can and will help me?' He stopped, aware that he had said more than he meant to and less than he could. He looked at her, shrugged his shoulders and showed the palms of his hands in a gesture of helplessness.

Dee picked up a sandwich, took a bite from it, cupped her elbow in the palm of the other hand and began her answer, emphasising her points by waving the sandwich towards him while swinging the crossed leg in counterpoint. 'Ok, serious stuff. Right! I was attracted to you and I was lonely. It sometimes

142

happens on tours. I was looking for company. Not sex, company. Conversation. I like conversation. Your next question, which you won't ask, would be about have I done it before or often. The answer is that yes, I have done it before. Not frequently but yes, the answer to your follow up question, which again you won't ask, is that on a few occasions it has ended in my bed. Last night I gave you all the signals and you either didn't see them or chose to ignore them. My bet is that you didn't see them until I kissed you goodnight.' She reached for another sandwich, 'up in the room half of me was hoping you'd try and make out and the other half was praying you wouldn't. You're a decent man Denton and I want to know more about you. I want you to know more about me and I do want to help you. I also want you in my bed but not yet and maybe not ever. So! Denton, it is for the moment. Ok? I've made a start with Julie. You wanna hear?'

'I don't know what to say.'

'Then don't say anything. Listen. Slammers is owned by an asshole called Woolley. He's a very serious, very connected, viscous asshole at the centre of drugs, prostitution, protection, people smuggling and every other kind of lowlife venture you could think of and some you couldn't. He's the big boy on the block in this little old burg of Manchester. You, Denton, are very, very seriously out of your league. But, here's the interesting bit. Woolley is in trouble too. He has a problem and your friend Andy Starmer and maybe Julie are part of that problem. He has another problem. The boys on the next ledge up in the food chain are pissed at him. I don't know why but I do know that he's had a visit from the top.'

'How the hell do you know all this?' Marvelled Denton.

Dee leaned forward and touched his lips with her forefinger signalling her need for silence and took the opportunity to brush a crumb from the side of his mouth. 'I've not finished. Woolley is definitely looking for Andy. So, the thugs that you missed at the house were working for Woolley. There's serious shit, and money on the street. They want either Andy or Julie or both badly. I don't know what they've done or what they've got but Woolley is promising a heaven filled with drugs, lap-dancers and loot to whoever finds them'.

Again, Denton asked, incredulous, 'how do you know all this?'

'How do I know? Musicians. The front end of any mob business can't work without them. Look at Vegas, Sinatra?

143

Musicians are like screen savers: Always around when it's not busy. Rehearsing. They see things. They hear things. If they've got any sense they keep quiet. But if they want a job and they're susceptible to the charms and subtle interrogation technique of someone as beautiful as your current companion, they talk. We've got a replacement drummer; you've got some information. He's a good lad. Local boy. Knows the scene.' As if to give emphasis to her account, Dee vigorously brushed her hands to remove crumbs, brushed a few more from her lap, picked up her glass, chinked it against his and said, 'impressed?'

She then leant back in her chair with a look of self-satisfaction that wouldn't have been out of place on the face of a small girl who had just given her teacher the right answer. Denton slumped back into his seat with a sense of horror that made him feel physically sick. Suddenly his mind was making connections to the part of the story of which Dee was completely unaware: McCarthy. For the first time in a very long time he felt fear. Alcoholics don't do fear. That's the whole point of being an alcoholic. Perhaps he wasn't alcoholic? He was frightened for Julie, himself, Andy and now Dee. He also began to appreciate that he had to tell Dee the rest of the story and was worried at what her reaction might be. Also, nagging away at the back of his mind was the effect that Dee was beginning to have on him and therefore his marriage.

'Dee. I've not been totally open, well, honest with you.'

'Denton, this had better be good. I know you're married, probably alcoholic and I suspect your marriage is in trouble. I think you're attracted to me and I've explained where I am with it. You've told me about Julie and I am trying to help. What else do I need to know?'

By the time he had finished explaining the events of the previous day he was looking at a chastened and pensive Dee Dee Wilson. In a desperate attempt to fill the silence he said. 'Some of this could be coincidence.'

She leant across the table her eyes wide with controlled fury and her forefinger jabbing at Denton. 'Denton, your daughter is addicted to drugs, she and her boyfriend are being chased by the mob, a friend of yours who may or may not be a policeman has been murdered, you've been hauled in for questioning and someone you worked with and who knows your daughter is connected with the mob and here in Manchester. What's more I'll bet a dollar to a doughnut that it's the same man who is the heat from outta town and the other guy you saw was Woolley. Denton there is no coincidence, it's all connected. There is some very serious shit goin' down here and you, little old 'mulling' you, are slap bang in the fuckin' middle of it.'

Her voice had been rising as she talked to a level that had attracted the barman's attention. He now occupied their end of the bar and had been polishing the same glass for too long while pointedly posing in a position of studied indifference. Dee and Denton's silence and stares, while they considered the eavesdropper, unnerved him sufficiently to cause him to move back down the bar.

'Denton, you are in a whole bunch of trouble,' she hissed.

They both leant back in their chairs and avoided each other's gaze. Dee folded her arms and breathed heavily while clenching and unclenching one fist. All thoughts of the relationship with her had been washed from Denton's mind by her outburst as the fear that he had felt earlier surfed back into his brain. He felt almost helpless, confused and very guilty. How the hell had it come to this and how had he managed to fail his daughter so badly? He was also conscious that it was his problem and not Dee's and to involve her in something that she obviously considered to be so dangerous would be very wrong.

He also judged from her composure and silence that the full enormity of the problem had hit her hard and that she would probably be grateful for a way out. He eased himself out of the chair and looked down at her. Her gaze remained fixed on a spot on the floor somewhere over to his right. 'I'm sorry Dee. This isn't your problem. I shouldn't have involved you. Thanks for listening and thanks for all your help. I'm sorry.'

Her gaze lifted and focussed as she looked up into his face and said very quietly, 'sit down Denton and listen. For the first time in a very long time a man has come into my life that I think respects me, a man who could and maybe would be a good friend and a man who perhaps wants to be with me because I'm me and not because of who I was, what I've got, what I do or what I may become. That's only happened once before in my life and I screwed it up. Now I've told you a whole lot more than I should have done. Right now, I wanna see how this plays out. That ok with you?'

145

He nodded numbly and quickly averted his gaze while he blinked away a sudden moistness around his eyes. Recovered, he looked back at Dee just in time to catch sight of a tissue being returned to her bag. She blinked a number of times rapidly fished again for the tissue and then giggled. 'We're a couple of Mary Ellens and we're goin' to take on the mob?' She said with the cadence of the sentence rising at the end to pose a question.

They both laughed.

'Look Denton, let me help. It seems to me that the key to all this is Julie. She's the connection between what happened back home and here. If we can find her, we can find out what the problem is. If we have her and know what the problem is we can work out the best way to protect her. And incidentally get her off drugs. But we've got to find her first. Before the mob.'

Nodding he glanced back over his shoulder at the sound of clinking glass and briefly caught the nervous eyes of the barman before he dipped his head below the bar to the sudden sound of rushing water. Denton stared fixedly in his direction until just his head appeared above the counter with the movement of his shoulders suggesting a frantic turning of taps.

Where would Julie go? Denton quickly realised that she was going wherever Starmer decided. Starmer was looking after Julie so, presumably, he was making the decisions. Starmer had avoided Woolley's first attempt to catch them so he must know that they were being chased. He'd be looking for a place of safety. Somewhere they couldn't be found. Somewhere that he could catch his breath, plan his next move. He was obviously a resourceful, capable and determined man. This thought brought the first real comfort of the day to Denton. If Julie couldn't be with him then Starmer was probably the next best bet. But where would he make for? He'd got a stolen car but if he had any sense he'd ditch that before too long. Denton tried to put himself in the man's place: If he were him what would he do, where would he go? He wouldn't go anywhere that he was known. He wouldn't go to friends or family, his or Julie's because they would be the first places Woolley would look. He'd try to get some distance in. Abroad? Unlikely. Passports, visas and the checks that could be made would keep him clear of airports and ports. So! Distance but not that far. Where? A place that he knew but which wouldn't be associated with him. If only he had known Starmer, even met him once or twice, knew a bit about him, he'd be in a better position even to guess. Christ! He hadn't even got a 'photo to show around. Denton suddenly stiffened in his seat. The computer. He'd got Starmer's computer in the boot of his car. Idiot!

Vaguely aware that he hadn't got Dee's full attention he was pleased when the distraction turned out to be a harassed looking Mathew Sinclair who asked if he might join them before pulling up a chair. He smiled recognition at Denton while opening an old-fashioned leather music case, which had a flap secured by a thin brass rod that passed through two brass eyes. From within he hauled a wadge of sheet music, an A4 pad, half a dozen pens held together by a rubber band and a Filofax. 'Sorry to interrupt but Dee and I have got to get a few things sorted out for this evening. I hope you don't mind.'

Denton said he didn't and sat back and watched them working together. It was quickly apparent that Dee respected and liked this earnest young man. The discussion ranged over practicalities for the evening's performance through to detailed examination of scores and arrangements and a slight disagreement about the running order. Dee seemed to want to leave it unchanged while Sinclair gently insisted that the change, of moving her new song to the middle of the set, was about marketing but that it was also about emphasising her new direction. Denton was surprised at how readily she accepted his direction and how warm the relationship appeared to be. He was slightly alarmed to note a faint twinge of jealousy. Several times Dee touched the young man's arm or hand while listening or making a point. Denton learnt that there was to be one performance in Manchester that night, followed by more in Edinburgh and the final concerts in Brighton and London to close this stage of the tour and other events to promote a record. When they had finished Sinclair carefully and methodically repacked his bag, thanked Denton and left Dee with clear instructions to rest before the performance.

'You seem to get on very well.'
'Hey Denton! There're a couple of really nice guys in my life at the moment. It'd be a shame if one of 'em screwed it all up by getting jealous.'

'I'm only jealous that he shares a part of your life about which I know nothing. That's all.'

Dee nodded, got up, gathered her things, leant over him and kissed his cheek.

'What's this about a record?'

'You heard the man. I've got to rest. I'll tell you all about it later. When will I see you? Will you come to the show? If you want to I'll leave a pass at reception.'

'Please do. I think I'll pay Jake another visit. He might be able to think of somewhere Starmer might go. I forgot to tell you that I've got Starmer's computer in the car, well the box bit at least, and Jake is a bit of a computer nerd. Maybe there'll be a clue there.'

Denton turned into Norman Road and immediately saw that there was a problem. While that was registering, and as he came opposite the house, he recognised the Mercedes from Slammers and Webber's designer attired frame in the porch. Praying that neither Webber nor the goon leaning into the entry phone panel would turn around, he accelerated up to the end of road and turned sharp right into Birch Grove. Blessing his luck for the second time that day, he parked. He assumed that Webber was at the house because it must have been listed somewhere as one of the addresses for Starmer and Julie. The obvious thing to do would be to turn the car round go back to the house, walk up to Webber, all innocence, and express surprise and pleasure at meeting him. After all, he reasoned, Webber might know that he was looking for Julie and was concerned about her but couldn't know that Denton knew about Slammers or that he had made the connection between the club and McCarthy. Chiding himself for a fool, he abandoned the idea because the less Webber knew the better it was likely to be for Julie and Starmer. He'd wait 'til they'd gone and see whether they'd met up with Jake or anybody else in the house.

It was nearly dusk and two furtive reconnoitres later before Denton felt safe to approach. The Mercedes had gone and Denton didn't have to ring the bell; the door was open. Jake was lying on the floor face down in the corridor, moaning. Denton gently turned him over and stepped back in shock. Half of Jake's face was one massive bruise with his features seemingly recessed into swellings and contusions that appeared to grow even as Denton watched. His left eye was completely closed by a swelling that was inches proud of his forehead and what looked like a fractured cheek-bone while his nose was split from nostrils to bridge and smashed over towards the right cheek. The left-hand side of his mouth was swollen past the profile of his jaw-line and Denton could see a glimpse of two of Jake's teeth where they had pierced his lower lip. The uneven swelling to his left jaw suggested a fracture and the blood oozing from his mouth indicated more damage inside. This couldn't have been Webber. Denton remembered him as being one of the few left-handed people he knew. The goon responsible had done all the damage with his right hand. Repeated, merciless, measured right-handers.

What frightened Denton more was the appreciation of just what sort of man Webber truly was: he had commissioned the beating and stayed to witness its calculated, cruel delivery.

He quickly appreciated that Jake was in no condition to answer any questions and more importantly needed urgent help. That thought was as quickly followed with another; waiting for help to arrive could see him involved in another brush with the law and the need to answer questions for which he could not provide answers. Every human instinct he possessed demanded that he stay and help Jake but every animal instinct in his body screamed at him to leave. Julie was his daughter and protecting her from the sort of people responsible for this sort of barbarity had to be his priority.

He stopped at the first 'phone box he came to and 'phoned in three nines. On an afterthought, he then 'phoned the Sachas and asked for Dee and was quite surprised to hear her voice.

'Hello, Dee.'

'Denton why the fuck haven't you phoned?' She barked.

'Dee,'

'Shut up Denton and listen. There've been people here asking about you. Mathew was at reception half hour ago, and overheard a guy asking for you and trying to get your room number. He was with what Mathew described as "very rough trade"; a big, brainless, bruiser. I've just checked you out of the Hotel. Well, Mathew did really, after they'd gone, he said you were with the tour and he'd sacked you and needed to settle your bill and send on your gear. He's taking your stuff to the concert.

Whatever you do don't come back here. The smart one is waiting in the lobby apparently.'

'What's he look like?'

'I don't know. I didn't go down and I'm not going to try and find out now. Ok?'

'Ok, sure, but how the hell did he know I was at the Sachas?'

'Who?'

'Webber, I've just missed him here. So, I'm pretty certain that's who it is in the lobby.'

'Perhaps he got it out of that Jake?'

'Jake didn't know.'

As one they reached the same conclusion.

'The barman.'

'Right', said Denton, 'In that case Webber might twig the connection and his next port of call might be you. Although I still can't work out how or why he seems to turn up wherever I am. What does he want with me? Anyway, I can't come to the concert Dee. Tell Mathew not to worry about the clothes; I've got everything I'll need. I'll call you when I've worked a few things out. Where'd you say was your next date?'

'Edinburgh. We're playing the Queen's Hall and we're staying at the Kildrumman Lodge, it's only just opened apparently.'

'Ok, I'll ring.'

'You take care Denton. Remember the things we said.'

'I won't forget.'

Chapter Ten

From leaving Dee to realising that he was in a state of shock saw nearly an hour of Denton's life drift as steadily by as the reflections on the windscreen while he drove aimlessly through Manchester. With his mind both buzzing and bruised from stress and lack of sleep he pulled into the curb, rested his head on the wheel and switched off the ignition.

Dee was right. It was all connected. She'd found out that it was Woolley who was looking for Starmer and Julie but part of that same hunt had seen Webber turn up at Slammers, Jake's and The Sachas hotel. He flipped his mind back to the scene outside Slammers where he'd first seen Webber in Manchester. He was sure that Dee had also been right in her assumption that the fat guy Webber had intimidated outside Slammers must, indeed, have been Woolley. But Webber knew Julie. Knew her well. Was he simply trying to find her? If so why? Did he have his own reasons or had somebody asked him to look for her and if so who?

Denton couldn't remember Webber cropping up in the interview he'd had with Church but the company they both worked for was obviously part of the enquiry. Something at Northern Mouldings Group had attracted the interest of a serious Customs investigation and that in turn had led to Mickey's murder. He'd been killed because, they, whoever they were, must have realised that progress was being made and collars that would be felt were getting itchy. He rubbed his gritty eyes and leaned back into the seat and considered lowering it to get a few minutes' shuteye. The thought that he was still in Manchester and therefore vulnerable to discovery straightened him up and he gripped the wheel and squeezed it hard as he tried to concentrate.

Julie, who knew Webber and had worked for NMG was missing and serious criminal effort and resources were going into finding her. Or, he mused, was Starmer the quarry who had dragged Julie into all this. Then there was the question of why Webber would seek him out at the Hotel. Assuming it had indeed been Webber what could he have possibly wanted with Denton? As he relaxed the grip on the wheel the tiredness returned and he leant his temple against the cold glass of the car window and realised that he wasn't far from where he'd started looking for his daughter yesterday. He stiffened with stomach wrenching panic as he realised that Julie was probably being hunted by the killers responsible for Mickey's death.

He couldn't go much further without sleep and food. He needed to find somewhere for both and that needed to be away from Manchester. But where? What general direction should he head off in pursuit of Julie? A cold weariness descended on him as he realised that he had no idea where to go or what to do next. A familiar, nagging feeling of loss or absence distracted him momentarily until he realised that his need for alcohol had fought its way through his preoccupations. It shocked him to realise that he hadn't had a drink for some time. A pint as a loosener and a large brandy for the glow just to settle him down wouldn't hurt right now. The thought brought with it opportunity as he realised that he had parked on a street corner outside a pub. A pub typical of the area in this city with a door in each street and the helpful sign on that nearest him to "use uvver door".

A street light flickered an orange cast onto soot stained red brickwork as he leaned forward and turned the ignition. A beep and a flashing fuel warning light gave the next few minutes purpose. Driving a few hundred yards to a junction he slowed just in time to make the turn onto the forecourt of "Blake & Co – Carriage Builders and Motor Traders" and pulled towards a centre island with a National Benzole canopy under which were a petrol, diesel and a hand operated paraffin pump. As he was unlocking the filler cap he spotted a portly, middle aged man in a brown warehouseman's coat, tucking a biro into a top pocket marked by the ink from hundreds of previous pocketings. The man walked towards the forecourt crossover and paused to stamp repeatedly on a cable stretched across the entrance. Obviously annoyed he turned to Denton.

'Petrol?'

'Please. Fill her up?'

There was a brief delay while the man fiddled with a counter on the pump. 'How many gallons will that be?'

'Not sure. Why?'

''Cos I set the gallons and it pumps them in.'

'Can't you just hold the trigger?'

'Well yeah. But then I've got to stand here.'

Denton sighed. 'Can't you lock it to pump and let the cut out take it?'

'Cut out. Do you know how old this pump is?'

He didn't but quickly scanning the site and taking in the general neglect suspected that the answer had to be thirty years at least. He nodded at the sign. 'Not a lot of carriage building about these days then?'

The man grinned wryly, 'that was Granddad. Eighteen ninety-six. Soon have the century up. If we last that long', he grimaced.

'Business not good?'

'Nope,' he shrugged his shoulders and nodded towards the street. 'Neighbourhood's gone down badly. Particularly the last five years or so. Few repairs, some servicing, a trickle of MOTs and the odd fill up. Sell a lot of paraffin though.' He grinned and rattled the pump nozzle in the filler housing to shake it empty, 'how are you paying?'

'Cash. While I think of it have you got any road maps, guides that sort of thing?

'Yeah, come over to the office and have a look. I don't know whether they are up to date but you're welcome to have a look.' They walked across the forecourt to a single-story shop front between a large workshop and an empty show room. As the man opened the door a bell rang. He laughed and nodded back to the rubber covered cable crossing the forecourt. 'That's what supposed to happen when you drive in. Bloody thing will probably ring as you leave now.' They both laughed.

'Maps are down there, 'the man said as he turned away to answer a ringing 'phone.

Denton marvelled at a collection of sun blanched Smurfs in presentation packs along the window sill as he walked towards a door at the end of the shop which was flanked on one side by mainly empty shelves, and on the other by a wire rack with a few curling maps and a couple of very old Shell guides. Hearing movement in the adjoining room he leaned slightly to one side to get a better view. A teenager in a maroon blazer with gold piping to lapels and cuffs was swivelling slowly on an office chair staring absently at a computer screen while impatiently circling a mouse on a magazine. 'Works better with a mouse mat.'

The boy turned cheerfully towards him and smiled slow and wide, 'that's what Dad would call a 'non-essential.''

'Knows a lot about computers, does he?'

'What do you think?' Said the boy with another grin.

'He sounds a bit like me is what I think.' As he said it a germ of an idea formed and grew, temporarily displacing his fears and indecision. 'What's the programme?' He squinted closely at the screen.

'Lotus 123. I do Dad's accounts with it.'

'Not that there's a lot of point to accounts with business as it is,' interrupted the father. 'The maps are out here, and you'd better get moving.' he added abruptly.

'What's up. What are you on about?'

The man looked at him then nodded an invitation for Denton to join him back at the counter and out of earshot of his son. As the cash register drawer rocketed open he leaned towards Denton and pointed towards his car. 'It seems one or two people are asking around about a car like that and a bloke who fits your description.' He glanced meaningfully at the 'phone.

Denton carefully scanned the street for any sign of anything unusual or different.

'Last week a fourteen-year-old kid called Benji was shot in a Take Away just around the corner from here. Drugs. Territory. We're just a quarter of a mile away from where the Noonans live and breathe their infectious little lives. Drugs are everywhere. It's infected this City.' He flapped his arms despairingly and nodded towards the back office. 'Robert goes to a good school. If I didn't take him there and back every day he'd get beaten to a pulp. Know why?' He didn't wait for an answer. 'That blazer, he's different see. The others round here haven't got a chance and that blazer reminds them of it every time they see him. They tried to get him on drugs.' He retrieved Denton's change and angrily slammed the cash drawer back into the till. 'If I could sell this place we'd go tomorrow, but we can't, so we stay. Like bloody hamsters on one of them soddin' wheels.' The man lowered his head then looked up slowly into Denton's face. 'So, you'll understand that if they ask if I've seen you I've not got a lot of choice. Probably best that you don't buy a map or tell me where you're going.'

Denton was stunned at the extent of the reach, power and resources these people had. 'What about the Police?'

He snorted dismissively. 'Contrary to what Mr Anderton, our last Chief Constable, believed, God was not on his side or that of the Greater Manchester Police and Judas Iscariot is in the ascendant.

'You mean they're bent or useless?'

'Probably both. How else do you explain that drugs are traded freely on the street, in the clubs, pubs and even the schools? Guns appear to be as freely available and are frequently used. People get killed and no one gets caught. Now they're killing children. Mark my words if this carries on you'll see kids emptying banana magazines into each other before long.' He snorted derisively, 'nobody can be that useless. They've gotta be bent.' He shrugged, embarrassed; probably more words than he'd used in a long time. He looked away from Denton and then quickly back. 'Look. just go.'

Denton locked eyes with him for appreciable moments and was encouraged by how his gaze was held. 'How'd you like to hit back?'

'I wouldn't, I've got too much to lose,' he waved down the aisle towards his son.

'Would you just listen to me before you make up your mind?' The answer was so long in coming that Denton had nearly reached the door.

'Put the car in the workshop. No point in waving a flag at the Bull.'

It was fully dark by the time that Denton had finished telling John Blake about Julie, the drugs, Andy's involvement and the fact that he had to find them before the Manchester mafia. He was deliberately vague about some parts of the tale and felt guilty that he wasn't more honest with this considerate man whose help he now sought.

'Where do I come in?'

155

'You don't. It's Robert's help I need.'

He went on to explain about the computer from Starmer's place and the idea he'd had to link Robert's monitor to Starmer's box to try and get at the information on the hard drive in the hope that it'd help him locate Starmer.

'I don't like it. But then I don't like the idea of your Daughter being hurt. I know how I worry about Robert. Come to that I don't like the idea of anybody being hurt,' he paused. 'God, I hate drugs. Maybe,' he mused, 'if we're careful,' he added distractedly. Suddenly, he straightened, decisively, 'ok here's the deal. Get the car in the garage. I'll get some food, fish and chips ok? Then you and Robert see what you can do. Once we've eaten we're going home. You can kip here if you like but be gone by first light. When you go make it look like you've broken in. Might be useful. Who knows? Deal?'

Denton shook the offered hand.

Robert seemed genuinely interested once Denton explained what he was trying to do and within minutes had hooked the box up to his equipment. They sat quietly in front of the screen as the computer booted up. Denton was furious with himself for not having anticipated the dialogue box demanding a power up password when it appeared. He grunted. 'Any ideas Robert?'

Robert paused thoughtfully and circled the dialogue box with the cursor. 'People are funny with passwords. They know they're necessary but somehow, they can't sign up fully to the idea. So, they use dumb combinations: "123456", "qwerty", "abc123", or even "password", that sort of thing. They're also scared that they'll forget the password. So, they tend to use something very familiar or something of which they can be readily reminded.'

'Like what?'

'Personal data or the name of something near to hand?'

'Let's give it a try then.' Denton realised that his main difficulty was that he knew so very little about Starmer other than his name and the suspicion that the man was in love with his daughter.

'Sometimes the obvious stuff works. Pets names, Birthdays, where they were born. That sort of thing?'

'Thing is Robert I don't know an awful lot about the guy who owns the box. Let's start with the obvious stuff I do know;

"Andy", "Starmer", "Julie", he continued to reel off words that came to mind. As Robert tried each in turn Denton, watching his hands flying over the keys, appreciated that the lad was a natural with this technology. 'You're a bit smart with this stuff aren't you Robert?'

'I enjoy it. I think I'm going to earn my living with this.'

'How the hell are you going to do that?'

Nodding towards the box and screen Robert said, 'in twenty years' time everybody will have one of these in their top pocket.'

'Bit of a stretch.'

'The whole kit and caboodle, as Dad would say, will be smaller than a packet of twenty Embassy. Any more ideas?'

'God knows. Try "Brailsford", oh I don't know, I'd rather hoped that you could get me in with some of your technical magic.'

'Maybe a few years down the line I'll be able to but right now we're stuck in a guessing game.'

Denton sighed, 'I know Robert. Look there's no point in keeping you here. Finish up your fish and chips and I'll give it some thought.'

John returned from cashing and locking up and sat eating his meal with a wooden two-pronged fork while they all sat looking at the screen blankly. 'He's right Robert. We need to go.' He screwed up the paper the fish and chips had been in and launched it at a bin by the door. He looked down at Denton as he rose from the chair and, again, offered his hand.

'Good luck and don't let me down.'

'I won't.'

Denton must have dozed for an hour after they had gone before returning to the computer. He idly tried Julie's birthday in all formats and any other number of random thoughts. By the time he got to "Manchester" and "Bromley" he knew he was clutching at straws but with nowhere else to go continued with the task. All that he knew about Starmer he had gleaned from Jake. He reviewed what Jake had told him: Starmer was a loner, in love with Julie and very anti-drugs. Denton spent the next half hour entering every combination of drug terminology that he could remember. He tried "heroin", "smack" and knew he was verging on desperation when he got to "syringe".

He leant back in the much-abused office chair and just thought passwords. Stella's, he knew was the name of their cat: "Treacle". His, which had to be changed monthly at work, had been a series of jazz artists: "Brubeck, Byrd, Coltrane or Thelonious", rotated through the year. He looked at his watch, stretched and then locked his fingers behind his head. Two hours had now passed. Desperately he cast his eyes round the cramped confines of the back-room office seeking any inspiration. Briefly, and more to keep awake and still thinking than with any hope of success, he pumped in random guesses prompted loosely on word association linked to Julie. Nothing.

Jake would probably not only have the answers but also a way round the problem but, in his current condition, was in no position to help. Denton retraced his time in Manchester seeking further stimulus. After Jake, there had been the encounter with Starmer's neighbour. What was her name? Had she said? His mind drifted to the encounter with matchstick man on the stairs at Brailsford Road. Starmer had marked his computer with his name. Denton entered every combination of Starmer's name to no effect. With hopes dwindling he tried the serial number of the computer recognising this a last resort.

As he contemplated disconnecting the box and packing up for the night his mind drifted back to his brief visit up to Starmer's room and Robert's assertion that password reminders were sometimes near to hand at. There'd been a shelf with CDs, which, he hadn't looked at too closely. Maybe Starmer used his system, Artists names. To check that out he realised that he would have to go back to Brailsford Road. Not a prospect he relished and one that would take time he didn't have. Disillusioned and now worried that he would never get a lead on Starmer and Julie from the computer he reached down to the floor to unplug the box. There had been an old enamelled sign lying down on the floor in Starmer's room. A sign advertising gravy. He typed in "bisto", he paused, snorted at his own foolish persistence and entered "Ahbisto". Maybe he should phone Stella explain the problem and see if she had any ideas. As he reached for the 'phone the black screen with the blue dialogue box still mocked him. In a final flurry of impatience, he tried again, "Aahbisto". Nothing. As a last resort, with the 'phone ringing at the other end, he dragged up a mental image of the sign and tried to picture the exact format of the letters and the case in which were printed; "aah!Bisto". The dialogue box disappeared, the screen turned blue, windows started to load to the mindless jingle of the Microsoft start up theme and a screen saver picture of Julie on a beach appeared with the desktop icons following. Denton slammed the 'phone back on the cradle. He couldn't remember when last he had felt so pleased with himself and marvelled at the sense of achievement this small triumph had afforded. He rubbed his hands together vigorously with pleasure.

He went straight to 'my documents' and reviewed the list of folders. Starmer, he noted was a very thorough young man. There were two main folders: "Personal" and "Uni". 'The first had three sub folders: "Bank", "Book" and "Letters". He quickly clicked on "Letters", then a subfolder, "friends" to find two further folders, "Jamie" and "Julie". "Julie", he decided, he knew enough about already. What about "Jamie"? Clicking on that folder revealed a list of WordPerfect documents; letters. Just over a hundred and fifty. Regular, one a week going back three years. Whoever Jamie was he was obviously important to Starmer. He also seemed to be the only person, other than Julie, with whom Starmer corresponded. Denton clicked the files into date order with the most recent first. It took no more than a few minutes to find that Jamie lived at a place called Findhorn, which meant nothing to Denton without a map. Then a passing reference to a protest against noise from aircraft at Kinloss had Denton mentally planning the journey to Scotland while he scanned through the rest of the files for further information. By the time he had finished he knew that the two were close friends. The intimacy of the correspondence, the shared confidences and exchange of advice and guidance spoke of a good and durable friendship. The sort of friendship you might need if you were in trouble. Not only that, Denton realised, if he hadn't heard of Findhorn, given that it was somewhere in the wilds of Scotland, it was likely to be just the place to hide out with little chance of discovery.

He looked at his watch. If he left just before dawn he had about six hours to get some rest and needed to be away by six if he was to leave in darkness. He let himself into the workshop got into the passenger seat, lowered it, turned up his collar, crossed his arms over his chest and composed himself for sleep by washing his mind with trivia. He slept fitfully, his tiredness not sufficient for sleep deep enough to be able to ignore the cold. At five, wide awake, he stripped to the waist at an old chipped Belfast sink and washed in cold water with the help of a cracked, split and grimed tablet of Pears coal tar soap. While carefully selecting the few unstained portions of an adjacent roller towel to dry himself he considered how best to fake the break in and decided to carefully ransack the shop and force the door on that and the entrance to the Workshop. It then dawned on him, with a sinking heart, that one of the few items of value was Robert's computer and that any local Herbert breaking in was unlikely to leave it. He retrieved a bill head from the counter for the telephone number and hid the computer under the counter behind boxes of old till rolls. He'd 'phone John Blake, tell him where it was and suggest he list it as stolen.

He was on the road by half five and reckoned he had a full day's drive ahead of him from Manchester to the Moray Firth. If he was lucky with the roads and the traffic he might get there by mid-afternoon. He decided to try not to think further about Julie but to rest his mind during the journey and to relax and enjoy what promised to be a scenic ride. It wasn't long before he started picking up signs for the Lake District and his mind, in serendipitous mode, had him back there with 'Aitch for the sort of holiday that only 'Aitch really enjoyed: canvas, compass & campfires. He'd been in his element and had delighted in showing off the skills he'd learnt in the Army.

'Do you know the most dangerous thing known to man young Paul?'

'No.'

'An Officer with a map!' He'd roared with laughter before reassuring Paul that as he was an NCO everybody was safe.

Denton, now hungry, pulled off the M6 into Penrith to get a meal with his mind gently returning to the problems that confronted him. One of his difficulties, he knew, was his complete inability to think like a criminal. He realised that he had no experience of criminality other than having lifted ten Senior Service from the Co-op in Torridon Road as a kid. He did know that Don and Ron moved around the fringes but doubted that these days they went very near anything would've resulted in much more than a fine if it all went bandy. He was therefore having trouble coming to terms with the fact that in recent years he had apparently been unwittingly stuck in the middle of mayhem that had already led to one murder. The question he repeatedly

160

asked himself was how he could have been so blind to so many things. Where had his head been that he'd missed all the crises with Julie and what, he now had to assume, was serious criminality within the company that he helped to manage? Certainly, drink had been part of the problem. What a boon his drinking must have been to the Webbers of the world; an absolute gift.

If he could get a grip on what Webber and Co were involved in and how that related to NMG he might just be able to figure out a way to use that information to protect Julie. Her addiction was no longer the problem. Saving her life was now the priority and he no longer cared about the drugs as much a securing her future; he'd deal with the drugs later. He needed help. Dee had helped with some of it but if push came to shove he could do with the sort of help that wouldn't balk at breaking bones or wrecking lives with the same casual indifference that seemed to characterize Webber's operation. Don and Ron had the muscle but not the heart for that sort of problem. Denton had met the sort throughout his life but had either avoided or subsequently regretted the encounters. What he needed was a friendly sociopath. A charmer not concerned by wrecking lives. He wracked his brains trying to think of anybody who remotely fitted that description?

The answer came many miles later on the outskirts of Perth and was prompted by a sign pointing the way to Rob Roy Country. Roy. Roy King. Son of Charlie and a practised nasty bastard from birth.

After the row about the Christmas trees on the Prefab Estate Charlie King's little world had begun to collapse. Being fronted out by 'Aitch' in such a gloriously public display of low cunning and nerve had reduced his credibility to zero, negated his influence and power to intimidate and made him a laughing stock now unable to do any business around the Estate. This had led in short order to an increasing desperation in Charlie that saw him move from the fringes up a level to play with the bigger boys in a lorry highjack. He hadn't had the sense to just take his cut. He'd lifted some of the load and when packs of two hundred cigarettes began to appear round the sides of Lewisham Market he was firstly beaten by the gang and then put in the frame for that and other jobs. When it came, the five-year sentence had been a relief to many on the Estate. Roy, meanwhile, sensing a slackening of parental discipline, such as it had been, took to the streets in a big way and began to run wild. A firework tossed into Denton's back garden that landed in the folds of his mother's best sheets had brought young Roy up against the first real discipline he had ever encountered.

Eleanor Joan Denton had a heart of gold but one that had been hardened by the sights and sounds of four years of fire watching through the Blitz. She rarely displayed tolerance or patience with anything she considered "frivolous" and out of season fireworks burning holes in her laundry she would not tolerate. Her fury over the sheets diminished slightly when Roy opened his back door an inch through which she could just about see his pinched features, snotty nose and sleep starved eyes. Joan had asked to see his mother but began to realise that the boy's reluctance to admit her was linked to the sound of a party coming from a room within. She pushed Roy out of her way and crossed the small kitchen in a few strides. Through the fog of cigarette smoke she could see Nora King on a settee on the far side of the living room, partially undressed and fully engaged with two men. Nora struggled to disengage when she spotted Joan.

'Oh, fuck me Lady Muck's here.'

'I'll talk to you later Nora.'

With that Joan, had grabbed Roy by the shoulder and dragged him home. A bath, egg and chips, three slices and most of a bread pudding later Roy had snuggled into 'Aitch's chair with a blanket round his shoulders, a mug of tea in his hands and a smile on his face as he listened to Journey into Space while his clothes were laundered.

Denton permitted himself a wry smile as he recalled the difficulties of living with Roy and the glee with which Roy viewed the occasional drunken forays that Nora King made to retrieve him. Forays which Joan forcefully and sometimes physically repulsed.

Denton had loved his Mum though she hadn't made it easy with her hard words and quick hands. He could remember being told that he had "transgressed" and that she was going to punish him with a slap. This meant a slap to the head. Further, she advised, if he moved he would get another. He'd always seemed to move and became reconciled to the left right routine. He'd struggled to get on the right side of her while Roy, the embryonic sociopath, seemed to have her complete attention and trust while she remained totally unaware that she was being manipulated by a clever, cunning and completely amoral child. He'd fallen further and further from favour as a series of thefts and vandalism were laid at his door by an increasingly favoured cuckoo. When the series of petty thefts and mischief stretched to burglary and serious harm that saw his very survival threatened he took it to 'Aitch.

'Christ boy. Why didn't you say something? I'm surprised you've stayed this quiet this long.'

'I thought you knew?'

'I had no idea. Look, I can sort it but it's you that'll have to live with the result. Might be better for you to tackle it. I'll have a word with your Mum and see if we can lift the rose-coloured specs from her eyes.'

Things came to a head when a good school friend was cut in Fosters Park and refused to say who was responsible. Denton had found the knife in the rabbit hutch. He had picked his evening and waited patiently on the waste ground next to St Michaels Church for King to appear. Denton blocked his path but said nothing.

'What's up with you?'

He'd not answered.

'C'mon. Stop mucking about I want me tea.'

He'd stayed silent.

'Fuck off or I'll do you Denton. Now get out of me way.'

Denton had taken a pace forward, remembering 'Aitch's tactic with Charlie and said, quietly, 'You're not going to do anything. 'Cos if you do the rest of the kids round here are going to find out what a bed wetting little turd you are. They're going to hear about your crying at night, how you shit yourself up the park and how mum had to throw all your clothes away because of lice. I've had enough. You're going.'

Looking back Denton realised that he hadn't thought it through and certainly hadn't been prepared for the assault that came without warning and with a fury and intensity that had overwhelmed him. At the time, he was dimly aware that he was in trouble but had no appreciation of just how bad that trouble was until, in hospital, 'Aitch had told him that two neighbours had dragged Roy King away from where he had been knelt beside Paul to hit him about the head with a half brick. The only consolation, in the weeks it took to get over the fractured skull and broken arm, had been that the attack had finally attracted the sort of scrutiny to Roy that saw him charged with Grievous Bodily Harm. A charge that was later quietly dropped when it was deemed that King was more in need of Care than condemnation and the sort of future that time in Feltham Young Offenders Institute would almost certainly guarantee. 'Aitch had never forgiven himself and the Kings were gone from the Estate within days. They'd bumped into each other once or twice through the years but King had always been polite, even a little reserved and always made a point of asking to be remembered to 'Aitch and Joan. Denton, pondered on his whereabouts.

As he neared Forres on the A96 he made a mental note to ask Don and Ron if they knew what had happened to King before his mind returned to the problems at hand. He gulped guiltily as he realised that his next thought had been of Dee, not Stella. She'd be frantically worried as he'd not 'phoned. Once he'd cracked the password he'd abandoned the call to Stella as he accessed Starmer's files. By now she'd be furious. He found a 'phone box, just outside Forres on the way to Findorn and was, again, relieved that the call went straight to the messaging service. He stumbled through a condensed version of events but assured her that he felt close to finding Julie and thought she might be with her boyfriend and staying with his friend Jamie at a place called Findhorn.

Findhorn, or more accurately The Findhorn Foundation' was a surprise to him. He felt very much out of place in what he appreciated was a worthwhile and earnest venture but one that had ethics and ideals very different from those he valued. Eventually he went into a sort of General Store on the site and was greeted warmly by a grey-haired woman dressed predominantly in purple who approached him nervously to ask if she might help. More to set her at her ease than anything else but also realising that a gift in the bag might be useful when next he was with Stella he enquired about a 'Findhorn Sanctuary Candle Holder' and was stunned by the animated but detailed explanation of their manufacture and popularity in the Community. He agreed to buy two and while they were being wrapped asked, 'I don't suppose you know a Jamie? I think he lives here.'

The woman froze with a partially wrapped holder in one hand before half turning towards him, thrusting the candle holder at him, seizing the notes he had been proffering, opening the till, thrusting his change into his other hand and ushering him to the door. 'There's no Jamie here that I can recall.' She opened the door, 'we're closing now. I'm afraid you'll have to go.'

A stunned Denton stood outside the shop in the late afternoon and realised that he may be getting closer to Julie; the woman in the shop had to be shielding Jamie for a reason and he'd bet money that Julie was part of that reason. He doubted, however, that he was going to get anywhere now it was starting to get dark. He decided to make his way back to Forres to find a place for the night. He'd be back very early for Julie.

Chapter Eleven

The camper van had been slow to start and reluctant to get anywhere near a speed commensurate with Starmer's need to get distance between them and whoever had been making the enquiries at Findhorn.

How in God's name had they been found, he wondered? For the first time since they'd left Manchester he felt fear, a fear which, overlaid with a sense of powerlessness, had numbed his brain. This was impossible. How could they have been found and so quickly when he'd only ever discussed his plans with Julie? He spoke sharply, harshly and without thinking as the suspicion surfaced, 'Have you been on the 'phone again Julie?'

A look of hurt quickly followed by the widening eyes of understanding answered his question. 'No Andy. Not guilty this time.'

He turned in his seat, looked across at her and realised that she was crying.

She sobbed. 'Christ Andy, if they're that well informed and organised we don't have much of a chance.' She dropped her head into her hands and gently rocked back and forth in the seat before grabbing his arm. 'Maybe if we gave them back what you've got in that rucksack they'll leave us alone,' she sobbed again.

Starmer's despair deepened as he realised how little she appreciated the danger that they were in and the ruthlessness they faced. 'That won't stop them. They've been shown up and they can't afford for anyone to get away with something like that. They don't just want back what I've taken they need to show they're not to be messed with and they need to stop their dirty little secrets getting out. Killing me will give them back their credibility on the streets and their stuff.' He glanced sideways to check her reaction just as the engine began to misfire. He slipped the VW into neutral, revved the engine hard, re engaged the gear and was gratified at the slightly smoother running. 'Yeah, they're going to kill me. Maybe not you, but me, they need to kill,' his voice trailed away.

She gasped and then lapsed into a shocked silence as Starmer continued to chase thoughts through his brain in never decreasing circles of fear and frustration. He was certain that the Filofax was the key to their survival; not its surrender but its possession. He doubted that Woolley would put this much effort into tracking him down just to recover the money. He was still convinced in his earlier thinking that Thompson's death would be seen as collateral damage and pretty sure that neither issue would move Woolley to this level of activity. No. Woolley was after that book first, the money second and wouldn't rest until he got both. There had to be a way to use the book to stop Woolley.

He dragged his mind back to the VW which was now firing in two four time with the uneven motion causing a cupboard door to open and close in sympathy while Julie rocked to her own rhythms in her seat. He risked another glance across at her, 'you ok?'

She turned with a worried, tight little smile. 'Scared. You?'

He grinned back as cheerfully as he could, 'scared too if I'm honest but more puzzled than anything'. He drummed a tattoo on the rim of the steering wheel with his fingers while urging the van forward, riding the seat like a jockey on a reluctant steeplechaser. The engine slowly died and in the silence that followed Julie said, 'I'm worried about Jamie'.

He exhaled loudly in exasperation. 'So am I but right now I'm more worried about us, yeah? We've got God knows what right up our chuff. Priority is to get some more distance in. Distance buys time. Time to think. Time to get you back on your feet. C'mon, get the torch; let's see if we can sort this out.' He lifted the engine cover at the back of the van, propped it up with the thoughtfully shaped and cut to length piece of batten left by the Australian and prayed for inspiration. He knew little about engines and experienced the hollowness in the pit of his stomach well known to any motorist stranded on a lonely road at night with a broken-down vehicle.

'Can you smell petrol?'

'Yeah, hold that torch steady.' The beam eventually settled on a damp and split hose with a loose jubilee clip sitting in the bend of the fuel supply line to the carburettor.

'We can't leave him, Jamie,' she added unnecessarily.

'I know that', he replied viciously, 'I need a knife and a screwdriver.'

On the drive back to Findhorn, he reviewed what he could recall of the layout of the Foundation and decided that his best and most secure approach would be from the beach. That way if the people making enquiries were still about he had a chance of avoiding them rather than driving straight into them on the approach road. He'd need to leave Julie with the van and sneak in and get Jamie.

Just after a wooded area and a few hundred yards from the bright lights of RAF Kinloss he swung hard right between two red and white painted oil drums holding posts and a height restricting cross bar. He turned past a dark green litter bin brimming with plastic bottles, a broken kite and a punctured beach ball to a point just out of sight of the entrance.

'I'll stay here then?'

'Might be best.'

'Be careful, won't you.'

'I'll try. Will you be alright?'

'I'll be better when you're back.'

He digested this for a minute then leant across and pulled her to him. They hugged with the desperation of those facing an imminent parting and an uncertain future. He held her at arm's length and looked into her eyes. 'Look Julie,' he paused, found her hands and squeezed, 'if you need a fix I'd rather you said so now than went looking for it. Jamie could wait a few hours until I get you sorted and then we'd come back together. Start coming off again when we next stop?'

'So, you have got some stuff left?' she levelled at him accusingly.

'Not enough to make much difference,' he lied. 'C'mon Julie. Do you want a fix now or not?' I need to get going.

'No. I'll be ok. I've got to be. I'm not going to give away the last two days just yet. Get Jamie but just hurry up. I'm worse when I'm on my own.'

He moved into the back of the VW muttering about the probable need for a coat and left by the side sliding door. He crossed the car park, paused at the litter bin, slid down the dunes grabbing clumps of marram grass to slow his descent and set out on the mile-long trek to the foundation turning up his collar against the stormy, cold gusting wind off the Moray Firth as he went. The receding tide had revealed a panoramic pattern of moonlit washed ridges, swirls and furrows laid across the wet sand like curdling milk beneath a sky of deep shades of blue, black and purple with the creamy aurora of the stars casting pale yellow reflections across the water as broken clouds chased shadows across the sand. He turned his body diagonally landward to shield his face from the booming wind and marvelled at the roar and the distant crashing of waves. He breathed deeply of the night air with its whiff of salty decay to calm himself as he neared the Foundation.

Coming at the Centre from the beach slightly disorientated him and on emerging from the dunes he found himself on an access road and to the rear of the Barrel Houses where Jamie lived. Recognising Melissa's home, he skirted round the vegetable garden that separated her home from Jamie's but froze at the sound of a door or screen slapping viciously back and forth in the storm. He back tracked and crept round to Melissa's front door which was held open by Melissa's head. One sightless eye stared up at the sky the other was obscured by her sheepskin helmet which had slipped down from her brow. Perhaps, dislodged by the bullet that had exited through her forehead taking most of the right side of her frontal bone with it.

Starmer, still crouched, spun away from the horror. As his back completed the one eighty and hit the wall of Melissa's home he slid down into a squat with his knees drawn tightly up under his chin and held there by his crossed and shaking arms. He shivered and tried to squeeze control back into his involuntarily convulsing limbs. The contractions shuddered to a halt as he turned to his left to check that he hadn't imagined the sight. The nightmare returned as he more calmly viewed the desecrated body of this gentle woman. A woman who had turned her life around and probably felt secure in her beliefs and her environment for the first time in her life. A woman who thought she had a happy and productive future in a near earthly paradise now laying there in a dark pool of blood in which he could see a reflection of the moon. She'd been killed with less thought than a midge gave to where it drew blood.

Scurrying, squealing noises from the vegetable patch and the rustling of wind swept winter crops focussed his mind on the plight of the hunted and the terror and despair of the caught. In nature, he thought, survival was pre- ordained by the food chain hierarchy but the fittest of any species could and did survive. The resignation that had plagued his earlier thinking gave way to an anger that bred defiance and a desire for revenge that was as pure as the life that Melissa had tried to lead in pursuit of her gentle beliefs. He would survive but now knew that he would have to kill again to do it. Time to hunt.

He crouched lower and crept back through the vegetable patch. As he neared Jamie's a widening pool of light from the opening door stretched towards him and he quickly slipped behind the compost heap. From there he peered over the top of the heap to see Osman, bloody Osman; Woolley's henchman. He watched the man walk down the path to the access road and carefully followed him back towards Melissa's, moving round the circumference of the Barrel house and keeping Osman just in sight on the tangent of the curve and ready at any moment to pull back out of the line of sight. Concentrating too intently he narrowly avoided a disaster with Melissa's bicycle propped against her wall and recovered just in time to see Osman approach a Mercedes parked under some trees on the main drive. The Turk opened the door, slumped in the passenger seat and pulled the door to but not shut. Turning to the driver he spoke a few words and then listened, nodding occasionally as though receiving instructions. As he sat there Starmer caught the profile of the driver, illuminated by the interior light, partly obscured by the head rest, but sufficiently clear to prompt the recognition receptors in his brain until the light switched off as Osman got out and quietly shut the door.

He swiftly returned to the compost heap and watched Osman go back into Jamie's home. A few minutes passed before a muffled cry brought Starmer from cover to the side of the living area window. With his back to the wall and leaning cautiously to peer round the jamb his view was blocked by an expanse of Prince of Wales check; Woolley. As he sank back into the shadows he heard the unmistakeably meaty sound of flesh being

170

beaten followed by cries and the insistent sibilance of Woolley's hissed enquiry. 'Where is he Jamie? Where is he? You can tell me and then we can all get on with what we were doing before. I mean, what sort of friend is he Jamie to leave you to deal with this? Eh? What sort of friend is that?'

Starmer edged to the window again and caught sight of Jamie as Woolley moved nearer to his victim. The little man was naked and propped, rather than sat, on a kitchen chair and held in place there by Osman. When Jamie didn't answer, Osman let him go and then punched him back into position with two blows to his ribs.

There was no spare flesh on Jamie and Starmer knew that these blows were cracking ribs. Blood and mucus from his broken nose and bloodied lips had run down his chest and pooled in the hollow of his stomach. Bruised ribs and a reddened, swollen torso shone beneath the glistening trail. Jamie's head lolled to one side and then fell forward and hung down as though it were simply too heavy for him. As Woolley turned towards the window Starmer dropped below the sill and wondered which of them had the gun that had killed Melissa.

'Is he dead?'

There was a pause while, presumably, Osman checked Jamie's vital signs before reporting; 'I don't think it'll be long'.

'Such a pity. An attractive boy. Who knows what might have been.' Woolley mused.

'I don't think he knows where Starmer is.'

'Academic now Mr Osman but on balance I think you're probably right.'

'Shall I search the place?'

'I can't see the point. He won't have left it here. They've cleared out.'

'Is it that important?'

Starmer raised his head slowly in time to see Woolley drop his considerable bulk onto the settee stretch his legs out in front of him and lock his hands behind his head. 'I'm afraid it is Mr Osman. If young Andrew works out what he's got hold of and has the balls to use it, you'll have a new boss because my Masters will not be pleased. Further, half of Manchester's finest may find themselves out of work or worse, sharing a cell with people who have long memories and time to turn their vengeful fantasies into fact. Even worse, if young Andrew and this Denton ever get to compare notes it won't be long before they put two and two

171

together which is going to cause all sorts of problems at the Amsterdam end. So, you see, Mr Osman, our futures are somewhat on the line and your stupidity with that woman hasn't helped.' Woolley levered himself from the sofa with Osman's help, shot his cuffs, straightened his tie and looked sadly down at the shorter man like a disappointed teacher with an errant pupil. 'Young Starmer has got to go.'

'I'm sorry about the woman. We were in the wrong house. She saw me screamed and ran. I panicked.' Osman blurted out as he paused to watch Woolley's reaction before pointing at Jamie and asking, 'What do I do with him now?'

'Well, get him out of here for a start. Take him down to the beach and dump him below the high-water mark. Dump her there too. With a bit of luck, they'll get washed away and that might keep it away from us and buy some time.'

Starmer crouched as he saw Woolley start for the door. A short time later the crunch of leather soles, a curse followed by a grunt and the sound of feet dragging on the ground receded in the distance as he heard the squeak of the porch door slowly closing. He inched his way round the house until he could see the front path and then crept a little further until he was concealed behind a large clay pot balanced on a column of dry laid bricks. Osman was across the path and on his way to the beach with Jamie's left arm hauled around his shoulder while Osman's right arm was round the unconscious man's waist. Every few yards Osman stopped to shrug Jamie back onto his hip as he dragged him toward the dunes. Just as Starmer slipped from behind the pot to follow Osman he heard the returning distant crunch of leather on gravel and sank back into position as Woolley reappeared. He heard him enter the roundhouse and the distant sound of doors being thrown open and the contents of drawers being emptied to the floor. Perhaps Woolley had changed his mind about the search or more likely received instructions from the guy in the Mercedes to make sure the Filofax wasn't there. Starmer crouched impatiently wondering whether he should take the chance and cross the open ground to the beach and risk being seen by Woolley. He was desperate to get to Jamie before more harm was done to him if it wasn't already too late. A large crash and the sound of breaking crockery suggested that Woolley would be engaged for a few more minutes and Starmer launched himself into the dark and ran over the uneven ground as fast as he could after Osman.

He crested the last dune and frantically scanned the beach. Far out to his left and near to the water's edge he could see a colony of sea lions or seals and another smaller group off to his right but no Osman. As he fought to get breath into his oxygen starved lungs he realised that he was looking too far out. They couldn't have got that far in the time and anyway with Osman half dragging Jamie he simply had to follow the tracks. He ran to his left along the dune and immediately saw a trail leading round a dune spur alive with the spiky fronds of wind lashed marram grass whipping in the freshening wind off the sea.

There, fifty yards out from the dunes, silhouetted against the reflections from the wet sand he saw Osman standing over a kneeling but slumped Jamie pointing at his head. The bang confirmed the flash that his disbelieving brain simply refused to register as Jamie's head jerked back and his body slowly toppled forward face down into the sand. Starmer sank to his knees, elbows in his stomach, clenched fists to his mouth and the flash searing the memory of Jamie's execution into his brain. He gently leant forward until his forehead rested in the sand in an unconscious re-enactment of Jamie's execution. All he could feel was contempt for himself and shame that he had abandoned Jamie and thus both he and Melissa were dead. Woolley had been right; he'd been no sort of friend.

In a lull between the gusts of wind he heard a muffled curse and raised his head slightly to peer through the grass clinging to the dune. Osman was immediately below him and slightly to his right clutching at tufts of grass to help him ascend the dune. Starmer edged back and to his right until he judged that he was about opposite where Osman was grunting his way to the top. He raised himself to a squat and waited. He tensed as the top of the Turk's head came into view but still didn't move. When Osman had both hands full of grass for the final heave to level ground and his head and shoulders rose above the edge Starmer rose, measured the distance, took two unhurried steps forward and place kicked Osman's head to the horizon. Stepping carefully down the slope he thoughtfully circled the unconscious but groaning Osman and silenced him with a kick to his right temple. Satisfied that he was now unconscious he relieved him of his gun, picked a tussock at the foot of the dune and sat down to wait.

He spent the few minutes it took for Osman to come round examining the gun. It was a small revolver and he found that he liked the heft of it in his hand as he spun the chamber and took practice sightings on the awakening form. As Osman groaned back to life and rolled onto his side to spit out blood and sand he ordered, 'don't get up'.

The man blinked unseeingly out of one eye at the stars, worked his jaw and moved a hand to his temple as he regained his senses, 'What the fuck.'

Starmer realised that with what looked like a fractured eye socket and a jaw lighter by some teeth but also certainly broken Osman was having trouble with both recognition and speech. 'Andrew Starmer,' he said by way of introduction, smiling grimly, 'you're looking for me. Remember?'

The open eye glinted and eventually settled on Starmer and then the gun. Osman hawked, coughed and spat blood and teeth onto the sand. 'You're fucking dead Starmer.'

Starmer smiled again and waved the gun. 'Not yet Mister Osman'

'You're fucking dead', Osman repeated looking past Starmer towards the Foundation and possible help.

'And you're wasting your time. They won't be expecting you for a bit. One more body to dump. Melissa? Remember? Nice lady, kind lady, gentle lady the one you shot in the head.'

Osman rolled half upright supporting his weight on his right elbow while gently exploring the damage to his face with his left hand. 'So, what now cunt?' He snapped.

'Nothing.'

'Nothing?'

'Well, nothing much.' Starmer smiled at Osman again before finishing quietly and calmly, 'I mean I am going to kill you. But as I said, nothing much really.' He looked down at the gun and then hefted it in his hand before sighting down the barrel at Osman with the vision of Melissa's broken head and Jamie's broken body floating between him and his target.

Osman laughed nervously, 'c'mon, for fucks sake. We can sort this out. Talk to Woolley with me. Do a deal. He likes you,' Osman babbled.

'No.' Starmer was determined not to give Osman an explanation. Any more than he was prepared to discuss what had now become a fact of his life: he was going to kill Osman. He got to his feet, looked down at the gun in his hand, carefully levered back the hammer with his thumb to cock the pistol, turned sideways and sighted down the full length of his arm at Osman.

'No, C'mon, let's talk.'

'What I'm wondering is whether shooting's too good for you. I mean it's a bit quick. I'd like to think you suffered. Like Jamie did,' he nodded to the distant moon washed form.

Osman groaned.

'I was thinking a couple in the legs just to stop you wandering off then one where it'll hurt and cause a lot of blood loss so that it becomes a toss-up as to whether the crabs or the tide get you and whether you'll be alive or not when they do. But whatever. It's going to hurt.'

Osman's face froze and as Starmer stepped forward he crabbed backwards, pushing his heels into the sand and holding one hand up in line with the muzzle. Starmer took another step and Osman dropped his hand almost in acceptance of his fate and then seemed to recover some of the defiance that Starmer remembered from the club.

'Fuckin' get on with it then you arsehole!'

The recoil surprised Starmer and sent the shot higher and more to his right than he intended, hitting Osman in the stomach. He stood looking down at him for a few minutes and saw his eyes flicker and his lips move as he tried to raise his head from the sand.

'Finish it you cunt!' The thug grunted, groaning as he rolled onto his side spitting and hawking blood onto the wet sand. He struggled to lift his head, grimaced and through teeth gritted against the pain said, 'Welcome to my world boy.'

Starmer put the second bullet into his head.

He pocketed the gun and started off along the beach at a jog, confident that the dunes and the storm would have muffled the sound of the shots; as they had previously when Melissa had been killed. Woolley wouldn't have been alerted and Osman wasn't due back at the Mercedes just yet. He felt a strange calm almost as though he had been released from a great burden. At first, he thought that this was maybe to do with Jamie's death and the realisation that someone as vulnerable as Jamie was always going to be at risk and that try as he might he would never have been able to have shielded him completely throughout his life. Now Jamie was dead and beyond any need of his help. There never had been any obligation but he felt that a weight had been lifted.

It had all started with Jamie. The violence; the killing of Randall at Loch Eil. He'd known before then that he was different. He'd had to learn that to survive you had to be able stare into an opponent's eyes and show no understanding of fear, defeat or pain and put out an aura of arrogant confidence. He did not consider himself violent but knew he had complete detachment from the consequences of his actions and that he never experienced remorse. He had also learnt that it was this detachment that terrified people. Uni had been the chance at a fresh start and again because of his feelings for another, this time Julie, he had been drawn back into the world in which he operated too well. Randall, Thompson and now Osman. He had killed three times.

Through difficult and dark times, he'd always thought that there were two of him. The one he was told he should be and the one he knew he was. He'd had no difficulty being the first while relying on the second to secure his position in the demi monde of institutionalised life by doing whatever it took to secure half a life. There was no further need for pretence. He was what he was. There had been no need for Osman to welcome him to his world. He had been there all his life. He was calm because he'd finally come to terms with himself.

He thought briefly about not having questioned Osman over the conversation he had overheard between him and Woolley in Jamie's house. That had, perhaps, been a mistake but he'd been determined not to allow Osman any bargaining space. Letting him die thinking he had nothing of value and would receive no mercy or answers had been an important part of avenging Jamie. Still at least he now knew the value of the Filofax and that his suspicions about corrupt Policemen in Manchester had been correct. He also knew that a 'Denton', presumably Julie's Dad, was looking for her. He needed to think more about that and the nagging sense that he knew the man in the Mercedes from somewhere.

As he crested the dunes and the white perimeter marking stones came into view he heard Julie scream. He saw that the VW wasn't where he'd left it but was halfway through the entrance and hard up against one of the forty gallon red and white oil drums with a Mercedes pulled across in front of it. Someone, not Julie, was inside the van and through the open back door of the Mercedes he could see Julie struggling beneath the weight of Woolley. He ran towards the vehicles frantically trying to pull the gun from his waistband as he went and picking up speed as it came free.   His first shot was loosed at the VW with no expectation of achieving much beyond announcing that he was there and armed in the hope that panic would ensue, Julie would be dumped and Woolley would drive off. He saw the man inside the van duck as the bullet smacked into something metallic. When the man jumped from the side door and scooted round to the Mercedes Starmer fired another shot and squeezed the trigger again to hear the hammer click on an empty chamber. Screaming and waving the gun he reached the boot of the Mercedes just as the driver floored the throttle and fishtailed a blizzard of gravel over Starmer sending him sprawling to the ground as the wheels got traction and the car straightened on the road to Forres.

He rolled onto his back in exhausted disbelief. It simply wasn't credible. Every move he made was thwarted at each turn. They couldn't have known Julie was there. She couldn't have told them and he certainly hadn't. He sat up and began to think it through. Reckoning that from when he'd left Woolley in Jamie's house to arriving back at the car park couldn't have been much longer than three quarters of an hour and that it was about twenty minutes since he'd shot Osman. It would have taken them less than five minutes to get from the foundation to the car park and they'd probably spent ten or so minutes searching the van and getting Julie into the car. That meant that they'd left Jamie's about the time he'd killed Osman. There was a chance they'd heard the shots over the storm and decided to bail out but he doubted it. Perhaps with two murders pending Osman's next usefulness was to be served up as the fall guy. Either way, he reasoned, looking again at where the VW was stopped, they had been passing along the road just at the moment that Julie, for whatever reason, had decided to drive away. She'd pretty much run straight into them.

Starmer stood up and walked to the camper picking up some of their belongings as he went. Outside the side door the ground was littered with cushions, clothes and food that had been simply thrown out as each cupboard, drawer and compartment in the van was searched. The head lining at one end had been ripped from the roof and the sink unit levered from the side panel as the van had been ransacked. If they'd had much longer they'd have got it back to bare metal. Starmer perched on the door sill and his peripheral vision caught a spreading darkness in the sand near the rear wheel of the camper at the same time as he smelt petrol. Bloody hose again. He lifted the engine cover but the hose was still firmly in place. Kneeling by the damp patch he could feel petrol running down part of the sub frame and as he pushed himself to his feet using the wheel arch he found the cause. A bullet hole.

He trudged across the car park tucking the now useless revolver into his waistband as he went. Reaching the waste bin, he carefully removed the broken kite and punctured beach ball and leant in to retrieve his rucksack. They'd got Julie but they still hadn't got the Filofax. They'd be in touch.

Chapter Twelve

Dee settled into the blue leather banquette seats on the splitter bus and tried to ignore the noise. The bus was a brand-new Van Hool from an entertainment transport company based in Manchester and was to be theirs for the rest of the tour. Behind her, to the rear of the bus and past the galley, the four curtained bunks and toilet and shower, was the rear lounge. It was from here that the racket was coming. Initially the low buzz of conversation from the band and some of the Roadies had not intruded but an argument about who got what bunk had degenerated into a noisy and petulant row that seemed never to end and was getting on her nerves. Again, the Drummer, another drummer, wasn't helping. What was it about drummers?

She tried to block it from her mind and her mood lightened as she allowed herself to savour the warmth of the reception she'd received in the Bridgewater Hall at the previous night's concert. She'd thought that Cambridge had been good but this had been better. The Cambridge concert had got a good review in the Guardian which had been picked up by the Manchester papers and she'd felt this had made a difference. She'd been more relaxed and thought that Mathew had also been less tense which had helped them all. So relaxed that she'd even had the confidence to kill a fumbled intro and start again with a joke at her own expense. This had been warmly received by the audience which had further cheered them both. Mathew had talked through the performance with her, after the concert, and they'd agreed that the band had begun to gel and been technically better than in

179

Cambridge. More importantly they were now working with, rather than around her and Mathew.

Loud raised voices from the rear dropped her back into the reality of a wet Monday morning on a tour bus ploughing its way up a congested M6. She half-heartedly held up a hand to restrain Mathew who had pushed his glasses more firmly onto the bridge of his nose as he rose from his seat and moved purposefully down the aisle towards the disturbance. His gentle entreaties were initially met with silence and then muttering to his back as he made his way back to the front followed by a distinctly audible, 'fuck 'im!'

Dee motioned Mathew back into his seat and walked determinedly to the rear making straight for the Roadie whose voice she'd heard.

'Fuck him? Really?' She waited head on one side, arms folded and foot tapping.

When pantomimed entreaties to his colleagues failed to produce any indication of support the Roadie blurted, 'c'mon Dee, don't get your knickers in a twist. Just a bit of fun.'

She looked at the bulked out and overweight slob between whose tattooed forearms resting on the table, was a bottle of Jack Daniels, some plastic cups and a pouch of rolling tobacco. As she raised her eyes back to his he hooked his hands behind his neck, locked his fingers together, flexed his shoulders and pumped his biceps seemingly unaware that this served only to draw attention to the expanse of creped and mottled gut that hid his belt.

'Listen Steroids, who said you could bring drink onto my bus?'

Embarrassed, the hands unlocked from the back of his neck and dropped into his lap, 'oh, c'mon Dee, dry bus? Not very Rock 'n Roll,' he guffawed and again looked nervously around for support.

Dee reached over for the bottle and handed it back to Mathew who she knew had followed her. 'For your information, retard I was Rock 'n Roll back in the day. Those'd be the days that you've dreamt about which'd be the closest you're ever goin' to get.' She could hear her accent going further south as she spoke. 'What you 'all know about Rock 'n Roll you done read in a book. Now I used to have coke for breakfast, JD on tap, guns for fun and a pet snake. That's one with two eyes. So, I've been around.' She smiled at the Roadie, leant in and upped the volume, 'but I've changed. I doan do dat no more.' She breathed deeply and made a conscious effort to get the accent back north of the Mason Dixon line. 'So, on my bus you will be quiet and sober. We clear on that?'

The Roadie nodded truculently.

'And while I'm on the subject there'll be no bus parties.'

The Roadie gulped but said nothing.

'We clear on that too?' She looked at each of them in turn. This time they all nodded. 'I thank you for listening Steroids,' that last bit, she realised, had been pure Steel Magnolia. She walked away to laughter and "steroids" being tried for effect and knew that the Roadie had a new nickname.

She returned to her seat and began to flick desultorily through that morning's tabloids. The front-page story for them all was the discovery of the body of the Merseyside toddler abducted in Liverpool a few days earlier. The inside pages did nothing to lighten her mood. She did briefly consider the standards in British journalism that followed a headline about a murdered child with a topless Cheri from Colchester on page three wanting to 'care for the children of the World.' Throwing the paper down in disgust she turned away from Mathew trying hard to ignore his patient stare.

'What?' She barked.

'I was handling that.'

'Not very well from where I was sitting.'

'That's not fair Dee and the way you've left it means it'll fester.' He shrugged, 'we're a small touring group. Tight. It must stay that way. That guy is what stands between you and equipment failure.'

'Yeah, well Mathew,' she could feel the South rising again, 'if it's such a 'small touring group' which I agree is what I had in mind why are we in this fuckin' great bus. We don't need it. Who is paying for it?' She held up her hand to stop his response, 'while we're on the subject I understand we are to be joined by a Tour Manager and a Sound Engineer. I had kind of understood that you were organising the tour and we were using house systems and staff. Whose idea was all this?'

'Well, David and I,'

'David?' She interrupted him.

'Well yes Dee,' impatiently, 'you know David's backing this. He thinks it's going really well and he wants to reinforce his investment.'

'Reinforce his investment? That'd be me. Right? I'm The Investment.'

'Yes, he thought I needed to concentrate on the creative side of the operation, and you, and that what we needed was someone who was more used to the touring side of the business to take on the day to day stuff.' He paused, 'don't you think it makes sense?'

'And the bus?'

'Well yes. Bit OTT perhaps?'

'OTT?'

'Quaint old English expression. Over The Top. Too much?'

'Yeah right. OTT, it is.'

'Well yes and no. You see the thing is that David has this business in Manchester. Production Company. Bought it when we were going to manage a boy band. They tour lots of bands and groups but always hire in transport. David decided that the Production Company should have their own. So, he bought this from a company in Belgium.' He held his arms wide and nodded appreciatively at the bus interior. 'It's brand new.'

'He just went and bought a bus?'

'Dee I don't know whether you've picked up on this or not but David does very well as an Investment Banker. He's always looking for companies in which he can invest. He has interests in lots of companies. He got into the Entertainment Industry because of me but he sees other opportunities there that simply wouldn't have occurred to me. He's always banging on about the need to reinvest and diversify. You wouldn't believe some of things he's into. I think he started with building and development which led to property and then student accommodation. Last time we discussed it he was talking about the need to extend his reach.' Mathew paused, smiling at a memory. 'You see,' he chuckled, 'most people see problems he sees opportunities; you see a derelict manor house out in the wilds and he sees a thirty-bed care home for the elderly.' he grinned. 'You know the hotel we're staying in tonight? Kildrumman Lodge? Well he owns that too; small four-star family boutique hotel. One of his companies was doing the refurbishment when the owners ran in to a financial problem. David did a deal and took it off their hands. I'm looking forward to seeing it.'

Dee nodded, not, she hoped, disdainfully, but she was less than impressed with Mathew's near worship of his partner's business acuity. Now, whenever she thought of Williams her mind drifted to the two encounters she's witnessed between him and the man with the scarred face. On both occasions Williams had shown none of the urbanity she'd come to expect.

'This isn't about the bus is it Dee?'

'Leave it Mathew. I don't want to talk about it.'

The logistics of parking, unloading and getting the gear into the Queen's Hall without bringing Edinburgh to gridlock had begun to further try her patience. There was also a continuing awkwardness with Steroids and the crew and she found her own way to the auditorium where she felt she had stepped back in time to the gospel circuit of the Southern States. She'd guessed from outside that the place had once been a church but was pleasantly pleased at how little had been changed from the original configuration; they'd left the pew boxes and the sweeping tiered galleries. She wondered briefly about the acoustics but was so taken with the ambience that with her hands clasped together behind her she slowly pirouetted drinking in the vibes left by earlier performers. This was a good place. She pirouetted again to the sound of Mathew's footsteps on the polished wood floor.

'What do you think?'

'Are we holding a Baptist revival or what in here,' she said sternly.

'You don't like it.'

She rushed to give him a hug. 'I love it. It has great atmosphere. This is a place for people who are serious about their music. Can you feel it?'

'I can,' he nodded enthusiastically. 'I've been here before. I even played here once. It's the home of the Scottish Chamber Orchestra but it's used for all sorts of live music and performances now. You're right though. The people who come here are serious about their music. Go well here and the word spreads. There's something about this place that makes the audience feel secure. It draws people in. A good artist gets a head start from that sort of audience. I'm glad you like it.'

'So, what now?' She slipped her arm through his and squeezed him to her.

'Well, I've got stuff to sort out here. Why don't you get a taxi to the hotel?' He paused before continuing shyly, 'I wondered if you'd join me for an early dinner. Long day tomorrow. Start rehearsing at ten, sound check at four, line check at eight and on stage at nine.' He smiled. 'Oh, and before I forget we're talking to a journalist tomorrow.'

'Now we can afford cars,' she teased.

He laughed. 'We've come a long way since then and David thinks we're going further.'

The hotel had been another pleasant surprise. A long way from the brash commercialism and chromed convenience of the Sachas in Manchester. The lobby was oak panelled with a deep maroon carpet that had a bold gold pattern of swirls and the small area was completed with wonderfully overstuffed sofas and leather winged chairs carefully placed so that the space seemed cosy but not cluttered. This was Victorian grandeur from discernible Scottish Heritage without recourse to even a hint of tartan.

Dee took her key from the woman at Reception, 'I'm expecting a call this evening. Could you make sure you come and find me if I'm not in my room please? Oh, and I'm dining with another guest; Mister Sinclair.'

The Receptionist smiled as she swivelled the register for Dee's signature, 'That's fine Miss Wilson. Will Mister Williams be joining you for dinner?'

Dee was slightly taken aback as she had no idea that Williams was in Edinburgh. 'I'm not sure,' she hesitated, 'is he staying here?'

'Yes, he's not here yet but he's booked in.'

'Well, I suppose if you own a great place like this you'd be a fool not to use it.' Dee smiled.

'Precisely,' said the woman in an icy tone that Dee felt did little to mask her feelings about Williams.

She felt relaxed as she joined Mathew in the bar for a pre-dinner drink and enjoyed his tales of attending the Edinburgh Festival when he'd been a student. They both knew, however, that they were treading cautiously around the issue of Denton. Dee was very conscious that she owed Mathew for his unquestioning help in getting Denton booked out of the hotel and a little puzzled that he hadn't mentioned it. From the dining room at the end of the bar she could hear cutlery and china being placed as the room was prepared for the evening diners and idly wondered what might be on the menu when to her surprise, she found herself blurting, 'I'm worried about Denton, Mathew.'

'I had wondered,' he said as he searched her eyes for a clue as to where the conversation might go next, 'can I help?'

'I don't think so. I mean everything else is going so well,' she hesitated, 'and I have so much to be thankful to you for that I don't want to let this get in the way.'

Sinclair took a sip from his drink and gently rotated and rocked the glass making the ice chink against its sides. 'Dee, I think you know there's a lot more to you and I than just the Professional side. If I can help, I will. If that's what you want.'

'I know. Thank you.' She took his hand and stared distractedly along a shelf line of single malts.

'Let me start then,' taking both her hands in his. 'Denton's in trouble. That much I understand. What I don't understand is that you are so concerned. You couldn't have known him for much more than twenty-four hours. What happened?'

Dee tried desperately to squeeze back the tears and was grateful when Mathew produced a spotless white handkerchief. She sighed deeply. 'Did you ever meet someone that you just knew was right? And,' she hurried on, 'if you have, did you know, right then, at that moment, that they were thinking the same thing?'

Sinclair smiled sadly, 'yes to the first no to the second. I think I've always loved more or too much. Means I get a lot of disappointment,' he smiled wryly.

'I know it's a cliché but I can't get him out of my mind. I just know that the sadness, loss, call it what you like, that I'm feeling now, not knowing where he is or what he's doing, is a fraction of what's going to hit me if it doesn't work out.'

'You're in love.'

'Sure looks that way honey,' she sniffed, grinned and handed him back the handkerchief.

'Are you going to tell me what sort of trouble it is?'

'Mathew, I probably will but can we leave it at that for the moment please? I need to think this through a bit more. She slipped from the bar stool also wondering how she'd ever explain her unease about Williams to this gentle man. 'Shall we go through?'

They were greeted at the Restaurant entrance by a trouser suited young woman who escorted them to a secluded table in a bay window. As they unfurled their serviettes and Mathew scanned the wine list Dee whispered, 'I don't think they get a lot of Black people up here.'

Mathew glanced around the room and smiled at each of the other diners before replying, 'You might be right. On the other hand, maybe one of us is so damned attractive they can't keep their eyes on their plates.'

Dee laughed and looked out through the window beyond the gravel drive towards the formal gardens and boundary wall which was just discernible beyond the fading pools of light cast by the estate lighting. She began to wonder just why she had been reticent with Mathew when dipped headlights, the crunch of gravel beneath tyres and the sound of marbles in a biscuit tin announced the arrival of an Edinburgh City diesel taxi. Her stomach lurched as she realised the passenger was Williams and failed to settle when it hit her that the reason she'd held back with Mathew was that she had developed an instinctive and deepening distrust of Williams that would always require her to exercise caution around Mathew. Especially where Denton was concerned. It fleetingly occurred to her that perhaps Mathew hadn't been entirely open with her and she wondered at his motives.

'David's here. You didn't tell me he was coming up.'

'He's here already?' Mathew peered through the window in time to see Williams back disappear through the entrance door as he rose from the table and hurried across the Restaurant to the lobby.

Dee realised that her heart was thumping with fear. Fear of what? Williams? Why? The fact that she had no answer to the question made her more anxious as she realised that the fight or flight instinct that had preserved her through the years had kicked in and she would do well to pay heed.

An ebullient Williams with outstretched arms loped across the dining room with a slightly embarrassed Mathew trying to keep up while nervously strangling the serviette he'd had in his hands as he'd left the table. 'Dee, my darling Dee, I'm hearing wonderful things,' he announced loudly before grabbing a chair from a nearby table, ignoring the soup spluttered protests of an elderly man dining alone while waving a hand in the air to attract service. Before Dee could acknowledge his greeting, he launched into a further address, 'Cambridge, Manchester and now Edinburgh. The reviews were good and are going to get better. This Guardian Journalist tomorrow will keep up the momentum. You must try not to let him side-track you to that historic stuff. This tour's about now not then.' He reached into his inside jacket pocket and retrieved a couple of sheets of paper. 'You need to read this. It's the release I prepared. He should have it by now. Try and keep to that if you can. You know if he wanders off message try to get him back on song. On song, oh I say, that's good, don't you think.' He guffawed as he handed the release to Dee.

'Good evening David, this is a pleasant surprise. Didn't expect to see you here. How are you?'

Williams smiled expansively at Dee and leant back in his chair to allow the waitress to set a place for him at the table. 'No big change of plan. Business really. Could have got someone else on it but saw an opportunity to combine business with pleasure, catch up with you both, and took it.'

'Someone else on what?' Mathew enquired.

'Ah ha,' said Williams rubbing his great hands together in mock glee, 'recording. We're going to record tomorrow night's performance.' Thumb and forefinger held apart and aloft he sketched an imaginary rectangle in the air. 'I can see it now on the sleeve, 'Dee Dee Wilson Live at Queens Hall. What d'ye think?' He paused at the look of shock on both their faces. 'I need this people. Some of the deals I'm looking at won't work without this. When you'd finished the tour, we were going into the studio anyway. What's the problem?'

The pair looked at each other, 'there isn't a problem David. It's just a bit of a shock,' said Mathew.

Williams nodded his understanding, returned to the menu and without raising his eyes went on, 'It's all set up. There really is nothing to it. If Dee repeats the performance she gave in Manchester, it's in the bag. Right Mathew?'

'Sinclair grinned at him, 'whatever you say David.

'It'll be good,' Dee smiled at them both.

'It'll be brilliant mes enfants, let's order.'

Despite her nagging disquiet Dee was able to enjoy Williams' company. She had to admit he was a born raconteur and the meal passed in a whirl of anecdote and gossip. The banter, empathy and affection between Mathew and Williams reinforced her concern about sharing any information on Denton with Mathew. As they were about to leave the table the Receptionist approached them. 'Miss Wilson, you have a call.'

With every nerve in her body praying that the woman wouldn't go on to announce the name of the caller Dee seized her elbow and steered her back towards reception where she was pointed towards a fin de siècle telephone booth near the main entrance. She closed the door behind her, sank on the buttoned leather bench and picked up the antique Bakelite hook and candlestick telephone from its scissor cross supports on the wall.

'Denton?'

'The same.'

'Where the hell are you?'

'I love you too.'

'Hey, I'm sorry. I've just been so worried.'

'How's the tour going?'

'Denton,' she hissed, 'the tour is going fucking brilliantly. Thank you for asking. Now, could we get to where you are, what's happened and have you found her?'

'Sorry Dee. I really wanted to say that I miss you very much.'

For the second time that evening Dee's eyes moistened and she coughed to release the lump in her throat before replying. 'Denton, you're a married man and I swore,' she sobbed, 'swore that never ever again,'

'Do you miss me?'

'You know I do you bastard,' she sobbed again.

Denton paused to let her recover. 'I thought I had her Dee. I'm sure I know where she is but the people I'm asking have just clammed up. So, I'm going back tomorrow to try a different tack. Whoever is chasing Starmer, for whatever reason hasn't caught them yet but maybe they're close. If I don't get a result tomorrow I'm stuffed.'

'Where are you?'

'Forres.'

'Where?'

'Forres, near a town called Nairn.' He spelt out the name of the small town.

'Is that far from here?'

'It's about a hundred and fifty miles. Say three or four hours in car.'

Dee paused to order the thoughts racing through her mind before asking, 'Does Stella know any of this? Has she heard from Julie?'

'I can't get hold of her. I keep leaving messages bringing her up to date but if she doesn't pick up its difficult for her to get hold of me while I'm travelling.'

Dee swivelled sharply on the leather seat as the door folded open to the sound of Williams' voice, 'Dee, Ok? Coffee's served.' She felt blood rush to her cheeks and thanked her lucky stars for her race as she forced herself to say, 'well thanks for the call. As I said tomorrow at Queens Hall and I'll leave a ticket on the door.' Williams held the door open as she made two attempts to get the 'phone back on the cradle.

'Friend?' He enquired.

'Sort of. What Mathew would call a musical mate,' she laughed.

The coffees were served in the lounge and Dee felt subdued and intimidated. Subdued at the wrench of having not finished the conversation with Denton and intimidated by Williams' blatant intrusion. He'd been desperate to find out who had called she concluded.

'So, Dee,' Williams leant forward and then glanced over his shoulder in pretence of secrecy, 'I hear you,' he mimed quote marks in the air, 'had an assignation in Manchester.'

'An assignation?'

'Met someone. Had dinner with said gentleman.'

Dee looked across at Mathew who was visibly embarrassed. She looked Williams firmly in the eyes. 'I had a pleasant evening with someone I met in the hotel,' she challenged.

Williams harrumphed, 'right, looking forward to seeing him again eh?'

Dee now knew her instincts were right and coldly stared him down using the coffee cup to shield her lips which she knew had set in a thin line with a faint tuck of disgust at one corner.

Williams looked away as Mathew, to ease what he felt was some sort of confrontation said, 'Tell Dee about the jazz festival at Nairn.'

'Nairn,' said Dee, ice gripping her heart which missed a beat until the power of vindicated instinct pumped blood to it through her veins in double time.

'There's a jazz festival there,' Williams continued evenly, 'I thought I might see if we could book you in there. On the fringe as they say up here. It can only help given the market we're aiming at.'

The interview with the journalist from The Guardian the next morning had not been as problematic as Williams had feared. To start with the 'him' was a 'her' and she had seen the set at Manchester. Dee had been advised that Ms Lockstone was a young woman in a hurry, parachuted into the music review role because she had a degree in English from Birmingham, an encyclopaedic knowledge of the ancestry, origins and potential of every band operating and had made her bones in pubs, clubs and dope filled lecture halls from The Hacienda to The Half Moon in Putney. Her opinions on the Music Business were said to be honest but often acerbic and were in danger of becoming the story. Dee was surprised to learn that Lockstone was tired of the current couple of dozen Britpop bands vying for her attention with inexperienced managers and Indie labels representing them. She saw Dee as something fresh and different and an opportunity to write about the Music and not the antics that had come to characterise the Business. They parted having enjoyed their time together and with Dee confident she would receive fair treatment from The Guardian.

The rehearsal had been difficult. Dee discerned a distinct atmosphere and knew that Mathew was aware of it also.

'What's going on Mathew?'

'Apparently, there was a real barney yesterday after we left.'

'The Roadie?'

'Yes. He got a few drinks into him and started mouthing off. One thing led to another and before you knew it there was skin and fur on the ceiling.'

'Well, he's got to go then.'

'He already has.'

'So, what's the problem?'

'The manner of his departure?'

'The manner of his departure? For Christ's sake, can't anybody in this country just come out and say what they mean?'

'Alright Dee. Don't have a go at me about this. I told you this would come back at us when you interfered on the bus.'

'Ok. I'm sorry. Just tell me what happened.'

Mathew sighed. 'David got to hear about it and two hours later we had a new Roadie.'

'So, problem solved.' Dee shrugged.

'Not really, as I said, it was the manner of his going. He left via the hospital.'

'Jesus Christ. No wonder there's an atmosphere. What did they do? Beat him up?'

'In the car park.'

'And the band thinks I commissioned this?'

Sinclair shrugged, 'maybe'.

'Ok', Dee sighed, 'find a restaurant nearby and book a table for you me and the band and ask them to join us at twelve thirty.'

Dee started the lunch by announcing that this was something that they should have done before starting the tour and apologised for not having done so earlier. Through the next two and a half hours she and Mathew deployed their social skills and half a case of fine Merlot to entertain, involve and entice the band back into her orbit. She praised their skills, hinted at her own vulnerabilities, sought their support and distanced herself from the Roadie and his departure. She went on to explain the plan to record that night's set and Mathew provided a timely assessment of how this would benefit them all financially. They all returned cheerfully for the sound-check but with Dee very conscious that she faced that night's performance under rehearsed.

She had always thought that while the set list varied little, all performances varied from location to location. Different ambiance, different audience, different atmosphere and different acoustics. In the case of the Queen's Hall this last, the acoustics, took her voice and emotions out into the intimate, darkened space and brought it back to her on a joyous wave of appreciation and love. The applause was rapturous from a capacity crowd who obviously felt they had been to a magnificent concert. She returned to the hotel with a post gig buzz that was going to make sleep difficult.

Dee hadn't been able to settle since coming up to her room some five hours previously. It was now nearly three and her mind was in turmoil. Her concerns and suspicions about Williams had been further fuelled by the story of the violence meted out to the Roadie and her suspicion that he'd been instrumental in that. Then the mention of Nairn was a coincidence too far and while she was having trouble pinning down just why it was that she distrusted Williams she was now in no doubt that he couldn't be trusted. The interruption of her call, the questions about who she'd met in Manchester and his tone had unsettled her. Circumstantial though it all may be it was beginning to build to a body of evidence that couldn't be ignored. What was now keeping her awake was what to do next. Above all she wanted to be with Denton but felt that there was little she could do until he had exhausted his line of enquiries in Forres. Neither did she want to disappoint Mathew and, were the truth to be told, she was desperate for her new career to succeed. The tension caused her to pace the room with hands that were at her mouth, clasped behind her neck, jammed into the pockets of her slacks or pushing her fingers through her tight curls. She needed to think clearly. She needed a cigarette and wasn't, any longer going to listen to maddeningly quiet warnings of that pious inner voice. There had been a vending machine in the bar. She grabbed a sweater and made for the stairs.

She was halted at the half landing above reception by the unmistakable rasping sound of Williams' hushed but forceful questioning of someone in the lobby. She dropped to her knees and inched further onto the landing and nearer to the balusters, raising her head slightly to see who the other person was. She crept a little nearer and broadened the angle between two balusters until she could just make out the back of the head and shoulders of Williams' companion. There she froze, like a small child eavesdropping on quarrelling parents. With every hissed question from Williams she could sense his rising anger and increasing frustration at the need to keep his voice down. She flattened herself to the floor and pulled herself along the carpet to a point directly above the discussion.

192

'Do you understand? Have you any idea what's at stake here? This is the biggest operation in Europe and its being fucked up by a boy, a girl and a drunk. If the Dutch find out what's going on we're stuffed. Starmer and Denton must be taken care of. If you can't do it I have people who will take that, and any other worry you may have, away from you. Am I making myself clear? You do realise what'll happen to you?' Silence. 'There was half a chance that if we could have got Denton his daughter back and straightened him out we could've got back on track. Now you've lifted her there's no way they're going back to play happy families is there you moron?' In the silence following the question Dee became fearful that the sound of her hammering heart might give her away.

Williams continued, 'Starmer should worry you because he worries me. He's become an operator. Above all I need that book and then them both taken care of. In that order. Starmer and Denton will both be looking for the girl. Sooner or later they are going to bump into each other. Use that. Follow Denton. Use the wife for Christ's sake. Sort this out. When you've done, get over to Amsterdam and get things moving there. Take the girl. Lose her. I don't want another body over here.'

Dee heard a rattle at the front door and raised her head in time to see Williams' acolyte turn to face the sound. She gasped as she recognised the hard and scarred face of the man she'd seen arguing with Williams in Docklands and talking to him in the bar at the Cambridge Corn Exchange. Through the door that he opened she caught sight of a middle aged blonde woman looking less than impressed at having obviously been kept waiting in a car outside.

The man glanced back over his shoulder at Williams then ushered the woman back into the night, 'Ok Stella, let's go.'

Chapter Thirteen

Denton sat on the edge of the bed staring at the 'phone in his hand until he was jarred back to conscious thought as the dialling tone was replaced by a looped recorded message telling him to "hang up the 'phone". He replaced it in the cradle, leant back against the headboard and swung his legs up onto the worn candlewick bedspread. It was obvious that Dee hadn't wanted whoever had interrupted the call to learn to whom she'd been talking. It had been a man's voice but he didn't think it had been Sinclair; deeper, gruffer and more authority. He stared moodily around the grubby little hotel room with its bedding that smelt faintly of nicotine, its tired and chipped laminated chipboard furniture and yellowing net curtains at the bay window overlooking Forres high street.

Queens Hall. She was at Queen's Hall tomorrow. Did she want him to meet her there? Could he 'phone there or would that add to the problem? What was the problem? He'd wanted to talk to her about Julie but was honest enough to admit to himself that he'd hoped for more. In all the years, he'd been married to Stella he'd looked at any number of women, flirted with some but never had he thought about leaving his wife far less contemplated starting a new life with someone else. How was it that today half his waking thoughts were about a woman he'd known barely a day and only the other half focussed on his missing daughter? He bounced himself from the bed and stood in the bay window staring down the street as the lights blinked on in sequence into the distance.

194

Forres had been a disappointment but then a town that prided itself on an annual flower display was never going to impress in February. Even in the fading light, as he'd driven into the town it'd been apparent that what had once been a thriving market town was now struggling with a different commercial future that had seen traditional shop fronts adapted for use as estate agents and building societies. Where the road narrowed from the old market square and just past a stone memorial he had spotted a pub with a bow front corner entrance off the street decorated with hanging baskets and long dead bedding plants. He'd slowed as he neared the heavily studded and forbidding timber entrance door with grimy bulls' eye windows to note the "Rooms to Let" card and marvelled at another sign attesting to two-star accreditation from The Scottish Tourist Board. Prompted by the impatient hoot from the car behind he'd swung sharply left into a narrow side street and through the high double gates into the car park at the rear of the pub. He hadn't thought he was paranoid but with Webber apparently dogging his every move off street parking was a sensible precaution.

He moved the net curtain to one side and squinted through the gap in both directions. Turning for the last time to look down towards the square he was reminded of another town and another time; Birchington on Sea. Another town with a history of better times and trades and industries long overtaken by general rural decline.

Denton grinned as he recalled 'Aitch's retirement to Birchington and how his Dad had embraced and signalled his new status with the purchase of short sleeved cotton shirts, sandals and a panama hat from the local "Gentleman's Outfitters est. 1897". Later that year the shop had become a "Pop in Parlour" a concept that had puzzled 'Aitch. Even this pub in Forres bore a striking resemblance to "The Sea View Hotel" that had become 'Aitch's local in Birchington. That too had floors of vacant rooms, roof leaks and an ageing clientele that clung grimly to privilege earned by attendance while drawing nostalgic comfort from the faded glory of the decor. The etching to the glass in the half-glazed entrance door advised that ale could be purchased "by the jug" while ornate mirrors above the bar advised that Coca Cola "relieved fatigue" and Marston's Old Empire was "particularly authentic".

195

'Aitch had not made himself popular on his first visit when, pint in hand, he'd announced that he'd seen more life in a Doctor's waiting room but his gentle good humour and tendency to seize upon every nod of greeting and turn it into an opportunity for a conversation had brought about a change. Within a few months' people who'd done little but nod at each other for years had begun to alter their routines to match 'Aitch's attendance. Crosswords were shared, produce from allotments exchanged, booze cruises organised, the billiard room was reopened and to 'Aitch's great satisfaction the Pop in Parlour closed.

It had been the booze cruises to Dunkirk that had started a chain of events that had led to Denton buying a boat. It had been quickly noticed that 'Aitch couldn't be tempted to join the group that twice a year took advantage of the Sally Line offers to booze cruise to the French port. No amount of cajoling could get him to change his mind and persistent attempts were met with a curt rebuff. This had puzzled many, including Paul. As the years, had passed Denton had joined a local sailing club and had managed to get a couple of days a month racing a small dinghy off Minnis Bay. Friendships at the club had led to him crewing a cruiser out of Ramsgate and after a particularly good year he had bought a second-hand Contessa 26. Two or three years of racing and cruising with the sort of obsession that he knew he applied to all new interests had started to cause friction with Stella. That and happy hours with 'Aitch in the Sea View while Stella suffered evenings of political diatribe and Eleanor Joan's forty a day habit had made a clash almost inevitable.

Things had started to come to a head, then not been helped much, the night that Paul, after more than a few pints, had offered to take a party of veterans on the Small Boats Association anniversary trip to Dunkirk. While 'Aitch had been playing billiards, Paul had revealed that his Father had been at Dunkirk and had been one of the last off the beaches in the retreat of The British Expeditionary Force from the Germans in 1940. A few more drinks had seen him foolishly assuring everybody that 'Aitch would be with them on the day of the Anniversary.

'You've done what?' expostulated 'Aitch.

'I've made you a member of The Dunkirk Veterans Association,' started Paul nervously, 'It's the fortieth anniversary this year and I'm taking the boat and a few friends over and I've said that I thought you'd come too.' In the silence that had followed the Landlord remained frozen in place with a glass an inch from the brandy optic, a man clutching two pints on his way back to his table paused as he reached 'Aitch, reluctant to step round him, when a woman at the far end of the bar broke the silence as nervous fingers inadvertently released ice cubes from tongs and scattered them along the bar.

'Let me explain something to you all,' 'Aitch swept the bar with a despairing look. 'Dunkirk, to you lot is a day out. Somewhere you go for Golden Virginia, litre bottles of vodka and moules et frites. In nineteen thirty-nine I went to France in a Bournemouth Greengrocer's lorry, with a pair of brown civilian shoes and a rifle without a bolt. There were just over a hundred in my company. By the time, I got to that beach I'd been fighting Germans and cursing the French for three weeks and losing just under a hundred mates. I was taken off the groin at Dunkirk by a Destroyer: The Anthony. She lost a gun turret on the way back to enemy aircraft while two hundred of us sat it out two decks below the waterline. And it didn't stop there. Did it? 'Cos four years later I'm dangling from a bloody parachute at Arnhem while the Waffen SS pick us off as we come down. And in the next few days I lost another couple of hundred mates!'

He could see that 'Aitch had been close to tears and had taken his arm to steer him towards the door. 'Aitch had straightened his back and thrown back his shoulders but had turned at the door to say, 'you lot have got absolutely no idea.'

Denton let the net curtain fall back and pulled the heavy drapes on the gloom of Forres after dark and decided on an early night.

The next morning, frustrated at the delay in getting an early breakfast, he checked out in a bad temper and then had to wait further minutes while the Landlord exacted his revenge hunting for keys to the rear yard gates that were eventually found to be unlocked. He roared through Springfield on the B9011, passed the airfield at Kinloss and had drawn level with the turn off for Sunflower Bed and Breakfast when he realised that there was a police car at the entrance to the Foundation. He coasted the Rover to a halt a couple of hundred yards short of the entrance, got out, went to the rear, opened the boot, pretended to rummage through its contents and squinted up the road.

He knew instinctively, given the experiences of the last few days, that to approach any nearer was to court the sort of attention he didn't need. He could just about make out a policeman huddled in a great coat leaning against the bonnet of his car talking to a small group of perhaps a dozen people. Looking past them he could see what looked like larger police vans further into the grounds and the unmistakable green and yellow chequer markings of two ambulances parked opposite them. As his gaze returned to the group at the entrance he saw an elderly man, wheeling a bicycle, turn in his direction and scoot along with his left foot on a pedal until he had enough speed to slowly swing his right leg over the fruit box tied to the rear pannier before he settled onto the saddle. Denton watched his unsteady progress down the road accompanied by a rhythmic metallic squeak as the inside of a pedal chafed against the outside of the chain guard.

As the man passed the front bumper Denton slammed the boot lid and stepped into his path seemingly oblivious to the approach. The old boy clutched painfully with arthritic hands at the levers of the rod brake assembly on the vintage roadster in a vain attempt to avoid a collision. Denton grabbed the handle bars as the front wheel stopped between his knees.

'Steady.'

'Och, ye gave me a fright. I didna' see ye there,' he said as he pulled an old cloth cap from his head and used it to wipe his brow.

'I'm sorry. I didn't see you either. Are you alright? You look as though you've had a bit of a fright.'

'I'm ok. I wasna' looking,' he pushed the cap back on his head and twisted sideways in the saddle to look back up the road to the Foundation. He turned back to Denton, threw a nod in the direction of the policeman and then reached back to the rear carrier to re-secure the old fruit box before sighing and putting both feet on the ground. He slumped forward, head bowed and forearms resting on the handlebars, 'oh God! What terrible, terrible news. That poor woman and that poor wee boy,' his voice caught in his throat, 'muddered, muddered by evil, evil people.'

Denton felt a chill in the pit of his stomach and had to fight for the breath necessary to ask the question, 'who was murdered? When did this happen?'

'During the night, I saw them both yesterday,' the old boy shook his head in disbelief while Denton steeled himself to ask the question again.

'Who was murdered?' He repeated patiently.

'Why Melissa,' the man sighed, 'my friend, we worked in the shop together. I was with her only yesterday. Such a gentle wee soul.'

At the mention of the shop Denton immediately thought of the grey-haired woman in purple who'd taken fright at his questions and had ushered him out. Guilt flooded his consciousness as he concluded that this gentle soul was almost certainly the Melissa and that his enquires may have played a part in her death. He hoped that the guilt he was beginning to feel had masked from the old man the overwhelming sense of relief he'd felt the moment he'd heard the name Melissa and not that of Julie. 'Who was the boy?'

'Och he was no boy really but he had a gentle innocence. Vulnerable, ye ken, like he'd not grown properly. Poor Jamie.'

'Jamie?' Denton gasped, unable to prevent a note of recognition creeping into his voice.

'Och, such a lovely wee laddie. Some friends had come to stay and he looked so happy with them. Out and about in their wee camping van the day. Laughing and joking. Aye, did ye ken the wee laddie then?'

Denton paused and considered his answer while fighting to control his emotions at the realisation that the friends had almost certainly been Starmer and Julie. 'A friend of a friend really. Never met him,' he added hastily, 'what happened?

I dinna' know and they're,' with another nod to the policeman, 'they're not saying anything. They won't let us in but one of the Councillors came out to tell us to go home for the day and that's when we found out. Three people had been shot.'

Denton's heart lurched again and a cold knot filled his stomach, 'three people?'

'Oh aye. There was another one, a stranger, on the beach with Jamie apparently.'

'A stranger?'

'Aye, I saw him being put into the ambulance. He was a stranger alright. He was in a suit.'

'He?'

'Aye, the cover blew away from his legs as they lifted the stretcher into the ambulance. He was wearing a suit alright. Ye dinna see suits here.'

Again, relief washed over Denton to be quickly replaced by the crushing worry that he still hadn't found Julie who was in the middle of viciousness beyond belief but who was hopefully, with an unsuited Starmer, still one jump ahead. His temples pounded with tension as he realised that not only was the situation far more serious than he'd thought but that the pace was accelerating. He had to get to Julie. He looked up the road thoughtfully to see the policeman looking back and realised that he was unlikely to learn more without drawing attention to himself. A thought that was quickly confirmed by the old man who gently but firmly pulled back on the bars until Denton released his hold.

As the man looked down to guide his foot to the pedal he muttered, 'someone was here last night asking for Jamie,' and he then raised his head to look straight into Denton's eyes. Denton followed his unsteady progress down the road and waved as the old man looked back, in a half-hearted attempt to give reassurance of his innocence to a man who'd obviously begun to have doubts.

He looked back up the road to the policeman and wondered whether a three-point turn would draw unwelcome attention at this distance. On balance, he decided that he had little choice. He passed the old man wobbling his way homeward and nearly clipped him as the old boy swung out towards the centre of the road to avoid a patch of gravel spilling onto the tarmac opposite the entrance to a car park. He was a hundred yards on before he realised that he'd seen a camper van. The old boy on the bike had mentioned a 'wee camping van'.

It was locked but a strong smell of petrol turned a cursory observation, with nose to glass and hands shielding against reflections, into a detailed search that revealed the bullet hole. The general mess in the van with the contents strewn everywhere, the broken fittings and the torn headlining suggested that the van had been searched thoroughly. A bra incongruously draped over a tap that looked as though it doubled as a hand pump confirmed his view that this was the van that Starmer and Julie had been in. He got back in the Rover and drove slowly away. Julie, he reasoned, had survived the incident in the Foundation and probably escaped at least as far as the car park with Starmer.

Which meant that she'd been here and alive a few hours ago. Then where the hell was she now? As he neared Forres he passed a sign for the railway station and it immediately occurred to him that the pair would now be on foot. In which case, they'd need transport. Public transport perhaps?

He pulled into the empty station car park and drew to the curb outside a sixties built brick single story building with a central entrance to the booking hall flanked on each side by Perspex protected timetables into which graffiti had been heavily etched. He was subconsciously concocting a story for the benefit of the booking clerk when he realised that the man struggling to hear directions while crouched at the semi-circular aperture at the ticket counter had repeated the word 'Manchester'. Denton slowly retreated to the other side of the booking hall near to the main entrance and studied him. His shoulders touched the brickwork reveals on either side of the ticket office window and as he stood Denton guessed he was just on six foot. He reached down between his legs and retrieved his rucksack which he swung up onto one shoulder while inserting a ticket into a wallet and pocketing some small change. Tucking the wallet into an inside pocket he hitched the rucksack strap higher on his shoulder, flicked his hair from his eyes and stiffened as he saw he was being watched. He returned Denton's unwavering gaze with a hard and challenging stare which he held long enough to push Denton to ask, 'Manchester?'
'What?'
'You bought a ticket for Manchester.'
'And?'
'My daughter was at University in Manchester,' Denton paused as the man's eyebrows narrowed in interest. 'Her name's Julie.' Any doubt he'd had about Starmer's identity vanished as he watched his shoulders drop in shock allowing the rucksack to slide down to the crook of his arm. 'You're Andy Starmer. Right?' barked Denton moving to confront him.
Starmer nodded.
'Is my daughter alive Mister Starmer?'
Starmer nodded again.
'You're sure?'

This time Starmer let the rucksack drop to the floor, lowered his eyes and made no protest as Denton grabbed his elbow and steered him to the car park.

Starmer sat silently in the front seat of the Rover with his rucksack on his lap wondering how any of the last two or three days could be explained to a man who was about to discover that his daughter had been kidnapped. A man who was barely in control of himself, let alone a car that was now barrelling along a country lane at over eighty miles an hour.

'Where is she?'

'Look Mister Denton,'

'Where is she?' the car swerved as Denton slammed his fist down onto the dash and screamed again, 'where is she?'

'If you calm down, slow down and pull over we can talk.'

'Don't tell me to calm down you piece of shit. Whatever has happened to Julie is your fault. Now fuckin' answer me,' he bellowed.

Starmer sighed, reached across, placed his hand on Denton's left forearm, squeezed hard and said quietly, 'I don't know where she is but I want to find her as much as you but neither of us is going to be much use if we end up having to be cut out of this thing by Trumpton. He squeezed again, much harder, 'are we?'

Denton looked at him sideways, breathed deeply and, finally, nodded slowly.

Starmer was relieved to see the speedometer start to move counter clockwise.

'Why Manchester?'

'It's a long story. One you need to hear. One you won't like. One that started in Manchester. There are people there that will know where she is.'

Denton's eyes switched nervously from mirror to road ahead and back to mirror as he considered what he'd heard. 'I think I know some of it, guessed some more and probably know bits you don't.' He scanned the mirrors again.

'Are we being followed?' Starmer turned in his seat.

'Not at the moment but nothing would surprise me. We need time for a conversation, don't we?'

From the change in tone Starmer began to hope that Denton had maybe begun to appreciate that he wasn't the villain in this piece. Guilt then gripped him as he realised that there were some elements of the story which decency prevented him from discussing with Julie's father, some that were better left untold while others needed to be thought through in more detail, including his instinctive reluctance to simply hand over the Filofax. The key to Julie's survival may be in the rucksack on his lap and Denton's paranoia about being followed while probably honestly felt was completely misplaced. Nobody was now looking for Denton or Starmer. Woolley was expecting Starmer to come to him if he wanted Julie back. That was why he had been going to Manchester.

Denton exhaled slowly trying to let the tension loose and allowed the car to drift onto a lay by on the A96 going towards Nairn. He slowly put the car in Park, engaged the hand brake, switched off the ignition, opened his door, stepped on to the gravelled lay by and slammed the door to his beloved Rover with all the force he could muster. Starmer left him to his thoughts for a few minutes before quietly approaching him as he stared into the middle distance across the roof of the car.

'Mister Denton,'

Denton whirled, grabbed Starmer by the lapels and completed the turn by slamming him into the car door. 'Talk to me you shit!'

There was a long silence as Denton tried to meet the unswerving gaze of the man in his grip. A man who seemed completely unconcerned, if not indifferent, to Denton's anger. Slowly Denton realised that Starmer's lack of resistance wasn't the result of fear or any form of submission. Starmer was allowing him his moment; a necessary indignity to be endured before an even more necessary conversation could take place. Denton released him.

'Mr Denton, can I start by saying that I think maybe I love your daughter?'

'So how in the name of holy fuck do we come to the pass where she is, apparently, on drugs, missing and one step in front of a bunch of seriously demented criminals who are hurting and killing people in their hunt for you both?'

'Mr Denton, my life with Julie wasn't idyllic but I'm pretty certain we loved each other'. He paused as though reflecting. 'Well, I certainly loved her. Then she went back down to London for the summer and something happened. Something changed her. She came back a different person.' He paused again as

Denton joined him, arms folded, leaning back against the car. 'I'm sure she was clean when she went home. I blame myself for not realising earlier, when she came back, that drugs had become a problem.' He paused again and glanced sideways at an unresponsive Denton for any clue as to the extent of his knowledge on Julie's problems. 'A big problem. Anyway, I think things must have become pretty bad for her because she slipped out of sight. Believe me I tried to find her and on more than one occasion I tried to help her.'

Denton nodded to himself in silent acknowledgement; Starmer's account fitted with what Jake had told him back in Manchester.

Slowly and not really trusting himself to deliver the next part of the story with the degree of delicacy to which a grieving Father was entitled, Starmer continued. 'She was in with the wrong crowd and they were taking advantage of her addiction and her' he hesitated, 'vulnerability.'

Denton swivelled, to lean his shoulder against the car and stared intently at Starmer who, now, refused to meet his gaze.

'What do you mean?'

'You know what I mean.'

The look in Denton's eyes confirmed to Starmer that this Father's worst fear had just been realised. 'I was trying to sort it out. Get her away but I seem to have stirred up a hornet's nest. If it's any consolation she'd been off drugs for three days.'

'So where is she now?'

'As I said, I don't know but I do know who has her and why and I had a plan to get her back.'

'So, let's hear it.'

Starmer took a very deep breath. 'I used to work with the people who have her. Not in any criminal capacity,' he quickly added. 'The same people who were taking advantage of her. Their boss was a man named Woolley and he had a particularly nasty sidekick called Osman; Manchester Mafia. In getting Julie away that night there was a fight. A man died.'

'You killed someone.'

'Not intentionally.'

'That makes it alright then, does it?'

'He didn't deserve to live but that's not the point. He worked for Woolley which meant that retribution would be swift and final and I had Julie to worry about. To get away, to put them off the scent, I made it all look like the dead guy had been doing

204

private deals and decided to take it on his toes with Woolley's cash. I didn't know how long it would stand up but there was an outside chance they'd buy it in which case Julie and I were clear and I had a chance to put her back together. I've tried everything since to throw them off the scent but they always seem to be just one step behind me. One of them tipped up asking questions at Jamie's place the other night.'

'That wasn't them. That was me.'

'What! How the hell did you know where we were?'

'I didn't. But I had liberated your computer, got in to it and took an educated guess based on your correspondence with Jamie.'

'But Woolley and Osman were there that night,' exclaimed Starmer, stopping himself from saying more. 'I saw them.'

'I know,' acknowledged Denton. 'I've just come from there. Three dead; the Lady in the shop that I spoke to, your friend Jamie I'm afraid and what I'm assuming was one of the Manchester mob.'

'I know.'

'Your doing?'

'Osman's.'

'And you killed him?'

'He killed Jamie and Melissa.'

'So, where was Julie when all this was going on?'

'Waiting for me in the van. I got back just in time to see them take her.'

A thought occurred to Denton. 'What does Woolley look like?'

'There's no mistaking him. Very pink, very fat and never been seen outside of a Prince of Wales check suit.'

Another piece of the jigsaw dropped into place for Denton; Woolley had been the man that had been arguing with Webber outside Slammers. 'Christ, this is horrendous we need to go to the Police.'

Starmer grimaced and rocked his outstretched hand from side to side in a gesture of uncertainty as he appreciated that he now had little choice but to tell Denton about his other suspicions. 'The thing is Mr Denton I also lifted a set of records from Woolley's office. Sort of Insurance. As near as I can work out he's paying off a lot of Senior Policemen in Manchester. If we go to the Police how do we know we are going to get a straight one?'

Denton pushed himself off the car, excitement and relief flooding across his face. 'We don't need the Police now then. We just give Woolley back all the stuff, including the records you nicked, in exchange for Julie.'

'I did think of that. Certainly, that's what Woolley is expecting. But he's lost two of his and he's now killed twice. There are no limits to what he and these people will do. I don't think we could trust him.' He paused, 'you found me through my computer. Right?'

Denton nodded.

'Then how did Woolley find me?'

Denton shrugged looking blank.

'Did you tell anyone where you were going?'

'No.' Replied Denton, looking away, as he recalled the message he had left for Stella.

A cold sense of foreboding overlaid with a feeling of helplessness flooded Denton's consciousness as he realised that several coincidences could be explained by Stella's involvement. Stella knew he'd gone to Manchester and she knew Webber. Webber had tipped up in Manchester within hours of his arrival, and, he now knew, was associated with Woolley. Apparently, Woolley had arrived at Findhorn within hours of him having left Stella a message. Perhaps Stella had initially, simply turned to Webber for help. Maybe, Webber's deeper, darker activities and involvement with Woolley were outside Stella's awareness. But then, if Webber knew Woolley what was the connection there and how did that tie into NMG? He slowed his breathing and fought to concentrate. He just had to assume that Stella had turned to Webber in all innocence; no mother could be implicated in the abduction of their daughter. No. If Stella was the source, then Webber must be playing her.

'Mr Denton?'

Denton snapped out of his reverie.

'Mr Denton, we're losing time. We need to decide what we are going to do.'

'"We", now is it?'

'You got a better idea?' snapped Starmer impatiently.

'Do you know a man called Webber?'

'Don't think so,' Starmer frowned, 'although there was a third man with Osman and Woolley last night.'

'That figures. I'd bet that was Webber. I know he's connected to Woolley. I saw them arguing outside Slammers in Manchester.'

'Is it important?'

'I think it probably is but I can't work out how,' said Denton painfully aware that with McCarthy's death, Custom's interest and his suspicions about Stella, he was being less that open with the man who'd tried to save his Daughter. 'Webber and I worked together in London.'

Denton leaned over to steady Starmer as the backwash from a forty-ton speeding articulated lorry rocked them both against the side of the Rover. Denton shoved Starmer towards the front of the car as he jerked open his driver's door.

'Get in the car.' Denton screamed.

'What.'

'Get in the fuckin' car,' yelled Denton as he keyed the ignition. He swung the Rover out of the layby onto the A96 heading back towards Nairn and floored the throttle in pursuit of the lorry.

'What are we doing?' Yelled Starmer above the throaty roar of the Rover's engine.

'That's a Van Doorn lorry.'

'And?'

'I told you I was in business with Webber. Well we brought products from Van Doorn in Amsterdam.'

'So?'

'We are their sole UK outlet. We are based in London. So, the question is. What's that fuckin' lorry doing in Scotland bearing in mind that Webber is somewhere up here too? Another coincidence. Somehow I don't think so.'

'And,' Starmer added, 'will it lead us to Julie?'

'Right, so we follow the lorry,' said Denton, easing off the speed sufficient to keep the articulated in sight in the distance.

Chapter Fourteen

Dee sat in the window seat of her room absent mindedly picking at a loose section of the piped cord edging to a cushion and watched the dawn break over the Pentland Hills. She leant closer into the window and rubbed at the glass with the heel of her hand to clear some condensation. The garden below was slightly frosted and at any other time she'd have taken pleasure in watching the shortening shadows reveal a pastel palette as the sun rose. A new day, she thought, as her fears crowded back in and threatened her composure. She returned to her bed, sat stiffly on the edge and began the breathing exercises she used to calm herself when waiting in the wings.

She and Denton had both begun to realise in Manchester that they were teetering, out of their depth, on the edge of something far reaching and dangerous. What neither of them had known at the time, she now knew, was just how deeply they would become enmeshed. The world she now contemplated was one of betrayal, corruption and evil that was complete, implacable and pitiless. There were no depths these people would not plumb, no crime they would not commit and no limit that they would recognise. The pair of them had thought they were dealing with a club owner who dealt in drugs, protection, prostitution and the type of criminal enterprise that required the sort of muscle he could deploy in Manchester. A sociopath but one localised to Manchester; a town that could be left behind with fresh starts beckoning from pretty much anywhere else in the World. Now it seemed that there were at least two levels of management above Woolley one of whom, operating internationally, was prepared to go to any lengths to protect his business. She'd never felt comfortable around Williams and had always had suspicions that there was a lot more to him than he allowed to surface. But, she now acknowledged, there was a big difference between the concern caused by suspicion and the fear that now threatened to overwhelm her with the revelation of his real character and the extent and reach of his power. She returned to the breathing exercises as the rising tide of panic brought bile to the back of her throat. Minutes later and calmer she considered what to do next.

Denton had to be warned and brought up to date. That had to be her priority. But warned about what? He already knew that Woolley and his thugs were after Julie and her boyfriend and that Webber was probably also on his tail. What he didn't know was that there was a Big Boss and a Middle Manager over and above Woolley, orchestrating that campaign and issuing death sentences on him, Julie and Starmer. She leapt to her feet and pasted a hand to her forehead, 'God dammit! You are one stupid broad. The guy in the lobby with the Blonde has got to be Webber!' Denton really needed to know that. More words scatter gunned from her as she began to pace the room. 'Stella! The blonde was called Stella. Goddammit Wilson get your act on,' she remonstrated to herself. 'You really are one dumb broad; Stella's the name of Denton's wife. What the fuck is she doing here?' The full import of Stella's presence gradually seeped into Dee's consciousness. If this woman was Denton's wife, and it seemed a scarcely credible coincidence that she wasn't, then Denton was in more trouble than he knew. He'd said that he hadn't been able to get hold of Stella but had left messages for her. She continued, 'damned right you couldn't get hold of her honey. She's been ridin' with the guys in the black hats.' Which meant, Dee reasoned, that there was a very good chance that Denton's present whereabouts were known to Williams? If that were the case, he was in real and imminent danger. She slumped back onto the bed and realised that she was frightened. Very frightened. Alone and frightened. But then, she reasoned, she'd been frightened before; terrified even. You couldn't be a black child of the sixties growing up in the Deep South and not have been frightened. The difference was that back then the very nature of the Civil Rights struggle meant you were never alone. The words of Martin Luther King drifted back to her across the years: "No individual can live alone; no nation can live alone. We are tied together." 'Damn right. Denton, we are tied together.'

Tied together. She'd seen violence before. The memory of a Mexican kid laying with the side of his face in the sand of an arroyo just south of El Centro, his hands tied behind his back with baling wire. Wearing a little check shirt and chinos with turned up sleeves and trouser legs; hand me downs that he'd now never grow into. One beautiful brown eye staring sightlessly from behind his fringe perhaps still with the last image of his massacred family fixed there for eternity. All bound. All with multiple gun shot wounds.

The Pianist had spat a long stream of tobacco juice onto the sand before gently pulling her into his shoulder and softly kissing the top of her head. 'I kinda thought I'd seen the last of this sort of shit in Nam.'

'What d'ye think happened?'

'Wet backs. Probably a little Mom and Pop operation running a few people across the Border; families mainly. Perhaps ran into a large coyote organisation running people and drugs? An argument. Something goes wrong and a couple of magazines get emptied.' He nodded towards several collections of brass cartridge casings glinting in the sun a few paces apart. 'Where there's drugs there's death.'

'Not for you Denton. Not for you.' Dee murmured emphatically. She returned to the window seat and checked her watch. Nearly half six. There were already distant signs of life in the hotel and she realised it wouldn't be too long before she was forced back into the company of Williams. Given what she now knew it was going to be uncomfortable and difficult to continue to act the Artist with nothing much on her mind but the coming performance.

She returned to the bed, unable to settle. How in God's name had she got into this mess? She'd been mildly attracted to Denton to begin with but whatever the attraction had been it had grown into something that was now consuming her emotionally. Her desperation to warn him, help him, protect him wasn't the result of a passing attraction. She began to feel she was playing against a stacked deck. From what she'd overheard in the early hours, Williams had known about Denton and his daughter well in

210

advance of her involvement, presumably from Denton's ex colleague, Webber. How these two worlds were connected or had converged was currently beyond her. Nonetheless, she now seemed to be the only one able to prevent that convergence becoming a collision.

She had to get to Denton. How? She was in a strange country, miles from the man with no idea as to how to get to him. There was an outside chance that he might ring again but she couldn't be sure. Anyway, she and Mathew were scheduled to be back in Edinburgh at ten for a meeting with another Journalist. How to get to Nairn? Who to ask? Mathew seemed the obvious choice but with her new-found knowledge of Williams she simply wasn't sure how much she could trust him. If at all. On the other hand, if she simply disappeared without offering some sort of explanation to Mathew then Williams would soon learn of it. Given he knew of her dinner with Denton he would doubtless put two and two together and set off in pursuit. No, a conversation, of some sort, with Mathew Sinclair was becoming essential and inevitable.

It was while she was showering, with her spirits slowly lifting beneath the pulsing cascade of the needle-sharp torrent, the thought occurred that if Mathew could be enlisted as an ally, many of her problems would become manageable. He could get, or guide her, to Denton, keep Williams at bay and perhaps shed some light on the connection between Williams and Denton. As she dithered over a choice of outfit; comfort for flight or full slap for the journalist, she realised that she had no evidence to connect Sinclair to any of Williams' nefarious activities or the suspicions raised by the early morning eaves dropping. Mathew had never shown himself to be anything other than a caring man with a passion and talent for music. If, therefore, she reasoned, there was no link to Williams' criminal activities, he could, surely, be persuaded to help her? The conversation with Mathew had to be sooner rather than later.

She returned to pacing the room and began to rehearse the pitch she would make, only to have her thoughts interrupted by distant sounds of bustle and conversation from the direction of the hotel entrance. She knelt up on the seat and pressed her cheek sideways against the glass to allow a downward and angled view of the area. Strain as she might she could see little except part of an overnight bag and the left shoulder of someone clearly taking their leave of another out of her line of vision. As she stood up on the cushion in the hope of a clearer view, a large black car entered the drive and crunched to a stop on the gravel. A large man un-jammed himself from the driver's seat flexing cramp from an extensive breadth of shoulder as he weight lifter waddled to the other side of the car. Dee's cheek slipped on the glass as the cushion beneath her feet moved slightly but not before she'd seen Williams hand the bag to the driver, hug Mathew and get in the car cheerfully waving a goodbye as the car accelerated away scattering chippings in its wake. She sat back down and gathered her thoughts. It was just gone seven. Williams had an overnight bag and had made an early start. She'd bet real money that he was joining the hunt for Denton. If so that was bad news for Denton but did afford her a chance to talk to Mathew and persuade him to help.

They met on the stairs. Dee startled him, 'Mathew, I need to talk to you', she announced abruptly and without preamble.
'Oh, hi Dee and a very good morning to you too', he grinned.
'Mathew, this is urgent. Can we please talk?'
Sinclair looked at his watch and then at her. 'Dee would this wait 'til breakfast? Let me get a shower? Yes?'
'No Mathew, this, as I said, is urgent.' She took him by the hand and began to lead him up the stairs, sensing initial reluctance being overcome by resignation. The nearer she got to her room the more unsure of herself she became. The carefully rehearsed pitch became a series of disconnected, contradictory and confused thoughts. She sat a puzzled but unresisting Sinclair in the window seat and began to pace in front of him. Muddled thoughts became clearer as she recalled Williams' instructions that Denton, his daughter and her boyfriend were to be killed. She stopped pacing, pivoted, seized a stool from beneath the dressing table, placed it in front of him, sat down and took both his hands in hers.
'Mathew. How much do you know about David?'
'What?'
'Bear with me. How well do you know David?'
'Dee, what's this about?'

'Mathew. Trust me. Please trust me. This is so very important. I need you to answer some questions and I am asking that you answer them honestly.'

Sinclair let out a long, exasperated breath. 'Dee, we're meeting a Journalist in a few hours to talk about your career and our music. That's got to be more important than whatever is bubbling away in that brain of yours at the moment. C'mon. We'll talk later.'

She leant forward, tipping the stool onto two legs, with her face now inches from his. 'No Mathew. We'll talk now. What I need to talk to you about could make the career and the music irrelevant for us both,' she hissed. Dee let the silence between them lengthen while she watched the full import of what she had said sink into Sinclair's mind.

'Why are you asking about David?'

'Because I don't think he's the man you think he is.'

'How do you mean?'

'Before I answer that can you tell me how David earns his living? From where does this seemingly limitless wealth come?'

'Dee, you know all this. He's an Investment Banker.'

'Which is?'

'Oh, I don't know,' he waved his hands, shook his head and looked to the ceiling for inspiration, 'people approach him with business ideas looking for funding and he invests. Or he sees an opportunity, a failing business, perhaps with a good property portfolio and he buys it up and strips out the stuff that's worth anything? That type of thing.'

'And does he do this for an organisation?'

'Dee, where's this going?'

'Stay with me please.'

'The answer is no then. As far as I know he is the business.'

'Hmm. As far as you know?'

'Dee, I've never really taken that much of an interest.'

'Have you ever, met any of his colleagues? Staff perhaps? Been to his office, taken a message, spoken to anybody he works with, bumped into them at lunch or met them socially?'

Sinclair stood up suddenly, throwing Dee's hands back into her lap. 'Dee, what's going on here? You know about David and me. He's the best thing that happened to me since I came out. He's given me everything I have. Love, security, confidence and an opportunity to pursue the career I've always wanted. What are you getting at?'

'He's not what he seems Mathew,' she said grimly.

Sinclair locked onto her gaze and through gritted teeth said, 'Then tell me what he is.'

'He's a career criminal Mathew. A 'Mr Big', a racketeer, a mobster or whatever you call them in this country. They're two a penny in The States but there is always a pattern, a modus operandi, modus vivendi. Believe me. I've been round the edges of this sort of crap since the first time I stood on a stage in a back-street dive as a kid. Somewhere at the top of the food chain, is the guy with the apartment overlooking Central Park, probably still married to the girl he met in College who thinks he's something in "Futures". Down through an unwieldy hierarchy of ever increasing violence you get to the crack addict whore pushing drugs outside her kid's school in the Projects. Drugs Mathew. Drugs. And the entire operation has a web of attendant businesses that are there with the sole purpose of laundering drugs money. Pubs, clubs, bars, taxis, construction, hotels, transport.' She paused before quietly adding, 'The Music Business?'

Sinclair gasped and spread his hands wide in amazement. 'So, because David has wide ranging business interests you've decided that he's a Gangster?' He snorted incredulously. 'Dee, are you sure it's not you that has the problem with drugs?'

Dee sought and re-secured Sinclair's hands, tugging him gently towards her. 'Mathew, last night I overheard your David issue instructions for Paul Denton, his daughter and her boyfriend to be executed. Is this what "Investment Bankers" do?'

Sinclair snatched his hands back. 'This is preposterous. Where was this? Where did this happen?'

'Here, in the lobby, early this morning. About three.'

'We were in bed.'

'Were you?'

'Yes. I'd have known if David had got up.'

'Would you?'

'Wait a minute. What's Denton got to do with David?'

'I'm not completely certain but Paul's daughter was missing. I'd helped him make a few enquiries in Manchester and the next thing we both knew all hell was let loose. Then last night David asked me about Denton. Did you tell him about us?'

'I'd told him you had dinner with Denton but no more than that. I didn't really know there was an "us" until you and I spoke last night and I didn't discuss that with David.'

'I thought so. So, why was he so interested to know whether I was seeing Denton again?'

'I'm sure there's a simple explanation. You could always ask him.'

'Yeah, right. Where's David now?'

'Oh, he's gone up to Nairn. He's going to talk to a builder about that place he's just bought and he's hoping to meet somebody about the jazz festival he mentioned last night.'

'Nairn?'

'Yes, Nairn.'

Dee decided to take a chance, 'Denton's in Nairn.'

Sinclair swallowed. 'Dee I'm sure this is all a coincidence. Anyway, as I said you've not got one piece of evidence to support these totally unfounded charges.'

'The conversation I overheard?'

'You must have misheard and the rest is pure speculation and supposition.'

'I did not mishear Mathew,' she shouted. 'Denton is in trouble and I want you to help me find him, warn him so I can help him before Williams and his thugs get to him.' In the stunned silence that followed Dee studied Mathew. Once or twice she'd had the impression that something she'd said had struck a chord with him. She'd felt that the questions about Williams' businesses had opened his eyes a little and that the litany of money laundering techniques had resonated, if his refusal to meet her eye as she'd listed them had been anything to go by. 'Mathew, in all the time that you've known David has there ever been anything, anything, that he's said or done that's worried you or caused you a moment's concern? Anything?'

'Well, no. Not really. But,'

'But?'

'There was the Boy Band, before you, that was suing us?'

'Yes?'

'Well one day it was a big problem.'

'And?'

'And, well that's it really. The next day it wasn't.'

'I'm not sure I understand.'

215

'One died of an overdose and another at a Pool Party. The other two disappeared although I did hear that one had surfaced running a bar in Thailand.'

Dee considered briefly how much of a coincidence it was that a contractual dispute should end in such a deadly fashion but now felt confirmed in her view that Williams was capable of anything. 'Mathew, I am not making this up. What possible motive could I have for doing that? Until this happened I was on cloud nine. My music has never been this good, I'm singing better than I ever have and my career is on the up. That is all down to you. I'm about to throw all that away because I'm convinced that David Williams is going to kill these three people and anybody else who gets in his way.' Pausing for breath she noticed that Sinclair was silently weeping and she reached out to put an arm round his shoulders. 'Come on Mathew. Are you going to help me?'

He stood, brushed at his tears, walked slowly to the door and opened it. 'Dee, I'm going to get a shower, have some breakfast and then order a car to take us back into Edinburgh for that interview. While I'm doing that, I'm going to think about all this. Quietly by myself.'

Taking advantage of what she guessed was an hour's grace before she was expected to join Sinclair at breakfast she returned to the lobby in search of the Receptionist. The desk was empty but the sound of bottles and glasses being moved and put away drew her to the bar. She rounded the corner in time to see the Receptionist taking a long pull from a large balloon glass. The woman's eyes defied her to comment as she took another, defiant slug. Placing the glass on the bar with the studied precision that only a drunk can bring to such a basic task she raised an eye in enquiry.

'Sorry to disturb you,' said Dee with a smile.

'S'not a problem. How can I help Miss?'

'Wilson?' Dee volunteered.

'S'right. Miss Wilson.'

'You took a call for me last night. I just wondered whether the caller left a number.'

'I don't think so. If I hadn't've found you I'd've asked for a number.' She giggled. 'But hey! I found you. Right?'

216

'Yes, you did.' Said Dee watching with alarm as the woman unsteadily worked her way towards the bar flap gaining support from fixtures and fittings on either side of the bar as she went. She lifted the flap, went through the gap, turned to lower it, realised she was beyond reach of any physical support and pitched forward onto her knees. Dee helped her to her feet and then got her into a chair. 'Honey, you need to sleep this off before Management see you.'

'I am management,' the woman announced proudly before emphasising the point with an imperious sniff.

'You're Management?'

'I am so. This,' she indicated her environs with a grandiose sweep of her hand, 'is all mine. Or rather it was.'

'You own the hotel?'

The woman looked at her in disgust. 'Like that's got anything to do with one of Williams' bimbos.'

'Honey, I ain't nobody's bimbo and David Williams is gay.'

'A gay crook then,' she slurred.

'Crook?'

'Crook, silvery tongued, slippery, lying bastard loan shark. Whassa difference?'

'I heard he invested in your hotel.'

'Invested?' She snorted, 'stole you mean.'

'Stole. How?'

'S'easy, take two naïve middle aged people with a redundancy package and a dream. Stay at their hotel. Get to know them. Listen to their problems. Lend a few thousand to get over a cash flow problem. Introduce a mate with a construction company. Lend a few more thousand. Twelve months later your savings have gone, you're in debt and that nice man has just explained that the interest rates that you agreed mean you now owe more than the hotel is worth. See if you can guess what happens next? You argue and a few days later a very big man starts a fight in your bar. You don't make the connection until a room gets wrecked, cars get vandalised and staff disappear. A month after that my husband went and I started drinking '

It took little persuasion for Dee to get the woman back to her room where she made her comfortable on her bed. As she opened the door to leave the woman stirred.

'Sorry about that. But thanks.'

'Advice. You listening honey? Good advice. When you wake up pack a bag and get as far away from this place as you can.'

They journeyed back into Edinburgh in complete silence. Dee's enquiries as to whether he'd thought any further about what she'd said were met with an obstinate, almost childish, turn of his head and studied indifference. 'Mathew. I do realise that you don't want to talk about it but if you get the chance, talk to the woman who is the receptionist at the hotel. She used to own the place. The story about how it was stolen from her by Williams should make even you begin to wonder. You remember that list on money laundering operations I gave to you? Well I forgot loan sharking. Or as Williams would call it Investment Banking,'

On arrival at Queen's Hall Sinclair directed Dee to the Café area having re briefed her on the points to stress in the interview with the Journalist and promised to return when the journalist had left. On his return, he seemed less stressed and even a little cheerful. 'Ok Dee. Time to go. Car's downstairs.'
'Mathew. What about our discussion. Denton, David; what we talked about?'
'We'll talk in the car Dee.' He smiled reassuringly as he ushered her across the pavement where a driver with broad shoulders and a weight lifters neck held the door for her. Vague recognition turned to alarm when the recent memory of another muscle-bound driver surfaced as she sank into the car's leather seat.

'Hello Dee. I hear you want to get to Nairn,' rasped Williams.

Dee, felt the shock of the betrayal hit her hard but knew that it was essential she maintain her composure and show no sign of weakness. 'You stupid asshole Mathew,' she spat at Sinclair as he tried to scrunch further down into the front seat.

Chapter Fifteen

'It's a DAF.'

'What?'

'The lorry we're following is a DAF. Dutch company. Well, Dutch and British Leyland.'

'What are you talking about?' said Denton impatiently.

'Just thinking. They, the Dutch bit, filed for insolvency last week and the British bit asked the government to bail them out. Heseltine refused. I cut the article out of the Telegraph. It was part of the research for my thesis,' finished Starmer quietly. 'Seems a long time ago now.'

Denton nodded in appreciation of another life dragged from normality and subjected to turmoil and found himself swept by guilt that he had not been open with this man who had tried to rescue his daughter and seen his life destroyed as a result. He looked sideways at Starmer, took a deep breath and went with his instincts. 'Tell me about it. A few days ago, I saw a friend of mine get his head blown off in a south London pub. A friend who was probably a customs officer. Hours later, having been interviewed by Police about the shooting and my company, I tip up in Manchester to search for Julie and nearly run into Webber. A man, it turns out, who has criminal connections with your mate Woolley and is also looking for Julie and me. Or both.' He thumped the rim of the steering wheel angrily with the flat of his hand. 'A man you now tell me was probably complicit in two murders. The same Webber who was employed by my company to arrange transport and storage from Amsterdam. Transport and storage with the company whose name is on the side of that fuckin' DAF,' he pointed angrily through the windscreen at the lorry in front. 'Don't tell me that's a coincidence.'

Starmer began to sift through this new information trying to make sense of it and work out what it meant in terms of his own recent experiences. He needed more time to think. 'Serious stuff Mr Denton. It explains a little bit more too.' He glanced at Denton's profile, 'if Webber was the man at Findhorn with Woolley and Osman, he was driving the car that lifted Julie from the car park.'

'Christ! It just gets better and better.'

'It could be worse Mister Denton,' he nodded up the road at the truck, 'we've got a lead.'

'Do you think you could call me Paul? You're Andy. Right?' Denton felt himself being appraised as his request was considered and sensed Starmer's resistance to over familiarity when no answer was forthcoming. 'Right. Starmer it is then.' Denton snapped.

'Whoa, hold up. He's stopping. No, no. Don't stop he'll spot us. Pass him. Take that round about and stop in a side road,' instructed Starmer.

Denton did so and they both turned back to see the driver's mate approach a woman in a bus shelter with a piece of paper in his hand. 'He's asking for directions. We must be close.'

'Yeah. And there's two of them,' added Starmer.

'Hang on, we're off again. Do you know where we are?'

'Coming in to Nairn. A day ago, Julie and I spent a good day here with Jamie. Nothing like her old self but she was getting there. You know?'

'Starmer, at the moment, I'm just hoping that following this DAF isn't a waste of time and that it will lead us somewhere I can find Julie. Once I've got her back you can leave the rest to me. I'll sort the rest out.'

'He's turning left, Mill Lane.' Said Starmer reading off the road sign as they followed the lorry's route up a winding lane and wondering what planet Denton was from if he seriously believed that rescuing Julie was going to be the end of their problems. 'You should slow down you're getting too close. He's too big to go fast down here and if he meets something coming the other way he's going to have to pull over and we'll be right up his chuff before we know it.' They followed the lorry round the twists and turns of the narrow lane with a waist high stone retaining wall to

220

the offside and neat whitewashed single story cottages with the dormer windows in their roofs level with the road on the nearside.

Denton slowed and watched the lorry slip from sight round a bend. As they reached the apex of the bend the brake lights came on as the DAF negotiated a narrow railway bridge. Denton was now less than twenty yards from the tailgate and they both sighed with relief as the lorry scraped under the bridge and accelerated away. Twice the DAF stopped, leaving the pair praying that no following traffic would appear behind to get impatient with their failure to pass the lorry. Their luck held.

'He must be nearly there. He's checking street addresses.' Almost as Starmer spoke the lorry lost speed and pulled slowly out to the right, gaining road room for a left turn into a property yet shielded from their view. They sat there for appreciable minutes before the lorry completed the turn into a drive that they could now see swept round to the front of a large two story stone built manor house with pitched and gabled slated roofs and in character extensions either side of the original main structure. As they slowly passed the entrance they could see that an extension to the drive returned down the side of the house towards some outbuildings at the rear. The drive to the front of the property was cluttered with building plant and materials.

'Speed up for Christ's sake and don't look,' snapped Starmer urgently.

Denton accelerated away but found it impossible not to glance to his left just in time to see Starmer slip from his seat into the foot well.

'Please tell me you didn't look?'

'Difficult not to with you hitting the deck like that. What's up?'

'The guy directing the lorry round to the back was Woolley,' said Starmer, resuming his seat, 'keep going.'

'Bingo,' Denton muttered with satisfaction.

The stone wall with cottage gardens balanced precariously above continued to their right but trees overhanging another wall obscured their view of the ground to Woolley's mansion on the left. They approached a slight rise in the road on a slow right hand curve with the roof of a cottage just visible in some low ground to their left. 'Ok. Keep going but we are going to need to turn around and go back. There's a track down the side of that

221

cottage that looks as though it might run back roughly parallel to the road but behind Woolley's house.'

The track didn't go far and was overgrown but seemed to be part of the old Manor Estate and perhaps an early access track or path for goods and services to the back of the house. They parked the Rover and followed the track on foot until forced by the undergrowth to leave the path. They entered a sparsely planted copse at the edge of which they could just discern brickwork through the foliage. As they cleared the copse they found the brickwork to be a boundary wall. At nearly ten feet high and moss and creeper covered they decided against scaling and continued along its length. The ground sloped away from the wall and down to their right for about fifty feet to where the sound of water and the odd glint of a reflection through the trees suggested a stream. After some minutes of struggling through undergrowth the wall turned to the left at an oblique angle which they sensed brought them more truly parallel with Mill Lane running past the front of the property. As they moved off through more undergrowth Starmer's rucksack caught on a branch and dragged him to a sudden halt making Denton slam into his back.

'What the hell have you brought that for?' He hissed angrily.

'It goes where I go.'

'You should have left it in the car.'

'We might not get back to the car.'

'Ridiculous to bring it.'

Starmer turned very slowly as he adjusted the straps on the rucksack. 'Mr Denton. Is there a point to this conversation?'

Denton sighed. 'Probably not. Sorry. Look, do we need a plan of some sort? I mean how are we going to handle this, them?'

Starmer looked slightly surprised at what he suspected was at the least a crisis of confidence if not a complete abdication of responsibility overlaid with discernible fear.

'I think the best thing we can do is check the place out, see what we've got and then take it from there. What d'ye think?' He encouraged cheerily.

Denton nodded.

As they progressed further along the wall they encountered the remains of collapsed or half demolished outbuildings that had used the boundary as a rear party wall. Starmer handed the rucksack to Denton and climbed a partially collapsed shed partition to bring him to a point just below the parapet of the boundary wall. After one quick scan of the area he pulled himself a little higher and spent moments scrutinising the grounds on the other side. He climbed back down took the rucksack back from Denton and struggled into the straps. 'Where we are now is roughly opposite the centre of the main house. Immediately on the other side of this wall is one of those Victorian timber greenhouses.' He waved towards the far end of the boundary. 'At that end of the greenhouse is some sort of plant room; machinery not marigolds, and somewhere just past that I think there's a gate in the wall.' He turned towards the wall, looked back over his shoulder to check that he had Denton's attention, and mimed positions with chopping motions of his hands. 'So, here is the greenhouse, then the plant room and off to one side of that corner is a set of sheds and a barn. The lorry is backed up to them. They're offloading it. Now the ground between the greenhouse and the main house is laid to lawn. Difficult to cross unseen. If there is a gate where I said, it's almost certainly locked and anyway it's in full view of the pair unloading the lorry.'

'Great. So, what do we do?'

'Get over the wall here and drop down through the greenhouse roof.'

'We'll get cut to ribbons and they'll hear us.'

Starmer grinned. 'Glass is long gone. The whole place is practically derelict or a building site. There's a lot of work going on in the house although apart from the two with the DAF there doesn't seem to be anybody else about.'

'Woolley, Webber?'

'Didn't see them.'

'Right. We're in. Then what?'

'We get Julie!'

'Yeah, but how?'

'Look Mr Denton. I can't tell you how and I can't tell you that it is all going to be alright 'cos I'm not sure it will be. Ideal, would be in and out without being seen and that way we avoid any confrontation.'

'And if it goes wrong?'

'Then we're going to have to fight for her Mr Denton. You ok with that?'

'Of course.'

'Good. If that happens hit first, hit hard and hit anything that moves with anything you can lay your hands on and above all keep moving. Got it?'

'Yeah.'

'Let's do it.'

Starmer sat astride the boundary wall and helped Denton over, then down into the abandoned greenhouse before joining him. The pair crouched behind the dwarf brick walls that carried the old cast iron heating pipes the length of the structure and peeped across the timber sill towards the main house. Denton quickly pulled Starmer to the floor.

'There's a man at the window. I think it's your man Woolley. He's watching them unload the lorry. He'll see us crossing that lawn.'

'Ok. No panic. We'll crawl down to the end of the greenhouse. Keep your head down.'

At the end a door opened onto a small courtyard between the greenhouse and the plant room that Starmer had previously identified. Hooked up to the house side of the boundary wall, at the end of the courtyard, was a set of ladders.

'Could be useful on the way out,' said Denton nodding in their direction.

'And that could be useful on the way in,' responded Starmer pointing to an alley that ran between the boundary wall and the back wall of the plant room. It looked as though at some time it had been used as a semi dry storage area with a lean-to roof cantilevered off the brickwork over the five-foot gap. Starmer started down the alley with the full expectation that it would bring him out very close to the gate in the wall and perhaps near enough to the storage sheds by the DAF to allow them to cross behind the barn and lorry crew, up towards the side of the house. He stopped to consider the uneven ground beneath his feet to see that under the general rubbish that had been dumped, the passage floor was convex. He was walking on the side of a slope. Before he could start off again he was yanked backwards. He wheeled to grab Denton as he was pulled up, back and across into Denton's arms.

'What the fuck!'

They both looked back to a small collapsed and missing section of Victorian, vaulted brick arch.

'Christ! What is that smell?'

'My guess would be a cess pit.' Denton peered knowledgeably into the hole. He picked up half a brick and tossed it into the pit, counting down to the splash.

'Fairly deep too. Place is falling apart. We'd better leave some other way.' He edged past Starmer and peered around the corner of the alley. The DAF was parked about forty feet away and backed up to within ten feet of the sheds with both the container doors open and folded back against the sides of the lorry. One of the crew was standing inside with a sack between his legs. The other appeared and the sack was shuffled across the floor to the edge where it was picked up and taken into the shed. 'Have a look. This could take fuckin' hours.'

Starmer edged to the corner in time to catch the return journey and another sack being offloaded and carried to storage.

'How many sacks in a load?'

'How the hell would I know? It depends on the job and I didn't know we even had a contract up here. And there's something odd about this anyway. That's a forty-ton truck and normal terms and conditions make the customer responsible for offloading and for a load that size we are talking mechanical; forklift. Otherwise, as you can see, you'd be here all day.'

'What's in the sacks?'

'Plaster, cement, grout in the smaller ones and those tubs.'

'Well we can't wait all day and there's no way we can get to the house with them still there.'

'You got any ideas?'

'Yup. Stay here. Don't move 'til I call you.' So saying Starmer stripped off his jacket, handed the rucksack to Denton, stooped to pick up an old piece of cloth from a pile of debris and stepped out of the alley. He walked towards the lorry whistling and industriously wiping his hands on the cloth while being careful to keep the lorry between him and Woolley's vantage point. He stepped up to the sweating crew and smiled.

'Want a hand?'

'You are sure?'

'Yeah, of course. Anyway, I'm between jobs and the Boss expects me to help out where I can.'

'Right this is ok. You, Mynheer, are earning drink.'

'What are we shifting?'

'All those.' The mate jerked his thumb in the direction of the lorry's interior.

225

Starmer stepped nearer. What remained of the sacks, a dozen or so, were stacked near the door. Behind were rows of ceramic panels and trays and sanitary fittings and maybe a dozen plastic tubs of grout.

'Ok. I'll give you a hand to shift the sacks then I'll go and get the forklift.'

'Forklift?'

'Well yeah. How else we going to shift that lot? Forklift? You Know? Small tractor, three wheels and a fork that lifts,' he laughed.

'That fat man. Woolley? Say there was not one.'

'He's the Boss. What does he know? C'mon, let's make a start on the sacks.'

'Oh, my friend you are saving lives here. I'll take care of the small sacks. The tubs, they're going up to the house. All the rest go on the floor at the back of this building,' he pointed to the open fronted shed behind Starmer.

Once the sacks were cleared the three of then stood at the rear of the lorry, resting their arms on the deck while they considered their next move. Starmer leant back slightly out of their eye line and studied the lorry doors. 'Ok lads, I'll go and get the forklift. Can I make a suggestion?'

They nodded eagerly.

'You see those shower tray type thingies on the right back there? Well they look like the biggest and heaviest. Let's take them first. Do you wanna get in and start moving them this way? We'll need to move these tubs first. He looked behind him, 'pass 'em down to me.' With the tubs on the ground Starmer gave the less than nimble mate a helping hand to get back in the lorry and waited patiently until they both had hold of one of the units and had taken the strain. He then dropped from sight, unhooked the left-hand door from the side of the truck, ran it round and slammed and bolted it on his way to retrieving the door from the right-hand side. As he got the door nearly closed a bellow of rage made him look up. The pair had dropped the load and were rushing the door. He slammed it shut, jumping to haul the cross lever and locking bar into place as a yelp suggested fingers had been caught. He leant back against the doors, let out a long sigh and listened to the muffled thuds and shouts coming from inside the container.

'Christ, that was brilliant.' Denton appeared.

'It worked and nobody got hurt. Well not really,' he said thinking of the Mate's fingers.

'Now for phase two.'

'Woolley?'

'Yeah. You got my rucksack?'

'Here. What next?'

'Well, we can't go to Woolley, he'll clock us from a distance and the game'll be up. We need him to come to us. We need him on our ground.'

'What have you got in mind?'

'Check if the keys are in the cab. Stay out of sight though. There's something I want to check out.' Denton went to the front of the lorry while Starmer made his way to the back and the tubs intended for the house.

Denton reappeared grinning and dangling a set of vehicle keys, 'Bingo.'

Starmer passed two of the tubs to him, 'give me a hand to get these out of sight.' They shuttled the ten sealed plastic tubs with wire handles, labelled "Waterproof Grout - 5KG" into the shed and stacked them behind several abandoned blue, plastic, forty gallon drums and their scattered lids. Starmer knelt and used the camper van key to break the plastic ring seal on one, levered off the lid and dipped a finger to gather a sample of the powdered contents. 'Heroin. Beginning to make sense,' he murmured as a quick calculation gave him a street value well in excess of a few millions. He waved the finger at Denton, 'grout?'

'Oh shit!'

'Probably.'

'Cocaine?'

'Heroin. Looks like you have been importing it.'

'No way.'

"fraid so.'

'To Scotland?'

'Geography wasn't the issue I had in mind. But why not? Glasgow is Drugs Central these days. Maybe Woolley was expanding or maybe he's warehousing for a Scottish mob. Either way there's enough stuff in that shed to begin to explain, perhaps, why we've been getting the attention and aggravation we have. This thing's big. Really big.' He looked thoughtfully up at Denton, 'maybe they think you're on to them? I don't know. Anyway, time for all that later. Now we need to get Julie.'

227

Denton looked defeated. Starmer took the older man by the shoulders and gently shook him. 'C'mon. Forget all that drug stuff, we'll sort it out later. What I need you to do now is drive the lorry, slowly, walking pace, round to the front of the house and then just sit there with the engine running. Can you do that?'

'Of course, yeah. But what about the racket?' Waving a hand in the direction of the trailer and the thumps and shouts coming from within.

'Adds sparkle to the lure. Can you do this?'

'Let's go.'

Denton had spent years moving lorries around to make room for other deliveries in the yard at Woolwich so moving this one was little challenge. As instructed he pulled up opposite but some distance from the entrance to the main house and sat there with the engine running in neutral. For three to four anxious minutes nothing happened. Then Denton saw the front door open and the fat man from Manchester appear. Sitting up on high, Denton watched him drop out of view below his sight line as he got nearer to the lorry. The banging and shouting from the rear increased as the passenger door was pulled open and Denton looked down at the florid, sweaty features of the fat man.

'What, in the name of all that is holy, is going on?' He lisped. 'And who, may I ask, are you?'

Denton felt under no pressure or obligation to respond as he watched the barrel of a revolver come into view and move slowly towards Woolley's head until it rested on his temple. Starmer followed the barrel into sight, hitching the rucksack over his shoulder as he moved closer to Woolley.

'Mr Woolley.'

Woolley's head began to turn but Starmer pressured it back with the barrel.

'Andrew? Oh, how unexpected. How are you dear boy?'

'Back to the house Mr Woolley.'

Woolley looked up at Denton, 'such a polite boy.'

Internally the house was as much of a building site as outside. Immediately inside the front door scaffold towers screened off the stairs with hanging polythene sheeting stretching to the ceiling some twenty feet up. Narrow walkways of scaffold boards had been laid across floor joists where the original boards had been removed. Loops of electric cable hung down from exposed joists at ceiling height and a mixing board coated with a mound of long since set plaster was propped in a doorway to one side. More plastic sheeting was draped over an ornate handrail and balusters to the staircase for protection and halfway down the hall corridor, leading to the back of the house, was a trestle table laden with gallon cans of paint and decorating equipment. Starmer pushed Woolley along in front of him with the revolver and Denton followed along behind checking side rooms for Julie as they progressed.

Starmer had been surprised at Woolley's compliance but was still caught off guard as Woolley, reaching the end of the boarded walkway, kicked one of the scaffold boards sideways from its support. Starmer lost his footing and slipped into the void between joists nearly to waist level. Woolley turned, for a big man he was unsurprisingly slow but his weight and gathering speed gave him momentum. He passed Starmer and barged into Denton who was knocked sideways onto the decorator's trestle table. Woolley was struggling with the catch to the front door when Denton, a gallon can of paint in his hand, caught up with him. As Woolley turned to face Denton, the can, at the end of an arm's length worth of swing, hit him full in the face.

Starmer stood next to Woolley checking abrasions and bruising to his legs as Denton knelt on the fat man's stomach and applied pressure.

'Paint can?'

'You said use anything,' grinned Denton.

'I did. Good thinking.'

'I see you're back with us you fat bastard.'

'Mr Woolley. Where's Julie?' said Starmer, quietly.

Woolley pushed himself into a sitting position, spat blood to the floor, looked up at the pair, shrugged and mumbled, 'kitchen.'

Denton ran nimbly down the hall skipping from one loose board to another. Starmer, limping, finally managed to push a reluctant and hurting Woolley into the room. Denton was on his knees by the side of a camp bed with an unconscious Julie in his arms. 'He's drugged her.' Denton nodded at the drug paraphernalia set out on a grubby towel on the floor by the bed.

Starmer glanced around the room. It looked more like the inside of a construction site hut than a domestic kitchen. It smelt of damp clothes, Calor gas and cigarettes. A free-standing sink unit had a water supply running in a hose from a hole in the ceiling above and a bucket beneath the waste pipe. There were two trestle tables and some benches, a coat rack hung fully with waterproofs, an electric hot plate and the Calor gas heater.

His gaze returned to Denton and he watched him gently lay his daughter back down on the camp bed, rise from his knees and advance on Woolley. Woolley was no coward and he'd been around long enough to have a few tricks up his sleeve and Starmer couldn't afford to have Denton hurt or dumped on his backside. Woolley, he thought, was just going to have to take this on the chins so that Denton got it out of his system. He went full stretch to pin Woolley's arms to his side and was surprised. The beating Denton handed out was delivered coldly and clinically without a word or any display of any emotion. Woolley suffered the further damage to his face and the pounding to his well-padded ribs in a silence punctuated only by grunts.

'Better?'

'I want to kill him.'

'I know.'

'I mean it. He deserves to die.'

'Right. Phase three?'

'Phase three?'

'Get Julie and get out?'

'Ok.'

'Look I want you to take the lorry back to where we found it. Then use that ladder to get back over the wall to the car. Bring the car back here but park it out of sight on the blind side of the lorry. You got that?'

'Yeah, yeah. What'll you be doing? What about Julie?'

'I think she's under pretty deep but she's breathing evenly. I'll try and bring her round.'

'And him?'

'Will you get going?'

Starmer watched the lorry reappear round the back of the house from the kitchen window and then just caught sight of a flash of aluminium as Denton got the ladder in place. He checked on Julie, kicked Woolley to his feet, and pushed him into the hall and out of the back door. Woolley puffed his way across the lawn guided in the direction of the plant room with prods from the revolver.

'Andrew, please Andrew,' mumbled Woolley through his damaged mouth. 'We can talk. There's really no need for any of this. Oh, do please listen. I've told you before there's a place for you in the business. You have a gift. That offer still stands you know.'

'Why were you chasing Julie and me?'

'Andrew, Andrew, you transgressed. You took my money.' He paused to spit another mouth full of blood and saliva to the ground. 'You had to be punished. You know that. I'd have had half the scum of Manchester taking liberties if I'd let you get away with it.'

'And Julie? Denton?'

'Dear boy. I'm not sure. I'm distribution not supply.'

They'd reached the corner of the plant room and Starmer prodded Woolley towards the alley.

'Andrew. Come and work for me.'

'Mr Woolley before I could come and work for you I'd have to kill you.'

'You killed Osman?'

'Yes.'

'You're going to kill me.'

'Yes.'

'It wasn't a question,' mumbled Woolley sadly through split and swollen lips. 'Why?'

'Jamie.'

'I understand.'

Starmer prodded him towards a right turn into the alley.

'Out of sight eh? Make it a clean shot Andrew. Please? A favour to an old man?'

Starmer had misjudged both the distance and the frailty of the brick vaulting and Woolley's weighty bulk crashed through the defective structure into the cess pit one pace in front of him. Forcing him to step back sharply to avoid Woolley's wind milling arms. The solid sounding splatter was followed by a howl of horror. Starmer stepped forward gingerly and looked over the edge. Woolley's head was just visible but surrounded by Prince of Wales check that had ballooned around his neck and shoulders with trapped air. One hand was scrabbling at the slimed brick sides in a futile attempt to gain purchase. With a surge of energy and a thrashing of his legs Woolley forced his head out of the semi liquid sewage and gasped, 'not like this Andrew. Please.' All energy spent the fat man sank back but his huge eyes, just above the surface, watched Starmer as he cocked and aimed at Woolley's head with the gun held at arms-length. The sound of the hammer hitting an empty chamber opened Woolley's eyes wider. Starmer smiled at the look of realisation, incredulity, anger and despair in those eyes and then tossed the empty revolver onto the spot where Woolley had disappeared.

There was no sign of Denton and the car by the time Starmer had got a still unconscious Julie to the sheds behind the parked DAF. He sat her with her back propped against a wall and made his way over to the plastic tubs and the blue forty gallon containers.

Denton drove into the yard too fast and came close to skidding into the DAF in his impatience to get back to Julie. He got out of the car and shouted for Starmer. As he rounded the end of the lorry he saw Starmer emerge from the shed.
'Where have you been? Where's Julie?'
Starmer pointed behind him.
'And Woolley?' he asked over noises and banging from within the container.
Starmer nodded at the lorry, 'in there,' he grunted. 'They're mates. They knew Woolley by name. Not your average truckers it would seem. C'mon. We've got to get out of here. I'm assuming that this place hasn't got a single builder on site because they cancelled today's work for this delivery. Just in case I'm wrong though, I'd like to get out of here before we're knee deep in workers.'

Starmer turned in his seat and reached for Julie's pulse. She pulled her hand away from his and, grunting, flopped onto her stomach from the recovery position in which she's been placed. Denton risked a glance over his shoulder to the back seat turning back just in time to negotiate the one-way traffic at the railway bridge in Mill Lane.
'How is she?'
'Coming out of it.'
Denton slammed his hand repeatedly against the steering wheel in rage. 'Why would anyone do something like that?'
'They knew she was an addict. It kept her compliant,' Starmer shrugged.

Denton renewed his assault on the steering wheel. 'She's not an addict,' he yelled. 'She may have taken drugs a couple of times but that doesn't make her an addict.'

'Mister Denton,' Starmer sighed patiently, 'she is an addict. She will tell you that herself. She will tell you that her life has become ruled by the clock. Tick, tock, tick, tock. Tick, you wake up, tock you need a fix, tick you need money, tock you do whatever you need to do to get the money, tick you fix up, tock, you wake up. Three times a day. If she's lucky.'

'What did she need to do?' Denton whispered.

Starmer ignored the question, 'we need to stop. You need petrol and we need food. I've not eaten in ages. We need loads of water, sugary stuff and loads of carbs.'

'Water? Carbs?'

'For Julie?' Starmer explained. 'She's going to need re-hydrating and feeding while we wean her off the stuff. Muscles are seventy-five per cent water. It'll help with the cramps. Some Imodium will help too. Carbs are for when she starts to get the munchies. Bread and peanut butter would be good too. Then bring the dosage down gradually, it was working before Woolley got to her.'

'Are you crazy? You're not giving her anything. She's coming off full stop.'

'You might want to talk to Julie about that.'

'Don't tell me how to deal with my daughter Starmer,' rasped Denton, gripping the wheel tightly but rocking in his seat in rage.

Starmer glanced sideways and said quietly, 'this is another one of those conversations, isn't it? You know the ones. Where you speak before you think and then won't listen? She's an addict. She's not mentally defective and the things that have happened to her because of that addiction haven't changed the real her. She still has the same values, hopes, loves and thoughts but they are all on hold while she deals with this thing. And she wants to deal with it. She really does. But, she feels totally alone, ashamed and abandoned. Yeah, so what she really needs now is for someone else not to listen and try to control her. Well good luck with that.'

Denton sat quietly fuming while he considered what Starmer had said. Yet again he realised that the absence of parental involvement or pretty much any contact with Julie in recent months let alone his lack of knowledge about the world that she now inhabited, poorly equipped him to deal with much of this. What had also irked him was the further appreciation that since he'd met Starmer it had been the young man calling the shots not him. Starmer seemed to have a presence and a natural ability to assess and act on situations that had left him hesitant and unsure. This, he was now sure, was probably the real reason he'd challenged Starmer's treatment plan; marking territory. 'I know you tried to help her and I thank you for that. I'm going back to Edinburgh and then I'll take her home and get professional help.' Guilt flooded through him as he realised that he'd put his need to see Dee before his daughter's welfare.

'Edinburgh?' Starmer slapped the dashboard, 'quick, turn here. There's a place where we can get petrol and supplies in Findhorn.' He directed urgently.

They pulled up in front of a collection of buildings that seemed to have been erected at different times, in differing styles from a wide range of materials to meet a variety of demands. On the central forecourt island were three pumps; petrol, diesel and an antiquated manually operated paraffin pump. Behind these and leading down to the foreshore, beach and estuary were a few sheds most of which seemed to have been built from tarred timber and corrugated sheeting. Between these were whaler sized boats chocked and blocked for the winter. Slightly in front but to one side of the sheds was the open front of a large Nissen hut, its curved tarred and corrugated sheet roof housing a car repair business and the cash kiosk for petrol sales. At right angles to these and parallel with the exit slip road was an L shaped building which judging from the goods on the pavement, the sign outside and the window displays was ironmongers, Post Office, provisions store and newsagents all in one.

'You deal with the petrol. I'll get what we need from the shop,' advised Starmer over his shoulder as he strode off giving Denton no time to debate the issue. He pushed open the door to the expected bell ring and paused on the threshold, motionless for a moment, breathing in the heady mix of smells, and listening to the hum of a refrigerator, simply staggered at the amount and variety of stock that had been crammed into every available space in the store.

He smiled briefly at the memory of a similar shop he'd frequented back in Manchester that had become the subject of a bet. He'd wagered that this shopkeeper could meet any reasonable demand. Five pints later, ping pong balls had been decreed the test. The next morning Ajay had enquired whether they had a colour preference while Starmer pocketed his winnings.

He turned right down the aisle leading to the back of the shop past fruit boxes of vegetables on one side with shelves of canned goods giving way to dry goods on the other. He turned left in front of the freezers at the end of the shop and left again up an aisle leading back to the counter. A large middle-aged woman in a day glow orange sailing top breathed in with a smile to let him pass in the narrow aisle.

'Excuse me. You will perhaps help me? Yes?'

'How?'

'This is for cooker? Or for the mickrowelle?'

'Mickrowelle?' Denton chuckled. 'Microwave?'

'Ah. Yah. The Microwave.'

Starmer carefully read the instructions on the packet and jabbed a finger at an illustration before declaring, 'either, both.'

'That is most helpful. Danke.'

Starmer collected two battered wire baskets full of cakes, biscuits, crisps, water and soft drinks and took his place in a short queue for the check out. The Postmaster, for that was the hat he currently wore, was carefully weighing and registering a series of packages that were going to Canada for an elderly and obviously flustered lady.

'Ach, he is patient with this old woman. Yes?'

Starmer turned to smile at the Sailor, 'probably the quickest way. If you're in a hurry you can go in front if you like.'

'No, I have time. We sail on the tide in an hour maybe?' She chuckled. 'My husband is in the pub. He very much likes your pubs. I am hoping to have an English gin and tonic with him before we depart. But there is not a hurry.'

'Where are you going?'

'The Kimberley pub. Our boat is moored at the jetty near there.'

Starmer laughed. 'No, I meant to where are you sailing?'

'Oh, I am not understanding. Kiel. We go home to Germany. After that storm, the forecast, for the time of the year, is gut for a few days. But we take our time though,' she laughed, 'like the shop. No hurry.' They chuckled together and he insisted she go first.

Exasperation had overcome the Post Master who had called for help and Starmer found himself leaving the shop immediately behind the Sailor. She stopped and tried, unsuccessfully, to light a cigarette in the freshening breeze. He took the lighter from her, mimed that she should cup her hands as a shield and shared her relief and some smoke as the cigarette lit. They both stepped back onto the pavement to allow a van driver entry to the shop. Starmer was vaguely aware that Sailor Lady was speaking but he was now totally focussed on Denton who was standing at the side of the Rover arguing with two men.

The older of the two seemed to be the main protagonist although the other, bigger man was the one that Denton pushed away as he made a grab. Taking advantage of this distraction, Starmer ran down the blind side of the van, parked on the other side of the fuel island, to the Rover which had a Mercedes behind it. Reaching the back, he peeped around the rear. On balance, he thought his chances of dealing with the pair were not good and practically nil if you considered the gun that the older one was waving about. He sneaked another look. He was positioned with what he assumed must be Woolley's thugs to his left, Denton, now on the other side of the island, by his car to the right and the pumps immediately in front of him. He slipped boldly out from behind the van.

'Mind yer backs lads. Make way for a working man.' Both thugs looked momentarily bemused but both instinctively stepped back as he took the petrol pump from its holster. As Starmer saw doubt enter the gunman's eyes and the gun begin to move in his direction he lifted the nozzle, aimed and pulled hard on the trigger lever. A twenty-millimetre diameter column of ninety-five octane petrol at a rate of forty litres a minute was hosed from the collar to cuff of the gunman. Starmer turned, and closer to this quarry, hauled the stunned, bigger thug closer by his belt and stuffed the nozzle with a now locked trigger down the man's waistband. 'Get in the car Denton. Now,' he shouted.

The older thug seemed to have recovered marginally and once more the gun was travelling an arc that had Starmer at its end. He opened the car door, got one foot inside, leant across the top of the door and flicked the Sailor's lighter to life. The thug and

236

Starmer locked eyes across the flame until Starmer chanced a look behind him as her heard the rear window winder motor whirr.

'Do it Andy. Do it. Light the cunt up. Burn him,' yelled Julie from the back of the car.

Starmer fell into his seat with the door slamming behind him as Denton accelerated fiercely, turned right across the front of the shop and left out onto the road.

'Webber?'

'Yeah. You recognise him?'

'Not sure. If he's mixed up with Woolley, he might have been in Slammers. I recognise that Merc though. It was at Findhorn the night Jamie was killed and I'm pretty sure he was the one in the car giving the orders,' recalling the face dimly lit by the interior light. 'What did he want?'

'Us,' he paused, 'oh, and some money and a book.' He said with a sidelong glance at Starmer.

'Watch out,' yelled Starmer, 'it's a one-way system past the pub, whoa, whoa, steady.' Denton was struggling to control the big car through a chicane formed by the corner of a big white building when Starmer shouted, 'stop, back up, down there,' urgently pointing to a slip road down the other side of the white building which led onto a grassed ramp and then to a jetty.

'Where the hell are we going?'

'Down that slip road and turn left at the bottom in front of this building and park up so we can't be seen from the road above. Then get Julie and follow me.'

Denton sat, stunned by the events of the past few minutes, then watched as Starmer retrieved his rucksack and ran down the grassed slope onto a stone jetty and then the hundred yards or so to a small fibre glass yacht moored on the seaward side of the jetty at its far end. As he pulled Julie from the car he heard the roar of an engine, a squeal of brakes and the sound of skidding as another driver unfamiliar with the road took the chicane too fast. He held his breath and prayed until he heard the car accelerate past their turning on the road above him. He struggled with Julie along the stone quay noticing the freshening wind was taking the tops from some of the waves caused by a fierce tidal race towards the estuary. To his right the buildings of the village gave way to scattered bungalows and then dunes as the shore line swept round in a hook of sandbanks narrowing the exit from the estuary to the sea. He arrived at the boat breathless to find Starmer trying to force a lock on the cabin door.

'Leave it,' he shouted, 'I know boats. Leave it. Cast us off fore and aft and push the bow as far past the end of the jetty as you can then jump aboard.' Starmer looked at him uncertainly. 'Starmer, I know about boats. Do as you're fuckin' told,' he bellowed, briefly aware that there had been a shift in his relationship with Starmer and then watching with satisfaction as his orders were carried out. 'C'mon get on with it. Forget the engine. The tide's nearly at full ebb, it'll carry us out.'

As Starmer dealt with the moorings Denton settled Julie in the impossibly cramped cockpit and unshipped and fitted the wooden tiller. As the bow cleared the end of the jetty he felt the ebbing tide push the boat to starboard but was fearful that being on the edge of the tidal stream it might just push them back into the slack water between the current and the shore. Starmer landing in the cockpit may have just provided the impetus needed to push them out into the tidal race. Denton pushed the tiller hard to port and steered them towards the centre of the ebbing race. As they neared the middle of the estuary he could see the entrance more clearly and picked out the first marker pole indicating safe passage round the spit of land hooking out into the estuary. Beyond that pole were two more and then the open sea.

'Look!'

Denton scanned the shore to where Starmer was pointing to see two cars racing along the coast road past the bungalows towards the dunes.

'Gotta be Webber. They won't get far it's a dead end. A car park for dog walkers,' advised Starmer.

Denton continued to watch the cars and as predicted they stopped in an open area with a few dunes between them and the channel to the sea. He saw Webber leap from the lead car and disappear into the dunes. He looked back at the second car where a group had gathered to watch Webber's efforts. None of the three men in the car seemed inclined to help and Denton was about to turn away when the biggest of the three went to the rear of the car opened the door and dragged out a protesting woman. A black woman.

'Get down.'

Denton felt as though the air between him and Starmer had split to the sound of torn silk. Probably twice if the two following cracks were anything to go by. Starmer risked a look over the gunwale to see Webber, pistol in hand, rabid with rage racing towards a point on the shore to bring him closest to their current course. 'Force that lock now. Get below. You've got about two minutes to get that engine started.' He looked back at Dee who was struggling with the man who'd pulled her from the car to retrieve her arm with which he was now forcing her to wave goodbye. For some reason he didn't feel a return wave was appropriate but rose from the bench seat in alarm as he saw Dee struck to the ground by the man who'd held her arm.

He was juddered from his state of shock by the Diesel thumping into life. With one last look at Dee he steered deeper into the estuary and set course for the North Sea.

Chapter Sixteen

As the car pulled away from Queen's Hall and out into the traffic of Clark Street, Williams leant across the rear seat and gently but firmly removed Dee's shoulder bag from her lap. 'Just need to check that there's nothing in there that can hurt either of us darling.' Dee saw little point in resisting and surrendered the bag without further comment. Williams scrunched over towards the door making room on the rear seat for the emptied contents and then proceeded to pick through them. 'Women's hand bags never cease to amaze me.'

'Why am I not surprised?'

Williams grinned, 'there have been times when it's been, well, necessary I suppose,' he grinned again. 'I must say Dee that in some respects you are a little bit of a disappointment. Keys, cosmetics, tissues, lozenges, tampons.'

'Turn you on does it David?'

'Hardly dear. It's just that given the recent exploits of your new paramour I'd expected something a little less mundane. A gun perhaps?'. Having finished sorting through the contents, he turned the bag upside down, inserted his hand and felt around the lining. A smile spread across his face as he turned the bag back up to reveal a zipped pocket. 'Hello. What have we here?' He unzipped the pocket and produced Dee's passport, some cash and a small wallet of credit cards. 'I don't think you're going to be needing this somehow now Dee.' He smiled menacingly as he carefully unbuttoned his overcoat to reveal a crimson lining and an inside pocket into which he inserted the passport, cash and wallet. This done he shovelled the rest of the contents back into the bag threw two sets of keys in last and handed the bag back to her.

Dee was still too shocked by Mathew's betrayal to be able to muster much by way of response as they travelled across the Firth of Forth. She wondered what "recent exploits" had drawn Denton to Williams' notice but was briefly distracted by the magnificent sight of the three great iconic supporting towers of the nearby railway bridge. The pale winter sun hanging low in the east backlit the great red girder framework of the towers leaving just a hint of a reflection on the slate grey waters below. Her mind drifted back to a restful evening she'd had with Mathew at the loft apartment when they'd watched an old film about a man on the run in Scotland. The hero, played by a tweed clad, terribly English actor, had far too much stiff upper lip for Dee's liking and had stopped a train on the bridge to effect his escape by climbing through the girders. She'd realised, the moment she saw Williams in the car, that she too, would need to escape but was hoping for an opportunity less challenging than having to tackle slippery steelwork hundreds of feet above a watery grave. 'Hey Mathew, you remember that film we watched where the guy escapes by climbing out the train onto that bridge?' She pointed out of the window.

'The thirty-nine steps.'

'Yeah, that was it. Do you think we'll end up handcuffed together on the run from the bad guys tramping across bleak Scottish moors like in the film? 'Cos, you do realise that these are the bad guys Mathew? Don't you?'

Williams grunted, 'be quiet Dee.'

'The hell I will. I'm being abducted. No way do you get quiet.' She caught a quick sight of Mathew's face in the wing mirror and was temporarily gratified to note worry and concern etched deeply into his features. 'Mathew, for Christ's sake honey, did nothing I told you make any impression on you at all. Your boyfriend here has instructed that other asshole to kill Denton, his daughter and her boyfriend. Listen to me,' she shouted

'I won't tell you again Dee,' said Williams in his soft, rasping, throaty voice, 'be quiet!'

'Go fuck yerself Williams,' croaked Dee, jerking back quickly in her seat in a vain attempt to avoid Williams' clawing right hand which then pinned her by the throat into the corner.

241

'Listen Dee,' Williams hissed, 'Mathew and I can't be separated by your flights of fancy and overactive imagination. Mathew understands that there have been some difficulties and that plans need to change and we need to move on. I've answered all the points you raised with him and he's satisfied with my explanation. Aren't you Mathew?'

It took for as long as Dee fought to recover her breath, as Williams released his hold on her throat, for Mathew to reply.

'Yes David,' he said, quietly and submissively while staring fixedly ahead though the windscreen.

'So why am I being abducted?' whispered Dee gently massaging her throat.

'You aren't. If you remember you asked Mathew to help you to get up to Nairn to meet Denton. That's what we're doing.'

'And part of the deal for this ride is that you get to steal from me and then assault me. Right? Well if it's ok with you sweetheart you can let me out right here. I'll grab a ride and make my own way there.'

'Don't be silly Dee. We haven't time. You need to be back for this evening's concert.'

'You expect singing after what you just did to my vocal chords? You can forget it. I just quit.'

'Dee, why don't you sit back quietly and enjoy the scenery. In a few hours' time, we'll catch up with Mr Denton, we'll clear up all the misunderstandings, I'll apologise for having lost my temper and we can all get back to normal. What do you say?' He smiled.

Dee began to gain an appreciation of just how Williams had managed to get Mathew on side. He was articulate, plausible and very manipulative. Given that there would also have been feelings and emotions involved, Williams would have been half way there before he started because Mathew would have wanted to believe him. 'But what do you want with Denton. He's done nothing to you. He's simply looking for his daughter.'

'It's never really that simple Dee. Is it? Enjoy the journey. I really don't want to have to ask you to be quiet again.'

Dee woke suspecting that the previous sleepless night, the comfort of the seat and the warmth from the car's heater had all contributed to lulling her to sleep and even as the reality of her position worked its way back to the surface of her consciousness she felt slightly refreshed. She caught sight of a battered metal sign advising that Drumochter Pass was fifteen hundred and sixteen feet above sea level as she sat more upright in her seat, ignored Williams' questioning smile and focussed on the passing landscape. A light dusting of snow and gusting flurries swept across the road down the steep slopes to the hummocks of grass near the bottom of the glen. The sheer sides of the surrounding hills reaching skyward gave the landscape a dark sense of drama. Not the sort of country, she reflected, to be a fugitive, handcuffed to company or not. Getting away from Williams had to be her priority and she prayed that she'd recognise an opportunity when presented. Forty minutes later they took the third exit off a roundabout signposted Nairn.

As the car started to pull round to the front of the house Williams leant urgently across the front seat and pointed through the windscreen to a large lorry alongside which stood three men. 'There Reg. Pull up by the lorry,' he instructed the driver.

Dee took advantage of the slight distraction to hit the electric window switch in the arm rest just as the car rolled to a halt alongside the lorry and the man she now knew to be Webber. She feigned disinterest as Williams left the car and walked the few yards towards the men.

'What's this still doing here?' Williams jerked a thumb at the truck.

'It's a long story,' replied Webber running his hands nervously through his hair.

'I'll take the short version.'

'Denton and Starmer were here. They've got the girl.'

'They've what?' screamed Williams. 'Where the fuck is Woolley?'

'We don't know. But he's not here.'

'Has Denton got him?'

'Could have but I really don't know for sure.'

'Who are these two then?' Dee saw both the other men start to shuffle their feet in the gravel and fidget as attention moved to them.

'Our Continental chums. The delivery?'

'They speak English?'

'Yes, I speak English,' replied the driver of the lorry.

'So, what can you tell us?'

'We arrived and,' he looked at his companion for support, 'the Fat Man?'

243

'Woolley?'

'Yes, Mister Woolley tell us to drive to here and unload all the stuff there and he would come back and tell us where to store everything,' he indicated the building behind him.

'And then?' Williams prompted.

'Well, we had unloaded the,' again he paused, 'special delivery, you understand the special delivery? When the man arrived to help us. He help out to get the rest of the special delivery off and then went to get the forklift for the big stuff.'

'Forklift? He went to get a forklift?'

'I don't know because then someone is shutting the doors and we are locked in the lorry.'

'You realise there wasn't a forklift?'

'Yes Mynheer. I do now know. It was a trick.'

'The man who shut the doors? Young, Old?'

'Not so old sir.'

'Starmer,' Williams muttered, 'the more I hear about this bloody man the more I begin to think I'd be better off employing him than you,' he said turning to Webber, 'so where's the "special delivery" then?'

'Gone.'

'Gone?'

'Well it's not where these lads left it and we've looked and can't find it.' Webber held his arms wide, hands palms upward and shrugged his shoulders in submissive puzzlement. 'Look Mister Williams, Woolley was in charge up here. Not me. I wasn't here. I left him in charge of the girl and the delivery and came down to see you. If I had've been here this wouldn't have happened.'

'I wish I had your confidence Webber. So, let me sum up.' His usually low voice rose in volume and harshened in tone as he enumerated his points. 'The only leverage we had; the girl, is gone. Woolley's gone. The consignment 's gone and I'm standing here with a truck full of building materials, two dumb Dutchmen and a man who's chosen fuckin' up as a lifestyle. If you were me Webber, what would you do? No, please tell me. I am really interested.' Williams snarled with intimidating intensity, grabbed Webber by the lapels, lifted him from his feet and slammed him hard against the car. Keeping him up on his toes he head butted him. 'Listen very carefully. Your future depends on it. That shipment was important for a few reasons. Its value alone is just south of five million. And now it's gone.' He pumped

Webber backwards and forwards against the car while he gathered his thoughts. 'Have you got that sort of money? No I didn't think so. Nor have I.' He lowered Webber to a sound footing, let go of his lapels and ostentatiously smoothed them back into position while thoughtfully picking a speck of lint from his collar and distractedly watching it float to the ground. 'We work for a large organisation. Worldwide. So, if the shipment is not recovered they will replace it. Then they will replace me. But not before I've replaced you. Do you understand "Replace" Webber? Let me make it clearer. We are not talking here about you quietly shuffling off this mortal coil. By the time I let you go. you'll be howling for your mother.'

Webber nodded grimly as he fished for a handkerchief to stem the flow of blood from his eyebrow. 'Mister Williams I am really sorry but as I said I wasn't here to stop any of this. We need to find them obviously. They've not been gone long so we might have a chance.' He finished lamely with a shrug that suggested little faith in the thought.

'And where do you think we should look? For them and the consignment?'

Dee saw him look in her direction and sensed that Webber had seen part of a solution and that it involved her. She quickly moved further inside the car and away from the window while straining hard to hear what was said.

'Well, we know he's cosy with her,' Webber nodded in Dee's direction.

Williams seemed to consider this for a moment and cast a look at Dee before turning back to the two hapless truckers. 'Ok you two can thank your lucky stars that you don't work for me. Now get this truck out of here and back to Amsterdam and explain to the boss what's happened. Tell him I'm coming over. Alternatively,' he laughed, 'you could just drive it off the edge of the cliffs at Cape Wrath. It might just be your better option.'

Dee sank back in the seat and watched the Dutchmen close the rear doors of the lorry, haul themselves up into the cab and manoeuvre past Williams' car and out onto the road. Williams and Webber were now talking quietly together while Reg sat impassive, solid, drumming his fingers on the steering wheel. She watched Williams move chest to chest with Webber so that their faces were inches apart with Webber flinching in the face of the tirade of spit and spite being launched at him. As she watched she saw the colour drain from Webber's face and a tic start to twitch the scar at the side of his face.

She was certain Mathew must have overheard some, if not all, of the conversations. Certainly, he must be witnessing the current showdown with Webber and be in little doubt as to Williams' control of and involvement with drugs and the criminal world that Webber represented. She wondered whether it would change his allegiance but feared that perhaps he'd always known the truth about Williams but had pragmatically elected for a life of comfort, protection and a strange love. She realised that she felt better now than she had for some hours. She now knew that Denton had found and rescued Julie and that they and this younger man Starmer had successfully eluded Woolley and were free. She had gleaned some information about Williams' intentions and a contact in Amsterdam. She now needed some time to process this new information in the light of what she already knew. Even the dawning realisation that Webber had highlighted her potential usefulness as a hostage, to secure she knew not what from Denton, left her less alarmed than it might have. After all, she reasoned, looking after herself was something she'd been doing all her life.

Williams tapped on Sinclair's window indicating that he should join him outside. Dee watched silently as they conversed out of ear shot. If she had been hoping for any signs of disagreement or challenge from Sinclair she was disappointed. He seemed almost compliant with acquiescent nods his only response to Williams forcefully expressed points. Finally, Williams turned to Webber and, Dee judged, from further nodding, that more instructions were being given.

As the pair returned to the car Webber and another over muscled minder led the way out onto the main road.

'Follow him Reg.'

'Ok Guvnor but we're going to need some petrol soon.'

'I know Reg,' sighed Williams with exaggerated patience, 'he's got the same problem, so as I said, follow him.'

'Right Guvnor.'

Williams sank back into the seat and turned to Dee. 'I'm afraid Dee that I'm going to have to ask you to stay with us a little longer.'

'What about the concert? My 'Comeback'?' She laughed hollowly.

'Cancelled and postponed I'm afraid Dee. In that order. As you know, you have a history of unreliability dear. A few words in the right ears and your public will understand. Mathew will go back to Edinburgh tonight and take care of the details.'

'Why are you doing this David? What is it that I have done, or know, that is such a threat that it warrants all this? What? Tell me.'

'You're an associate of Mister Denton are you not?'

'Ok but apart from setting out to look for his daughter, what is it that he has done?' Dee hadn't really expected an answer and wasn't disappointed.

Dee's reverie to the gentle ticking of the turn indicator was sharply interrupted by Williams jumping forward in his seat, smacking Reg hard on the shoulder and shouting, 'don't follow him. Keep going.' Reg pulled out of the turn into a garage, narrowly avoiding the rear of Webber's car and fishtailed back onto the road. 'Keep going 'til you find a place where we can pull over but out of sight of that garage.'

'It's a one-way system Guv and it's a bit on the narrow side.'

Williams had turned in his seat to look out of the back window and shouted instructions over his shoulder, 'ok, go back round the system and see where it brings us out. And slow down. Last thing we need is an accident.'

Dee turned to the rear window as Williams sat back down, 'what's going on?'

'Life suddenly got better Dee. That's what happened. Webber seems to have spotted a car at the pumps which has a young woman in the back seat, a man who, unless I'm very much mistaken is Denton and a younger man walking from the car across the forecourt. Full house!'

Dee was swung across and forward onto Williams' lap as Reg braked hard into and out of a chicane around a large white building in the road.

'Ease up Reg.'

'Sorry Guv. Came up a bit sudden like.'

'Go back to where we were; just before the garage and park up. Let's see if Mister Webber can redeem himself.'

Reg pulled the car into the kerb about fifty yards back from the turn into the garage.'

'Switch off Guv?'

'Yeah. We need to keep some distance. Here will do for the moment.'

Williams leant intently forward between the two front seats with an elbow on the back of each. 'You drove for a little crew out Essex way didn't you Reg? Back in the day?'

'Yes Guv. Had its moments. Few more years working the doors. Never dull Guv.'

'Before that?'

'Two Para Guv.'

'As you say, never dull. You happy driving?'

'For the moment guv.'

'Might be able to put a bit of work your way. Interested?'

'Always interested Guv.'

'Right, I'll bear it in mind. Trick here though Reg,' he nodded towards the garage, 'isn't speed, its control. When they come out of there I want to be near enough to exercise my options and far enough away to leave it. Got it?'

Reg was spared the need to consider this complex equation by the screeching appearance of a car fighting to gain traction through an impossibly fast exit from the garage. Dee's pulse soared as she caught a glimpse of Denton fighting to keep the car on the road through the turn. Appreciable moments passed in silence and consideration of the unmet expectation that Webber would be right behind in chase. When his car did appear, it stopped at the crossover onto the road and Webber got out of the car, tore off his jacket and threw it into the back. 'What is he doing,' Williams muttered irritably, 'Ok Reg go.'

Dee's pulse was throbbing in her ears while her eyes sought another glimpse of Denton and her mind puzzled at Mathew's continued silence in the face of Williams' admission that he employed a getaway driver as a chauffeur. She wondered just how much more proof was required before Sinclair questioned his allegiance. Red brake lights seen through the cloud of sand kicked up by the sideways drift of Webber's car, out of the chicane and round the white house, put them closer to the action than Williams wished.

'Pull back Reg.'

Reg eased back to the twenty miles per hour limit deemed sensible for the cramped lanes by the Findhorn Parish Council and they turned back into the start of the one-way system to see Webber running towards them from his parked car. Williams lowered the window.

'Have you seen them?'

'Not since they came out of the garage,' Williams paused, 'Christ, you stink of petrol.'

'They've gotta still be back there then if they've not passed you going in the other direction.' Webber ran back to his car like a man possessed.

'Follow 'em Reg.'

Dee grabbed for her seat belt as Reg relived his past and floored the accelerator in perfect synchronization with the release of the clutch, changed gear and double de clutched back down as Webber's car skidded to a halt on the exit from the chicane round the white house. She looked on intently as Webber ran down a slipway to a jetty, turned out of sight, reappeared, and then ran a few steps onto the jetty gesticulating frenetically in the direction of a small boat in midstream. As they all craned to see what was animating Webber, he ran back up the ramp and threw himself into his car. This time Reg, freed from all restraint, pinned the car on the bumper of Webber's as it entered a single-track road off the one-way system running parallel with the shore. As Webber's car ploughed through puddles Reg hit the wipers and washers to clear the muddy spray. Dee braced herself on the back of Sinclair's seat as the car lurched to a halt alongside Webber's in a circular parking area with dunes partially obscuring the seaward view.

'It's Denton,' screamed Webber over his shoulder as he ran from the car and scrambled to the top of the dune before slipping down the other side and out of sight. Williams slowly got out of the car walked round to Dee's door, opened it, grabbed her elbow and yanked her out of the car and to her feet. 'Wave goodbye Dee. You've just been dumped.' He hoisted her elbow into the air and jerked it back and forth in a parody of fond farewell. Dee abandoned her initial struggle and focussed her attention on the small boat now beginning to struggle against heavier seas as it left the shelter of the inlet. A second man joined the one at the helm and she saw both duck in unison shortly before her ears registered two sharp cracks. As the helmsman

249

straightened up and looked towards the shore she resisted the urge to wave at him and cleared her face of all expression. She was damned if she'd give Williams the satisfaction of knowing that Denton meant anything to her and focussed on her relief that he and his daughter were now out of William's reach.

'Reg, get down there, get that fuckin' gun off Webber and bring him back up here.'

'Not going too well is it David?' said Dee snatching her arm out of his grip. 'D'ye ever get that feeling that things are getting away from you? Out of control perhaps? Face it. It's all slipping away from you. Show biz? Gone. Drugs biz? Busted. Relationships? Over?' She looked towards Mathew to see if this last jibe had any effect and her spirits rose as she saw him fail to meet her gaze and deliberately look away. As she turned back she moved straight into the path of Williams' sweeping open right hand that struck her to the floor. Dazed she pushed herself up onto an elbow, cupped her hand to her mouth then spat blood onto the ground. A handkerchief hovered in her peripheral vision and she snatched it from Williams's hand, accepting this apparent courtesy much as the victim of the executioner received a blindfold. This man was going to kill her. All doubt now gone she realised that, like Denton, she had to take any opportunity for escape. She hauled herself to her feet and slumped onto the back seat of the car.

'Slipped through your fingers again then Webber?' Williams fanned his hand beneath his nose, 'Christ, have you had a bath in petrol?'

'That cunt. Starmer? Got us both in the garage.'

'As I said before. Eminently employable, that young man.'

'Mr Williams, they can't go far. They've got to land somewhere.'

'Webber,' said Williams sweeping his hand in an arc across the horizon, 'out there is the North Sea. He can land anywhere between, oh I don't know, Bergen and Brussels or Cape Wrath and Ramsgate. We have more chance of meeting God in an Amsterdam brothel on a wet Thursday than we do of being there to meet him when he lands. Unless,' he mused, 'unless, perhaps,' he pulled his overcoat more tightly around him against the freshening breeze, 'unless he's cuter than we think.'

'How'd you mean?'

'Where's Denton?'

'Well on the boat,' replied a puzzled but cautious Webber. Still mopping at his head-butted nose with a very bloodstained handkerchief.

'Where's the boat?'

'The North Sea?'

'What's on the other side of the North Sea?'

'Europe?'

'Specifically?'

'You've lost me.'

'Holland?'

'Sorry, you've lost me again. Why would he go there?'

'Think about it Webber. He knows he's not safe here. Everywhere he goes we've been right behind him. So far, he's been lucky. He knows about the operation. He knows about the consignment 'cos he's lifted it. It had to be him. He knows where it came from 'cos it's painted in bloody great letters on the side of that lorry; "Van Doorn". He knows the people in that company 'cos all NMG kosher gear is transported by them. So, if you were fighting to survive what would you do? Where would you go?'

'Amsterdam?'

'Right. Cut a deal or cut off head of the snake.'

'Hang on a bit. Denton must have stolen that boat on the spur of the moment. An hour ago, he didn't know he was going to be on the North Sea with an opportunity to go to Amsterdam. Christ, I wouldn't want to try it at this time of year.'

'You see, there's the difference between you and that pair,' he pointed savagely at the disappearing yacht. They don't think. They act. Judging by the way Denton got that boat out of here I'll bet he's got a shelf full of sailing trophies and if it hasn't yet occurred to him that he has an opportunity to cause me grief in Holland it will by the time night falls.' He paused to collect his thoughts. 'Ok, here's what we're going to do. I was already scheduled for Amsterdam and Mister D and that stands. I need to buy some time while we try and recover the load. Webber, you'll come with Reg and me. You drop me at Glasgow Central for London and then you can take her,' jerking a thumb at Dee nursing her jaw in the car, 'well, anywhere you want really. Lose her. Are we clear on that?'

'You could fly out of Glasgow.'

'Passport?'

'Right.' Webber half turned and stopped hesitantly with a visible effort at steeling himself before facing Williams again. 'Stella's in Edinburgh.'

'I'll get Mathew to take her back to the flat. I might want to talk to her. He's got to go back to Edinburgh to sort out the band and the cancellation of Madam's tour. And you need to get a crew up here to find those drugs. I doubt they had time to get them onto that boat and I somehow doubt they'll be in their car. So, they could be at the house or they've been dropped off somewhere between here and there. Find 'em. It's your only hope, believe me.'

Dee had endured the car journey to Glasgow sat in the rear with an overpowering level of petrol fumes barely kept in check by partially open windows. She had resigned herself to the journey on the realisation that any chance of escape was unlikely from a moving car and pinned her hopes on seizing an opportunity at the Edinburgh stop. It had been almost as though Williams had read her mind. She had pleaded for a toilet stop mainly out of necessity but with a half-formed plan to seize the moment if an opportunity arose. Webber had escorted her into a public lavatory, stared down the outraged glares of middle aged Scottish matrons and chosen a cubicle without a window. Now she reviewed the likely opportunities of the Glasgow stop convinced that psyching herself up in preparation to act decisively and quickly was the key to her survival.

For some minutes the car had been stalled in heavy traffic in Gordon Street on the approach to Glasgow Central Station. They'd also been surrounded by hordes of celebrating Scots noisily making their way to catch trains.

'What's going on?' asked Webber impatiently.

'Football. Scotland versus Malta. Scotland won three nil. McCoist scored twice,' volunteered Reg pointing at the radio that had been quietly playing in the background.

'I'm going to hop out here. Can't hang about any longer. Pull over Reg.' As the car cruised into the curb Williams opened the door carelessly scattering a group of fans who were partly dissuaded from carrying out their threats to "do 'im" by his size, his look and his half-hearted apology.

'Ok Reg, let's get out of here,' instructed Webber.

'We've still gotta go past the entrance, It's one way.'

'I need the toilet,' interjected Dee beginning to realise that an opportunity may be there for the taking.

'Not again.'

'Up to you honey. Do you really wanna spent the rest of the journey sitting in a puddle? I'm past caring.' Dee shrugged.

As the car pulled onto the station forecourt Webber walked round the back towards Dee's door. She quickly checked through the rear window that the crowd of supporters they'd cut in front of to let Williams out were still on track to arrive at the car as she exited. Providing she got the timing right that was. The small crowd of about a dozen supporters was led by a diminutive man in a kilt wearing a Tam O' Shanter and sweeping a large blue and white flag from side to side in front of him as he walked chanting she knew not what. She took a deep breath, opened the door and jammed her shoulder into Webber as she stood up. He stepped back into a swirling blue and white cloud which he attempted to claw from his face while seeking to grab Dee's arm.

'Get that fuckin' rag out of my face,' he finally yelled at the small Scot.

'Did I hear that weegie bampot right Dougal?' said the kilted standard bearer turning to address his nearest companion; a man as large as he was small.

'Aye, ye did wee Mungo. Ye did.'

'He insulted the Saltire?'

'Aye he did wee Mungo. He did.'

'Will ye hold ma flag there Dougal?'

'I will wee Mungo. I will.'

'Fuckin' Krankies,' said Webber, still grabbing for Dee's arm while he threw a roundhouse right at the furious little Scot. Mungo simply ducked and stepped inside where, from his crouched position, he jabbed a solid right to the left kidney and a quickly straightened knee into Webber's wide open crutch. As Webber fell to his knees the Scot took a contemplative step back, measured his man, stepped forward and delivered a stunning, clubbing right hander to the side of Webber's head.

Reg struggled to shift his bulk from the car seat but once released moved quickly and purposefully towards Mungo who turned to greet him with a smile.

'Dougal will ye nae show willing here?'

'Aye. What exactly would you like me tae do?'

'I dinna know. Put him in the boot mebbe?'

253

Dougal stepped in front of Reg put the palms of both hands on his chest and pushed. Like a schoolboy, Reg instinctively responded in kind, except that Douglas wasn't there to halt his momentum. Reg just had time to realise that while his right arm was still in front of him his left was locked up his back before Dougal, now breathing down his neck, kicked his legs apart, turned him and smashed his head down on the car roof.

Dee was very conscious that the priority for Webber, once he extracted himself from the fight, would be finding her. Crossing the concourse, she was therefore keen not to assist him in any way by drawing attention to herself further by running. She was already aware that heads were turning as she moved through the crowd. 'Goddammit, surely to Christ I'm not the only black woman in the whole of this damned country,' she muttered to herself.

The long hours spent in silent thought and preparation on the back seat of the car were now paying off. Williams was on his way to Amsterdam. So was she. Williams was going back to his flat to pick up his passport. She was on her way to find Williams and retrieve hers. He was catching the London train. So, she had to be on that train. Dee stopped in the centre of the concourse beneath a huge four-sided clock suspended from a maze of girders in the roof where pigeons noisily changed perches. She searched frantically for departure indicator boards and a clue as to the track she needed for the London train. Her eyes swept across the facade of the ancient wooden panelled ticket office and various shopping outlets and back again towards crowds moving slowly through ticket barriers. Finally, she caught sight of a destination and track indicator which seemed to consist of a set of rolling shutters that clattered sequentially and vertically downwards revealing a new set of destinations as each train left. Standing beneath the board and craning his neck to view the detail was Williams with the station crowd breaking around him like a river round a rock. Dee froze but continued to scan the board establishing under an "Intercity" heading both the time and track for departure. They both realised at pretty much the same time that they had only minutes to spare. As Williams hurried to a gate over on the left of the station Dee timed her own approach to the same gate to give him a thirty second lead. As she approached the barrier she cast a last anxious glance towards the entrance where she'd left Webber still fearful that he might yet intervene. Williams was entering the last car on the train as she reached the final hurdle between her and that London train.

A lean, cadaverous man in an oversize grey uniform with blue piping to collar and lapels, a strange high fronted cap with an "Intercity" logo smiled charmingly and snapped a chromium plated ticket punch playfully in the air. 'Tickets please,' he grinned.

Dee dropped back into her southern belle routine and returned the smile with genuine warmth before uttering breathlessly, 'honey, I done just arrived here and I'm gonna miss my dang connection if I gotta go get a ticket. I declare that train is gonna go anytime now.'

The man's smile slipped slightly. 'I'm sorry madam but you need a ticket to board the train.'

'How about I buy a ticket on the train from the brakeman or the conductor?'

'Brakeman, Conductor?'

'Guys on the train. They look after passengers?' She volunteered. Dee never caught his reply. A man with a flag had appeared from the rear car and was fishing a whistle on a chain from his waistcoat pocket. She launched herself forward covering the intervening forty feet to the encouragement of the man with the flag who seemed oblivious to the shouts from his colleague at the gate. The train door slammed shut behind her and she relaxed with her back to it as the train jerked into motion.

As the tensions of the escape eased from her she began to think through what she needed to do next. This far, she reasoned there hadn't really been a plan just an acceptance that she had to be constantly alert and ready to seize any opportunity that came along. The same principles still applied but she thought that maybe the odds had moved slightly in her favour. There was the element of surprise; Williams had no idea she was on the train. She also had Williams in an environment where the very proximity of the public would restrict his options considerably Back in the car, on the way to Nairn her only real plan had been to get away from the whole gang and find Denton. What had happened to her since had hardened her resolve and a rage was slowly building in her. A rage now directed solely at Williams. It was he who had ordered Denton's death, he who'd wrecked her burgeoning and sweet relationship with Mathew, he who'd cancelled her tour and he who'd casually handed her over to Webber and an uncertain fate in Manchester. 'Oh Williams. Man, are you going down or are you going down baby'.

She walked through the hissing automatic doors into the next car on the train and a vision from a bygone era. She passed three sets of seats using alternate hands on their backs to check against the violent sway of the train as it clattered over a never-ending series of points. At the fourth set a man with a belly, a beer can, a football scarf and a brogue so thick she couldn't initially understand a word, rose from a nicotine fug and stood across her path in the aisle.

'I ken ye wee lassie. Youse the Singer Dee Dee Wilson.' He swung round triumphantly, slopping beer from the can, inviting his fellow football supporters to share his encounter. 'Raise your glasses this here is Dee Dee Wilson. Ye hear? A Goddess.'

Dee looked at this middle aged, overweight, happy little man and her heart swelled with pride. A true fan. Somebody she'd reached through her music. She leant forward and kissed him on the cheek. 'Hi there, what's your name?'

'Davey. Davey Brown Miss Wilson and I'm very pleased to make your acquaintance.'

'Davey, honey, I'd really like to stop and talk but I'm in kinda a rush here. Could you write down your address because I'd like to meet with you some time? Maybe you could come to a concert?'

After more autographs than she'd signed at many concerts Dee was escorted by Davey through another smoking carriage full of supporters to the articulated platform connecting to the next carriage.

'Davey, it has been lovely to meet you.'

'The pleasure has been all mine Miss Wilson.' He purred.

'Davey, do you think you could call me Dee?'

'Och no,' he hesitated, 'Are ye sure?'

'I am Davey. We will meet again and, to you, I am Dee,' she kissed his cheek and went through the hissing doors to the next car. As she moved hand over hand from one seat back to the next along the swaying car she reflected that the meeting with Davey had reconnected her to values that she'd recently thought lost. She determined that she would survive this and one day she would watch Brown drink champagne in her dressing room.

The next communicating door hissed open to reveal a Police Sergeant and a man dressed in the livery that she now recognised as the "Intercity" brand. 'Your ticket madam?' Said the Conductor.

'God. Am I pleased to see you? I didn't expect Police on a train,' said Dee breathlessly to the woman wearing the sergeant's epaulettes.

'I, and my colleagues, are a calming presence when there's a match on,' the young woman grinned, 'but how can I help you?'

'I've been mugged,' stated Dee baldly.'

'Mugged?'

'Yes. I was in a queue for the washroom. Talking to the man behind me. I came out of the toilet and went to my bag for a tissue and my wallet was gone.'

'And you think it was the man that was standing behind you?'

'Yes.'

'Would you recognise the man again?'

'I would.'

'What was in your wallet madam?'

'Pretty much my life? My credit cards, passport, cash, oh,' she paused and looked at the Conductor, 'and my ticket.'

'Unfortunately, we get a lot of opportunist theft on these football specials. Follow me madam. Stay close. When you see the suspect tap me on the shoulder, point him out and then step back. Do you understand?' You will need to step away,' she added sternly.

As they reached each new carriage the Sergeant got Dee to look through the glass door panel into the car for a sighting of the suspect. As they reached the end of the dining car Dee saw Williams swaying his way back to his seat clutching a polystyrene coffee cup.

Dee tapped the Sergeant on the shoulder, 'that's him', she indicated.

'Ok, stay here with the Ticket Inspector'

Dee wondered how a thug like Williams would react to the icy calm and natural authority of the Sergeant and watched with her breath on hold as the Policewoman began to speak with him. The man's bluster, protestations and angry reactions caused concern to appear on the faces of surrounding passengers but fazed the sergeant not at all. Williams was obviously protesting

257

his innocence but seemed to be complying with the instruction to turn out his pockets onto the table between the seats. The Sergeant examined some of the contents of Williams's pockets and then fished out a notebook and began writing. Williams stood with barely contained anger until she finished and, tucking the notebook away, obviously apologised, before returning to Dee.

'I'm sorry Madam; he has none of your possessions and protests his innocence most vehemently.'

Dee stepped out of the shadows with the bitter taste of defeat in her mouth to see Williams far down the carriage staring at her with a look of shock and amazement freezing his features into a mask. She began to walk away and as she did caught a flash of crimson above Williams' head.

'You didn't check his overcoat. The one in the rack with the crimson lining.'

'His?'

'That's what he was wearing.'

Not a word passed between Dee and Williams as he was led past her in handcuffs towards the rear of the train. The Policewoman had the overcoat over her shoulder and Dee's wallet in the hand that wasn't pushing Williams forward. 'Perhaps you'd like to take your seat Miss Wilson. I'll be back with your belongings once I've secured the suspect.'

Dee sat quietly watching her own reflection in the train window against a darkening panorama of shadowy distant hills and star studded skies knowing that this triumph over Williams wasn't there to be savoured. This was only really the beginning of a longer struggle.

'Miss Wilson,' Dee turned as the Policewoman sat beside her, 'I'm so sorry I didn't recognise you,' she said as she placed Dee's passport on the table.

'Honey that really isn't a problem. As they say back in the States, "British Police are wunnerful", but no money, no ID and in a foreign country I consider myself fortunate to have met you.' Dee smiled, 'particularly as I'm supposed to be in Amsterdam tomorrow.' She picked up the passport. 'What'll happen to that man?'

'Well he's strangely quiet at the moment. Not saying anything,' she paused, 'runs a bit against type for a dipper really. But there you are.'

258

'What will happen to him?'

'He'll be taken off the train at Crewe, charged and arraigned before Magistrates tomorrow morning. He'll then be bailed and you'll hear from us about attending Court as a witness.'

'I'm touring.'

'Right, I'll take a statement now. I've got all the other details I need from your passport.'

Dee took a cab back to Williams's flat secure in the knowledge that she was safe from his further attentions for at least the next twenty-four hours. As she turned the key in the lock she wondered back to Williams' search of her bag on the way to Nairn and her surprise that he'd not recognised his own door keys but had handed them back to her. The priority now was sleep and then a thorough search through the flat to find any information that might help her or Denton or shed more light on 'Mister D' and the Amsterdam connection. She went to the seating area at the farthest end of the spacious apartment, threw her bag onto one settee and herself onto another.

She knew from the light of a pre-dawn sky that she's slept for five or six hours but that wasn't what had awakened her. She'd heard a door close. A heavy door. A front door. She levered herself up so that her eyes were level with the top of the settee and then bolt upright.

'Dee?'

'Mathew?'

Chapter Seventeen

'Did we just get shot at?'

'We did. That bastard Webber. It's getting serious.'

'Getting? You're only just beginning to realise that?'

'Listen Starmer, can I remind you about the shooting back in London?' snapped Denton. 'Watching Mickey McCarthy's brains drip from the optics sort of focussed my mind just a little bit,' Denton barked

Starmer locked eyes with him for appreciable moments before answering softly, 'sorry, yeah, but the thing is, I know why they're after me but why you? I mean obviously, drugs are the link between London and Manchester,' Starmer's voice trailed off as the deck went from under him and he dropped hurriedly onto the padded seating that ran around the sides of the cockpit, searching for a handhold to secure against the boat's unpredictable motion.

'They're after you because of the money and those records you took. The connection is Julie. Because of her we're together and so I'm what they'd call collateral damage.' Denton shrugged dismissively.

'I'm not so sure,' Starmer turned from his study of the receding shoreline and braced against the constant pitch and roll of the short choppy waves by jamming himself into the fore port corner of the cockpit. 'There's got to be more to this,' he sighed thinking back to the last conversation with Woolley who'd seemed to see him and Julie as two separate problems; Starmer being his and Julie being a problem for 'Supply', probably the London end of the operation. He glanced again at the shore, partly to gauge progress but mainly to find a fixed point of reference on the horizon to offset the nausea of sea sickness. To keep the contents of his stomach off the deck he took in several large gulps of salt laden sea air, 'anyway what now?'

'I have absolutely no idea,' muttered a now deflated Denton no longer boosted by the adrenaline rush of their escape.

'You sail then?' said Starmer, appreciating a change in mood but wanting to keep Denton engaged, nodding towards the tiller in Denton's hands.

'Bit of cruising. Cross channel mainly. You?'

'Dinghies.'

'You could helm this then?'

'I think so, yes.'

'How did you know it was at the jetty?'

'Wife of the owner was in the shop at the garage. We chatted while we queued. They were sailing back home to Germany. After that business in the garage I couldn't see us getting out of Findhorn by road.'

'True. Quick thinking. Nice work.'

Starmer felt the beginning of a warm glow as he realised that Denton had praised him but he determined to keep him talking, 'we need a plan.'

'You're right,' replied Denton almost visibly pulling himself together. 'First things first though. Can you go and check on Julie? Then have a scout round and see how we're fixed for food, water and fuel,' he shivered slightly as a spray laden gust showered across the cockpit. He shook water from his eyes, jammed the tiller beneath his arm and vigorously rubbed his hands together. 'While you're there can you see what we've got in the way of any warm or waterproof clothing?'

Starmer prised himself from the security of his position wedged against the cockpit bulwark, and briefly stood upright before being dropped to his knees as the rolling deck fell away beneath him. Levering himself upright he tried to anticipate the boats next roll but this time was caught out by the pitch.

Denton laughed, 'when you get your sea legs perhaps you could also see if you can find some charts? Oh, and about Julie,' Denton looked away briefly and paused, 'I did listen. She must decide what's best for her,' he paused again, 'treatment, you know? I'll be guided by you. Ok?'

Starmer nodded his appreciation.

Denton began to get a feel for the boat. Like a lot of designs of her size she had a tendency, under power, to slap down onto a sea rather than slice through or ride over. She'd be better under sail he thought. The boat was probably close to thirty-foot long and fibreglass built. He suspected that below decks there would be two and a bit bunks, a galley consisting of a two-ring burner and chart table close enough to the toilet to allow a course to be plotted from a sitting position. As he began to get the rhythm of the sea state and the balance of the boat he noted from the compass on the cockpit bulwark that he had a heading a few degrees north of north east, a course dictated by their exit from the harbour. A glance at the masthead pennant confirmed that the wind had moderated slightly and moved a shade south of west coming at him over the aft port quarter. He eased his shoulders, jammed himself into the leeward corner of the cockpit, wiped the spray from his face, tasted salt and grinned.

He'd not felt like this for a long time. All his anxieties had been reduced to basics. He was now in his element. The elements. Him, the sea; wind, waves and weather. Tangible problems, physical problems with solutions. Solutions that depended only on skill, knowledge, experience and the courage to act on his instincts and senses. Clean solutions. He had found Julie and she was now safe and in his care. As he watched water wash past his feet on its way to the self-drainers in the cockpit floor, reality flooded back and his mood darkened. Julie might be safe but Dee very obviously wasn't. Seeing her on the harbour spit had shocked him. Thinking about the implications of her presence there with Webber and a man he was sure was Sinclair while trying to work out where the thug who'd pulled her from the car fitted into the equation left him totally bemused.

His previous good mood was partially restored by the sight of Starmer, arms full of clothing with a chart case clamped between his teeth, struggling through the companionway back into the cockpit. 'You'd better fit that washboard the sea is picking up a bit.'

Starmer muttered something through clenched teeth but eventually fitted the board before making his precarious and unsteady way to the transom bench; his burden denying him hand holds. 'Try this. It should keep you dry,' he mumbled through the chart case as he dropped onto the bench. 'Looks a bit like some sort of immersion suit.'

262

'Take this then,' Denton said handing over the helm, 'it'll take your mind off the sea sickness.'

'I'm ok.'

'The colour of your face is telling a different story. Did you get sick sailing dinghies?'

'No. Too much going on.'

'There you are then. Hold this course while I have a look at the chart,' grunted Denton as he shrugged his way into the top half of the suit and zipped it tight. He unfolded the case to view a full chart of the North Sea from Norway to the Netherlands complete with a pre-marked course and way points from the Moray Firth to The Baltic. He sighed contentedly, very much a man who appreciates the certainty that a map or a chart can bring to an otherwise disordered world. 'Aitch would be proud he thought. 'Right,' he announced, 'according to this they were making for Wilhelmshaven which is, sort of, southeast from here.' He paused and traced his finger back from Wilhelmshaven along the intended course running north of Dogger Bank and south of the vast swathe of oil rigs that stretched diagonally down across the North Sea from Shetland to Rotterdam.

Starmer leaned into him, wiped the Perspex cover clear of spray, briefly studied the chart over Denton's shoulder and jabbed a finger at some chart markings. 'What are they?'

'Shipping routes.'

'Christ almighty but that looks totally mental. You mean that couple of pensioners were seriously considering a crossing in this? Have you seen the size of those North Sea ferries?'

'Spirit of Drake and Frobisher Mister Starmer, or their German equivalent,' he mused as he studied the chart again. 'Safe enough providing you follow the rules.' He lapsed into a thoughtful silence, glanced at the bulkhead compass and noticed that Starmer was occasionally off course but handling the boat well. 'Did you check the fuel?'

'Well, tapped it. Sounds about half full.'

'No gauge?'

'Not that I could see.'

How big is the tank?'

Starmer tucked the tiller under his arm and quickly indicated sizes with open palms on extended arms before seizing the tiller back to meet a quartering wave.

'Can't reckon on more than about six to eight gallons then. Say eight or nine hours?'

'Well, that'll get us down the coast a bit. Safely back on dry land?'

'You reckon?'

'Well, don't you?'

'No. I don't. Think about it. So far, everywhere you and I have been they have turned up. Now I'm not sure how they are doing it and until I do I'm steering very clear.'

'So where are we going?'

Denton leaned back against the side of the cockpit, braced his feet on the edge of the windward seats and looked hard at Starmer. 'Amsterdam,' he held up his hand to silence any protest, 'let me explain. One,' he peeled back a finger to mark the point, 'there's this business of them seeming to know our every move. We're not safe here. Two,' another finger, 'that DAF belongs to a company Webber deals with and that company is based in Amsterdam. I know that company and some of their people. If we're to stand a chance of finding out what's going on, I can't think of a better place to start. Three,' a third digit, he paused, and sighed, 'well I'm sure there is a third but I'm just too bloody tired to think of anything. Apart that is from following me old Dad's maxim of taking the fight to the enemy.' He sighed, relieved that he'd not given voice to the third concern; the possibility that Stella was passing on information about their whereabouts.

Starmer looked at him sympathetically. 'There's a lot to be said for that approach but look, if I've got that chart right North is Norway and south is Scarborough. So, obviously, south it is. Why don't we just head that way for the time being, use the time to think it through and keep our options open?'

'Well south south east.'

'Right, south south east it is then Skipper,' replied Starmer sarcastically.

'No,' said Denton opening the chart case again, 'we're going to need to continue on this course for a bit until we're far enough out to clear Kinnaird's Head,' he jabbed his finger at a point on the chart. 'There's enough fuel for that and then we'll hoist sail and use this west, ish, wind and turn south east on a reach.'

'So, what do I do?'

'I'm going to check on Julie and maybe get some sleep. We're going to have to set up watches anyway. Might as well start now. Will you be alright? Call me in a couple of hours?' Denton began to divest himself of the sailing suit to hand it to

Starmer, 'don't leave it any later it'll be getting dark.' Denton took the tiller while Starmer struggled into the suit.

'If we go to Amsterdam how long would it take?'

'Nearly four hundred miles? Say at five knots? I don't know. Three maybe four days?'

'Four days?'

'You had other plans?'

'Can you do this?' Starmer snapped back waving his free arm at the general expanse surrounding them. 'Weather, shipping, sailing, navigation oil rigs and all that?'

'We haven't got much of a choice really,' Denton grimaced wryly. 'Have we?'

Starmer nodded grim acknowledgement.

As Denton closed the hatch he sensed Julie, behind him; watching. He took longer with the catch than necessary desperately trying to think what he could or would say to her. Leaning against the hatch with his forehead moist from the condensation on the surface of the bulkhead he breathed in the fug of all small boat cabins; wet wool, diesel, bilges and chemical toilets. A particularly violent lurch to starboard dumped him onto a bench in front of the chart table. Julie was sitting opposite with her knees drawn up to her chest wrapped in a blanket staring at him with eyes that had never been that big. The guilt returned; a tide of emotion swirling up through him and bringing with it a series of wracking silent sobs that he struggled to hide behind very deep breaths. He blinked rapidly through tear blighted eyes and looked across at his daughter who regarded him with a look of puzzled concern.

'Julie, I am so sorry.' This time the sob escaped the deep breath.

She shuffled across the bunk and reached a hand followed by a painfully thin arm through the blanket and gently rested it on Denton's knee. 'What have you got to be sorry about daddy?'

'Everything, everything,' he crassly mimed a syringing motion with his thumb and two forefingers, 'the drugs, not being there, being a drunk,' he shuddered to a halt.

Julie shed the blanket put both her arms around his neck and pulled him to her. She could feel his shoulders shaking as he fought to suppress his sobs and reaching a hand up to the back of his head pressed it firmly onto her shoulder. As the dry sobs subsided she gently eased back, dropped her hands to his shoulders and looked up into his tear sodden eyes. 'It's not your fault daddy. How could it be?' She used the heel of her hand to wipe tears from his eyes and reflected briefly on the transposition of roles.

'It is my fault. I didn't look after you. I was never there.' He straightened up, cuffed his face clear of tears and looked into her eyes. 'Julie, I've been in an alcoholic fuzz for years. I missed you growing up and when you needed help I just wasn't there.'

'Oh, come on daddy,' she smiled half-heartedly, 'you weren't that bad.'

'That's not what Stella says.' He felt Julie go rigid in his arms and watched, puzzled, as she withdrew to the bunk and wrapped the blanket back around her. 'What's up Julie? What did I say?' Neither question prompted a response from his daughter and he crossed the gangway and sat at her feet on the bunk. 'C'mon darling tell me.' Julie lowered her head onto her arms and pulled the blanket even more tightly around her. Denton struggled to keep his impatience from showing but was only partly successful, 'for Christ's sake Julie what is it?' He leant in towards her with his arms stretched wide and palms up in supplication. 'C'mon, tell me,' he attempted a reassuring smile that tension turned into a grimace, 'what could possibly be worse than the mess we're already in?'

The big eyes reappeared, two dark circles of sadness, 'Stella is having an affair.'

Denton realised that, bizarrely, his first thoughts weren't those traditional to the newly advised cuckold but the reshuffling of a series of other thoughts and memories that now made more sense that they ever had previously. As he pretty much instantaneously worked his way through this review he was surprised that the announcement hadn't hit him as hard as Julie had obviously feared. Whether this was because of some years of pretty loveless marriage or attributable to his feelings for Dee was a thought he decided to set aside for the moment. 'How long?'

'Couple of years I think. Maybe longer. I'm not sure.'

'Is it someone I know?'

'Yes,' she murmured.

'Who?'

She looked at him with fear and tears in her eyes, 'Webber.'

This time the shock did hit Denton, hard. Through a tangle of thoughts fighting for consideration one hammered into the forefront of his brain. Why Webber? A man he disliked and despised. A view he'd thought Stella shared. 'Oh God, how could I have been so deluded?' A second later the memory of Stella dismissing him from the car in Bromley with the words, "And if I have to get drunk myself to talk to you, I will", pierced through him. She hadn't wanted to talk about his drinking or starting a new life together; she had been going to tell him about Webber.

'It's not your fault daddy. You didn't do anything wrong.'

'Didn't I? wandering around, giving it the big I am, the Lush in the loop, "have a drink on me Denton", Christ, how they must have all laughed?'

Julie reached out for his hand and squeezed it, 'maybe all that didn't help but I don't think that was what caused it. I think Stella was going anyway.'

Denton noted the distance implied by the second use of Stella's name as opposed to the 'mummy' he remembered. 'How did you find out?'

Julie pulled her hand away, shrank back into the corner of the bunk and, again, drew her protective blanket tighter to her shoulders and then Denton knew. He knew that his wife's affair wasn't the secret that Julie had been protecting him against. Whatever this last secret was it was the reason for her decline into drugs and God knows what else. He took several very deep breaths, reached across the bunk, pulled her to him and nestled her onto his lap with her head just beneath his chin and his arms encircling her. 'Julie, in the last few days I've seen a man killed, been told my daughter was missing, been shot at and learnt that my wife has been unfaithful. In short, my whole life has been turned upside down. But I've found you.' He stroked her hair and gently moved a lock from in front of her eyes. 'This is to do with Webber isn't it,' he guessed.

She half turned towards him and raised her face to look at him. 'Why do you say that?'

'Back at the garage when Starmer doused Webber in petrol you screamed "light the whotsit up Andy", do you remember? Even as he spoke he marvelled at the paternal self-censorship to avoid the use of the actual word she had used. 'You've really got to hate someone to wish that sort of death on them. You want to tell me why?' he asked quietly.

267

Julie tucked her head back under his chin. 'This is really hard daddy. You are not going to like this. You'll hate me.' This time, she sobbed, 'I hate myself.'

Denton chucked her under her chin and gently turned her face to his. 'I love you. There is nothing you have done or could ever do that will ever change that. Do you understand?'

She nodded. 'You remember I went to work for NMG in the holidays? Well after a few days working for that idiot Henfield with his halitosis and high opinion of himself I'd had enough. One afternoon Webber came looking for him and stopped to chat. He made me laugh about Henfield and it was very easy talking to him. Obviously, he knew who I was and he'd often say nice things about you and how lucky you were to have a daughter like me. He sometimes asked me about you and your friends and what you were up to.' she laughed hollowly.

'Anyway, at some point he seems to have arranged with Henfield for me to work with him but the thing was he didn't seem to do anything. He was either away or on the 'phone. A couple of weeks went by and I was bored and I told him so.' She sighed, 'so we started going places; meeting people in clubs and bars. Then we spent one afternoon with some of his business partners in a loft apartment in Wapping. There was this famous Boy Band there and I suppose I was impressed.' She paused. 'I mean I'd smoked pot. Everybody has. But, up until then, that was it. Anyway, one of these guys had some coke. That's where it all started really.

On the way back, I suppose I'd started to feel bad about the coke and Webber said not to worry it was only 'recreational'. It would be our secret.' She shrugged. 'When it was time to go back to Manchester I was hooked; totally drug dependent and Webber's.' She stopped, wondering whether he had appreciated the full import of her words. She realised he had, as she felt the muscles in the arms around her tense and watched the hands clasped in front of her waist clench and unclench, again and again and again. She hurried on, 'I didn't know about Stella then.'

'He did,' grunted Denton.

'I know.'

'So how did you find out?'

'He told me.'

'He told you?'

'Oh, daddy it was horrible,' she paused, sniffed and began rocking backwards and forwards on his lap. 'We were in Amsterdam. Webber had been out all day at a Suppliers and when he came back to the hotel he said we were going to a party. We went to this place out in the country somewhere. He said it belonged to a Supplier. There were drugs and drink, girls, women even boys, you name it and it was there and available.' She stopped and then laughed ironically. 'Hark at me, "there were women" like I wasn't one of them. Anyway, I was pretty high and I went to a bedroom with Webber.' She paused again and stopped rocking and became as still as a high diver focusing before the plunge. 'At some point, I realised that we weren't alone; there was an audience. Then Webber explained what he wanted me to do. I refused. Back then I had standards,' she sobbed, 'oh daddy.'

'Hey C'mon. You're still my girl. Remember that. Don't ever forget it. I love you. Unconditionally. Ok?' He held her tighter. 'So, let's get this out the way.' He hugged her to him, 'let's get this out there and then bury it.'

Julie gathered strength from resources she thought she'd long since lost. 'He smacked me about. Then they joined in. You know what I mean. That's when I found out about Stella. As they left the room he said, "next time you can have the mother, she's in training" and they all laughed.'

Denton felt his arms loosen in despair but quickly tightened his hold less Julie misinterpret this as judgement or disapproval. He hugged her tightly as she sobbed into his chest and they both rocked gently to and fro together. He stroked her hair and murmured half remembered reassuring nothings from her childhood and was surprised how calm he was. Something inside may have died but something else now burned deep. There was now one very simple objective in his life. To kill Webber.

Starmer dragged his eyes away from the compass, looking up sharply as he heard the washboard lift to reveal Denton struggling into the cockpit. 'She ok?'
'She will be.'
'You ok?'
'I will be.'

269

'Right', said Starmer, wondering what to say next and concerned that Denton's joy at Julie's release seemed to have evaporated.

'Sorry', said Denton quickly turning his back on a spray laden gust while straining to stay upright in the quickening seas.

'That's ok.'

'How's it going?'

'Well, I'm having all sorts of fun with this compass. I'm not used to it. In a dinghy, you have a bloody great orange buoy to aim for. The needle on this soddin' thing never stays still and I'm not handling this being under power thing very well. I've had the prop out of the water and racing, twice.'

Denton took a quick look at the compass heading, 'it's probably about time we changed course anyway and started heading south south east. I've tapped that tank a couple of times and I'm not convinced it's much more than half full. We'll get some sail up. Save the fuel for when we need it. We also need to set some running lights.' He glanced back over Starmer's head in the general direction of the now out of sight coast and the sky on that western horizon. 'It'll be dark very soon. We need to set sail now before we lose all the light.'

'What do I do?'

'Stay as close as you can on this heading while I investigate the sail lockers and get that sorted. You sit tight. Luff up when I shout. You ok with that?'

'I'll be fine. Good luck.'

In a remarkably short space of time Denton managed to rig the fore and main sails and sort out the lights. He then sat, shivering, with Starmer, giving quiet advice on keeping to a course and handling the yacht under sail until he was satisfied that Starmer could stand a watch on his own at night. 'That's good. Ok on my command bring her to south south east.

They sat in companionable silence taking quiet pleasure from the way they had worked together to master their situation, listening to the creamy hiss of the boat slicing through the waves and the thrum of the wind in the sails.

'It might be an idea if I take the first watch tonight. Give me that suit then go below and get warm. See if you can prepare some food and a hot drink for us all and then try and get some sleep. We're going to need you both fresh tomorrow.' Denton hesitated, almost as though in two minds as to whether to say more before looking back over the stern and running a hand over his face to clear another shower of spray and freely flowing tears from his face. It was a grim-faced Denton that advised, 'if you'll take my tip, you won't ask Julie too much.'

Starmer looked long and hard at the red eyes of a very distressed father, 'ok I understand.'

Starmer sat uneasily on the edge of the starboard bunk struggling hard to contain the seasickness that had returned the minute he'd lost sight of the horizon. 'How are you feeling?'

'Better than you look.'

'Your dad says its best we don't talk.'

'What do you think?'

'I think we should.'

'Okay.'

'But when you're ready.'

Julie's half smile reassured Starmer that he had called it right. He levered himself upright and made his way forward to the bow cabin.

'What are you doing?'

'Looking for sailing gear. Your dad says we should do watches but I can't be sitting here. I need to be outside. I am going to try and find some waterproofs and stuff so I can join him. Then, I'll get us something hot to drink and maybe a bite to eat.' Starmer recalled the provisions bought in the store that had never made their way onto the boat and hoped that there'd been an earlier re-provision.

Julie sat back on the bunk as he disappeared into the forward cabin and began running her fingers through her hair and rubbing her hands up and down her thighs. She struggled to divert her mind from the returning cravings back to what was going on around her but failed. Her desperate eyes flashed around the tiny cramped cabin looking for Starmer's rucksack. She pulled herself upright and furniture walked a few steps from one end of the cabin to the other, opening lockers and checking behind cushions as she went. Exhausted and exasperated she returned to the bunk and waited for Andy.

The forward cabin door crashed open to reveal a bizarrely dressed Starmer wearing a huge orange lifejacket. 'Ta Da', he announced, attempting a theatrical entrance spoiled by being swept back into the forward cabin as the little boat dropped off the top of a rogue wave.

'Andy, I need a fix.'

Starmer saw no point in any comment and eventually reappeared from the forward cabin with what she needed. He sat gently next to her on the bunk and watched her prepare the fix. She reached out her hands. And took his.

'Andy, first we need to talk.'

Denton huddled down into the suit and tried to organise his thoughts into some sort of order that made sense. He struggled to stop his mind flitting from one aspect of the problem to another as fast and as confusingly as it was. Why would Webber target him? Okay, maybe he had loved Stella and wanted Denton out of the way, although given Julie's story he doubted that was the case. Anyway, if she'd really wanted to go she knew he would never have tried to stop her and was sure Stella also knew that. No, there had to be more to it than that to explain Webber's murderous onslaught on him and his family. He ducked below boom level to avoid another face full of sea water and caught a glimpse of the beginnings of a full moon on the eastern horizon. The wind had picked up a little and the relatively smooth passage so far had now changed to a challenging crash through short, choppy and wet seas. He stared up at the masthead to see spindrift floating through the shrouds, visible in the beams from the running lights. With each gust those shrouds thrummed, the little boat healed and Denton fought to ease her through successive crests while keeping her as near to her planned course as he dared. He eased the main sheet a little in a trade-off; comfort for compass points.

How in God's name had Webber acquired sufficient hatred of him to abuse his family so badly. Being doused with petrol had obviously fuelled his anger to the point of pushing him to take a shot in public. Even from a distance his rage on the sand at Findhorn had been plain to see and the second shot had come perilously close. His mind slipped back to his last day at work; the last time he had seen the man under normal circumstances: The day McCarthy had been killed. There was obviously a connection between all that had happened since and McCarthy's death. McCarthy, it would appear, was investigating NMD, Webber was running a drug operation from within NMD. Denton knew them both. Webber, knowing of his friendship, might have assumed he was working with or for McCarthy. Maybe that was his motivation? Perhaps, he now reasoned, they all thought he knew more than he did? Maybe, just maybe he was beginning to know, now.

He glanced aloft at the masthead again and sheeted the mainsail to bring the tell-tales streaming back aft from the leech of the sail. As always, when sailing, he quickly adjusted to the rhythm of the sea and the demands of the boat and took time to appreciate the odd star peeping from behind dark, scattered, scudding clouds and the occasional reflections of moonlight in the troughs.

He smiled as the first lines of 'Aitch's favourite song came to mind; "we were sailing along on Moonlight Bay", and the politically incorrect and mischievous use of the original lyric; "We could hear the darkies singing, they seemed to say". 'Aitch and Joan had been happy in Birchington until frailty had overtaken them and residential care raked them and their savings into a world of barely warm food, community singing and incontinence pads. 'Aitch had handled it well but Eleanor Joan had died shortly after entering the home. So, 'Aitch soldiered on for a few years more and died one cold winter night. Denton had driven through the night to be with him but had arrived too late.

He remembered the matter-of-fact attitude of the matron as she handed over a tin cash box, a pro forma advice sheet on funerals and benefits and a plastic bag with some cash and 'Aitch's spectacles. He'd been ushered from the premises so fast he'd half wondered whether someone was due to view the now vacant room that morning. Sitting in the car he had absent mindedly fondled and fiddled with the spectacles. The last time he'd seen 'Aitch he'd promised him a new pair and had attempted a running repair with Elastoplast to the bridge piece to keep him going in the meantime. The box revealed a collection of ancient documents; 'Aitch's army pay book, marriage and birth certificates, his first driving license and his campaign medals. In a small sliding try in the lid of the box was his much-prized silver Para Cap Badge. Denton had always been proud of his dad's Army record particularly his escape from Arnhem after the disastrous assault on the bridges over the Rhine. 'Aitch had always spoke fondly of the courage of the Dutch people who had rescued, hidden and then restored him to safety with the advancing Allied Armies.

The noise of the Washboard being slid open pulled him back to the present and he leaned as far forward as the tiller and the motion of the boat permitted, to accept the mug offered by Starmer. He watched in amazement as he finally dropped onto the bench seat with half a mug of something, wearing not so much a life jacket as a flotation device over a yellow waterproof peeping from behind which could be glimpsed a pink cable knit sweater all topped off with a bright yellow woman's hat with earflaps.

'Big woman then.'

'German.'

'Oh. Julie asleep? She say anything?'

'Some.'

'You want to talk?'

'No. You?'

'No.'

Denton sensed the tension and easing back from further comment nodded at the life jacket. 'Bit Titanic. All those white straps and packing.'

Starmer shrugged his neck uncomfortably in the horse shoe neck of the life preserver. 'You should wear one. They might be old fashioned but they work.'

'We need a plan.' Denton shrugged and nodded towards the lightening eastern horizon. 'It'll be dawn in an hour. The wind is pretty constant, the sea has moderated slightly, if it stays like this we could be at the German's third waypoint by tonight.' He jabbed a thumb at the chart in its Perspex case.

'We're still going to Amsterdam then?'

Denton slid his gaze from the compass to meet Starmer's quizzical challenge. 'Did she tell you?' He looked up at the tell tales, 'about Webber?'

'She did.'

'About the party at that house in Holland?'

'What about it?' Starmer snorted his impatience and frustration. 'That wasn't Julie. How many times must I tell you? That is the addiction. Her only sin, if you could call it that, was getting addicted. Whatever happened from then on was consequence. Outside her control.'

'I didn't mean that.' Denton hauled on the tiller to steer a course down the side of a wave and marvelled at the rise of the strange beauty of the scattered oil rigs profiled on the horizon in the dawn light. Somehow the gargantuan structures, looming in the distance, lit by their perpetual flares, provided a dramatic opposition to the ocean. 'I know that House. Is what I meant.'

'How?'

'I've been there. Went as a guest of the Van Doorn family. A day's clay shooting; we were good customers of theirs,' he shrugged.

'Where is it?'

'Not far from Arnhem.'

'Where?'

'Oh, spare me.'

'And that is where we're going?'

'As I said before, you got a better idea?'

'No I haven't but I'd like to know a bit more about what you've got in mind.'

Denton checked the compass and lifted his feet to avoid a small wave working its way down the cockpit to the self-drainers in the stern. 'What have you noticed about the events of the last few days?'

'Not sure I understand Mister Denton.'

'We seem to be involved with a group of people who have no values and no inhibitions. They consider themselves to be above the law and they act accordingly. Worse, they seem to be remarkably well informed and resourced. So far, they have been one step ahead of us all the way. We've been reacting. We need to take the initiative.' Denton paused, realising that what he meant was that he wanted to go after Dee.

Starmer looked sceptical to tease out further discussion but was relieved that Denton had finally reached the conclusion he'd arrived at back in Manchester. 'Mr Denton, all I want to do is to keep Julie safe.'

'We both do. But how?'

'Trade on the records in that Filofax?' Starmer offered, hoping for further confirmation of his own conclusions.

'Won't work. The minute they've got that we will lose all leverage and then they lose us. And Julie,' he added. 'We need to be as ruthless as them. We need a plan that considers no half measures.' Denton looked sternly at Starmer. 'Do you understand what I mean?'

Starmer wondered briefly whether Denton had forgotten about the killings at Findhorn and his dispatch of Osman. Patiently he replied, 'I think I got that, but what exactly are you proposing?'

'Well I'm beginning to think that Webber wasn't even middle management and my bet would be that the big bloke with Dee at the harbour was maybe executive level. Now they are both in trouble at Board level. Sorry about the business hierarchy terminology but it helps me to have a structure to work with. They are both in as deep a trouble as us. They must know what will happen to them if they fail. Why have they acted as they did? Maybe because of this Filofax, maybe because of you and Julie or even perhaps because they assumed that I knew what they were up to and so I, and any witnesses, have got to be stopped.'

'Why would they assume that?'

'Perhaps because I was friendly with the guy who was investigating them? Maybe, because I worked for them? If I'd had more of grip I might have really worked out what they were up to.' He breathed out slowly, 'they weren't to know that some of the time I didn't even know what day of the week it was.'

'Right.'

'The thing about violence is that it can command respect, it can intimidate, it can silence, but it can also draw attention and a whole load of unintended consequences. My bet would be that the Board won't have liked the way they've handled things. I am going to introduce myself to the Board as the unintended consequence.'

'That should impress them,' said Starmer sarcastically and instantly regretting it.

'It will when I kill Webber,' growled Denton viciously.

'Won't they see all this coming?'

'Depends how we arrive. I wasn't intending to ring the bell.'

'Look, I know I advised against it before, but don't you think the police, Metropolitan not Manchester, might be a better option?' ventured Starmer seeking agreement for the last conclusion he'd reached in Manchester.

'No I don't. I don't trust anybody anymore.' He briefly considered the suspicions he'd earlier entertained about the then possibility that Stella had leaked his whereabouts to Webber. In the light of Julie's revelations, he now felt vindicated, surprisingly saddened but certain that Stella had been the source. 'We can't trust anyone, least of all the Police. I am surprised you'd even consider it now.'

'Okay, how do we get into Holland?'

'Eh?'

'Passports?'

'I have no Idea,' grunted Denton, sawing the tiller from side to side to keep the boat right side of a cresting wave. 'If push comes to shove we'll just have to beach this.'

Starmer crossed to the windward side, braced his feet across the cockpit, scrunched down on the bench and gathered his thoughts. There were gaping holes in Denton's plan but try as he might he failed to come up with an alternative. Denton was right about one thing; if they were caught they would die. Taking the fight to the enemy did now seem their only chance. He stared moodily under the boom across the port side as the horizon struggled back into view and was surprised to see a sizeable ship on a parallel course. 'What's that?' He pointed.

Denton looked. 'Battleship grey, probably the Navy, maybe fisheries protection?'

Starmer, knowing he was in a stolen boat, watched with increasing alarm as the now blue-grey ship narrowed the angle to their course and slowed to a stately wallow.

Denton eased the sheets and luffed up a hundred yards off the vessel's beam.

'Heave to Mr Denton and prepare for boarding.'

Denton traced the source of the megaphoned voice to the duffel coat huddled figure on the open bridge of HMC Sentinel.

'Oh fuck! It's Church.'

Chapter Eighteen

'Dee. You're here.'

'Surprised? You bastard.'

Sinclair stood in the doorway to the apartment and took one step towards her. Concern creased his strained features and he held his arms away from his sides with palms facing outwards and towards her in supplication. 'Dee please listen to me. Will you just give me a chance to explain? Please?'

'You must be so surprised that I'm still here,' she snapped. 'What did you think your murderous buddy Williams meant when he told that creep Webber to "lose" me? In Mathew world, you know that world where you wander blindly around not seeing, hearing or believing, did you think he meant me to be abandoned in Scotland to see if I could find my way back without a fuckin' map? Is that what you thought?' She snorted, 'no I didn't think so.'

'Dee please, please listen to me.'

'Mathew, Shut the fuck up,' she screamed, 'I'm long past listening to you. I asked for your help on at least three occasions while your fuck friend Williams was attempting to have me murdered or attempting to kill Denton and not once, not once,' she paused to draw breath before screaming again, 'did you raise a fucking finger to help me. You asshole.'

'Looking back Dee, if I had helped we would have both been', he paused, 'dispatched.'

'"Dispatched"? Is that the new word for recreational murder? What is it with you people and your fuckin' language, why can't you say what you mean?' She sniffed, brushing tears of rage from her cheeks, "dispatched" indeed.'

278

'Dee. Please calm down and let me talk,' he pleaded, advancing towards her with hands now steepled beneath his chin as though at prayer.

'I don't think there's anything that you can say to me Matthew that will change my opinion of you. You are a rat; the lowest form of life. Somebody that I no longer wish to associate with. You sat back when my life was threatened and did absolutely nothing.'

'What exactly did you expect me to do Dee?' He shouted, exasperated and close to joining her in tears. 'How could I have helped you? Had I said a word or done anything, anything whatsoever, they'd have been all over me and it would've been the finish for both of us. If you think about it, you know that to be true. A lot of what you said to me in that hotel room made sense but as you now know, when it comes to David, I can be gullible and susceptible. He talked to me during your interview with that reporter and convinced me that you were paranoid and probably back on drugs. He got me to the point where I simply didn't know who to believe and much of what he was saying made more sense than what you'd said. Think about it. I go to bed with everything in my world better than it has ever been and I wake up twelve hours later to a barely believable story that casts the man I love, not just as the villain of the piece, but a homicidal maniac to boot. That's a lot to take in Dee.'

Dee shut him down with a viscous chop of her hand across the space between them. 'So, it was easier to believe that I was in a drug induced hallucinatory state that in the same twelve hours had rendered me psychotic and paranoid?' She laughed dryly, 'Really?'

He slumped onto a couch, gulped nervously and looked up at her pleadingly. 'Dee, I didn't want to have to believe you,' he shook his head sadly. 'But, during that day in Edinburgh I began to learn, to my astonishment and horror, that all of what you had said could be true. As the day went on I became more certain. I then spent every opportunity throughout that day looking for a way out, a way to help you.' He shrugged, 'I was pretty powerless. My fall-back position, once I left you to cancel the concerts, was to go straight to the police and report what had happened.'

'So, why didn't you?' Dee watched Sinclair look down at his feet and gently shuffle them back and forth on the floor before resting his elbows on his knees and dropping his head into his hands.

'Because I thought I'd give him a chance to explain. I'm here to persuade David that this was all a big mistake and the best thing we can do for everybody is to get back on track with your career and our lives,' he mumbled into his hands.

'So, now you believe him.'

He raised his head to meet her eyes. 'No, but maybe, just maybe, I can get him to change.' He raised his head and looked at her with tear filled eyes, 'I still love him Dee.'

Dee took several deep breaths to calm herself and considered the pathetic state of Mathew and the relationship that she'd enjoyed with him when they'd rehearsed. The piano behind him stood as a solid, silent symbol of what they'd enjoyed and achieved together just a few weeks previously. Sighing as she felt her anger subside she dropped to her knees in front of him, took his damp face in her hands and placed her forehead against his. 'But does he love you?' she murmured gently. 'Didn't you listen to anything that was said on that journey up to Scotland? Didn't you see him knock me to the ground at that harbour? Didn't you hear him tell Webber to "lose" me? Didn't you see them shooting at Denton?' Having enunciated the points slowly and carefully, she pulled back to look into his eyes, 'forget what you thought he was and think about what he is; a killer and a big-time player in what's beginning to look more and more like organised crime. Is that really the future you want? There is nothing that this man will not do. You simply cannot be this naive.' She gently rocked his face from side to side, 'Mathew, don't believe me. Believe the evidence of what you've seen and heard in the last couple of days.' She stood, walked to the window, turning her back to him and looked out across the river with arms folded across her chest. The anger that had coursed through her veins dissipated as she balanced his misplaced loyalty and betrayal against his sensitivity, vulnerability and dedication to her career. She stepped away from the window. 'That man will not only kill me Matthew he will kill you also once he realises that you have now seen through him.'

'Dee, I am sure that I can convince him that this is all wrong; that it's not too late to stop. When he gets back here I am determined to discuss it with him.' He tossed his head defiantly, 'I am confident I will get through to him.'

'Matthew, at the moment, he is in police custody on charges that'll slow him down for no more than a few hours, up in a one-horse town called Crewe. Charges initiated by me to buy a head start to go look for Denton. I do not know how long that'll keep him in custody. I suspect that he'll be released on bail sometime mid-morning. That means we have got a couple of hours to get away from here. If you value your life I suggest you join me. Because Matthew we are now talking survival. Yours as well as mine'. She slumped down beside him on the couch and studied the careworn face of this gentle, sensitive man to whom she had grown so close and regretted her anger. 'I can use that couple of hours. Hopefully, with your help I can find out something, anything, about David's connections and business interests. Look at his papers or his computer perhaps?' She gently put her arm around his shoulders, all rage at this innocent abroad now gone, 'help me go through his things. See what we can find? You heard him say that he was going to Amsterdam. He's not going to Amsterdam for the red-light district, is he? He's going to Amsterdam to report, talk to his connections and because he's convinced that's where Denton is going. I want to find Denton before he does. So, I'm gonna get there first. What are you going to do?'

'Oh, God Dee I don't know.'

'Well while you make up your mind I am gonna turn this flat over from top to bottom and see what I can find that gives me something, anything, of a clue as to where to start looking for Denton in Holland.' Dee's shoes clacked their way across the stripped oak floor to the spiral staircase.

She had never been into Matthew and Williams' bedroom and was quite surprised at the austerity of the furnishings. Two walls were lined with black hardwood built-in wardrobes with matching bed head and shelving. Four circular hardwood bulls eye windows and two dormers in the mansard roof flooded early dawn light across a floor scattered with hand knotted wool oriental rugs. She quickly established which unit belonged to Williams and slid the doors wide. From an array of hangered suits she ignored those in Dry Cleaner's bags and threw the rest on to the bed. She abandoned the search through dozens of pockets realising that she could not afford to continue on the off chance of discovering the clichéd vital train or cinema ticket, beloved of crime writers, in the time available. She turned her attention to a stack of shoe boxes in the bottom of the wardrobe but was disappointed to find only shoes. She was not sure what she was looking for although had been half hoping for a briefcase, a box of papers or even a small hotel type safe. Finding nothing she turned her attention to Matthew's area. She treated his possessions with slightly more respect but no less thoroughness and with the same result. Standing fretfully with her hands on her hips viewing the mess across the bed and floor she accepted defeat. She quickly moved from room to room on the upper floor, checking each room for potential hiding places, again with no success. Sensing the passage of time and the need to complete her search and leave the building before Williams returned she made her way downstairs to find Matthew sitting where she had left him.

'Matthew where does Williams keep his personal effects and papers?'

'What do you mean?'

'Papers? You know what I mean Matthew. Where does he keep his personal items of correspondence and other documentation; passport, birth certificates, bills, receipts? That type of thing? Does he keep any business papers here? Is there an office I don't know about?'

'No.'

'What you mean "no"?'

'I mean that he doesn't keep any papers here. Or at least if he does I've never seen them.' He shrugged, 'I had always assumed he kept him at his office.'

'Okay,' she breathed deeply to calm her nerves. 'What about the computer,' she said, pointing to the twin computer towers half way down the room.

'The one nearest is mine.'

'Ok, let's look at the other.' Matthew rose and went to the PC to switch it on. Dee tapped her foot impatiently and watched the hard drive indicator light blink its way through the start-up process and the Windows screen and start menu appear. With a few clicks of the mouse, Windows Explorer appeared and he stepped back and waved towards the screen inviting Dee to take a closer look. Dee studied a sparse file structure tree before turning to Matthew, 'no password?'

'Apparently not.'

'Then my bet would be there is nothing on there of any significance to us and certainly nothing that will lead us to a location in Holland.' She pulled the office chair from beneath the computer table and leant on the back, 'is there anywhere in this flat that you or Williams use to keep items secure; jewellery, passports, cash? That type of thing?'

'Well there is the safe,' he chuckled.

'For fucks sake Matthew, what do you think I'm trying to do here? What safe?'

'It's not really a safe. You'll see what I mean.' He grimaced apologetically, 'I'm sorry Dee I am really not thinking.'

'Just show me to this "safe" Mathew.'

He led her across to the kitchen area and the vast expanse of stainless steel work surfaces and appliances. He opened the top compartment of the industrial sized fridge freezer and began removing boxes of frozen ready meals to reveal a sealed plastic container the size of a shoe box which he handed to Dee. She quickly removed the lid to reveal passports, a few bundles of cash in a variety of currencies and an automatic pistol. Picking up the gun she waved it in Matthew's face. 'Still not convinced?'

'Dee I had no idea that was there?'

'But you knew about the stash?'

'Yes, but I have never seen the gun before.'

'It's a drug dealer's thing Matthew. Sort of last resort. You keep a gun with your stash so if ever you're forced to reveal it you've got one last chance to stop it being stolen.' She looked down at the ageing US Army Colt pistol in her hand and rubbed her thumb over the circular, silver, prancing colt logo button set into the hardwood grip.

As she did so she marvelled at the remembered skills from her days in the desert with the piano player. She racked the slide, caught the ejected round and played with it. Tossing and catching it repeatedly. She paused, picked the bullet up from her palm and rotated it between her thumb and forefinger before bringing it up to her face and studying it more closely. Pensively, she removed the magazine from the pistol and thumbed out another round. Placing the gun on a kitchen surface she carefully compared the weight of each round; one hand against the other. She flicked more rounds from the magazine and checked the weights again. Unless she was very much mistaken some of the rounds were Reloads.

In some parts of the States Reloads were common practice and made properly not a problem. But, getting the powder weight wrong could see a round with insufficient power to drive it through the barrel resulting in the slug getting stuck. Follow that round with another, fully powdered or not, could see an explosion in the barrel. The pianist had called them Squibs and they had once spent a frustrating afternoon twice rodding barrels to remove squibs during range practice. She squeezed the trigger while supporting the hammer with her thumb, lowered it into place, reloaded the magazine, homed the clip and wondering briefly about the weapon's poor maintenance condition. 'You can put that back.' She collected the passports and cash and made her way back into the main room.

Mathew followed. 'Dee what are you doing?'
'What do you mean what am I doing?'
'I mean why are you taking David's money and his passport?'
Dee was busily riffling through the pages of each of the half dozen or so passports. 'You still don't get it? Apart from yours the rest, judging from the photographs are all David's; all in different names!' She handed him his passport. 'I'm taking the money because I need it and he owes me. I'm taking his passports so that he can't follow me. Or at least, if he tries it's gonna slow him down a little.' She looked sympathetically at Mathew, 'you really are having trouble coming to terms with this. Aren't you?'
Tension pulled his face into a brow furrowing frown and he slowly shook his head from side to side, 'not any more Dee. I think I've seen enough now.'
She clasped his hand firmly, 'good, now we need to go.'

With a hastily packed shoulder bag Dee stood patiently by the open front door while Matthew juggled two sets of keys searching for the one to the dead lock. She reached round behind him and switched off the lights to hurry him. As he found the key, stepped into the corridor and pulled the door towards the jamb Dee was distracted by a red light blinking back in the main room.
'Matthew, have you got an answering machine?'
'Yes.'
'Wait here.' She dropped the shoulder bag and ran across the room to the machine blinking away on the occasional table beside a settee. Within seconds of her hitting the replay button a sonorous, faintly American voice but with accented English enquired; "David, I begin to worry man. I have not heard since two days. You have solved problems, yeah?" There was a long pause, "you are still expected at Warnsborn." Another long pause,

"David, you are friend, it is necessary we talk," a longer pause, "but", followed by silence and a final few words that trailed off as the caller spoke to himself, "this is fubar man." Dee looked down at the machine as a series of clicks and then a pre-recorded announcement was followed by the dialling tone. She pressed the rewind button and then replay as Matthew joined her. 'Who is this Matthew?'

Sinclair listened intently before replying, 'I don't know.'

'You've never heard that voice before?'

'No I don't recognise it at all.'

'You're sure?'

'Yes. What is that accent? American?'

'Yeah, but not from the US of A. Could be a Dutchman. Many of them speak English with a faint American accent. If you listen to the phraseology it has got a bit of Dutch running through it.'

'How would you know?'

'I spent some time in Holland during one of my,' she chuckled, 'disappearances'; Amsterdam, and round about.'

'What's Warnsborn? A place?'

'You're asking me? But we now know that's where Williams is expected and that he's not particularly popular at the moment. C'mon now we can't hang about here any longer. Let's go.'

Dee stood by the lift impatiently fiddling with the strap on her shoulder bag as she watched Matthew work his way through the bunch of keys yet again looking for the one to turn the deadlock. She froze, immobile, knowing that something important had just happened. Matthew turned to her with alarm his eyes widening, 'the lift.'

'What about it?'

'It's coming,' he hissed frantically stuffing the keys into his pocket.

'It's coming here. Look,' he pointed to the floor indicator, 'It's David.'

'How the hell can you know that?' She asked, marvelling at Mathew's fear of a man that minutes previously he had been considering giving a second chance.

'Who else would it be Dee?'

'Somebody visiting another flat.'

285

'There are only two apartments on this floor and the other one is empty.'

He grabbed her hand and pulled her towards the staircase. They raced down the first flight, rounded the corner onto the half landing when Dee, on the outside, stopped dead in her tracks and yanked Matthew back hard and out of sight. She peered back, down to the street below, through the glazed screen that ran the full height of the staircase, 'that's Reg.'

Matthew cautiously moved forward until his eyes reached an angle where he could also see down to the pavement. He quickly stepped back stretched out his arm and swept Dee hard back behind him against the wall. 'Reg with David's car,' he affirmed. 'Oh, God what do we do now?'

'Well, we can't go up and we can't go down. Our best bet is to go halfway back up the stairs and wait.' Cautiously they re-ascended the first few steps of the flight leading to the apartment and pressed themselves as far back against the inside wall as was possible, barely daring to breathe. They heard the ping announcing the lift arrival and the hissing of the opening doors followed by the sound of a few footsteps crossing the corridor to the apartment door. Muttered curses followed as keys were jangled, one selected and then skidded around the escutcheon before finally entering and turning the deadlock. All doubt as to the identity of the visitor disappeared as Williams' harsh growl echoed from within the apartment, across the corridor and down the stairs. 'Matthew, are you there?' Followed by the sound of the apartment door slamming shut.

Dee and Matthew exchanged looks of horror as their joint appreciation of the predicament seeped in. Dee from the higher step looked down at Matthew and whispered, 'is there another way out?' Matthew simply shook his head and raised his forefinger to his lips. She resigned herself to a long wait before it occurred to her that were Williams intending to stay in the apartment for any length of time it was unlikely that he would have left Reg waiting outside. No, she reasoned, Williams was there to collect whatever he needed for the journey to Amsterdam and no more. Reg was there to take him on the next leg of his journey. Whilst this thought, initially, brought some comfort, she began to regret the bravado with which she had removed all Williams' passports from his cold Safe Deposit. She feared that within a

286

very few minutes the results of that decision would be visited upon her and Matthew in the form of an enraged Williams.

Almost as that thought began to give way to the next she heard the door to the apartment open. At this point she knew that her and Matthew's future existence depended on whether Williams left the apartment and turned left down the stairs or called for the lift. The sound of an almost continuous flow of foulmouthed invective from Williams as he repeatedly jabbed at the lift button served to both terrify and reassure her in the same moment. She reached for, found and squeezed Matthew's hand and was reassured when he squeezed back. The hiss of the door closing matched their collective sigh of relief as they felt the vibration of the lift passing down the shaft at their back. Matthew squeezed her hand again and she looked down as he raised his finger to his lips and gently pulled her up the few stairs to the landing. They both breathed in deeply as down the stairwell, some two floors below, they heard lift doors open, footsteps crossing the lobby, the main entrance door being flung back and a yell as Williams began to shout across the pavement to Reg.

Matthew held Dee by the shoulders, 'stay here and do not come down whatever happens.'

'What you going to do?'

'I'm just going to see if they are still there. I'm serious Dee. Do not follow me. Stay where you are until I come back.' He stepped cautiously down to the next landing, lowered himself to his knees and then flattened himself to the floor before crawling his way to the edge of the landing. There he cautiously raised his eyes level with an inter floor timber transom of the story height screen and peered down. Williams was standing by the car, Reg seemed to have been dispatched to look along the street. Matthew watched him return shaking his head only to be dispatched in the opposite direction. Meanwhile Williams was venting his rage on the car by rhythmically hammering the undersides of his clenched fists down onto the car roof and shouting at the top of his voice. Mathew dropped his head below the line of the transom and waited. A very few minutes later he heard doors slam, the car start and the scream of tyres as the car pulled away from the curb. He sensed Dee's presence. 'Do you ever do as you're told?'

'I heard the car go.'

'What now?'

'The airport I think.'

'Are you sure?'

'What do you mean?'

'I mean that my bet would be that David was intending to get to Amsterdam via City Airport. It's less than a few miles from here and he uses it frequently. That's where he'll be going.'

'I don't think so.'

'You don't?'

'Passports? We've got all his passports. Now I don't doubt for one minute that someone with his organised-crime connections will soon find a way of leaving the country, either legally or illegally, and making his way to Amsterdam. But what I do know is he won't be doing it through City Airport this morning. Can we agree on that?'

'I suppose so.'

As they approached the airport Dee had been more than a little alarmed watching the arrival of aircraft and, the what she considered to be, insanely steep angle of descent necessary to land on the short runway of this busy hub. The taxi drew up outside the two and three storey boxy structure of the terminal and she and Matthew made their way immediately beneath the entrance canopy past the stainless-steel support pillars onto the concourse. As they crossed the floor towards the check-in desks she was firstly surprised by the relative smallness of the amenity compared to other airports that she had frequented and then amazed at the sight of bamboo trees growing from circular beds set in the floor and reaching up the full height of the three-storey atrium building. She strode purposefully towards the Lufthansa desk with passports and Williams' cash in hand with her confidence growing at the bemused look of dawning, but not quite realised, recognition from the check-in clerk.

With an hour to wait before boarding, the pair made their way towards the Meridian Line restaurant and thankfully sank down into a couple of leather accent chairs. Within minutes they were approached by a young waitress whose cheerful enquiry as to their needs nearly fell on stony ground. Dee, finally, dragged herself back from her worries, quickly gathered her thoughts, forced a smile and looked at this bright young woman with her black waistcoat, white shirt, elasticated sleeve garters, black bowtie and starched white apron. She glanced at her name tag and smiled again, 'Well Monica, can we get some coffees and croissants please?'

They sat back in a companionable but concerned silence as they waited for the order to be filled; reflecting on the near miss with Williams and their good luck. Dee gazed back across the concourse to the clock above the Lufthansa desk and stiffened. 'Matthew look, who is that by the Lufthansa desk?'

Sinclair leant back and looked over his shoulder. 'Oh god! It's that reporter that we met in Edinburgh.'

'I thought it was. God she's looking over here.' Dee gathered her wits and composure, partly assisted by Monica's delivery of their order, while keeping an eye on the tall, confident young woman now striding determinedly across the concourse in their direction with a wide smile of recognition upon her face.

'Hey, what a lovely surprise. I didn't expect to see you here. Are you meeting David as well?'

Dee and Matthew exchanged horrified looks as the forward Miss Lockstone pulled a chair over to their table and instructed Monica to return with another coffee and a Panini. 'I had heard that you were unwell Dee.'

Dee paused for the briefest of moments, 'artistic differences.'

Miss Lockstone helped herself to one of Matthew's croissants and munched contentedly with the pastry held just in front of her mouth while considering her next question. Carefully picking a small crumb from the corner of her mouth with her little finger she sucked the full force of her charismatic personality into a disarming smile and enquired with steely resolve, 'no truth in the rumour that the old problems have returned then?'

Dee met her head on, 'you mean drugs?'

'Not necessarily but you have had, shall we say, management problems before.'

'Are you here to interview me?'

'No, no, as I said, I'm meeting David.'

'And then?' Dee ventured.

'Oh, we're off to,' she bent to her bag and retrieved a spiral bound notebook, flicked through the pages and then phonetically and laboriously read out, 'Langoed Groot Warnsborn.' She turned her attention back to the croissant and missed the look that Dee and Sinclair exchanged at the mention of Warnsborn. 'David and I had a long discussion up in Manchester about the music business. I think he feels I have a lot to offer that fits with his plans and ambitions. Anyway, it never hurts to get another iron into the fire. Does it?' She laughed again, 'so a couple of days of plum beano at this place is eagerly anticipated. I take it that's where you're off to?'

'You're meeting David here?'

'Yes, but if he doesn't get here soon he's going to miss his flight and I'll have to find my own way there,' she laughed.

Dee experienced the same sense of helplessness that she'd felt when they were trapped on the staircase and, she judged from the look on Mathew's face, she wasn't alone. She was still confident that Williams wouldn't be able to fly out from the airport any time soon but now feared that he might turn up to make his apologies to the young reporter. On the other hand, she reasoned, he'd left the apartment before them and if he'd been coming to the airport should already have been there. She glanced nervously around and saw the check-in clerk on his way across the concourse and heading in their direction. That was all she needed right now; a star struck fan. The clerk smiled at her sweetly but turned to the Reporter.

'Miss Lockstone. I have a message for you. A Mister Williams advises that he'll not be joining you on the flight but has arranged for you to be met at Schiphol and looks forward to seeing you tomorrow.'

Dee sank back into the back-seat cushions of the taxi, content to let her mind drift while she marvelled at the number of people on bicycles in Amsterdam. She felt completely exhausted, not just because of the events of recent days but also because of the sheer effort of fending off the inquisitive attentions of the young reporter on the flight. Although she couldn't be certain, Dee had been sure that her curiosity was focused on the possibility of a story about Dee's cancelled tour, fall from grace and possible return to old habits. She felt, however, that she had managed to leave her with the impression that her difficulties were temporary and soon to be resolved in discussions with Williams. She even went so far as to hint that the trip to Langoed Groot was at Williams invitation and that she had been disappointed not to have met up at with him at the airport. The resultant offer of a lift by the gracious Miss Lockstone had barely ruffled her, by now, polished, skills of dissembling and the explanation of her need to get some rest and hotel pampering before such an important meeting with

Williams seemed to have been accepted. They had parted with show bizz hugs, air kisses and sisterly anticipation of good times to come.

'So where are we going?'
'Zutphen.'
'Where?'
'Small town on the river, a few kilometres north-east of Arnhem.'
'I thought we were going to Amsterdam.'
'So did I. But we never knew exactly where in Holland we could find Denton. But if our young reporter friend says that Langoed whatever it's called is near to Arnhem then we are heading in the right direction.'
'Right. So, how do you know Zutphen?'
'I stayed there. Few years back now.'
'So, that's how you come to know Holland and Amsterdam.'
'Partly.'
'Why Zutphen?' He chuckled quietly at his own mimicry of a mittel European accent.
'Friend had a boat.'
'Oh.'
'I am sure there must be many more questions in your mind Matthew and it's unlike you not to ask them,' she responded impatiently.
'Dee that's completely unfair and you know it. How do you know your friend will still be there?'
'I just do.'
'And he will welcome us with open arms?'
Dee giggled. 'he'll welcome you with open arms Mathew.' She placed her hand on his and squeezed an apology for the embarrassment his blushes suggested she had caused. She hurriedly continued, 'it's an old ljsselmeer converted seagoing fishing boat. I think it was refitted back in the 60s. Bit like a barge. It's got a fairly big cabin, kitchen, all the usual amenities, couple of bedrooms and an additional sleeping area in the cabin that can be used at a push.'
'Do you think Lockstone will tell Williams about our meeting?'

'Bound to. But she is unlikely to run into him until he sorts out his passport problem. Which, she reflected, 'gives us a little time to find Denton.'

'And how are we going to do that?'

'I am working on the assumption that Denton is coming to Holland to confront and deal with Williams or his Boss. Williams was absolutely convinced that was the case. The chances are, therefore, that we're all heading in the same general direction. Quite how we go about finding him I am not sure. Maybe Jonny can help.'

'Johnny?'

'Jonny van Rijn.' She smiled. 'It's his boat.'

Chapter Nineteen

Denton huddled down in the jump seat facing forward as the Rib skidded across wave crests, bouncing its way over an increasingly choppy sea with a now noticeable swell, towards the looming hull of Her Majesty's Customs launch, Sentinel.

He looked down moodily at the top of Julie's head as she crouched between his knees on the rough slip proofed surface of the Rib floor, partially sheltered from the gusting wind and spray. Glancing back over his left shoulder he moodily viewed the now captured yacht and wondered at its future. He didn't envy the "Prize" crew, now aboard, their task in the worsening weather conditions although when he'd left they'd seemed more concerned with ransacking the boat than any imminent threat from the prevailing weather. Despite his previous confident assertions to Starmer about his navigational and seamanship skills, his doubts had been growing in the hours leading up to the boarding of the yacht and a part of him felt relief at having been released from that sea of troubles. The rest of him fretted about the confrontation with Church that awaited him on the cutter. As he swivelled back to face forward he briefly locked eyes with Starmer and reflected on the short conversation they'd been able to have during the interval between being hailed from Sentinel and the arrival of the Rib crammed with Customs Officers. They had both struggled to come to terms with, yet again, having their plans disrupted by apparently omnipotent forces that seemed to know their every move in advance. There had been a brief accusatory challenge from Starmer who'd been convinced that the link between Denton and the shooting in Bromley must have meant contact, if not collaboration, with the forces of Law and Order. Denton had been unable to completely convince him that he was as much in the dark as to the sudden arrival of the customs cutter as anybody else.

He returned his gaze to the fast approaching blue grey slabbed side of the Cutter. Any number of combinations of thoughts, plans and suspicions raced through his mind but none provided any sort of understandable explanation for the sudden arrival of Church. Of one thing, he was sure; it wasn't coincidence. He looked across at the faintly ridiculous sight of Starmer huddled in the old-fashioned lifejacket and the woman's yellow hat. He was still clutching his rucksack and they exchanged looks of grim resignation as the Rib swept from a wide circle into an approach alongside the cutter. Denton watched with slight amusement at the less than able skills of the various seamen attempting to secure the Rib as the deck crew above prepared to lift it from the water. The coxswain seemed to be having some difficulty keeping the boat in position alongside the cutter while lines were attached fore and aft to maintain stability during the lift. He looked up towards the crane type davit and the lifting tackle hanging above their heads swinging in wide circles over the Rib. On the end of the tackle was an orange floatation buoy below which was suspended the lifting hook and safety grab handles. A worsening sea and a gusting wind was now forcing the Rib into the hull of the cutter while the Rib was defying the boatswain's attempts to centre the lifting point beneath the suspended lifting tackle. Denton despaired at the ineptitude of the crew. The lower the hook descended the more nervous became the receiver, standing legs astride braced against the boat's movement while anxiously casting his eyes aloft. With one hand held skyward the man signalled to the crane operator while shielding his heavily bandaged other hand behind his back. After several attempts, during which the boatswain's patience reached its limit, the boat was finally secured to the central lifting hook and hoisted into position on the side afterdeck of the cutter. As they waited to disembark Denton looked across at the man with the bandaged hand, smiled and said, 'you didn't catch that in the gate, did you?' Pointing at the hook and lifting point assembly.

The man looked angrily at Denton and snapped, 'it's a new fucking system and we haven't had time to train with it.'

294

Starmer chipped in cheekily, 'Christ, if it's that difficult getting it out of the water I really don't want to be in it when you lower it off.'

The man turned towards Starmer looking him over scornfully, 'that's a real jacket you've got there. Haven't seen one of them since I was a boy.'

Starmer grinned and shrugged his shoulders within the spacious confines of the orange jacket, 'how did you do your hand?'

The man's irritation briefly flared before he recovered his composure and looked down at his bandaged hand. 'It's a new crew and we were rushed out mid-commissioning,' he grinned ruefully. 'Nah, lowering you off is not a problem providing we're secured fore and aft. As it hits the water you just hit that orange lever,' he pointed up at the lifting tackle, 'and bosh, bosh, ting a ling, it releases the hook.'

'And your hand?'

When you hit the water the Rib moves aft of the cutter. I was a second late hitting the release. It came out under tension. And I got this,' he waved the damaged hand in the air and looked aft to the frowning boatswain, 'come on you lot over the side.'

Starmer shrugged as sympathetically as he could and turned to help the man get Julie onto the cutter deck, 'let's hope it doesn't happen again,' he offered.

Starmer helped Julie over the transom through the watertight door from the boat deck, brushing up against the wheeled locking handle with the rucksack on his shoulder as he went. He came to an abrupt halt in front of a small man with a navy blue woolly pully complete with cloth patches and epaulettes and a white peaked cap emblazoned with the gold crested cap badge of Her Majesty's Customs. He and Julie shuffled further forward as Denton careered into them when the ship turned hard to port.

'Good morning I am Coxswain 'edge. That's 'edge with an 'Aitch. You are now on my war canoe. To ensure your continued safety you will follow my instructions at all times. Do you understand?' The little man stepped smartly back one step as though his statement needed the emphasis the movement provided. He clasped his hands rigidly behind his back and rocked up and down on his heels as he surveyed this intrusion into the pristine confines of his domain.

Denton stepped round Starmer and Julie and approached to within a few feet of the little man. 'Mister Starmer, my daughter and I are cold, wet and tired. Would it not be a good idea for you to provide us with some warm clothing and a hot drink before you start issuing your orders?'

The Coxswain went back up onto his toes and leaned forward aggressively,

'That, Sir, was my very next intention. Kindly step into the drying room and remove your outer garments.'

Denton stepped over another transom into a storage space lined with pine slatted benches and lockers with hooks above holding a variety of dry, and wet, suits and sundry waterproofs with assorted rubber footwear below each set. He struggled out of his dry suit and watched in amazement as Starmer peeled off layer after layer of the German woman's clothing. Finished, they made their way to the passageway and the quizzical gaze of the Coxswain.

'You, sir', he barked.

'Me?' enquired Starmer with his arm round a now shivering Julie.

'Yes, you sir. You will not need that life preserver sir. Oh no. We are not going to sink.' He sniffed disapprovingly in the direction of the neat pile of clothing that Starmer had left on the bench. 'Leave it with your other things,' he paused, 'sir'.

Starmer remained motionless for appreciable seconds before turning slowly back into the drying room and carefully placing the jacket under the bench where his clothes were stacked. He returned to Julie, hefted his rucksack onto his shoulder, draped the other arm around her and smiled disarmingly at the little man.

'Follow me', barked the Coxswain stepping smartly forward into the passageway and the unhappy trio followed in his wake. Starmer was aware of a heavy vibration beneath his feet and the adjacent hum of machinery. Farther away he could hear faint noises of static and radio chatter and from close by, the smell of cooking was overlaid by wafts of electrical heat, oil and disinfectant all combining to pervade the enclosed space of the passageway. Running below the high notes was the unmistakably and acrid smell of fresh paint. So fresh that he trailed his fingers along the unblemished bulkhead and was quite surprised when they came away dry. They passed a companionway and stairways giving access above and below the deck on which they stood and were halted opposite an open galley on the port side with banquette seating on the starboard where they were instructed to sit.

Almost as if by magic a rating appeared from behind the Coxswain clutching three blankets. Two of which he handed to Starmer and Denton while the third he folded, over solicitously, around Julie's still shivering shoulders. The Coxswain indicated his approval to the rating and dismissed him with a jerk of his head while raising enquiring eyes to the chef behind the spotlessly clean stainless steel galley counter. 'Three very large hot chocolates, when you're ready Cookie. Thank you.' He returned his attention to the now seated trio, 'I shall leave you in the good offices of Cookie. You're free to order whatever you should require I shall return in forty-five minutes precisely with further advice and instruction.'

Starmer sat wedged into the corner of the banquette desperately trying to overcome the all-consuming tiredness that threatened to pleasurably overwhelm the thoughts and fears racing through his brain. He looked across the small table at Julie, scrunched into the opposite corner alongside her dad. Both seemed to be suffering the strains of exhaustion. As he watched he saw Denton's eyes begin to close and the arm that he'd placed around Julie's shoulder began to drop down to her waist. Starmer shook himself awake reached over the fiddle rail running around the edge of the table and shook Denton's elbow. 'Mr Denton wake up', and again, 'wake up now,' he pleaded urgently. Denton's eyes struggled to focus, 'what's the matter?'

'Who is Church?'

Denton visibly gathered himself together, dropped both elbows on the far side of the fiddle rail and quietly cautioned Starmer about volume with a raised finger to his pursed lips. 'I told you before about the shooting in the pub in Bromley, right?' Starmer nodded. 'After the shooting, I was interviewed by that man up on the bridge, the one who hailed us? His name is Church. He is an Officer in Customs and Excise. Ok? As I tried to tell you before I have no idea how he got from Bromley to here. I am sure there is some rational explanation but I am absolutely buggered if I can think of it now,' he ended sourly.

'Mr Denton, you must have begun to wonder how it is that we seem to be continually wrong footed. It's becoming much, much more than a coincidence that every time we move forward we bump into another group of people lying in wait. Surely to God you don't think that Church and his "war canoe" just happened to be out on a day trip and chanced to bump into us in the middle of the North Sea. That is no coincidence. Someone worked out, or was told, where we were going. Someone with the access to enough connections, power and resources to be able to whistle up an HMC cutter to chase us down.'

Denton rested his elbows on top of the fiddle rails and dropped his head into his hands shaking it silently from side to side. He felt that his thinking was probably quite a bit in advance of Starmer's. He'd already established in his own mind that the source of the intelligence that had dogged their tracks from start to finish had, initially, been Stella. Now he was being forced to the conclusion that the those pursuing them had access to resources and power way beyond his earlier imaginings. He looked up at Starmer. 'You had a suspicion, from the stuff in the Filofax, that these people are heavily involved with at least the Manchester police force. Correct?' Starmer nodded. 'Well it's not much of a leap from there to Customs, is it? Customs cover supply, Police cover distribution?'

Starmer looked thoughtful. 'It's possible but I refuse to believe that they can suborn the entire crew of one of Her Majesty ships for the pursuit of us and their interests.'

Denton looks across at him. 'But they don't have to. Do they?'

'How do you mean.'

'All it takes is for one very senior officer, Church, to instruct the cutter to chase and find us. He doesn't have to explain anything to the officers and crew. Does he?'

'So, what now?'

'They were searching the yacht as we left.'

'They won't find anything.'

'I was going to ask you about that.'

'Best you don't know,' grunted Starmer.

'Okay, let's work with the assumption that Church is bent. I think that he's alone on this boat in that enterprise. As I said, the whole crew can't be crooked, surely to God? That limits his options. It's unlikely that he can do anything to us while we're on this boat. It would require too much explanation and I suspect that the little Coxswain is as straight up and down as a ramrod.' He leant back in the seat moving his hands to massage his temples. 'No. Our problems will start when we get off the bloody boat.'

Starmer nodded, 'so wait-and-see?'

'Do we have a choice?'

'Three chocolates as ordered.' They all looked towards the end of the table where a slim young man with freckles and a shock of red hair had carefully clasped three Styrofoam cups between his hands while advancing unsteadily across the moving deck towards the table. Starmer reached forward to take one, Denton took the other leaving the sailor to position the third in front of Julie. 'Is there anything else I can get you?'

Starmer looked at Denton and then at Julie. 'I would really appreciate something filling. We haven't eaten for some time. Perhaps three platefuls of toast with butter dripping from the edges,' he smiled up at the eager young sailor.

'Not a problem. Coming right up.'

As he moved away back to the galley Starmer called out. 'And have you got any bottles of water?'

'Need to go to the stores for that. Back with you in a jiff.'

'Before you go, is there a chance you might have some Neurophen?'

'Not a problem. I'll talk to the Coxswain.'

Starmer leaned across the table and took Julie's hands in his and gently shook her awake. 'Julie, Julie, come on wake up time to eat.' She awoke with a shiver and immediately pulled the blanket tighter over her shoulders and tucked her chin beneath the folds. Starmer could see her hands moving beneath the blanket as she scratched at her arms and shoulders. 'It starting again?'

She nodded. 'I am not gonna get a fix here am I?'

'I am afraid not Julie.'

The conversation came to an abrupt halt as the unbending little Coxswain snapped into position at the end of their table. 'I hope you're more comfortable than you were when we pulled you from the sea. Is there anything else I can do for you at the moment?'

'Mr Hedge. A word if you please.'

They all turned and Denton immediately recognised the small, chubby, pink and sweaty figure of Church through the numerous folds of a vastly oversized duffel coat as he struggled to restore his comb over to some semblance of order while demisting his glasses.

The Coxswain faced smartly about, 'Sir?'

'Have the prisoners been searched Mr Hedge?'

Hedge looked puzzled. 'I wasn't aware they was prisoners. Suh!'

'I repeat,' intoned Church, 'have they been searched?'

'No Suh!' barked the little Coxswain with alacrity bordering on the dumbly insolent. 'Immediately Suh!'

'I'll wait,' said Church sharply stepping back to avoid the seemingly careless placement of Hedge's heavy sea boots. The little Coxswain visibly bristled at the misshapen lump that was Church as he carried out his instructions.

'Please forgive me lady and gentlemen. Could I ask you to step into the passageway?'

Denton looked sternly at Hedge. I do hope you're not going to attempt to body search my daughter?'

'No Sir, if the lady will just remove the blanket a visual appraisal will suffice. Thank you. Suh.' Hedge threw Church a look that challenged any other interpretation.

Duly searched, all three returned to the table as the young cook reappeared with the buttered toast a bottle of water tucked beneath each of his arms and a packet of Neurophen. Hedge smiled at him and helped to serve the trio. 'Before I go perhaps you'd like to pass me the rucksack?'

Starmer looked at him blankly. Hedge smiled, 'the one beneath the table. Between your feet?'

Starmer slowly fished the rucksack into sight, painfully aware that two other pair of eyes were following his every move as he passed it to Hedge.

The Coxswain rummaged through the two main pockets and deposited the contents; a couple of dirty T-shirts, some socks and an old Ordnance Survey map onto the table before turning his attention to the side pockets and the lid flap pocket. Further searching produced nothing of interest. He returned the rucksack to Starmer who carefully stuffed it back under the table between his legs painfully aware of the quizzical glances from Julie and the transparent disbelief worryingly apparent on Denton's face. He straightened up, smiled and said, 'what are you looking for Mr Hedge?'

'Contraband Suh! Been my life. Man and Boy. Contraband is my job Suh!'

Denton followed Church down the passageway and marvelled at how little control the man had over his legs. He seemed to bounce from one bulkhead to the other along the corridor, completely out of sync with the motion of the ship. He suddenly staggered from view, propelled through an opening, narrowly avoiding tripping over a transom and into what Denton took to be the wardroom. He entered the small but plushily furnished space in time to see Church regain his equilibrium by grabbing a large carver chair and dumping himself into its seat before further upset befell him.

Denton viewed the room from the doorway. Long and narrow with the outboard bulkhead contoured to the shape of the hull, the compartment contained another banquette dining arrangement down one long and one short side. This time with a plush buttoned blue leather finish for the fixed seating and matching leather upholstered chairs for the head and remaining side of the table. He was surprised to see that the deck was carpeted and that the theme in general was dark oak panelling to wainscot level. There was a small quadrant bar and serving counter gracing the fore end of this small wardroom.

Church, equilibrium restored, stood and made his way towards the banquette seating where he selected a corner and positioned himself immediately beneath a porthole. As Denton, still standing, waited for further invitation or instruction Church struggled from out of the depths of the duffel coat removed a sodden scarf from around his neck and again attempted to reposition his combed over hair across his thinning pate.

'Sit down Mister Denton', he instructed, waving his hand at the chair he had just vacated, 'I have some questions for you.'

Denton sat as instructed, crossed his legs and leant back in the chair hoping his nervousness wasn't apparent and said, 'and I have some questions for you Mister Church.'

Church waved his hand dismissively, 'I think I'll go first Mr Denton. The yacht? Yours?'

'You know it isn't.'

'Where did you get the yacht?'

'You know where I got the yacht.'

'For the record?'

'Findhorn.'

'You stole the boat from the harbour?'

'You knew that.' Denton decided to take the initiative, 'how did you know where we were?'

'I am a customs officer Mr Denton. It is my job to know.' he groaned through tightly clamped lips.

'You see Mister Church I am puzzled. Some days ago, whenever, I've lost track, I witnessed a brutal murder in a pub in Bromley. A few hours later I was interviewed by you. Since then you simply would not believe what has been happening to me, my family and my friends. You would not credit the sorts of people that I've had to deal with in those few days. Or perhaps you would? Perhaps you know better than I what has been happening. Because it seems very strange to me that you were there at the start and here you are,' he paused, 'yet again.'

'Mister Denton please don't flatter yourself. I am a senior customs officer engaged on an important and far reaching Investigation,' he intoned pompously. 'Those enquiries took me to Scotland. Word came through of a disturbance in and around the Findhorn area. Shots fired? I had a flag on your car and, hey presto, there it is abandoned in Findhorn with no sight or sound of you but with a yacht disappearing into the sunset. It didn't require a Poirot to make the connection. HMC Sentinel was in the area on commissioning trials out of Kinlochbervie; just up the coast. I was able to secure her services in the search for the yacht abroad in the North Sea, which I was pretty certain contained you or others important to my enquiry.' Church paused as he struggled to remove a handkerchief from his trousers pocket and mop his heavily sweating face and forehead.

Denton realised that Church was suffering badly from sea sickness. 'Are you feeling alright?' he enquired solicitously.

Church ignored him and continued to mop his forehead and swallow hard against the rising tide of bile before launching himself from the banquette across the small wardroom and into the passageway in search of the heads.

Denton reflected on his wise choice of the seat opposite the porthole where occasional glimpses of the horizon stabilised his own inner gyro sufficiently to ward off seasickness. So far, the conversation had produced little that he didn't know or could not have guessed. He appreciated that he needed to steer the conversation towards establishing the extent of Church's knowledge and involvement.

Less than happy, Church returned to the wardroom and made his way to his corner seat now clutching a plastic bottle of water. 'You know a Mr Webber.'

'Is that a question?'

'No, we established when we first met that you knew Mr Webber if you recall.'

Denton hesitated. He was certain that Webber's name hadn't come up in that first interview but Church could have made the connection through McCarthy. 'Yes, I know Webber,' he admitted.

'And Mr Webber was at Findhorn?'

'Yes.'

'And it was Mr Webber from whom you sought refuge by stealing the yacht and attempting to cross the North Sea?'

Denton breathed deeply before answering and considered the fact that Church had no way of knowing his intentions other than by an educated guess or advice from elsewhere. 'Why do you think I was crossing the North Sea?'

Church's attempt at a sardonic smile faltered as his brain reminded him that only his lips stood between him and the upward rush of his stomach's contents. He gulped himself back into control. 'Because you were heading in that direction?' He concluded lamely.

Denton decided to try a different tack. 'Mr Church, for reasons that are entirely beyond me I seem to be mixed up in something that is very much outside my experience. I've told you some of what happened since we last met. Not all. I have a range of suspicions about what may or may not be happening but no clear picture. I am completely out of my depth.' He leant forward earnestly, shaking his head in helpless disbelief while looking entreatingly at Church. 'Essentially, what I am trying to achieve here is to secure the safety and future of my daughter, my family and myself. I have no idea how I'm going to do that but I am pretty certain there is a connection between Webber, his boss and the man at the top of the tree. I have reason to believe that man is in Holland; Webber spent a lot of time there when he worked for NMG. So, my thinking was to take these problems to the top of the management structure and to reassure them that I know little about their business, wish I knew less and that I have no interest in their activities, no knowledge of their plans and in no way, represent a threat to them.'

Church looked archly thoughtful, 'I suspect that may not work but I do have an idea.'

Denton barely managed to conceal his delight as Church allowed a self-satisfied smirk to cross his features as he bit into the hook that Denton had so carefully baited.

'Work for me.'

'Work for you?' Denton shifted uncomfortably in his seat buying time while he struggled to muster a look of surprise and concern at this not unexpected proposal.

'Yes Mr Denton. Work for me. Think about it. Your plan has a serious and fundamental flaw. You have nothing to offer. Unless you have acquired some evidence or intelligence that you can trade for your future security I fail to see how you hope to succeed.'

Denton, marvelled at Church's disingenuous attempt to get him to reveal the only card that he and Starmer still held. 'I see what you mean, Mister Church,' he answered ruefully wondering, again, where Starmer had left the Filofax.

'You are right. This is an organisation of committed criminals. They are ruthless. Without the sort of protection Her Majesty's Customs can offer you wouldn't stand a chance. All that you have is some knowledge of the people involved and half an idea of how to go about following up some of those connections. I need information about the continental end of this business. I know how it works and operates in the UK but I have little, or no, idea about those involved or the structure of the organisation in Holland. It seems to me that you, in the guise of an innocent abroad, seeking to secure the safety and security of yourself and your family and knowing some of the key players may be able to furnish me with the information I need to shut this organisation down.'

'And how would that work?'

'Before I answer that, how were you intending to get into Holland?'

'I haven't really thought that far ahead.'

'I understand but, presumably, unless you have passports in your back pocket,' he chuckled, 'which I know you haven't and money available, you'd have struggled?'

'As I said I hadn't given it that much thought.'

'Working with me those issues will be resolved. We can take you into coastal waters in the cutter and land you from the Rib. I can provide you with funds and documentation. You can do pretty much what you intended. But,' he paused for emphasis, 'with back up.'

'And the detail of how that would work?'

'Details we can work out. It is the principle of working for me that I seek to establish.'

'Okay I agree in principle.'

'Good, now before we go further when you were in Nairn were you at an old House in Mill Lane at any point?'

Denton didn't hesitate. 'No, why?'

'You said you rescued your daughter from Webber?'

Denton racked his memory but recalled no such admission. 'Did I?'

Church dismissed his answer with a wave of his hand, 'no matter. We know he was at that house. Did you go anywhere else in the area while you were up there?'

Denton struggled to see where this was going but determined to play along to find out. 'I went to the Findhorn foundation. My daughter had been there for a brief period and I thought that she might have gone back there.'

'But she didn't?'

'No, she didn't.'

'So where did you find her?'

'I didn't. She found me.'

'So,' Church hesitated, seemingly choosing his words very carefully, 'apart from the Foundation at Findhorn and the harbour you went nowhere else?'

Denton nodded.

Church continued, 'and all that you have is what you stand up in, the stuff on the yacht and what you left in the car?'

Denton sensed the desperation in the question and could only guess at the pressures behind it to have prompted such a revealing line of questioning. 'Sorry?'

'Nothing, don't worry.' Church hurried on, 'okay I think we know where we're going. There's probably time for you to get some sleep. While you're doing that, I'll work out the details of how, when and where we'll work together.

Denton moved slowly back down the passageway towards the galley and messing area with the rolling gait, now necessary to maintain some sort of stability to counter the cutter's motion. Starmer was stretched full length on the banquette seating with

305

his back and shoulders against the bulkhead, his eyes closed, mouth slightly open and arms folded across his chest. As Denton attempted to sit gently at the end of the bench, so as not to disturb him, Starmer's eyes flickered open and he sat upright.

'How did it go?'

'Okay. I think.'

'Just okay?'

Denton grimaced, 'I think you're right.'

'Church?'

'Yes.'

'What did he say?'

'Enough for me to consider that on the balance of probabilities he is in this up to his neck.'

'You sure?'

'Pretty much. He let stuff slip that he wouldn't have known were he kosher. He wants us to work for him. Gathering intelligence on the Dutch end of this operation and report back to him.' Denton looked thoughtfully at Starmer, 'he seemed particularly interested in where we were in Scotland; where we went, what we did.'

'Really?'

'Really indeed. Anyway, he's offering to put us ashore in Holland so we can follow up from where we left off. But working for him.' Denton paused thoughtfully. 'What I think he actually wants, is us off this ship. He's done what he was told to do; he found us. Now he's got to find a way of delivering us into the hands of his Dutch mates and that bastard Webber. And all that has to be done away from prying eyes. Or at least away from the eyes of the legit officers and crew on this ship. That's what I think he actually wants.'

Starmer grinned, 'well, we were going to Holland'.

'Yeah, we were. Now we're going first class. Well Rib class. I don't suppose he can deliver us straight into the arms of the ungodly from the deck of one of her Majesty's Revenue Cutters. This way at least we get there safely and dry.'

'My thinking exactly.'

'But, there's a problem.'

'There are two!'

'Yeah, the first is the Rib crew and the second,' Denton's face screwed into a puzzled frown, 'is the reception party'.

'If we can deal with the first we can avoid the second.' Starmer swung his legs to the deck, bent down and retrieved his rucksack from beneath the table. 'What do you think of this?' He said pulling the old Ordnance Survey map from the rucksack and pointing at the front cover.

'Land Ranger 41? Ben Nevis, Fort William and surrounding areas?'

'Not that. The symbols beneath the titles.'

'Information, caravans, vista and camping?'

Starmer snorted and unfolded the back to the inside leaf and indicated a more detailed table of ordnance survey symbols, 'no these. What's that one?'

'What it says? A church?'

'Exactly, that symbol appears in Woolley's Filofax against a whole schedule of transactions.'

Denton looked thoughtfully at the map and then at Starmer. 'Church? Are you thinking the same as me?'

'Almost certainly.'

'While I think of it, where is that book?'

Starmer grinned, 'remember the lifejacket you took the piss out of?'

'Seriously. You put it in the lifejacket?'

'Yup,' he laughed, 'while I was getting changed into that gear you found so amusing. Now all we need to do is make sure that I leave with it.'

Denton leaned over across the table to look down at Julie stretched full-length along the bench, still swaddled in her blanket. He sat back down, 'how's she been?'

'Not good. The crew have been really helpful. Cookie keeps the nibbles and water coming and Chalky came through with a bottle of Neurophen which might have taken the edge off just a little bit.'

'Chalky?'

'The guy with the damaged hand? In the Rib?'

Denton was pondering the continued worry of Julie's condition when his next question was forestalled by a warning glare from Starmer as Church lumbered into view grabbing at the end of their table as he passed to halt his slide aft. He grasped at the table with both hands and spent appreciable minutes gulping, swallowing and sweating his way through another attack of sea sickness. Finally, the words came, 'Have you briefed Mr Starmer?'

'Nearly.'

'Right, well here's the plan.' He spread a carefully folded nautical chart cross the table and turned it round that Denton might view it. He jabbed a finger into the middle of a stretch of Dutch coastline, 'Zandvoort.'

'Seems to be miles from anywhere,' said Denton.

Church gulped quickly, several times, before replying sharply. 'What did you want? A welcoming committee?'

Starmer and Denton exchanged looks at what they both considered a Freudian slip.

Church hurried on, perhaps sensing his slip, 'Okay let's get to the arrangements for when you're in Holland. What seems to have happened in the UK is that you stirred up a hornet's nest. Agent Provocateurs in a way. That's going to cause them to make mistakes. We'll be waiting and watching.'

'How do I get in contact with you?'

'At the risk of sounding like a very bad spymaster you don't. I get in touch with you.'

Denton and Starmer exchanged further brief but meaningful looks, both reaching the conclusion that this lack of commitment to contact was further proof of their suspicions and Church's intentions. Denton pulled the nautical chart closer towards him and placed his finger on Zandvoort. 'How far from there when you launch the Rib?'

'I'd like to stay outside territorial waters.'

Denton returned to his study of the chart and mentally traced a route north from Zandvoort.

'You need to be ready to go at first light tomorrow morning which means you've got eight hours to rest and recover from your exertions.'

Denton smiled as he looked up at Church and returned the now neatly folded chart.

The three of them gathered in the passageway near the drying room looking out through the open water tight door to the heaving boat deck and the crew struggling to prepare the Rib for launch. Julie had been provided with a full dry suit, Starmer was attired in his German garb complete with the lifebelt while Denton had retained the German sailor's suit.

'You lot sure you're ready for this,' enquired a cheerful Chalky as he approached them across the rain and wind lashed deck.

'Gonna have to be really, Chalky,' said Starmer.

'Okay, let's get you on board one at a time. There's nothing to worry about.'

'Is the cutter going to stop?' shouted Starmer above the gusting wind.

'Nope,' shouted Chalky, 'smoother launch on the move.'

Starmer waited quietly at the top of the access ladder leading up to the suspended Rib as Denton was assisted down into it and across to the far jump seat positioned immediately in front of the crew cockpit, seats and controls. Julie was lifted from her feet by an over considerate Chalky and positioned in the second jump seat. Chalky stepped into the Rib and busied himself strapping his passengers into their seats.

Starmer took the opportunity to review the layout of the boat. There were two powerful Evinrude outboard motors over the stern with the crew cockpit immediately in front of them. The cockpit had two crew positions; back rests and jockey seats for the crew to sit astride. The Pilot's seat was on the starboard side with a wrap-around spray screen and the throttles and wheel easily to hand. In front of the crew on the other side of a low bulkhead, housing the launch and recovery lifting assembly, were the two jump seats occupied by Denton and Julie. Chalky offered Starmer a hand to ease him over the side and he carefully made his way down onto the deck area in front of Julie and Starmer, only slightly impeded by the bulky lifejacket. Once on the deck he sat between Denton's knees on the port side of the Rib; that nearest the cutter's hull.

He watched as Chalky braced himself with one hand on the hook assembly while the other held a stabilising line from the ship. He looked down at the deck below him as the Rib was swung out over the sea and then round over his shoulder, watching the Boatswain using his right hand to gently indicate with circular motion of his extended forefinger the extent and speed of descent required. Starmer got to his knees, leant in towards Denton and whispered over the sound of the Rib's idling outboards, 'brace yourself.'

With the boat still a good metre off the water, Starmer stood upright, reached over to the hook assembly and hammered down on the orange release lever with the flat of his hand. Instantly Chalky, who had been firmly gripping the hook protective cage was launched into the air as the Rib fell away beneath him.

The Boatswain screamed something unintelligible as the boat hit the water and Starmer, briefly clutching at Denton's shoulders to steady himself, reached over the spray shield, grabbed the wheel and turned it with one hand while hauling both throttle levers fully towards him with the other. Hanging on to both as the Rib made a fully powered skidding turn to starboard away from the cutter, Starmer only narrowly avoided the flailing arms of the Boatswain as he slid from his seat and over the side. He breathed a sigh of relief as Denton clambered into the cockpit, mid-shipped the wheel and eased the throttles.

'Some warning would've been nice.'

'It worked.'

'It did.' Denton scanned the instrument panel looking for the compass. Right, we're heading North. Den Helder here we come.'

'Den Helder?'

'Dutch naval base on the Ijsselmeer estuary.'

'Won't this stand out a bit if we leave it there?' Starmer waved his hand from fore to aft over the side of the Rib. 'Says 'HMC Sentinel' on the sides?'

'Courtesy visit maybe?' Denton shrugged, 'anyway, I'm not planning on hanging around long enough to find out.'

Starmer looked back nervously at the cutter behind him.

'Stop worrying. By the time they fish Chalky and the Boatswain out of the drink we'll be out of sight.'

Chapter Twenty

Dee sat on the bollard despondently viewing the chocolate waters of the Ijssel swirling and eddying round the hull of Jonny's barge. She eased her position slightly, gingerly, aware of the pitted and red rusted surface of the bollard and the effect that it may be having on her clean and tightly creased trousers. Her gaze swung moodily along the length of the hawser rope stretching from the bollard to the bow of the barge. She watched idly as the catenary curve of the rope alternately bellied and tightened with the eddies, squeezing a trail of droplets from the sisal as each tensioning lifted it from the water. Across the river, the bare branches of semi submerged trees marked the line of a flooded road, beyond which she could see swamped water meadows where a skein of ducks took flight to be briefly silhouetted against a blood orange sunset. Her attention was briefly diverted by a plastic bag which ballooned past her in the cold but light breeze, parascending down a set of granite steps to a stagnant dead pool of still water with the rainbow stains of fuel spillage and flotsam of waterlogged timbers floating in near perfect herringbone symmetry at the harbour's edge. Prompted by the slow clanking and rattle of a train crossing beneath the steel bow-spring arches of the bridge over the river to Hoven, she swivelled to follow its progress, lifting her gaze and panning round to view the town of Zutphen behind her.

She'd always thought of the town as ancient but somehow ageless in a way that she'd never experienced in The New World of The States that had sometimes nurtured her. Here, she'd found respite from the hard heads and harder hearts of the world she'd come to hate. Here, she'd found a balm for her wounds; a place to heal. A place where the history, ancient buildings and cobbled lanes of the old town dictated a pace and a tempo that matched her slow reawakening and her need to return to living and life. The isolation of the desert had been her previous salvation and living there with the extremes of temperature and climate had provided a discipline that had underpinned her recovery. Her arrival in Zutphen had been the continuation of that journey.

Amsterdam had been just a little bit too much for a fragility that saw her treat every encounter with a suspicion bordering on hostility. Her early attempts to secure work there had foundered in a confusion of exigencies; settling in while learning and surviving exposure to a very different society and culture. A day trip to Zutphen, a chance visit to the Café de Deur, a helping hand to a harassed waitress and Jos; the proprietor with the sense to recognise salvation when he saw it, brought her to live and work in this little town. Work that had been hard but rewarding, with sleepless nights becoming a thing of the past and new days being greeted with a sense of purpose and anticipation.

She'd found the changing clientele of the little bar, through different phases of the day, a source of quiet pleasure; the elderly taking lunch, with the time and the need to chat, the homeward bound in the early evening and the dedicated drinkers who didn't make it home and were then joined by the late crowd. She'd preferred those late shifts, particularly when Jos had organised an 'Event' or live music. Some of the acts had fallen far short of her own standards, even those she'd drifted down towards when at her worst. Somehow, though, it didn't seem to matter. The atmosphere, appreciation and support from the partisan clientele encouraged the mediocre towards the magical. She'd suspected that many of the performers finished their evenings convinced that the stars were inches from their grasp. She'd enjoyed her time on the other side of the footlights taking pleasure from the pleasure of others; performers and audience. Not once, during the busy summer months of that year had she felt the urge or the need to sing. For the first time since the death of her desert pianist she'd felt, if not complete, then at least content.

Some acts had appeared regularly and arrived complete with an entourage of aficionados. Others, less well supported, appeared earlier in the evening as supporting acts, setting up nervously before a gathering audience, that, whilst forgiving, had certain expectations of all performers. Several times Dee had watched one such act with interest. The pair wore matching outfits; crimson shirts with black pencil skirt and trousers. He, bearded and Beatle bobbed, on guitar and stool she blonde, chignoned and elegantly much taller than he. Their repertoire was limited to folk songs and a few standards and Dee had felt there was some commercial potential if only their harmonies had extended into their personal relationship. The on stage smiles and air kisses at the end of their set gave way to either silence or her tantrums when they returned to the bar. From a professional standpoint, Dee, had sympathised with the patient little man whose talent and musicianship underpinned the act and whose harmonies often covered her tendency to drift a semitone in either direction. She smiled to herself as she recalled that the same advice Mathew Sinclair had given her only a few days back, about her material and application, could equally have been applied to 'Nightshift'.

A particularly disharmonious rendition of 'I got you babe' with the chignon being vigorously shaken loose in a sulky display of misplaced artistic temperament as she left the small stage, had found the guitarist having to finish the duet solo without her 'little hand in mine'. Dee's heart had gone out to the man and she'd smiled encouragingly as he'd made his way through the crowd to the bar. He'd grinned and shrugged off his embarrassment, 'I don't suppose you can sing?'

Dee had laughed, 'not those sort of songs. No.'

His eyes had widened and for the first time, she'd seen him smile. 'What sort of songs do you sing?'

'Mainly Blues. Some standards but more West Coast than where you are.'

He'd rested the guitar case against the bar and leaned in earnestly, his face alongside hers, speaking into her ear over the noise from the bar. 'Seriously?'

She'd nodded, realising as she did so that she needed to perform to complete her return to the world. She could never be quite whole unless she were performing. 'Seriously? Yes, seriously. But I don't duet.' She'd paused, waiting for his response, then continued, 'you have a good voice but mine is better. You are a very good guitarist. We should play to our strengths. Don't you think?' She'd begun to move away, 'anyway,

313

tomorrow it will all seem different and you'll be back with your friend.'

'Nina.'

'Again, seriously? Nina? And I suppose you're Frederick?'

He'd laughed, no I'm Jonny but she is a Nina.' He'd gently taken her arm and had looked up earnestly into her face, 'I just know this could work. Look, I have a barge. We could practice there. Will you come?'

She stood, shrugged her coat collar up to her ears against the chill that had come with the loss of light and walked the few steps to the barge. Even in the gloaming it was possible to see the signs of dereliction and lack of maintenance to a craft that she suspected was no longer seaworthy. She recalled her earliest sight of the boat as she'd walked down the quay to that first rehearsal. All the paintwork had been in bright primary colours with carefully picked out mouldings in contrasting shades. The deck had been scrubbed to a snowy whiteness, brass fittings had glowed and glinted in the sunlight and ropes had been neatly laid in concentric circles with unattached ropes hung in gasket coils. The roof had been an ever-changing display of brightly coloured and decorated pots, pans, kettles, watering cans and flower pots filled with geraniums and trailing lobelia. One watering can now remained, on its side, gently rolling with the movement of the boat, its original station marked with a rusty ring on a, now, yellowing deck.

She glanced back down along the quay towards an old steam powered wharf crane with a lowered derrick overhanging the water. She watched a bird fly through the glassless window of the rust streaked corrugated iron cabin as the dying sun silhouetted the leaning, cranked, stove pipe chimney and jib against a clear cold sky. Sinclair came into view in the distance making his way back down the line of moorings towards her.

'Any luck?'

'No, nobody has been seen on that boat for weeks, although I'm not sure they'd have told me if they had. Whatnext?'

'I don't know,' she sighed, 'I really don't know.' She looked back distractedly towards the crane, trying to conceal her concern from Sinclair.

'Dee, why are we here?' He fidgeted as he struggled to keep the impatience out of his voice, 'remind me.'

She sighed, 'I've told you Matthew,' replying as patiently as she possibly could while feeling increasingly frustrated at his questioning. 'Think of Jonny as a local contact. Someone who might help us find a way through all this.' She looked wistfully over the moorings, remembering better, happier times and wondered whether she would ever find Denton and a chance to share that sort of contentment again.

'Well, we can't stand around here all night. Can I suggest we go and find somewhere to stay and rethink our next move somewhere warm?'

Sinclair offered his arm and they walked, in time, together, carefully stepping over mooring ropes, until they reached the steps that led back up to the main road. He hesitated on the first step, 'you know Dee, the more I think about this the more convinced I am that there is another way. A way that doesn't involve all of this running around, secret squirrel, cops and robbers stuff.' He glanced at her nervously, 'it's just I've been thinking that David is probably as much caught up in this as we are.' He gulped as he saw embryonic suspicions at the enormity of his proposal register on Dee's face. He hurried on. 'If only we could get him on his own, give him a chance to explain himself. All this' he flapped his arms, 'is a little outside my comfort zone.' His voice trailed off when he sensed her disapproval and he continued up the steps.

Dee didn't move follow but dragged him back viciously to a halt before pulling her arm free of his. She spluttered in disbelief, struggling to marshal thoughts into some sort of coherent response and failing. '"Outside your comfort zone"? What about the gun, false passports, all that cash and the assault on me? Is all that in your comfort zone? I thought we agreed that this was about survival. Is death in your comfort zone Mathew?' She slowed and breathed deeply to control her anger. Failing, she looked up at him, 'for fucks sake Matthew, I thought we'd been over this and you understood? Back in the flat we talked about survival. Have you forgotten them trying to shoot Denton?' She was surprised that he stood his ground in the face of her increasing anger and saw, again, a glint of the steel she'd seen him deploy when he'd forced her to consider her career choices all those weeks back.

315

'Dee,' he continued patiently, 'I have known David for some years now and he's just not like this.' He ran his fingers through his hair and knuckled his brows in frustration. 'This is simply not him. Maybe, just maybe, he started out doing a few dodgy things on the side and it grew a bit and then, maybe, it got out of control. Then before he knew where he was, he was up to his neck in trouble and fighting to save his business and look after his interests.'

'And "maybe, just maybe",' she parodied, 'he's a double dealing, slimy, bushwhacking, drug dealing, skunk motherfucker of a bastard who thinks nothing of dealing drugs on an industrial scale, getting people whacked and ruining people's lives. Someone who also, "maybe, just maybe", went out of his way to keep you in cloud cuckoo land where reality is kept at bay with little musical distractions, a riverside love nest and golden handcuffs.' Dee, could feel her voice continuing to rise with her anger. 'You stupid, stupid man. You cannot seriously be considering a reconciliation with that bastard, again. Surely to God, even you must realise by now what sort of man he is.' She knew she was out of control when Sinclair stumbled up the next step, now retreating in the face of her onslaught, as she shrieked, 'he's a fucking killer Mathew. He ordered my death for Christ's sake.'

'Hello Dee. The voice. You still have the voice. Yes?'

They both started and peered through the dark up towards the road where a small man dressed entirely in black sat at the top of the steps watching them.

'Hey, Jonny. Been there long?'

'Long time maybe yes.'

Dee knelt with her arms stretched wide in apparent supplication, holding a newspaper to the grate of the log burner to nurture flames from barely glowing embers. She looked along the length of the converted hold of the barge towards the eight steps leading up to the wheel house at deck level. Rising slightly on her haunches she could just about see one of Sinclair's brown brogues idly propped on the stainless-steel foot-rail to the Captains' swivel chair with the other rested in the lower segment of the ships wheel. Again, she wondered at his mood and attitude, one of which had darkened while the other had worsened. The argument on the quay, she knew, was the root cause of the problem but she suspected that Jonny's arrival had not helped, although was at a loss to know why. What she did know was that that Sinclair's truculence was making matters worse with every passing minute.

With the roar from the hearth and the crackle of flame consuming paper as the fire took, she crumpled the singed remains of 'Nederlands Dagblag' into a ball and tossed it onto the crackling logs. When first she'd followed Jonny below deck there had been an airlessness, a faint whiff of bilge and a musty smell to the cabin which she now hoped the heat would dispel. She was thankful that the external neglect that she'd noticed earlier hadn't reached the inside of the barge. The two ergonomic, leather recliners covered with the throws they'd found in the old van they'd used were still there along with one of the original seats. Everything else seemed to be much as she remembered although the Bang and Olufsen sound system was missing and where there had once been a large television there was now only a tangle of cables. Her slight sense of inebriation was finally explained when she noticed that the level of the dirty water, barely covering a collection of used crockery in the sink, wasn't parallel with the deck. She hoped the list was due to tight moorings and not a problem with the hull.

She'd had good times in this cabin, she reflected. Their first rehearsal had been more enjoyable than productive but she had been enthralled by Jonny's guitar skills. It had quickly become apparent that he'd dumbed down for the sets in the Café de Deur, presumably in deference to Nina's assumed lead role. His technique was essentially classical but adapted to his musical tastes that saw jazz expression applied to near primitive finger picked blues licks. There were Charlies, Christian and Byrd, with more than a nod to Django and Segovia in his work. He had a reverence for, and an ability with, the un-amplified instrument that put mellow gut way in front of plectrum picked steel. He'd backed her through some standards and while they'd both been pleased they hadn't been delighted. Instinctive but consummate musicians both, they'd realised that the line-up didn't work. They'd needed a percussion, rhythm and a horn section and Dee had been surprised to learn that Jos, the proprietor, played saxophone and his sister bass.

317

The first set, at the café, had been one of the more amazing performances of her career. She'd opened with Fitzgerald, eased onto Simone, wandered through her own arrangements from 'Tapestry', upped the pace with Etta James and haunted her way home with 'Cry me a River.' She'd been pleased with her performance but what followed had kept her firmly anchored in the anonymity she'd originally sought in Europe. As the applause had died with her passage to the bar, Jonny had started a solo performance that had stunned her and the packed house. There had been reverential silence as he rolled into a series of themes and variations around Byrd's 'Blues for Night People'. Jonny wove his way through the tripartite suite with due deference to the composition but with an interpretation that embroidered, enhanced and enthralled. The second half of the set had struggled by comparison and, lesson learned, in the busy months that had followed they'd revised the set list to build to that climactic finish and she and Jonny had become Stars.

From then until the following summer their little band had wandered the province of Gelderland, courtesy of contacts provided by Jos, playing small clubs, hotel bars, Universities and the odd chi chi watering hole. Jos had taken to management with a vigour that suggested he was more interested in volume than value and what, for Dee, had originally been a delight, began to remind her of the grind from which she'd walked away. During the long hours of the early morning return journeys in the clapped-out Citroen H van she'd begun to feel less and less a part of the group and more of a disapproving onlooker.

She'd expected drugs to be part of the scene but had been surprised how quickly they'd become a major part of Jonny's life. Things had come to a head in Amsterdam in a club off Leidseplein when she and Jonny had realised that they were not being paid but auditioned. The consequent argument with Jos and the resultant tensions ruined the set. A maliciously, malevolent agent had delighted in what he recognised as Dee's fall from fame to a level where his opinion mattered. It had taken a coked-up Jonny appreciable moments to realise that Dee was known, not only to the agent, but to a far wider audience. At the dawning realisation that she had once occupied the heights to which he now aspired, and with fuel being added to the fire by the odious little man, Jonny had hit her. She had returned to The States that night.

318

She stood at the foot of the companionway leading to the deck house, leant forward, rested her elbows on the fifth step and craned her neck upwards to see Sinclair. 'It's warming up a bit. Why don't you come down?'

Sinclair appeared, rested his elbows on the hooded entrance hatch and looked down. 'Dee I'm not comfortable with this.'

'Not comfortable with what precisely?'

'Your position on David, your refusal to listen, the whole situation that we're in, your little friend. You name it really.'

'My "little friend"?'

'Oh right, let me be more precise,' he said impatiently. 'Your scruffy, unwashed, drugged up mate with the alcohol problem, halitosis and attitude. The friend who you thought,' he snorted, 'I would warm to instantly because we are both gay? Gays, of course,' he ranted sarcastically, 'all being promiscuous, fickle and incapable of commitment. That little friend. Ok?'

'Have you any idea how camp that sounded?'

'Have you any idea how insulting it is for you to assume that I'd be interested in any man other than David? Do you think I'd risk what I have with David for that,' he sat down suddenly on the top step and slapped his knees repeatedly in exasperation, 'that oik!'

'I'm sorry,' she acknowledged, 'it was a mistake to mention the gay thing. He is gay, yes, but he is also a very gifted musician, a talented man and normally clean and tidy. But that's not what this is about is it?' She moved up a step and took his hand. 'Mathew, none of this is our fault. We are where we are because of the actions of others. As for you risking "what you have with David", it's gone Mathew. If it was ever there. You're angry because you don't want to accept it.'

Sinclair looked down at her and slowly released her hand. 'Dee, I'm sick of having these sorts of conversations with you.'

'What sort of conversations?'

'The ones where you're right and I'm stupid.'

'You're far from stupid Mathew but you are seeing this from way too close. Back up and test what I'm telling you against the facts.'

He sighed, 'maybe, I just don't know anymore.' He propped his elbows on his knees and dropped his jaw into his hands. 'Do you think your little friend will come back with all that money you gave him?' He laughed, 'my bet is that he's face down in a puddle of Amstel with a needle stuck in his arm and a big butch gay basher biding his time.'

'He'll be back. We needed supplies and somewhere quiet and out of the way to stay. He needed help. But then so do we. He'll be back. Trust me.'

Dee looked across the table to Jonny who was toying with the remains of his meal. Sinclair had been right. The man hadn't been looking after himself at all. There were deep shadows under his eyes and his unshaven cheeks were sunken and sallow. His hair was unkempt and streaked with grey and his eyes were the shade of yellow that haunts the mirrors of the alcoholic. The collar of his shirt was frayed and grubby and the sour smell of his unwashed body was winning the battle over the whiff of bilge and bolognaise sauce.

'You can still cook,' Dee smiled.

'Glad you enjoyed it,' he nodded towards the wheelhouse, 'your friend? No hungry?'

'Been a bad few days.'

'It sound like it.'

'How much did you hear?'

'Most? You want to tell? Why you are here?'

'Let's talk about us first. What happened after I left?'

'It all falls apart. What you expect?' He slapped the kitchen counter in disgust.

She waited a moment to let his anger subside, 'well to start with I hadn't expected you to act as irrationally as you did that night, and I certainly hadn't expected to be assaulted.'

This time a fist came down hard on the counter, rattling the dishes, 'Dee, it come like thunderbolt to hear that I had been playing with the second fiddle to a Superstar.' He paused, shook his head slowly from side to side and took a deep breath. He then looked across at her and grinned ruefully. 'I'd been sort of thinking I was hotshot; you were newbie studying ropes; you were below my wing. When I hear who you are I feel deceived, betrayed, a fool, stupid. Stupid was worst part. When you gone, I kept thinking and asking myself how could I have been so stupid to think little Jonny van Rijn from Zuptphen had discovered and nurtured this talent.' He smiled sadly, 'Oh Dee, I had such plans. It was going to take us to such places.'

'Jonny, I was in Holland, in the first place, to recover from a whole series of disasters that had overtaken me during my time as a,' she mimed air quotes, '"Superstar". I was in Zutphen recovering. And doing quite well. Then the chance came along and it was good to be able to get back to performing. How the hell was I to know that I'd linked up with one of the best guitarists in Europe?'

'One?'

She laughed, 'I had no interest whatsoever in taking it further than gigs in bars and clubs. It was you, and Jos, that had the big ideas. Not me.'

'You could have told me Dee.'

'And I regret that I didn't. So, what did happen after I left?'

'I am four years in de gevangenis.'

Dee was suddenly reminded that while Jonny sometimes spoke perfectly idiomatic, if slightly accented, English, when upset he slipped into Dutch. 'In prison, why?'

Jonny shrugged. 'Jos sack the group. I stay on in Amsterdam for some months but I couldn't get gigs. Those I get I mess up.' He began toying with his uneaten food again, 'drugs became a way of my life. I need gigs to pay for drugs and drugs to do gigs. Believe me Dee, you know you hit bottom when they shout in a brothel at you to go. I can't stop, I don't know how to stop and then I don't want to stop. But, eventually, I clean up my act and for many months I take not drugs. But no money I have. Then dealing I begin.'

Not for the first time in her life Dee wondered at the idiocy of an industry that failed to find and nurture talent and then destroyed those that did accidentally make it with the stardust of substance abuse. How many times had she heard of or witnessed the destruction of a talent by the excesses of the world of show business? To then see the poor souls who had slithered to death or oblivion glorified as icons of rock 'n roll was the ultimate obscenity. 'When did you get out?'

'I am two months here.'

'How's it going?'

'I am everyday working for my father. Him you remember? He still owns farm. He is pleased. I think. He knows I struggle with booze and sometimes the drugs but he asks just that I come each day to the farm and work some hours. That is helping.' Jonny, leant back and waved his arm around the cabin, 'my father, he care for barge for me while I am in prison. But I have very little.' He vaguely waved at the spaces previously occupied by the television and stereo. 'I have to sell things to live.'

'Your Guitars?'

'Yes, them also I sell.'

'Oh Jonny. We'll get them back. I promise.'

They both looked up sharply at the sound of the wheelhouse door opening and then sliding shut with a rattle of glass. 'This Mathew, he is your friend?'

She nodded. 'Yes, a good friend,' she brightened, 'and a musician. Gone to get some air I expect.' She smiled, disguising her concern, as she wondered just what was going through Sinclair's mind.

'He doesn't like me. It is because I am gay. Ja?'

'Oh, if only it were that simple Jonny.'

'So, Dee, now you tell me about this man who ordered you to death and then I will know why you come to see Jonny.'

Dee pushed back and stood up from the kitchen counter to make her way across the galley to the sink. There she started the barely remembered sequence for pumping water from tank to tap. She looked back over her shoulder, 'coffee?' Johnny didn't answer. 'Did you hear me Jonny?' He seemed to slowly gather his senses as he swivelled on the stool to face her, his arms crossed defensively and his face conflicted with expressions ranging from perplexity to concern. She wasn't surprised. The retelling of the story had taken over an hour. An hour during which his frustration at what he considered to be her stupidity had seen heated exchanges between them.

'Which way I look at this Dee I cannot make it sensible. I am not sure how I understand such a story. Why you get involved with this? Do you know how dangerous these people are? You crazy?' He paused to collect his thoughts then slipped from the stool and made his way to stand beside her at the sink. Carefully he reached up, placed an arm round her shoulders and pulled her to him. She slipped her arm round his waist and squeezed to acknowledge his concern, glad, if for nothing else, that events from the past seemed forgotten. At least for the moment. He released his hold as memory and instinct saw her reach for the coffee in the right cupboard.

'The bit that I not understand is why you want so much to rescue this man Denton. You are knowing him for how long? Years? No. You know him days only. You could place in danger you and Mister Sinclair for this? Why you do this Dee?'

With one hand on the handle of a kettle she took several deep breaths waiting for it to come to the boil. She fought hard to control her rising impatience as she considered the best way to respond to the not unreasonable questions that Jonny was asking. There had been times during her explanation when he had been openly scornful of her involvement and motivation. She realised, now, that if she were to enlist his help she first had to gain his understanding and sympathy.

'In a sense, Jonny, it sort of crept up on me. I told you about Denton's daughter, I told you about the race to try and find her and out of that one thing led to another. You are right though. Considering the short time that I knew Denton there was no relationship worthy of the name. Certainly not one that can explain to you why am I here and trying to help him. Except,' she paused to pour the water over the coffee granules, 'for two reasons. First, he is a decent man, an honest man and I know that all he's trying to do is protect his family from harm. He is in the middle of something that he probably doesn't understand and he needs help. I offered that help. I can't walk away now. Can I? I know that world Jonny. I've lived there.' She found herself absent mindedly waving the teaspoon at him as she tried to marshal her thoughts. 'But yes, I was,' she paused, 'am, attracted to him. It would be nice to think that there could be some sort of future with him but I'm not doing this with just that in mind.'

Jonny took the coffee to the counter and hiked himself back on to the stool. 'So, then you find Denton. What you do then?'

'Jonny, I don't know. I wish I did. I wish I had a plan but I don't really. What I do know is that these people are vicious. I don't think Denton is and I don't think he has any real idea of what he is up against. Maybe, I can talk him round. Maybe there's a way to stop this? Walk away perhaps?'

'What you want for me to do?'

'Help me?'

'How?'

'Well, you'll remember that they held me against my will and that Williams ordered me to be got rid of? That means I really don't think it's safe for Mathew or me to be wandering around near this place at Warnsborn that I told you about. So, I thought that maybe, because you live round here, you could, oh, I don't know, reconnoitre? Maybe, you could find Denton before he runs into trouble and bring him here? Do you know this place? Warnsborn?'

'Very well.'

Dee, paused, momentarily confused as to whether Jonny was agreeing to help or conceding knowledge of Warnsborn. 'I'm sorry Jonny, what do you mean?'

'I will help. Also, I know Warnsborn; Langoed Groot.'

'That's it. That's the place.' She laughed with relief. 'How do you know it?'

'My father's farm is on the estate. I grew up there.'

'Jonny, that's marvellous.'

He shrugged, 'not so marvellous. It is a bad place. The people are not good people. The house was sold and the new people are not for my father liking.'

Dee digested this information and for the first time since she'd escaped from Williams felt a sense of achievement. 'Could we go to your father's place?'

'That is what I am thinking. Yes, we go there. From there we will find this marvellous Mister Denton who I think you must love. Yes?'

'If'n I was a little ole white girl there Mister Jonny Sah! I might just have blushed,' she giggled. From the bemused but serious look on his face she guessed that he harboured real concerns about the task in front of them and that she would be well advised to mark those fears. She coughed away the rest of the giggle and straightened her features. 'Can we see the house from the farm?'

'No, but to get to the house you must first pass farm. Now we need to sleep I think. Your friend, he will come back?'

Dee looked at her watch, 'he should be back by now. He only went out to get some air.'

'Getting air? This is an English thing? He walks at night when it is freezing?'

Dee acknowledged his comment with a shrug, 'mad dogs and Englishmen eh?' and wondered at Sinclair's continued absence.

'Ok, tomorrow, at early dawn, I will go to see Jos. I will borrow his van. Then we can go to the farm in private.'

'In secret?' She smiled.

He laughed, 'in van.' He looked down at his feet swinging twelve inches from the floor and sighed, 'you know Dee I am sorry for what happened. For every day, I think of you. Every night, in prison, I think about the time we have, good times.' There was an appreciable period of emotionally charged silence and then he quietly sobbed, pulled a dirty handkerchief from his pocket and said, 'I think I used to love you a little bit Dee Dee Wilson.'

Dee pulled him roughly from the stool and into her arms, 'just a little bit?' He tried to answer but was overcome by sobs. She bent and kissed the top of his head, beginning to realise just how much of an impact she had made in the little man's life and he in hers. 'I love you too Jonny. When this is over we are gonna tour big time. And I mean big time. There is a world out there that needs to hear you play.'

She wasn't sure whether it was the dawn light streaming through the opening lights at deck level or the sound of the car door slamming that woke her. She dressed hurriedly, hoping that Jonny would make some coffee while she took the chance to shower and change. She emerged from the sleeping cabin into the saloon with a wash bag in one hand and a towel in the other to the sound of the wheelhouse door sliding open.

She shouted up the stairs, 'Jonny, get the kettle on I'll be with you in a minute.' She paused on her way forward to the heads, puzzled at the lack of response and looked up the companionway to the wheelhouse. Her heart hammered in her chest and double timed adrenaline to her brain at the sight of the highly-polished Oxfords and a shin's length of pinstriped trouser. As the rest of Williams came into view, slowly, step by step, she retreated aft down the saloon towards the cabin.

'Good morning Dee. I trust you slept well,' he rasped.

'Fuck off David,' she fired off desperately, still retreating and foolishly but furiously annoyed that she had countered his urbanity with profanity.

'Oh Dee, ever the Lady.'

'What are you doing here,' she burbled, wondering at the inanity of her question almost before she'd finished asking it.

'You got screwed again Dee.'

'Mathew?'
'No, your little Dutch friend.'
'Jonny?'
'Jonny the dealer.'

Chapter Twenty - one

Denton swept his gaze across the harbour and out towards the entrance half expecting to see HMC Sentinel looming through the mizzle.

'They won't come in here.'

'How'd you reach that conclusion,' Denton snapped.

'They'd have too much to explain?'

'That won't stop that devious little bastard Church.'

'Think about it?' Starmer suggested.

'I have.'

'Then think again Mister Denton,' replied Starmer as sharply. 'If we were right, that he was sending us to Zandvoort to meet a reception committee, all he has to do now is redirect them here.'

'How will he know we're here?'

Starmer sighed, 'The Rib bobbing around in the harbour might be a clue. Remember?'

Denton's shoulders slumped in tired recognition of Starmer's logic. 'We don't have long then.'

'No, and there's a lot to do.'

'What?'

'Well, at the, moment we look as though we've just been plucked from the Belgrano.' He opened his arms wide inviting Denton's appraisal of the brightly coloured seafaring attire that he'd looted from the German's yacht. 'We need fresh clothes, money and a quick way out of here. We're already attracting attention.' He nodded back along the jetty towards a dockside bar where two men stood outside, smoking, while a third leant against an old Ford, all eyeing their little group with the hollowed hungry eyes of those used to living on the fringes of society.

Denton pivoted quickly on his heel and pointed up a pedestrianised street to a large, squat, circular brick water tower that struggled skywards in a half-hearted attempt to bring some height to an otherwise drably horizontal town. 'There,' he pointed, 'that looks like the town centre.'

'Yeah, and if that sign is right there's a railway station up that way too,' advised Starmer waving at a municipal tourist board. 'So, that's the way out. Now what we need is money,' he nodded at Julie, 'and maybe some stuff?' He shrugged the rucksack higher onto his shoulder while his mind raced over possible ways to convert some of the money it contained into Guilders. 'Make your way to the station and lose the waterproofs on the way.' He instructed.

Julie turned back from her study of the street, 'where are you going?' Julie demanded.

'To take care of business,' he grinned. 'Don't worry I'll be back with you before you know.'

She looked pleadingly at him.

'I know. That's where I'm going.'

She smiled.

Starmer hitched his arm through the other ruck sack strap and marched straight through the two at the entrance to the little bar, brushing one aside and barging the other into the door frame on the way. They bridled but Starmer caught the look from the man by the car that stopped them both from reacting further. Now he knew who he would have to deal with. It took a few moments for his eyes to adjust to the gloom within the narrow bar which consisted simply of a counter and a long alley, barely six feet wide, lined with stools, leading to toilets and a kitchen at the rear. From out of the gloom a woman with the yellowed, deeply etched and dried parchment face and yellowing beehive of the committed smoker wheezed her way towards him. As she neared Starmer saw her eyes flick towards the door and was reassured to see that the driver had followed him in. She leant forward across the dimpled, sheet copper counter, taking her weight on sizeable forearms while displaying expanses of desiccated cleavage. She nodded an invitation for him to place an order.

He stooped and, from his sock, withdrew a quarter brick of sterling which he slapped on the bar between her elbow and an old-fashioned soda syphon in a scruffy, lattice worked, metal ewer. 'You speak English?' The woman's eyes narrowed as Starmer continued, 'I want to buy some drugs.' The woman gave no sign that she had heard but placed her palm on top of the bundle, riffled the notes with her thumb and glanced knowingly at the driver who now stood five feet away with his elbow resting on the bar. If this guy was a dealer, Starmer guessed, he was also a user. He was tall but gaunt and there was not an ounce of spare flesh on him. The assured stare from the bloodshot eyes suggested street credentials but the constant tapping of a shoe on the foot rail hinted at a chemical boost to that confidence.

'What do you need?'

'What have you got?'

'Whatever you need.'

'H?'

'How much?'

Starmer nodded at the money on the bar, peeled off two hundred pounds, pocketed the rest and enquired, 'how much'll that get me?'

The cadaver looked at the woman who nodded and disappeared towards the kitchen while he counted the cash and tried hard to ignore the much larger wad just visible in Starmer's pocket. On her return, she handed a freezer bag containing sachets to the dealer. He opened the bag and began to count packets out onto the counter. Starmer reached across, firmly removed the freezer bag and its contents from his grasp, scooped up the sachets on the bar and stuffed the lot inside his jacket. 'I think that's a fair price,' he said, nodding towards the two hundred, 'specially at the current rate of exchange. Gonna use your toilet?'

The stunned silence followed him all the way to the washroom. There were three cubicles and a urinal with a window above. He quickly unlatched the window, pushed it up to open it wide and then retreated to the cubicle nearest the door. He'd planned for a two-stage operation and wasn't disappointed when the two acolytes appeared. The first in, seeing the window, rushed forward, stepped up onto the urinal step and strained to see out. The last twigged that there was somebody behind him just as Starmer's kick to the back of his knees dropped him to the floor. He grabbed the fallen man by the collar as he stepped over him and ran his head into the urine stained porcelain.

Unconscious, the man dropped into the trough, limiting the options of the other, still at the window, who stumbled backwards over his fallen mate. Starmer assisted him further on his way with a vicious backward elbow to the throat as he struggled to rise. Leaving one unconscious and the other gasping for breath, fighting to force his Adams apple from his trachea, Starmer opened the door to the bar.

He'd reckoned that the shock factor of his reappearance in good shape should be good for five paces but in the event had to run two of those and sprint the remaining three. He grabbed the soda syphon in passing and broke the arm holding the knife before reversing the swing and silencing the scream by smashing the siphon into the driver's face. He picked up the knife and turned to the woman behind the bar. 'Open the till.'

Not a flicker of emotion crossed her face as she moved slowly to the old-fashioned cash till and stabbed down on a key to open the draw. 'There is not so much,' she shrugged, 'it is early.'

Starmer nodded thoughtfully, waved her away from the front of the till with the knife and pointed to some blue and white bank bags on the shelf below. He slipped one of the bags open saw a wadge of sun flowered fifty Guilder notes, knelt by the driver, stuffed bags, drugs and cash from the till into the ruck sack, then went through the man's pockets to find his keys. The driver groaned into consciousness and tried to lever himself from the floor with the wrong arm and screamed again. Starmer leant over him speaking quietly and considerately, 'you really need a new line of work. You are not very good at this.'

Denton sat on a slatted steel bench outside Den Helder station watching the hands on the station clock crawl sluggishly towards the half hour. He had promised himself that if Starmer hadn't appeared by half past he and Julie would have to make a move. He was reluctant to admit it but he felt vulnerable without the younger man's support. Some of the fire and determination behind his intentions for Webber seemed to have slipped from him as he fought against exhaustion. Julie was also showing signs of fatigue which, overlaid with signs of withdrawal, left her alternately agitated and withdrawn. The thought that the Zandvoort reception party might be heading his way caused a rush of fear that very nearly overwhelmed what little resolve he had left.

He and Julie had shed the waterproofs which, while aiding their concealment, had done nothing for their comfort in the cold air. Julie was shivering uncontrollably and he was chilled to the bone. For the hundredth time, he scanned the station car park for a sign or sight of anything unusual. Quite what he was looking for or expected to see wasn't clear. He turned to put his arm around Julie and cuddled her to him. Over her shoulder, he saw another vehicle enter the car park. The thought only hit him after it had passed; left hand drive and a GB sticker. He watched as the Range Rover completed a circuit of the car park and headed towards the exit. He began to breathe a sigh of relief, then held it, as the vehicle turned back on the road, towards the entrance. He pulled Julie to her feet and took a step forward before leaping back as a battered old Ford screeched to a halt in front of him and a door swung open.

'Get in! They're here!' As the doors slammed shut Starmer let the clutch out against a screaming flywheel and the Ford fishtailed towards the exit scattering a group of uniformed Royal Netherlands Navy personnel on the way.

The Range Rover had, eventually, been lost after a virtuoso display of full throttle reversing, hand brake turns and a sequence of wrong way travel down semi pedestrianised streets. Denton's anxiety had been palpable and then vocal as they came to a skidding halt at a level crossing. 'For fuck's sake!'

Starmer glanced in the rear-view mirror and saw panic and uncertainty flicker across Julie's eyes at her father's outburst. 'Mister Denton you need to calm down.'

'Calm down, fucking calm down. Are you serious? We go from one disaster to another. We get through one then we hit another.' He rocked in his seat, then rose out of it and slammed his hand down hard onto the dashboard, 'when's it going to end?' As he sank back in the seat, exhausted, a huge blue and yellow double decker train thundered down the single track, its turbulence rocking the little car as it passed. As the silence returned Denton half turned in his seat and addressed them both, 'I'm sorry.' His subsiding fury was gradually replaced by a nagging sensation that something was missing. Something that would ease the emotions and slow his racing brain; the buzz that only that first drink could bring.

For the next twenty miles, the road paralleled the railway with an algae and pond weed smothered ditch between it and the bund carrying the track. Denton noticed that the fields on the other side of the road were waterlogged and in the lower areas flooded. As they hit the ring road round Amsterdam he picked out the first signs for Arnhem and the memories of his last visit drifted over him.

After Eleanor Joan's death 'Aitch had become withdrawn, almost melancholic and no number of visits seemed to make very much difference. Occasionally he'd venture out for a pint, or two, but he seemed to have lost his conviviality. The enforced sociability of lunch in a pub had only served to emphasize his loneliness. 'Aitch's sullen responses to Denton's conversational gambits had discouraged him from arranging more trips. Then, a chance comment from a colleague, in a Territorial Parachute Regiment, about the celebrations planned for the fortieth anniversary of the Battle of Arnhem, had got Denton thinking. Forewarned by the failure of his earlier attempt to get 'Aitch over to Dunkirk he had approached this venture more carefully. In the event, it had taken little persuasion. Denton had wondered whether the loss of Joan's company had pushed 'Aitch to consider revisiting a time when comradeship of a different sort had been vital to his survival.

Denton had been staggered at the numbers attending the commemorative parachute drop over Ginkle Heath. Serried ranks of veterans gazed skywards as seven hundred parachutists dropped from equally venerable Dakotas or the more up to date Hercules. 'Aitch had stood in silence throughout, occasionally moving his stick from one hand to the other in silent rebuke to those in folding chairs. Whether intentionally or not, he stood slightly apart from his fellow veterans. His refusal to wear "another uniform" of blazer, beret and campaign medals served to exclude him from the beery company of his contemporaries whose presence in their hotel was another cause for grumbling.
They'd returned to the hotel bar where 'Aitch's usual reluctance to socialise or converse shrivelled before the wide and adoring smile of a young Dutch barmaid. 'Aitch, in response to her enquiry, acknowledged, not altogether reluctantly, that he was indeed a Veteran and spoke several, halting sentences in Dutch.

Denton smiled to himself as he recalled the conversation and what he had later come to see as a turning point in 'Aitch's grieving for Joan.

'I didn't know you could speak Dutch.'

'Had to learn,' 'Aitch smiled and took a sip of his beer, 'at least well enough to get by.'

'You ever gonna tell me about Arnhem?'

He had seemed genuinely surprised and a little puzzled, 'do you really want to know?'

'Not just me. The kids would like to know and in a sense, I think that you owe it to me, and them, to tell us.' Denton remembered a long moment of silence before he continued. 'We're all very proud of you. You did some amazing things and stuff happened during the war and it would be nice to know a little bit more about it.' Denton had noticed a look of poignant sadness settle onto the old man's features.

He'd sighed and taken a deep breath, 'It was a war. None of it was amazing,' he'd said sadly. 'It was pretty much what everybody expected a war to be; strange, bloody, inhuman, frightening and dirty. But mostly it was confusing.' He'd looked over at a table of veterans and their families. The men neatly attired in their navy blazers and regimental ties and proudly sporting the maroon beret, their prouder wives, in summer Sunday best.' He'd nodded towards them, 'to listen to them talk you'd think we'd all understood on the day what was going on. Oh, we all knew we had to take a bridge and I knew roughly where it was but by the end of the first day that was not the problem. From then on, all I knew was what was happening in the next hedge or house. Hindsight makes it sound different from how it was.' One of the blazered brigade had noticed his scrutiny and gave 'Aitch a cheerful wave. He had waved back, 'brave lads though. All of 'em,' he'd muttered and sniffed.

'You make it sound as though you weren't,' Denton had offered.

'Aitch had grinned, 'I had me moments,' the set of his features hardened, 'I was lucky. Many weren't. You see,' he had continued, 'hindsight is not always a bad thing. At least I now know what went wrong which means I can make a little more sense of what happened to me.'

He had taken another pull on the Amstel, 'the Army has a saying, "No plan survives implementation". So, they came up with a plan and gave it a bloody stupid name; "Market Garden". Well,

Intelligence was wrong, the plan was flawed, we got shot out of the sky and then we bumped into an SS Division that wasn't supposed to be there.' He clunked the empty glass back on the table and laughed, 'I remember a Major telling me it was "frightfully bad luck them turning up" as though it was all a game. We fought long and hard for maybe seven, maybe eight days. I can't remember. Towards the end, me and a couple of mates had fallen back to the edge of a copse with a small track behind leading down to a church. Somewhere along the way I had inherited a Polish machine-gun crew. So, we dug in and waited. We didn't wait long. A couple of tanks, along with what looked like a company of SS advanced towards us.'

'Aitch had sighed and pulled a snow-white handkerchief from his pocket, removed his glasses and mopped his ever-watering eyes. 'You need to remember that we were only supposed to be there for forty-eight hours. So, by this time we were out of food and very low on ammunition. Water was the main problem though; we were all dying of thirst.' The word had prompted 'Aitch into action and he had swung round in his chair and waved his empty glass in the general direction of the young Dutch barmaid who rushed fresh supplies to the table. 'When their ammunition went, the Poles retreated and we weren't very far behind. We scarpered into the copse where we got split up. I was with two others and suddenly from about twenty-five yards away a machine gun opened up.' He chuckled, 'being machine gunned from twenty-five yards is a sobering experience; trees got chopped down. Christ knows how they got so near without anybody bloody noticing. Anyway, by the grace of God, that had to be the worst machine gunner in the Wehrmacht. We dived behind a mound which turned out to be a dung heap.' He laughed bitterly, 'didn't matter, all I needed, at the time, was somewhere between me and that bloody Spandau. He might have been the worst machine gunner in the world but he knew we weren't going anywhere and he fired a couple of bursts either side of the mound; an invitation to surrender. So, we gingerly stepped out and walked towards him. He and his mates sat us down and gave us cigarettes and water.'

He had paused in his account and then glanced across at the veterans table as one of their number concluded a story by waving his beret in the air. 'Aitch had continued, 'that's the strange thing about that battle. There was a sort of weird element of chivalry, respect, between us and the SS; strange considering

334

what I learnt later.' He mused. 'Anyway, from there we got carted off to a place they used as a hospital; The Tafelberg hotel. A lot of the wounded from the battle seem to have been taken there and I and another guy were put up on the first floor. It had been our Aid Station but, a few days after I got there, the Germans arrived and started clearing the wounded away. I thought that the flesh wound in my thigh wouldn't be considered serious enough for me to be kept in a hospital. And there was talk of the lightly wounded being shipped out to Germany. So, I decided to escape.' He took a long draft of the Amstel and wiped froth from his upper lip while he considered the next part of his story.

'That night I, and this other bloke, carefully unpicked some cord that was decoratively stitched along the bottom of the curtains. We collected enough to lower ourselves down to ground level. Then we started to walk.' 'Aitch, had slapped his thigh and then kneaded the muscles as though reliving the discomfort of that night. 'Well, I had seriously underestimated that wound,' he chuckled, 'and I was delaying him. After what seemed hours I decided that he should go it alone. I sat on a wall outside this big old farmhouse at the foot of a lane while I decided what to do. This is now maybe an hour before dawn. I had this feeling I was being watched and I turned around and there, peering round the slightly open door was a young boy. Behind him was a couple in night clothes; Mum and Dad. They took me in.' He examined his empty glass from all sides before setting it down on the table.

'By this time the area was alive with escaping squaddies and the Germans had mounted an operation to sweep up as many as possible. I later got the feeling that the Dutch resistance was swamped and didn't really know quite what to do with all these soldiers. Anyway, it was pretty obvious I was gonna be a liability until my leg healed so I was hidden behind a false wall in some outbuildings behind the farmhouse.' He had sighed and then chuckled again, now plainly enjoying the retelling of his escapades, 'The boy would bring me food and drink, mum would redress the wound and I would come out in the evenings and play cards with them and smoke. God, how I loved that first fag of the evening.'
'Aitch had paused reflectively and Denton had then seen the muscles in his jaw tighten. 'It would all have been quite peaceful but for the fact that news began to filter back that the

Germans were taking reprisals on all Dutch civilians who had been caught helping any escaping British soldiers. By this time my wound had begun to turn septic. There was no way I could escape down the usual routes and so had to simply stay put until I had healed. Andries, the farmer, was so concerned that he sent the boy to fetch the local doctor. This was a massive risk for them all. But they took that chance. They risked everything for me.'

'Aitch had slipped into a companionable silence and Denton had taken the chance to consider the progress that seemed to have been made. On balance, he had been pleased; they had had a conversation; the first in many years.

The next morning Denton had been surprised to find 'Aitch already at breakfast and enjoying the ministrations of his favourite barmaid. He'd barely had time to sit before 'Aitch had enquired, 'can we hire a car?'

'Of course, where would you like to go?' Denton had replied, more than delighted that at prospect of further conversation with 'Aitch.

It had taken time for him to orientate himself and eventually they'd had to return to the 'Hospital' near Oosterbeek from where he'd escaped to retrace the route back from there to the farmhouse. Denton had been amazed, when, eventually, they had located it, at just how far 'Aitch had dragged himself and his flesh wound that night. As instructed, Denton had pulled up in sight of, but some distance from the house. 'What do you want to do?' he'd enquired.

'I'm not sure,' the confidence that 'Aitch'd displayed at breakfast seemed to have deserted him. 'The thing is Paul, they might not want to see me.'

Denton, chancing all, seeing his Father's obvious distress, had taken his hand. 'Why ever not?'

The old man had sharply retrieved his hand and stared down the road at the farmhouse. 'You'll remember that it was decided that I should stay where I was until I was fully healed. By that time there was no chance of escape back to the Allied armies. The North of Holland had effectively been shut off and the Germans were starving the population. They'd taken all the supplies to feed their retreating troops. So, as I recovered and began to feel stronger, I took an interest in what was going on around me. Which is another way of saying I got fed up with hiding and began to take chances,' he had frowned, 'and I'd learnt some Dutch by then.' He'd sighed heavily, 'Andries was away somewhere with the Resistance, the boy was at school and, instead of being hidden I was in the barn when the Germans came,' he shrugged.

It had taken Denton a few minutes to appreciate the real depth of his Father's concerns, 'so, if we're not going in, why are we here?'

'To see if I've been forgiven,' the old man had grunted as he'd levered himself from the car.

They had slowly made their way across the farm yard towards the rear of the house where the top section of a half glazed stable door afforded a glimpse into a large kitchen. As they had neared the door both halves had swung open to reveal an elderly woman with an unwrinkled, broad, fresh, smiling face framed by a shock of silver hair held loosely off her brow with a brightly coloured headscarf. She smiled enquiringly at them both as she stopped the swing of the upper door with one hand and hefted the washing basket higher up on her hip with the other. Denton had felt 'Aitch slump against his side as the old man had gasped, 'Hallo. Grietje, is dat echt u?'

The basket had dropped to the floor as the woman's hands had flown to her face and her eyes had widened, 'Beste Harry, oh beste Harry, je lieve man. U bent terug gekomen.'

'Yes, Grietje, it is Harry.'

Denton started from his reverie to the sound of klaxons, followed by the sideways lurch of the small Ford, pushed sideways by the slipstream from a large articulated truck now passing impatiently on the inside. 'They drive on the right here.'

'Is that meant to be funny Mister Denton?'

'No, but you're in the fast lane and with this car, on this autobahn it might pay us to get on the inside.'

Starmer risked a quick sideways glance at him, 'oops. Mind elsewhere. You're right about the car though. Thank God Holland's flat.' He leant forward and tapped the speedometer, 'pedal to the metal and seventy-seven kilometres per hour top whack. Mind you, I don't want to push it too hard. Have you heard that engine? Sounds like someone's dropped a bag of marbles and half a percussion section in that gearbox.'

Denton peered down into the foot-well at Starmer's feet. 'Might go a bit faster if you pulled that rucked up car mat out from under the accelerator.'

Starmer studied him in amazement but reached down and yanked the mat back into position to be rewarded with another eleven kilometres per hour.

'Boy, you're on form.'

'Not really,' Denton turned in his seat. 'I've been thinking about what we do when we get there.'

'There, being where?'

'Just keep heading for Oosterbeek,' Denton replied enigmatically.

'You were pretty emphatic on the boat about what you were going to do when you got hold of Webber. Have you changed you mind?'

'No.' Denton hesitated, sighed and then snorted, 'maybe, oh God,' he paused, 'I don't know. The more I think about all this my main objective is to get Dee away from them. The thing is, I feel responsible. If she hadn't have met me and tried to help, she wouldn't be in this mess. I'll do anything necessary to achieve that but,' he paused and looked at Starmer, 'I'm no killer. And, even if I was and did kill Webber, would it end there?'

'Probably not,' Starmer ran a hand over tired eyes, recalling his earlier doubts about Denton's original plan. He'd used the journey to consider their predicament from every angle and particularly against the background of Denton's wavering commitment. If the plan, he reasoned, was simply to release Dee there was, maybe, an outside chance of success. What worried him was the scale and extent of the involvement of the Authorities. Organised crime on Woolley's scale was one thing. This was corruption beyond belief and he suspected Denton had reached the same conclusion and it had frightened him. There had to be a way. Denton's idea of approaching the "Board" on a business-like basis was patently ridiculous but, he thought, there might be half an idea there.

Denton slipped into a very poor imitation of Sean Connery, "They pull a knife, you pull a gun, he sends one of yours to the hospital, you send one of his to the morgue". Madness. There's got to be another way.' As he developed the idea, his enthusiasm for this new strategy became tangible as he hurried to get his thoughts heard. 'I'll talk to Van Doorn; I'll explain that this is all one glorious cock up. That we have no interest in him or his business,' he rushed on, 'that we'll give him back his wretched Filofax and walk away. We'll leave it there.' He stuttered to a halt before finishing desperately, 'I'll give him my word.' Almost, as though sensing the pitiful weakness of his strategy, he sought to re-establish his credibility with a new show of bravado, 'I'm still going to beat that bastard Webber to a pulp though.'

The thought of a hardened killer standing still and allowing Denton to administer old school pugilistic retribution just so he could restore his sense of violated honour and injured pride was too much for Starmer. 'For all the reasons we've been through before,' he shouted, 'that isn't going to work.' He hammered on the steering wheel in time with the last five words.

Both were shocked into silence by the barely audible yet firm voice from the back seat, 'If you don't kill Webber, I will.'

Starmer completed the turn into the farmyard and switched off the ignition with visible relief. For the previous ten miles or so the car had been showing signs of serious distress with the needle of the temperature gauge sat stubbornly on the limit pin and a small collection of warning lights advising imminent disaster. They sat in a silence punctuated by a series of clicks and hisses watching steam curl gently into the cool evening air from beneath the bonnet. 'This is the house?' Starmer opened the car door and looked back over his shoulder at Denton, 'The one you know about?'

'No. That house is about a mile up that lane to the side of this.' They both turned and studied Julie. She was still lying half across the rear seat, huddled in a down jacket and swaddled in a collection of coats and clothes they'd bought on the journey. The lower half of her face was concealed by the hood on the jacket but her un blinking eyes shone with a bright, hard intensity back at them both.

'You recognise, remember, it?' Starmer asked Denton.

'Before all that other stuff happened, Webber and I once walked down here through the woods and then back up the lane one afternoon.' He shrugged, embarrassed. 'Early days. Didn't know him that well then.'

Starmer turned to Denton, 'and you were at that house on business?'

Denton studied him, weighing his words, 'not initially no. The first time I came here,' he pointed at the farmhouse, 'was with my Dad; part of the fortieth Arnhem commemoration. Dad had met the farmer here during the war and we looked him up on that trip.' They both looked across the yard to the house as a door opened and an elderly man, supporting himself with a stick and the door jamb viewed them suspiciously. 'I came back on a business trip a few years later with Webber.' He shrugged, 'I should have looked in on Andries and Griejte then but,' he looked apologetically at Julie, 'those were the days of thinking backwards and screaming in bars. Come on, let me introduce you to Andries.'

Andries apologised for not having recognised Denton but it quickly became apparent from his faltering steps around the big kitchen that it was eyesight, not memory, that was failing. Eventually, seated around a huge, scrubbed pine table, each with a coffee bowl of aromatic aroma with freshly baked bread and large slices of maasdammer in front of them, Denton began to explain the purpose of their visit. Gentle enquiries had already established that Grietje, like 'Aitch, had passed away. Andries then explained that he now lived alone but with help from the village and his son. With the farm managed by a cooperative he had little to do but watch the seasons and the occasional passer-by.

Starmer coughed and Denton picked up on the clue, 'I expect there's a few comings and goings up the lane to the big house?' Andries face creased with incomprehension and Denton, wondering at language difficulties, started again, 'Do you see many people?' He raised his voice in case hearing was another problem, 'do many people go up to the house?' If anything, the levels of bafflement seemed to increase and Andries looked to each of the others in turn, slightly mystified, but anxious to help and seeking clarification.

'Why you have interest in house?'

Denton could think of no reason to lie to Andries but did feel that a little evasiveness at this stage might suit his purpose better. 'I used to do business with the man who owns the house; Mister Van Doorn?'

'Is not possible. Van Doorn is dead long time.'

'Surely not. I have been using the company Van Doorn for supplies and transport for a long while.'

340

The old man fretted with the impatience of the long lived anxious not to waste any remaining time on idiocy. 'The company lives. Van Doorn is dead. When he is dead the business, the house, the land, everything sold.'

Starmer and Denton exchanged looks, 'does it make any difference?'

Before Denton could answer the old man stirred, 'Van Doorn was a good man. These people,' he waved in the general direction of the house, 'are Klootzakken'.

'What?'

'Bastards,' the old man translated.

'Again, does it make a difference?'

Denton looked thoughtfully at Starmer then at the old man, 'only that I thought I knew what we were dealing with and that maybe that gave us some leverage. Now,' he shook his head sorrowful, 'now I don't know.'

Andries stood, 'we drink Peket now Denton and you tell me why you are here.' The old man, in standing, somehow grew in presence, shedding the years; Operational again. A Resistance Leader.' The girl,' he nodded towards Julie's slumbering form, 'your daughter? She needs sleep,' he smiled sympathetically, 'and maybe a fix?'

Denton and Starmer exchanged looks; the old man was a Player. While Andries fetched bottle and glasses Denton decided that, with this man, honesty was, probably, the only policy and steeled himself for Andries' return.

The old fighter edged between them, 'Denton,' he began, leaning his hips against the table to steady himself while he dispensed Peket, 'did 'Aitch talk of the war?'

'Some.'

'He not tell you about Grietje?'

'I met her but no, he didn't talk about her.'

Andries sat and nudged a glass of Peket towards Denton as he gathered his thoughts. 'An SS Obersturmfuhrer and his driver, in a Kubelwagen, came to the farm. They wanted what they could get.' Andrei, paused and looked hard at Denton. 'They saw Grietje.' The old man considered the contents of his traditionally tulip shaped glass, swirling the spirit around the bowl, 'you understand me Denton?'

Denton nodded, marvelling at the man's emotional control.

'They finished with her. Then they looked for Peket, food, I don't know? This is when 'Aitch find them. The Feldwebel he killed with spade. He then take the man's Schmeisser and Walther. He make the Obersturmfuhrer beg, to Grietje, for his life.' The old man paused and fixed a mask over his features, 'even after what they did,' the old man took a sip of Peket, 'she forgive, give this man back his life.' Andries reached for the bottle and poured another slug, '"Aitch took him outside. Made him kneel in the dirt. Execute him.' He looked across at Denton who lowered his eyes in expectation of an unpalatable truth. 'Now you have problem? Ask yourself. What would 'Aitch do?' The old man sighed as he finished his account, 'so, Denton, maybe now you start to tell me the truth? Why you really here?'

'He didn't talk about that bit of the story,' Denton offered. 'He did say he wanted forgiveness. Not much else.'

'Not big talker, 'Aitch.'

'True.'

'He blame himself for what happened to Griejte.' the old warrior scowled at Denton, 'I blame Germans.'

Denton smiled sympathetically and looked hard at the glass of Peket and wondered, as always, whether one drink would do any harm. Still reeling from Andries' revelations, part of his mind was attempting to apply this new knowledge to his understanding of 'Aitch and the relationship he'd had with him. The other half of his brain struggled with the realisation that there'd have been no execution had it been he and not 'Aitch in that farmyard. He'd always known that his father had loved him but long suspected that he'd fallen short of 'Aitch's uncompromising values and demanding standards. 'As I said he came to find out if he'd been forgiven.'

Andries smiled gently, 'he felt that if he not here, Germans not here and Grietje not harmed. As I say, he blame himself.' Andries seemed to sense Denton's unease, 'what I am saying Denton, is that I work for 'Aitch, and you, Ja? With this problem you have?'

As Denton considered this they all turned to the sound of a less than healthy diesel engine powering into the yard. Long after the ignition had been killed a bodywork rattle persisted as the dieseling engine shook itself to a halt. Andries rose slowly from his seat and made his way around the room, via a variety of handholds, to the door. He reached to his right and flipped the outside light switch as the others gathered behind him to watch a small figure in black walk across the yard. Andries, swung both halves of the stable door wide and ushered the visitor into the kitchen with a beaming smile. 'Denton, you never met my son?' The old man beamed with pride, 'he was in Resistance; a friend of 'Aitch.' The younger man shook his tousled, greying hair, partly in embarrassment and partly to lift the fringe from over his eyes. 'This is my son, Jonny.'

Chapter Twenty - two

Dee reached across the armrest and took Mathew's hand in hers. 'I'm sorry Mathew. I just don't know what's happened with Jonny, I trusted him.' She ran her other hand through her hair seeking some relief from the stress that was beginning to consume her. 'I can't think what made him do it.'

Mathew turned towards her, 'drugs I should think.' He smiled sadly but unsympathetically, gently withdrew his hand and returned his gaze to a countryside barely visible through the rain streaked windows of the Mercedes. She leant sideways in her seat, stretching to see round the bulked mass of ridges and rolls that was Reg's neck, for a glimpse of the road ahead. Sensing the movement, Williams twisted in his seat, eased the belt and turned fully to face her.

'We must stop doing this Dee,' he chuckled. She sat back, wedged herself in the corner of the seat, again, staring fixedly at the rolls of flesh threatening to engulf the Driver's collar and determined to ignore Williams' gibes. She closed her eyes at the sound of his deep, throaty, rasping voice, 'must hand it to you Dee, that was a neat trick you pulled on the train. Didn't think you had it in you.'

'Oh, you'd be surprised what I'm capable of David,' she spat, furious that she'd bitten on the taunt.

'Now. Here's the thing Dee. I would have been surprised. But not anymore. You have become a threat. A threat I must respect.'

'Well, we know what you do to threats David, don't we?'

'Not at all Dee.' His features relaxed slightly and, for the briefest of moments, she noticed signs of worry and concern in tired and bloodshot eyes. Concern for her, Mathew or his predicament she wondered? Williams looked down at the walnut centre console and idly pushed the cigarette lighter fully into its socket. He exhaled deeply, his lips vibrating with the expulsion of air, seemingly showing fatigue or an uncertainty foreign to Dee's experience of him. The lighter popped up from the console, Williams retrieved it and waved the glowing heated element at her. She shrank further back into the seat not at all surprised that Williams might consider inflicting pain upon her given the problems she knew that she and Denton had caused. Sensing her discomfort, he laughed and replaced the lighter. 'Oh, please Dee. What do you think I am?'

'A killer,' she shouted and felt Mathew shift nervously in his seat.

'Dee, I've told you that David isn't like that.'

'Are you saying that for my benefit or to get back into this Motherfucker's good books? They were shooting at Denton. Trying to kill him. You were there for God's sake. Or has that convenience store you call a memory sold that little fragment to the highest bidder. Then, what about this asshole,' she jabbed her forefinger at Williams, conscious that her anger was rising, 'telling the other asshole, the one with the fucked-up face, to "lose" me? That's "lose" as in whack, Mathew.' She stopped, slumped forward and rested her head on the back of Reg's seat. 'How many more times have we got to go over this Mathew?'

She was surprised to find that the hand she felt on her shoulder was Williams'. He coughed uneasily, 'Dee, listen to me. The shooting at Findhorn was a mistake and let's be honest,' he ventured apprehensively, 'the chances of hitting anyone at that range were pretty slim.' He smiled, 'tempers were frayed.' He turned his palms up and inclined his head to one side, inviting her understanding. 'That man has been spoken to.'

Dee snorted in disbelief, '"spoken to"? Did you have a word with yourself, while you were in speaking mode. A few words about it not being the best of manners to terrorise a woman before punching her to the ground, perhaps?'

Williams inhaled slowly, 'Dee, I said, tempers were frayed, I cannot apologise enough for what happened to you.' He opened his palms again to reinforce his peaceful plea for understanding. 'Your friend Denton and his troublesome mate have got themselves involved in a world that has rules they don't understand. They have something of mine. I want it back. It's a

345

business, not a war. I get back what they've taken and we can all go back to normal. And that,' he added, 'can include you.' His eyes widened inviting a response.

'Listen, to David, Dee. He's trying to help you. I've been trying to tell you that David can sort this out.'

Dee marvelled at Sinclair's gullibility as he smiled earnestly at his lover; inviting his approval for that support. Her lips set in a tight, hard line as she bit down on her anger and the words she could feel rising in her throat. To herself, she conceded that Williams was good. Very good. She now understood how he had maintained his hold over Mathew throughout their relationship with his scheming psychology, plausible explanations and the sheer force of his personality. She had, she reasoned, little to lose by going along with his explanation. The alternative seemed to be fraught with complications, unpleasant consequences and the certainty of confinement or worse. All best avoided if possible. 'What about Denton?'

'You must be very important to him Dee. He seems to be going to considerable lengths to get you back. We're pretty certain he's on his way.' He grinned ruefully, 'pity he didn't know you'd got away really. Would have saved you both a deal of trouble.' She studied his face, warmed by his assessment of her importance to Denton but wary of his intentions. Again, she noticed that the bullish confidence of their first ever meeting seemed to have diminished. The man before her was worried, frightened even, under pressure certainly. 'What about Denton indeed?' His features set, masklike, as he considered, 'if he gives me what I want, as I said, we all get to walk away.' She felt the hand on her shoulder patting re assurance. 'Dee, for Christ's sake, it's not even beyond the bounds of possibility that we pick up where we left off; you and Mathew? What's to stop us?'

Dee looked down at her shoes and marshalled her thoughts. She couldn't think of a worse prospect that going into partnership with Manchester's made men. She'd seen how that worked in Vegas and simply wasn't prepared to meet the inevitable demands of such an association. She breathed deeply and slipped into show time mode. 'I'm not sure. Would you like that Mathew? Maybe we could make that work?' She smiled across at him, trying hard to embrace her new role with the determination of the deviously desperate. Mathew reached for her hand.

As Williams straightened in his seat and faced forward and Sinclair removed his hand from hers, she reflected on the last car ride she'd shared with these men. So much had happened and so much had changed since then that it was difficult to accept that only a few days had passed. There had been the elation of her revitalised career, the highs from those early performances, the excitement of meeting and helping Denton and the lows of the two betrayals she had suffered at the hands of people she trusted. She had always led her life with a big heart sown high on her sleeve and suspected that the easy award of her trust would ever be an invitation to treachery. She doubted that she'd change but was equally convinced that recent events had taught her valuable lessons. She'd take a chance with Denton but Williams was beyond redemption and there to be taken down. She was convinced that her determination was the key to her survival.

She gradually became aware that she was passing through familiar territory and sat up to take more interest. As the car slowed to pass through the town square of Brummen she recognised trees growing from circular beds set into brick paving and the, still, skew whiff 'Grolsch' sign outside the bar where she and Jonny had lunched. They had once padlocked their bicycles to the railings protecting the trees and then lost the key. On sunny, summer Sundays they had got into the habit of cycling out and exploring or sometimes taking the train from Zutphen for more serious sightseeing. Jonny had been an informed and solicitous guide anxious to give a good account of his country and its history and those days had always been a delight. His recent deceit and deception had hit her hard and she wondered, again, what had prompted his change of heart. She'd thought, after their evening together, that they'd re-established their friendship but now supposed that the wounds of her abrupt departure, all those years back, had cut too deep. Or maybe, it was just all about the drugs. If, as Williams asserted, Jonny was a Dealer there'd be any number of incentives for his duplicity.

The road swept up to a bridge over the river and she glanced to her right at the magnificent seventeenth century manor house that was Kasteeltuin Middachten. She and Jonny had spent a glorious afternoon there picnicking on the banks of the moat and admiring the brick built manor house that rose off buttressed foundations out of the water. She'd used nearly a full roll of Jonny's film trying to get the perfect picture of the house and its reflection on the water complete, with an island of brilliantly pink water lilies in the foreground.

They sped round Rheden and on and through Velp and she suspected, from sketchy details gleaned earlier from Jonny, that they must be nearing their destination. Minutes later they passed a deserted camping site, mothballed for the winter, then turned sharp left into a narrow lane darkened by a tracery of bare winter branches swaying gently above the narrow road. A few hundred yards ahead Dee could make out a clearing with the steeply pitched roof of a traditional Dutch farmhouse with outbuildings, all set back from the road. Reg slowed the car as they neared the house to take a right-hand turn into an even narrower lane heading off at right angles. As the car swayed around the corner Dee turned her head curiously to look at the farmyard. Reg picked up speed and they were back in the curtained dimness of what was now little more than a wide track when she realised that the van she'd seen, to the side of an old Ford saloon, had the battered, traditional, corrugated panelling of the Citroen H that had belonged to Jos; the one they'd used to tour. The van that Jonny had gone to borrow before he'd decided to switch sides.

Dee reached for the grab handle as the Mercedes lurched out of a pothole and crawled its way down the undulating and unmade track. She gazed silently through the windscreen at two ornate gate pillars on either side of the drive, each topped with lichen smothered stone orbs. She wondered at their history and whether the barely discernible letters on a shield to the centre of the remaining gate had any current significance. Hanging on one hinge at an angle, with the lower scrollwork hidden by undergrowth there was barely enough room for the car to pass. She pondered over the age and history of the house that she supposed to be at the end of this rolling and winding approach road. As if anticipating her thoughts, the winter tracery of bare branches thinned as they left the woodland behind. The track gave way to a metalled road flanked on either side by once neatly trimmed and frost dusted privet hedges. As they cleared the end of the formal hedging a large stately building with the beautifully impressive and monumental architecture of bygone years came into view.

The main part of the house was two stories, although the ox eye windows and mansard roof suggested a further occupied floor above those. Probably a floor for servants where the windows in their quarters were above eyelevel, preventing their masters being overlooked when at play in the grounds below. At the farthest end of the building was a circular, ornately finished tower with a conical roof and castellated parapet which extended a further storey height above that of the main building. Arrow slit windows spiralled down the side suggesting a staircase inside. At least, she thought, a modern-day Rapunzel wouldn't have to lower her hair to her lover; provided she had a key. She stretched further forward and looked up through the car window at the pitch slated roofs leading down to baroque cast iron gutters and rainwater outlets in the form of gargoyles at regular intervals around the parapet. The car crunched across the gravel in front of the house and she glanced up the six marble steps leading to the portico and a plain double oak door set below a gothic arch with a stained glass borrowed light.

The car continued across the front of the house and turned left around the corner of the tower and headed towards a single-storey quadruple garage set between the side of the house and the encroaching woodlands. Given its style she assumed this to have been the original stables or coach house. There was a momentary distraction as Reg felt around in the car door pocket and eventually produced an electronic door control. As the garage door rose jerkily he edged the saloon inside and brought the car to a halt in front of a cluttered workbench that ran the full width of the building. At the far end and to one side of this cavernous garage was a side door next to which, bizarrely, was a small dinghy with several fishing rods laying across the thwarts. Williams got out of the car and carefully, courteously, even, opened the rear door for her and held it while she stepped out. 'Well here we are Dee. Your new home for a few days.'

'A few days only, one would hope, David?' She smiled.

'Indeed Dee. I think that you will be comfortable here. I know that Matthew will.' With which he flashed an embracing smile towards Matthew who, Dee noticed, seemed uncomfortable and turned his head away in apparent embarrassment. 'I am pretty sure we can find time for you and Matthew to rehearse in the music room and I'm sure you'll be impressed with that when you see it. Come on let's get inside. I do believe it is getting colder.'

He set off back towards the house, obviously expecting others to follow. Dee was very conscious that Reg did not move until he was satisfied that both she and Matthew were trailing in Williams' wake. As they crossed the space between the garage and the house she noticed a lake in the gap between the two which explained the dinghy.

She had half expected the door to be opened by a uniformed flunky of some description and was therefore surprised when upon reaching the top of the steps Williams hesitated and began searching through pockets for keys. While she waited, she studied the front of the building and noticed that this had once been a very fine building indeed. Once, being the operative word. She doubted that it had received any serious care of attention for many years and was now showing signs of age and the decay consequent with lack of maintenance.

Looking upwards she traced the origin of the green streak of algae at the side of the portico to a defective metal gargoyle hanging loosely from the parapet guttering. Swivelling and ignoring the curses from Williams as he sought for the right key, she surveyed the grounds immediately to the front of the house. She suspected that these had been the sometime pride of the Lord of this particular manor with carefully designed parterres hedged with miniature box, each displaying a variety of flowers and plants in serried ranks for his viewing from the overlooking windows. Now most of those areas were smothered with the detritus of fallen leaves from the previous autumn, lying in windswept heaps, occasionally pierced by stunted, straggling perennial plants and weeds pushing towards the light. Many of the stone balustrades and decorative supports had fallen from the edge of the drive onto the garden below and lay abandoned, partly hidden by weeds. This house, she thought, in its day, would have been much loved. A house, however, that now, required considerable love and affection and a great deal of money to restore it to its former owner's pride.

This, she reflected, had not been what she'd expected. From the brief conversation, she'd had with Lockstone at the city airport, she'd got the impression, that the young woman had been invited to a place where movers and shakers gathered to consider

350

talent and deals. The sort of place that would attract the young and the beautiful and where expensive cars were driven into swimming pools. If that had been Miss Lockstone's expectation she was about to be, or already had been, disappointed.

With a loud, protracted groan the heavy oak doors swung open and Williams stood back to usher the small party inside. If the outside of the house had disappointed the inside didn't. The entrance hall was fully marbled with a grand stylish spiral staircase sweeping away and up to a wrought iron and opaque glass dome skylight. A crystal chandelier, picking up the weak winter sun through the open door, made rainbow colours dance across the luxurious lobby. Off in a room to one side, she could just make out one end of a billiard table behind which were shelves filled with leather-bound volumes flanked by exquisite paintings in ornate gilt frames. On the other side of the hall, through an open pair of pristine white doors with golden handles and ornate hinges, she could see a room high marble fireplace with a brick inset inglenook, complete with red leather seating set atop brass fenders. Above the mantle of the fireplace were some antlers flanked by ornate candlesticks, while a cast iron wood burning stove would be a source of comfort for those who chose to sit in the two embroidered silk sofas on either side of the hearth.

'Dee let me show you to your room,' she felt a hand gently but firmly take her elbow and steer her towards the foot of the marble stairs. As they neared the first landing she looked back to see Mathew looking at the pair of them as the sound of her heels clacking on the marble echoed around the vestibule. He offered a half smile which she didn't return.

'I think you'll find everything you need here,' rasped Williams, taking a proprietorial stance as he waved towards the en-suite and encouraged Reg to place her small case on the stand at the foot of the bed.

She smiled again, reflecting that her new-found role required a degree of submission that was beginning to grate, 'thank you David.'

'Try and get some rest Dee. I'll come and let you know when dinner is ready.' In an almost choreographed move, he and Reg withdrew backwards from the room, swinging the door closed behind them. Before she really had time to consider this structured departure she heard the key turning in the lock.

'So, we "can all get back to normal", can we David?' She muttered viciously into the silence.

She stood facing into the room, her palms pressed flat against the door at her back as she surveyed what she now accepted as her cell. It was a large room on the corner of the manor house nearest the tower with two windows overlooking the neglected gardens to the front and another with a view of the garage to the side. The furniture and furnishings were dated but of fine quality and she suspected that, given the layout and amenities, the room had served as a joint study come bedroom for a previous occupant. A large four poster bed with maroon velvet drapes and a patchwork quilt dominated the windowless wall while an antique mahogany desk with twin three draw pedestals, a red leather covered captain's chair and a cherry wood stationary and pen holder sat beneath the window overlooking the garage. In one corner were chairs and a low rosewood coffee table covered with lace doilies and off to her left was the en-suite. The other corner wasn't a corner; here the arc of the tower protruded into the room. An arc with a beautifully radiused but small access door. Islands of parquet flooring were scattered between an expensive collection of worn but beautiful hand woven rugs.

She wondered about the previous occupant of the room and wandered over to the two photographs on the desk wall. Both were formal; a man and a woman, posed in the garden, by a rose arbour with the manor in the background. As she had suspected, the house had indeed been in a beautiful setting in those days. Fluffy white salts lifting the wallpaper behind one of the photographs and black mould and water stains stretching back up to the cornice, also confirmed her earlier views about the current condition of the house.

She gripped the back of the Captain's chair and leant forward to look down through the window. To her left she could just catch a glimpse of the lake. She swept her gaze through one hundred and eighty degrees and across the woodlands on the far side of the garage. Somewhere, through that wood, at the other end of the drive, was a farm and in that farmyard, was the van that she Jonny and Jos had used for gigs. The Citroen H; Jos's van. The van that Jonny was going to borrow that they might reconnoitre the property where she was now held prisoner. There

352

simply weren't that many H types in use any more and it was too much of a coincidence that the van intended to bring her to this location should now be parked less than a mile from where she was being held. The farm, must be the one belonging to Jonny's dad; the one where he went to work. Why, she puzzled, would the van be parked at the farm? Once Johnny had betrayed her to Williams she wasn't going anywhere with him; he had no need of the van. Perhaps, today was one that he visited his dad?

Her mind drifted to thoughts of Denton and Williams' conviction that he was on his way to find and release her. How, she wondered, was Denton expecting to achieve this miracle. She had few doubts now about his determination or his ability to look after himself but worried at the wisdom of bracing Williams and his cohorts on their home ground. Despite her forced acceptance of Williams's olive branch and promises of a fresh start, she knew, beyond all doubt, that her survival was, again, hanging by a thread. She did not believe, for one minute that William intended to allow either her or Denton to walk away from any of this alive.

She paced for what seemed like an hour to the point where curiosity and boredom had seen her begin to catalogue all the faults in the room and the en-suite. Damp, mould and crumbling plaster had not been confined to that one window and the bathroom revealed a catalogue of defects and sanitary horrors confirming the complete lack of care and cleanliness the property had suffered for some years. Such was her disgust at the condition of the shower and the torn curtain loosely suspended from a few remaining rings that she decided against Williams's advice to "freshen up".

At one point her pacing had simply aggravated her frustration to the point where, against her better instincts, she hammered on the door, yelling at the top of her voice to be let out. With no response, she concluded that her attempts to deceive Williams into accepting her acquiescence as submission and her apparent commitment to the promised future under his management, had simply failed. Had they worked, she reasoned, there would have been no need to secure her in this room. He'd been playing her. Again.

As a deeper appreciation of her predicament took hold she began to search for a way out. She took her small bag and emptied it onto the bed, searching for anything that could be used as a weapon or tool. A make-up bag provided a long nail file and a small pair of tweezers. Fantasies fuelled by years of watching film actors pick a lock with a hair grip in minutes, saw her on her knees at the bedroom door for the best part of another fruitless hour. Rising wearily, she pulled her top loose from her trousers and stuck the nail file down the waistband.

Slowly, she made her way back to the window overlooking the garage, swung the Captain's chair around, sat and began to idly swivel to and fro, brushing her knees against the three draw pedestals. She reached across to the rosewood stationery holder and pulled out one of the few remaining, yellowing and curled pieces of writing paper. The crest at the head of the paper was immediately recognisable as being the same as that on the gate hanging loosely from the entrance pillar on the drive. Pushing herself away from the desk to arm's length she looked down at the sets of drawers and tried each in turn. They were all locked. Between the desktop and the first drawer she noticed a timber pull-out shelf which revealed tooled insets for pens and trinkets. There, nestling alongside an Indian rubber was a small brass key. She quickly unlocked each draw in turn. One set of drawers contained files hung in a metal frame. On the other side, the upper two contained leather bound volumes with marbled page edges and collections of legal looking documents secured with ribbons and seals.

The lower drawer contained a tin box. A locked tin box. Quickly, nearly frantically, she searched each of the drawers for a key to the box. At the point she was considering retrieving the nail file and forcing the lock she wondered again at the progressive and simple security measures the owner had taken to protect his possessions. That man had perceived no real threats to the security of his records but had taken the precaution of placing keys one remove from the locks. It followed, therefore, that the key to the tin box would be close at hand. As that thought chased another she found herself staring at the stationery rack. Lifting it from the rear of the desk she shook it. She allowed herself a small cry of satisfaction as the rattle confirmed suspicions and she tipped a key onto the palm of the hand.

It was difficult to hide her disappointment as the lid opened. It was jammed with large brown envelopes, folded to fit and jammed on edge into the box. Each envelope, seemed quite bulky and she removed the first to read, on its side, in beautiful black copperplate, "Koethuis". She felt the envelope and her heart soared. These were keys. She frantically riffled through the envelopes discovering, in turn, "Keller", "Huis", "Toren" and "Cottage". From her days working in the bar with Jos she knew that "Keller" was the basement and "Huis" was obvious. She seized that envelope and ripped it open, emptying the contents onto the desk. Two dozen, or more, keys, each carefully labelled, glinted in the low winter sun straining through the window. Sorting through the pile she found eight keys labelled "Slaapkammer" and set these, bedroom keys, to one side. The third key that she tried fitted her door. Her elation quickly dimmed as she realised that this escape route would involve her descending a wide staircase into a vestibule open to all the rooms on the ground floor. Her chances of making it to the front door unnoticed were very slim. Sat back in the desk chair she began carefully replacing the envelopes in the tin box. "Toren", she looked sideways at the curved corner and the small door that it contained. 'Tower', she muttered. She re locked the drawers and replaced all the keys except those for the tower and bedroom doors.

Leaning back in the Captain's chair she sighed and offered a silent prayer of thanks to the meticulous little man from the photograph and pictured him sitting at the desk managing his household and estate. She sat on the bed and carefully reviewed her position. She now had the means to escape and all that she required was the opportunity. If she could make it from the house into the woods beyond she was convinced she could avoid capture and perhaps make it to a nearest town. But what then? Alternately, she might be able to make it to that farm and tackle Johnny about his betrayal. Understanding that to do so would invite further betrayal and accepting that this was a plan fuelled by anger not reason she reconsidered. She eventually rejected both options when she realised that a major concern in all that was happening, was her concern for Denton. Somehow, she had to prevent him from getting to Williams. There was no point in securing her own safety if Denton was left at risk. If, as Williams claimed, Denton was, even now, on his way to find her, she needed to be here either to help or stop him. She needed to wait for an opportunity, recognise and seize it without a moment's hesitation.

Pleased with her decision she moved towards the front windows and heard a car crunching through the gravel below and coming to a halt. Peeping around the curtain she saw the passenger door of a large silver-grey Jaguar open and a short swarthy, oriental with dark hair and a goatee beard step out of the car and move off towards the house. Moments later the driver's door, of the left-hand drive car, opened and a tall, florid faced, heavily built man, dressed in a pale, pastel checked sweater, burgundy slacks and cherry red tasselled loafers, stepped out and round the car to speak to the passenger; stopping him in mid stride. She then heard the groan of the front door opening and was not surprised to see Williams come into view at the foot of the steps and make his way towards the new arrivals with his hand outstretched in greeting. In what seemed a synchronised movement, the driver got quickly back into the car, and swung it in a gravel spraying u turn leaving the new arrival staring after it before he ignored Williams' outstretched hand and made for the house.

Dee descended the tower's last three steps cautiously with her back hard up against the inside stone curve of the spiral staircase. She bent her knees and lowered her head to peer down through a stone arch into a large basement kitchen that stretched towards service stairs on the far side. To her right, she could see a back door that appeared to open onto another flight of stone steps up to ground level. Cautiously, she crossed the floor, passing sinks, drainers and drying racks dimly lit by borrowed lights at ceiling level; stealing daylight from the gravelled drive above. Conscious of the uneven stone flags beneath her feet she steadied herself on the, once, polished brass rail running along the front of a massive cast iron range. Somewhere above her she heard again the groan of the front door opening. She paused beneath rows of copper pots hanging from hooks above a chopping block, waiting until silence returned. As she neared the staircase the sound of distant voices floated towards her and she inched out of the kitchen and onto the stairs where she paused, puzzled.

She could no longer hear the voices. She retraced her steps and looked down the dark corridor between the kitchen and the stairs. From the dim light through another borrowed light she saw a battered serving trolley positioned beneath an aperture in the wall. As she neared, the voices became clearer. She slowly moved the trolley, quietly opened a hatch door and placed her head inside the dumb waiter. One voice was loud, insistent and very angry and it wasn't Williams, Sinclair or Reg. She assumed she was listening to the voice of the new arrival with the goatee beard.

'Let me see I got this right. I make you boss in UK.' Dee heard Williams start to say something as she puzzled over the new voice. 'Shuddup. You doan speak. You fuckin' listen. You, boss in UK. Hokay?' Again, Dee heard Williams try to speak. 'Fuckin' shuddup,' the newcomer shrieked. 'First, you kill Customs man, then you let Fat man in club fuck up. Then guy working at club steal Fat man money. Fat man kill people who not soldiers. This stupid. Only kill soldiers. Then, thief kill Fat man friend and then Fat man disappear. Then you kidnap man's daughter. Why? Why fuck you do that?' The man pre-empted Williams again, 'shudda fuckup. Hokay. Man get daughter back so you kidnap,' he paused, 'oh that right, you kidnap hinternational fuckin' singing star. Then you lose hinternational fuckin' singing star. Then what you do?' again Williams started to speak, obviously having trouble with the concept of the rhetorical question, 'shuddup. You fuckin' listen. Then you bring hinternational fuckin' singing star to my house.' There was a long pause, one which Williams, this time chose to respect.

'David I begin to worry', Dee started as the first words of the answerphone message in Williams flat re spooled through her brain. The same words. No longer sonorous but still faintly American. Goatee continued, 'Oh, and long away you lose near five million sterling in drugs. Five fuckin' million. Asshole!' There was a loud crash as something heavy and fragile hit something unyielding and shattered. 'Then, peoples say, thief also got details of who we got on take. Fat man write this in book?' The little man's voice reached a pitch that reflected his incredulity. 'Why he do that? He fuckin' stupid?'

'I didn't know about the book.'

'What else you didn't know asshole? What else I gonna find? Why this hinternational fuckin' singing star here in my house asshole?'

'As I tried to explain Mister Duong,' Williams paused, perhaps expecting another tirade before hurriedly continuing when none came. 'Denton must know where that shipment went.

Denton and the Singer have a thing. He knows we have her. He will come for her and we can do a deal.'

'You think he stupid? The man and this thief they run the circles round you. You think he gonna walk in here and give up, you asshole? You know, in Saigon we kids play with rats. You wanna see a fight you put rat in corner.'

Not Dutch American, concluded Dee but the accent and argot of a South Vietnamese in daily contact with US ground forces during Vietnamization. "Fubar", he's used the word, common in the military, when he'd left the message; "Fucked Up Beyond All Recognition", a phrase she was familiar with from her days protesting against the war.

'It won't come to that Mister Duong,' Williams re assured, 'we have people here to take him before he can hurt us. Then we do the deal.'

'Then?'

'Then,' Williams paused, 'then we don't need him anymore.'

'And the hinternational fuckin' singing star?'

'Perhaps you have a place for her in Saigon?'

Dee felt the fear take a grip as the little Vietnamese cackled, 'perhaps I meet her first.' Breathing deeply, she tried to control the fear and disgust rising in her throat. She had to get away and get to Denton before they got to him. Hearing footsteps in the room above she realised that were someone to be sent upstairs to fetch her she would lose the only card she had to play; the freedom of the keys.

She ducked her head out of the lift shaft and cannoned straight into the trolley, sending it careering down the corridor towards the foot of the stairs where it crashed to a halt as she tripped and fell heavily to the floor. She didn't need the lift shaft to hear the voices raised in alarm and enquiry. Someone rattled the handle of the door she supposed was at the top of the stairs and she heard a further muffled enquiry from the vestibule. Scrabbling to her feet she launched herself, at a run, into the kitchen, making for the tower staircase and the relative safety of her room. The need for speed overcame her previous caution and she tripped on a flag and felt herself losing her footing. Her heart hammered in her breast as hands grabbed her shoulders and steadied her. 'Hello Dee.'

358

'Denton?' She shrieked.

'Who else were you expecting?'

'What are you doing here?' She burbled.

'Come to get you.'

'How did you,' she paused as she caught sight of the open kitchen door up the stairs behind him and answered her own question, 'get here?' They both looked upwards at the sound of a key in a lock and an ill-fitting door being kicked open at the top of the stairs. 'Come on.' Dee grabbed his hand and pulled him towards the spiral staircase leading back to her room.

Chapter Twenty - three

'You are Denton,' a statement laden with incredulity and concern.

'Yes.'

'Dee Dee's Denton?'

Denton exchanged glances with Starmer, 'how do you know about me?' Again, he looked over to Starmer, sharing his suspicion.

'Dee, she tells me last night.'

'You were with Dee last night?' As Starmer tried to speak Denton quickly interrupted, holding up a silencing hand, 'where is she now?'

'Last night she is saying she want to come here,' he waved in the general direction of the lane outside, 'up to the house. She is thinking she find you there. Yes?'

'Jonny, let's get this right. Last night, she was with you? Last night? You're sure?' repeated Denton, too quickly. He appreciated his eagerness and concern were being analysed when he caught Julie's quizzical stare. At some point, he realised, he'd need to sit and talk with her about Dee. A task, perhaps best left until he'd managed to untangle his feelings for Dee from those emotions and the hurt caused by Julie's revelations about Stella and her affair with Webber.

'Yes, Mister Denton,' the little man said impatiently, 'she was with me last night. We are together on my barge. We are talking.' He frowned at Denton's apparent struggle to accept this fact. 'We talk of old times. She ask for Jonny's help. My help,' he thumped his chest proudly, 'me, she ask me for my help,' he emphasised to clear any remaining doubts that may have been clouding Denton's mind.

'Where do you know Dee from? Where did you meet? How do you know her?'

'We are friends from the past.'

In the last twenty-four hours Denton had rerun every conversation he'd ever had with Dee, seeking comfort, reassurance and some promise of a future and he vaguely recalled her speaking of having spent time in Amsterdam. 'Who else was with her?' he demanded but seeing confusion, wariness and the start of hostility cross the Dutchman's face, backed off with, 'so, you were friends?'

'She was with her friend only; the Gay man?'

'Sinclair,' Denton muttered, ' but where is she now Jonny?'

'Men come and take her this morning. I am not being there. I am away borrowing truck to bring her here. When I return to boat I see men put her in car.'

'What men?'

Jonny puffed his cheeks and spread his hands in frustration, 'a big man and a bigger man.' The little guitarist indicated height an arm's length taller than himself with a proportionate width. 'Bigger man could be outside of doors on Clubs,'

'A bouncer?'

'Ja, he is Bouncer.'

Starmer interrupted, 'sounds like those two merchants on the quay; the ones that drew up behind Webber in Findhorn.'

Denton, anxiety and frustration beginning to affect him, barked at Starmer, 'quiet for a minute.' Realising his error, he waved a hand in apology and returned to his questioning of the little Dutchman. 'When we last saw Dee, she was being held by men, like those you describe, they were in Scotland.'

The little man smiled, 'Yes, this also she tell me. Too, she is telling me how she get away and how she think you come here and how she is helping you. Ja?'

'So, how did these two men, the two that took her, know where to find her.' Denton exchanged a glance with Starmer who nodded his acknowledgement and understanding of the question.

The Dutchman paused, ran his fingers through his hair, swallowed and carefully addressed the space between Denton and Starmer. 'Her friend. He is English Ja? This Sinclair, he say, last night, he "going for a breath of the fresh air", Jonny attempted to mimic Sinclair's strangulated vowels and clipped speech, Ja? The English are mad, yes?' He laughed nervously and shook his head, 'not that mad. It was very cold, freezing, it was raining and was dark.' Johnny looked at Denton and Starmer quizzically, 'not for fresh air he go. No, he make call. I bet. Ja?'

Starmer ignored Denton's scowl of displeasure as he joined the questioning, 'how well do you know the house, the area?' He circled the index finger of an upright hand, 'round here?'

'I grow up here,' the Dutchman shrugged, 'I play in the woods, play up at the house with their children.' He laughed, 'hide from Germans.'

Starmer turned his back on Jonny and stepped between him and Denton, 'could be useful.'

Denton, was still considering his response when Jonny shoved Starmer roughly aside, 'you guys gonna help Jonny get Dee or you gonna talk more.'

'That's sorted then,' Starmer grinned at them both.

Denton leant forward to secure one corner of the linen backed German campaign map that Andries was attempting to spread out on the large kitchen table. He looked behind to a plate filled dresser for some heavy object to secure the corner of the map nearest to him as the farmer bent to retrieve a lumpy object being used as a doorstop and dumped it onto the offending corner. Denton stepped back in alarm and pointed, 'that's a hand grenade.'

Andries smiled, 'you observe well Mister Denton. It is a British Army hand grenade number thirty-six with four second fuse.' He smiled proprietorially.

'Deactivated I hope.'

'I do not think so. It matters not. The pin is there.'

Denton glared at him, 'but it's nearly fifty years old. It could be unstable.'

Andries barely concealing his impatience, leant across to the grenade, picked it up, squinted at it and then slammed it hard down on the corner of the map. Denton jumped back in alarm, 'it is stable,' Andries announced.

Denton looked towards Starmer, for support, who simply shrugged and returned his own attention to the map covered with chinagraph markings but showing the farm, house and surrounding areas. Denton persisted, 'why do you keep a live grenade in your house?'

Andries now seemed to be nearing the limits of his patience, 'it is aandenken.'

Johnny translated, 'keepsake; souvenir.'

Denton ignored Starmer's restraining hand on his arm, 'you keep a live hand grenade in your house as a souvenir?' He spluttered.

Andries could stand no more, he snapped, 'Mister Denton your father and I fought a hard, dirty war against Germans. These were the best and the worst times of our lives, I think. Sometimes, I sit and I hold this bomb and I think back to that time. It is a link to the past.' He sighed, 'now would you like me to explain the house and how safely you go there to find your friend?'

Denton nodded and Andries' meaty fist smoothed the folds of the battered campaign map and flattened it down on the table. The old man then swayed to and fro and up and down trying to bring the map into focus before abandoning his spectacles and lowering his face to within a foot of the map. One thick forefinger stabbed at a cluster of small black blocks in the lower left-hand corner. 'We are here,' from that point he traced a wandering contour line north-east towards the pale blue of a lake ringed about with paler yellow denoting beaches.

Denton placed his finger on the house in front of the lake and some more chinagraph markings in German, 'Is this the house?'

'Yes. This house was headquarters for SS Division during the later battle for Arnhem,' Andries explained. 'This,' he tapped the map, 'was among the things that 'Aitch took from the German Feldwebel that was coming to the farm that day.' He paused and Denton guessed he was recalling one of the "worst times." Andries continued, 'I suggest you come to the house through the woods by following this track,' his finger returned to the wandering contour line stretching towards some outbuildings south of the main house. 'It's not so much a track as a ditch for drainage. 'Aitch he call it "culvert", we used it when we are keeping observation on the Germans in the house.' Again, he paused, long enough to signal another reverie.

'Then one day they think we are watching and they send a patrol to farm. 'Aitch decide to booby-trap culvert so that at least we had warning of them if they come again.'

'Landmines?'

'Grenades.'

'Grenades?'

'Yes, 'Aitch he make the booby-traps with grenades. He take out pin, hold lever tight then put grenade in empty food can.' He pointed to the grenade on the table, 'so the firing lever held down by sides of tin. Then he tie can to bottom of tree. He take tripwire from the top of grenade, over branch and across culvert. Patrol is trip over wire, grenade pulled from tin, firing lever fly away and boom.'

Denton considered this new information about the father that had raised him as a child: a man he had considered to be a good, gentle, if a little distant, man. Again, he wondered at his own abilities to continue with the rescue suspecting that he lacked the resources, determination, ruthlessness and, he regretfully acknowledged, probably the courage that 'Aitch would've displayed in similar circumstances.

Johnny coughed as he leant forward across the table and placed a finger at the intersection of the culvert and the drive where it approached the house. 'Sometimes, there are some men who are standing in these woods. If you drive along the road they come from the woods and ask you questions. We need to go very carefully. Perhaps I should go first. Ja?'

Denton nodded thoughtfully, 'we?'

Again, Starmer placed a restraining hand on Denton's arm, 'Jonny knows this place.'

'Okay,' Denton acknowledged reluctantly, 'Jonny and I will go to the house.'

'No chance. You are not going without me,' Starmer exploded. He moved away from the table in exasperation and sat down on the overstuffed and ancient sofa next to Julie who was doing her best to control shaking limbs.'

Denton looked apologetic, 'I thought you'd want to stay and look after Julie.'

Before Starmer could reply Julie spoke, 'you're not leaving me here.'

Andries looked at her dispassionately, 'you need fix before you go anywhere.'

Denton snorted his exasperation, 'we can't all go traipsing through the woods to this house. The bigger the party the greater chance that we will be spotted before we get there.'

Starmer shrugged, 'I don't think so. If we're careful and we follow Jonny's lead I think we can get there safely. Numbers will always give us options if we use them intelligently.'

They walked in single file; Jonny leading, then Starmer and Julie with Denton bringing up the rear. At some places the shoulder high, moss covered banks and ice covered puddles from the recent rains and heavy frost, lulled Starmer back towards a world where continuity and seasons were life's governing factors. Glancing over the top of the bank to his left he was, again, momentarily distracted by a display of early snowdrops and one or two wild primulas.

The nearer they got to the road the more cautious they became and progress slowed with Johnny and Starmer leaving Denton and Julie while they reconnoitred a couple of hundred yards ahead. Denton sat with his back to the side of the culvert looking out over the opposite bank and onto the woodland. He thought about 'Aitch, a bag of bombs over one shoulder, creeping through these woods, almost under the noses of an SS Division, quite prepared to risk his life to protect others and kill his enemies. The concept of defeat wasn't one that 'Aitch seemed to have understood. They might not have triumphed at Arnhem but that was no reason to give up. He tried hard to put himself in his father's position wondering at the emotions that he might've experienced while trapped behind enemy lines in this out of the way place in Holland. Cut off from friends, surrounded by foes and not content to just sit out the war but determined to take the fight to the enemy. Andries' account of his execution of the German had shocked but not surprised Denton. 'Aitch's life, as Denton remembered it, had been characterised by a natural sense of justice and fair play. Anything that contravened, contradicted or got in the way of that set of values was challenged and checked without fear or favour. While he doubted that he would have been as ruthless, in that situation, he did understand how it could happen in a time of war. His spirits lifted as he began to realise that perhaps his earlier doubts about his own abilities were maybe misplaced. He did not possess the combat hardened skills that 'Aitch had acquired through five years of war but he'd begun to appreciate that since Julie had gone missing he'd certainly shown the will and determination to see this thing through.

'Time to move,' a returning Starmer announced.

The culvert took a gentle turn into a broad clearing at the far end of which was a brick buttressed entrance to some form of underground working, sealed off with a cast iron grille. Jonny turned and whispered to Starmer, 'it is old place for store of ice blocks for the house.' Starmer nodded his understanding and they continued through the clearing into a deeper section of culvert where trees encroached right up to the edges of the bank. Jonny waited for Starmer to reach him, 'I will go ahead,' he volunteered eagerly. 'If there are men on the road it will be at the end of this stretch of culvert.'

Starmer nodded his understanding but restrained Jonny. 'I'll go.'

Starmer was guided to his quarry along a waft of cigarette smoke. Nearing the point where the culvert disappeared under the road he crept cautiously out of the ditch and crawled forward, trying hard to maintain cover on his approach to the man that he could now clearly see. He paused, keeping a large oak between him and the sentry while he studied the approach. Watching the man, he suspected that long hours of sentry duty had taken a toll on his commitment and that boredom had begun to take an equal toll on his attention span. With his arms folded across and cradling a shot gun, the guard was wandering aimlessly across the road kicking at stones as he went. Starmer inched forward, spread-eagled, clearing twigs and brush from his path as he went, conscious that, in the frozen quiet of the wood, the slightest sound would alert the man on the road. There were two or three yards of open ground between the edge of the road and the treeline and Starmer needed his quarry to be a lot nearer.

As if in answer to that thought, he heard, then felt, the spattering of raindrops through the bare branches above and watched as the guard moved across the verge into the tree line to take shelter behind the oak against the side of which he leant the shotgun as he pulled another cigarette from a pack.

He nearly made it. Starmer was within three feet of the tree when the guard, perhaps sensing his presence, leaned round, looked back, saw him and began a grab for the gun. Starmer took two paces and with the third smashed the heel of his right foot onto the breach of the shot gun before launching himself across the final yard into the midriff of the guard. His momentum, however, took him through and over the man who, turning quickly, dropped on top of him and began flailing wildly, but effectively, at his head with fists the size of cobbles. The force of the first blow left Starmer semiconscious, only vaguely aware of the second and a subsequent hit before his world went dark.

The sound of Denton's voice and the sharp pressure of his assailant's belt buckle pressed into his forehead convinced him that he was at least conscious and his opponent was not. He rolled from beneath the unconscious man to see Denton standing above him holding the barrel of the broken shot gun from which trailed the fractured, splintered and blood stained remains of the butt.

'Is he dead?' Denton enquired nervously, 'have I killed him?'

Starmer reached across and past the blood and matted hair and checked the man's throat for a pulse. 'No. He's alive. Come on, help me get him away from the road.'

'That's the second time I've saved your bacon,' Denton grinned, not trying to hide his pleasure at having come successfully to Starmer's aid.

'Really?'

'Fat man? Can of paint? Nairn?'

'Right,' grunted Starmer as he cupped his chin and rotated his jaw. checking for damage, 'I must remember that.'

Starmer reappeared on the far side of the large garage to join the small group concealed between the garage wall farthest from the manor house and the encroaching wood. 'It all seems very quiet. I haven't seen anybody.'

Denton nodded, okay, so how do I get in?'

'I thought you'd stayed here?'

'Yeah, I went through the front door then. You think that'll work today?'

Starmer shuffled impatiently. 'OK, it's not so much how you get in as what you're gonna do when you get there.'

Denton threw an angry glance in Starmer's direction, 'I'm going to get Dee out.'

'What about all that stuff around doing a deal so that we all get left alone in the future? What happened to that?'

'I'll think about that when I got Dee free. She's the priority.'

Starmer exploded, 'think about it? Denton think about this. Think really fuckin' hard for Christ's sake. There's a house full of people over there, probably armed, who are almost certainly expecting you, and who would dearly love you to walk straight into their arms. What sort of plan is that?'

Denton eyed him evenly, 'I have no intention of walking like a fly to the web. Johnny suggests getting through the kitchen at the back. I am simply going to reconnoitre. If an opportunity presents itself, I'll get Dee. If it doesn't, I'll come back here and we can decide what to do then. Okay?'

Starmer sighed with resignation and turned to the Dutchman, 'I suggest, Jonny, that you go back to the farm and wait. On the way check the icehouse to make sure that bozo is still secure where we left him. You're gonna be our fall-back position. You okay with that?'

'Yeah fine,' Jonny nodded, not meeting Starmer's gaze.

Starmer looked at a still shivering Julie huddled in an old quilted parka provided by Andries. 'Julie, you and I are gonna hide up in this garage. Wait until your dad comes back, with or without Dee. There's a car in there we can use to get away if push comes to shove.' He looked straight at Denton, 'so if you find Dee, and you manage to get away, make for the garage. You understand? You've got an hour.'

Denton nodded and stood up.

'I need a fix,' Julie nodded at the rucksack between Starmer knees.

'It'll be the last one.' Starmer stood from where he had been sat leaning back against the front bumper of the Mercedes in the garage, moved a few paces from Julie and delved into the rucksack.

'You never go anywhere without that rucksack, do you?'

'I keep a few things in there, as you know.' He handed over the gear and turned away, unable to watch her as she prepared and then injected. He wandered around the garage idly picking up items from the bench and replacing them.

'All done,' her voice was quieter, less edge and she managed half a smile as she looked up at him.

He returned to the car and joined her, squatting down again and leaning back against the bumper. Julie's eyes were closed, her limbs stilled and her breathing even. 'I am not sure that your dad knows what he's doing.' He sighed, 'I'm not even sure he's up for it.' He briefly wondered why he'd voiced the thought; Julie was plainly out of it'

'And you do know what you're doing?'

He twisted round and returned her sleepy smile, 'I think so. Yes.'

'Yeah, I think that you really do know what you're doing,' she whispered as the high replaced the rush. 'In fact,' she giggled, 'I think you've got a plan.'

Starmer chuckled, 'what makes you think that?'

'Well maybe not a plan but I'm pretty certain,' she waved her forefinger under his nose, 'that you know something that the rest of us don't.'

'All I know, at the moment is that your dad is ten minutes out of time.'

'What are we gonna do?'

'We, are not going to do anything. And this time I am not up for any argument. This is about to get very serious.'

'What do you mean?'

'I mean that I'm gonna have to go and find your dad and you're staying here.'

'Andy, if you think you are leaving me here alone wondering what's going on you are very much mistaken. I am coming with you. If you try and leave I will follow.'

'Julie you're high.'

'I'm a functioning addict.'

'You've made up my mind then,' he grunted in resignation.

They were caught, half way between the garage and the house, when Starmer glimpsed the glint of sun from a car roof above the hedged drive on the approach to the house. What, chance, he wondered, that it would stop in front of the house? If it didn't, at the speed it was travelling, it would catch them in the open. They ran back to the garage but as he pulled the side door closed behind them, the glaring flaw in his thinking became apparent. If the car continued, past the house, it could only be going to the garage.

The door motor whirred into life and the garage door began to jerk and rattle, unsteadily upwards. He pulled Julie down beside him in front of the Mercedes, slipped the rucksack from his shoulders, pushed her lower and risked a peep over the bonnet as light flooded into the garage. The new arrival was gently edging a Beamer into position on the far side of the garage. The sharp twist in Starmer's stomach was one that he recognised. It was accompanied by a stiffening of the muscles in his shoulders and an increase in his heart rate. It was fear. That moment of recognition. Fight or flight? As with so many other occasions in his life he knew there wasn't really a choice.

The last time he'd seen the Face behind the wheel it had been contorted with anger as he'd hosed it with ninety-five octane; Webber. He signalled Julie to stay put and with two walking fingers mimed his intention to move. Webber, he now knew, was a seasoned operator, one unlikely to be easily taken out. Worse, the encounter with the guard on the road had taken something out of him and knocked his confidence a little. He half re-considered the 'flight' option but knew a reckoning with this man was inevitable. While there was any kind of chance, however slim, he knew it had to be taken. Anyway, he thought, unusually seeking to justify a course of action on which he'd already decided, in the garage there was nowhere to really hide; they were bound to be discovered. The element of surprise with an attack launched from concealment was their only hope and might just succeed. Though, he'd need to stack as many odds as possible in his favour to overcome a man almost certain to be armed.

He began to duck walk down the side of the Mercedes and paused as he heard the Beamer door open. When this was followed by a beep and the sound of lock springing he risked a long enough look to see the boot lid rising and Webber making for the rear of his car. With speed essential for surprise he crouched at the rear corner of the Mercedes, coiled to spring when Webber reached the BMW boot. Judging the moment, he launched himself around the corner into a slow-motion world of defeat and despair as one foot skidded from under him. He lurched towards the open boot of the Beamer, Webber, almost unhurriedly, drew a pistol from his waistband, levelled it, laughed at him and growled, 'well, that's saved me a job. Oh, I am so looking forward to this you cunt!'

Starmer knelt on one knee at the corner of the open boot and looked up at Webber with the boot lid framed behind him. Gritting his teeth, he deliberately lunged forward, inviting the blow, drawing Webber in as he caught a movement out of the corner of his eye. Webber took the bait, viciously pistol whipping the crouching man but bringing him just close enough for Starmer to rise through his pain and knock him back off balance. As Webber struggled with one arm inside the boot attempting to lever himself

370

upright, Starmer saw Julie rise from the car roof and launch herself, feet first onto the boot lid. Starmer was pretty certain the scream followed the crack of the arm breaking but very certain that it was him breaking the finger entwined in the trigger guard as he seized the pistol, that caused the second scream. As Julie slid to the ground, he freed the trapped arm, pulled Webber towards him by his hair and smashed the gun barrel across his temple. He looked at Julie and grinned, 'thanks for that. I was nearly in trouble there.'

She didn't smile, ' nearly?'

He nodded towards the bench at the end of the garage, 'see if you can find anything we can use to tie him?' As she squeezed between the two cars Starmer hauled a groggily conscious Webber to his feet, slammed him against the garage door and, with thoughts of Julie's degradation spinning in his brain, kneed him between the legs. As Webber slowly straightened from the doubled over centre of pain, the hand on his unbroken arm cupping his violated genitals, Starmer studied him briefly, dispassionately, then took the hand hanging limply from the broken arm and pulled the man fully upright. There was not a sound as Webber fainted into unconsciousness. At the first sign of returning awareness Starmer pulled Webber towards him and hissed, 'I don't want to have to do all that again. So now you answer questions. Understand?'

He was only a little surprised and even a little impressed at the hardened thug's instinctive lunge with a determined but uselessly slow attempt at a head butt. 'You can go fuck yerself!'

Starmer grabbed the broken arm and pulled. This time Webber remained conscious but slumped forward so that his head rested on Starmer's shoulder in seeming surrender. 'Last chance. I'll ask questions. You'll answer.'

Webber licked dry lips set in a face the colour of parchment and slowly nodded. His eyes told Starmer that he understood but a brief glint suggested he wasn't quite finished.

'Hurt him again Andy.'

Webber strained against the pain and raised his head to look over at Julie. He knew he could expect no mercy from either of them but also knew that Starmer would despatch him without a second thought. He knew the type. They were both the type. It was business. The girl would want more. Much, much more. He shivered.

371

Starmer stared hard at Julie. Given her experiences at the hands of Webber he'd expected to see anger, rage and hatred. The hate was there, in the eyes; bleak, hardened pinpoints focussed on retribution. But no anger. There was a cold, almost clinical appraisal of a trapped animal that she was about to put into misery. He looked at Webber whose eyes flickered tired acceptance of a fate he hoped wouldn't be in the girl's hands and then held out his hand for the electric cable, gaffer tape and fishing line she offered. 'Shut the door and go and keep a lookout.'

'What are you going to do with him?'
'Find out who is in the house?'
'Then?'
'Find your Dad.'
'Then?'
'Have maybe have another chat with Mister Webber here.'
'What about?'
'This and that,' he replied evasively as ideas and opportunities assembled in the back of his mind only to be swamped by thoughts and strategies to deal with more immediate problems. He looked hard into her face and when she refused to meet his eyes chucked her chin, lifting her face up towards him. 'So, when I come back I want to find you here and him still breathing and I don't want to hear any more about you coming with me. I'm better on my own.' He hauled Webber over to the Beamer and dumped him into the driver's seat. Webber grunted in pain as his jacket and shirt sleeves were rolled from his wrists which, in turn, were secured, with several lengths of tightly wound gaffer tape, to the steering wheel. Starmer then shoved the seat as far forward on its rails as it would go. A complex series of turns with electric cable behind the seat, complete with tensioning knots, secured Webber's elbows and a loop around his neck and the headrest completed the job. 'So, who is in the house?'
'How would I know, I just got here.'
'Fair point. Take an educated guess.' Starmer watched the man's face muscles tense; preparing a lie or steeling himself for more pain? 'Mister Webber, you are a very small fish in what's beginning to look like an ocean. Do yourself a favour.'
Webber nodded slowly in final submission. 'Williams, Sinclair and the Singer that I know of.'
'Back up?'
'A Face in the woods on the approach road maybe?'

372

Starmer grinned, 'yeah I know about him. Anymore?'

Finished with securing the information he needed from Webber, he handed back the tape and fishing reel.

Julie studied him, her lips in a tight line with just a hint of a forlorn smile. Tenderly, she raised her hand and touched the side of his head just below where Webber had hit him, quickly removing it as he winced, 'your face is a bit of a mess Andy.'

'I'll live. Don't forget. Stay here,' he instructed as he pushed Webber's gun inside his rear waistband. He gently brushed her lips with his and chuckled, 'fishing line?'

'It was in the dinghy,' she shrugged, 'long and strong.'

Five minutes later as Starmer crossed from the garage to the house armed with the knowledge he needed, Julie opened the door to the Beamer. 'Comfortable?'

Webber, tried to turn his head to look at her but the restraint around his neck limited movement. 'Julie, you don't have to do this,' his voice strained out through his constricted throat. 'I can put this right,' he struggled to look at her. She moved into his line of sight.

'I was seventeen.'

Webber struggled to raise his head, and, in Starmer's absence, some of his earlier defiance returned, 'old enough then.'

She took a deep breath and surveyed him calmly. 'You have no idea what you've done. Do you?' she said quietly, 'you nearly destroyed me. You've broken my family. You killed Andy's friend and you're just going to keep on. Right?' She snapped the last question out knowing now that Webber would never express remorse. That realisation was pushing her towards completing the threat she'd made a day or so back; she would kill him but, she realised, she wanted more than his death. She wanted to see him suffer but knew she had to suffer more first. My mother? she gently enquired and as the question left her so did the tears.

Webber's defiant shrug barely concealed the fear that was beginning to overwhelm his pain. He launched a desperate ploy, 'c'mon Julie we had some good times. Didn't we?' He swallowed hard against the restraint around his neck. 'The early days? The show biz stuff? The Boy Band? Pop Stars? We had fun. Didn't we?'

'Yeah right. Then you brought me here. Remember?' She hissed through gritted teeth as she struggled to compose

373

herself, 'you know, I was so out of it I don't remember this place at all.' She sniffed and waved an arm in the direction of the house, 'I do remember those men though. You know what they did to me. Don't you?' Her shoulders heaved as she struggled to hold down the sobs, realising just how stupid the question had been. 'It was all a game, wasn't it? All about control. I'll bet there's a trail of girls like me. Parties, drugs, important people, more drugs, favours, more favours, even more drugs and then more and more men. Then one day they find themselves with a hundred pound a day habit and only one way to pay for it.' She paused to wipe tears from her face with the sleeve of her jacket. 'But by then they're no good to you. Are they? All used up. Only good for tremblers round the back of one of your skanky clubs. Right?' With her face inches from his, her hand searched for the break. As he screamed she stepped away, pleased that she'd got a reaction but far from satisfied that it was anywhere near enough. She stepped back, uncertain, fearful that if she didn't exact revenge she'd spend the rest of her life regretting it. She idly spun the fishing spool on her little finger and wondered whether her subconscious had led to her picking it up from the bench. She fumbled at the zip on her parka pocket and wrestled the object there into view. 'Do you know what this is?' She shoved the object to within inches of his nose. He didn't reply.

'It's a, "number thirty-six British Army hand grenade". Left over from the war apparently. So, nearly fifty years old.' She paused, turning the grenade over in her hand flicking the ring on the end of the pin up and down with her thumb. 'Apparently, if I pull this ring, the pin holding that handle thingy down, comes out and the handle thingy flies off and it explodes.' She looked at Webber, almost conspiratorially, 'it's on a spring see.' She offered the grenade for his inspection.

'I know how it works.' Webber grunted.

'Ah, but did you know they could be used as booby traps?' She noticed a flicker of fear in the eyes that followed the grenade as she tossed it from hand to hand. 'See, you take the pin out and slip the grenade into a container that'll hold that lever thingamabob in place. Could be a tin can or a mug,' she paused, 'or even the door pocket on a car.' His eyes swivelled down and to his left. 'I think it'll fit, don't you?' She added. 'Look there's just the space there for a bottle or a cup.' This time the fear wasn't just in his eyes; it was in the stress lines etched into his face.

374

'C'mon Julie,' he gulped. 'You don't really want to do this.' He tried to shift in the seat and grunted with pain from the arm. 'Just walk away. I swear to God you'll never here from me again,' his voice had risen in pitch, not quite a whine but moving that way, as the imminence of his fate began to fully hit home, 'for God's sake listen to me. Please.'

'I don't think you're going anywhere near God. Do you?' She weighed the grenade in her hand. 'The thing is you haven't shown any remorse. That worried me. Most people in your position would have, even if they didn't mean it. Then I realised. You don't think you did anything wrong. Do you? As I said, it was all a game to you, wasn't it?' Her lips tightened into a thin line and she shuddered as the need for a fix resurfaced and itched away at her, reminding her of the very dark days.
'You want me to say sorry? Ok. I'm sorry.'
'But you're not. Are you?' She tossed the grenade from one hand to the other. 'Oh, you're sorry you're here, now,' she stopped for appreciable moments, 'with me, knowing you're going to die.' She looked at him thoughtfully, ' and it's probably hurting that it's me that's going to kill you, but you're not sorry. To be sorry you'd have to be a human. You are an animal.'
'What, you want me to beg?'
'Wouldn't make any difference. Now where was I? Oh yes. We put the grenade in the door pocket to hold the firing lever thingy in place. Then we tie a line, or something to the top of the grenade. Then we take the pin out and sit back and wait for someone to pull on the line.'

She left Webber's side, retrieved the fishing reel, stripped several yards of line from the spool and, eventually, bit a length free. She slowly wound turns of line round the neck of the grenade, securing each turn with a half hitch and completing the knot with a reef knot remembered from the innocent days of Akela and the Wilberforce Scout Centre. She dangled the grenade in front of Webber's eyes, 'seems secure.' She walked round the back of the car and opened the rear door behind the front passenger seat. Leaning over the seat she carefully placed the grenade in the front passenger door pocket. Gently, she threaded the line from the top of the grenade up to roof level and through the passenger grab handle on that side. Struggling slightly with a nylon line that seemed to have a mind of its own and a tendency

375

to bird nest she eventually threaded the free end through the grab handle above the driver's door next to Webber and then secured and tensioned it to the door handle. The irony of the enforced intimacy with Webber while she completed the operation was not lost on her as memories were stirred by his aftershave. 'Nearly there, anything else to say?' Without waiting for a reply, she pasted gaffer tape across his mouth. Then, leaning in to the front of the car and the grenade she muttered, 'now the tricky bit.' Slowly she removed and discarded the pin but kept her fingers pressed onto the top of the firing lever. Then gently she released her grip until the spring forced the freed lever hard up against the restraint of the side of the door pocket.

'Right, if anyone opens the doors you have four seconds to enjoy their company then it's all over for you both. Let's hope it's a friend of yours.'

Chapter Twenty - four

Dee hauled the puffing Denton up and over the last few steps from the tower, across the threshold and into the bedroom. She turned back to the door, closed it gently, leant against it with her ear pressed hard against the timber surface and held up her hand up to caution him to silence.

'For Chrissakes, they must've heard that trolley crashing around,' she whispered.

'Difficult not to,' Denton agreed.

Dee tapped a foot impatiently on the timber floor, 'Goddammit, why didn't we go out the back?'

'They'll think we have.'

'Huh?'

'I'd only just got here. I'd left the door open. They'll think we've legged it.' He moved to the window overlooking the garage hoping not to see a stranger on the way to investigate further. Reassured, he went to Dee and took both her hands in his. 'Should give us some time,' he smiled. She looked at him briefly then turned away but not before he'd seen eyes that were too bright with un-shed tears. He pulled her gently towards him, bizarrely, momentarily distracted by the thought that he'd never embraced a woman his equal in height. She placed both palms flat against his chest and gently pushed him away.

'Denton, now is probably not the time. We are in a whole bunch of trouble here.'

'I had sort of worked that out,' he grinned to reassure her with a display of confidence that he was far from feeling. 'We seem to have been chasing each other around for days now. I really can't believe some of the stuff that's happened.'

377

She nodded, 'tell me about it. But you found Julie? How's she doing?'

Denton held out his hand and rocked the down turned palm, 'she's trying, that's the main thing but it's not easy and all this crap isn't helping.' He smiled, briefly reliving the reunion with Julie but wondering just how much safer his daughter was now than when he'd started out on his search to find her.

'She'll be better when she gets into Rehab,' Dee reassured.

'Apparently, "Rehab's for quitters"' he laughed. 'And, Andy? Turned out to be a good guy. You remember Andy? The guy I thought had sort of kidnapped Julie?' Dee didn't respond and he wondered whether she was listening or even hearing. She seemed distant, vulnerable, hurt. He cupped her cheeks in his hands and found his thumbs gently caressing the lobes of her ears. 'The last time I saw you a man hit you. On the quay at Findhorn?'

'Williams.'

'Sinclair's mate?'

She nodded.

'Pair of vipers.'

'What?' She stepped back, puzzled.

'You were grabbed from Jonny's boat, right?'

She nodded, 'God help that low down double dealing little Dutch bastard if I ever see him again.'

Denton shook his head, 'no Dee, it wasn't Jonny that set you up. It was Sinclair. It was Jonny that brought us here to get you. He's been telling us about his time with you; all the stuff you told him that had happened since Scotland? He told us about this place and how to get in.' He watched her eyes widen in surprise at his revelation and felt the weight of her despair as she slumped back against him.

'Christ, it's getting to be that I just don't know who to trust anymore.'

'You can trust me.'

'I know Denton, how did you meet Jonny?'

'He found us really,' he offered a sympathetic look, 'I'd never have guessed about Sinclair.'

'Christ Denton, I got that so wrong.' She straightened up, 'I gave that musical Machiavelli a second chance too. He only needs one more betrayal for the Judas bumper sticker,' she concluded ruefully. Suddenly, her body tensed, her arms stiffened and her fists clenched with rage, 'I can't believe I called it so ass backwards. Not just once but twice,' she hissed through clenched teeth.

'Forget it. We are where we are.'

'And that is where exactly?' her anger unabated, she waved her arm around the four walls indicating their confinement, 'I mean in terms of our current predicament?' She concluded bitterly.

'Well,' he ventured quietly, 'we're together.' He smiled, nervously, 'at last.'

She slipped her hands up between his, cupped his face in turn, kissed him and gently rested her forehead against his, 'Denton,' she sighed, 'we're practically strangers.'

Denton closed his eyes as a surge of emotion threatened to overwhelm him. The one constant in all that had happened in recent days had been his thoughts about this woman. The woman who now seemed to see him as a stranger. He'd not just been motivated in his search for her by a sense of responsibility for having involved her in his affairs and endangering her life. Nor was it even just the need to find her and make her safe. There'd been more. Or at least, he now realised, he had been hoping for more. Much more.

He knew that whatever he said next would change his life forever. He ran his tongue over lips dry with anxiety until the lingering taste of her all too brief kiss freed his thoughts. 'I'm not sure we were ever strangers.' He started carefully. 'I think, that day we met, we both saw something in the other that we recognised. There was something there. I knew it. You knew it.' He paused, desperate to ensure, having got this far, that his emotions didn't get in the way of expressing his thoughts and then he decided to simply stop thinking. 'This may sound fanciful, but meeting you was like time had stopped and then started again. There was no past anymore. Only the present, 'he took a deep breath, 'and maybe a future. Then it all went bandy and we got separated and I couldn't stop worrying about you.' He held his hands up, palms open, in supplication, head slightly to one side and a face clouded with doubt as thoughts and feelings tumbled through his mind. 'It was as though a light had shone on both of us but only we could see it. Oh, God, that sounded awful,' he acknowledged as he grasped her shoulders, 'but I know you saw that light.' He sighed, hating her silence, exasperated by his inability to articulate his emotions and feeling faintly and ridiculously like a teenager experiencing all the vulnerability of a first love, 'how the hell else can you explain the pair of us racing around after each other through all that has happened?' Throwing caution to the winds he abandoned his attempts at reasoned explanation, 'when I saw that man hit you on the foreshore at Findhorn,'

'Williams.'

'Yeah okay, Williams,' he conceded and continued, 'I just knew I would do anything, give anything, to keep you safe. How do you explain that then?' He stammered to a despairing halt.

'Love.'

'Love?'

'I love you Denton.'

'But that's what I was trying to say to you.'

'It seemed to be taking some time,' she smiled, 'thought I'd take a short cut.'

He kissed her and the world that had moments ago, been a confused sea of troubles, slowed and calmed as they ebbed and flowed on a tide of gentle passion. The kiss was soft, sensuous, unhurried and comforting in a way that he doubted he could ever describe but would always remember. Their breathing quickened, as hands instinctively wandered and they pulled each other closer until there was no space left between them and he could feel her nipples against his chest. Her lips parted, their breaths mingled, he slipped his hand up under her top to her breast and massaged her hardened nipple with his thumb, conscious that she would be aware of his own arousal. Then, he felt her body tense and she eased away from him, head to one side, her eyes bright and the beaming smile he remembered from Manchester spreading slowly across her face.

She, almost shyly, glanced down and smothered a chuckle with her hand, 'hell, Denton, you sure pick your moments.' She took him by the hand and led him over to the bed, 'don't get your hopes up Mister,' she teased, 'we need to talk.' She patted the bed, 'you English eh? First "mulling" then "fanciful", and now "bandy", you sure know how to romance a woman with that fine language of yours.'

He laughed, 'you remembered "mulling"'. He realised that he was taking an unreasonable amount of pleasure from the fact that she'd salted away a memory from their first meeting.

'Mulling,' he chuckled. 'Foreigners always underestimate an Englishman. It is not only words with which we have a way.'

'"With which"?'

'Well, you wouldn't want to end a sentence with a proposition.'

Again, Dee smothered her laughter and Denton now noticed how much he enjoyed making her laugh. She turned towards him, the laugh gone and a frown spreading across her face, 'Denton, I found out about something on my travels.' She lowered her voice, 'something about Stella.'

'She was having an affair with Webber?'

'Screwed up face?'

'Yeah. Webber.'

'You knew?'

'Not until Julie told me a couple of days ago. I've found out a lot about stuff that was going on in my life that I was too drunk to notice.' As his fists clenched to force himself to focus and halt the slide towards self-pity he felt her hand grip his forearm.

'Easy done Denton. Easy done,' she repeated emphatically. 'Us addicts, "we are where we are", right?'

'The thing is Dee, I once had a very good and loving wife and I didn't notice because I was a drunk. I was careless with her love.'

'Denton, addiction is the explanation, not the cause.'

'Counselling?'

'Yeah, sorry about that.'

'It makes a weird sort of sense. Or does it?' He mused. He took her hand from his arm and held it up to his cheek, 'jars a bit with an Englishman though. Englishmen don't talk; they tell jokes.' He turned the hand and kissed the centre of her palm, 'I've found out things too. Things that happened to Julie.' He caught the sob before it reached his eyes but as her lips met his on the other side of her hand he knew she was feeling his pain. She knew that his worst fears for Julie, shared with her back in Manchester, had been realised. 'I'm going to kill Webber.'

Dee wondered why she wasn't shocked that an urbane Englishman from what he considered to be the cradle of civilisation should share the same visceral, gut wrenching, need for revenge that she had witnessed so often in the madness of Vegas and the Badlands north of the Mexican border. She came from a country where violence was pretty much a right assured by the Constitution. Denton didn't. But then, she thought, everybody has their limit. The point beyond which they will not be pushed.

'I haven't seen him here.'

'He'll turn up. I'll kill him. Then we do a deal with the rest of them and get on with our lives.'

'Do a deal?'

'Yeah, Starmer, Andy, has got stuff on them.'

'Stuff?'

'Yeah, records. Details of transactions, deals, incriminating the Authorities. Police, Customs,' his voice trailed off as though contemplating the forces ranged against them had weakened his resolve.

Dee made no attempt to hide her complete scorn and disbelief at what she saw as Denton's naiveté. 'Denton, I don't care if he's got the Dead Sea Scrolls and Hitler's diaries with signatures and full provenance. Chips like that only work if the opposition are prepared to bargain for them.' She shook her hand free of his, 'but they don't have to bargain. They will secure your silence by killing you and anybody else who might get in the way.' She sighed, 'killing Webber won't make any difference to them. They might even appreciate it; he and Williams don't seem to have been much of a success. Back in Scotland I overheard Williams balling Webber out, telling him they were in trouble because of you. You might be doing them a favour, without those twos' involvement they wouldn't be getting all this attention.' She got up from the bed and began to pace. 'No, we need to get the hell away from all this.'

'That's what Starmer says,' he admitted ruefully.

'Then for Chrissakes listen to him,' she shook her clenched fist at him with frustration; desperate to get him to agree. 'Denton,' she continued, 'from down in that kitchen I overheard a conversation between Williams and a Mister Duong who is from Viet Nam. My bet would be that Duong is on the supply end of this whole thing. The real Mister Big. Trust me Denton; that's where the power is. That's where the money is. And,' she paused to emphasise her point, 'if they're out of Viet Nam they are psychotically, murderously, ruthless. Up in The Triangle, in the mountains on the borders of Laos and Thailand, these people have wiped out whole villages to secure harvests. To them, life is cheap. Any life.' She stood up from the bed and began, again, to pace backwards and forwards in front of him; deep in thought, considering her next point. Decided, she sat back down and clasped his hand in hers, 'Denton, they were discussing what to do with me.' She looked into his eyes not attempting to hide her disgust, 'first Duong was to have me and then I was to be shipped to a "place" in Saigon.' She squeezed his hand, 'do you understand what I'm saying?'

He nodded.

'They also talked about you. According to Williams they were simply waiting for you to turn up to rescue me at which point they would do a deal with you and then, when they didn't need you anymore they would kill you. Get that Denton? They wouldn't need you anymore!' Her voice rose in exasperation. 'They know you have the details of who is on the take and they think that you can tell them where the missing drug shipment ended up.' She stopped, shocked by the look of incredulity that crossed Denton's face, a look quickly replaced by a fixed stare of puzzled concern above a mouth hanging slack with surprise.

'What shipment?'

Dee snorted, 'I have no idea but it's worth five million, it's missing and they are convinced that you know what happened to it.'

Denton shook his head, 'well I don't.'

She scanned his face but his obvious openness convinced her. She shrugged, 'I believe you, though I'm not sure that you not knowing is much of a chip to play. But you do know about the paper trail to their people on the inside?'

'Yeah, Starmer has those.' He paused, took two deep breaths, raised his eyes to the ceiling, shut them and laughed quietly while shaking his head from side to side.

'What? Is this about the shipment? You know where it is?'

'Nope, but I think I know a man who does.'

'Starmer?'

'Yup.'

Dee stood and resumed her pacing. 'I don't think that changes anything. We know that even if they get everything back they still intend to kill us, regardless.' She knelt before him and looked up into his face, 'I can't think of a way that we can use what we've got to secure our future.' She placed her hands on his shoulders, 'you can't do a deal with these people. We've got to run.'

Denton reached up and carefully took her hands from his shoulders and placed them back by her side. 'No.'

'What do you mean no?'

383

'I mean no. We don't run. They'd find us.'

'So, what do we do?'

'Kill them,' he announced with icy calm.

She studied his face. There was fear in his eyes, sadness at the corners of his mouth, worry etched into his forehead but determination written large across his features. Her brief reflections on a side of Denton she'd not anticipated were interrupted by the distant, closing, worrying slap of leather on stone as someone with a heavy tread ascended the stairs. 'You gotta hide, someone's coming,' Dee hissed in alarm.

Denton spread his hands wide and looked at her incredulously, 'where?' Not waiting for an answer and painfully aware that the steps were now very close, he ran to the door and flattened himself back against the wall alongside. Coming out from behind whoever opened the door, he reasoned, would give him the advantage of surprise and he was painfully aware that when it came to a fight he needed all the help he could get. Particularly against people who seemed to use violence as a first resort. He heard the key enter the lock and leaned slightly forward to watch the handle turn when a thought that had been nagging him since he took up his position reached the front of his brain. He could see no hinges; the door opened outwards. As the handle turned further, he took three paces back into the room, turned, faced the door and at the moment he saw the gap between the door and the frame reach six inches he launched himself at it.

He felt the wood impact on flesh and bone, heard a muffled shout and kept shouldering at the door to clear a gap to get access to the fallen thug. A man was flat on the floor with his head up against the marble balusters to the landing with blood pouring from his nose when Denton's knees landed in his midriff. He launched a roundhouse right that connected better than he'd expected and as his opponent slumped into semi consciousness Denton crouched over him and tried for a left hook. Too close, the blow glanced off the chin and Denton's forearm landed under the man's jaw, on his throat. Every iota of emotion that had been churning his guts in recent days, anger, grief, frustration and fear seared through his body in a last gasp explosion of violent energy as he leant his full body weight into forcing his forearm down onto and through the throat of the man who had struck Dee.

Denton was vaguely aware he'd heard a scream but could not, would not, loose his hold. Not until the second scream did he turn to look over his shoulder to see a very large man, almost gently, fending off Dee's attempts to stab him with a nail file. Tiring of her attentions the tough elbowed her aside and, barely missing a beat, advanced on Denton. As Denton struggled to his feet the man slipped a small revolver from his jacket pocket and levelled it at him. 'Time to stop I think. Don't you?' He said very quietly.

Denton nodded.

'Back in the room for a minute, yeah?' He smiled and waved them both back towards the bed with the gun while reaching out a supporting hand to the man on the floor. 'Up you come there Mister Williams.'

Sat on the bed, Denton turned to Dee and jerked his thumb in the direction of the smiling giant and breathlessly enquired, 'where the fuck did he come from?'

Dee nodded to the tower and the open door to the staircase descending to the kitchen, 'They must have heard us earlier.' She smiled ruefully, 'mind you there was a moment when I didn't think he'd fit through that door.' She nodded towards Williams, 'you had him.'

Denton basked in the warmth of her gaze and appreciation, 'why thank you ma'am! He had it coming.'

'Well thank you Sir.'

'Don't mention it. The nail file?'

'A little something for emergencies?' The start of a wry second smile froze on her face as Williams entered the room.

'Mister Denton.'

Denton looked up. Williams was bigger than he'd expected though a man now diminished, in his own eyes by defeat and dirty, torn and blood stained suiting. He watched calmly as Williams struggled to draw an automatic from an ostentatious shoulder rig with his left hand while trying to stem the flow of blood from his nose with the right cuff.

Dee pulled Denton protectively nearer while noting the prancing colt emblem on the grip and wondering, idly, whether Williams had cleaned the automatic since she'd last seen it at his home.

'Get up Denton,' Williams whispered through a damaged, swollen and constricting larynx, 'I am going to hurt you.'

'Not now Guv,' the large man interjected, 'Mister Duong is waiting.'

Williams looked long and challengingly hard at his underling for appreciable moments before turning to leave, 'okay Reg, bring them downstairs.'

For reasons that he knew he would struggle to explain if ever a chance for quiet contemplation occurred in later months, Denton found himself advancing across the room, hand outstretched, towards the oriental man who hesitantly rose from the depths of a silk covered sofa. As he reached the Vietnamese who seemed confused and a little alarmed at this approach, he announced, 'Denton.' Duong looked at him blankly. Denton tried again, 'Paul Denton, we need to talk.' He waved at the sofa, 'please sit down, I understand you've been expecting me.'

Duong, slowly recovering his composure, looked at Denton and then across the room at Williams who seemed preoccupied with the expensive suit jacket hanging from his forefinger which he was brushing with the other hand while ruefully viewing the torn top pocket and lapels. Alerted by the silence following Denton's greeting and a warning cough from Reg, Williams, eventually, looked up.

'Wadda fuck go on here Weelyams? Why this guy think he own fuckin' place?' The initial look of bewilderment on Duong's face was almost instantly replaced by one of irritation fast moving to rage. 'You go to fetch singing fuckin' superstar, you come back with face like mango, croaking like frog and with this Den ton.' Duong paused to consider then turned back to Denton studying him for appreciable moments before turning back to his henchman, 'where you find him Weelyams? Wadda fuck goin' on here?''

Williams cleared his throat, or tried to, 'err, he was in Miss Wilson's room,' he whispered.

Duong persisted like a schoolteacher tracking missing homework. 'Howda fuck he get there Weelyams?'

Williams attempted to ease his throat with a series of swallows, 'I'm not sure Mister Duong, but you may remember that I did tell you we could expect him.'

'Not sure,' Duong shrieked, 'you not fuckin' sure?' The swarthy little man scratched at his Ho Chi Minh beard, 'You, "not sure", you "not know", wadda fuck I need you for Weelyams? You 'spec him to beat crap outta you? Eh? That part of your fuckin' master plan?'

Williams tried again, 'I did say he would come here and he did. I also said he would do a deal Mister Duong.'

Denton, took advantage of Duong's preoccupation with Williams to smile reassuringly at Dee who was staring contemptuously at Sinclair perched on the fender in front of the inglenook. Reg, he noticed, was stood, impassive, immobile and massively taking up a lot of the width of the pair of entrance doors. 'He's right about one thing Mister Duong, if I may,' he interjected.

'Whass that?'

Denton paused, painfully aware, given Dee's convincing arguments, that their survival now depended on the destruction of Duong and his followers. There was no other way. They had agreed. Any proposal he could put, any chip he played could only buy time. Time to wait for and then seize any opportunity that presented. He bit on his lower lip to focus his mind on improving the proposal that was already ringing hollow as he rehearsed it in his mind. 'Firstly, may I apologise for this unseemly intrusion into your lovely home and the harm that I appear to have inflicted on your associate Mister Williams.' He stopped wittering in anticipation of a response. He was not disappointed.

'Are you for fuckin' real?'

Denton smiled, he knew he was unsettling Duong. The man was used to being in control and Denton's faux upper class twittery was unnerving him. He bit down hard on his lip again, this time to ward off a smile prompted by the look of complete disbelief on Dee's face. 'Here's how I see it Mister Duong,' he sat on the sofa opposite Duong and graciously waved him to take a seat.

Duong's knees had started to bend when he realised his acquiescence, 'doan fuckin' tell me what to do. You listen, you hear?'

'As you wish, I was just thinking of your comfort,' Denton advised wondering how he was ever going to parley this conversation into any sort of an opportunity. 'I have, how shall I put this, access to information that could prove to be, shall we say, an embarrassment to your operation. How to explain?' He chuckled, desperate for an idea or intervention; any intervention.

'Let me s'plain something to you Den ton. You listen Den ton? Drugs is a business. You have profits,' he rubbed his thumb against his first two fingers, 'and you have, sometimes, loss. You have peoples who work for the business and peoples who are the business. The workers,' he shrugged, 'they can be replaced.' Duong cast a quick glance in Williams' direction. This information you think help you. About these Police who is crooks. What you gonna do? Tell Police?' He cackled, 'maybe, you get lucky; you get honest Cop.' He laughed at this unlikely outcome. 'Honest cop, he put them all in Jail. Maybe.' He shrugged again, 'maybe not. It doan matter. They Workers. I get more Workers. More Cops. You unnerstan Den ton? You look at me,' he demanded, 'you unnerstan?'

Denton looked and knew that while it would be easy to write off this, irascible, seemingly disorganised little man with his faintly ridiculous goatee beard, one look in those hard, unblinking eyes changed any such misapprehension. These were the eyes of an intelligent perhaps unhinged man. Eyes that had only seen fear; never shown it. There was focus and determination but a complete lack of soul, understanding or compassion in those eyes. Denton struggled on, 'of course, I appreciate all Intelligence is time limited but rather thought you might see the benefit of not having to restructure your entire Protection network just for the sake of letting me and mine walk away never to trouble you again.'

Duong interrupted impatiently, 'you got this book?'

Straight to the point Denton thought and looked away and then firmly back, 'no, but I know where it is.'

'Whaddabout my drugs; the shipment. You got that?'

'Again no, but I know where it is.'

'Where?'

'Aye, there's the rub, Mister Duong.'

Duong looked at Williams for guidance, 'whadda "rub"?'

'Hamlet?'

'I mean,' announced Denton, slowly and emphatically, staring straight into those unblinking eyes, 'I need some assurances to be in place before I tell you.' He shrugged, 'If I tell you all now we'd all be floating from weights in that lake or buried in the woods within the hour.'

'Whad sorta peoples you think we are? Whad you think I am? You think I am thug?' He came closer, his voice hardening. 'I am Professional. Doan kill civilians for nothing. Bad for business.' He thumped his chest, 'I am businessman.' He smiled, revealing teeth that owed more to a goldsmith than a dentist. 'Den Ton,' he smiled, 'we both want same thing, the peace and the quiet, yeah?' He paused and put the dentistry on display again. 'C'mon, what you think we are here?'

'Killers.'

The angles to Duong's face sharpened as his emotions tightened the muscles holding the smile fixedly in place. He chuckled, 'you civilians. Bad for business kill civilians. Trust me.'

'I know you're a killer Duong and you get fuck all 'til I get some assurances agreed.' Denton picked up on Dee's sharp intake of breath and wondered if he'd overplayed his part. Risking a reassuring glance in her direction he was pleased also to see a degree of confusion in Duong's eyes as he continued. 'You see Duong, the more I look at your organisation the more I think you're struggling. I mean, Williams here, has not exactly covered himself in glory. More trouble than he's worth I'd 've thought. I mean, why are you here? Shouldn't you be in on a beach in Phuket, drinking Mia Tais, counting your money and fighting off the Lady boys?' He slowed to gather his thoughts wondering whether levering a breach between Duong and Williams could work to his advantage. 'Let's face it if Williams is the best you've got for this end of your operation things are not going too well are they? You need all the help you can get.' Thoughtfully he took a step closer to Duong and tapped the man's chest with his forefinger. 'More particularly, the last thing you need is another fuck up,' he concluded quietly as he threw a meaningful look in Williams' direction.

'Don't listen to him Duong.'

'Shuddup Weelyams.' Duong looked back at Denton. 'How you wanna deal?'

Denton looked over at Dee, perhaps seeking inspiration, reassurance or even hope, he knew not. He let out the deep breath he had been holding, 'you get us all back to the UK. When we land, you get the Filofax and my party is released. Then two senior serving police officers, names from that book, names I will choose plus someone from your side and I, all go to get the shipment.'

'Why?'

'Why what?'

'Why cops?'

'You tied them into a life of crime. I'm going to tie them into my continued survival.' Denton knew it sounded impressive but suspected it wouldn't take a lot of unpicking if Duong was given time to think.

389

Duong, however, didn't hesitate. 'Weelyams thas whad we goan do.' The little Vietnamese clapped his hands, 'c'mon, let's go.'

'Hold on Duong,' Williams croaked, swallowed hard and massaged his throat, 'we need to talk about this.'

'No more talk.'

'Listen Duong, I've got a stake in this too. It was me that set the UK distribution up. It was me and my contacts that sorted out the Police and Customs. Me who got the London mob to work with the Manchester boys and me who got both to start talking to the Glasgow crowd.' He paused to massage his throat again before croaking, 'everything I have is tied up in this and I won't let this smooth-talking bastard sweet talk his way home.'

'You work for me,' Duong uttered impassively.

'Duong, my bet would be that Denton doesn't know where the book or the shipment are. He's stringing you along. Don't forget, we've only got half of them here. Somewhere, and I'd bet, not very far away, is the daughter and that bloke that started all this in the Manchester club; Starmer. He's here, I know he is and he's the one that took the book. We know that.' The fast closing trachea rendered the last three words barely audible and Williams began to cough. Eventually, after a struggle to get his breath and several more swallows Williams wheezed out a plaintive, 'Trust me,' to Duong.

Denton seized the initiative, 'Mister Duong,' slowly, patiently, 'I can get you the book and the shipment. It's me you should trust not someone who seems to continually let you down. Believe me.'

Duong's head turned from Williams to Denton and then back to Williams, 'No more talk. We do as I say.'

The painful roar that escaped from Williams badly damaged throat surprised them all. Dee looked on in amazement as the big man's rage consumed him, resulting in a series of uncoordinated hops as he fought to free the automatic from the shoulder rig. As the gun came free Williams waved it around wildly before levelling it at Denton. 'Tell Duong where that fuckin' shipment is. Now,' he hissed as he thumbed back the hammer, 'or I blow your fuckin' head straight off your shoulders.'

Everybody, except Williams, turned at the slapping sound of accelerating, soft shoed feet crossing marble. Denton saw Reg half turn in the doorway just in time to miss Julie, on a run, squeeze between him and the door frame and launch herself at Williams. As her arms closed around his hips he staggered sideways and began to fall. The sound of the shot smothered that of three bodies hitting the floor. Julie fought to extract herself from a tangle of limbs, Williams got to his knees with shock and horror written large across his face and Mathew Sinclair sighed once as he examined the bloodstained fingers covering the bullet wound in his chest.

Williams heaved himself onto one knee rage, incomprehension and loss fighting for room on his face. 'You cunt Denton,' he slowly levelled the gun and sighted along the barrel, 'this is your fault.'

Denton felt almost as though he wasn't present but observing what was happening from some high place where all was calm and the key to survival was the acceptance of the inevitable. He, almost meditatively, watched Julie hammering at Williams with her fists and calmly noted the tightening of Williams' finger on the trigger. He became vaguely aware that he was still alive as he watched a perplexed Williams try, and fail to rack the slide and sounds began to intrude on his almost hallucinative state.'

'It's jammed,' Dee yelled. 'It's fuckin' jammed,' she repeated wondering at her own prescience back in Williams' flat when she'd considered the possibility and causes of misfires in poorly maintained weapons.

As Williams dropped a hand to the floor to lever himself upright, Denton stepped forward and kicked him in the stomach. Taking a further step with the intention of administering the coup de grace with the other foot he stopped as Reg pressed the barrel of a gun to his chest. 'No more.'

'Leaving us mister Duong?' Reg waved the Vietnamese away from the door and back towards the sofa as Williams finally recovered his breath, stood and hurled the useless automatic across the room.

'Okay Duong, now we've got the daughter. Either she'll tell us where everything is or she'll tell us where her boyfriend is. Either way we get what we want.'

'You can go fuck yourself,' Julie yelled.

'Everybody shaddup. You no listen Weelyams? I already tell you what we do. You do as told,' Duong finished uncertainly.

'No Duong, we're going to do this my way. You may not have noticed but you're here on your own. So, what I say goes.'

Williams paused and took several breaths to ease his throat, 'I wish you no harm and when this is over you will thank me and we will go back to normal.'

Duong looked at him sourly, 'you think?'

Williams turned to Reg, 'where's Webber?'

'I saw him drive up Guv. He must be over in the garage.'

'Go and get him. Leave the gun.'

Denton reached down to his daughter, took her hand and helped her to her feet. She embraced him with the sort of desperate need he'd not experienced since she was a nightmare afflicted toddler. 'Thank you,' he muttered while gently caressing her hair. 'I'm not sure quite how that would've worked out if you hadn't turned up. Thanks.' He looked down to see very wide eyes searching his while fear and uncertainty stared out from hers. 'It'll be alright.' He kissed the top of her head, 'I promise.'

'No, you don't understand,' she craned her neck back, straining to look out the window and pushed him away, 'I've done something,'

Denton grunted, pulled her back into his arms, idly looking across her head and through the window as Reg opened the garage door and disappeared inside. He dreaded Webber's appearance. Being in the same room, helpless, with the man that had seduced his wife and abused his daughter was an appalling prospect.

For an instant, he thought he'd returned to the transcendental state of consciousness that had shielded his mind through Williams' attempt to kill him. Then the sound of the explosion served to partly explain the split second earlier sighting of Reg and a car door appearing horizontal in a cloud of dust, flame and debris before landing two yards outside the garage.

Denton and Williams rushed to the window, enmity temporarily set aside, as both attempted to make sense of what they were seeing. When the smoke cleared and the dust settled it was evident from the set of one of his legs, the complete absence of clothes from the upper half of his body and his bloodied scalp that Reg, if alive, was seriously hurt. Denton dropped his hands to the window sill, leant forward, rested his head against the glass and let his gaze drift across the debris scattered about Reg. He gave his mind time to reconsider what it thought it had registered by focussing elsewhere for a long moment before returning to check.

He was indeed looking at a man's forearms gaffer taped to the steering wheel of a Mercedes. He turned towards Julie and then quickly back to the window as the tops of three white cars with flashing light bars followed by a blue and red diagonally striped van, emblazoned with the motive "Politie", and a Jaguar drove towards the house.

Chapter Twenty - five

Starmer was hurting. As he crossed the kitchen he glanced quickly into a cracked, plastic framed mirror hung crookedly above a large porcelain sink and was shocked at what he saw. Adjusting his position and selecting the largest image of himself from the several on offer in the dislodged shards he carefully explored the wound with his fingers. The blow from Webber's pistol, while partially dodged, had opened his scalp and blood had dried above and around his left eye while continuing to seep from the gash to his head. Worse, the blows to his face from the sentry on the road had caused a swelling that was closing his right eye and he suspected, from the tenderness and slight deformity, that the cheek bone below might be fractured. Julie had been right; his face was a mess. He yanked an old fashioned striped roller towel from its wooden rail, wiped himself clean with a sink cloth and pat dried his wounds as best he could. Still damp, he moved towards the far end of the kitchen and slipped.

He stretched out his left hand to prevent a fall as searing pain shot through his right side and doubled him over. Gasping in agony he slowly straightened and carefully lifted his top. His side, from just above the hip to immediately below the armpit was marked, inflamed and swollen. The flesh covering the lower ribs was covered with blueish yellow bruising. Gingerly he walked his fingers down his ribcage probing for damage. He found it at the eighth and ninth. Probably not broken he thought, but cracked. Either way he wouldn't be throwing many right hooks for a few weeks. He had no memory of incurring the injury; it could have been Webber or the Sentry. It mattered not. What now concerned him was that he was in no shape for any further such

394

encounters. He reached behind him and tapped the reassuring weight that was Webber's gun pressing against the small of his back in his waistband and began, subconsciously, to adjust his mindset and adapt his plans to take account of these constraints.

As he reached the foot of the stairs leading up from the kitchen to the ground floor he heard the buzz of conversation and quickly tracked the source to the dumb waiter in the basement service alley. He settled to eavesdrop but his vigil was halted before it started by a distant crash, muffled sounds of struggle and a woman's screams from upstairs. Clutching his ribs, he moved as quickly as he could back to the kitchen where a further shout, nearer this time, allowed him to track the source to an open door in the tower in the far corner of the kitchen. Pausing to consider his best option, the sound of someone stomping down the staircase above that serving the kitchen pulled him back in that direction. He peered around the corner at the foot of the enclosed staircase and could see a patch of light at the top. Carefully, conscious that if discovered mid-flight he was a sitting duck, he drew the gun and inched up the stairs until his eye line was level with the top landing. Leaning, slightly to his right he could see a door, leading to a marbled entrance hallway. The door was half open and by leaning further he could see across the hall and part of the room opposite. Reaching out, while ignoring his protesting ribs, he pushed the door closed enough to leave just a small gap. Dropping back to his knees, then belly, he carefully stretched himself across the top five treads and risers with his eyes at floor level to get a clearer view across the hall to a room he could now see beyond.

Trying hard to protect his ribs by taking the weight on his elbows he was shuffling for position when he heard more feet on the stairs above his head. He drew back, out of sight but inched up to peer through the gap when he heard the steps moving away from the foot of the staircase and across the hall. There was no mistaking Denton and the woman, he knew, had to be Dee. He pulled back out of sight and, having seen the mountain of muscle waving the couple forward with a ridiculously small revolver, looked to his own weapon and decided that size was important.

Try as he might he could make little sense of what conversation he could hear. He could distinguish Denton's voice with the occasional word in measured tones, a sibilant, authoritative and sometimes louder voice with an accent and the more emphatic but strangulated tones of a man struggling to grate out thoughts from a sore throat. He edged nearer to the door and quickly poked his head out. To his left the marble staircase swept upwards while to his right was the main door and entrance lobby. An instinct, a sound from the staircase or a change in the set of the shoulders of the lump guarding the room, spooked him into a hasty retreat.

Without knowing who was in the room and where they were situated he could see no percentage in an intervention at this stage. There was little hope of a successful outcome. Even if he shot the man in the door from behind and then rushed the rest while hoping that his injuries didn't slow him down, he knew his chances were slim. As his eyes rose above the landing level for another check on the room opposite, he froze. He had, indeed, heard something previously. So had that guard. He sank back, shut his eyes and listened. He heard the noise again. The soft whisper of clothing rubbing against plastered walls. Someone was on the staircase above him, just on the other side of the wall that hid him from view. He checked again. The guard hadn't moved.

He ducked back to process this new information when a shout, a yelled threat, a cry of alarm and the sound of feet moving fast prompted him to rise to his knees in time to see Julie, running, slip round the man in the door and on into the room. The big man lunged to follow but stopped in his tracks at the sound of a shot. Starmer froze but then breathed again, recognising Julie's voice over the sounds of alarm and struggle. As he began to a move another female voice, louder, deeper, dominant shouted. The guard disappeared further into the room and he heard Julie tell someone to go fuck themselves. The babble of heated exchanges died down and the voice that croaked and struggled appeared to have taken charge. Starmer decided that he could wait no longer but quickly sank back out of sight as the ponderous tread of the large man announced his return to his post. Having decided that he now had no choice but to act he risked a last look to check the man's position, just in time to see the thug's feet plod past his hiding place on their way to the front door.

As near as he could judge the odds were now stacked in favour of intervention. The large guard had gone; he'd only ever heard three male voices, one of those had belonged to Denton and the guard had never spoken. Someone had a gun but so had he. Two to one and he had surprise on his side. He looked down at the automatic pistol and realised that he still knew very little about its' operation. The SA80 rifle had been his personal weapon and in Iraq, such had been the kit shortages, he'd had to fight to hang onto that. The revolver he'd walked Woolley to the cess pit with had been a far simpler proposition. He looked down at the automatic in his hand, gripped the slide, pulled and an ejected bullet flew past his ear as the wall against which he was leaning shook noticeably, seconds before the crump and rumble of an explosion.

He checked himself as he realised that part of his brain hadn't caught up and was still considering the search for the ejected bullet. He hauled his body, despite his protesting ribs, up and out and into the lobby where he padded slowly towards the two white double doors. As he came close he noticed a strange blue flickering reflection on the metal door handle. At the sound of slamming car doors, he turned towards the lobby to see the stained glass borrowed light above the oak doors alive with the fluorescently glimmering blue light mandatory for Police vehicles on serious business. He leapt back towards the kitchen stairs.

With his ribs now causing him real pain rather than considerable discomfort he sank gratefully back into his hiding place. Gritting his teeth, he reached up to the door and held it a half inch from closed. He then shuffled on the stairs until his line of sight ran clear to the front door. In less than seconds the door swung open to reveal a tall blonde young woman with an ID badge swinging from a lanyard struggling to be the first in as a phalanx of armed, booted and overalled policemen stormed past her. They were followed at a more measured pace by two older officers with bars and crowns on their epaulettes. Bringing up the rear was a Home Counties apparition straight from a golf course in red shoes, maroon trousers and the sort of sweater that men were given at Christmas. He and the young woman briefly conversed in passing and Starmer saw that the man also had an ID badge. As he shifted his weight to ease his discomfort he felt something digging into his buttock. He reached behind and retrieved the errant bullet. With the lightest of pressures from his fingers he edged the door towards its jamb, stopping it just short of engaging the catch and thereby avoiding a consequent click. He then carefully wedged the bullet between the underside of the door and the landing floor. Satisfied that the door would stay put and that his ploy might even delay an attempt to open it he made his way back down to the kitchen.

He took a circuitous route around the back of the house, away from the garage and the general direction of the Andries farm and on into woods running down to the shore of the lake. From there he skirted the end of the drive before looping back towards the farm. He dived into a ditch at the edge of a clearing opposite the house as an ambulance with full lights and sirens careered down the road and onto the house. He then moved deeper into the wood while maintaining a course parallel to the road.

As he trudged through the darkening woodland he felt a deep sense of disappointment and failure. He'd had every expectation of getting Denton and the woman away from the house and had been confident that he'd have been able to deal with whoever had got in his way. Busted ribs or no busted ribs, right up to the police bursting in, he'd been sure that one way or another, he'd have finished it. Now, he was simply at a loss. Why, he wondered were the Dutch Police all over the place? Who were the two civilians? Probably not civilians he concluded but what were they doing there and, now, how the hell was he ever going to sort out this new mess? And from where, he wondered, in the name of all that he held dear, had Julie come? She'd defied him and left the garage and must have somehow got upstairs. Probably, he guessed, from the open door to the tower in the kitchen.

He stumbled down a bank in the gathering darkness and slid to a halt in an ankle-deep mess of composted leaves and mud. Looking up through the trees he couldn't see a cloud in the darkening steel grey sky and suspected that a frost would return with sunset. He carefully picked his way around the morning's frozen, now thawed, puddles as the ice house loomed into view. He approached cautiously, fully expecting to see the sentry from the road still secured where they'd left him after the fight. It didn't take much more than a cursory look around to discover he'd gone. Starmer dismissed a nagging concern about the man's absence, assumed that Jonny had moved him to the farm house and picked up his pace hoping to get to the farm before the light went completely.

He reached the top of the slight rise at the edge of the woods overlooking the farmyard and began his descent when he heard voices; two people in conversation. The experiences of recent days had instilled in him a caution that now prompted him to halt, duck into some brush and move slowly on his hands and knees to a covert vantage point. He noted, with some satisfaction, that the beaten-up drug dealer's car from Den Helder was still there and that Jonny's van hadn't moved either. The voices were coming from the other side of the van and he was sure he recognised Jonny's. Relieved, he rose from the bushes and then froze. The owner of the second voice had appeared at the back of the van, opening the doors, where he was then joined by Jonny. Starmer shrank back out of sight. Jonny's companion was the sentry from the road. The sentry that Jonny had been supposed to have kept secure.

He sat back on his haunches and considered yet another puzzling twist in the days' events. Hoping that he had, perhaps, been mistaken and wrongly identified the man as the sentry, he combat crawled along the rise to a point nearer the vehicles. The two men were in earnest conversation but hidden from sight by the open rear doors of the van. If, Starmer reasoned, the man was indeed the sentry and he was now here, unrestrained, talking to Jonny, then Andries' son had a lot for which to answer. Starmer straightened as Jonny stepped back into sight to swing the door to the panel van shut. This revealed the sentry offering a cigarette with one hand while he slammed his door and turned the handle with the other. The flare of a match and a cloud of cigarette smoke followed by a companionable silence confirmed Starmer's worst suspicions. They'd all been conned. It had been Jonny who had delivered Dee into the hands of the crew up at the house and Jonny who had then very nearly finessed their own delivery to the same fate with his helpful guidance and assistance.

He frantically back tracked over recent events, reviewing Jonny's actions since they'd met in the light of this new discovery. He recalled that on their way to the house it had been Jonny that had offered to check whether there were men on the road and he who'd stopped him. If the little Dutchman had been intending to warn of their approach Starmer had inadvertently thwarted him.

Then, it had been Starmer who'd decided to send him back to the farm before they'd approached the house. Further thwarting any attempts at an early warning. 'Devious little bastard,' Starmer muttered.

The blinking and flickering of head and blue lights on the uneven road filtering through skeletal winter foliage energised the pair to hide themselves behind the van. Starmer stood for a better view as the police vehicles careered around the corner on their way to he knew not where with Denton, Dee and his Julie presumably under arrest. As the light show faded in the distance the two remerged from around the van and walked out from the entrance to the farm and onto the road where they took up station looking back towards the big house. 'What the hell are they waiting for?' Starmer mumbled as he struggled to see the pair through the evening gloom. As if on cue, a powerful set of headlights clawed their way skywards as a large saloon crested a bump in the access road before returning to earth to fully illuminate the two waiting men. The car had barely stopped before the doors were open and another two men joined the waiting committee in the pool of light. Starmer didn't recognise the smaller man but there was no mistaking mister Home Counties in his red trousers and that sweater. Discussion seemed one sided and animated but it was the golfer that seemed to be doing most of the talking. As conversation ceased, three of them took a step back as the man in the sweater produced a gun and fired shots into, windscreen, headlight and radiator of the car. Immediately, Jonny's companion, got into the car and backed it some distance up the lane. As it passed from sight whining backwards in full reverse Starmer began to have an inkling of what might be afoot. As if to confirm his suspicions he heard the car start its return. As it passed the entrance to the farm the driver rolled clear from the open door and watched the Jaguar miss the turn, clear a bank and bury its front in a ditch and a cloud of steam. While the driver stood dusting himself off the other three made their way towards Jonny's van. Jonny opened the rear doors and from the light cast by the interior light Starmer got his first look at the mystery fourth man. The face wasn't one he knew but he'd remember him as Ho Chi Minh.

With the tail lights of the van disappearing into the distance Starmer crossed the farmyard. Cautiously, he palmed the stable style door open and leant around and in to scan the kitchen from the threshold as the gap widened. Andries was slumped in the ancient sofa, his elbow propped on the arm and his hand supporting the side of his face. As Starmer neared he could see tear tracks on the old man's face.

'Andries, are you alright? Are you hurt?'

The old man looked at him soulfully, 'No.'

'No?'

'I am not alright. I am very hurt in here,' he tapped his chest above his heart.

'Ok,' said Starmer hesitantly. He stopped in front of the man and stooped, 'your son, Jonny?' He reached out and placed his hand on the old Resistance Fighter's shoulder not asking the question for which he had now guessed the answer.

'He betray me,' Andries sobbed. 'He betray you. What must you think of us?'

Starmer shrugged, 'people change?'

'No!' The old man shouted, hammering his clenched fist up and down onto the arm of the sofa. 'Drugs change people.' He sobbed again, 'if you had seen him when the Germans were here, then, you would have said, "there is a very brave young boy, fooling these Germans under their very noses." His mother and I were so frightened but so proud of him.'

'Rightly so. As you say, "Drugs"'

'Drugs, greed, easy life. Anything but work hard. And always the lies,' he sighed, 'I thought he had changed.' He brushed away his tears with the back of his hand, 'he is dead, ya? You come to tell me he is dead.'

Starmer, looked at him, puzzled for a moment, 'oh, the shots?'

'Ya. He is dead, you kill him for he betrays you?'

'No Andries, Jonny is very much alive but probably in more trouble than he realises. The shots were him and his friends staging an accident.' He stopped, momentarily considering what might have been the motive for the piece of pantomime he had witnessed. 'I'm not really sure why but Jonny is not dead I can assure you.' He shook the old man's shoulder reassuringly as he saw tears well up in his eyes. 'Have you got a telephone?'

The old man didn't seem able to make eye contact but pointed to a Bakelite rotary dial telephone on the dresser.

'Did you get a call in the last hour?'

Andries nodded.

401

'From the house?'

'For Jonny?'

'Ja.'

As he'd expected, Andries nodded again, confirming his suspicion that Home Counties man had 'phoned ahead to plot his little charade and the escape. 'I expect the Police will be here soon with some questions. It would help if they didn't know I had been here.' He watched the old man's shoulders straighten, his back stiffen and his head raise to look Starmer straight in the eye.

'You have my word.'

And Starmer knew he had.

Starmer tried to ignore the fussy little Station Master at Den Helder waiting to lock up for the night as he stored the rucksack in the locker. Incurring the man's displeasure was a small price to pay for security through the night. He thanked the man courteously as he was ushered out and onto the pavement to the sound of the retractable trellis security gates slamming together and padlocks snapping shut behind him. He stood, leaning against a light standard, and idly watched the swaying navigation lights of a boat entering the harbour in the distance as a cold wind from the sea rattled the lamp fittings above him.

He had used the time during the drive from Andries' house, in the clapped out old car he'd had to nurse all the way, to analyse his predicament. Whichever way he looked he could not see a clear way forward, let alone a solution. With Denton, Dee and Julie in custody there was now nothing to keep him in Holland but returning to England presented a whole new set of problems. Not the least of which was the absence of a passport and the probability that all ports would have his description and probably a copy of a warrant. He knew he had enough money in the rucksack to disappear but his feelings for Julie and his conviction that his predicament was not of his making were driving him to seek some permanent resolution and natural justice. That could only be achieved in England.

He shrugged down deeper into his jacket and walked towards the battered old Ford on the fringes of the station car park. He needed sleep and here was as good a place as any. He wondered briefly about the scattering of cars and whether their owners had missed the last train as he passed a brand new red Audi Cabriolet convertible parked a few rows back from his car.

402

He levered open the stiff door on the car, sank onto the seat, reclined it and closed his eyes. As he relaxed the muscles in his neck, breathed deeply and tried to clear his mind of thoughts a sound intruded into his consciousness. Heels, he could hear a woman approaching. He sat up, checked to his front and then caught a glimpse of movement in the wing mirror. A woman, in a leopard print belted trench coat, a windblown beehive and stiletto heels was keying the lock of the Audi. He turned for a better look, checking his first impressions. As she got into the car she faced front and even in the poor light he recognised the barmaid that he'd robbed in the portside bar. He started his engine as he watched her tail lights pass through the barrier and turn onto the road leading out of the town.

He ignored the puzzled stare of the Station Master as he retrieved the rucksack and slammed the locker door. He drove through the shopping centre, crossed the bridge and turned onto the quayside knowing that the bar would be open. He had, after all, followed the barmaid from her home. He was hoping that it was early enough to catch her on her own without her attendant goons and hangers on. He parked the Ford where he'd originally stolen it and walked into the gloom of the long narrow bar. The rustle and clack of a beaded curtain parting announced her entrance. She stopped when she saw him, her face expressionless, one hand holding the curtain aside the other clutching a pen. He smiled, pulled out a stool, sat, dropped the rucksack to the brass foot rail, winced and slipped his left hand inside his jacket to shield his ribs from possible contact with the bar.

'What do you want?' She stepped towards him, now with anger flushing through her heavily made up cheeks. 'I have no money.'

'I don't want your money.'

'So, why you here,' she snapped, 'apologise perhaps, pay me back, what?'

'I'm sorry. How much do you want?' Starmer saw a brief look of disbelief followed by satisfaction glint in her eyes and realised that he may have given away too much too early.' He watched as she studied him, the bruises and the dishevelled appearance of someone who'd not slept, showered or changed his clothes since last they'd met. He could almost hear the calculations as he waited for her response.

'You're running.'

He nodded, 'I want your help.'

'Why you think I help you?'

'Because you and I are in the same business. Because you are a business woman. Because you are too intelligent to let a small disagreement stand in the way of a good deal and because you have no choice.'

'I have no choice?' She bridled. 'I am not a business woman. I just work here. A barmaid?'

Starmer chuckled, 'a barmaid with a very nice house and a stud farm down the coast?' If he'd been expecting a reaction, he was disappointed. He continued, 'oh, and a top of the range brand new Audi convertible to get you back and forth.' He saw a perceptible change in her demeanour and deportment. The previous air of vague submission and sullen servility seemed to fall from her to be replaced by a body language that screamed of initial uncertainty fast being overtaken by determination and an innate and growing sense of her own power.

She smiled, stepped forward, leant her elbows on the dimpled sheet copper counter, poked the biro into the beehive and pointed to the door. 'Keep running.'

Starmer took a deep breath, 'the two children. The ones you waved off this morning. Granddaughters?'

They locked eyes from a distance of less than a foot for appreciable moments. He felt her nicotine laden breath on his face, sensed her fear, her anger and her resolve. He struggled to keep a lid on his own fear, knowing the chance he was taking with a woman he'd begun to think he'd totally misjudged. She blinked and stepped back, 'what do you want?'

'To get to England.'

'Why me?'

'Because, my bet would be that this little bar, slap bang alongside a thriving port, is more than a penny ante, mom and pop operation. You couldn't afford your lifestyle if it was. No, Madam, you are up to your neck in anything and everything crooked that goes in and out of this port and I will pay for that expertise.' He looked around the bar, 'I think the Mafia call it hiding in plain sight. Nothing ostentatious. Stay in the neighbourhood; Godfathers and goatherds, yeah?'

'You are young for this.'

'No, I have always been old. I just look young.'

She nodded.

404

He shifted on the seat, winced and repositioned the hand inside the jacket.

'What's inside the jacket?'

'Cracked ribs.'

'You're not having a good time, ja?'

They both turned as the door to the bar slammed open and the Cadaver and the two wingmen that Starmer had previously beaten in the toilet advanced on him in echelon. The woman held up a warning hand in their direction, 'I've got this.'

Ignoring her they crowded around Starmer at the bar. Plastered nose to his rear, bandaged head to the left rear quarter and the Cadaver, with a plastered right arm, so tight up against his left side he could smell his foetid breath.

'You go now.'

'No Mia, this is personal.'

'Ya so is this personal. Very fuckin' personal. Go, get out! I won't tell you again.'

'You should listen to her,' Starmer added, wincing as his ribs pressed up against the gun in his left hand, 'she's trying to help you.'

Starmer just knew it would be a knife and it had to be the left hand. As the light caught the blade he relaxed his left arm and let gravity drop it and its extra weight out of his jacket down to his side. With the blade inches from his throat he squeezed the trigger. The Cadaver went into shock, uttering not a sound as he fell to the floor where he stared at his shattered foot in disbelief.

'That was necessary?'

He looked at her and smiled sadly, 'no.'

The barmaid looked at the other two, 'get him out of here, shut this place up and send Bernard to me at the house.' She glared at Starmer, ' you, come with me.'

He enjoyed the ride, she was an accomplished driver but the real delight had been her ditching the beehive wig, the make-up, the heels and the artifice that had been the barmaid. He glanced to his left and wondered at the history that had brought this mature woman with the short bob, the strong, striking features and the vulnerable nape to such a position of respect and dominance in her chosen world. 'Thank you.'

'For what?'

'Helping me?'

'You will pay a price.'

'I know.'

'You threatened my family.'

'Someone is threatening mine.'

'People are looking for you.'

'I know.'

'Serious people.'

'I know. Friends?'

'Not in this lifetime.'

'Does that mean I can trust you?'

'No, you threatened my family.'

'I was desperate.'

'I know,' she turned and studied him, 'that's partly why you're here. I can maybe use your desperation but you will also need whatever's in the rucksack.'

'Not love at first sight then?'

'You said I was a business woman? You were right. You have a talent. I have also a talent; I recognise and use talent wherever I find it. So, when you have sorted all this out, maybe you come back. We can do business. In the meantime, stop shooting people. It is bad for business.'

Starmer digested this information and decided to deal with what he assumed to be a serious offer by ignoring it, 'who is Bernard?'

'My Consigliere?'

'James Caan?'

'Robert Duval.'

He looked away, along the coast road that in daylight seemed a lot less isolated than it had when he'd followed her last night. 'I'm sorry for robbing you,' he confessed.

'You had your reasons.' She studied him again and smiled ruefully, 'okay, I forgive you,' she paused, 'maybe.'

'How much do you want for all this?'

'Ten thousand pounds.'

'Not that forgiving then?'

She giggled, 'Ten thousand and then we make love.'

Starmer blushed and looked away.

She convulsed with laughter, 'okay, let's call it twelve thousand.'

'I'm sorry, I didn't mean to be disrespectful. It just came as a bit of a surprise.'

'You don't fancy me?'

Starmer coughed, 'well, you're a very good looking woman but…err, I'm with someone.'

'You have morals?'

'Well yes.'

'But they don't stop you shooting people, dealing in drugs and setting fire to barges?'

'There's Business and there's Family.' He tracked back, 'what barge?'

'Zutphen?'

'I know nothing about a barge,' he declared wondering whether Andries had restored the family honour with arson.

She dropped a hand to his thigh and squeezed, 'ok, so anyway, leave my family alone.'

He lifted her hand and replaced it in her lap, 'it's a deal.'

'I am Mia.'

'Charlie.'

'Charlie? You don't look like a Charlie.'

'I'm beginning to feel a bit like one,' he muttered quietly to himself. 'So how are you going to get me to England?'

He'd been surprised at just how easy it had been to talk to Mia. With little prompting other than the provision of a much-needed cooked breakfast and a bottomless coffee pot he'd unburdened himself, gradually. She now knew that his involvement with "serious people" was largely accidental and that his main motive was the rescue of Julie. She'd seemed particularly interested in his disavowal of the life he'd been forced to live in recent days. She'd been sceptical, pointing to the contents of the rucksack, his willingness to use violence and the obvious discrepancies in his account, to suggest an instinctive affinity with that world. Her world. She didn't press him on the inconsistencies but unpicked enough to demonstrate that she also wasn't without a certain natural cunning.

She sat on the stool at the end of the kitchen island, crossed her legs and lit the ninth cigarette of the breakfast. Seeing Starmer's eyes drift towards her, she re-crossed the legs, smiled and enquired, 'you sure you don't want to save that two thousand?' She grinned as he blushed. 'Here's the problem, Charlie Starmer.' She laughed again at the stunned look on his face. 'You think I am hick from Belgium, Andy?'

'You knew?'

'Of course.'

'I feel like I've been auditioned.'

'You got the part.' She frowned, 'I won't say I was expecting you but I was not surprised.' She sighed, 'you were nearly right about the Mom and Pop operation. We are a little bigger than that but not as big as the people you have been messing with. My problem is that they are beginning to think that they can push people around. They want my contacts, my routes and maybe my people. Who knows? I must decide, soon, do I join them or fight them. One thing is for sure. I can't stay as I am.'

'Why not?'

'They see me as competition. They are not satisfied with a reasonable profit. They are not happy unless they have obscene amounts of cash that they haven't got room to store, let alone spend.' She viciously stubbed out her cigarette and reached for the tenth.

'Well, now, they're in trouble. They've attracted a good deal of attention and their protection doesn't seem to be working too well.'

'Protection?'

'Police?'

'Never, never, ever deal with Police. They are too greedy and you get very little for what you pay. However,' she reflected, 'I would pay real money for their Customs connections.'

'Why?'

'I'm import and export, not distribution. I don't need Police. I don't do sachets.'

'The Cadaver in the bar?'

'Is tolerated.'

'And there was me thinking he was running things.'

'Rook en Speigels.'

'Huh?'

'Smoke and mirrors. As you say, hiding in full sight.'

'Now, let us talk about your trip. You have heard of Hoverport in Boulogne?'

'Used it once; school trip.' he shuddered with the memory.

'Good, it is one of our routes. They are running down the operation. Already they do not so good. Next year the Channel Tunnel is open. Then they do more not so good. They are stripping plant and equipment from Boulogne and taking it to a place called Pegwell Bay. My shipment goes as well. You go with shipment.'

'When?'

408

'Tonight. You go as a monteur?'

Starmer shrugged quizzically.

A voice from the open kitchen door supplied, 'Mechanic, you go as a mechanic.'

Mia swivelled on her stool, 'ah Bernard, meet Charlie or Andy.'

Starmer stretched out his hand to a tall, painfully thin man with a grey and yellow complexion in his late fifties. A man who struggled to fill both his collar and a superbly cut tweed jacket and who chose to ignore Starmer's greeting. He sat back down, slightly embarrassed, as the grey-haired visitor moved slowly and painfully to Mia's side and kissed her on both cheeks.

'He is what the fuss is all about? He doesn't look old enough.'

'Yeah, okay Bernard, I've done all that. He might not look old enough but he seems to have made an impression on the opposition. They've posted big money on this boy.'

'How much?'

'More than twelve grand Charlie.'

'So, why not turn me in for the money?'

'Giving you to them doesn't solve my problem. I'm sort of hoping that you might be part of the answer to that problem.' She paused and looked across at Bernard as though seeking his endorsement. He nodded, almost imperceptibly, 'I need someone on the distribution end in the UK. Someone smart enough, connected enough, determined enough and maybe desperate enough to take it on.'

'Not in a million years. I've told you. I just want to get Julie back and get on with my life with her.'

'And you think they're going to let you?'

Starmer shrugged, uncomfortable with a truth he'd already accepted and one that he knew was about to be reiterated.

'The thing is Charlie; you have got a few million pounds' sterling of their product. They are never going to let that go. You do know that, don't you?'

He nodded, reluctantly.

'You work with me and I deal with them. Who else you gonna get to help? The Police? Think about it. Come back when she lets you down. She will let you down.'

'What makes you think that?'

'She's a Junkie.'

Starmer's frustrations got to him and he began to pace angrily, 'how the hell do you know all this stuff; the shipment and my name? How do you know?' He demanded.

Bernard clicked his paper dry fingers to gain Starmer's attention and to distract him from his rising anger, 'that's my part of the operation. Intelligence. Was any of what you we told you today wrong?'

Starmer shook his head.

'So, will you consider my Sister's proposition?'

'I will think about it yes. I take it that if I say no my trip is off.'

Bernard smiled sadly, 'that isn't how we work.'

'Ok I will really think about it.'

'Thank you, please don't take too long. Time is short.'

'It is?'

'Bernard is dying,' Mia murmured. She moved behind her brother and slipped an arm around his shoulders. 'He wants to leave me with good partners.' She looked at her brother, 'will he do Bernard?'

'There would be work to do. But yes, I think, once he realises that he really has no choice, he will do.'

Starmer reached down to his feet, pulled the rucksack onto the kitchen island, unzipped it and retrieved a brick of cash, 'twelve thousand, yeah?'

Mia waved a dismissive hand, 'there is no charge.'

'Really?'

She laughed, 'well maybe now we have to be making love six times to settle the debt.' She walked over to him and kissed his cheek, 'you will think about our offer?'

Starmer nodded.

'Good, we are looking to set up in Manchester.'

Bernard moved towards Starmer with his hand outstretched, 'There's a place we now have an interest in,' a smile played at the corners of his mouth, 'the previous owner is missing.'

'Slammers?'

Bernard laughed. They shook hands.

Chapter Twenty - six

Denton pushed back, rocked the chair onto its two rear legs, hooked his ankles around the front ones and propped his knees against the hardwood lipped edge of the table in the interview room. It seemed less than hours since he'd last spent time in a Police Station, being interviewed about the shooting in the Dukes Head, although he knew it was nearer to just over a week. Reflecting on his experiences from then he could scarcely believe all that had happened since. Now, though, he felt an overwhelming sense of relief. Relief that it was over, relief that he was in the safe hands of the Authorities and relief that he would soon be able to surrender to the exhaustion that was threatening to overcome him. This release from the all-consuming tension and uncertainty of recent days had started the moment the first uniform had burst into the house at Warnsborn. He'd realised immediately that the arrival of Uniformed Police was the best possible outcome for him, Julie and Dee. Sure, there would be questions but he was confident he had the answers and was determined to mount staunch and maybe, indignant defiance in the face of any interrogation.

Since the Police assault on the house in Holland he'd been handcuffed, separated from the others, driven by fast car to Schiphol, lugged across the tarmac at City Airport and driven to the underground car park of Police premises somewhere in London. He guessed he'd now been confined to this room for a couple of hours. The handcuffs may have been removed but so had his freedom. Like many of his generation and upbringing he'd never had a real reason to doubt the Police and his trust in them, while not absolute, was sufficient for him to be reasonably confident of a good outcome. On balance, he had faith in them and the justice system and the more he reviewed the events of recent days the more convinced he became of his ability to defend himself against any allegations and charges. He firmly felt that he had been an innocent reacting to circumstances, imposed by others, in the only way he knew how and in the best interests of the safety of his family and Dee.

He unhooked his ankles, dropped the chair back onto all legs, sat up and addressed the Policeman stood by the door with his arms folded, legs astride and gaze unfocused somewhere on the middle distance. 'Any chance of a cup of tea?' The eyes focused, briefly, but not on Denton, before the brain switched back to neutral and the contemplation of whatever delights policemen distract themselves with while on such demanding duties. Denton studied the man; knife edge creases in both trousers and shirt while a bristling moustache and a campaign medal bar suggested ex-military. A paunch, burst capillaries to his nose and flushed cheeks hinted that his more active years were behind him. 'How about telling me the time then?' Denton enquired conversationally waving an empty wrist at the Officer to indicate his watch had been confiscated. The man didn't move and gave absolutely no indication that he he'd heard. 'No? So, I suspect that telling me where I am and how long all this is going to take is a bit above your paygrade also. Right?' This time the Officer blinked, gazed at him through bloodshot eyes and sniffed before slipping back into a reverie that was brutally interrupted by the door opening and slamming into his back.

Denton recognised the man as one of the British Detectives who'd accompanied the Dutch Police at Langoed and now, as then, was vaguely aware that memory receptors were at work somewhere in the far reaches of his brain. The man had substituted a dark grey suit for the maroon trousers and pastel checked sweater he'd worn on their last encounter and walked purposefully to the table, tossed a pack of cigarettes down, nodded to Denton and invited, 'help yourself.' Turning to the uniformed Officer he instructed, 'ok you can go,' before pulling out a chair and sitting down. Both, looked up as the guard coughed. 'Yes?' The Detective barked.

412

'Suh, protocol requires that I, or another officer, stay in the room to accompany you during interview,' he tensed and came to attention, 'Suh!'

The Detective swivelled to look at Denton with a faint look of quizzical amusement playing across his features. He turned his back on his colleague and grinned at Denton. 'Do you know who I am Constable?' He enquired, turning to stare the man down.

'I do sir.'

'And?'

The Constable coughed again, 'you are Detective Chief Superintendent Roy King. Suh!'

'Right, so fuck off and organise some tea.'

'Right you are sir.'

A slow smile spread across the Detective's face as he looked at Denton, 'you didn't recognise me then Paul?'

Denton slowly shook his head from side to side while he studied the man opposite as the full import of the revelation seeped into his brain where it filtered through recent memories, cross matched with experiences and perceptions, before finally reaching farther back. As far back as his childhood. His eyes glinted at King, 'I'd always sort of assumed that you'd end up on the other side.'

'I might have done but for Joan and 'Aitch,' King acknowledged with a rueful grin.

Denton continued, 'in fact at one point in this sad and sorry mess I seriously thought about tracking you down and asking for your help.' He laughed sardonically, 'I was sure you'd be something in the Mafia, or close, and might have helped me, or at least made some sense of what was going on. How wrong can you be?' He shrugged and sighed, 'though it's strange, when I saw you at Langoed I had a feeling I knew you from somewhere. Just couldn't place you.'

King grinned, 'well, here I am now and not in the Mafia.' The grin slipped from his face as quickly as it had arrived, 'I will try and help you Paul but you are mixed up in a very serious investigation and you have questions to answer. I hope you understand that. We're a long way from the pre-fab estate now. I regret that our history buys you very little in this situation.'

Denton, again, rocked the chair onto the back legs and took a good look at Roy King who endured the scrutiny good naturedly. 'No, I'd never have recognised you anyway. You're far too well fed these days. What happened to that skinny kid with the criminal tendencies and the massive chip on the shoulder?'

"Aitch is what happened. Sat me down and laid it all out for me. Chapter and verse. Then he kept an eye on me through various foster homes, visited occasionally, remembered my birthday, Christmas, that sort of thing. He came to see me after a couple of run ins, nothing too serious and suggested the Army. Best move ever. So, I joined up. Then left that gang and joined this one.' He leant back looking pensive, 'Yeah, I owe a lot to 'Aitch. And Joan, of course. I went to her funeral you know.'

'Didn't see you.'

'Saw you. Didn't hear about 'Aitch's funeral until too late. Real shame. I admired him and owed him a lot. I'm sorry.'

Denton wondered again about 'Aitch and what he'd now come to think of as his father's little secrets. 'So, Detective Chief Superintendent? Married? Kids?'

King chuckled, 'I'm supposed to be asking the questions.' He paused reflectively though, 'married, separated, two kids and living a couple of miles from you. Now, let's make a start.'

He briefly mirrored Denton's actions as he pushed himself back to balance on the rear two legs of the chair before suddenly dropping forward with the thump of his forearms hitting the table, 'you've been a busy boy Paul. Let's see, you first "come to our attention"', he mimed mid-air quotes with his fingers, 'as a witness "stroke" suspect in a shooting in Bromley. Then before we know where we are mayhem breaks out in Manchester; a body is found in a car boot and two well-known local reprobates are put in the hospital.' He held up a hand to halt Denton's angry response, 'no, hold up. I haven't finished. Then the action moves to Scotland where, in Findhorn, we have the bodies of one very nasty and well known little Manc scrote and those of two very unfortunate civilians. Not to mention various reports of a missing Manchester crime boss.' Again, he held up a hand to stem any outburst from Denton, 'then, Paul, you go all nautical on us. You pinch two boats, embarrassing Her Majesties' Customs and Excise Service in the process, enter Holland illegally and tip up at the place of an international drug importer where, somehow, your ex colleague, Webber, manages to blow himself up with a hand grenade. What was going on Paul?' He spread his hands wide inviting a response.

'Are you suggesting that I was responsible for the shooting of Micky McCarthy, the deaths of those other people and Webber?' He stood up angrily and leant over the table furiously waving a clenched fist beneath King's nose, 'because if you are,' he stuttered to a halt and slowly sank back down on the chair as the enormity of the explanation now required of him began to seep in.

'You need to stay calm Paul. Another outburst like that will see you back in cuffs. Do you understand?'

Denton nodded.

'Good. No I don't, necessarily, believe you were personally responsible for all that. Although, given the,' he mimed the quotes again, "history", 'between Webber and your wife, there is motive. No, what's intriguing me is that McCarthy was investigating the company of which you were a Director. A company under suspicion and investigation for the importation of drugs into this country. You, your wife and daughter were "known associates"', he, again, mimed the quotes, "of a convicted drug dealer"; Webber? A man you employed? Doesn't look good, does it?' He inclined his head to one side and offered a sympathetic smile.

'I didn't kill Mickey', Denton hissed savagely through teeth gritted in frustration.

'Maybe not, but you might have arranged it or know who did.'

'Do you seriously believe that?'

'Again, not necessarily, but maybe you can begin to see why you are in a very difficult position here. You see Paul, you may well protest your innocence but when all these things happened you were either at the scene or very nearby at a time when you were already under suspicion and investigation.'

'Look, for Christ's sake listen. I am a victim of circumstance. Until I was interviewed by that dodgy Customs Officer Church, I had no idea that NMG was a front for importing drugs.'

'Dodgy Customs Officer?'

'Church?'

'Church is not dodgy. He's played a pivotal role in this Investigation,' King snapped sharply.

Any doubts that Denton may have had about his opinion of the Customs Officer's probity were immediately dispelled by the sharpness of King's response. Church was in it up to his neck.

415

He hurriedly returned to his account to distract King from further query. 'That same night, I was told my daughter was missing. I went straight to Manchester to find her and to try and sort out that problem. I eventually traced Julie to Findhorn, found her, rescued her and then got chased and shot at by a bloke that, until then, I didn't like, but had no idea was a gun toting crook. That was Webber? Right?' He paused for breath and to gather his thoughts. 'That's why I stole the boat. To get away from Webber and his trigger-happy mates. Apart from the theft of the boat I have committed no crimes whatsoever.' Before King could interrupt again he held up his hand and declared, triumphantly, 'and I didn't enter Holland illegally, I was taken into territorial waters by Her Majesty's Customs.' He dropped his face into his hands and massaged some relief into tired and prickly eyes, 'a hand grenade?' He muttered, his thoughts returning to Andries' farmhouse, the paperweight, Julie's interest and her whispered declaration to him immediately before the explosion at Langoed.

King leant forward, propped his chin on his intertwined fingers, closed his eyes briefly, ignored the question and asked softly, 'who is Andrew Starmer?'

'Julie's boyfriend,' Denton responded quickly, seeking refuge in an answer for which he could see no harmful consequences.

'No, I mean, "who is he?", what's his background, where did he come from, what do you know about him?'

Denton let his mind drift back to his first meeting with Starmer and then on and through the various experiences that they had shared in recent days and realised that he knew very little about the man. 'Julie's boyfriend, a student at Manchester,' he stumbled to a halt, 'someone who helped me get Julie back?'

'Did he tell you that he worked at a night club in Manchester; Slammers?'

'I knew he worked there, I think he mentioned it, but I'm not certain', replied Denton wondering at his own caution and reminded of the old churchgoer in Manchester who'd told him about Starmer and Slammers.

'Did he ever mention any names?'

'Not that I recall,' again Denton wondered.

'Mention any records, a book, register, notes, accounts, that sort of thing that he may have found or seen at that club?'

This time Denton knew what had prompted his caution and started the warning bells that had been increasing in volume throughout the interview. The book contained information about payments and arrangements with corrupt Police Officers and here was a Police Officer who knew of its existence. How many times had Starmer had to explain that one of their major problems was never knowing who could be trusted? He shook his head slowly realising that perhaps his earlier faith in the Police and the criminal Justice system may have been premature. 'He never mentioned anything.'

'Do you know where he is?'

'No.'

'That didn't sound very much like the voice of an innocent, concerned citizen "helping the Police with their enquiries", did it?'

Denton was beginning to find the air quotation marks irritating, 'As I said, apart from borrowing a boat, I have committed no crime. Now I want to see a solicitor.'

King sighed, 'yeah, about that, I am going to charge you with the theft of the yacht, escaping from lawful custody, theft and misuse of property belonging to her Majesty's' Customs and illegal entry to the Netherlands. You'll be charged and released on bail.' An apologetic smile flicked along his lips. 'You will be recalled for further interview. Your wife is waiting for you downstairs.'

Dee Dee Wilson felt tired, dirty and a burning sense of injustice. Bad enough that she had been manhandled into a car by policemen who'd ignored her protests, worse that she'd been recognised, under escort, on the flight back by a fan and completely, gut wrenchingly, unacceptable that she should now be interviewed, for the second time, by a woman she'd trusted as a respected music journalist. 'So, you're no reporter?'

'Sadly no. I'm Detective Inspector Kate Lockstone.'

'Don't give me that prissy, goody two shoes "sadly" crap you two timing piece of work. What the hell was all that about back in Manchester? What happened to Kate Lockstone music journalist? How did you get the reporter gig?'

'My DCS set it up.'

'Your what?'

'My Detective Chief Superintendent. Mister King.'

Dee studied the young woman long and hard, 'I just knew you weren't the real deal.'

'You did. How?'

'You listened. Reporters don't listen they come with pre-conceptions they want confirmed.'

'Sadly,' Kate Lockstone smile briefly at her own temerity, 'my guise then was a necessary subterfuge in an ongoing investigation.' She did her best to arrange her features in some semblance of a sympathetic smile in a doomed attempt to assuage the now visibly angry singer. 'You became "of interest" because of your connection to Mister Williams. I needed to know the extent of your involvement. So, the aid of,' she laughed, 'a "well-known national music journalist" was enlisted, or rather invented.'

'Yeah, you sure as heck ain't no reporter.'

'Did you get to read the article?'

'You wrote an article,' Dee exclaimed incredulously.

'I did, and I think you might even be a little impressed.' She shrugged, 'there was no knowing how long I'd need to use that cover back then. We might have needed to keep that line of communication open. The absence of an article might have got you, or others, wondering.' She looked over reflectively at Dee hoping the news that the interview hadn't been a complete scam might placate the singer. 'Anyway, I need to ask you some questions.'

'Am I under arrest?'

'Not at the moment, I am simply hoping that you will help me with our enquiries.'

'Hope on Sister and show me the way outta here.'

'Miss Wilson, I said you weren't under arrest. Please don't think, however, that I won't arrest you if I need to. I'd rather not but I will if pushed.'

Dee took refuge in her deep breathing while she tried to gather her thoughts and some level of control. She ignored the irritatingly composed and confident young woman sitting at the other end of the leather look utilitarian office sofa and glanced across the polished meeting table to the windows beyond. It had not escaped her notice that she was not in a standard Police interview room and that she had, at least, been accorded some courtesy and spared some indignities. Still seething though, she rounded on the young woman, 'if'n you planning to arrest me you damn well better be fixin' to get somebody from the embassy down here pretty damn quick. You gonna drop the dime? Make the call? You hearing me?' she demanded. Dee witnessed an almost imperceptible change in the young woman. She watched her features harden as sympathy and understanding were chased from her face by tightening jaw muscles, narrowing eyes and a look of determination that barely concealed the detective's anger.

'I hear you,' Lockstone sighed, looked hard at a pad on her knees, crossed and re crossed her legs, picked up the pad and then slapped it down hard on the sofa. 'Miss Wilson neither a personal entreaty from your new President Clinton nor the combined intervention of the United States Marine Corps marching down Whitehall with a wing of B52s overhead and all of 'em whistling Dixie will see you released from this room until I am finished. You, perhaps unknowingly, wandered into a long, complicated and very expensive investigation. Unless and until you tell me everything you know about what happened, you are not leaving this room. Now,' she paused, 'are you hearing me?'

Dee nodded. Eventually.

'Good, can we now get out of this pissing contest?'

Dee slowly smiled, marvelling at the young woman's chutzpah. 'Okay, you got a deal.'

'Thank you. Start at the beginning?'

Dee wondered just where that beginning to this latest chapter in her life was. So much had happened in such a short space of time that her mind was a whirling kaleidoscope of experience and emotions. Denton was where it had started she concluded. 'I met a guy in a bar in Manchester. His daughter was missing and he was looking for her. I helped him out with a few enquiries on the club scene.' She paused, struggling to remember how, from such a relatively innocent start, events had spun so far out of control. She continued with a voice slowed by exhaustion, 'then, along the way, I realised that my new Manager was up to his neck in all sorts of crap. He realised I was becoming a problem and sorta hijacked me. That was just after that interview with you.'

'So, the guy looking for his daughter was Paul Denton?'

Dee nodded.

'And the Manager was,'

'Williams,' Dee supplied.

'They, hijacked you to where?'

'Scotland. That's when I knew I was in some pretty serious shit.'

419

'Yeah?'

'Yeah, they shot at Denton.'

'And then?'

'Well, I got away from them at a station in Scotland and made my way back to London.'

'Getting Williams arrested on the way?'

Dee smiled, 'you know about that?'

'Neat trick. I'd have been proud of that one,' the detective smiled back.

Dee chuckled, 'so by then I knew that they were after Denton and I knew they were going to Holland and that he and his daughter were in danger. So, I decided to get over there and see if I could help him.'

'Why?'

'What do you mean, "why"?'

'You met this guy a couple of days previously and suddenly you're crossing borders for him?'

Why indeed she wondered. Not for the first time. 'Love?' She ventured slowly, looking at Kate Lockstone and hoping to see, if not complete acceptance, at least a degree of understanding in the other woman's eyes. And she did.

'It happens,' the Detective's face relaxed and a broad smile briefly replaced the official face. 'I'd like to keep you for a couple of hours and get a detailed statement from you. Times, places, people? That sort of thing?' She grinned, 'would you help me with that? Or do I need to phone Mister Clinton?'

Dee laughed, 'I think he's probably kinda busy now, right after the Inauguration. Does this mean you believe me? I'm free to go?'

'I think so. For the moment, at least. Certainly, I'd find it difficult to charge you with anything that'd stick and I can personally corroborate some of your story.' She leaned intently towards Dee, 'my guise wasn't just to check you out. Mister Williams was a major part of the investigation. That's how I got the invite to the place in Holland. Remember? Our chat at the airport?'

'Was that coincidence? Meeting at the airport?'

Kate laughed, 'not entirely. We picked you up as you left Williams flat.'

'Ok I'll help.'

'Thank you. Oh, and when you get a minute read my article. It really is rather good.' The young woman threw a smile

420

over her shoulder and Dee could hear another chuckle as the door closed behind her.

Denton squeezed his legs into the front of Stella's car painfully aware that on the last journey he'd taken in this car, they'd argued fiercely. The irony was that, back then, it'd been him, his lifestyle and shortcomings under attack from her. Knowing now what he knew about her and the affair with Webber, he wondered whether her audacity at fronting him out then was born out of fear of discovery or a desire for some sort of reconciliation. Perhaps, with him leaving NMG she'd seen a natural conclusion to the affair? They sat in awkward silence, the only intrusion on their self-conscious solitude being a "top of the hour" news summary from Capital Radio. He learnt that in his enforced isolation from Current Affairs a newly elected Bill Clinton had appointed a woman as US Attorney General and a three-man IRA gang had been arrested in Warrington for bombing a gas works and shooting a policeman. As an over excited, adenoidal young man with an estuarial accent talked over the intro, the words, "If I should stay, I would only be in your way" and Whitney Huston's haunting delivery concentrated his mind on his present predicament.

He glanced sideways at Stella's profile. She'd lost weight. Her face was gaunt and there were deep shadows under eyes that seemed to have receded to the deepest recesses of the sockets. Her usually impeccably coiffured hair was scraped back into a bun, serving further to sharpen and harshen her features while her normally flawless complexion was marked with blemishes partly concealed with carelessly applied make up. She looked as exhausted as he felt.

'Did you know that your lover was sleeping with our daughter?' He shifted in his seat that he might study her reaction. Initially there was none. Then he noticed her shoulders were quivering, her grip on the steering wheel had whitened her knuckles and she was swallowing great gulps of air. 'Did you?' he shouted. The sobs fought their way past the swallows, her shoulders began to shake and she had to use her sleeve to wipe the fast-flowing tears from her eyes. 'You'd better pull over,' he advised. She eventually pulled into the large car park in Norman

Park, coming to a halt alongside an overloaded skip by the entrance to the running track.

'Did you hear me?' he barked.

She pivoted in her seat and turned on him, spitting fury, 'Yes. I heard you. What sort of mother do you think I am?' she screamed at him, 'of course I didn't fucking know.' Her forehead dropped onto the top of the steering wheel which she held with both hands in a ceaseless twisting, turning, tightening grip. She straightened up, retrieved a tissue from her sleeve and attempted to stem the tears and sniffles with a scrap that had neither the size nor the absorbency necessary for the task. 'I knew nothing about Julie's experience,' she fought to regain her composure, 'until she told me,' she sniffed. 'That was last night,' she added emphatically, her restless fingers turning the remains of the damp tissue into a tightly wound twist.

The release of such fury from a woman he'd never known to lose her temper was all the validation he needed; she hadn't known about Julie's experience. Denton felt a sense of relief he hadn't expected. The subconscious logical side of his brain had never accepted that Stella could have been involved or complicit in Julie's degradation. The emotional side, however, bruised by her infidelity with a man he despised, had been prepared to believe the worst. He looked at her as tears coursed runnels through the poorly applied make up and felt a stirring of sympathy and affection that he fought to swiftly dispel. 'Webber?' He studied her face for a reaction with disbelief and scorn written on his. 'And please don't tell me he made you feel alive.'

'Why not? Oh, that would really offend your proprietorial sense of 'droit de soigneur' and male pride, wouldn't it? You being the only one capable of making me feel alive.' she laughed, 'Newsflash Paul; you haven't managed that in a very long while.'

Denton began to see past the practical consequences of his errant behaviour and absence to an uncomfortable appreciation of his failings, not just as a husband, but as a man. Worse, he could feel the moral high ground shifting from under his feet and longed for the buzz and reinforcement of his securities that a drink would deliver. 'Don't go there Stella. You committed adultery behind my back. With fucking Webber. For Christ's sake. He must have been laughing himself sick at me.'

'You pompous pratt. I committed adultery right in front of your unseeing eyes; not behind your back. How many times

Paul,' she shook an admonishing finger in his face, ' how many fucking times did I ask you to think about us, our lives, our futures,' she sobbed, 'our family? How many times did I say you needed treatment for alcoholism?'

'I haven't had a drink for ten days.'

'Am I supposed to be impressed?' she snorted loudly, 'but, hey ho, I'm pleased for you. But, you are an alcoholic and you fucked up our lives and the question you should be asking yourself is will you ever get to day eleven?'

Denton was distracted as an estate car reversed alongside and a middle-aged woman in an ankle length waxed Barbour riding coat with a flowing skirt, green wellies and several leads bustled to the tailgate of her car. His distraction turned to amazement when several dachshunds launched themselves to the ground where they proceeded to tie a besotted dog lover in knots. The corollary of the tangled canine relationships and his own did not escape him. 'But, was any of that an acceptable reason to have an affair?'

'Of course not.' She snapped, as she in turn was distracted by the woman returning to her car with several tethered, yapping dogs in tow, to retrieve her keys and lock up. The woman smiled nervously at her perhaps fearing she had interrupted a tryst. Stella returned the smile, wondering why she was attempting to reassure a stranger as she struggled with Denton. That brief contact with a world going about its business had, she realised, only served to emphasize her own isolation. She looked over at Denton, 'have you any idea how lonely I was?'

Denton struggled for a reply, 'c'mon Stella, you make it sound like it was all bad.'

'Just as I thought,' she tossed her head in disbelief. 'you have no idea.' She turned to the front, adjusted the rear-view mirror, glanced across at the wing mirror to see dog woman fighting to untangle her legs from criss crossing canines and sucked in a breath. 'It wasn't "all bad". Just the last ten years.' She laughed, 'you only get nine for murder. You sucked the life out of me Paul, with your behaviour. You know, there were times when I'd, maybe, wake as you came home and the only clue to your commitment to me was another dirty shirt in the laundry.' She laughed quietly, poignantly, 'you know, I used to be so much in love with you.' She tried to untwist the nearly shredded tissue

423

to mop her cheeks and sobbed, 'then as you disappeared into a pint glass my love sort of dribbled away.'

Denton's assertiveness and his certainty vested in the moral outrage of the cuckold had begun to desert him in the face of this factual and emotional onslaught. Worse, he was beginning to feel guilt; guilt on two fronts. Guilt because of his declared feelings for Dee and guilt for his reawakening feelings for Stella. 'But for Christ's sake Stella. Webber?'

'Would you like to hear how we got together?'

'Not particularly. No!'

Stella dragged her eyes back from the distraction of dog lady and her erratic progress across the park, 'we met because of you.'

'Really?' Denton snorted.

'Yes really. You were, apparently, at a sales conference in Birmingham. That's what you told me.'

'Right?' He replied hesitantly.

'For eight days?'

'And?'

'I was worried. Webber answered the 'phone.'

'And?'

'He found you. In Downham.'

'In Downham? What the fuck was I doing in Downham?'

'Exactly.'

'So, this arsehole does you a favour and you drop your knickers?' He regretted the words the minute they had left his mouth and Stella's look of disdain and disgust began to give him an insight into her frustration and despair. Why, he reflected, was it always thus? That this instant, irrational, impulsive, destructive side of his nature took free reign over his deeper, considered and heartfelt feelings. Why did he hurt those he loved?

'I'm sorry,' he muttered, wondering whether his apologies had currency any more. He could vaguely recall periods when constant badgering about his lifestyle had been a part of his life, when every departure from the house had been accompanied by a crescendo of complaint and when he'd felt nothing but relief as he'd sat in the car contemplating the next drink. He'd begun to listen but only on the day that Julie had disappeared; the day that Stella had told him that she would talk to him whether he liked it or not. Perhaps she had been going to tell him about Webber?

'Paul, I was alone. Not lonely; we have friends and acquaintances. I was alone. If we went anywhere I was constantly on edge; would you go into your one-man show, insult someone or argue a lost cause of no interest to anybody. How many looks of patient sympathy from other wives would I harvest in an evening? Then, this man, George, helped me find you. He came to reassure me that you were okay and that he would keep an eye on you. Then, he listened and he talked a little; asked what I thought or felt and took me places you never would, dined me, danced me and listened some more.'

'Did you love him?'

'No,' she enjoyed the sense of relief he fought to hide, 'but I enjoyed him in every sense.' She knew that it wasn't only the hint of sexual satisfaction but also the triumphant accent on those last few words that had made her husband turn away.

'And now?'

'And now he's dead. Julie told me,' she explained.

'Did she tell you she killed him?'

'She did. She wasn't sure you knew.'

'I worked it out. Where is Julie?' He slapped the dashboard angrily, 'what I meant was how is Julie?'

'I've booked her into the Priory at Hayes. She needs time, space and expert help with the addiction. I thought it was for the best.'

He nodded, the Hospital certainly had a good reputation, although, locally, it had, in the past, provided some amusement in local hostelries when drying out pop stars had got over the wall. 'How's she doing?'

'Not too well. I think the drugs are the least of our problems.'

'And our worst problem?'

'What Webber did. That's going to be with her a very long while. Maybe forever. Hopefully she can learn how to deal with it in the Priory.' She reached across for his hand and squeezed it, 'few people deserve the sort of death that Webber had. He did. I understand what she did and why she did it. She needed that.'

She dropped the hand and stared distractedly through the side window at a waxed milk carton teetering on the brink of being dislodged from the edge of the skip by a strong breeze. 'Paul, I made a big mistake with Webber. Looking back, he took advantage of my vulnerability.' She reached for the wheel and the comfort of the twisting grip and release. 'I am not offering that as an excuse but briefly,' she breathed deeply, very deeply, 'briefly, I was free. I could see a different way of living.'

425

'With the bastard who went on to seduce your daughter?'

She shook her head sadly, 'I couldn't have known that was going to happen. I never thought George was the future but he'd pointed me in the right direction.'

'George?'

'Yes, 'she murmured, 'such a re assuring name. Un-prepossessing.'

'He was a killer.'

'Apparently.'

'You realise I have grounds for divorce?'

'Almost certainly.'

Denton paused while he puzzled over the monosyllabic responses from the woman whose previous response to any challenge would have been a calm dissection of his argument and a firm rebuttal. His thoughts drifted to Dee and his feelings for her which, he realised, strongly conflicted with his re-awakening feelings for the wife that had so stoically suffered his apparent inadequacies. But, he recalled, she'd been aiding and abetting Webber while he'd been trying to find Julie. 'You were with Webber in Scotland.'

'I'd asked him to help find Julie. You'd disappeared, hadn't 'phoned and I was desperate. Remember, he'd helped before?'

'And when he found me he tried to kill me,' Denton took some satisfaction from Stella's audible intake of breath.

She reached across and took his hand again, easing her other hand up to his cheek. She slowly turned his head and earnestly locked onto his gaze, 'Paul, I had no idea. I'm sorry.'

Denton sensed approaching absolution and an obligation to address unresolved responsibilities to an unfulfilled family butting up against his feelings and hopes for a relationship with Dee. The return of Dog Lady and her apologetic grimace as she sought to load her Germanic hordes and squeeze past abutting wing mirrors gave him time to consider. Guilt and a sense of how things were, how they could have been and how they might still be began to damn any lingering hopes of a future with Dee. He coughed apologetically, 'Stells, we've both made mistakes. But, we can work through this, can't we? I mean, the day of my retirement you were going to put the heavy word on me. Right? And I'd've left work and we'd have worked it out. Right?'

426

Stella looked past Denton to Dog Lady in her car and her final apologetic parting glance as she drove away and then gave her full attention back to her husband. 'No, I was leaving you. That's what I was going to tell you. Let's get one thing very, very, clear here Paul. I am not asking for your understanding or acceptance; I am certainly not asking for your forgiveness and I have no intention of apologising for my actions. I want one thing and one thing only from you. My freedom and, of course, your help with Julie. We need to work together on that,' she added. 'However, be under no illusion, we are finished. It is over.'

She lowered the car window wiped her swollen eyes with the now tattered and shredded tissue and tossed it to the ground. As she watched the discarded scrap lift on a breeze and drift away she felt a calm certainty and she dropped Denton's hand, 'we were finished a long while ago.'

Chapter Twenty - seven

Starmer sat in Woolley's old chair, idly swinging from side to side as he looked down onto the floor of the empty club from the place he'd begun to think of as his eyrie. He'd been surprised at how fast Mia and Bernard had moved. Slammers had already been acquired and within weeks of his return to Manchester refurbishment was well under way. Staff had been hired and a grand opening night had seen the relaunch. He'd taken an active part in the redesign and Mia had seemed content to give him his head. Her only objection had been to the 'eyrie' which she saw as a waste of space. In the end, she'd bowed to his experience and assertion that the control and management of such a venture was about visibility; seeing and being seen to see. Looking down through mirrored glass he could see the full length of the main bars opposite and all the floor space from the entrance to the stage area. He'd also insisted on lightening the Maginot look with several coats of pure white over the old purple and had upgraded the lighting; he wanted visibility in all areas and those that weren't covered from the eyrie had camera cover. He glanced over at the bank of monitors on the end wall that completed his surveillance precautions. Leaning forward he rested his arms on the sill and idly watched a heavily built young woman in leggings, T shirt and head scarf swing a floor bumper and polisher in wide arcs on the floor below. He could hear the faint whine of the electric motor and snatches of tuneless song as she accompanied her Walkman.

He swung the chair full circle and pulled it up to Woolley's old Partners desk. He'd installed many touches of his own in the eyrie; paintings, Chesterfields and a magnificent Tabriz carpet but had decided to keep the desk. Partly as a reminder that, in this new world, mistakes, as Thompson had discovered while perched on its edge, could be fatal. He'd not heard from Denton since his return but had managed to discover that Julie was being cared for in a rehabilitation facility. His initial instinct had been to visit her but Mia, whose advice he'd come to respect, had cautioned against. He had, however, 'phoned Julie's home in Bromley, spoken, very briefly, to a hostile Stella and enquired after Julie. The response had been less than helpful and he'd been asked not to call again. In the brief time that had passed since he'd last seen her his feelings for Julie had remained undiminished but, he thought, were probably unrequited. Worried how she might view his present lifestyle he'd decided not to pursue her. He reasoned that she'd find him if she wanted to see him. He would then have to decide, as would she, whether his chosen path was for them both. He had no doubt that it was she who had been responsible for the explosion that had killed Webber and wondered whether that responsibility was now weighing heavily upon her. However briefly, she'd entered a world where nothing was off limits; his world. Perhaps they could both make a life there?

He'd been surprised that, apart from a desultory interview with the locals a few days after his return to Slammers, the Police hadn't come calling. He knew they were struggling to make the connection between him, Thompson, Osman and the still missing Woolley. He sensed a distinct lack of endeavour with the interviewing Officers readily accepting that while he knew all three men he was not involved in their alleged activities. Part of their difficulty, he understood was, that apart from Denton and Julie, the only other people to have seen him in Findhorn at the time of the murders, were Woolley with Osman and poor Jamie and Melissa; the missing and the dead. He'd puzzled, briefly, as no mention was made of his time in Holland but eventually concluded that as he'd escaped the arrests at the house, they were unaware of his time there. The fact that the officers were seemingly ignorant that he'd been held by Church on the Customs Cutter, tended to support his earlier view that Church was bent and keeping that titbit of information to himself. Thankfully for Starmer, being interviewed by bent Policemen had certain advantages; they had a vested interest in not asking questions that could lead to compromising answers.

He'd also accepted Mia's explanation that the Police knew where he was and would already have been back had they any definitive evidence of his involvement. While Woolley's empire ran courtesy of Police corruption, Mia scorned such involvement as costly and counterproductive. She was, though, very interested in the Customs connection. With his new-found respect for Bernard's abilities and connections he'd wondered whether Church had already been got at to ensure he didn't speak of Starmer's detention on HMC Sentinel?

His greater, current, concern was that Manchester was fast turning into the Wild West with gun battles between rival gangs a regular occurrence. Bernard's Intelligence briefings kept him up to speed on the different operations, the key players and particularly the two families vying for supremacy in the drug supply chain. Some members of both families, on different nights, were regular attendees at Slammers and Starmer knew some of them as old acquaintances of Woolley. Overall, they were reasonably behaved, while in the club, and seemed to have accepted his new status although he knew that would change the minute Mia and Bernard decided to open for real business.

Bernard's strategy was based on a simple supply and demand model. He knew that Manchester was about to suffer a drastic drop off in supply and in a city fuelled by drugs, proposed to keep a stranglehold at the Dutch end until demand had reached unprecedented and unfulfilled levels. This, Bernard explained, would cause a turf war that could be exacerbated and exploited to their advantage by pitching one family against the other. At a certain point Starmer was to then approach the surviving family and offer them a new arrangement. He'd argued that they should use both families but Bernard had pointed out that to effectively control one they had to destroy the other; "pour encourager les autres". Once the surviving family realised that their old suppliers were no longer coming through they'd have little choice but to sign up to the new deal. The trick, Starmer realised, was not to get caught in the middle.

His gaze returned to the floor below as the motor on the floor bumper cut. The young woman flicked a long length of cable from the path of a big man in an oversize suit padding his way across the floor towards her holding a plug in his hand. Starmer stood and leaned in closer to the glass for a better view. He sat back down and reached behind him for the PA mike.

'Send him up Josie.'

The door opened and he studied the man standing there. He'd had only the briefest of views of Williams' minder; on the quay at Findhorn and while crouching on the stairs at Langoed.

'You've lost a lot of weight.'

'We've met?'

'Not really. You been on a diet?'

'No.'

'What do you want?'

'I'm looking for Williams.'

'What makes you think he's here.'

'I thought you might have heard from him by now.'

'Why?'

'You've got his gear.'

'Last I heard he was under arrest.'

'He got away.'

'How?'

'Injured in custody.'

'So?'

'They gave him crutches.'

'And?'

'Cuffs and crutches?'

'Right. So, he wasn't injured?'

'And he wasn't cuffed. Skipped from the bail hearing.'

'Why do you want him?'

'He owes me.'

'Much?'

'Enough.'

'Right. How are you now?'

'What d'ye mean?'

'Last time I saw you, you'd just been blown out of a garage in Holland.'

'You were there?' The big man's eyes narrowed and a puzzled frown creased his forehead

Starmer nodded, 'close as we are now.'

The man grunted, 'I was lucky. Grenade was rigged to the car door. Webber's eyes were all over the place for four seconds. Door took most of it. Banged about a bit. Burns. Hospital for a few weeks. Healed now.'

'Lucky indeed. Well I've not seen Williams.'

'You will.'

'You reckon?'

'What you're holding is all he's got left.'

'What am I holding?'

'A shipment.'

'What do you know about me?'

'You ran Webber ragged. Williams reckoned you were an Operator. I've spent quite a few days chasing you for him.'

'What would you have done if you'd caught me?'

'What I was told.'

'You up for a bit of work?'

'No. I just want to get what's mine. What I was promised. Then I'm out.'

'Think you'll get it?'

'Maybe not.'

'So, as I said, want a job?'

'Doing what?'

'A one off. A Spectacular.'

'They don't come cheap.'

'That's not a problem. Know any Manchester Faces?'

'Some. The ones Woolley dealt with. Not all.'

'Any from the two families?'

'The Reynolds.'

'Get a job with them. The Woolley connection should swing it.'

'Not what I'm looking for.'

'No, but it's what I want.'

'An Insider?'

'Agent Provocateur.'

'You want me to wind them up into doing something stupid?'

'Not them. The McGuigans.'

'How?'

'Do you use a gun?'

'Apart from Goose Green? Once or twice. I don't kill civilians.'

Starmer nodded, viewing the man with a new respect. 'I want you to get a job with the Reynolds. Once you're accepted get known around town. As a nutter. You know the routine; chat up the wrong bird, row in a club, shoot out a window, hold up a dealer, anything to get you noticed. I leave it to you. Just make sure you're recognised, that they know you're with Reynolds and that you're a nutter.'

'Will I get time to write the note?'

'What note?'

'The suicide note?'

Starmer's mind was racing through the possibilities and opportunities that could come from having someone on the inside. 'When you're well known, we'll make the move.'

'The move?'

'The one off. The Spectacular.'

'And then?'

'And then you'll disappear.'

'I'll need to.'

'Pays well.'

'It'd need to. Enough to retire?'

'Ten?'

'Thirty.'

'I could get six Turks for that.'

'Yeah, but you want it done properly.'

'Twenty.'

'Deal.'

'You've got three weeks.'

'Gun?'

'You'll need one. MAC 10s seem to be very popular around here. Get two thirty round magazines. One to get you in the other to get you out.'

'Spray and pray.'

'Yup. I'll be in touch. What's your name?'

'Reg. Reg Boulter.'

Starmer felt an increasing sense of satisfaction as he watched Reg cross the floor below, take the plug from Josie and then stoop to re insert it into the socket on his way out. For the first time in some weeks he felt he was moving towards taking control rather than acting at Mia and Bernard's direction. He liked them both but felt he could only work with; not for Mia. He'd been amazed at the change in the woman. Getting her away from the dockside bar and the persona, character and clothes that went with it had seen a transformation. She'd all but stopped smoking, started to take care of herself and had surprised him with her business acumen. As Bernard's cancer, had progressed he'd visibly declined and Starmer expected that Mia would come to rely on him and knew that this was Bernard's wish. He now felt he'd taken an important step towards implementing the man's plan to destroy one of the families and isolate the other. The news that Williams was on the loose was a concern but not one that he could allow to divert him from the more immediate problem of establishing control in Manchester. Briefly considering Williams' position, he realised that the man's options were limited all the time he held on to the shipment. He'd also have great difficulty coming at Starmer from outside Mia's operation but there was always the possibility he might try for leverage by intimidating Denton or threatening Julie.

Reg Boulter sat in the window of the old Victorian pub in Walmer Street, Rusholme, took his third gulp from his second pint of 'Hyde's Original' and wondered whether he could trust Starmer. On balance, he felt he had little choice. Recovering what he was owed from Williams depended on Williams recovering the shipment that Starmer held. At least, he reasoned, if he was working for Starmer he'd be nearer the money. Of more immediate concern was what was expected of him in the next three weeks. There was also the disquiet that Starmer didn't seem to have much of a grip on mob dynamics. You didn't get into a firm by targeting their opposition and hoping you'd get noticed by the home team. Forced entry was the only way into an outfit; displacing a current middle ranker by force of arms and extreme violence. Once established, and only then, could you reinforce your position by targeting the opposition.

He looked down again at the headline in the Daily Mirror that he'd been using to screen himself from view; 'Huge IRA truck bomb in Bishopsgate.' He'd served with men who'd been with two Para at Bloody Sunday and wondered, not for the first time, whether it had all been worth it. He lifted the paper and looked over the top through the rain splattered window as he watched two smartly but casually dressed men carrying holdalls, leave a dry-cleaners opposite. They moved a few yards up the road to a Jaguar, XJR S Coupe, parked half on the pavement where the older man deposited both bags in the boot. The younger shadow boxed his companion playfully before shaking his hand and making his way to a Porsche 911 a few cars in front. Now, thought Reg, would the late Saturday afternoon habits of a lifetime come into play or would the Mark break with tradition. He saw the man look at his watch, pause, turn up his collar against the rain and look over at the pub as the outside lights switched on and flickered inviting orange reflections across the wet pavement.

As the man skirted some pavement works and made for the entrance, Reg tucked himself out of sight in the Snug end of the bar at the rear of which was a door leading to the toilets. He knew that, in the Saloon Bar, on the other side of the central bar island, was a similar door leading to a corridor and the same toilets. Reg had often had to acknowledge that he was not one of life's great planners but, since he'd left the Army, he'd often found that the Para standby of extreme aggression and shock overwhelmed most opposition. His original plan had been to tackle the man in the toilets but being a "nutter" on the loose required an audience and witnesses to spread the word. He finished the pint of Hyde and made his way through cartons of stacked crisp packets along the corridor to the door for the Saloon. He slipped his watch into his pocket, flexed his fingers, shot his cuffs, took a deep breath and quietly opened the door. The Mark was standing with his back to Reg talking to two punters playing crib at a table to one side of a Juke Box. Ten paces he estimated. As the Mark raised his glass to his mouth with his right hand, Reg launched a low powerful right into his kidney off the back of the ninth stride and fifteen stone's worth of momentum. The man crumpled as his legs weakened and Reg helped him down, and, mercifully, out, with a re cocked right to his temple.

He knelt beside his victim searching through his pocket for keys and looked up to see both card players in a frozen tableau; one with matchstick poised above crib board and the other in mid count. Reg smiled, pocketed the keys and a wallet and enquired, 'one for his nob?'

Outside he paused as he came level with the pavement works, bent down, picked up a piece of broken flag and walked purposefully over to the Dry Cleaners.

Three miles away and thirty minutes later, in an underground hotel parking lot to the north of the centre, he retrieved the holdalls and caught a bus to the centre of town and his hotel to the south. There he retrieved close on seven thousand pounds and some product from one bag and a MAC 10, five magazines and a couple of hand guns from the other.

An hour later he walked into the Sheer Khan restaurant on Curry Mile, carefully arranged his raincoat on the seat next to him, ordered a Balti with Naan and waited. He lounged back in his seat trying to look more relaxed than he felt and watched the party get out of the Limo. The man and a woman from the back seat and their passenger were followed by two goons from a car behind. The woman entered the restaurant first, holding her hand forward to be fawned over by an obsequious Indian in full fig. Reg had always been amazed by gangster's women. He couldn't remember ever having met one that wasn't blonde, buxom, brassy and bronzed. Lee Reynold's wife was not the exception to prove any rule. These women amazed him. Most were married to serial adulterers whose main, sometimes only, concession to their spouses was a Saturday night meal and visit to a club where they were expected to say little, show a lot, stay sober and sit with the women, while the men talked at the bar. Boulter suspected that Reynolds could lay hands on a million in cash at any time but lived in an over extended terraced house, holidayed in Majorca or Marbella and spent more money on his mistress in a month than on his wife in a year. He waited and watched as one of the goons whispered in Reynold's ear. As the mob boss turned he was ready with a smile.

'Lee.'

'Reg. Fancy seeing you here.'

'Lee, how the devil are you?'

'You've lost weight you fat tosser.'

'Harsh.'

'You ill?'

'No, been on a diet.'

'Suits you. You was getting podgy. Need a new suit though.'

Reg sat quietly waiting for the man's brain to kick in and make the connection between this chance encounter and the events of the afternoon. He smiled as he saw uncertainty, realisation and then a flash of fear suddenly flicker across Reynold's face.

'You bastard. I suppose I've got you to thank for that stroke this afternoon?'

''fraid so.'

'Why?'

'Make a point?' Boulter smiled enquiringly.

436

'Which is?'

'You're getting slack.'

'Williams put you up to this?'

'No.'

'So, what you after then?'

'Job?'

'So, you turn me over and I give you a job? Yeah right.'

'In less than three minutes Lee, I had your boy, his car and the weeks take.'

'And you think you're going to walk out of here you Muppet? Seriously?' Reynolds, turned to the minders behind him and jerked his head towards Boulter, 'get him outside.'

Boulter watched the nearest minder slide a hand towards his armpit and dumped his raincoat on the table with a clunk. He flicked a fold in the coat aside, just enough, to reveal the bottom corner of a box magazine for a MAC 10. 'Just want to talk Lee,' he spread his hands wide, 'you need help. Trust me son.'

Reynolds looked down at the barely concealed machine pistol tucked under the raincoat and then waved the minder off. He turned to his wife who plainly didn't appreciate her evening being interrupted by business, ushered her to a table and then positioned his men strategically behind and to the side of him. 'Talk.'

'Think about it Lee. If I can take part of the operation in three minutes, how long d'ye think it'd take the McGuigans to roll the lot up? You've got soft Lee. Where did you get that plonker? You're trusting people and they're not delivering. You need a Capo.'

'That "plonker" is in ICU on a drip,' Reynolds snapped back before lowering his voice and looking nervously towards his wife, 'and just happens to be Lotte's brother. You fucked his kidney you arsehole.'

'He'll mend.'

'You better not be around when he does.'

'Oh, Give over. Get real Lee. Wannabe faces like him are two a penny.' He grinned, 'so do I get the job?'

'Do I get my money back?'

'Call it a signing on fee? Expenses? Might buy a new suit. Yeah?'

'So, what you heard about the McGuigans then?' Boulter watched the calculations behind the eyes. 'You're looking for a job. Why didn't you go to them?'

437

'Your little firm are an easier touch.'

'Fuck you Boulter.' Reynolds paused and looked around him slowly, beginning to realise the truth of Boulter's observations. It dawned on him that with this encounter he was being shown just how vulnerable he and his wife were. This meeting could just as easily have been a hit. He took a deep breath, 'see you at Slammers. Monday afternoon.'

Boulter stood and caught a slight movement from the minder with the swollen armpit. He reached for his raincoat, 'don't twitch again son. Be a pity to spoil a Saturday night out.' As he reached the door he let the raincoat fully unfold and an empty box magazine drop to the floor. He side footed it up the aisle towards Reynolds and laughed.

'You're mental, you cunt.'

Boulter laughed again, 'be lucky Lee.'

Starmer stood propped against the door frame of the newly commissioned men's shower and locker room watching a small, delicate, middle aged man with a perm and thick eye shadow mop the floor. 'You don't have to do that Justin. Josie will be in soon.'

The man paused in his swabbing and coyly looked back at Starmer over his shoulder, 'you can't do enough for a good Guvnor Mister Starmer. I mean, you turned that dirty old office of Mister Woolley into this lovely facility for us. The least we can do is look after it.'

Starmer smiled ruefully, partly wishing that his motive for providing the new facility had been solely that of Staff Welfare. In truth, the stripping of all plaster and the cement screeds at the start of the work has been the only way to ensure the eradication of any forensic evidence. He could be tied to the club at the time Thompson disappeared but he couldn't be tied to the murder if there was no forensic to connect him to the crime scene. 'C'mon Justin, leave that. Go and open your bar. There'll be a few drifting in for a quiet Early Doors.'

'Ok Mister Starmer,' Justin hovered in front of him, shifting from foot to foot in the doorway, wringing his hands with obvious embarrassment before blurting out, 'can I just say what a difference you have made.' He flapped his hands, rolled his eyes and flicked away a stray lock, 'I mean, it's my happy place now.' He reached forward, squeezed Starmer's forearm, tossed his

438

head again, paused to appreciate his own exit and delivered the line, 'I just love what you've done with the place.'

Starmer roared with laughter, tucked his clipboard under his arm, clamped his pencil between his teeth and enthusiastically clapped Justin on his way up the corridor. He then wandered through the locker room compiling a desultory snagging list to present to the builder and wondering when the jet setting lifestyle of the international drug dealer would kick in.

As he reached the stairs leading to the main floor he could hear the sounds, instantly recognisable, of a small group that had gone from raucous to rowdy. It was all part of the game although he would have preferred that 'raucous' had gone through his tills. He rounded the corner to see three men at the bar. One standing and the two on either side of him on stools. They all looked up at his approach but his initial focus was on Justin. A look of complete terror was fixed on the little man's face. Had he been able to shrink further out of sight he'd have been behind the optics. Starmer slowed his pace. The stool on the left thought he was the muscle; big enough but with a button bursting belly, weak jaw, three stone overweight and a massive perspiration problem that would see him swimming from his suit if he didn't remove his jacket soon. The power was in the middle; expensive, if badly creased suit, heavy lidded, deep set eyes that peered myopically through steel framed glasses and a slow lupine smile that revealed slightly protruding and yellowing teeth. Starmer dismissed the third man as an appointment that only a police force with a slavish compliance to an Equal Opportunities Policy would appoint; the detective was old and infirm enough to draw a pension on both counts. He caught Justin's eyes which swivelled from one bottle of Krystal to a second, further along the bar, before looking back at him with an embarrassed, helpless shrug and a moue of apology.

'Gentlemen.' Starmer congratulated himself on winning his bet as Buttons piped up.

'Wondered when you'd tip up.'

Starmer ignored him and turned to the Suit, 'Detective Inspector Stead, to what do I owe the pleasure?' If Stead was nonplussed at being named, he didn't show it but Starmer made a mental note to thank Bernard for his Intelligence briefing folders. Bernard had seen these as an essential part of their strategy.

439

"Know thine enemy." Nonplussed or not, he could see that Stead was discomforted by his knowledge.

'Now you've re opened, thought we'd pop by. Talk about the arrangement.'

'Arrangement?'

Both turned as Buttons, forefinger inserted in the neck of an empty Krystal bottle tapped it on the bar, and shouted at Justin, 'another bottle Justine.'

Justin, tears in his eyes, looked over to Starmer.

'Don't look at him you deviant. Open another bottle.'

Starmer slowly but steadily locked eyes with Stead and allowed his facial muscles to tighten and clear any emotion from his face. He felt the silence stretch but maintained the stare.

'Leave it Lazzer,' Stead finally instructed Buttons before looking back at Starmer. 'Lazzer there is the bag man. You settle with him when he visits and if you need me you tell him. Ok?'

Starmer could feel his eyes re engaging non-blink mode, 'I won't be needing you or him.' He paused, enjoying the confusion registering in Stead's eyes. 'Finish your drinks and leave.' Over Stead's shoulder he saw Justin's jaw drop in amazement before clamping shut as Buttons spoke.

'You want me to sort this out Guv?' He lurched drunkenly towards Starmer who didn't move. Stead, quickly did, moving between them to head off the confrontation. He turned his back on Buttons, placed his palm on Starmer's chest and, again, attempted a thousand-yard stare.

Starmer gently levered the palm from his chest with his thumb and looked over to Justin, 'print the bill Justin. These gentlemen are leaving.' He turned back to Stead, 'you want to pay the bill before you leave or would you like me to send it to your Chief Constable asking whether he thinks the public purse should meet the entertainment bill for three underworked, pissed up detectives drinking champagne all afternoon at his expense?'

The heavy lids behind the steel rims flickered and the stare hardened. 'You don't know who you're messing with.'

'Neither do you.'

Stead blinked. Again. 'Larry, pay the man.'

Buttons, eventually, pulled a crush of notes from his, now sodden, jacket pocket, threw them at Justin and advanced on Starmer. With his face a foot away he spat, 'I'll be back.'

Starmer decreased the distance between them, 'I'll look forward to it Detective Sergeant Clarke. Though, next time, have a bath, use mouthwash, tidy yourself up and I might let you in.' He pushed the DS, gently, away. 'Now fuck off back to Angela, Lazzer.' Again, he took quiet satisfaction from dropping that personal detail into the conversation. As Clarke struggled to regain his composure Starmer added, 'you are still with Angela, aren't you? Only she was in the other night with a young Uniform.' Starmer stepped aside as Clarke, partially held back by Stead, lurched at him. Starmer didn't bother to hide his amusement as two of Manchester's finest struggled to restrain one of their own. He ceremoniously waved all three to the exit with a bow and sweep of his arm while Clarke wriggled in Stead's grip and screamed abuse over his shoulder as he went. Starmer went over to Justin, 'you alright?'

The little man, frozen in the pose of an angelic schoolboy; fingers steepled, head on one side, freed his hands and came back to life with animated fanning of his cheeks as he mouthed, 'my hero.'

Boulter snicked the gear lever down into second and gunned the Jaguar around a kerb crawler with one hand on the horn and the other waving various insulting hand signals at a bemused taxi driver.

Starmer turned in his seat, cast an eye over the luxurious interior and sniffed the heady scent of the new leather upholstery. 'Nice car. New?'

'One previous owner.'

'Family man, was he?'

'Why?'

'His wife's dry cleaning is on the back seat.'

'Ah.'

'Lee Reynolds know you're driving around in his brother in laws' car?'

'Probably.'

'Where are we going Reg?'

'Thought I'd show you the sights.'

'Sights?'

'Yeah, sights of Manchester,' Boulter laughed, 'the underbelly.'

'You know what really pisses me off Reg?'

'I don't Guv.'

'People who take me for a cunt.'

Boulter risked a collision with another taxi to glance across at Starmer, 'you don't mean me Guv, surely.'

'I do Reg. Ever since we met you have gone out of your way to make out you're the thick. Muscle. Nothing else. But you're not thick. Are you?'

'Very kind of you to say so Guv.'

'You want to know what else pisses me off?'

'I do Guv. I do.'

'Monosyllabic answers.'

'Monosyllabic?'

'Yes. Always enjoyed a conversation Reg.'

'Did you know Guv that the languages of China and South East Asia are sometimes referred to as monosyllabic languages? Although both languages are considered phonetically complex.' Boulter looked across at Starmer as from deep inside his massive chest there came a low gurgling that became louder as it reached the back of his throat and flooded forth like a burst water main spouting up into the sky. The unrestrained gales of laughter reduced the big man to a helpless, shivering, thigh slapping lump. Eventually he shuddered into silence and wiped his eyes. 'Sorry Guv. Couldn't resist.'

Starmer chuckled, 'and can we lose the "Guv"?'

'Sometime yeah. Thing is, I don't know you from Adam. I was just keeping my cards close. I mean, Respect. You offed Woolley and Osman and tied Williams in knots. No way was I taking you for a cunt. Believe me.'

'Offed?'

'Now you really are taking me for one.'

'I am?'

'You are. Three groups of people. One group dead or missing; Thompson, Osman and Woolley, the other group chasing; me, Williams and Webber. Then there's your little team. We didn't whack Thompson and Osman.' He looked across at Starmer. 'Had to be you.'

'Who else knows?'

'Williams will have worked it out.'

'The Police?'

'Not really looking. Someone did 'em a favour would be their take.'

'Ok, Respect all round then. Now where are we going and why do I need to see the underbelly of Manchester?'

'Let's get a beer and a bite to eat first.'

Starmer reached to unclip his seatbelt as the car slowed to a halt, 'where are we?'

'The Underbelly.'

'Geographically?'

'Hulme.' Boulter had parked the car in a street to the side of a flat iron shaped pub that filled the acute angle between two narrow streets. He leaned forward to look towards an undeveloped area at the end of the road. 'You heard of The Crescents?'

'Some.'

'Well that's where they were,' he pointed to the end of the road. 'In the sixties, they demolished the terraced slums and built "Cities in the Sky"; Deck access flats. Modernist and Brutalist Architecture.'

'Wow. Monosyllabic to Polymath.'

'You taking the piss?'

'No, just struggling with your new-found erudition.'

'I read a lot. Anyway, by the late eighties this place was like the wild west. Nobody paid rent, Council made no attempt to collect any and the place was filled with squatters. Crime and drugs took off.' He sighed, 'now they're demolishing it. Might get it right this time round eh?'

Starmer stood on the pavement and while Boulter locked the car he looked at the grim, dirty, crumbling and unloved edifice that was The Junction Hotel. In its day, the colourful exterior wall tiles with their intricate patterns and shapes would have made the pub an inviting proposition. Above the door the Brewer's logo was tiled in bas relief, the design matching that etched into the part frosted windows. The main entrance door, on the apex of the triangle, opened onto a small, Snug type bar with a couple of tables, some stools at the bar and half a sheet of unglued, nicotine stained, Lincrusta wallpaper that threatened to further unfurl and envelop the unwary drinker. 'This is where we're having lunch?'

Boulter hovered over the small circular table near the window with three pints clasped between his massive hands. He nudged the spare chair, over which he'd draped his raincoat, to one side with his knee and gently placed the pints on the table.

'Someone joining us?'

'Got a bit of a thirst. Lovely beer; Hyde's Light Mild.'

'So, talk to me.'

'Right, with Drugs there's a top and a bottom. The slope, in Holland, Duong, is at the top. That poor bastard in the lilac shell suit at the end of the bar over there is at the bottom. With me so far?' Reg, quaffed two thirds of the first pint as Starmer ignored his sarcasm. 'So, you supply to Reynolds and McGuigan. They cut the product and franchise it to little teams that put it into clubs, pubs and the next tier down the food chain. Probably cut again. Now it gets like those Russian dolls; you open one and there's another. So, those little teams have their own little teams and so on. Babushka! By the time it gets to Shirley Temple,' he jerked a thumb in the direction of the shell suit, 'it's been cut to a price he can afford but because he's so skint he burgles to buy. He sells what he steals back up the chain. Black Economy.'

'And your point is?'

Reg finished the first pint and made a start on the second while he considered Starmer's question. 'Which part of what I've described is organised? As in "Organised Crime"?'

'Down as far as the Reynolds and McGuigans?'

'No. They're both a couple of chancers that cruised in on Woolley's coat tails and just happened to be connected to the areas where there was the greatest demand. The Estates, like The Crescents?' He clicked his fingers at a shadowy figure lurking behind the bar, 'three more pints,' he continued without checking for a response. 'They cut it, mark it up and move it on. What happens after that could not be called Organised in any sense of the word.'

'And that affects us how?'

'I'm liking the "us".'

'Well, don't dine out on it,' Starmer looked around, 'well not here anyway.'

Boulter smiled, leant into the curved timber back rest of the small wooden chair that his bulk overflowed and emptied his lungs in exasperation. 'Listen, you talk about "The Families" like they were running the five Boroughs in New York; Mafiosi. Now that is Organised Crime. This isn't. This is a loose collection of brain dead bozos who made their bones busting Post Offices, earnt a few bob, bought pubs or taxi companies and funded little bits of work. Drugs came along, they got involved 'cos they saw an earner. These people are not business men, entrepreneurs or

444

managers. They're disorganised, careless and stupid. All they've got is a little cunning, connections, a gut instinct for the market and a dime bag network to feed it. Now, it's grown too big, too fast and they are out of their depth. They're not managing it. There's no discipline. MAC 10s everywhere. Gunchester. Right? Even Woolley was struggling. Williams wouldn't have put up with him for much longer.' He finished the second pint and looked for the delivery of the next as it appeared at the bar. 'Did you see the going of Shell Suit behind me?'

'A few minutes ago.'

Boulter nodded thoughtfully, rose, went to the nicotine grimed net curtains, pulled them to one side and looked both ways, up and down the streets. He sat back down, 'given a nudge, Reynolds would leg it to the Costa tomorrow. Last time I saw him he had the haunted look of a man at his own hanging. And,' he looked towards the street with his head cocked to one side, listening, 'I'm in there. Reynolds is finished. When he nods his head, he'll realise I've cut his throat. Then his boys are all ours.'

'The McGuigans?'

'Should be here any minute.' He smiled and shrugged ruefully. 'This is their pub.'

'I think I preferred monosyllabic. How we going to handle this?

'Quickly. Very, very quickly.'

Starmer heard two cars screech to a halt in the small street outside and counted three, followed by two, doors slamming. 'Five.'

Boulter nodded, reached for the raincoat, quickly slipped his arms into the sleeves and sat back down, 'let 'em get right in.'

Were Starmer less apprehensive he might have enjoyed the small comedy moment as two men fought with a red velvet, draught excluding curtain, hung from a circular brass rail above the door. Eventually, one side, the wrong one, was yanked clear and a powerfully built man of medium height in waistcoat, shirtsleeves, a green trilby hat, red neckerchief and moleskin trousers barrelled into the small pub. His eyes quickly went to the only customers and he spread his arms wide holding back the four younger men behind him.

'Would dat be yer fuckin' Jag outside?'

445

Boulter wiped beer from his lips with the back of his hand, 'who wants to know, you Pikey bastard.'

The closer of the younger men tried to force his way pass the leader, edging around him and swinging a baseball bat out from behind the curtain. 'I got this Da.'

The older man swept his son back into place with a forearm the size of a leg of mutton without taking his eyes off Boulter, 'that's a Reynolds car out front. You with Reynolds? Do I know you?'

'Shouldn't think so you Irish cunt. Who are you?' Boulter leant back in the chair and watched the Irishman's complexion move through a palette of colours until it matched the red of his scarf.

The man seemed momentarily stunned but recovered quickly and sound and spittle flew from his mouth as he screamed, 'I'm Dermot McGuigan and this,' he nodded proprietorially towards the bar, 'this is my pub. Now who da fuck are you?'

'The man who's going to put you out of Business.'

As the son tried to push past his father with the bat raised, Boulter stood up, let the raincoat swing clear, cocked and raised the MAC10, swung the suppressor fitted machine pistol in a high lazy arc and pulled the trigger. Thirty brass jacketed empty cartridge cases arched and then fell to the beer stained and cigarette scarred carpet as did the young man when Starmer lifted him from the floor with a vicious kick between his legs. Boulter used that distraction and the shock of the thirty-round burst to fit a replacement magazine. As it clicked into position he re cocked and levelled the gun at the older man who had bent at the knees, pulled the sides of his trilby down over his ears and clamped his eyes tightly shut. He dropped his aim and walked half a magazine across the floorboards six inches in front of McGuigan's feet. As the Irishman hopped from foot to foot Boulter turned, emptied the magazine along the optic shelf and reloaded.

Pivoting Boulter then made for the door where McGuigan was now on his knees, sobbing. The big man hauled the Irishman to his feet, dragged him out into the street and threw him across the bonnet of one of the cars. Turning to the second car he opened fire and watched two of McGuigan's men dive for cover beneath showers of glass and metal shards while a third tried to squeeze under the car leaving behind a trail of blood from a

446

shattered leg. Again, Boulter reloaded, stepped away from McGuigan, took careful aim and stitched a colander's worth of holes through the bonnet on which he lay. He watched McGuigan's head bounce in time to the staccato hammering on the steel. The sound of impact drowning out the burring buzz of the bullets leaving the suppressor as they punched dents and holes into the bonnet. Tears from red rimmed eyes joined snot and saliva in a trail down the bodywork as McGuigan moved a finger to the edge of the nearest nine-millimetre diameter hole, inches from his face.

The emptiness of the silence that followed was gently and slowly filled by a hissing radiator, the tinkle of cartridge cases rolling down the slope of the bonnet and the cries of the wounded man. Boulter unclipped the magazine, stowed the gun in the raincoat pockets, pulled McGuigan up by his collar and spoke quietly, 'so, Pikey. I see you again it'll only take one bullet. You understand?' McGuigan tried hard to still the shaking and quieten the sobs but failed. He knew he'd lost control of his bowels as well as his little empire and, strangely, regretted the former more than the latter.

If anything had struck Starmer about the events of the last ninety seconds it wasn't the speed and the fury but the calm that followed the storm as they, unhurriedly, walked to the Jag, unlocked it, settled in and gently pulled at their seat belts. Boulter leaned towards Starmer as he fumbled to find the seatbelt socket, 'spectacular enough for you?'

Starmer grinned, 'will it do the job?'

Boulter laughed, 'it'd better. Only one magazine left.'

'Reg.'

'Yes Guv.'

'Don't ever try a bottle test on me again.'

Boulter met his gaze evenly, 'you got it Guv.'

'Time for a low profile, I think. Couple of days Reg. What think you?'

'Before or after I get paid?'

'Don't you trust me Reg?'

'I do Guv but I'll trust you a lot more when you pay up.'

'Take a couple of days.' If Reg had a fault, Starmer noted, it was that his face registered his emotions; wrinkled eyes for thought, widening with realisation and then darkening with suspicion. They darkened.

'You're going to blow me off. Right?'

'No, I think I just offered you a job.'

'You trust me then.'

'As much as anybody.'

'Williams?'

'I think you've probably worked out which side your bread's buttered. Anyway, Williams is finished,' Starmer settled down into the seat, closed his eyes and mumbled, 'or soon will be.'

Chapter Twenty - eight

Denton walked quickly across the cobbled yard, shrugging into his raincoat as he went. He rounded the side of the ancient, overloaded and seriously unroadworthy lorry to find the Bulimias sheltering in the lee from the rain lashing in sheets across the river. He nodded to them both as he sorted through a bunch of keys for the padlock securing the large double doors to a steel freight container. As the hasp came free the Bulimias hauled the doors apart and they all sought shelter inside.

'That thing legal?' Denton nodded back at the truck.

'Oh, he's still a joker Don.'

'He is Ron, he is.'

Denton patiently shook his head as the two big men exchanged high fives, 'can we lose the double act for a minute and do some serious stuff?' The pair looked down and shuffled their feet in ways much practiced over the years at times when called to account by Authorities. Denton jerked his thumb at the tarpaulin covered load, 'I'm assuming that lot is kosher. Right?'

'It is Paul,' confirmed Ron.

'Sweet as Paul,' added Don.

'It had better be. Since that night in the Dukes I've been knee deep in Policemen and it's not over yet. The last thing I need is to find I'm sitting on half of South London's hooky gear.'

'It's all sweet Paul. It's a mixture, stuff that's out of season, stuff that didn't move, new stock, bits of kit. Nothing shonky. I promise.' The two looked at each other and Denton knew that a rehearsed set of questions was on the way. 'So, heard you'd been a bit busy Paul.'

'You could say that.'

Don, nodded through the rain at the yard, the factory and the warehouse beyond, 'back here in Woolwich then? Back at NMG. All settled now then?'

'Nearly.'

'You back in charge?'

'Yeah.'

'Henfield?'

'Gone.'

'Webber?'

Very gone.'

'Yeah, we heard a little bit about that,' the pair exchanged another look.

'So, you're alright now, then, like.'

Denton snorted, 'yeah Don, I'm alright. My wife has left me, my daughter is being treated for severe depression, this business is pretty much on its knees and I'm still bailed to appear weekly. Yeah everything is just tickety boo.'

'Stella gone then? For good?' Don probed gently.

'Looks like.'

The pair looked quizzically at each other. 'Heard you was playing away though Denton.'

'Where?'

'Eh?'

'Where did you hear that?'

'Well it was all over the papers weren't it. You and that Dee whassername leaving the nick with Stella, her at 'er flat in Wapping. S'obvious.' Don concluded lamely.

'Seriously?' Denton snarled. 'I mean seriously. I'm struggling with putting my life back together, working my arse off and I take time to help you, and all you two want to do is gossip about stuff you've read in the papers?'

The pair looked crestfallen and went back to their foot shuffling before Don stepped out of the routine, took a step forward, wrapped his huge arm around Denton, pulled him into a hug, pinched his cheek playfully between two massive fingers and chuckled, 'you have, you have, though haven't you? You've 'ad a dabble.' He shook Denton's cheek and then gently pushed him away, laughing, 'you little scamp.'

'Playing away. Oh, dear, oh dear,' added Ron.

Denton couldn't help but laugh at the irrepressibility of the pair, 'pack it in both of you. Yes, there was maybe something.

But,' he hesitated, 'who knows now after all that's happened? Anyway, I think I blew it.'

'Looking forward to hearing all about that Denton. Duke's tonight?'

'Don't drink Don.'

'D'ye hear that Ron? Reckons she don't drink.'

'Leave it Don.'

'Yeah, leave it Don. You're one sentence away from a storage problem.'

'Okay mate.' Don gripped Denton's shoulder, 'you need anything, you bell me. Yeah?'

All three looked up, and shrank back as a three and a half litre V8 Rover in Metropolitan Police "Jam Sandwich" livery swept into the yard. Denton's heart sank as the passenger opened the rear door and carefully selected a dry patch of ground on which to lower a loafered foot.

'Fuck me, King of the Yard,' Don murmured sardonically.

'You know him,' Denton enquired earnestly.

'Not really, made himself unpopular up at the Warren, Police club up on Keston Common, you know it? So, for a bit, he used to drink in the Legion at Hayes. Until he made himself unpopular in there too; giving it the big I am. Then didn't see him for a bit. Next thing he tips up back at the Warren. Heard tell he's plotted up in a cottage in the grounds with some bird who works in the club. Nasty bastard.'

'How nasty?'

'Well, according to those in the know, up The Warren; coppers like, he's a very nasty bastard. I mean there are some right cases get in that place and if they don't like him there's something very wrong with him. Drinks alone. Says it all really.'

'What are you doing in a Police Club for Christ's sake?'

'We play in their bowls team,' Ron volunteered waspishly, aggrieved that their admittance to a Police establishment should be looked at askance because of their presumed social standing; rather than the social acceptance that he felt their new-found commitment to the traditions of Middle England should have bestowed.

'How well do you know him?'

'Well enough to stay clear. Mate of yours?'

451

'No. Look lads, I've got to go. I'll be in touch, stay here, out of sight. Last thing I need is another bloody interview about my criminal connections.'

'Harsh Don.'

'Very harsh Ron.'

Denton, slipped round the back of the Bulimias' truck, picked his way through the puddles and made his way towards the Police car as weak sunlight struggled through the clouds and the rain stopped. 'Roy.'

'Mister Denton.'

'Business then?'

'Few loose ends and a development. Somewhere we can talk?'

Denton threw open the boardroom door briefly reflecting on the events that had taken place since he'd made his retirement speech there. He marched to the far side of the room, gazed through the still grime coated windows to the Bulimias in the yard below, hoicked a chair out from beneath the polished yew table with his foot, sat with his back to the window and tiredly contemplated a smiling King opposite. He glanced idly at motes of dust dancing in a strengthening beam of sunlight and took some satisfaction from King's discomfort as the same crepuscular rays forced him to shield his eyes. 'A development?' He prompted.

'Yeah, I'll get to that in a minute.' The Policeman, perhaps recognising the irony of conducting an interrogation while shielding his eyes from bright light, impatiently sought shade in another chair before continuing. 'How are things?'

'Oh, just peachy.'

King either missed or ignored the barb, 'you've gone back to work then?'

'Looks like.'

'How long?'

'Few weeks or so.'

'Your business?'

'Was.'

'And now?'

'In the absence of a clear trail through several offshore holding companies to establish ownership, I'm claiming salvage

452

rights.' He laughed grimly, 'If for no other reason than the future security of my pension.'

'How's it going?'

The truth, Denton mused, was that he wasn't sure. 'It's interesting. When I walked back in the entire NMG Management Team had gone but the workforce, my originals, were carrying on as per. Orders were being processed and delivered, materials and components are still coming in and financially, at the moment, we're ok.' He laughed, 'they took off in so much of a hurry they neglected to cancel me as a Signatory.'

'I thought it'd been bought out by Northern Mouldings Group.'

'So did I,' he mused, wondering how King knew. 'Fact is, NMG doesn't exist. I checked back to when they bought me out.'

'And?'

'Cheque came from a Bank in the Cayman Islands. Paperwork from a shell company registered in Holland. Both dead ends.' He waved a curious hand in the air and watched the motes of dust obediently and indolently scatter and reform like a shoal of fish disturbed by a predator. 'If you came for the crooks they're all gone Detective Chief Superintendent. There's just little old me and even you must be beginning to realise that I was never part of any of the crap that was going down here.'

'Our enquiries are ongoing.'

'I'll bet they are.'

'What does that mean?'

'It means that you must be purblind if you can't see I wasn't involved,' or, he soliloquised peevishly, 'in it up to your neck and you're just down here fishing.'

King seemed to sense his unease and looked away, breaking Denton's angrily unflinching gaze and taking appreciable moments before speaking. 'How's Julie and Stella.'

'Have you met Stella?'

'Pardon.'

'Simple question, have you met my wife.'

'Well, no.'

'Then wouldn't the question have been more appropriately phrased, "How's your wife?" The use of her Christian name implies acquaintance. Don't you think?'

'Not, sure,' he stuttered to a halt.

Denton interjected viciously, 'you knew she was having an affair with Webber, didn't you?' He didn't give King a chance to answer and stored away another little piece of evidence against the man. He suddenly felt the strain of recent days as he thought of his difficulties with Stella and his concerns for his daughter, 'Julie's up at The Priory in Hayes,' he blurted out with instant regret.

'I'm sorry to hear that. What's the problem?'

'Addiction, Depression and what's beginning to look like Post Traumatic Stress. She is not very well. Not very well at all.' His eyes drifted back to the dancing scintillas trapped in the brightening shaft of light and he wondered whether somewhere in the universe a superior being was watching him cavort for forces beyond his control. 'Was there anything else?'

'Ah, the development. Yes. Mister Williams is back in the community.'

'I thought he was arrested.'

'He was. He then escaped.'

'Escaped?'

'Yes, an unfortunate mix up at the bail hearing.'

'Unfortunate?'

'Yes, I just wanted you to know. Hopefully he'll not bother you but you needed to be told. Best to be on the safe side. I think he's probably more interested in your side kick.'

'Starmer?'

'Yes.'

'Have you told him?'

'Someone will be in touch with him.'

'Have you told Dee? Miss Wilson?'

'Yes. I doubt that she'll be troubled. She's living in Williams flat. He's hardly likely to return to old haunts. Anyway, we've got a guard on the place.' King treated himself to a knowing smile, 'but then you know where she is. You've been to see her. Right?'

Denton, ignored the jibe. The memory of his visit to Dee was still painful. He'd wondered whether her feelings may have been changing when they'd both been released from Custody and Dee and Sella had spent appreciable moments silently assessing each other in the reception area while he'd looked on embarrassed, wondering whether to effect an introduction. During his visit to her at Sinclair's flat, he'd been received courteously, politely even but she had coldly rejected his explanations and pleas. At the start, he'd determined to be totally honest with her and had spoken of his feelings about Stella being tangled with his concerns for Julie's recovery and treatment. On reflection, he knew that his explanation of those feelings and doubts and his account of his rejection by Stella had been presented clumsily. He knew too that, inadvertently, he'd left Dee with the clear impression that she was his second choice.

He looked over at the detective, 'anything else? Only as you can see I'm busy.'

King looked pensive, 'nice little operation you've got here,' he waved an almost proprietorial hand through the still dancing motes. 'Be worth hanging on to.'

'Im trying.'

King nodded, 'yeah, I can see that.' He paused and blinked light from his eyes as the rays crept further round and into the room. 'Seems to me Paul, you've got a lot on your plate at the moment. Last thing you need is trouble with the Law.'

'I didn't realise I had any.'

'Maybe you'd like to keep it that way?'

Denton's eyes narrowed as he began to take on the full import of King's line of questioning. He now knew that all his earlier concerns and uncertainties about King's probity would be resolved in the next few minutes. 'What do you want King?'

'Paul, come on. No need to be unfriendly. I'm talking about a little cooperation. That's all.'

'Cooperation,' Denton snorted. 'You mean at best turn a blind eye or at worse be your new Webber. Am I right, you bent bastard?'

King stood slowly, 'think about it Paul. Big boy's rules now. You've seen how it works. Right?'

Denton nodded, 'I have indeed.'

King turned back when he reached the door, 'I'll be in touch.'

Denton opened the door and nearly fell out of the car which he had parked with the near side wheels half way up a bank in the narrow country lane that was Hayes Grove. He cursed as the edge of the off-side door, because of the angle, fouled the tarmac below and wondered, again, why the parking facility in The Priory was so inadequate. As he looked up the lane, hedged in by the woodlands of Keston Common, he couldn't help but remember a picnic he'd had up here with Stella, the kids and their friends. Somewhere, he knew, there was a super eight cine film of that picnic. He still treasured a slow motion shot of Julie on a Space-hopper bouncing across a clearing with her hair floating unhurriedly out of sync behind her in mesmerising waves of sunlit amber and honey. Those were the days; the days before the serious drinking. The days of good memories.

He trudged through the entrance and turned left down the access lane that led to the main house, storing that memory away to discuss with Julie should the opportunity arise. He had visited her every night since her admission and every night he had struggled. There had been nights when he'd sat in the sparsely furnished room and just watched her sleep, kissing two fingers and then touching them to her forehead as he left. Other nights they'd sat in what he'd hoped, but doubted, was companionable silence. He knew that Stella visited her in the afternoons and wondered whether her visits were more productive than he felt his to be.

He and Stella had been briefed by Medical Staff during the assessment and admissions process but, after three weeks, he was unclear as to Julie's progress or even what treatment stage she had reached. There had been a careful avoidance of detailed discussion on prognosis with refuge being sought through reference to therapeutic environments and the management of associated physical symptoms. He did know that Julie had been through a medical detoxification and wondered at his, and Starmer's, ignorance and arrogance in thinking they could ever have weaned her off drugs.

He nodded to the duty receptionist and briefly wondered whether this large, cheerful man was Security. The visit from King had left him more concerned than he cared to admit and he was uncomfortably aware that he'd volunteered Julie's location to King, without prompting, at a time when his suspicions should have stopped him. He turned the corner at the reception desk, passed an old fashioned red fire extinguisher and walked slowly down a blue carpeted corridor. He trailed his fingers along the top of a latticed timber radiator cover, absent-mindedly staring down the passage at a window sill laden with flowering orchids and on out to the gathering gloom of the evening beyond. He stopped at the last door in the corridor, knocked and went in.

Julie was sat on the bed propped up against pillows and lilac scatter cushions. Stella occupied a maroon velour tub chair between a bedside table with a telephone and a sash window that overlooked the garden. Feeling an intruder but reluctant to relinquish any of his time with his daughter, Denton grabbed a chair from beneath the veneered chipboard escritoire and plonked himself down near the foot of the bed.

'How are you feeling?'

'Bit better. I went to a Yoga and Relaxation session this afternoon. Met some other people.'

'Good,' Denton nodded at his wife, 'Stella.'

'Paul.'

He nervously rubbed his hands together, entwining his fingers and cracking his knuckles, trying to think of something to say and stumbling over the recently stored memory. 'I was thinking as I parked the car about that picnic we had on the common. The one we filmed? Do you remember?'

'I'm surprised you do,' Stella sniffed.

Denton ignored her and persisted, 'do you remember that slow motion scene; the Space-hopper? You used to love that bit.' He chuckled, gratified that the memory had earned him a smile. He sensed Stella's irritation and wasn't surprised when she rose to leave. 'I've been meaning to ask you,' he held up a hand as she rounded the bed, 'when Andy Starmer phoned, did he leave a number?'

Julie snapped upright, 'Andy 'phoned?'

'He did darling, I was going to tell you when you were a bit better.'

'What did he want?'

'To talk to you?' Denton helpfully volunteered.

'You didn't tell me mum.'

'As I said darling, I was waiting 'til you were a bit better.'

Julie studied her mother without expression, 'and have you got the number?'

With Stella's departure Denton took her chair and reached across for his daughter's hand, 'How are you really?'

'Really?'

He nodded.

'I don't know. Today was good,' she shrugged, 'one day at a time eh?'

'It's the only way my darling.'

457

'I mean, I feel better. My mind doesn't race as much and the edge has gone off a bit on the drugs thing.' She squeezed his hand, 'mind you, that could be the medication. Couldn't it?'

He nodded again, content to let her talk.

She took several deep breaths, 'the thing that worries me is how I'm going to feel without the drugs.' She took another deep breath, held it and then exhaled slowly, 'all those things I did,' she rushed on, 'how am I going to cope with the memory of all that and everything else, off drugs?'

Denton held her tightly and stroked her hair as she sobbed into his shoulder, 'well my darling, we're going to have to do a lot more of what we're doing now.'

'What?'

'Talking?'

'That easy?'

'Nope.'

'I killed Webber.'

'I know.'

She sobbed, 'I tortured him. I set it up so that he knew he was going to die and had time to think about it.'

'It's not worth thinking about and whatever encouragement you get to talk about issues while you're here, you can't ever mention that. You do understand that Julie, don't you?'

'But I did it.'

'He deserved it.'

'He did?'

'Julie, you got there just before any one of several other people, including me.'

'I ought to thank you.'

'Well go ahead,' he smiled, 'but what for?'

'Finding me? Fighting for me?' she sobbed, 'being here now.'

'I couldn't have done any of it without Andy. He was the one that really got us through it all.'

'I'll ring him.'

'Can I make a suggestion? Wait until you get day release from here. Wait until your mind has finally stopped racing. Use this time to think. About you, about him,' he laughed, 'life and the universe?' He hugged her to him, 'but most of all wait until you've worked out how you really feel about him. He deserves that.'

'I know, thank you daddy.'

Denton padded back along the blue carpeted corridor towards the sound of voices at the entrance. The Receptionist was quietly but firmly advising the man with his back to Denton that admission was not possible without authorisation. He was making his case by reference to an open ledger, 'I'm sorry Sir, but you are not on the list and this is a Hospital where admission to patients is by permission only.' As Denton neared, the Receptionist looked up, recognised him and smiled. 'Ah, Mister Denton, your daughter has another visitor but he's not listed.'

Denton didn't need the man to turn. He knew it was Williams and he knew why he was there. Julie. For Williams, Julie was the lever that could open the box that contained the missing five million shipment. With Julie under his control he could force Denton to get Starmer to hand back the shipment.

Somehow, this Williams looked bigger than the man he'd surprised and nearly throttled back at Langoed. Denton could feel his resolve being seriously strained as he pulled on Williams' right shoulder with his left hand to turn him into the path of the right he'd already launched. Williams stepped smartly back and inside the swing smashing the back of his head into Denton's face. As Denton dropped to his knees he could see, but not avoid, the slamming right hand that Williams jack hammered down onto his temple.

He struggled back to consciousness and the sound of an intruder alarm, attendant flashing strobed lights and the sight of the Receptionist hovering over him with a fire extinguisher dangling from one hand. He levered himself upright with his back to the corridor wall and struck his head against the wall bracket that had once held the extinguisher. 'Where's the fire?'

The man looked momentarily bemused before glancing down at the heavy red appliance in his hand. 'No, no fire. I thought he was going to kill you. I couldn't get him off.' He looked soulfully at Denton, then at the empty bracket, finally at the red metal cylinder in his hand and shrugged, 'what else could I do?'

'You did ok. Where is he?'

The man waved the extinguisher at the entrance doors, 'he went.'

Denton eased himself upright, gently explored the ridge on his broken nasal bone and slowly opened, closed and rotated his jaw, checking for effect on his jaw. As he widened his eyes to offset an attack of dizziness he caught sight of his daughter standing, rigid with fear, both fists clenched and held in front of her mouth and eyes that were filling with tears even as he watched. He struggled to his feet, 'we need to go Julie. It's not safe here.'

He sensed his daughter's unease as he gunned the car up the ramp from the Rotherhithe Tunnel and made for Wapping Lane and Williams' and Sinclair's apartment. 'You'll like her.'

'I don't know her.'

'She knows about you.'

'But she doesn't know me. I've seen her briefly. Twice. How do you even know that she'll help us?

'I don't know,' he acknowledged, 'but she helped before. It was she who stepped up when I was trying to find you up in Manchester.'

'Mum thinks you're having an affair with her.'

'That's a bit rich after her and Webber.' The minute the man's name had left his lips he realised his mistake and her shudder completed his discomfort. 'Sorry.'

'Did you have an affair with Dee?'

Denton treated himself to a brief rueful grin as he recalled one missed opportunity in Manchester and the urgent, but chaste, embraces and declarations in the Langoed bedroom. 'Technically no. An affair of the heart perhaps?'

'You mean you didn't do it?'

'Yes, thank you, young lady. Stop there.'

'Do you love her?'

He nodded, 'Can we leave it there?'

'Not really,' Julie persisted, 'if you love her why are you with Mum?'

'I'm not with Mum. I'm,' he hesitated. 'we, rather, we, are working together.' He dropped a hand to her knee, 'we're trying to get you better.'

'So, it's me that's keeping you together, and apart from Dee?'

'In a way but that's not really how I'm looking at things.'

'But temporarily you and mum, you're sort of together?'

'What?'

'Well you live in the same house but different rooms, separate lives and tonight is the first time I've seen you together since I was admitted to The Priory.'

'It's difficult but you are what's important here.'

'Does Dee know why you're not with her?'

460

He pulled in front of the warehouse apartments, switched the engine off and shifted in his seat to face her. 'I did try and explain but I made a pretty poor job of it.'

'Did you tell her that Mum wants out?'

'How do you know that.'

'Mum? So, did you tell Dee?'

'Yes. But it came out all wrong. Maybe I should have kept that to myself?'

'Did you tell her that you love her?'

'It didn't really come up.'

'Unbelievable, "didn't really come up"?' she snorted 'and you think, after all that she did, after the way she's been treated, she's now going to welcome you with open arms and offer us refuge?'

'She might take some convincing,' Denton acknowledged. He looked down Wapping Lane as he saw an interior light flicker on and off as a man opened and shut a car door and crossed the road towards them. 'She's under Police guard and surveillance,' he jerked a thumb at the Policeman approaching the offside window, 'so if you're here I know you're safe. Anyway, the last place Williams will tip up is at his old flat.'

The Policeman who'd escorted them to the apartment door stood aside as it opened and ushered Julie and Denton forward. Denton looked up as he crossed the threshold at the man who'd motioned Julie on through, 'Christ, I thought you were dead.'

Sinclair smiled wryly, 'as did I.'

'But you were shot.'

'I was. Not fatally though,' Sinclair managed a slightly forced but defiant smile that suggested damage other than physical, 'as you can see, alive if not exactly kicking. What is called a "through and through sucking chest wound", I believe, and I can even say that in Dutch now.' He winced when he turned to allow Denton to pass, 'I was very fortunate that the Dutch Police had an ambulance nearby. Otherwise I'd have quit this world in a strange house that had seen better days leaving behind a woman who was owed a massive apology.' He gently patted his chest, 'I'm still getting a lot of trouble from the ribs but consider myself very lucky.' He paused for a couple of deep breaths which he drew while holding his chest with both hands. 'How are you Paul. It seems a lifetime since I interrupted your supper with Dee up in

461

Manchester and I just missed you on your last visit; still in hospital.' he offered his hand.

'Does Williams know you're alive?'

'We hope not.'

'Denton was shocked but genuinely delighted to see the gentle man who, he knew, was so important to Dee. He looked over Sinclair's shoulder, down the long room, along the line of cast iron columns trying to ignore the picturesque view of the broad, black and gold crushed silk that was the river mirroring a waxing moon. There, at the end of a vast expanse of stripped oak floor stood Dee, looking back at him but making no move to reduce the distance between. He began the journey holding Julie's hand, past the work stations and the piano towards the settees and occasional tables and Dee. As he neared, he placed both hands loosely on Julie's shoulders and walked her towards Dee, knowing that the feelings he had for this woman could never have been replicated in any future life with Stella. The feeling was deeper than any he could recall and his sensitivities were more heightened now than ever before in his life. A sensitivity that had given him a level of perception that took him past Dee's frigid hauteur to see the hurt she struggled to hide. 'Dee, this is Julie.'

The internal struggle was written all over Dee's face but courtesy and concern won through. She stepped forward, embraced Julie, kissed her on both cheeks before holding her at arm's length for a moment, 'Julie, it sure is good to meet you properly. I won't count the brief encounter when you crashed the party at Langoed. How are you? Your Pa told me so much about you.' she looked at Denton, half expecting a comment.

'Can I call you Dee?'

'Sure Honey.'

'Well, Dee, I know you mean a lot to my Dad,' Julie looked back over her shoulder at Denton, before returning her earnest gaze to Dee, 'and I think we're asking an awful lot of you coming here.' She swallowed hard to force saliva into a mouth dry with apprehension, 'I really only agreed to come because I think you two need to talk.'

Denton looked helplessly at Dee, 'that wasn't my plan Dee, I just need somewhere safe for her to stay until that nutter Williams is caught.'

'He do that to you?'

462

'Caught me unawares Dee,' he laughed, 'he's still on the loose and I heard you'd got Police protection so this was the safest place I could think of.'

'That the reason you came?'

'Not the only reason.'

'The other?'

'To see you.' She turned away quickly but not before he'd seen just a little of the tension released from her features.

'What are you gonna do?'

'What do you mean.?'

'Well, Julie stays here, what are you going to do. You figuring on staying too?'

'I'd like to but I need to get hold of Starmer. We need to sort this Williams thing out. I can't go on like this.'

'I don't know how you're fixed viz a viz the Police. You might want to leave now. There's a detective on her way over. I expect she's fixing to bring us up to date on this Williams business.'

'Then maybe I'll stay and talk to her.'

'While you're waiting, talk to each other.'

Dee laughed wearily before responding, 'Julie, honey, you look tired. Would you like to freshen up, lie down, eat, sleep,' she laughed again, 'give your Pa and me some space?' She called out to Sinclair and waved in the direction of the spiral staircase, 'Mathew, can you show Julie to the washroom please?'

Denton, crouching on the corner of the settee, sighed and went to massage his eyes and pinch the bridge of his nose before he remembered it was broken. He suddenly felt exhausted and twenty years older and for the second time that night, sensed his resolve beginning to drift away. He looked over at Dee, draped across a chair, languorously tapping one velvet brocaded slipper against the other while studiously ignoring him. He addressed her profile. 'That was a shock.'

'Mathew, you mean?'

'Yes.'

She nodded but didn't turn to look at him, 'he gets better every day and we've started to work again. Gently, nothing strenuous.'

'Has he forgiven me for thinking it was him that put Williams onto you in Zutphen?'

463

'After all that's happened I don't think he's too concerned.'

'Well, I'm sorry but that's the way Jonny told it to us. Wasn't 'til later that I got the right picture.'

'He's getting there. There's quite a bit of interest in us you know. I'd like to think that it had to do with the concerts that we did before the world went mad and maybe the recording of the Edinburgh gig.' She sniffed dismissively, 'but I suspect it's got more to do with the press attention since the bust in Holland. Anyway, I'm not going to look a gift horse in the mouth I still need to earn a living. We've been offered three nights at The Roundhouse.' She sighed, 'I just hope we can be ready in time, 'cos that could kick start us all over again.'

He leant forward, dropped his elbows onto his knees and massaged his hands together desperately trying to marshal his thoughts. He knew that she'd given him a chance. A chance to explain or attempt to excuse himself from the God-awful mess he'd made of their last meeting. There wouldn't be another opportunity. He smacked a clenched fist into his open palm, 'Dee do you still love me?'

She swivelled to face him, uncrossed her legs and fixed him with an icy glare until he lowered his eyes, 'how dare you?' She stood, took a step towards him and shook a finger furiously at his now downturned head. 'How damned dare you, after what you said, you have the nerve to ask me that? After all that happened, after all that we said to each other in that bedroom in Langoed you turn up here, ask me, again, for my help and expect me to forget that pathetic performance where you explained that you'd have gone back to your wife if she hadn't dumped you first. I thought I'd gotten to know you Denton. I was wrong. Very wrong and you're way outta line here man.'

'So, you do.'

'You Bastard Denton.'

'I love you. I never stopped.'

'You were going back to your wife, the wife that had betrayed you,' she shouted.

'Dee, I could give you all sorts of excuses; I was exhausted, worried out of my brains and frightened. But the truth is more prosaic; in one weak moment, I settled for peace, quiet and the relative security of what I knew to give me time to mend Julie.' He shook his head in exasperation at his inability to articulate his feelings. 'Love for a Daughter hollows out your heart

464

Dee, love for a woman fills it. I was desperate for your love but prepared to sacrifice it for my Daughter. She had to be the priority and there's some good history between me and Stella. Just enough, I thought, for us to get Julie well.'

'So, I got dumped?'

'At least I was honest with you Dee. I didn't have to tell you any of that. Could have just tried to pick up where we left off and not mentioned Stella or the fact that she binned me.' He reached for her hands, 'I don't suppose I'll ever to be able to really explain it.' He lifted a hand up to her cheek, 'I do love you and I'm sorry. Is there a chance for us?'

She pulled away from him, returned to the chair, pulled her feet up onto the cushion, clasped her knees to her chest and gazed moodily, silently, at the river.

'Dee?'

'I don't know Denton. I need some time. I need to think.'

'I'll go then?'

'Like I said, I need time to think. I'll let you know.'

He chuckled wryly, 'you going to mull it over?'

'That word came from a good time Denton.'

'Sorry, so, can Julie stay here?'

'Of course.'

He heaved a sigh of relief, not just at having found a secure place for his daughter but also at having maintained a relationship, however tenuous, through Julie to Dee, 'Ok I'll get out of your hair.'

He heard the hiss and clunk of the lift doors closing behind him as he crossed the lobby buttoning his coat on his way to the entrance. He looked up just in time to avoid the opening door.

'Mister Denton, how are you?'

Denton recognised her immediately as one of the team of detectives on the raid at Langoed. He looked impatiently past her to the back of the Uniform stationed outside, feet planted firmly and arms folded; the reassuring presence that had prompted his request of Dee to let Julie stay. 'You're expected,' he nodded at the woman and made to move around her.

She smiled but didn't budge, 'have you got a minute Mister Denton?'

'Is there a choice?'

'There is always a choice,' she snapped. 'Yours is, do you help me with my enquiries and in so doing help to stop further attacks on you and your family, or do you go on stumbling from one crisis to the next in the vain hope that it'll all be alright in the end?' She smiled again, stepped to one side, opened the door and waved him on his way, 'your decision.'

He looked at this tall, stylishly, if practically, dressed young woman with her blonde bob and her beautiful, yet serious, face and somehow felt drawn to those silent features and wide, thoughtful eyes. 'You are?'

'Detective Inspector Kate Lockstone,' she held out her hand, 'I've heard something of you, from Dee,' she added, nodding up towards the apartment.

He shook her hand, 'good things?'

Lockstone laughed, 'she seemed impressed. So, you bumped into Williams tonight? What did he want?'

Denton gently caressed his broken nose, 'we didn't talk a lot.'

Her full lips tightened into a thin impatient line. 'well what do you think he wanted?'

'Oh, I don't know. Perhaps he just dropped by to give me tips on how to escape from custody.' He was sure he caught a flash of frustration and anger in the DI's eyes.

'That should not have happened. Unfortunate, careless or what, do you suppose?' She looked closely at him, inviting a response.

He sidestepped the opportunity, 'am I still a suspect?'

She frowned, 'technically yes; you're bailed without charge with investigations pending.' The frown deepened, 'that means there wasn't enough evidence to charge you. For my money, you'd be more useful as a witness.'

'That's not what your boss thinks.'

'Boss?'

'King?'

'Ah,' the frown returned. 'We are part of separate Investigations that,' she hesitated, 'might be linked? He tells me you are old friends though.'

Denton's bitterness over his recent treatment at King's hands, the threats and the memories of the man's childhood machinations at his expense surfaced through the throbbing pain of the injury to his nose. 'He's been a wrong 'un since he got out of short trousers,' he barked, wondering how he could ever have

466

set aside his original impressions of the younger King and bought into the born-again version the DCS had recently provided. 'Aitch, he concluded, would be turning in his grave.

"Aitch?'

'My dad,' he grimaced, 'gave the bastard a second chance when he was a kid.'

'I see,' Lockstone studied him thoughtfully for a moment, 'interesting.'

'Oh shit, forget I said that. It's been a crap day.'

'A "wrong 'un"?'

'Forget it.'

'I'm afraid I can't. Have there been aspects of Detective Chief Superintendent King's recent behaviour that have added to this childhood impression of yours?'

'As I said, forget it.' He looked again at her beautifully serious face and this time felt drawn by the clear concern in her eyes. This woman, he realised, already had her suspicions about King. He now knew King was bent, did she, he wondered? Now he needed time to think and a conversation with Starmer before he would be pulled into further discussion on the subject. 'Have you caught Williams?'

'I'd love to be able to say that "we are confident of an early arrest". But I'm not. It would help me considerably if I knew what he was up to. What he's after. Might help you too.'

'As I said, he didn't say anything while he was trying to kill me.'

She leant back against the glazed, curtain walled front of the lobby, her hands behind her back pressed up against the glass, levering herself gently to and fro with her fingers; deep in thought. 'Let me tell you what I think is happening here. Williams wasn't at the Priory for you. You just got in the way. He was after your daughter.' She pushed herself fully off the glass and began to pace the lobby. Returning to stand in front of him she studied his broken nose and bruised face, 'now, was he looking for a lever or information? You understand where I'm going with this?'

He nodded and realised that he had completely underestimated this young woman.

'What does your daughter have, or know, that he needs?'

Denton considered several answers to avoid the trap but exhaustion and concern forced each aside, 'nothing. She knows nothing.'

'Then he wants her as a lever.' The detective didn't wait for a response. She resumed her pacing this time stopping several paces away before turning to speak. 'You love your daughter Mister Denton.'

He nodded in agreement.

'So does the mysterious Mister Starmer. Am I right? I mean, I can understand a father chasing half round Europe in pursuit of a missing daughter but Starmer? Love explains all, right?' She walked slowly towards him, 'so, Starmer is the key. He's got what Williams wants and our fugitive was after what Starmer values; your daughter. Right? So, what has the one got that the other wants? Do you know?'

'I think so. What I don't know is where it is.'

She nodded. 'Have you discussed any of this with Mister King?'

Denton thought back and compared Lockstone's forensic dissection and interview technique to the several clumsy early attempts that King had made during their first interview in pursuit of this knowledge. 'Not really, no.'

'I was looking for a yes or a no.'

'I didn't trust him. So, I was careful what I said.' He paused thoughtfully, 'I sometimes thought that he knew more than he let on. And,' he added pensively, 'Williams tipped up at The Priory a few hours after I'd told King Julie was there.' He checked closely for any reaction from Lockstone and ventured, 'maybe, he knows what Williams is after. Have you asked him?'

'Let me ask you again. Do you know what it is?'

Denton sighed in resignation, 'Dee, heard something while Williams was holding her. They've lost a drug shipment. A big one.'

'And, therefore important. Perhaps to them both?'

'Probably.'

'So, Starmer knows where it is?'

'I assume so.'

'You "assume so"?'

'Yes, I don't know for a fact.'

'You didn't discuss it?'

'No.'

'Have you spoken to him recently?'

'No, but I've got a number.'

'Manchester number?'

'You know where he is then?'

468

'Let's just say he blew a beautifully maintained low profile a few days ago.'

'Now I've got Julie settled I'm thinking of going to see him. I can't carry on with my life on hold while Williams plays havoc all around me.'

'No, Mister Denton. Stay here. Go back to work. Leave this to me.'

'You're going to see him?'

'Yes, he's long overdue for a chat.'

Chapter Twenty - nine

Starmer checked his watch. He'd been looking at her now for some twenty minutes. She sat on a stool, back to the bar, long legs stretched out in front of her holding a tall iced drink and idly twirling a twizzle stick. Occasionally, she took a thoughtful sip through a straw and let her gaze drift upwards to his eyrie. Twice she'd been approached by barflies playing out of their league. She'd spared each a single glance, a slight shake of her head and then silently ignored these deluded suitors until they withdrew, embarrassed. He picked up the 'phone and watched Justin walk the length of the bar below to answer the ring.

'Blonde, tweed jacket, polo neck, jeans and boots.'

'Yes Guv.'

'Seen her before?'

'Twice.'

'She say anything?'

'Tonic water ice and lemon?'

He was half way into the long walk across the floor from the stairs to the bar when his earlier suspicions were confirmed; she had been part of the Police raid at Langoed. He'd seen her burst through the front door when he'd been hiding on the stairs. She turned slightly, smiled and then looked away. 'Mister Starmer.'

'And you are?' he enquired with an air of innocence.

'Detective Inspector Kate Lockstone,' she murmured quietly, 'and I have a suggestion.' Again, she looked away from him, seemingly preoccupied with the contents of the bar shelves.

'I'm listening.'

'Point me in the direction of the Ladies and then, in fifteen minutes meet me in the lower lounge at the Sachas Hotel.'

Starmer nodded, extended an arm, waved in the general direction of the lobby and muttered, 'what's this about?'

She smiled, 'fifteen minutes.'

She was waiting at a table towards the far end of a pretty much deserted bar watching a liveried bar man in a claret waistcoat vigorously polish a glass while pretending not to be looking at her. She smiled as Starmer approached, leant forward and gently pushed a pint of beer across the table towards him.

Starmer dumped his overcoat on an adjacent chair, 'beer drinker am I?'

'So I'm told.'

'What else have you been told Detective Inspector Lockstone?'

'That you need help.'

'I've been through this once with your colleagues. I won't be shaken down.' He paused long enough to take a long pull on the pint. 'I don't like bent coppers.'

'That's good. Nor do I.'

'So, what do you want?'

'I want to put away a very bent copper and I need your help to do it.'

Starmer realised he was nonplussed when he found himself taking another long pull from the pint he didn't want to mask his confusion and buy time. He lowered the glass and raised his eyes to a slightly cocked blonde bob and a confident smile.

'Would you like me to start?'

He nodded and took further refuge in the beer.

'Lecture first. Police corruption in London and Manchester is endemic. To the extent that Government sees it as a threat to the social fabric of society. Concerns began to surface, in London at least, after a private detective had an axe buried in his head in a pub car park in south London. He was investigating a group of police officers. What's worrying about that is the amount of interference that was run to hinder a successful prosecution. Then, there's a DCI in a town west of here found not only taking bribes from a drug baron but also running a goodly part of his empire. In North London, there's a drug squad that uses the Evidence Lockup for storing drug shipments and here, in Manchester, there's a squad of detectives that run their own dealers.'

She looked at him, waiting for a response. 'But then, you know about DI Stead. Don't you? Incidentally, he's the reason we're talking here and not at your club.' She sighed, reproachfully, at his lack of response and waved an arm in the general direction of the busy upstairs bar. 'The public either don't know or don't care as long as it doesn't affect them. At the moment, a lot of this is under the carpet and would probably have stayed there but for drugs.' She smiled grimly, 'back in the day, taking a bung from an armed robber and allowing him to go free had a limited effect on society. Policemen being complicit in the introduction of drugs to our inner cities and the chaos that's causing is killing our society. Something has to change.'

Starmer sensed her passion from the rising inflexions and her look of exasperation at his lack of response.

She sat back in her chair and puffed out her cheeks in frustration, 'There is so much money out there that it's changed the rules.' She leant forward and stared into his emotionless face, hers creased with concern and irritation, 'last week I was called to a semidetached house in Tilbury. Belonged to a middle-aged detective constable on a drug squad who was under investigation. He was hanging from the loft hatch. Do you know what he was using for loft insulation?'

Starmer shrugged.

'Bundles of notes. With the money, he had in that loft he could have bought every house in his street. But then he couldn't, could he?' She enquired, waiting for some, any, response from Starmer. 'There was just too much to spend. Christ, he couldn't even have burnt that much without getting nicked on a nuisance charge. Pointless. Fuckin' pointless and meanwhile whole neighbourhoods are sinking into poverty and prostitution levels not seen since the gin craze of the eighteenth century.' She paused to compose herself, 'is any of this getting through to you?'

'What do you want?'

'You were in Holland.'

'I was?'

'You were. I can't prove it and I don't intend to waste my time trying. But you were there.'

'Ok.'

'But, it didn't start in Holland,' she mused. 'That's where it ended. No, it started here in Manchester. Something happened, maybe at Slammers? Whatever it was saw you head for the hills with several Manchester notables on your heels and a certain Mister Williams in hot pursuit close behind them. Right?'

'Is there any point in me saying anything?'

'No, not yet.' She reached both hands behind her, scraped her hair up onto the top of her head, held it there and closed her eyes. A few moments later she opened them and smiled, 'they used the girl before, didn't they? And Williams is on the loose and trying to do it again.' This time she got a reaction.

'What do you mean?'

'Stop being an arse,' she barked, 'you know what I mean. Don't try and tell me Paul Denton hasn't been in touch. But just to be clear, Williams escaped from custody and tried to abduct Julie Denton from the Priory Clinic. He thinks she is important to you.'

'She is.'

'So, give him back his shipment.'

'Denton told you about that.'

'He did.'

'It wasn't a question. I'm puzzled. I've just sat through your impassioned commentary on the ills being inflicted on society by drugs flooding into the community and now you want me to add to the problem.'

She laughed, and fingered air quotes, 'in a managed way.'

'You want me to set him up.'

'That wasn't a question either. Was it?'

'You got a warrant card?'

'All coppers have. Including the bent ones and what you're wondering is whether I'm corrupt. Right? If you'd allowed me to finish my "impassioned commentary" I'd eventually have got to my membership of a specialist squad set up to tackle Police corruption in the Met.'

'Another "specialist squad", he mimicked. 'Well that's going to make all the difference. Crooks to catch crooks.'

'I understand your cynicism. But this is very different. This is more than anything before. Much more. Working title "Ghost Squad".

'"Ghost Squad", are you serious? Bill Murray a member, is he?' Starmer guffawed.

She sighed deeply, 'I'm very serious. So is the squad. A squad with a very strong interest in a particular senior detective at The Yard.'

'Pringle sweater and maroon trousers.'

'You were in Holland then.'

Starmer chuckled grimly, 'long enough to be able to tell you something interesting about him.'

'Go on,'

'He let the big fish out the net.'

'He did?'

'Claimed he was ambushed?'

'Lucky to have escaped alive.'

'And you believed that?'

'Did I say so?'

Starmer sat back in his chair, crossed his legs and looked absently at the shoes of the occupants of the bar up on the mezzanine floor. In his guts, he'd known it wasn't over even before he'd heard about Williams reappearance and the threat to Julie. He'd spent nearly an hour on the telephone reasoning with Denton and trying to calm him down. Knowing Lockstone was on her way and that King was making overtures and heavy threats about reopening for business had given him some thinking time but not enough. What he didn't know and now needed more to time to work out was how to use this earnest young woman to best effect. Somewhere in all of this must be an opportunity to finish it. He rolled his lower lip into his mouth, biting it gently, pensively, 'I'd need to get in touch with Williams. You know where he is?'

'I do.'

'So, nick him.'

'Too easy and not enough evidence. He'd walk, and anyway I'm more interested in using him to get to King. I need something that's going to stick big time to both. All I've got now is terrified witnesses.'

'So, what next?'

'I hide in the bushes. You deliver the shipment. We take it from there.'

'Better if he collects.'

'Why?'

'Trust me?'

'OK.'

'Then what?'

'The big fish.'

'Maroon trousers?'

'Detective Chief Superintendent King.'

'Aren't there some laws about Entrapment?'

She held his gaze a full moment before answering, 'as The Chief Inspector of Constabulary said only last year it's "Corruption in a noble cause".

'You're serious about all this.'

'I'm glad that wasn't a question.'

Starmer, convinced, leant over to his overcoat and puled the Filofax from a pocket, 'that might interest you then. I think it's a record of payments to Police Officers in Manchester. Some of it is coded with symbols and stuff. Like those on Ordnance Survey maps. There's a church and a crown,' he added.

'King?'

'I wondered.'

'And a church.'

'The Customs Officer?'

'Where did you get this?'

Starmer put the coat back on the chair, 'renovations at Slammers. Ripped out an old safe. It was in there.'

She grinned, 'yeah right. Just left there for you to find. How careless.'

'So, where's Williams.'

'There's a Police social club in South London, The Warren. Cottage in the grounds. Currently occupied by King's girlfriend and a guest.'

Starmer nodded, pleased that her answer had checked out against Denton's intelligence. Perhaps she could be trusted? He stood and retrieved his coat, 'how fast can you move?'

'I need twelve hours' notice to scope and set up.'

'I'd make that twenty-four. You're going to Scotland.'

The increasing closeness between Mia and Reg Boulter was beginning to get on Starmer's nerves. Initially the embryonic romance had brought some relief from Mia's, half serious, coquettish attempts, to seduce him. There had even been some light relief in watching Boulter's clumsy attempts at courtship and his arrival in the offices with an expensive bunch of non-seasonal birthday flowers was still talked of, out of his hearing. When Mia had responded to these overtures there had been a moment when Starmer had seen the rare sight of fear in Boulter's eyes as he'd witnessed Mia's impassioned, not quite desperate, rush to engage. They seemed, now, to have settled in to the first flushes of an affair with open displays of affection; girly blushes and boyish mischievousness and the delusion that it was their secret. This new relationship had changed the dynamics of that between Starmer and Reg. Having proved himself in the competition wars, Reg had offered to stick around and Starmer had, initially, been glad to have him on board. Lately, however, Boulter had begun to use his relationship with Mia to mark his territory and twice Starmer found it necessary to remind him that he was neither the brains nor the boss. The last occasion had seen Mia intercede on Starmer's behalf but walls were being written on as far as Starmer was concerned.

He stood, moved around the desk to face the door, leant against its edge and pasted a smile on his face as the giggling pair entered the office. Mia reached behind her, slapped Boulter's hand from her backside, sashayed across to the chesterfield, slumped down and breathed Rioja into the room. Boulter dropped to her side taking a moment to appreciate the gentle bounce of her flaunted embonpoint as his weight hit the cushions upon which she sat.

'Good lunch?'

'What's that supposed to mean?' slurred Boulter sullenly.

'I need to talk to Mia, Reg,' his eyes narrowed as they locked onto Boulter, 'leave.'

Boulter was still angrily struggling to get out of the low chesterfield when Mia's mighty forearm dropped across his knees and pinned him in place. 'You could not think of a nice way to say this thing? Ja?' She glared at Starmer.

'Mia, I need to talk to you,' he looked over at Boulter, 'not the help.'

The Help brushed aside Mia's restraining arm and lurched out of the chesterfield. Starmer stayed motionless, propped on the edge of the desk, legs stretched out in front of him, crossed at the ankles and his arms folded. Boulter lurched to a halt, face furiously red, spit flecking his lips and a pulsing vein in his temple signalling rising blood pressure. He repeatedly jabbed a forefinger to within inches of Starmer's face, 'so help me Andy.'

Starmer didn't flinch, 'think about it Boulter.'

With vein bursting concentration, he did. Slowly the big man regained and kept control of himself. Right up until he reached the door.

'Do you trust him?' Starmer enquired over the echoes of the still vibrating partition.

'You have reason for which I should not.'

'I have a reason that says you need to be very sure Mia.'

'Charlie, there is here business and there is fun. I do not confuse the two. Tell me.'

'Williams is loose.'

'So?'

'Well, apart from anything else, this is, maybe, his club.'

'No longer is this his. Trust me. And Reg?'

'Was his driver.'

'And?'

'I've been thinking.'

'Tell me these thoughts.'

'Well, Williams is connected to a Senior Policeman. Hand in glove. Bloke called King. At the moment, that Policeman is also sheltering Williams. The same Policeman is putting pressure on Paul Denton to pick up where they left off; use his business to bring in drugs. The pair have already had a go at Denton's daughter and it won't be long before they come this way.' He paused, wondering if she was beginning to see it. 'Reg tipping up here when he did was a coincidence too far.'

'And you know this. How?'

'Partly from Intelligence that your Bernard provided before he went to hospital, partly from Denton but mainly from stuff I saw in Holland. This isn't going to go away unless we send it.'

'And the young Policewoman in the bar?'

'And partly from her.'

'You know what you are doing?'

'I think so.'

'And you have plan.'

'I have a plan.'

'Your plan or Policewoman's?'

'Mine. It seems to me that we can either fight a series of battles or,'

'We fight one. With one stone, we kill the two birds in the bush?'

Starmer chuckled, 'that's the idea. The key is timing. Williams is after the missing shipment. It's about all he's got left and he's desperate.'

'I was wondering when you would get to that. You still have his shipment.'

Starmer paused briefly before replying, 'well, he thinks so. I am thinking of drawing him out with that and a deal that sees him going away in return.'

'He never go away.'

'I know. It doesn't matter. Once he's in the open, game over. The bigger threat is King. We use Williams to get to King and then we lose him. Williams will have dirt on King and we use that to ramp the pressure up. King will then make a mistake.'

'Why we no just kill him?'

'The heat from killing a top cop would cause problems we don't need and anyway, there is a better approach. We get Williams in the open with the shipment and I'll deal with him then. With him out of the way we go after King. We get on his case; surveillance and searches. Everything he has. Everything he's ever done. We take what he's got and then fit him up. Think about it. Every copper on the take anywhere will think twice after that. Yes? You've always said that corrupting Policemen wasn't worth the money.'

'This is true. But this one is already corrupt. If we control him we no need to pay him money. Ja?'

'I disagree. We don't need him. He's a threat. Too much of a threat.'

'Him you might fix. The rest will take a holiday and then come back as greedy as before. But, if this man is threat to business it is start. How you do this?'

Starmer levered himself from the desk, crossed the room, sat beside her and rested his hand on her arm. 'That's where Reg comes in.'

Mia moved her arm from beneath his hand, sat forward, adjusted her décolletage and addressed the middle distance. 'You will tell Reg where is shipment. Yes?'

He nodded.

'Then if Williams, he collect, you will know. About coincidence? Ja?'

Starmer nodded again looking for, but not finding, any sign of emotion on the big woman's face. In the weeks that'd passed since their meeting in her bar he'd come to like Mia. Outside of her self-inflicted gangster moll character he'd found her to be a warm woman with a big heart and he was sure she'd fallen for Boulter.

'And you will deal with them both then? Ja?' She looked distractedly at the door which Boulter had slammed behind him, 'it is a pity. Ja.'

He patted her arm.

Starmer sat at the bar watching Justin polishing glasses and holding them up to the light to check for smears. He'd found, in recent weeks, that half an hour chatting to the barman each evening was an investment well worth making. It was where he'd first learnt of Boulter's interest in Mia. There wasn't much that went on the club that didn't pass under Justin's scrutiny. The man not only had a keen ear and sharp eyes but also an instinct and ability to store seemingly random pieces of information until a pattern emerged that turned dross into Intelligence. It was from the threads and snatches of conversations that Justin had overheard at the bar that he'd first begun to have doubts about Boulter. Mutterings about the man's behaviour on the patch had begun to build to a level of discontent that he couldn't ignore. Some of those whispers had begun to confirm his suspicions that Boulter was skimming way beyond accepted margins and giving the impression that he was in charge. He watched Justin hold a glass aloft and squint for smears, holding the pose for slightly longer than functionally necessary as he polished the gem he was about to deliver.

'Tweed jacket and polo neck. Blonde.'

'Yes?'

'She didn't use the Ladies.'

'And that's important because?'

'You directed her to them.'

'Right.'

'Then followed her out the club.'

Starmer studied the little man's face for a clue as to where this might be going. 'You know Justin, sometimes it pays to keep stuff to yourself.'

'So, you don't want to know who followed you?' The pout was replaced by a grimace and a muttered, 'speak of the devil and he will arrive.'

Starmer watched Boulter cross the floor now knowing the source of Mia's intelligence about Lockstone.

'I owe you an apology,' grunted Boulter as he pulled up a stool.

'You do.'

Boulter struggled for a moment before shooting a cuff and thrusting a meaty hand and a surprisingly weak handshake forward, 'Sorry Boss.' He avoided Starmer's gaze, withdrew his hand and muttered, 'won't happen again.'

'I know that Reg,' Starmer offered graciously but with a hint of menace that Boulter couldn't fail to notice.

'Anyway, I'm sorry. Let things get on top of me a bit. Been overdosing on the booze too. What with that and,' he chuckled, 'Mia, my head's been all over the place. Thought I might take a bit of a break. Just another couple of days. If you could spare me.'

'Good idea. Where you off to?'

'Well, I've been thinking. Maybe down the smoke. Look up a few faces,' he chuckled, 'tell a few lies, sink a few beers.'

'Your mate Williams is on the loose down there. Had you heard?'

'Who me, no not me, not a word.'

Too many negatives, thought Starmer. Not only had the devious bastard heard, he'd been talking. 'Good Guvnor, was he, Williams?'

'Turned me over Guv, didn't he? Turned me over big time, the bastard.'

'Never met him. Saw him from a distance a couple of times.'

'Yeah, right, you was in that boat that Webber took a few shots at off Findhorn, weren't you? Christ, that was a day. Never seen Williams so mad. That Webber was a fuck up from beginning to end though and between him and that fat bastard Woolley they'd managed to lose the girl and that shipment.' He glanced slyly at Starmer, 'he knew you or Denton had it you know. He just didn't know how you did it or where you put it. Drove us fucking mad searching that place.'

Starmer laughed, 'that a fact.'

Reg studied him closely, 'I'm not daft Guv. I know one of you had it and I worked out that you didn't have a lot of time to do much with it. It's up there somewhere ain't it?' He laughed nervously. 'C'mon Guv, Professional interest nothing else. You pulled a right stroke. I'd just love to know how you did it.'

'You been giving it a lot of thought Reg,' thinking that somebody had jacked the pressure up if Boulter was risking asking so openly about shipment.

'It's been bugging me.'

Starmer let his mind drift briefly back to Woolley's despairing last moments in the cess pit and his subsequent return to the alley struggling with the blue forty-gallon container into which he'd then jammed the ten plastic tubs of drugs. It had taken several attempts to submerge it sufficiently to keep it below the rim of the pit. Twice, Woolley's body had surfaced alongside and had to be pushed back with a length of timber. Eventually satisfied he'd loaded planks and debris over the hole to conceal the breach. 'Well, as we're partners I suppose you had to find out sooner or later.' Boulter looked stunned and for a moment Starmer wondered whether he'd overplayed his hand. 'I was going to send you up there to get it next week. Doesn't matter, it'll wait 'til you come back now.' Starmer thought back to his conversation with Boulter outside The Junction Hotel where he'd first noticed the man's inability to conceal his emotions. Yet again, his face registered them fully; the eyes wrinkled in thought then widened with realisation as the lips moistened in anticipation.

'Whatever you say Guv. So, where is it?' he enquired eagerly.

Starmer hesitated for effect with an almost comical check to either side for eaves droppers before replying. 'There's an alley between the back-boundary wall and the boiler house. Half way down there's a cess pit. Take rubber gloves,' he laughed.

'That house in Nairn?'

'Where else?'

'You bastard. You cunning fucking bastard. Oh, Guv what a stroke.' he slapped Starmer's back enthusiastically in apparently genuine admiration, 'respect Guv, respect, what a stroke.'

'Our secret?'

'On my life, Guv.'

'Enjoy your break Reg and I'll see you in a couple of days. Then off to Jock land, yeah?'

'Right Guv, I'll get a few things together and be on my way,' he caught one foot in the leg of the stool in his eagerness to leave.

Kate Lockstone was nervous and the brisk tones of Sue Lawley interviewing Ken Livingstone on Desert Island Discs was doing little to soothe her anxieties. Even Livingstone's surprise opening choice of one of her favourite Tina Turner tracks failed to lift her spirits. She twisted in her seat to ease the cramp in one buttock and sighed impatiently as Red Ken rambled on about a bedroom full of newts and being bullied at school. Surveillance had always been her least favourite part of Police work and four hours had stretched her tolerance to its limit. As Maria Callas reached the end of Ken's second choice she reached for the car radio and killed the broadcast before the politician's drawling monotone drove her to further despair.

She considered another radio and readiness check with each of the several Highlands Police Officers dotted strategically around the house but suspected that this would only add to their irritation at the intrusion from South of the border. The Scottish officers had made little effort to hide their irritation at the briefing and had questioned her instructions to a point that would have been considered insubordination in her own Force. After a particularly truculent interruption from an Armed Response Officer she'd let them all have it with an acerbic series of put downs that'd even managed to drag in a reference to Culloden. In the stunned silence that'd followed she had reiterated her instructions that nobody moved until the Spotter gave the word and that would be when Williams had loaded his vehicle and not before. Rationally, she knew, she had very little about which to be anxious. She knew from surveillance, at the Warren back in Hayes, that Boulter had met up with Williams and that the two of them had left hurriedly, together, the following day. There was, she reasoned, only one place the two of them could be going together and she was three hundred yards down the road from it.

The radio crackled into life, 'white ford transit turning into the drive. Two on board. Standby.'

She thumbed the Push to Talk Button, 'hold your positions. I repeat, hold your positions.' She held the handset closer to her ear, anxious not to miss anything among the distorted crackling hisses and whines and cursed the poor reception in the area. She waited anxious minutes before the radio spluttered back into life.

'Spotter to Red one. They are in the alley. I repeat, they are in the alley. Wait one.'

Lockstone started the car and crept slowly forward out of the side lane leading to the woods at the back of the perimeter wall and turned right, back onto the Nairn Road back towards the house. 'C'mon,' she muttered, 'c'mon you bastards. Hurry it up. Move it, move it.' A loud blast from a set of two tones and a flash of lights from a motorist behind, impatient at her carefully timed and measured rate of progress, forced her to a stop and an exchange of insults. Just as she was considering flashing her warrant card the radio crackled to life, 'load on board. I repeat, load on board.' She thumbed the PTT button and yelled, 'all units go, Go, Go, Go,' as she accelerated round the impatient motorist to the accompaniment of "La Cucaracha" and a squeal of brakes.'

Driving quickly between the entrance pillars she noted piles of what looked like abandoned plant and construction materials as she turned left across the front and then right down the side of the main house towards the outbuildings and the Ford Transit. She opened her door to a shout followed by the sharp bark of two double tapped shots echoing around the buildings. Ducking round to the other side of the car she raced to the side of the van. Peering around the back she saw the Fire Arms Officer, standing over a body, shuffle a foot sideways and kick a MAC10 several feet clear. She ignored the Officer's shout and stepped between him and the van towards the sound of a struggle. Williams was on the ground face down with one Policeman's knee on his neck while another sat on his legs and a third attempted to cuff him. She moved back to the rear of the van and swung the doors fully open to reveal a blue plastic drum. She nodded to the Policeman who'd just cuffed Williams, 'get that open, would you?'

'What happened?' She enquired of the stunned looking policeman holding the Heckler and Koch.

He looked over at the MAC10, 'he had that in the back of the van. I shouted the warning but he just kept coming.'

She nodded and turned away as the Spotter appeared at her side.

'Guv, you'd better come and have a look at this,' he nodded in the general direction of the alley behind the boiler house.

She carefully picked her way over the builder's plant, rubble and debris and followed the young detective along the alley.

'Watch your step Guv. I'm not sure how stable this lot is. Here hold onto my hand,' gripping her wrist he moved her past him and anchored her as she leant forward to peer into the exposed cess pit. She drew back quickly, heaving and gagging while desperately sucking nearly fresh air through her tortured nostrils to clear the stench and taste from her mouth. 'Jesus Christ, what is that?'

'You alright Guv?'

'I'll be fine. Give me a minute.' She took several deeper breaths before gripping his hand and edging over the breach in the broken brick vaulted roof to peer down at the pit below. She gripped the detective's hand tighter and leaned further out. It took a moment for her brain to make sense of what her eyes were seeing; a bubble of Prince of Wales check suiting, the outline of an arm a few inches below the surface and the back of a head just above.

As she approached the table Starmer swivelled the Manchester Evening News around with the flat of his hand to face her. 'Your work?'

'"Manchester Detectives suspended in Corruption Investigation",' she read, removing her jacket and sitting down, 'interesting.'

'And your work?'

'Indirectly. Problem?'

'Could be if they make the connection.'

'They won't.'

'You seem confident.'

She nodded at the newspaper. 'there is no link from that to you. You weren't the only person they were shaking down you know and there were other investigations ongoing.' She paused to scan the room, the pink pleated wall furnishings, the pink back lit corner bar and the autographed show posters breaking up the tedium of the pink flock wallpaper in the Manchester Press Club. 'You a Member here?'

'Connections. I'm told that there are nights when you can't move for Coronation Street stars.'

'Always a draw.'

'He swivelled the paper back to face him, 'nothing in here about Williams, and it's been a week.'

'There won't be.'

'Because?'

'He's been persuaded to think about his future place in Society.'

'Meaning?'

'He's in secure custody; talking.'

'Christ, you've offered him a deal.'

'Not much of one. He's grassed up his mates and the drug business bigtime and he's still talking. Sort of Super Grass. For that maybe he'll get a reduced sentence but he'll spend the rest of his life looking over his shoulder.'

'Does King know?'

'Oh, I do hope so. It won't hurt if he does. All part of piling on the pressure.'

'Boulter?'

'Dead.'

'Dead?'

'He bought a MAC10 to the party. He'd used it before apparently,' she eyed him with a faint smile playing at the corner of her lips. 'Did you know about that?'

Starmer stared at her in silence, his face expressionless, taking some small pleasure when she finally averted her eyes, 'have I upset you?' he enquired.

'Why do you ask?'

'A bit smart arse?'

'Starmer, you're a crook. We both know it. Perhaps a crook by force of circumstances but a crook none the less. You helped me put another crook away. But you're still a crook. And,' she returned his stare unflinchingly, 'you're a crook with questions to answer.'

'Such as?'

'We found a body in that cess pit. Your predecessor from Slammers; Woolley. We also found a revolver. The two bullets found in the body of a Mister Osman, on the beach at Findhorn, were fired from that gun. Two more bullets recovered from other victims were fired from that gun.' She searched Starmer's face for any sign of emotion, stress or anxiety and found none. 'People who know about these things tell me that Woolley drowned. His lungs were full of fluid and liquid crap. They also tell me he went in alive.'

485

'And this means?'

'Well,' she drew the word out into a drawl, cupped her chin in her hand and studied him, 'you knew about the shipment and where it was.'

'I sure did. I told you. Remember?'

'So, the question is, did you push Woolley or did he fall?'

'Neither. When I stashed the stuff, there was no sign of a body. There was crap to within feet of the top leaving just enough room for the drum. No body to be seen.' He sighed, thinking briefly of Woolley's last seconds but remembering that when he'd left the alley there had, indeed, been no sign of the body.

'So, when you were in the alley there was slurry to within feet of the top of the pit?'

He nodded, 'about that yes.'

'And no body?'

'No.' Starmer was struggling with a plan that now looked as though it was about to backfire on him spectacularly. The idea behind returning the drugs had been to get Williams lifted at the scene of Woolley's death. He'd thought that the natural bloating of the decaying body would eventually bring Woolley to the surface thereby implicating Williams in his death as he recovered the drugs with Lockstone there waiting to spring. The link from the gun to Osman and back to Woolley could then have further incriminated either Williams or Woolley in Osman's murder. He simply hadn't bargained for the sort of methodical analysis that Lockstone was applying to each fact and account. He realised that, again, he'd underestimated her as he fought to marshal his thoughts. 'Williams was up there at the time, as was Osman, Webber and Boulter. Let's not forget that Woolley had cocked up big time as far as Williams and Webber were concerned. Osman was Woolley's boy. Perhaps Williams or Webber or both did for the pair.'

'Its's an explanation certainly. If I'm to believe it, I'd have to accept that the body went into the pit, sank and some hours later you stored the container in the same pit and there was no sign of the body. Because,' she screwed he eyes up in concentration, 'if anybody had put Woolley into the pit after you hid the container they'd have found the shipment. Right?'

'Correct.'

'Without a detailed account of your, and Mister Denton's movements while you were in Nairn it'll be difficult to prove,' she twirled a lock of her hair round a finger; deep in thought, 'or disprove for that matter.'

'Well, you could talk to Paul I suppose.'

'No, I think you'd better. I'm going to charge Williams with Woolley and Osman's murder and probably the two others. So, sort it out. Soon as. Right?'

He nodded, hoping that he'd given no sign of the immense relief he'd felt at her decision. 'What about King?'

'Right now, he's pulling every string he can get his grubby little fingers on to try and find out what happened to Williams. Or more particularly, that shipment of drugs.' She puffed out her cheeks as a frown creased her forehead, 'by the way, there is a discrepancy.'

'In what?'

'The drugs. According to Williams there was one hundred and fifty keys.'

He nodded, 'and?'

'There's fifty missing.'

'And you think?'

'There's fifty missing.'

'He could be lying, they shipped less or he could have been stiffed along the way. Who knows?'

'You don't then?'

'No. Why?'

She smiled and then began to chuckle, 'only if King thought you'd got the fifty keys we could go fishing again.'

They both paused as a small group of chattering theatricals released from a nearby matinee delivered their lines to each other and the barman while checking their performances in the mirror at the back of the bar. One, a large man with a loud check suit and a perspiration problem that was leaving furrows like culverts in thickly applied stage make up, occupied centre stage. His voice enveloped the room in tones of deep base velvet that ebbed and flowed like the tide. Noticing Starmer's interest he inclined his head, looked for recognition, bowed from the waist and raised his glass in a toast. Starmer smiled and returned the gesture. 'All the world's a stage,' he muttered. Lowering the glass, he waited for Lockstone to turn back from her own scrutiny of the actors. 'Why would King be that desperate?' he mused.

'That was a large shipment by any standards. And it's missing. He's probably being held responsible.' She pursed her lips and blew out her cheeks, 'he's also the last man standing and someone's got to pay. He's close to desperate. But then, King is only part of the problem here. He works for others. His job is to facilitate the supply of drugs into the country. So, we know, at the moment, with his Vietnamese supply line maybe out of commission, he has another problem. Plus, he must have realized that he's on his way out and he's looking for a last payday.'

'You knew about King and Duong, didn't you?'

'Suspected', might be more accurate.'

'Well you know that Duong wasn't rescued from that car in Langoed. King let him go.'

'You definitely saw that?'

'I did.'

'Would you testify to that?'

'No.'

'Well fifty keys might draw him out but only if we really ramp the pressure up.'

'Where are all the ill-gotten gains though? Think about it, he's camping out with a girlfriend. That's not exactly the high life. What's he done with all the money? Where is it?'

'None of the usual places. We checked.'

'Did you try the loft?'

She chuckled, 'Funny man. He'll have some house and fuck off cash maybe but the rest will be offshore. Somewhere he will have stashed some serious money.'

'How do you open an offshore account? I mean you can't just tip up at Credit Suisse in Geneva and say tuck this lot away for me. Can you? Surely to God?'

'Well no. You'd have to present some form of identification, accreditation.'

'Like a passport?'

'Probably, but not his own. Then once the account is open presumably there is some sort of pass card or letter of credit that can be presented for withdrawals. I'll find out.'

'So, if he loses the accreditation, he's in deep trouble with nowhere to go and under really big pressure.'

'And we get hold of that,' she encouraged him with a bemused smile, 'how exactly?'

'He's expecting to have to run. All that stuff will be close, near to him.'

'Again, how do we get hold of it?'

'"We" don't. I do.'

Starmer stood in the open door and scanned both sides of the island bar. A woman rocked herself backwards and forwards on a stool behind the bar to gain sufficient momentum to break the seal between the stool and her vast bottom. As she waddled towards him she stuffed a pencil in her chignon, recovered her spectacles from where they hung over the shelf of her bosom, cracked the make up with a semblance of a smile that revealed nicotine stained teeth and grimaced an invitation to order a drink.

'It's ok Margaret. I've got that.'

Starmer peered further into the shadowy depths of the Dukes Head and picked out Denton on the far side of the pub, flanked by two heavily set men who were eyeing him with suspicion and a hint of hostility. 'Mister Denton.'

'Paul please, I'd like you to meet Don and Ron.'

Starmer nodded, 'I came to see you.'

'Trust me. The boys are good. They've been helping me.'

'Good to hear. But I talk to you alone.'

Denton looked at the Bulimias and offered an apologetic shrug while ushering Starmer towards a banquette.

'Tell me.'

Denton paused, wondering whether to challenge this new, confident, authoritative version of the man he'd shared so much with. 'King has been back again. He really means business now. He wants the stuff you've got or else.'

'Or else what?'

'Or else, he'll fit me up, close me down, disappear me, go after Julie. I just don't know. What I do know is he's not gone away and he wants an answer.'

'You frightened?'

'Wouldn't you be?' He nodded towards the Bulimias, 'I'm keeping them close as witnesses in case he goes the fit-up route and they're also a bit handy.'

'Ok, we know King lives in a cottage on the grounds of that Police Social club near here. I need to get in. How?'

Denton nodded again at the Bulimias who were trying hard not to appear to be listening, 'they know the place well.'

'Ask 'em over.'

Denton and Starmer slid tight up into the corner of the banquette, on opposite sides of the table, in a doomed attempt to make sufficient room for the Bulimias.

Starmer offered a hand to Don, 'pleased to meet you. What's the security like in this Warren place?'

'There isn't any.'

'No security on Metropolitan Police premises? You sure?'

'I'm sure. Anyone can come in the rear entrance, from Holland Way, past the old stables, the cottage and the tennis courts and you're up at the main house.'

'Cottage is on the service road?'

'Yeah, you pass it on the way up to the house.'

'What do you know about the woman who lives there?'

'Nice girl who has made poor choices and is living with a tosser. Works shifts, mainly eleven to three and early evenings.'

'Can the cottage be seen from the club?'

Don paused and looked at Ron who shook his head. 'Don't think so.'

Starmer looked at Denton, 'is King there during the day?'

Ron chipped in before Denton could answer, 'he's been about quite a lot lately. Like he's not got regular hours.'

'That figures,' grunted Denton as he looked over at Starmer, 'what are you thinking?'

'I'm thinking I need a couple of hours in that cottage without being disturbed.' Starmer pondered the silence and what appeared to be a process of telepathic communication taking place between Ron and Don. 'Ideas Lads?' he enquired, catching a slight nod of agreement between the two.'

Don coughed, 'we used to know a couple of blokes that worked a sort of scam.'

Starmer looked from one to the other, 'big blokes, were they?'

'You interested or not?' Don demanded sharply.

'Very.'

'No one looks twice at a Builder. You leave the front door wide open, lean a new bath in its wrapping up against the wall, dump a broken bog on the path and a few bags of debris in the road and you're invisible.'

Starmer stood in the tiny hall leaning against the kitchen door frame watching Denton lower himself from the cottage roof access. 'Anything?'

'A wind-up gramophone, a cot and some very old porno mags.'

'Did you check between the joists?'

Denton dropped to the floor and dusted himself down, 'you want to look?'

'No. It's just that I was bloody convinced King'd stash his stuff here, close by.'

'He's gonna know we've been here you know,' Denton looked through the door to the small living room and the jumble of upturned furniture with ripped linings.

'That won't hurt. I want him to know. It'll jack the pressure up.' Starmer turned back to the small galley kitchen and stared gloomily at the gas boiler as a pump hummed into life, a thermocouple sparked and the boiler fired. He pushed himself away from the frame, 'sod it, come on, time's up, we need to go.' He edged round Denton in the small hall, brushed by a storage heater on the way to the door and stopped dead. 'That's an electric storage heater.'

'So?'

'That's a gas fired boiler in the kitchen.' Starmer, stuck his head through the living room door, 'and wet radiators in the rooms.'

'And?'

Starmer kicked the electric storage unit. 'You don't have both. Those storage cabinets were useless; filled with bricks that were heated by electric elements.' He kicked the cabinet again and smiled at Denton, 'why keep a redundant bit of kit?'

Denton looked at the screws securing the lid of the steel cabinet and grinned. 'I'll get a screwdriver.'

Don drove the builder's truck carefully up the service road, past the tennis courts and the club house and down the drive towards the main entrance.

Starmer looked up from the contents of the small suitcase on his lap to enquire, 'did we have to go out through the main entrance?'

'It's One Way.' Don laughed, 'wouldn't want to break the law.'

491

Denton nudged Starmer as the turn onto the main road jostled them together on the bench seat, 'is that what you were after?'

'It's more than that.'

'How do you mean?'

'If I'd lost this lot, I'd be more than desperate,' he grimaced at Denton, 'I'd kill to get it back.'

Chapter Thirty

Dee stood, arms folded, staring through the apartment window and out across the river. She flexed her shoulders and reached up to her neck to massage and ease tensed muscles. 'A week to go Mathew,' she said brightly, turning and trying hard to hide her frustration and impatience as she listened to him repeatedly practice shifting harmonic progressions up through the scales. He seemed to have become obsessed with his ability to play piano and the fear that his talent had been damaged by his experiences and injuries. At breakfast, she'd caught him obsessively practicing finger and thumb positioning on the table.

He looked at her briefly, lowered his eyes and slowly, carefully, closed the fallboard, 'I can't do this Dee.'

She walked around the baby grand, made room on the stool by shuffling him along with her bottom and put an arm round his shoulders. 'Mathew, honey, you can do it, you really can.' She gathered her courage. A lot, for her, was riding on Sinclair giving the sort of performance he'd delivered in Edinburgh. She could do it without him but didn't want to. 'Mathew, before all that stuff went down I'd never heard you practice scales. Since we got back, you've done nothing else. It's like you're locked in. You've been through a hell of a lot I know. I'm guessing you've gotten yourself emotionally exhausted. Nobody should have had to go through what you did with Williams.' She hugged him closer and smoothed a lock from his forehead. 'He was cruel and heartless and you deserved so much better honey.' She smiled, 'you still do. You need rest, how about you take a nap? You'll feel better. Then we'll try again,' she added hopefully.

'Dee,' he interrupted sharply, 'I think it best you accept that I won't be playing with you at The Roundhouse,' his voice shook with supressed emotion. 'I haven't got the confidence and I simply can't focus.' He looked absently down at the hands in his lap, 'I was such a fool. How can you possibly forgive me for betraying you?'

'You loved him Mathew.'

'But if only I'd listened to you.'

'You've heard the expression, "blinded by love"?'

'God, I could've got us all killed.'

'But you didn't.'

'Oh Dee, how can you ever trust me again? How can you ever forgive me?'

'Because you're my friend?'

'Still,' he looked into her eyes, 'I'm still your friend even though I can't play at your concert?'

Her head dropped with resignation but she hugged him closer to her, 'You'll always be my friend. Will you tag along though? Stay with me? Just be there? I really don't want to do this without you at least being there.'

He nodded and they both looked up as static on the intercom was followed by Denton announcing his arrival, 'hi Dee, come to see Julie if that's alright.' Mathew rose from the stool and hurried for the stairs and as Dee reached out for the intercom she heard his bedroom door slam.

Denton's despairing tread reached the foot of the spiral staircase where he saw Dee standing in the kitchen in front of the coffee machine. Hearing his footfall, she turned, 'coffee?'

He struggled to keep the surprise and delight from his face. Since Julie had moved to the apartment he'd visited every day, seen Dee on several occasions and been ignored on all. 'Sure,' he nodded gratefully, 'that'd be great.' He studied her profile as she busied herself at the machine and noticed the lines under her eyes and the fatigue evident in the slumped shoulders. 'How are you doing?'

Dee turned, offered the steaming cup, leant back against the kitchen worktop and sighed heavily, 'not brilliantly, if I'm honest. You?'

He snorted, 'I know how you feel.'

'Julie?'

'Yeah. She was doing reasonably well at The Priory but since I moved her here she's definitely regressed.' Catching a look of vague hurt and puzzlement on Dees face he hurried on, 'I mean I can't thank you enough and I know you're doing all you can but she needs full time Professional care.'

'I've tried Denton. God knows, I've tried.'

He put the cup back on the counter, reached out and placed his hand on her arm, 'I know Dee and I am so very, very grateful.' She pulled away from him and cuffed a tear from her cheek. He gently gripped her arm and drew her slowly towards him and she buried her face in her hands and sobbed. With a damp cheek pressed against his and her breath on his neck he enfolded her in his arms and gently rocked comfort into her trembling frame. She nestled into his neck and he could feel warmth radiating from the spot where her lips brushed against his skin. He ran his fingers lightly down her spine and felt the trembles turn to shivers. They moved slowly apart and he rested his forehead against hers. Her eyes moved from left to right and back; focusing on each of his in turn. Searching, hoping, he didn't know, wasn't sure, didn't care. She gasped as he leant forward with the answer, capturing her lips, stopping time and taking them to a place where there were no worries or problems; just the two of them.

As their lips parted he took her face in his hands and looked intently into her eyes. 'I love you Dee. I never stopped.' He paused, waiting for a response and then gambled it all, 'do you still love me?'

She broke away, cuffing more tears from both eyes and reached for a hank of kitchen roll, 'no, I hate you, you bastard!'

He smiled, 'well thank God for that.'

They both laughed, 'I think we better go and sit down.'

Denton nodded and led her by the hand to the settee opposite the grand piano. 'No Mathew?'

'Thereby hangs a tale.'

'So, tell it.'

'He's got cold feet, nerves, post-traumatic stress, who knows? He's also suffering from masses of guilt and nothing I say seems to make him feel any better. Anyway, a week away from the Roundhouse Concert he's pulled out. He's there in the background doing the Manager bit but he will not get up on that stage. He's sort of way back there inside his own head.' She sighed, 'it's interesting, he and Julie seem to spend quite a bit of time together and I don't think it's doing either of them much good.'

'Can he be replaced?'

'Yeah, he has been, someone he brought in, but it won't be the same.'

Denton leaned forward and clasped both her hands in his. 'You're the star Dee. You're the talent. It's you that carries the show.'

'Denton, you are so good for me,' she giggled and moved onto his lap, 'can we do that thing again?'

'What thing's that,' he smiled.

'You know. The thing with the lips,' she giggled again, 'that was so damn good.'

He laughed, 'yes we should do that some more but then we need to talk,' he added sternly, pulling her to him.

Starmer walked up from the car park towards the turn of the century, three storied, red bricked, ornamentally roofed and gabled house with its mock Tudor chimneys and York stone porticos. The Metropolitan Police had done rather well for themselves he thought; the lot of the Policeman at The Warren was indeed a happy one. He crossed the vestibule, pushed open a heavy oak panelled door and started the journey to the polished oak bar, ankle deep in blue Axminster, past oil portraits of politicians, towards the equally unsmiling face of a uniformed barmaid. He pasted a cheerful grin across his features, determined not to add to the woes of King's paramour if possible.

'May I help you sir?'

Starmer surveyed the array of pumps, 'pint of Directors please.'

'Are you a Member sir?'

'I'm not,' Starmer affirmed affably, nodding at two men propping up the far corner of the bar. 'I'm a guest of a Member although perhaps I'm a little early.' He turned at the sound of a swish as the door sashayed over expensive pile, 'and here she is.'

He watched her settle back into the plush red leather armchair as she tucked her warrant card back into an elegantly and expensively slim lizard skin shoulder bag. The bob now had a fringe and was slightly lighter in colour and the make-up was sparingly but skilfully applied. She was wearing a tailored tweed suit, three button high with a velvet trimmed collar and four inch heels that matched the bag. Around her neck was a single strand of pearls. He remembered having been previously impressed by her composed beauty and having caught himself, on several occasions since, wondering. Wondering at a future he knew just wasn't possible. He suddenly realised that she was aware of his scrutiny, 'you're looking good,' he exclaimed.

'Are you for real?'

He grinned, 'so, you've not made an effort on my behalf?' He realised his mistake as the pearls achieved a greater lustre against the background of an increased blood flow to her neck which developed into a charming but revealing blush.

'Don't be ridiculous.'

He hurried to hide the moment, 'is it wise, meeting here?' He nodded back towards the barmaid.

'Why not?' She shrugged, 'if you're referring to the burglary, she's not reported anything.'

'King?'

'Gone off the grid.'

'And that means?'

'He's not here, he's not at work and he's not been seen. Is that what you found?' She pointed to the case at the side of Starmer's chair.

He nodded.

'All of it?'

'What do you mean?'

'Well, forgive me for asking but your record precedes you. I haven't forgotten the fifty keys.'

'See what you think,' he dumped the small case on the table, 'I'm going to get another pint. Anything for you?'

She shook her head, pulled the case to her side of the table, flipped the latches, opened the case and began arranging the contents in the lid, making notes as she went.

Starmer moved the case slightly to set down his pint, shifted his chair to shield her actions from scrutiny and enquired, 'what you expected?'

'No cash?' She returned the contents, but left the case open and pushed it back across the table.'

'Expenses.'

'Seriously?'

'Yeah, seriously. That's what you wanted isn't it?'

'Not exactly. What I wanted was for it to be stolen from King; jack the pressure up. As evidence, this is inadmissible; "unlawful search or seizure",' she intoned. 'You'd better take it with you. I will not compromise this investigation,' she added firmly.

'Right, I get it,' he nodded at the case, 'I'm the live bait.' 'How's he going to know it's me to come after?'

'He's an intelligent man, but if that doesn't work the two at the bar will tell him.' She stood sharply, smoothed her skirt, looped the bag over her shoulder and leant down towards him, 'when he makes his move, when you're handing that stuff over, I'll be there.' She patted his shoulder reassuringly, 'take care.' With that, she swivelled the lizards and made for the door, noticing but ignoring the looks of contempt from the two in the corner.

Starmer raised his glass and proposed a toast to a picture on the wall, 'bit like you Winston; bold, ballsy and more brains than I'm ever going to have and,' he finished the pint, 'a fine strategist.'

Denton pulled his car into the kerb and cursed the neighbour who'd chosen to show off his new purchase by parking a Land Rover Discovery across his drive. He made his way wearily to the front door, hoping that Stella was out or in bed. Recently she'd taken to ambushing him in the hall, knowing that he'd been to the apartment and, wrongly, she'd thought, to Dee. Except tonight she'd be right.

He entered the house to complete darkness. As he began the journey to reach the switch the hall was suddenly flooded with light. He blinked furiously and opened his eyes to the sight of King leaning against the door to the lounge.

'Good evening Paul.'

Denton's brain raced to overcome the shock and was at least one move forward when he responded, 'where's Stella?'

'Safe.'

'Why?'

'You know why. You get her back when I get my stuff back.'

'What stuff?'

'Don't fuck me about Paul.'

'I haven't got it.'

498

King inclined his head and clicked his tongue in sympathy, 'I know, but you know the man who has.'

'So, talk to him.'

'My erstwhile colleague, Detective Inspector Lockstone, would just love that. Starmer is under surveillance Paul. Her surveillance. I go near him I get lifted. You just got elected as the intermediary. Behave and Stella will be fine.'

'You hurt her and I will kill you,' Denton spat.

King grinned, 'you'll try, but even as a kid, I could turn you over.'

Denton was surprised at how hard this hit home. He remembered the hours his mother and 'Aitch had invested in this no hoper kid with a mother that'd eventually slipped into full time prostitution and the father who'd returned from prison and pimped her. 'You know, when I heard you were a Policeman I remember muttering a prayer up to 'Aitch: "you called that right Dad, saved him from a life of crime."' He laughed, 'what happened, why the fuck did you throw it all away?'

King threw back his head, genuinely amused, and laughed out loud, "you think I joined the Police Force to "Serve and Protect"? He chuckled, 'oh Paul, bless you. You really are naive. I was, shall we say, encouraged to join by a group of people who were far thinking enough to see the advantages of having an ambitious, ladder-climbing, career copper on the books. Someone to give them a heads up, someone to lose or manufacture evidence, point out the pressure points, grease the wheels? You know the sort of thing.'

'And what's it all got you?'

'Something you'd never understand.'

'Try me,' Denton prevaricated, desperate for time to order his confused thoughts.

King smiled slowly, 'It's a game.' He shook his head, seemingly baffled by the question, 'power without responsibility and absolutely no rules?' The smile widened, 'instant gratification for any need or desire?' He laughed quietly, to himself, 'your mate Starmer would understand.'

'I think there's slightly more to him than that.'

'You'd like to think so, wouldn't you?

As King mused, Denton tensed and moved to reduce the distance between them. King lazily returned his full attention to the situation and held out an upturned palm to halt the movement, 'even if you knock me senseless, which you won't, that leaves poor old Stella swinging in the breeze. If anything happens to me and that includes getting lifted by Lockstone, you lose Stella. Please don't let this urbane discussion fool you. I will get what I want.'

'And that is what exactly?'

'Are you thick?'

'No, I understand; you get your stuff back but then what? I mean you're finished in this country.'

'I have certain skills and a knowledge of a business that is the biggest growth industry in the world. I will not be unemployed.' With a push from his hip he levered himself from the door and advanced on Denton. 'Here's what's going to happen Paul. I'm going to check on Stella, you're going to get in touch with Starmer and get my stuff back. At three thirty tomorrow afternoon, I'll ring you here to explain the plan and give you instructions. By then you must have my stuff.'

He prodded Denton in the chest with his forefinger, 'that's all my stuff; fifty kilos and the suitcase he lifted from the Warren. I'll tell you where to take it and you're going to need to be ready. There won't be a lot of time before it gets dark.' He made for the door fishing keys from his pocket as he went. At the threshold, he turned back, 'and, between now and then, if I see Starmer or Lockstone you won't see Stella again.' The corners of his mouth drooped and his face assumed a baleful glare, 'I don't want to hurt you or your family Paul. But, I'm tired and I need to get away and I'll go through anybody who tries to stop me. Do as I say and this time tomorrow it'll all be over and you can go back to normal.'

'Starmer If he clocks us Stella is dead.'

'Mister Denton,' Starmer protested, 'the sun has only just risen, it's barely daylight, we are out of sight, if we go much further we'll be in the middle of the Thames.' He glanced behind him, theatrically, for any sign of King, his cohorts or covert observation. They were on the tow path between Denton's factory wall and the river. 'Get a grip, if, as you say, he knows I'm under surveillance he's not going to put himself anywhere near me where he can be plotted. Is he?'

He drew the collar of his coat tighter to his throat against the brisk easterly whipping white tops onto the waves lashing spray over the stone, algae covered slipway. Looking down at the green and red, rust and weed encrusted bollard at the head of the slipway he decided that sitting would provide a lower profile against the biting prevailing wind. As his feet went from under him he seized Denton's arm to steady himself.

'Careful, we lost a bloke on this.'

'Yeah?'

'Slipped on that algae, smacked his head on that granite wall. Brain damage. Died a few days later.'

'Seriously?'

'He thought so.'

'What was he doing down here anyway?'

'Webber had a Rib. Flash sod used it to ferry him over from City Airport.'

'And it never occurred to you that this wasn't maybe kosher?'

'Leave it. We are where we are.'

'True.'

Starmer stuck his hands into the slash pockets of his Pea Jacket and looked idly at the weed trailing from a rusty iron anchor ring fixed to the side of a timber stanchion some fifty feet from the slipway, 'What's the tide here?'

'This time of year? Fifteen feet.'

'Does it come to the top?'

'No, about half way up the ramp.'

Starmer looked back at the stanchion, noting that the outgoing tide washing up against the upriver side was at least six inches higher than that downriver and a chocolate whirlpool had sucked flotsam into a vacuum on the lee side. 'How fast is the tide here?'

'Faster than you could swim.' Denton snorted in exasperation, 'fuck the tide Starmer. What are we going to do about King?'

'Calm down. We'll get Stella back.' Starmer nodded reassuringly, 'we just need to give him what he wants. I give you the stuff, you take it with you and you do the exchange.'

Denton grunted in relief.

'Except, I don't trust him.'

'And?'

'I'm going to be there.'

'Why?'

'I'm better at this sort of crap than you are.'

'He said as much.'

'There you are then.' Starmer shrugged deeper into his coat, 'go through it again. Tell me again what he said. Everything.'

'How many times,' Denton huffed, 'he'll ring at three thirty and I've got to be ready to move.'

'Exactly. Is that exactly what he said?'

'For fuck's sake.'

'It's important.'

Denton dipped his chin below his buttoned collar to get some shelter for his face against the wind. 'He said,' he paused, considering, trying to remember, "I'll ring at half three, be ready with the stuff, you'll have to move quickly, there won't be a lot of time", I think.'

Starmer tapped his pursed lips with his forefinger, inflated his cheeks and slowly expelled the air, 'he's time critical.' He shoved his cold hands back into his pockets.

'Meaning?'

'He's got to be somewhere at a particular time. He does the deal and he'll have what he needs for the great escape. Now, he knows half the world is looking for him so he doesn't want to risk two trips; doubles the chances of being seen.' He pulled his hands from within the pea coat, rubbed them together, blew on his chilled fingers, looked at Denton and allowed a slow smile to spread across his face. 'So, the exchange and the getaway are part of the same operation. He'll continue on his way after he's got his stuff.' He looked at Denton. 'What's the matter?'

'I've just remembered something else.'

'What?'

'Before dark. He said, "before it gets dark", I remember now.'

'What time is sunset?'

'Half five?'

'Wherever he's going then he wants to be well on his way before it gets dark.'

'He's given himself two hours.'

'So, he rings at three thirty. Very precise timing that. Let's say he allows an hour for your journey and the exchange. That gives him an hour before dark.'

'What's he going to do in an hour. I mean I sort of assumed that he'd make for an airport or the channel ports and use his fake IDs to get him out of the country.'

'He doesn't need dark for that. But you're right. He should be making for the exits. Why,' he mused, 'does he need daylight?' He stuffed his hands back in the slash pockets and idly watched a de Havilland Dash sideslip a cross wind, eliminate the crab and flare out of the steep approach. He grabbed Denton's arm excitedly, 'how long does it take to drive from Bromley to here; Woolwich?'

'That time of day, opposite direction to the rush hour, thirty, forty minutes?'

'Here just after four then, half hour for business,' he nodded at the slipway, 'quick trip in a Rib across the river to City Airport. Nice time for Customs and Duty free and Amsterdam for tea.'

Comprehension dawned and Denton grinned, 'City Airport shuts at sunset. So, he'd just be in time for the last flight.'

'Bingo. And, if they're watching the Airport entrance they won't see him arrive from the river.'

'So, what now?'

'Take the stuff, go home and wait. Then you do exactly as he says. If I'm wrong and he's not using your slipway and you're somewhere else, you're just going to have make the exchange on your own and do your best.'

'If you're right?'

'I'll be here, waiting to make sure we get Stella back.'

'How you going to stop the Police following you. He said you were under surveillance.'

'The same way I did this morning.' He nodded back some hundred yards down the tow path to the end of the factory perimeter wall and a beat-up builders truck.'

'The Bulimias?'

He nodded.

'You seem to have it all covered.'

Starmer looked at him carefully looking for any sign of sarcasm. Finding none he wondered just how re assured the man would feel if he knew that he was making it up as he went along.

Denton looked down at his feet, huddled deeper into his coat against the chill and looked over hesitantly, 'I need a favour.'

'Ask.'

'Go and see Julie?'

'She asked?'

'No, but the state she's in she probably won't.'

503

'OK, I'll go this morning. I take it she doesn't know about Stella and King?'

'Wouldn't help. Would it?'

'Probably not. You clear on everything else?'

Denton nodded, 'thanks.'

I didn't know you knew them,' Julie glanced towards the Bulimias. Don was clearing condensation from the café window and Ron was buried in the sports pages of the Daily Mirror.

'Only through your dad. They're helping us. Don will take you back to the apartment, when you want to go.'

'Helping with what?'

Starmer looked down at the steam curling from the coffee cup and the undissolved granules of instant coffee floating on the surface and considered his options. 'There's a bit of tidying up to do Julie. Nothing to worry about.' He saw new concern reflected in the dull eyes buried in kohl dark sockets and hurried on, 'the Police are on it. Nothing for you to worry about,' he repeated, 'honestly.' He reached across the chipped Formica table, gently removed the spouted sugar dispenser from her hands and gripped them both. 'How are you?'

'Well I'm clean, if that's what you mean,' she pulled her hands away from him.

'It wasn't.'

She raised her chipped mug to her lips and sipped the tea. 'You've talked to Dad?'

'He's worried,' he leant back in his chair. She'd lost weight she couldn't afford to lose and looked gaunt and exhausted. 'I think, in a day or so, it'll be safe for you to go back to the Priory.'

'And that'll make it all alright, will it?'

'Nothing is ever going to make it "all alright" Julie,' he replied, surprised at his own testiness.' 'Stuff happened. Treatment will help you deal with it. Put it in perspective. Stop it ruining the rest of your life.'

'You have no idea,' she spat savagely.

He sighed, 'probably not. What I do know is that if you don't make an effort and start trusting the people who love and care for you it'll go downhill fast and you do not want to go back there. Surely?'

She lowered the cup and stared at him intently, 'do you "love and care" for me Andy?'

He met her penetrating gaze evenly, knowing that the time for truth had arrived and they both knew it. 'I tried Julie. I really tried. You didn't make it easy and I never really got much back from you. Did I?'

'It wasn't love if you had to try.'

'Is that what you thought when you were trying?'

So why did you trail all over Europe after me?'

Starmer recovered a damp teaspoon from the table and encouraged recalcitrant granules towards dissolution in his luke warm coffee while he took time to think. He was surprised how far only a few moments conversation had gone to rationalise emotions and feelings that had worried and puzzled him for so many days. He took a deep breath. 'I thought I loved you.' He shrugged, 'but then I thought you loved me. Maybe we were caught up in the moment? Then, I suppose, circumstances took over. You were in trouble, your Dad seemed like a nice bloke that needed help, we had to get you back and neither of us liked being pushed around.'

'Thank you for helping my Dad.'

'That's Ok.'

'Thank you for helping me.'

He leant forward, 'I'll always care for you Julie. You do know that?'

She smiled diffidently, 'I do now Andy.'

'Advice?'

'Go on.'

'Do your time in the Priory. Go back to Uni in the autumn. You need Objectives.'

'You're probably right,' she dropped, then raised her eyes shyly, 'I do love you Andy.'

'I know,' he grinned, 'but not in that way.'

'Not in that way,' she repeated with a smile.

Starmer stood on the beach his eyes level with the top of the convex concrete seawall and tucked himself into the right angle the wall formed with the weed covered slipway. From this position, he could just about make out the lamp standards on the top main Woolwich road and most of the service lane that ran down from there to Denton's factory. The wind off the river and the spray being whipped off the waves of the incoming tide had chilled him. He shuffled and squelched his feet in the Thames mud to restore some circulation and tried to marshal thoughts that were beginning to spiral out of control. Since Boulter's death there had been several occasions when he'd missed the man's ability to plan and set an operation. His current problem, he knew, was that there were far too many variables. Starting with, was he even in the right place? If it was the right place was his assumption that King was going by Rib to City Airport correct? If so, when would King make his way to the slipway? The plan, such as it was, assumed that King would arrive at the factory with Stella, make the exchange and then get himself down to the river. He and Denton had decided that it was best he wasn't visible at that stage as it would spook King into looking for a Police presence. Denton had seemed sure, after his meeting with King, that no harm would come to him or Stella. King, he advised, was tired and beaten. He would just go when he'd got what he needed. Not convinced, Starmer had placed the Bulimias in the freight container in the yard.

He dropped back down into the shadows, conscious that, if he was right, there were two directions he would have to cover; the road and the river. He rose and peeped back over the sea wall. Denton, he knew, had arrived some minutes back; King was late. Not convinced by Denton's sanguine assessment of King's intentions and his state of mind Starmer had set himself as backstop. If all went well he'd let King pass, go back to Denton's office, ring the Police and tell them where they could collect their current most wanted. The conundrum of what he'd do if King played rough was sending scenarios and solutions across his synapses faster than his brain cells could process them.

He turned to face across the river, brushed spray from his face, looked over the water and marvelled at the steepness of approach as a plane seemed to drop from the sky onto the tarmac at City Airport. To his left, across the top of the slipway, the seven silver shell structures of the Thames Barrier with their yellow hydraulic gantries caught the low rays of the setting sun. He scanned east, towards the estuary, looking for any sign of a boat making for the slipway. Moving his feet, he felt the tug of suction and a sucking squelch as his shoe broke the vacuum with the now saturated ground into which he'd sunk. Since he'd last looked the tide had advanced several feet and was now covering half the length of the slipway. Strands of green weed clinging to the granite block surface and sides were washing on and off the slipway with successive waves.

At the sound of a faint single beep on a car horn Starmer swivelled and checked the service road. There, roughly opposite where he knew the yard gates to be was a white Discovery with its offside indicator flashing. The driver flashed the lights twice, seeking entry and almost immediately the car moved out of sight and into the yard. His sense of relief was palpable; his basic assumption had been correct; King was on site.

So far so good, all he had to do, he reasoned, was stick to the plan. Impatiently he set aside one of Boulter's military maxims that no plan survived implementation and focused on the next steps. As he considered the remaining elements of his strategy a nagging worry surfaced. There had been no sign of Stella. King had been the only occupant of the car. Starmer forced himself to slow down with a series of deep breaths as he reasoned that she was probably on the floor or in the load compartment.

He knew he was in the worst of all his worlds: placed in a situation where he could give free rein to his cold-blooded instincts, instant aggression and ruthless determination he'd back himself every time. This waiting game with time to think wasn't working for him at all. He consoled himself with the thought that you could overthink these situations.

The wait ended with a single shout, followed, ten seconds later by two more from slightly farther away, then three gunshots and the metallic clang and buzzing whine of a ricochet. He tried to lever himself over the top of the sea wall but struggled to gain sufficient purchase with his mud caked and sodden shoes to complete the manoeuvre. As he tried, again, to swing a knee up onto the tow path, he heard an engine roar into life, tyres squeal, gears crunch, the impact of metal on metal and the sound of cornering at speed. He froze as he saw the Land Rover leave the service lane, fishtail pass the factory perimeter wall, bounce over an apron of rough ground and head for the slipway.

He dropped back down to the beach, ducking as the vehicle skidded on the weed covered granite above his head and come to a crabbing, sliding halt part way down the slope. He might have been right about King's escape route but was sure they'd all been sold a dummy on the exchange. As he considered

507

what to do next the water breaking over the slipway was illuminated by successive flashes from the Rover's powerful headlights. He moved down the beach until he was level with the front wheels of the car above and peered beneath to the river beyond. Just visible, about a quarter of a mile out, shaping an elliptical course to counter wind and tide, was the bow wave of a small boat.

He returned to the sea wall and launched himself at the concrete with a desperation that tore fingernails as he scrabbled for a grip on the granite sets of the tow path to haul himself over. Slithering at full length along the path behind the car then down the near side until he reached the passenger door, he paused to catch his breath and check on the Rib. It hadn't moved as fast as he'd feared and was making very heavy weather as it slammed bow on against the flood tide with wind against. He hoisted himself into a squat and reached for the door handle. As it opened he grabbed the passenger seat headrest and the top of the door and levered himself up and into the seat in one movement. Before King could react Starmer swivelled left in the seat, to generate power and momentum, pivoted back and, off the end of the swing, propelled his right elbow into the man's temple. As King slumped forward into the seat belt the small case with his possessions slipped from his lap into the foot well. Starmer retrieved the case and reached down between King's feet gathering up loose documents and cards. Checking for any signs of a return to consciousness and finding none, he flicked through the cards, looking for one that had caught his attention when Lockstone had made her cursory examination of the case contents up at the Warren. He sensed, rather than saw, the movement and was surprised that King didn't anticipate and block the elbow's return journey. The man's hands flew to his now shattered nose and Starmer casually reached across him and retrieved the gun that had fallen with a clunk back into the door storage bin.

'Who got shot?' He jerked his head back towards the factory. King continued to massage his nose. Starmer reversed the pistol in his hand and swung the butt down hard onto the man's kneecap. 'What happened back there?'

King rocked in his seat trying to control the pain from the blows, 'stupid bastards tried to jump me.'

'Who did?'

'Those fucking idiots that you've been towing around since you got down here.'

'What happened?'

King sighed, then rocked his head back onto the seat rest to stop the flow of blood from his nose. 'Denton got upset because I didn't bring Stella, he shouted and made a grab. I had to bowl him over. Next thing these two gorillas swing from a freight container and are coming at me.'

Denton waited briefly and impatiently, 'and?'

King sniffed blood, 'I let off a couple of shots to keep 'em back.'

'Did you hit anybody?' Starmer watched the man's eyes defocus and then drift off to the left and knew somebody had been hurt. 'So, where is Stella?'

King pointed to the Rib that was now less than a hundred yards from the slipway. 'I never had her. The exchange was always going to be here.' If they'd kept their cool nobody would have been hurt.'

'And you'd have been on your way to the airport.'

King turned towards him, 'you're Starmer right? Heard about you.' He studied Starmer over the top of the hand covering his nose, 'look, there's no reason why we can't just finish this as planned,' he mumbled. He waved towards the Rib broaching a wave onto the slipway, 'Denton's wife is there. Look. I just take my stuff and we all walk away. What do you say?'

'Maybe.' Starmer looked down the slipway to where the man in the rear of the Rib was struggling with throttle and steering while the other held a terrified woman by the collar up in the bow.

As he watched he felt a strange disorientating sensation. Something had changed. Something had moved. He leant forward and looked through the windscreen at the granite sets in front of the vehicle. Almost imperceptibly they were edging from view. The Land Rover was moving. He bent over the large centre console, yanked on the seat belt, felt into his coat pocket and then fiddled with and checked the belt tongue was engaged. 'Stay put,' he waved the pistol under the damaged nose to reinforce the instruction, 'I'll be back.'

As he side slipped down the algae and weed covered granite he held the pistol away from his body; making sure it was clearly visible. The man holding Stella was sat astride the Rib side tube with one foot outside on the slipway. As Starmer approached the man hauled a terrified Stella over his lap and dumped her at Starmer's feet.

'You the passenger?' He shouted above the wind, waves and a revving engine.

Starmer leant down, grasped Stella by the arm and pulled her to her feet, 'change of plan mate. Best you get going.' The man nodded, shouted at the helmsman, pushed off with his outboard foot, circled his arm in the air and with a flourish pointed the helmsman out to mid river.

Starmer pulled the soaked and trembling Stella into his arms, 'Listen Stella, I'm a friend and you are now safe. Listen,' he urged again, pushing her to arm's length to check if she understood. She was staring fixedly at King over in the Range Rover with a look of hopeless and wretched terror. 'He shook her. Don't look at him. He's over. Finished.' He shook her again, 'Look at me and listen,' he barked. 'I want you to make your way up to the tow path and then over to the factory. Paul is up there.' He wrapped an arm around her shoulders and began to walk her up the incline. As he neared the top he heard marbles bouncing in a biscuit tin as the diesel engine fired. He pushed Stella across the tow path and yelled, 'run, go on run. Don't look back.'

He looked down to the Land Rover and the ghostly outline of King's face as he peered backwards, round the driver's seat, through the misted rear screen. King released the handbrake and the car rolled a few inches forward as he missed the biting point on the clutch. He then tap danced between the foot brake and accelerator as the vehicle continued a slow slide. With the water coming ever closer, and as the slip continued, King let the clutch out fully, too quickly and floored the accelerator. The rear wheels began spinning and then tracked sideways over the algae, veering towards the edge and failing to stop the inevitable slide down towards the water. Starmer walked towards the tailgate and peered over the spare wheel clamped there to see King struggling to engage the four-wheel drive. He stepped back and to the side, expecting to see the Discovery reverse by him as traction bit. For a moment, all tyres did grip and the slide was halted. Hoping to build on this success King then put his foot down. The rear wheels skidded uselessly and tracked sideways again while the front wheels, up to their hubs in the water, spun hopelessly in the tide.

Starmer turned, squatted, positioned his back against the spare wheel, placed his heels in a joint between the sets and slowly extended his legs. It was easier than he'd thought. The spinning wheels reduced friction to a minimum and once moving, momentum took over. Denton had said there was a depth of fifteen foot at high water here and Starmer had expected the Rover to sink from sight as it slipped into the water. He watched as the tide caught the front of the car and pushed it into a current that gyrated it some fifty yards further from the shore. With each rotation Starmer could see King becoming more frantic; pushing at the doors, hammering on the windows and yanking over and over on the seat belt. As the current released the car into the calmer, mid-stream the front began to sink and the Rover canted over onto its nearside. Waves broke over the roof and he could just see the white blur of King's face with palms alongside, all pressed flat against the top of the window as he sucked desperately on a small bubble of air before the car capsized and sank.

'That's that then.'

Starmer looked back over his shoulder at a dirty and dishevelled Denton sitting on the bollard. 'Looks like. You alright?'

'He jumped me.'

'It's ok. Stella ok?'

'She will be. Thanks.'

'Bulimias?'

'Don's got a nasty splinter wound from a ricochet on his forehead.'

'Lucky old Don.'

'Yeah that's what he thinks. God I could murder a drink.'

'How long has it been?'

Denton looked at him and laughed, 'weeks? Feels like a year.'

'C'mon, we need to get out of here.'

'Is it over?'

'Yeah, it's all over.'

Epilogue

'She's back.'

'Thanks Justin, I'll come down.' Starmer didn't need to peer down from the eyrie. He'd been expecting her for some days. He used the walk towards the bar to watch her studiously ignore his approach and prepare to be discovered. The bob and fringe were the same but the tweeds, shoes and bag were gone. Strapped ankle boots, skinny jeans, a double-breasted navy blazer with rolled cuffs over a cashmere sweater and a silk scarf loose at her throat.

'Back to business then, DI Lockstone?'

She turned, a prepared, quizzical frown creasing her face, 'what?'

'The outfit,' he smiled, 'very "NYPD Blue.'

'What is it with you and my appearance?'

'Just showing an interest.'

'Well don't.'

'No pearls. I liked the pearls. Nice touch,' he persisted, pleased with her reaction and another slight blush.

'I'm not here to talk fashion.'

He twitched the corner of his mouth and clicked his tongue, 'did you pay for that drink?' He caught the slight shake of Justin's head from the corner of his eye, 'only I'm not in the business of giving freebies to Policemen.'

'Cut the crap Starmer.'

He grinned, 'so what are you here to talk about?'

'Somewhere less public perhaps?'

'Is this where I direct you to the toilets and we meet down the road?'

'Your office.'

'Got a warrant?'

'Oh, trust me, if I need one it'll be here within the hour.'

'My office it is then.'

Starmer sat behind his desk idly swinging the chair from side to side as much as the pedestals and his knees would allow. His elbows were propped on the arms, his hands steepled and his forefingers tapped at his lips. He realised that the swing of the chair was synchronised to Lockstone's pacing of the floor. 'You seem upset.'

'Furious would cover it better.'

'Really. Why?'

'Oh, give it up Starmer, nobody is buying the wide eyed innocent routine.'

'I have no idea what you're on about.'

She stopped pacing, rested her palms on the desk, leant towards him and fixed him with a penetrating gaze. 'The idea, you may recall,' she turned her head away in mock disbelief and laughed sardonically, 'was that we, let me say that again, "we!". We,' she shouted, 'would use King's getaway pack to entice him into the open where he could then be arrested and subsequently subjected to the due process of Law. Right?' She barked.

'Seemed like a plan.'

'I am not joking Starmer. Believe me.'

Starmer returned her stare and allowed his features to harden, 'I can see that DI Lockstone. If you've got something to say it's best you get it off your chest.' This time the blush wasn't embarrassment it was rage.

'I don't need your fucking permission Starmer. I can get you banged up tomorrow and the key thrown into the Thames.'

Starmer sighed and held up his hand, 'no you couldn't. If you could you'd have been here a couple of days ago, and we'd be having this conversation under caution at the Station. You've got nothing and you know it. And this hard arse act really isn't you,' he smiled.

She slammed both hands down hard on the surface of the table, 'you know nothing about me.'

'I'd like to,' he allowed the silence to lengthen and watched her face relax marginally as the rage was challenged by a series of very different emotions, 'know more about you, that is,' he offered, watching as she resumed her pacing and tried to recover her composure.

She came back to the desk, 'you know we recovered the body of DCS Roy King from a Land Rover washed up at Barking Reach?'

'It was on the News.'

'Death by drowning but fractured nose and temporal bone. He went into the river at Denton's premises. There's wheel tracks all over the place.' She wagged a forefinger at Starmer, 'but here's the puzzle. Whichever way that car went into the river there was never any chance of him getting out of it. Was there?'

'Because?'

'Because someone had fixed the seat belt. There was no way he was ever going to be able to get out of that car as it sank.'

'Oh dear.'

'Don't fuck with me Starmer. Someone had jammed a plastic shim between the red release button and the tongue of the belt.' She glared down at him, 'you know what the shim was.'

'I've no idea.'

'It wasn't a question. It was a bank card; one from King's stuff. The stuff you lifted. The stuff we agreed to use as bait. Remember? It was in that case at The Warren. The same case we found floating, empty, in the back of that Land Rover. Last seen, before that, in your possession. Care to explain how it got there?'

'I have no idea. I thought I was under surveillance. Did you see me anywhere near King? Did you?'

She ignored that question, 'but then the stuff in the case would've been no use to him anyway. Would it?'

'You've lost me.'

'You'd already cleaned him out.'

'I did?'

'The day after we met at The Warren your partner at Slammers, the Dutch woman, left for Holland.'

'Mia? It's where she lives. Her brother is dying and she's decided to retire.'

'Not surprised she can retire with the money she's got.' She stamped her foot on the floor, 'c'mon Starmer, Amsterdam via Zurich? Please. She cleared King's accounts. Didn't she? Fifty-fifty, was it?'

Starmer stood, impatiently kicked away his chair and rounded the desk, 'can you prove any of this? Because I'm getting tired of your theories. This is the second lot of accusations you've come up with. You were wrong before. You're wrong now.'

'No, I'm right. I'm right on both counts,' she crossed the room and sat on the arm of the chesterfield. 'But you're right too.'

Starmer cocked an eyebrow.

'I can't prove it.'

He smiled.

'But I don't have to.'

'You don't?'

'No, I don't. All I have to do is put you on the list.'

'That list?'

'That list. Every Coppers got one.'

'Yeah, I know how it works.'

'I have a proposition.'

'I thought you might.'

'Work for me.'

'With.'

'For.'

'Doing what?'

'We'll start with Mister Church, shall we?

'I see, "Corruption in a noble cause".'

'You could agree,' she paused, 'or, on the other hand, you could agree.' She smiled.

'Is there a choice?'

'Always.'

'In that case let me buy dinner.'

'Dinner?'

'I have a proposition of my own,' he opened the office door and stood aside for her to pass, 'I really did like you in those pearls.'

Denton scrunched further down into the seat, embarrassed to be on such prominent display in the front row and very conscious that he was the only person, other than Security, wearing a suit and tie. As seats filled up around him, with greetings being exchanged, late comers being excused for disturbing the settled and furled coats finally tucked away, he sought refuge, again, in the programme.

He skipped the section on the history and heritage of The Roundhouse; he needed no reminding that the place was a converted tram shed. It was cavernous. He glanced up at the circular steel tracery of iron girder work, looking for all the world like the central hub for cell galleries in a Victorian prison and wondered again. He knew Dee was concerned about the acoustics. There were sixteen songs on the set list and some demanded an intimacy with the audience that she might struggle to achieve in this industrial cathedral. Rehearsals had only partly helped and that afternoon he and Mathew Sinclair had spent time reassuring her and bolstering a faltering confidence.

It all depended on the opening number; Nina Simone's, "Feeling Good". The first dozen bars were acapella followed hard with heavy brass triplets leading in the rest of the accompaniment. It was intended as a Show starter and stopper but would require poise, artistry and nerve. He shuffled in his seat, closed the programme, folded his hands in his lap and started slightly as cool slim fingers enfolded his.

'She'll be fine Paul', Sinclair squeezed again, 'all Artists get nervous before an opening night. The minute the house lights dim the nerves will go.'

'I hope you're right.'

'Paul, she'll be fine. She's got great musicians, a great set and,' he waved his good arm behind him at the now full auditorium, 'an audience that came to see her. It'll be great.'

The house lights dimmed, the floor mounted spots speared upwards and the stage seemed to drift on clouds of dry ice. As a hush settled over the audience Dee Dee Wilson, in a tailored white satin trouser suit, stepped forward. As the uplighters were killed and a single follow spot beamed down from above, she stood, head bowed beneath the light, raised her right arm, pointed an imperious forefinger heavenward and poured out her soul. Denton's eyes drifted back up to the steel tracery almost expecting to see the "birds flying high". He and the audience gasped at this tremendous vocal outpouring of the lyrics of Newley and Bricusse roared as a defiant message of hope and renewal into the rafters as she held the last note over the sound of their applause. Dee raised both arms on high and the audience rose from their seats and clapped, hooted, whistled and roared their approval. Denton, stunned, hadn't realised he was the only person still in their seat until Sinclair loomed over him.

'Feeling good?'

'That was amazing.'

'And it'll get better.'

'Yeah?'

'She'll ride the wave.'

From the gentle, tinkling, almost whimsical keyboard intro to Labi Siffre's "So strong", Dee soared up onto a tide of raw vocal indignation, challenging the "Barriers" with the sheer power of her voice. Then she drew her audience closer in with a throaty, haunting rendition for the "lost and the lonely" with Elkie Brookes' "Pearls". Twice, in this tale of the failed nightclub singer, Dee used her own name. Watching closely, Denton was sure the slip was subconscious but tellingly the audience had noticed and the second slip was applauded. As she acknowledged the applause and gathered her breath she peered down in Denton's direction, shielding her eyes with her hand and just for a moment looking lost and vulnerable.

The moment passed as bass and guitar laid out the gentle, haunting opening bars to "Cry me a River". She stood, feet from Denton, microphone held in both hands, head slightly to one side, eyes closed, gently swaying in time until the last line; her eyes opened, focused and pinned him to his seat. "I've cried a river over you."

As the band took a moment to change instruments and Dee sipped some water, Denton turned to Sinclair, 'you should be up there.'

'I am. In spirit.'

'And the body.'

'It wasn't the body Paul. It was the mind.'

'And how's the mind now?'

Sinclair grinned, 'after tonight? Mending.'

'And you and Dee?'

'Will work together.'

'And you and Dee?'

Before Denton could answer the punchy E and D chord intro to JJ Cale's "Cocaine" split the air and regathered an audience that had drifted into a mindset and expectation obviously not shared by Dee. Denton marvelled as a flaxen haired hang over from the sixties delivered the solo from a low slung Gretsch while Dee matched his every move with enthusiastic and joyous air guitar. The pair took a joint bow and Dee stepped forward.

'The Day Lee Mail,' she announced, pausing to shield her eyes with her hand while attempting to scan the audience through the stage lights. 'Y'all heard of "The Day Lee Mail?'

Distantly, from the audience, 'It's a shit newspaper.'

'You ain't wrong brother. You folks may have been wondering where I been. Well according to the Day Lee Mail, I'm a criminal, an addict, a dealer, a supplier, a fugitive from justice, a home wrecker and,' she assumed an eccentric English accent, 'an all-round bad egg.' She waited for the applause and whistles to subside. 'Oh, and I damn near forgot, I'm a gangster's moll.' Again, she timed the interval, 'Ladies and Gentlemen, I'd like to introduce you to the Gangster that never was. Denton,' she instructed, 'stand up, take a bow, wave your arms about so these good folks can see you ain't in cuffs.'

Denton, in a state of complete bemusement, did as instructed, reflecting, as he sat back down, that this was the only standing ovation he'd ever receive.

As the crowd settled, a different, softer, gentler voice soared over the four-bar intro before sliding down to meet the opening lyric of "Wind beneath my wings". Denton sat, mesmerised, as he realised that this amazing, beautiful, talented and loving woman was singing for an audience of one. As she reached the final verse she leant forward slightly, reached out her hand and whispered the lyric; "did you ever know that you're my hero?' This time Denton knew he was the only one still sitting. He used the applause as a diversion while he wiped away the tears and struggled to prepare for what he was sure would follow.

'Paul, take a bow.'

He stood, clenched hands held above his head in a boxer's salute, acknowledged the appreciation and sat as soon as he could.

'Guess that's settled then,' laughed Sinclair hugging him.

Denton smiled a slow, lazy, relaxed beam of smile and looked up at a backlit Dee, hand still outstretched, 'She called me Paul!'

Dee watching the pair hug, felt the tension fall from her shoulders and relaxed back into her concert. She dreamily reintroduced the audience to the Great American Songbook using Sinclair's arrangements of "Love for Sale" and "I've got you under my skin". With the help of the small string section and her two backing singers she belted out a version of "At Last" that would have had Etta James looking over her shoulder. She was surprised how well the small acoustic section of the concert was received by the crowd. She, the two singers and the flaxen haired troubadour, this time with a Gibson Les Paul acoustic, harmonised, palm slapped and jammed their way through "Ring of fire" and "All shook up" to deafening appreciation.

As the concert neared its finale she was confident that she hadn't made the mistake of letting her jazz soul distract too much from the melody and meaning of the songs. She did not want to be known only as a performer of other people's songs but was pleased that her personalised renditions had found favour with her fans.

With the band settled and waiting her cue she thought back to the mantra that had got her from the dark and out into light. In the dark she'd fought despair and found distraction from an incantation that solemnized a ritual and in the light turned into a redemptive expression of triumph over despair. A song; her song.

She nodded at the drummer, took the mike from the stand, pivoted and looked at Paul Denton.

'You take a little pain
You draw a little blood
You breathe a little air
Rise above the flood
And that feeling starts over again
Backtracking…………..ooh…………Backtrackin
g.

You feel a little love
You go a little ways
You cling a little long
Fight a burning blaze
And that feeling starts over again
Backtracking…………..ooh…………Backtrackin
g.

519

You seem a little strange
You're a little sick at heart
You give a little bit
As you start to fall apart
And that feeling starts over again
Backtracking……………...ooh…………..Backtrackin
g.

You feel a little lost
You hope they're gonna care
You light a little fire
Pray a little prayer
And that feeling starts over again
Backtracking……………...ooh…………..Backtrackin
g.

Printed in Poland
by Amazon Fulfillment
Poland Sp. z o.o., Wrocław